The Tyranny
of Gods
and Men

True Tree Chronicles:

by G. S. Scott

Sorrow's Heart

(A True Tree Chronicles Origins Story)

The Chaos Trilogy

Cleansed

Chaos Reigns Vol 1: The Hand of God

Chaos Reigns Vol 2: The Tower of Time

Restoration Trilogy

The Tyranny of Gods and Men

The Tyranny of God's and Men

True Tree Press
TrueTreePress@gmail.com

The Tyranny of Gods and Men
by G. S. Scott
Restoration Trilogy: Book One

Cover design and art by Christy Hans and Khandaker Ashiqe

Editing by Melissa Ringsted and There For You Editing

Published by: True Tree Press
PO BOX 70052 Lansing, MI 48908
TrueTreePress@gmail.com

ISBN: 1-7337092-6-2
ISBN-13: 978-1-7337092-6-2

This is a work of fiction. All characters and situations appearing in this
work are fictitious. Any resemblance to real persons, living or dead, or
personal situations is purely coincidental.

For Sarah,

my Angel Eyes

Chapters:

I am the True Tree

The Mother of all

I am the wellspring from which all life flows

From my branches and roots

come the seeds and pods of birth

Wherever there is life, I am there

Wherever there is death, I am there

Life and death are one

What is returned to me in death

shall be brought forth once more into life

I am the mighty

I am the meek

I am the one

I, am singular

I, am True

Prologue:

Reign Fall

(522 years after the start of the Reign of Chaos)

The stench of fish and sewage assaulted the priest of Chaos, the light wind tussling his jet-black hair as he made his way from the river docks into the city of Cross Corners. The cries of fishmongers mingled with the cacophony of livestock passing through the city, as did the clacking of wagon and cart wheels on the paving stones. Reminded of home, he smiled. In the South, every city was coastal, so the only thing missing was salt air. He found it reassuring, and far better than the Westlands, with nothing but grass for leagues and an occasional tree line.

When he reached the major road running through the city, the smile slipped as he examined the surroundings with black eyes, his inner-fire smoldering. Clean, neat, tall buildings of brick and stone lined the street. They all sat on foundations ranging from five to ten feet high, while small lanes—all meeting at right angles—crisscrossed the wide road. The place stank of latent Order. He clutched his multihued robes, wanting to lash out, burning the blasphemy all around. It would be easy. The Breath of the Lord floated all around him, visible through his third eye, the essence of Chaos just waiting to be used. Grasping it with his will, he drew it in, filling him with the power of God. With it he could do anything. But to what avail? If anything, it would slow he chase, and Concord would be that much farther away.

They're not worth it, he thought with a sneer.

Reaching a large, city-square bazaar, paved in red and black brick, his gaze went to the temple directly in front of a major intersecting street. *Why do they allow such disrespect of The Great Lord of Chaos? I didn't bathe myself in the blood of children all those years ago for* this.

Mounting the steps, he marched to a priest in gray robes standing next to the main doors some twenty feet above street-level. "I would have words with your High Priest."

The brown-haired priest smirked. "And you would be?"

"My name is Calidos Flint."

Calidos fumed, staring with contempt at Rendell Morgan, the over-stuffed High Priest and City Master. The man's office took up several suites in the west wing of the temple, overlooking the bazaar below. Sweet incense burned from a half-dozen diffusers scattered about.

"Why such vehemence in a search for a single man?" Master Rendell asked. His robes were large enough to be a tent. He reeked of perfume, and bejeweled rings donned each thick, sausage-like finger.

Calidos had idled on the other side of the Cunning River for a week, unable to cross due to recent treacherous currents. Then, this fool made him wait another three hours for an audience. Now, the man had the nerve to dismiss Calidos' concerns as flights of fancy. "I told you. I'm seeking a man, possibly the most dangerous ever born."

"Surely, you overstate yourself," Rendell said with a flip of his hand. "Nothing is more dangerous than the Lands of the Dead, beyond Gate Hall, with its time-twisting spirits and mad ghouls."

"The man I seek escaped the Cleansing with the aid of Ukase."

Rendell's eyebrow twitched up. "The God of Order? No

one's heard a peep out of that cult in … well, longer than I can recall. You've proof of this?"

"I've heard it from the lips of over a dozen," Calidos Flint lied. He'd heard many things while putting people to the question, searing their flesh with his Chaos-infused fire, but none directly mentioned Ukase. Yet, Calidos knew he was right. "The man I seek is a Traveler going by the name of Ellis Concord "

The fat man's face darkened. "Meddling with Travelers is a dangerous business. The roaming entertainers are the Lord's favorites."

Calidos suppressed a snarl. "Be that is it may, I still want him. It took far too long to cross that cursed river, and I'm losing time. I've been tracking these Travelers since the Cleansing. God demanded the lives of all children under two, and I'll not lose Concord now."

Rendell's eyes widened. "The Cleansing? That was twenty years ago! Such persistence is not very becoming of a disciple of the Lord of Chaos."

This wasn't the first time Calidos had heard the like. His drive left him an outsider, shunned by his fellow priests. His most burning regret and humiliation was when he'd had Concord in his hands when the Travelers was only a boy. Then letting him go out of ignorance for fear of harming one of *the Lord's favorites*. Calidos had killed the boy's parents in his hunt to retrieve the young Concord, but it was a hollow solace.

The memory made Calidos grind his teeth. "I want this man. All I ask is—"

"I don't care what you *want*," Master Rendell said, his face a thunderhead. "You obviously hold ill will toward these Travelers, and I'll not have the Lord's wrath fall upon *my* city when you disturb one of his favorites. You'll receive no aid in Cross Corners."

Calidos shook in rage. "The Lord's wrath? You must be joking. If there's any place more deserving of His judgment I don't know of it."

Rendell Morgan held up a finger. "You watch your tongue."

"You speak of things that are not becoming of the Lord? This city is rife with Order!" Calidos stabbed a finger toward the City Master's window. "Roads that run in straight lines? Schedules? *Strict districts*? This city spits in the eye of the Lord of Chaos."

"That's it." The large man stood and bellowed toward the door, "Raaz! Get your imp ass in here and remove this fool."

Calidos Flint grinned. "I've had enough of this as well." He channeled the Lord's Breath through his inner inferno. It coalesced in his hand ... and dissipated. He stared, open-mouthed at his empty palm. He grasped for Chaos again but found nothing. "How?"

The City Master let out a chuckle. "I possess the ability to cut others off from the Great Lord. How do you think I took this position?"

Chaos coalesced, wrapping around Calidos' chest and lifting him into the air. It flung him across the room. He slammed into the wall next to the door and stuck in place as though glued.

Randell waddled across the room to stand in front of Calidos. "You're not the first I've dealt with."

The door next to Calidos opened, and a waist-high person in black robes glided in.

Randell addressed the newcomer, "Raaz, take this fool to the street."

A hand, covered in green and gold scales, reached out from the little man's sleeve and touched Randell Morgan on the leg. The High Priest shrieked, sending a chill down Calidos' spine. Morgan fell to his knees, trying to pry the little hand off his leg but couldn't. He flopped to his back and bellowed and thrashed. The scaled hand then moved to Morgan's throat, whose scream became a high-pitched squeal. His neck turned black, cutting off the howls.

"Hush now," the little man said, his voice sounding like charred leather. "We don't want anyone disturbing us-ss, now do we?"

The Chaotic bond around Calidos vanished as the rest of Randell Morgan's body blackened and quivered. Morgan's eyes popped out of their sockets and his tongue grew, filling his mouth. His hands, puffed with blackness, then began to shrivel, his arms and legs drawing into his body as though all the blood and water within him was being sucked out. Within moments, Morgan was nothing but a withered, twisted husk.

The little man turned toward Calidos. Its face was covered

in the same scales, and a long, sinuous tongue flashed between spiked teeth. "My master sees-ss great promise in you," it hissed.

Calidos tore his eyes off the decrepit corpse of the former City Master and shied away. "Who are you?"

"I am Raaz. I am a servant of my master."

Calidos frowned. "Who is your Master? And what does he want?"

"My master's-ss name is Dekriot. He's an ardent devotee of the Lord of Chaos. As for what he wants?" The little beast smiled. "That, I'll explain on our way to Gate Hall."

The charred ruins of the amphitheater used by a portion of the Travelers no longer smelled of smoke and ash—after so many weeks it wouldn't—but Calidos still sensed the fire that caused it. All he needed do was reach out to rekindle the blaze, regardless of the lack of fuel to make it burn. That fuel lay within him. He wanted to do it anyway, but what good would it do? The people he wanted answers from there were long dead.

His stomach knotted with frustration. He arrived too late. The rest of the Traveler caravan had moved on a week before these fools died. The only thing that kept Calidos from chasing after the caravan was the fact that the man he pursued, hounded since the man was an infant, hadn't gone with them. For some reason, Ellis Concord had gone into the Lands of the Dead, and Calidos was forbidden to follow.

"That bastard Karados," he spat.

When Calidos first arrived, he explained his hunt to Gunther Karados, the High Priest of Gate Hall. "The man had laughed," he said to Raaz. "Laughed! He said Concord had entered the Lands of the Dead as though it were an afterthought. He said it was 'being taken care of by others,' like it was an afterthought." The High Priest then forbade Calidos from going after Concord and dismissed him with a wave of the hand.

The ever-present warble and whine of the barrier to the Lands of the Dead to the north filled the air seemed to mock Calidos, its swirling colors looking like oil atop water. He grasped the Lord's Breath and funneled it though him, melding it with the fire in his core, and shoved it into the pile of blackened-stones and charred-timber. The stones glowed and cracked before turning to dust. Heat poured off the heap in waves, threatening to set nearby buildings, already sooty and blacked, on fire.

"Why does that bastard refuse me?" Calidos bellowed.

"Gunther Karados-ss is nothing if not consistent," Raaz hissed. "He holds these lands in his fist and is very protective of them. Lord Heartless, the Champion of God himself gave Karados the stewardship of the prison that is the Lands of the Dead. Heartless wanted to make sure no minions of the God of Time escape."

"Karados is an ass! I'm more than capable of protecting myself from those ghosts in there and he knows it. I asked around. He sent in two acolytes and a tracker to fetch Concord. I'm far more skilled than two helpless whelps and a weakling. So why refuse me?"

"Those whelps, as you put it, are far from helpless. One was Karados' own daughter, Mangin, and the other was, well, let's just say he's probably the most powerful man in the entire region. Perhaps the entire world."

"Who?"

Razz's lips smiled a toothy grin. "Betal."

Calidos rolled his eyes. "Never heard of him. If anyone that powerful existed, I'd have heard of them. And who names someone *the Hand of God*? Puffery." He turned to the imp. "Are you sure there's no way you could get me in there?"

"Again, I cannot. The prison is an amalgam of Chaos and the powers of my master. I am not allowed to enter."

Calidos' head swiveled toward the half-demon. "Not allowed? Before you said couldn't, and now it's not allowed?' What are you playing at, you little snake? You said you'd tell me of this demon, but thus far I've heard nothing but vague notions and hot air."

Raaz's mouth curled into a smile, exposing his needle-like fangs. "The machinations-ss of my master are beyond one such as yourself." His catlike eyes held a menacing glint.

Calidos took a step back, out of the reach of the little monster, and drew in Chaos. "Do not threaten me—"

His eyes went wide as the flows of the Great Lord, the very essence of Chaos, dissipated, winking out as though they no longer existed. His mouth gaped. "It was you. You are the one who cut me off back at the Corners."

Raaz's laugh was like the crackling of glass shards. "No. I lack that gift. This is something far more significant."

The hiss of the prison grew sharp and piercing. The skies above it, the swirling clouds of every color dancing across its surface grew thin, as though their color was being drained away. A massive boom shook the air and reverberated through the ground as the shell containing the Lands of the Dead popped like a massive bubble. Buildings all around them groaned and collapsed, their dust and debris carried away in a gale flowing from the former prison.

Raaz stood still, unmoved by the destruction all around. He tilted his head as though listening to something and smiled again. "It would seem that the time of Chaos is over, my friend," he said. "Edis, your Lord God, has been banished. If I were you, I'd not tarry here. With your Lord's reign over, the other gods have returned, especially Ukase. He already has a strong presence here and his retaliation will be swift and violent."

Screams erupted in the city and smoke billowed up in several locations. Calidos saw none of it, the cacophony of a city in riot registering only a buzz. He was empty inside, a shallow husk to be blown away in the slightest breeze. "How can this be?" He felt cold; his bones ached as though they'd turned to ice. "What do I do?"

"You go to The South," Raaz said.

Calidos shook his head. "Why go home? What difference does it make? The Lord is gone. One place is no different from the other."

"Oh, but there is-ss a place, my friend. One unlike any other," Raaz hissed. "There, you will find a connection to power undreamed of. You can take back what was yours and punish those who wronged you." He patted Calidos' leg as though consoling an invalid. "Trust me. In the South, you will find what you ss-seek."

Chapter 1

The Return of Order

Dirge's boot crunched on a piece of small, dry brush. The gateway Betal had created—a shimmering orb connecting the ancient chamber to the outskirts of Gate Hall—winked out, leaving Dirge and Mangin blinking in the bright light of day. Sunlight bathed Dirge's ebony skin with warmth, soaking through his short, tightly curled, black hair. A light breeze, filled with the scent of wildflowers, blew through the surrounding waist-high grass, making it dance and sway. Birds sang and flitted about. Belying the tranquility around them, smoke billowed up from several places in the city of Gate Hall.

Searing agony flashed high on Dirge's chest, as though red-hot irons were pressed into his skin. Tearing open his shirt, the old brands of the Lord of Order—the ones he received when consecrated as a Warrior of the Righteous decades before— flamed to life. A presence filled him, swelling in his chest, and then suffusing his every fiber, one of divine nobility and honor, one right and true. Dirge had no doubt it was his god, the Lord of Order, Ukase.

The voice of Ukase exploded in Dirge's skull, "*I HAVE RETURNED. YOU HAVE MUCH WORK TO DO.*"

Dirge's head rung as though struck by a hammer Swallowing, he asked, "What work must I do, my Lord God?"

His god didn't reply, and his holy presence faded.

"What was that?" Mangin asked, eyebrow cocked.

With a shake of the head to clear it, Dirge ignored the former priestess of Chaos, and pondered Ukase's ominous message. The world had just changed dramatically, and pain and death would soon follow. How would Betal and Daylin fit into it all, being gods in their own right?

He pulled out the bronze sun pendant from the pocket of his black coat which covered his scored, leather chest-piece. The medallion glinted in the sun. It had belonged to Ellis. He wondered how the young man would feel now that Chaos was gone. Would he truly be happy with the violence that would come? The scene flashed through Dirge's mind: Ellis' body lying on the ground … the blood pouring from Ellis' neck where the Chaos paladin Hogar had ripped out. … the shrieks of Daylin kneeling at the lad's side … the knowledge that he had failed to stop Hogar, failed to save the young man he'd promised to give his life for.

Dirge squeezed his gray eyes shut to try and erase the memory. It didn't work.

Mangin huffed. Pursing her lips in annoyance at being ignored, she asked a different question, "What's that in your hand?" The waver in her sweet, melodious voice made him look at her. She came up only to his chest, and her long, undulating red hair nearly looked afire against her alabaster skin. But her green eyes held worry.

"Daylin gave it to me," he said. "For remembrances, and so that I would always have a piece of her."

Lifting one of her strong, supple legs out to the back from beneath her knee-length skirt, she stretched forward to peer into his hand. The motion caused her low-cut blouse to expose her full, pale bosom. "Didn't that belong to Ellis?"

Knuckles cracking, Dirge squeezed the pendant in his huge fist as he did his best to ignore the wanton woman. "Yes," he said. "It was his mother's, before that."

Dirge's hand shook. "As if I would need something to remember my failures." He failed to save Ellis from the hulking paladin, Hogar. And years before, when Ellis was a child, Dirge saved his life, and in so doing, left the boy's parents to die at the hands of a priest. Dirge's mistakes rushed at him: his wife's death along with those of his comrades in arms, the murders he committed while on the road with Jacob … the abandonment of his faith. "I am surrounded by death and failure."

Mangin pursed her ruby lips. "What are you talking about? Daylin is alive. She's the Hand of the Mother in the mortal world. She may no longer be mortal, but she is alive."

"I failed her and let that monster kill her."

Moving close, Mangin placed her hand on his. "If not for you, we would all be dead. You drove that blade into Heartless' leg, causing him to flee." She paused. "Though I'm not even sure Heartless is there anymore. That thing is a puppet of Dekriot, now. Twitch is a fitting name for what he's become."

Mangin's warm, soft skin made Dirge think about the cavernous room where she tried to seduce him less than an hour before. He still hated her; a vile temptress who stood for Edis, the Lord of Chaos. But then, with the god now banished, she was no longer a thing of Chaos. She was only a woman now, beautiful and vulnerable. She needed his protection—as he swore to do so.

She gazed up at him, a slight smile playing on her lips.

Why was she doing this, trying to ease his conscience? Was it comfort, or manipulation? He took a step back, out of her reach. "I have promised Daylin I would protect you with my life, but it would be wise if you kept your distance."

Mangin stood tall, pressing her chest out, and said with an air, "You find me pathetic and disgusting?"

Staring at her, his blood coursed, and his ardor rose. "No, only a fool would think that." He stomped his lustful thoughts down. "If you get too close to me you may well die. As I said, I'm surrounded by death. My mother died when I was a child. My wife, her parents, everyone who followed me in my war with Chaos died because of me."

When she asked what he was talking about, he told her of his youth, his early apprenticeship to the Brotherhood of

Assassins, of Ukase's calling him to fight Chaos, and the ensuing destruction of his army at the hands of Chaos.

She waved her hand. "You can't blame yourself for that. The gods war and we are but—"

"I killed my best friend ... someone I'd known since childhood. He saved me in that battle, dragging me to safety. I repaid that kindness with my sword through his back."

Tilting her head, she frowned, looking at him as if for the first time. "Why?"

"We became thieves afterward. One day we came across the Traveler troupe when Ellis was a child. Jacob wanted us to rob them. He tried to kill Ellis and—"

She flung up her hands. "Oh, for the Mother's sake! And for a moment I thought you had it in you to be a scoundrel." She stomped off toward Gate Hall.

"Where are you going?" He started after her.

"I'm going to see what's happening in the city. My father may need help."

The dead littered the streets—some mangled, some charred, while others were little more than piles of bloody rags. Fires raged throughout most of the city, choking the air with smoke. Shrieks echoed down the passing alleys along with the roar of mobs, like beasts on the prowl. Yet within the destruction lay pockets of undisturbed buildings, whether only a pair or entire city-blocks, as though the desolation dared not enter.

Dirge had seen it all, years before. "It's like the Cleansing."

"Come on," Mangin said, her voice filled with worry, "we have to get to the Citadel."

Dirge did not increase his speed, his boots crunching on the gravel at a measured pace. "We need to use caution."

Her eyes flitted about, and her feet skittered forward, then stopped like a dance. She obviously yearned to hasten ahead yet didn't want to leave Dirge's side. He wanted to tell her to go, at least part of him did.

As they turned a corner, ahead of them, a group of men wielding spears, wood-axes, and clubs stood over a bloody and broken body. With the roar of a beast, they charged Dirge and Mangin.

Stepping forward, Dirge drew his sword. "Halt!" The brands on his chest pulsed with heat and it was as though God touched him again.

The mob stopped and bowed—their backs rigid and eyes burning with a zealous fire.

"What did you just do?" Mangin asked, trembling against his back.

"I'm not sure," Dirge said.

A tall man with short-cropped, black hair stepped forward and bowed again. "We seek out the wicked, those who did evil during the time of the Depraved One. I ask you to step aside and let us dispense justice upon this woman."

Dirge kept his sword in a guard position. "Justice?"

"She is a defiler," the man said. "See how she flaunts her flesh to entice a man."

"You can't be serious?" Mangin said with a wavering voice.

"Shut your mouth, harlot!" The dark-haired man waved at those behind him. "Take her."

Dirge knew the man spoke the truth, but he held his head high. "This woman is under my protection, and you will not harm her."

The man's eyes grew hot, and his knuckles went white as he clenched his club. "I said, let us have her." He stepped forward.

"Stand down." Dirge's brands flared once again, and heat pulsed through him.

The fire in the man's eyes dissipated and his shoulders relaxed. He bowed. "As you say, so we obey." With a chopping gesture, the man turned, and the group went on their way.

"How did you do that?" Mangin asked.

Dirge knew it had something to do with his connection to the Lord, but not exactly what. "I'm not worthy of this," Dirge muttered. Memories flashed in his mind, a long list of misdeeds that damned him and stained his soul.

He dismissed them, having more important things to do than worry about the past. "Let's go. And stay close."

Mangin crept through the shadowed hallways of the Citadel, the cool air pimpling her skin. She'd not seen a single living soul thus far, neither priest nor servant who usually bustled to and fro with their busy lives. Slipping away from Dirge had been easy within the twisted halls. The problem was she felt naked without him. It churned her stomach, needing aid of any kind, let alone his. Unfortunately, with the Lord's Breath gone, she had little choice. That would change when she reached her father's office and what lay hidden there. She could go back to her old life, doing as she wished.

Turning a corner, she froze. Three bodies lie in pools of their own blood—two wearing priestly robes. She shrunk into a squat. Who had done the killings? The rampaging mob from the city? Mangin doubted it. She'd seen none of them inside. Then who? The bodies gave off the sickly-sweet stink of death, so the killing hadn't been too recent. She peered into the gloom, straining to make out potential assassins lying in wait. But the corridor ran straight with no doorways or alcoves for someone to hide in. Taking a steadying breath, she stood, keeping herself small as she crept away from the corpses. *Soon*, she reminded herself, *soon I'll be free of worry, free of doubt.*

The final corner loomed ahead, her heart fluttering, Mangin peeked around it. The door to her father's outer office was closed. Easing up, she slowly turned the handle and inched open the door. The room was empty. After closing the door behind her, she went to her father's door, but her hand hesitated on the knob.

Mangin shook her head in disgust. "Stop it. What happens happens." With a deep breath, she opened the door and peeked in. Her face went slack and her heart broke. "Father?"

Dust motes filled the room along with the stink of char. Furniture was strewn across the floor, most broken or in pieces. Her father sat behind his desk. At least, she assumed it was him. His arms lay at his side, ending in black stumps, as black as what remained of his chest. He had no head. Atop the burned desk sat the Chaos Orb, the focal point of the prison, split into two jagged pieces.

Mangin wanted to check if it was indeed her father, but her feet refused to move forward. Her heart ached, and her hands shook, but she couldn't go to him. It was as though a part of her had died. Tears streamed down her face as she turned and left her father's office and entered the hallway. She'd never felt so alone.

"I am sorry for your loss," a woman's voice said from her right.

Mangin jumped and squeaked. "Follett?"

In a long, coal-gray dress, the raven-haired former priest of Chaos stepped out of the shadows and into the lamplight. It seemed like months since Mangin had last seen her friend, when they gossiped over the latest intrigue within the Citadel. Follett had also been teaching Mangin about the world beyond the Reach, trying to prepare her the potentiality of a world without the Great Lord of Chaos. It had seemed silly to Mangin at the time. Not any longer. As hollow as Mangin felt, she knew Follett must feel the same. Yet, her friend looked so confident, as though power still coursed through her.

"All is not lost, Mangin," Follett crooned. "Your father was a great man, but the time comes when we must choose what we do next."

"What choice? What are you talking about?" Mangin didn't want to hear of choices and decisions. She had no future, and at that moment she just wanted to curl into a ball and cry.

Follett glided closer. Though of only medium height, the former priestess seemed to loom. "We all have a choice, my dear." Follett's voice droned and her dark-brown eyes seemed to pulse. "All you need do is embrace the future, embrace what is already in your heart."

As Follett reached out, her mouth opening, Mangin sagged. Life made no sense; it was a worthless shade of its former glory. Why should she care what happens next? But Follett was so beautiful, full of strength, vitality, and power. Perhaps the woman did have something for her?

Follett stopped, her eyes going wide. She spun and darted down the hallway, disappearing in the shadows.

"I told you to stay close to me," Dirge said behind Mangin.

She jumped with her heart in her throat. "Don't sneak up on me like that." Dazed, her head felt thick as though she were drunk.

"Who was the woman?" he asked.

She tugged at her blouse. "She's … no one. Someone who

doesn't matter anymore."

"Do not trust her." His voice was like a stone. "She has a darkness in her as black as the abyss."

"How do you know?"

"I saw it, a shadow encompassing her like a shroud of evil." He started to put a hand on her shoulder but pulled it back as though she were covered with sewage. "Come, we must be going. This place is not safe."

She turned and followed, not caring where they went, but a stubbornness yanked her out of her doldrums. "I want to go to my rooms first to get a change of clothes."

"Yes, that would be best. You need something more ..." his gaze traveled down her body, pausing at her chest, then quickly averted, "more modest."

Chapter 2

The Magnus

Dirge watched over the red-haired woman as she rummaged through bureaus and dressers, pulling out dresses, blouses, and boots, adding them to a trunk containing books of all things. The new outfit she wore was far better than her previous, which exposed her to mid-chest and showed far too much leg. The problem was, her new sky-blue dress—though covering from neck to ankle—was so tight it left little to the imagination. He tore his eyes away from her posterior as she bent to rearrange the trunk.

"You've no porters, and I'm not about to carry your bags, so take only what is necessary and appropriate," Dirge said with a scowl.

"It's all necessary." She glanced back, a smile playing on her lips. "As for appropriate … Do you not like this one?" Her smile faded, and she stood as uniform marching echoed down the hall. She fidgeted as the footfalls grew closer.

A man turned the corner, head held high in a black surcoat over shining steel armor, with a red Star of Ukase outlined in white below his left shoulder. Ten men in matching armor followed him in tight two-by-two formation. Stopping just short of Dirge, the man put a fist to his chest, and bowed to Dirge. "Righteous Warrior Tegan, at your service, Righteous Captain Dirge."

Dirge turned slightly. He'd never seen the newcomer before, but something told Dirge he could trust him. "How do you know my name?"

Tegan laughed. "You are a legend, sir. I don't believe there is a man in all the Righteous Legion who doesn't know who you are." Clearing his throat, he stood tall, and his face turned stoic. "The Magnus has summoned you, Righteous Captain Dirge, and it is my honor to escort you to him."

"Who is the Magnus?"

Tegan turned sideways and extended an arm down the hallway. With a uniform snap of boots, his men stepped aside, giving room. "The Magnus will explain everything you need to know."

When Mangin approached and grasped Dirge's arm in trembling hands, he turned to her. "Everything will be all right. Just stay here until—"

Tegan interrupted, "Your woman is to come with us, Righteous Captain Dirge." The corners of the man's eyes tightened when he looked at Mangin.

Dirge patted Mangin's hand. "Stay close to me." When she opened her mouth to speak, he forestalled her. "Best to not say anything. Just walk behind me, do as you're told, and speak only when addressed."

Her eyes hardened and back stiffened, but then she wilted with a nod.

One of the guards sprinted ahead of them and quickly cut of sight as Dirge marched down the hall, uncertainty gnawing at his gut, but so did a sense of premonition, of destiny. His life was about to change forever.

At Dirge's side, Tegan pointed the way with the rest of the men behind Mangin. Dirge did his best to think of the men as an escort, and not a guard. *Who's this Magnus, another Prophet like the one from my youth?* Considering how that turned out, Dirge was not optimistic. But then, Ukase had returned, of that he'd no doubt. Could the Lord see into his heart, see the debauchery he'd sown after the Prophet's army fell in the battle that cost him Lynette? Or worse yet, could the Lord God Ukase see Dirge's devotion to a woman who was now a god herself?

He cursed himself, trying to quell his doubt. After all, he wasn't devoted to Daylin. He just made a promise to her. And when one made a vow, it must be followed through. No matter the consequences. The realization put him at ease, for some reason. His mind, heart, and spirit were aligned. Like they had been all those years ago when he pledged himself to Ukase.

After countless turns, they approached a set of open, dark-wood doors at the end of a long hall. A line of men filed out, their arms filled with books and scrolls. Upon passing through the doors, Mangin gasped. The three-story tall, six-sided room was the size of a city's central square. Bookcases, stretching to the ceiling, filled the space. The room was a buzz of activity, with men scrambling up and down ladders, pulling out books and scrolls, and taking them out through doors at each wall. A circular room lay at the center of the library with a set of ivory-white doors guarded by over a dozen men.

Mangin asked what they were doing with the books, but was ignored. She huffed, frustration tugging at the corner of her eyes.

Dirge spoke up to keep Mangin from bursting, "Where are the men taking the books?"

"They're filled with blasphemy," Tegan said, "so we're burning them. We shall create a fire so bright it will lighten the world with the glory of God."

Mangin's jaw dropped, her eyes flashing with rage, but then her face grew worried. When he asked her what was wrong, she shook her head, seeming to look inward as she chewed on her lower lip.

Shrugging, Dirge turned back to the doors in front of them. His future was beyond those doors, a glorious life filled with virtue and glory, one of confirmation that he'd been right from the start. He thought of all the people who doubted him and the righteousness of God. He then frowned, because he also might end up with his head upon a pike for his own blasphemies during the long days he was lost. God told him he'd much work to do.

But what if he was wrong, what if it wasn't Ukase, and instead some old trickster god he'd heard?

His past failures and crimes flashed through his head. The deaths of his wife and his comrades during his failed war against Chaos … The prostitute he beheaded. Granted, she'd been sent by Kellen to kill him, but he took her life instead of simply disarming her. The look in Jacob's eyes after Dirge stabbed him in the back … The drug-fueled night of debauchery. The last one struck him the worst. He'd been enchanted by a priestess of Chaos. Dahlia still haunted his nightmares: her bright green eyes, the taste of her lips, the feel of her silken skin beneath his calloused hands, her golden hair sparkling in the lamplight as she rode him. He hated himself for succumbing to Dahlia's bewitchment, but even more so, because he enjoyed every moment. So, the closer to the door he went, his foreboding rose, heart thudding like a giant's footsteps leading to his doom.

No. It *was* Ukase who spoke to him. The new warmth suffusing his soul confirmed it. But that didn't mean his soul wasn't damned by his past deeds. *And if that's what Ukase demands, then so be it.*

The dozen men guarding the door—in gleaming plate armor, with snow-white surcoats and cloaks trimmed with black and red piping—snapped their heels and saluted with fists to chest. Tegan bowed and saluted the guard-captain, a man with golden, seven-pointed stars on each shoulder. "I bring Righteous Captain Dirge to the Magnus," Tegan intoned.

The guard-captain nodded and returned the salute. "He is expected. He is to enter at once, but the woman is to stay."

Mangin let out a small squeak as the doors opened and Dirge followed Tegan into the circular room. The doors closed behind them with a soft boom that echoed in the small, nearly empty room. However, Dirge didn't hear it. He'd stopped dead, his jaw falling open.

Behind a large, oak desk sat a man in pure-white robes trimmed with black and red. Light from a glass-domed ceiling bathed the man, making him almost glow. A tall, elm-leaf shaped hat topped his gray-haired head.

Dirge was at a loss for words. The last time he saw the man's hair it had been brown. The eyes were the same though: strong and determined, yet filled with caring and love.

Just like Lynette's.

"Mister Malik?" Dirge locked his knees to keep them from collapsing in shock.

Duncan Malik, radiating righteous might and authority, rose and approached with his arms out. He clasped Dirge on the shoulder. "Hello, son. It's so good to see you."

Dirge's mind swam and the ground seemed to tilt. "How ..." He faltered. Duncan Malik, the father of his late wife, had died when the minions of Chaos destroyed the city of Tuilar twenty years before.

Duncan smiled. "How am I here? We are here at the behest of the Prophet. Before you left Tuilar on your holy quest with the Army of God, The Prophet told me to gather the family, the remaining Rods of Order, and select members of the revolution. He bade us go north with all stealth and set up the sanctum here in Gate Hall, right beneath the nose of the enemy, and await the fall of Chaos." He let loose a laugh. "I must confess, I did not expect it to take this long to come to fruition."

Dirge shook his head. "The Prophet? Mister Malik—"

Duncan interrupted, "Magnus, my son. You must refer to me as Magnus from now on. I am the head of The Righteous Truth of Ukase, and the voice of God in the mortal world. He tells me what needs be done."

Shocked, Dirge knelt and bowed his head. "I apologize, your eminence."

Placing a hand on Dirge's head, the Magnus intoned, "Rise, my son. Again, it's good to see you. Elli with be thrilled to see you."

Dirge's heart sank as realization struck. "It will be good to see her as well." If the Magnus' wife still lived, then it meant the rest of the Malik household came as well. He recalled the last conversation he had with the now Magnus. The man begged him to allow Lynette to stay behind in the city when Dirge went on his crusade. That meant if Dirge had acquiesced ...

Lynette's last words to Dirge echoed in his mind: "*Until tonight.*"

His stomach clenched and he shook, tears flooding his eyes. "She'd be alive if not for me."

"No, my son." The Magnus clasped Dirge's shoulder again. "It was God's will."

Lips trembling, Dirge squeezed his eyes shut. "Then why not let her stay behind in the city?" A rage started to boil in his gut. "Why make her come along at all? She would be here now, alive if not for that!"

"Dirge," the Magnus snapped. "Calm yourself. You cannot know the mind of the Lord. Moreover, it is not your *place* to question him. Do you hear me?"

Taking hold of himself, Dirge stood tall, his face like stone. "Yes, Magnus." Yet, deep down, he still flayed himself. Lynette was dead, and it was his fault.

"Good," the Magnus said. "You must not blame yourself. You could not have done what was necessary, otherwise. You would have sought her out, to protect her. You know this. Now, what happened in the Lands of the Dead, how did you end Chaos?"

"I didn't," Dirge said. "That was done by a god."

He told the Magnus everything that seemed pertinent: the chaos paladin Hogar killing Ellis and Betal, Betal coming back to life and revealing he was actually an ancient god named Gabriel, the Arbiter of a council of gods in Taneer, and of Gabriel ending the reign of Chaos.

Smiling, the Magnus shook his head. "Remarkable. You have been far and seen much, my son. You were with a woman when Righteous Warrior Tegan found you. Was she with you the entire time?"

"Yes, your eminence," Dirge said.

The Magnus nodded to Tegan. "Have her brought in. And, Righteous Warrior Tegan, be gentle with her."

The man returned with Mangin in tow. Behind them was a tall, slim woman of middling years in pure white robes. She looked vaguely familiar, something about her black and white hair in a tight bun. Next to her was a young man in a black surcoat with a red Star of Ukase, outlined in white over a vest of chainmail. He had short-cropped, black hair, and blue eyes that held a zeal Dirge found unnerving as the young man rocked back and forth on his toes as though ready to leap.

Mangin stopped next to Dirge, her back stiff, and head held high, with a stoic expression as though she were the one about to pass judgment. But Dirge saw the fear in the corner of her eyes, a tightness that came into being since she lost her power. Dirge admired her sprit. Where most would be a blubbering pile, Mangin faced what was about to come head-on.

Scowling, he stomped down the feeling down. She was a monster, with a past so vile to be beyond redeeming. How many minds had she bewitched? How many lives had she taken? How many others had she ensnared into her bed, like she had Daylin? Mangin did not deserve his respect.

"What is your name, child?" the Magnus asked her.

"Mangin Karados."

Tegan grabbed her by the shoulder and shoved her to the floor. "Show the Magnus respect, you miserable—"

The Magnus held up his hand. "That's enough, Righteous Warrior Tegan. I said to be gentle with her. Until the time is appropriate for her to be handed over to the Seekers and put to the question or to the Immaculates for correction, you will show her a modicum of dignity."

He then turned to Mangin. "You will forgive Righteous Warrior Tegan for his vehemence. The time of reclamation is early, and he is adamant to see the guilty punished." He cocked an eyebrow. "This is strange. You are Mangin Karados, the daughter of Gunther Karados, am I right?"

"Yes," she said.

Tegan drew back an arm to slap her, but the Magnus lifted a hand to stop him. The red-haired woman had shied away from the oncoming blow, but only in the slightest, and again Dirge had to quell his respect for her.

"You will show me respect," the Magnus said, "and call me by my title or I will be forced to let Righteous Warrior Tegan teach you deference." Pursing his lips, he tilted his head. "What I don't understand is if you are who you say, then why do I see no guilt in you? Your crimes are nearly beyond counting, yet you are clean in the vision bestowed upon me by the Lord."

Dirge spoke up, "Your eminence, she was pardoned by Gabriel, the Arbiter. He said though her crimes were against Ukase, they were done during the time of Chaos, and were not crimes in the eyes of the other gods."

The Magnus nodded. "Fascinating. Every word of that is true. We have two things coinciding yet diametric: she is not guilty, yet she is. I then must decree that by her being innocent in my eyes she is also innocent in the eyes of God."

"How can that be, your eminence?" Tegan asked. "She's a priest. And look how she flaunts herself."

"Because," the Magnus said, "the Arbiter absolved her of her crimes. And as Ukase is below the Mother and the Council of Taneer, He abides by their decision. As for her garments, she will need something more fitting." He then gestured to the woman in the salt and pepper bun. "Immaculate Clara, along with my wife's servants, will aid the young woman with this."

The hard-faced woman curtsied. "I will see to it at once."

Dirge watched the woman exit. There was something about the Immaculate—her looks and voice—that make Dirge think he should know her.

The Magnus turned to Mangin. "The world has changed, my child. You will need to dress more appropriately and adhere to the Laws of God. You will find your life onerous, I'm sure, but if you stay true in the eyes of God, you will flourish."

Mangin lowered her head, her eyes wet.

"Dirge will look after you." The Magnus' eyes were warm and welcoming. "He's a good lad, the best I've ever known; there's nothing he can't do. So, you needn't worry."

A hint of a smile played on Mangin's lips when she glanced at Dirge out of the corner of her eye. "Yes, your ... eminence. He is indeed a marvel."

Magnus Malik then turned back to Dirge. "As a Righteous Captain, you normally would be placed at the head of a squad of Righteous Warriors, but I know your road has been an arduous one. We here have been training and preparing for twenty years, whereas you have been languishing, lost in a world ripe with Chaos. You will need time to get acclimated. If you wish to retire, I will grant it to you. In the meantime, you will require a squire."

He pointed to the young man in chainmail. "This is Estonia. He grew up in the clergy, but now that he's old enough, I believe he will make a fine Righteous Warrior one day." The Magnus glanced at the young man and grinned. "He's a fine one with books, but he's too wild. He's heard all the stories of *Dirge the Magnificent* and has it in his head to be just like you."

Dirge shook his head. "The *Magnificent*?"

"Yes, Dirge. You are a hero. Our members talked to the Travelers you were with. Now I know some," he pointed to

Tegan, "think all Travelers are spawns of Chaos. But just because Edis favored them, does not necessarily make them damned ... these especially. I met several. They possessed a great will and strength. Some even spoke of your Ellis, and how he was meant to end Chaos. I saw your influence in them."

Realization dawned on Dirge. "Your eminence, are you saying you knew I was here in the city? Why didn't you come to me then?"

"I didn't dare approach you for fear of interfering in God's plan. I could not hear His voice then, as I do now, so I went on instinct. I'm glad I was right.

The Magnus paused. "One thing more. You will need a last name, as all Godly men do. What would you like your last name to be?"

A mixture of loss and love filled Dirge. "Your eminence, if I am not overstepping my bounds, I would consider it an honor to take yours—to honor Lynette."

A warm smile spread across the Magnus' face. "The moment you married my daughter, you became like a son to me. It would be my honor to name you Dirge Malik. I will let it be known to the Grand-Consul Donavan, and he will pass it on to Veridical Barnhold in Cross corners."

"*Veridical*, Magnus?"

"Yes, they are the shepherds to the people, overseeing their day-to-day lives. Estonia will fill you in on the hierarchy of the True of Ukase."

The Magnus then bid him good day, and Dirge left with Mangin and Estonia on either side, a pace behind.

Dirge's mind whirled and the back of his neck itched as though he had a target on it. Stopping, he spun on the other two. The young man stared at him with reverence, whereas Mangin held her old sly smile.

"What?" Dirge asked.

"Let us head back to my room," Mangin said. "Now that we have a porter, I can get all my books and we can head out." Her smile deepened. "Unless you want to rest up there first? The bed is quite comfortable."

"Hold your tongue, woman," Estonia barked.

She flashed the young man a wicked grin. "Actually, my tongue is quite talented. It would be a waste for it to be idle."

Estonia drew his arm back to strike Mangin, but Dirge grabbed it. "Don't ever let me see you raise a hand to a woman again. You get me? They are to be treated with respect and care. I don't know what they've been teaching you, but you never strike a woman." He then turned to Mangin. "And you, stop it. Don't think I won't take you over my knee and paddle you."

Mangin's eyes went wide and a full smile bloomed on her face. "Is that a promise?" Her smile slipped, and her eyes grew concerned. "You're right. I'm sorry. I just want to get out of here. I do hope you aren't planning on staying long."

Dirge's mind went back to Magnus Malik, and Lynette's words once again drifted though his head: "*Until tonight.*"

He shook his head. "No, I've no desire to stay here. We'll get your things and go." He paused. "The only question is, where?"

Mangin smiled once more. "May I make a suggestion?"

Durgian

Tresenda Forest

Empire

Gate Hall

Kirks Knob

Timsdale

The Westlands

Fars Glen

Cross Corners

Cool Winds

Talendor Mtn

The Great Waste

The Reach

Kindermark

The Cunning River

The Searing Sands

Chapter 3

Going Home

Trees and hills rolled by the carriage window, the smell of the river having faded long ago. Mangin suppressed a sigh as she fidgeted with the long sleeves of her full-length, black dress. Her four other dresses were in the trunk at the back of the open-front carriage, each as dark and drab as the one she wore. When they arrived at her rooms, half-a-dozen women already occupied it. Her clothes were long gone, along with half her books, with the rest in the process of being carted away, until Dirge stopped them. She owed him for that. Without those books, she'd be truly lost. Not that she wasn't already. With each passing day, she missed the Lord's Breath more and more, the raw brutality and mischievous twisting as you forced it to do as you wished gone now. She never felt more barren. She also owed Dirge for agreeing to go to Cool Winds and check on Adel. Mangin didn't trust those village idiots, especially now with Chaos gone. They were likely to try something stupid—or worse yet, violent, like those at Cross Corners and Gate Hall.

Thinking of the Corners, she tugged her cowl up farther, lest a potential passerby recognize her. Their stay had been brief but it was too long as far as Mangin was concerned. The destruction wasn't as rampant as in Gate Hall, but bodies still littered the streets, many wearing multi-hued robes.

"How much longer until we get there?" the squire asked from the driver's seat ahead of her. His horse clopped behind them, tethered to the back.

Clicking her tongue, Mangin turned back to the window. By her estimate, they'd reach Cool Winds that day, but she wasn't about to tell him. The boy was a nuisance, but more than that, he was a sycophant, fawning after Dirge like a puppy.

"I asked how much longer, woman."

Mangin ground her teeth and continued to ignore him. Oh, how she wanted to take his mind and teach him some proper manners.

Estonia's leather armor beneath his surcoat creaked as he turned—the red, seven-pointed star of Ukase outlined in white at its center, seeming to mock her. "By Ukase, you had better answer me—"

"Enough, Estonia!" Dirge rode up next to the carriage, his steel-plate armor jingling, and shining through the gaps of his surcoat. "You will start treating her with the respect due a woman, or I'll have you digging holes and refilling them from sunup 'til sundown."

"But I was just trying to find out—"

Dirge held up a gauntleted hand, cutting the boy off. "We will get there, when we get there, and not a moment before." He turned to Mangin. "We must all learn to get along."

"I've said nothing to him since this morning," Mangin replied.

Dirge scoffed. "Your silence is often as contentious as your words."

She smiled and looked him up and down, enjoying his regal visage. "What can I say, I like getting a rise out of people."

Dirge ignored her taunt. "Will we need to find a place to set up camp before dark?"

"We're not far now. I'm looking forward to sleeping in a bed." Mangin had spent enough nights on that stiff cot to last her a lifetime. But in truth, she looked forward to more than a bed. Adel was in Cool Winds, and Mangin ached to see her beautiful face, to hold her lithe form once again.

She chewed her lip with worry while thinking of their parting—she treated Adel harshly. Straightening, she smoothed her dress. *Adel has seen through that by now*, she thought. *She's realized I was only trying to protect her from those in Gate Hall—as well as cretins like Cobb and his associates.*

As least that's what Mangin hoped. All the time she spent teaching Adel to read by tuning her mind, Mangin had also been accentuating her intellect. The last knowledge bundle Mangin had placed boosted Adel's cognitive ability. *Hells, she's probably running that flyspeck of a town by now.* Adel belonged to her. She was Mangin's beloved, a gleaming light in the darkness of Mangin's heart. And nothing would keep them apart.

They cleared the forest, and Estonia pulled the carriage to a stop, pointing ahead. "Is that normal?"

Mangin peered past the young man and her heart clenched. She put a trembling hand to her mouth. "No, no it's not."

Twenty pikes lined the street into town, and upon each was a head, fresh blood seeping down the shafts. Stomach churning, Mangin swallowed bile so as not to throw up as she searched the faces, but Adel was not among them. Fear and worry clutched her throat as she whispered, "You fools. What have you done?"

"This was done recently," Dirge said. "I recognize the one on the left. Adam Killington, am I right? He was in your party when we met on the road."

She nodded.

"If I recall, he was close to Betal." Dirge snarled. "Do you know the others, were they friends of yours?"

"My only friend here was Betal," Mangin croaked. "But yes, I've known these people most of my life. Each man and woman up there were friends and backers of John Simmons."

"Who is John Simmons?"

She pointed. "The first on the right; he was Town Master." She then turned to Dirge. "He was Betal's adoptive father."

Dirge's eyes burned in anger, but his voice remained even when he stated, "We shall investigate." He urged his horse forward down the lane and through the open gate.

Estonia flicked the horse's reins to follow. "You'd best stay quiet and hidden. Something tells me you'll not get a good reception here."

Sinking back into the seat, she clutched herself as they passed Simmons. His eyes were vacant, but to Mangin they stared at her with a mixture of sorrow and blame.

As they entered town though, she couldn't help leaning forward to peer out the windows. She had to find Adel, yet part of her feared she would. "What am I worrying for? She has Worm to protect her, after all," she murmured.

They thought she returned her former slave, Worm, back to his old self when she left Gate Hall with Betal. But that was impossible. She was thorough in his conditioning and control. Her entire time with Cobb, she sifted his memories—as well as those of his friends—to build a replica of the man Worm was before, Jason. He would act and talk Jason, but deep down the man was still Worm, and her final command to him had been to protect Adel at all costs.

They rolled up to the Village Green where a large fire roared. People streamed in and out of the temple, those coming out held books and scrolls, which they then tossed into the pyre.

"Ignorance begets ignorance," Mangin muttered. During the reign of Chaos, reading was discouraged, because illiterate people were easier to control. Like the fools at Gate Hall, they willfully destroyed knowledge in the name of purging the past.

When Dirge pulled up his horse halfway to the temple, five men approached, each wearing leather armor, and four held spears at the ready. Their leader, Erin Cruchfield, rested his hand on the pommel of his sword while holding up the other. "What business have you here?"

Mangin pulled back farther, surprised Erin's son, Cobb, wasn't with him. "Where is that boy?" she whispered.

Dirge straightened in the saddle, putting his head forward. "I seek the man who now calls himself Village Master."

"That would be me," Cruchfield replied, holding his head higher. "What do you want?"

Dirge dismounted and approached Cruchfield in a smooth, deadly pace. The four spearmen readied their weapons and took up a defensive stance, while Cruchfield simply tried to make himself seem taller. The rest of the village now took notice and crept closer. But not too close.

Dirge removed his full-helm. "What is the meaning of the display on the road?"

"Because Chaos is over," Gordon, the blacksmith shouted, jabbing his hammer in Dirge's direction.

Cruchfield's eyes went wide. "Dirge. I didn't recognize you. Yes, we got word a couple of days ago that Chaos' reign of terror is done."

"So, you killed those people," Dirge said, his voice low yet sharp. "Where they priests or creatures of Chaos?"

"We did to them that had it coming," Gordon shouted again

Dirge asked again, harder, "Were they priests, or ardent followers of Chaos?"

"They were under the sway of the Beast," Cruchfield said. "All of them, ardent followers and backers of Betal. He was a monster. You of all people know that."

Cable, one of the herdsmen, inched closer to the carriage. Mangin tried to shrink from his sight, but the man still saw her. "It's the red-haired witch," he shouted. "It's Mangin!" He turned on Dirge. "You're in league with her!" He stabbed at Dirge with his spear.

Dirge drew his sword in a blur, knocking the spear aside and stabbing Cable's shoulder. The man fell to the ground yelping and grabbing the wound. Dirge took half a step back and pointed his now bloodstained sword at the villagers. "If any of you lay a hand on her, I will remove it."

Cruchfield drew his sword and took a step back, in a defensive posture. Mangin couldn't help but respect the man for holding his ground. The others, on the other hand, took several steps back, half of them running away.

A man Mangin didn't recognize sprinted up through the crowd, waving his hands. "Stop, you fools, stop! He is a man of Ukase! Look at the symbol on his coat. That is the Star of Order, the sign of God." Panting, he stopped next to Cruchfield and fished out a wooden, seven-pointed star from around his neck He held it up to Dirge. "See! We are all men of God, worshipers of Ukase. We did not mean to insult you." He took a step forward, his eyes filled with zeal. "I am Lermin, up from Cross Corners. Are you here to cleanse our spirit in the light of God, to lead us in all his glory?"

"I have come here to see a woman named Adel Floweret,"

Dirge said.

Lermin's head bobbed up and down. "Yes, the one they have locked away in the cursed temple. She lay with the witch." He pointed at Mangin, and then turned to the villagers. "You see? I told you to kill those two as well. They were tainted. A Seeker is sure to come and put her to the question, but you no longer need wait. Here is a Warrior of the Righteous. Our secret Veridical at the Corners told us about them, the Warriors. They are the Righteous Hand of God."

Cruchfield lowered his sword. "Is what he says true? If so, then why does the witch still live?"

Estonia spoke up, "This is Righteous Captain Dirge, the first to know the touch of God from the time long before the fall of Chaos. It is he who led the army of God in the South. It is he who went into the Lands of the Dead to end Chaos. It is he who—"

Dirge held up a hand. "Estonia, stop. That's enough." He then focused on Cruchfield. "The Magnus absolved Mangin of her past crimes. She is clean in the eyes of God. By my authority, you will take us to Miss Floweret." He stepped forward. "Now."

Every man stopped their fidgeting and stood at attention, their eyes growing sharp. Even the air seemed to grow still, yet held a crackle as though lightning were about to strike.

"This doesn't look good," Mangin said. But, to her amazement, they all bowed in unison.

"Yes, Righteous Captain," Cruchfield said. "This way." He pointed toward the temple doors.

Dirge waved behind him. "Estonia, bring her." He turned his head. "Respectfully."

"Come along, miss," the squire said, his voice holding only the slightest bit of conceit. "Let's not keep him waiting."

Mangin exited the carriage, her head down, and followed Estonia and Dirge, as Cruchfield led them into the former temple. Mangin's unprotected back itched, awaiting an arrow from one of the villagers, but it didn't come. The men remained where they were, as though rooted in place.

Light streamed through broken windows in the worship-hall, illuminating broken benches, the shattered alter, and pools of blood. They traversed the hallways to the kitchen and then down into the cellar. The cramped stairs, along with the smell of mold, left Mangin a little claustrophobic. She'd never been in the cellar before. Why would she? The close confines and the stink left her feeling soiled.

At the end of a short hall, a man stood next to a barred door with only a single lamp illuminating the area. It took a moment for Mangin to recognize Cobb under the battered and rusted helm.

"Father," Cobb said. "Does this mean you're finally taking me off guard duty? I swear, I'm starting to feel like a prisoner my—" His eyes went wide as he spotted Mangin in the back "You filthy bitch! I'll kill you!" He started to draw his sword.

Erin grabbed Cobb's arm and slammed the blade back into its sheath. "Shut up! You'll do no such thing." He indicated behind him and introduced Dirge. "He is a Righteous man of God, here to see Adel."

"But, what is that witch doing here?" Cobb asked, his mouth hanging open.

"The Magnus, the very Voice of God, has absolved Mangin of her crimes," the elder Cruchfield said.

Cobb shook his head. "But … how? She is vile—a stinking whore of Chaos!"

"Your place is not to question the word of God," Estonia said.

"I will explain everything when we leave," Dirge said. "Now, the two of you, go. I would have words with Miss Floweret in private."

"What about Jason?" Cobb asked.

When Dirge turned to Mangin with a raised eyebrow, she said, "Yes, we should see Jason as well."

Cobb snarled. "You're taking orders from this demon? He's under her control, Father," he said as his hand went to his sword again.

Stepping forward, Dirge smacked Cobb across the face and drew the boy's sword, handing it to Estonia without looking. "Hold this. He gets it back when we leave." Dirge then pointed at the two Cruchfields. "Out, both of you."

Their eyes both went sharp. With a salute—clutched fist to chest—they marched out of the basement.

"That's the second time you've done that," Mangin said.

"How do you do that … make people do exactly what you say?"

Dirge raised an eyebrow. "I honestly don't know."

Estonia smiled. "It is the Word of Will, a power handed down to you from God—through the Magnus, and then through our superiors in the Militant Sect. All Men of God have their powers thusly." When Dirge raised an eyebrow, Estonia continued, "I'm to instruct you in all the ways of the Lord. That's why the Magnus picked me, with my initial scholarly training."

Dirge grunted and seemed to look inward. "Strange. I never noticed those powers before." He closed his eyes and concentrated, then opened then, looking confused. "I can't speak to the Magnus with my thoughts like I could the Prophet. Why is that?"

"That was something only instilled through the Prophet. As to why? It is one of the many glorious mysteries of God."

Mangin wanted to scream. She wanted to dash past the two of them and throw open the door, but part of her was afraid at what she'd find. "Can we—" Her voice faltered. "Can we talk about this later? They might change their mind and come back with more."

Estonia narrowed his eyes. "You doubt the power of God?"

"Enough," Dirge said. He threw back the deadbolt and opened the door. The inside was black. Grabbing the wall lamp, Dirge strode in with Mangin close on his heels.

Chapter 4

In the far corner of the cellar, Jason stood in front of sacks of grain, his fists raised and eyes keen. His shirt and pants were bloody and torn in several places. He had a black eye, scabs at his lips, and a broken nose. "Stay back. You'll not have her."

Adel peeked around his legs, her blonde hair in disarray and covered in dirt, but she appeared unharmed. "Who are you?" she asked. "Are you here to kill us like they said?"

Mangin sped across the room. Jason stepped aside as she fell to her knees in front of Adel. "Oh, thank the Lord you're alive." When she reached for Adel, the girl drew back. Tears filled Mangin's eyes. "I'm sorry for what I said. I didn't mean it. You know that."

Adel stared at Mangin, her eyes keen and attentive. "No," she whispered. "Not here, not where they can see or hear." Her lips trembled. "Perhaps never again. Not if we want to live."

Standing, Adel walked around Mangin, making sure not to make contact, and addressed Dirge, "I ask again, what would you have of us? We are true to the Lord Ukase. What she did to us was not of our accord. She bewitched us. But with Chaos gone, so is her touch. I beg you, please, let us go."

Dirge paused a moment. "We will get your things, and I'll escort you both out."

"We have nothing," she replied. "They burned it all before throwing us down here. Poor Jason." She grabbed his hand when he came abreast with her. "They beat him terribly when he tried to protect me. Can he come as well?"

"Of course." Dirge stepped aside. "Estonia, lead the way. If anyone tries to bar the way, hold them until I deal with them."

With a salute, the squire drew his sword and marched out of the room. Adel followed him out without looking back. Mangin's heart crumpled. Jason, on the other hand, paused, glancing at Mangin.

"You've done well," she whispered.

The young man went sharp. With the slightest nod, he turned and hastened after Adel.

Dirge strode up to Mangin. "What was that about?"

She wiped her eyes. "What? I just wanted to thank him for keeping our friend safe."

The hard, dark warrior stared at her, his eyes seeming to pierce her soul. "He's still your creature, isn't he?"

"I don't know what you're talking about." She held out a hand. "Would you please help me up? I'd like to get out of this filth."

Dirge clasped her hand and helped her up. "You will listen to me," he said. "No more lies. One of my gifts from God is the ability to see the guilty. Lies are a sin, and any Man of God can see that guilt. Do you understand? I cannot protect you if you don't protect yourself. Silence is better than a lie."

Mangin's stomach clenched. "What about Adel?"

"What she said was true ... all except the part of your touch no longer being on her." He scowled. "I don't know what you did, but she is a pure soul. And I've seen far too many good people die for what amounts to nothing. But when the Seekers get here?" Dirge shook his head. "I talked to some of them in Gate Hall before we left. They won't be as forgiving."

Tears streamed down Mangin's face again and she trembled. "Is there anything you could do? I already owe you, but I'd do anything for this. I'd ... I'd die if anything happened to her."

Dirge's eyes softened a brief moment, and then turned hard once more. "I will take care of it." Turning, he muttered as he left, "The things I do for her."

Mangin hurried after him, scrubbing away her tears with her sleeve. The others awaited them at the top of the stairs, with no locals in sight. They exited the temple, where it looked like the entire village awaited them.

Dirge pointed at the carriage. "You will both have to ride inside. It will be a bit of a tight fit for the two of you, I am sorry, but I'll not risk you out in the open." He pointed to Jason. "You will drive. Estonia will ride on the other side."

As the young squire trotted to his horse and untied it from the back of the carriage, Dirge turned to the gathered crowd. "I am taking them with me."

Lermin stepped forward and bowed. "Are you taking them to be cleansed?"

"Don't ever use that term!" Dirge trembled, eyeing the villagers. "Have you so easily forgotten that name? It was an atrocity."

"We have not forgotten," the elder Cruchfield said. "We could never forget what was done in the name of the Beast." He stabbed a finger toward the village gate. "Unlike them. They accepted that monster as one of us. Well, the time came, and they paid for it."

"You killed your Village Master," Dirge said, "people you knew for decades."

"We did as the Lord would have wanted," Lermin said.

"John was my friend." Erin Cruchfield crossed his arms, his head high. "But time and again, he protected the Beast, Betal. He needed to pay. I saw the hate in your eyes when he took up with the young woman in your troupe. Do not deny it."

"I do not deny it," Dirge said, "to my everlasting shame. And it will haunt me forever."

Erin looked perplexed. "What are you talking about, man?"

Dirge looked to the ground. "Do you want the truth?"

"Of course!"

"It will burn you," Dirge sneered. "I went into the Lands of the Dead with Ellis and Daylin. Our plan was to lure Betal there and kill him. But it was there that I learned the truth. Betal was not a beast of Chaos. He was a god—*is* a god."

"Chaos, incarnate," Lermin said, trembling.

Dirge shook his head. "No. He was not Chaos. He *ended* Chaos."

The people murmured and shuffled as Dirge continued, "His real name is Gabriel, sent by the Council of God to end the reign of Chaos. He is a god higher than even Ukase, for the Lord bows to the will of the Council. Gabriel is older than time itself. He is the first born of the True Tree, Mother's first child in the multiverse." He stared at them all, one by one, letting it sink in. "And you killed the man who he saw as a father."

Fear filled their eyes and some wept openly.

Dirge mounted. "I would pity you." He spun his horse and rode to the gate. "But you do not deserve it."

Estonia booted his horse forward. "*Revenge is mine,* says the Lord. *For a crime upon my people is a crime upon me. Praised is he who strikes down the wicked in my name, for those who do not obey my word are below my sight and shall be punished accordingly.*" He pointed a finger at them. "*But he who strikes down the just, the innocent, or the true in my name, he shall know my vengeance tenfold, for he is damned and death eternal awaits him.* Lo, but this is a village of the damned, for you did slay the innocent. In due time, a Seeker shall come. For the Seekers of Truth always come before one of the Lord's Veridicals, to tend his flock. The Seekers of the Lord always find the truth, and pain is their tool. Only through pain will one know purity of the Law. Prepare yourselves, for Order now rules this land. The Word of Ukase is Law, and he has no pity for those who deserve none."

Estonia motioned Jason to move out, keeping behind the carriage as they left the stunned village behind.

They made camp that night, with Adel taking Estonia's tent and cot—the men lay out in the open. Mangin yearned to go to her, to lie in her arms. The entire trip they sat side-by-side, Adel's body heat radiating like a furnace, her smell like flowers and musk making Mangin wet with desire. Yet they could do nothing. It was torturous.

Mangin twisted and turned all night. When she got up to relive herself, Dirge insisted on going to the forest edge with her, but kept his back turned, for "your modesty," he said. She was so aroused she almost asked him to take her, then and there. But she knew it would only cause animosity—that, and it would embarrass him. Gone were the days when she could flaunt her sexuality and take whomever she wanted to bed. When she returned to her cot, she didn't know whether to laugh or cry. She did both.

In the morning, after breaking camp, Estonia approached Dirge. "Where are we taking them?"

Dirge's gaze went to Adel and Jason, and then to Mangin. "We are taking them to Cross Corners and putting them on a ship downriver."

The squire's mouth fell open. "Out of the lands under God's sway? Our control doesn't reach far enough yet. They may well die out there."

"If they stay around here, they'll die for sure. You saw what happened in that village. Word will spread about these two, and someone, sometime will think they can judge them as minions of Chaos."

"We should take them to a Seeker ourselves," Estonia said. "Let them prove their innocence or guilt."

Mangin's hair stood up on end. She stared at Dirge, pleading with her eyes not to let that happen.

Dirge shook his head. "I'll not take the chance. Something could well happen between now and then."

The squire stepped forward. "But, sir—"

"Are you questioning me?" Dirge's voice was like iron.

Estonia shook his head. "No, sir."

Tears in her eyes, Mangin wanted to kiss Dirge. Adel would be safe, and that was the only thing that mattered. Mangin went to the carriage to await another long day of frustrated, sexual agony.

Mangin stared at the receding boat, doing her best not to cry, yet tears fell, nonetheless. Adel didn't say a word to her the entire trip, not even to say good-bye. Adel walked head high and eyes forward as Jason escorted her to the ship.

"Farewell," Mangin whispered.

Wearing a scowl, Estonia strode down the dock toward her and Dirge. "I do not envy them. It is a dangerous world down south."

"Everywhere is dangerous," she muttered.

"Where were you?" Dirge asked.

"I spotted a man on the wanted list, but he ran off into the East Warren."

Dirge grunted. "We've plenty of time for that later."

The squire saluted Dirge. "As you say, sir. What now?"

"I honestly don't know," Dirge replied.

Estonia bowed. "Then if I may make a suggestion?" When Dirge nodded, the man continued, "The Magnus said you needed to speak to Veridical Barnhold here in the Corners."

"Do you know where he is?" Dirge asked. When his esquire nodded, Dirge sighed. "Take me to him."

Dirge sat at a table of a tavern called God's Glory, with Estonia and Mangin standing behind him. Across from him, Veridical Barnhold wore the customary attire for a holy man of Ukase who oversaw a congregation: white robe, with the Star of Ukase in black, outlined in red. His graying, black hair was cut uniformly, as though a bowl was used.

"I apologize for having to meet you here," the Veridical said, "but we are not yet finished purifying the former temple to Chaos. Normally, we would simply destroy it, but like in Gate Hall, it was fortified with spells to strengthen its defenses. The Magnus decided it would be foolish not to use it ourselves. This establishment's owner swore his devotion to God the moment we arrived, as did most of those here in the Old Town quarter. The rest of the city is still in need of purifying."

Not caring about the local politics, Dirge asked, "Why did you want to meet me, Veridical?"

"Well, it's about your estates."

Dirge cocked an eyebrow. "I have no estates."

"Actually, you do." Barnhold pulled a rolled parchment from one of his satchels. "The Magnus set it up for you—to contemplate your future. It's just south of here, at the edge of the floodplain near the woods. A family has been keeping it up for you. They'll stay on and farm the land for you."

Dirge's mouth opened and closed a couple of times. "How did he even know about me … that I would even need it?" Dirge asked.

"Well, the people aren't specifically keeping it for you. But the Magnus has given you the papers to the land. Cross Corners has always been rather tidy in the ways of business and land management." The Veridical grinned. "After all, I did, and still do sit on the board of Land Management."

"What about me?" Mangin asked. "Where does that leave me?"

With a frown, The Veridical's eyebrow rose. He did not reply.

Dirge turned to her and said in a low voice, "You must watch your tongue." He turned back to the Veridical. "Is there any position for this woman under my care?"

"She is to stay on as your maid," the Veridical said

Mangin groaned, and Dirge shot her a glare.

"You don't have a wife, do you?" Barnhold asked

Dirge frowned, not likening where the conversation was going. "My wife passed quite some time ago."

"Well, the Lord says that a man must have a wife. You should take the woman as yours. She is quite comely, I must admit. And her hips were made for bearing children."

Mangin made a slight choking sound.

The Veridical continued, not seeming to notice. "What better way to protect her than to make her your wife? Provide her your home and hearth where she will raise your young. That way you could hire a proper maid who would do a much better job. After all, it has been said that pretty women often make terrible housekeepers." He grinned. "This one has fire in her eyes. She would make a good mother and strong mistress of the house. Though I think I'll have someone teach her the ways of decorum." He spread his arms. "I could wed you now, if you like?"

Dirge was at a loss for words. The very idea was abhorrent, given her past. But the Veridical was right. It may well be the best way to keep Mangin safe. "I'll think about it."

Chapter 5

Blackest Winter

Kenja Badell crouched behind a wobbly table, his right hand on the black leather dagger at his belt—it was the only weapon he had now. He stared out the window, the hanging shutters blocking part of the view of the street. His brown hair was singed and sooty, as were his tattered shirt and pants; only a great fool wore their priestly robes now. He'd been hiding from the roving mobs and warriors of the cursed god Ukase for days.

He'd fled his previous hiding spot, a cold, ground-level storeroom of an inn whose owner still believed in Chaos. It had been perfect. But then he spotted Mangin with a group headed for the river. Shocked at seeing her alive, he had gone after her. Halfway there, he realized a pair of Ukase warriors escorted her. When the younger of the two turned and went after him, he fled into the East Warren. After dodging down alleys and climbing through ruined buildings, he'd run into the back of a dozen, black-shirted men wielding makeshift weapons—Militants of

Order. He darted into the house before being spotted.

"Fool," Kenja muttered. He nearly died over a woman who no longer mattered.

He didn't love Mangin, but he'd had plans for her going back more than a decade. Kenja spent years courting her, gaining her trust before he started bedding her. He'd planned it all: bribed the herbalists and midwives to ensure she would come with child, and then once it was born, have the Brotherhood kill her so he would get control of the child. Unfortunately, she'd all but stopped coming to the Corners, having taken several lovers in Cool Winds. When word came she was being called to the Citadel, he'd grown desperate, planning on taking and drugging her until she gave him the child he wanted. But then she showed up with *him*, and he nearly shook from the cold hatred in his heart. Some whispered for years that the Beast was actually a man, but he'd laughed them off as fools.

"Betal," he growled. "I should have killed him."

"You would have died trying," someone whispered behind him.

Kenja spun, his guts icy with fear, and his jaw dropped. "Kek?"

The mousy, former priest huddled in the shadowed corner of the room, his dark clothes, hair, and complexion fading to match his surroundings. "Hello, Kenja," he whispered.

"How are you still alive?" Kenja asked. "I heard everyone in Gate Hall died."

"Not everyone," Kek said. "I donned servant's garb and blended in. I saw it all, privy to all but the most secret meetings."

His eyes went wide and he shrunk in on himself as the crunch of boots came from out front. Kenja turned back and crouched even lower, but kept an eye on the street as a contingent men marched down the street. They all wore black uniforms with a white, seven-pointed star on their chest. The man at their head made Kenja grunt. It was Devin Reich, the former Captain of the City Guard at Cross Corners.

After they passed, Kenja let out a breath. "How could Devin be with them? I've known the man for years—he's true to Chaos."

"Not anymore," Kek said, keeping his voice low. "I was there when it happened. I stowed away with some camp followers when the Magnus—their head, high priest to Ukase—sent men to secure the Corners. They had men with them, Truth-Seekers. They brought Reich to the Truth-Seeker in chains. The man touched Reich and changed him, made him see *the truth*, as they call it."

A shiver ran down Kenja's spine. "Truth-Seekers?"

Kek nodded. "They look into your mind, your soul, and decide if you are worthy."

"Worthy of what?"

"Life."

Kenja looked inward, knowing full well what would happen if a Truth-Seeker laid hands on him. "What did they do to Reich?"

"After Reich writhed and screamed for a time, the Truth-Seeker deemed him an *orderly man*, and charged him with seeking out those like us. That's when I went into hiding."

"How could this have happened?" Kenja asked, his voice raspy. "How could the Great Lord of Chaos abandon us?"

"It was bound to happen," Kek said.

"What?"

"I told you, I was there. I heard it all from a man named Dirge, a hard, dark-skinned fellow who came out of the Lands of the Dead—which now teems with life, by the way." Kek adjusted his feet, his eyes flicking toward the window. "He arrived with Mangin Karados in tow and told them Chaos was supposed to give up his hold on the world over twenty years ago."

Kenja shook his head, his mind going back to the man he spotted with Mangin. "She was with him, a man of Ukase?"

Kek nodded. "He came from the South originally; the first Warrior of the Righteous in over five-hundred years. A true man of Order."

Snarling, Kenja remembered the way Mangin looked at Dirge. "She's fucking him, I know it; all to save her skin."

"Dirge told the Magnus … well, he said many things, but chief among them was that Betal was the one who ended the reign of Chaos."

Kenja's head snapped to Kek. "What?"

"It is how I know Betal would have killed you. He was not The Hand of God. He *was* a god, the first born out of the Mother.

You see—" Kek's eyes jerked to the window as the sound of crunching boots returned in the street.

Devin Reich appeared once more at the head of a column. He stopped, put a hand to this chest, and bowed at the waist. "Righteous Warrior Fennec."

A man approached from the opposite direction, with seven men at his back. He wore a black surcoat with a red star over plate armor that shone like a mirror, and carried a long, black rod in his right hand. "What news, Head Militant-Seeker Reich?"

"This place is rife with those who worshiped Chaos," Reich said. "We have rounded up all those who came willingly, but will need to root out those hiding in the hovels."

The officer shook his head. "That is not needed. I will bless the area. Those who live through it will have the Lord Ukase in their heart."

The Warrior raised a rod. "By Ukase, I consecrate this ground in your name." The rod glowed red as though freshly plucked from the smith's fire. "Your Righteousness will be upon all those near."

He slammed it into the ground.

A blast wave hurtled in every direction, slamming into Kenja's building which promptly collapsed. The room above fell, and Kenja dove under the table as the rest of the building followed suit. But the table didn't hold. It collapsed onto Kenja, leaving him in darkness.

Kenja took a step and the ground crunched beneath his foot. His eyes snapped open. Dark rolling hills of snow and jagged mountains of ice surrounded him. There were no trees or buildings, only vast tundra stretching to the horizon. "Where am I?" His breath left a heavy white mist in the air.

The cold sank into his bones, but it didn't bother him. He relished in it. He loved how the cold bit at his skin and leached into his body. Most preferred heat, racing for a burning hearth in the dead of winter, but not Kenja—cold was when he felt most at ease. In the height of summer, he found no respite from the damnable heat.

A voice, sharp like an ice crystal, called out to him from the distance, "You need not fear, my child." A skeletal figure grew out of the snow, arctic-blue and white, with sharp points protruding from its skin as though made of ice. "I have returned. Come, embrace me, and take me into your heart. You have always been mine, my child. You know this."

The creature was right. In his heart, Kenja loved the cold. When he manipulated Chaos, he used it to chill and freeze, sometimes to lethal extremes. As he took a step forward, a black figure appeared, and clasped his hand. Pain shot through him, lancing into his soul.

Blinding light woke him. He coughed from the dust as hands pulled him from the rubble. His eyes went wide at seeing who had rescued him. "Follett Dinar? What are you doing here?"

Of only middling height, the dark-haired former priestess stood with her arms crossed in dead-black robes with the hood up, and a smile on her spotless face. "It's good to see you, Kenja. How have you been?"

"How have I been? How do you think?" He coughed again.

A woman stepped up next to Follett wearing equally black robes and scratching at a pink, four-pointed star tattoo on the inside of her left wrist. "We must be quick, Mistress. Ukase's people are everywhere."

"You look lost," Follett said.

Kenja shook his head in dismay. "I'll be fine, so long as I can kill that man Mangin brought through here. He brought this on us. I'm sure of it."

"Always the jealous one, Kenja. But, in this case, you happen to be right. You want revenge. I can help you with that." Her dark-brown eyes seemed to pulse. "You need not worry." Her voice droned, erasing thought. "You can once again know the touch of power." She moved closer, her face looming large.

Kenja couldn't move. Couldn't think. His eyes were locked on Follett as she glided up and caressed his face.

"I have a kiss for you, Kenja," she said, her voice almost sounding like a hiss. "Just a single kiss and you will know power again. And then you can have your revenge." She opened her mouth, and a tube-like tongue snaked out, the tip opening into a four-pointed star.

Kenja trembled. *Succubus*, he wanted to scream, but nothing came out but a squeak.

The tongue slithered under his neck, and then drifted behind his ear. It latched onto his skull, and his mind exploded in agony. The ecstasy of her touch set fire to his loins, while the misery of her devouring his soul sent him into a pit of despair, a blackness where nothing existed. Yet, something did dwell there, a decrepit entity, foul and wizened and crackling as though existence had rotted into a shell of nothingness. Time lost all meaning. *He* lost all meaning when the Abomination swallowed him.

A hiss brought him back to the world, the slithering voice of Follett as she caressed his cheek. "You are now sealed to our Master," she said. "Through Dekriot, you will know revenge."

"Yes, Mistress," Kenja croaked, his throat so dry he thought it had withered with his soul.

"The master has a task for you."

"Yes, Mistress."

"You are to go south," Follett said, "to the city of Kindermark. Seek out G'Klaas. He will take you into the heart of the Great Waste, to Moira who now revels in what is left of his Lord. She will not accept your aid—not the aid I want you to give, anyway." She handed him a dead-black stone. "Touch this to her crystals—you'll know which ones I mean. You will give our master the souls he demands."

Kenja smiled, once again fill with a purpose. His heart felt as though it lay at the center of the blackest winter, a place he belonged. "Yes, Mistress."

Chapter 6

Purging of the Westlands

Truth-Seeker Evram Kirkadite's hard, brown eyes surveyed the village of Rosedale, as the wind tussled his short-cropped, black hair. His uniform—tight, red pants and coat, with a white Star of Ukase outlined in black in the center—fit snug on his tan, gaunt frame. Rosedale was no different from most villages in the Westlands. Sitting atop a modest hill, its wheat, corn, and rye fields hugged the village's tall, wooden walls. Thick hedges, lined with low, stone walls, surrounded the fields, as well as their corresponding lanes to the village. Wide, but low sally gates allowed access to the fields, while still providing protection for the village.

Bells tolled as Kirkadite rode his dun up the road to the village's only external gate. Men with crossbows watched his approach from the towers on either side of the gate. Kirkadite led his squad of Militant-Seekers, along with a company of Righteous Warriors, their steel armor glinting in the sun. As the campaign was one of purification, the Seekers had the command.

Kirkadite addressed the bowmen, his voice strong and hard, "In the name of Ukase, the Lord of Order, I demand entrance. We are here to purify you in the name of Ukase and rid you of heretics."

"We've no heretics here," the left guard shouted back. "No one here worships Chaos—the world is well rid of his scourge. And we've no desire to join Ardentia, we're happy as we are. Now, if you've proper business here, we will welcome your leader and his retainers, but the rest must stay out."

Kirkadite scowled. "I will be the judge as to whether you harbor heretics. Now, open the gates or we will open them."

The left guard rang a bell next to him and shouted an alarm to those behind the wall, while the right guard hunkered down.

Kirkadite snorted. "So be it." He spun his horse and rode back down the road. Passing Righteous Warrior Kent, Kirkadite said, "Open those gates. Do whatever you need."

Kent whistled, whirling his arm over his head. Dozens of Righteous Militants in plate armor marched up the road with heavy crossbows, their boots hammering in unison. Behind them, six men in sloping, broad-brimmed helmets hefted a steel-capped battering ram. The village guards fired, but their bolts ricocheted off the Warriors' thick, steel armor. Four more bowmen joined those in the tower and fired, but the result was the same. Twenty yards from the gate, the Warriors stopped, and fired in unison, six at each tower. The bolts slammed into the villagers and punched through the thin, plank walls, sending men screaming as they fell. The ram slammed into the door and wood flew. They hammered the door again, and again, chips flying with each stroke. With a great crack, the door burst in, and the rest of the Warriors charged with swords drawn.

Kirkadite turned to Righteous Warrior Kent. "Follow me and set the Divinity Rod in the center of the Green."

He then started his horse at a walk. Screams sprang from within the village as Kirkadite passed through the gateway. Inside of the wall, bodies of men and women littered the ground, the men wearing simple leather armor. Each villager missed limbs or sported gashes in their chests and bellies. His eyes lingered on the bodies of the women. Their deaths were regrettable, but it was their own fault—they should have been in their homes.

Kirkadite approached the Righteous Militants encircling the Village Green, as they cleaned blood off their weapons. "Where are the rest?" he asked.

"Holed up in their homes," a Militant replied.

Righteous Warrior Kent marched to the center of the Green, hefting the Rod high. "In the name of Ukase!" He slammed the Rod into the earth, and a tone of perfection filled the air, a calming ring some called *The Voice of God*. A blast-wave of the might of Ukase radiated out, suffusing the village. Doors shook and dirt flew, and then all was calm.

Kirkadite turned to the Head Righteous Militant. "Drag them out."

The men hauled the villagers to the Green. Thanks to a blessing from the Lord, Kirkadite saw their crimes, of which there were many. Symbols of fornication, self-abuse, sodomy, theft, and worst of all, heresy, floated over the heads of many. One trembling young woman with long, blonde hair appeared clean, but Kirkadite wanted to be sure. The militant knelt the woman in front of Kirkadite where she sobbed.

"I am here to purify you," he said. "If you are true with God, you've nothing to fear." He grasped her by the head, sending the power of Ukase into her.

The woman's eyes rolled back into her head, and she sucked air through her teeth. She flailed her arms and shook, and foam frothed in the corners of the mouth. When Kirkadite let go, she flopped to the ground, moaning.

"You are pure, my dear. Go with the Lord." He then turned to his Truth-Seeker in training. "Pursuant, have her taken to the recovery area and bring the next. I don't have all day."

They plopped an elder man before him, and he snarled. The symbol of the god Enlil floated over the man's head—a ball of swirling winds.

Kirkadite scowled. "There is no place for heretics in the lands of Ukase." Grabbing the man's head, he let God's might flow through him. The old man shrieked and quaked, his body lunging forward but his head didn't move, causing his back to arch and nearly double over. When Kirkadite released him, the old man flopped to the ground, his eyes glazed with death.

A sneer playing on the Truth-Seeker's lips. "One less heathen to poison the minds of others." He turned to his Pursuant. "Throw the Purged onto the pyre and bring the next."

Evram Kirkadite rode away from Rosedale, his body and mind exhausted. It took two hours to Purify the village and he needed food and rest. At his tent, he climbed off his horse and handed the reins to his Pursuant. Kirkadite couldn't remember the lad's name, having only been under his tutelage a few weeks. Not that it mattered. The lad was beneath him. "Bring me a hot meal, then feed and curry my horse. After that, you may stand down." He paused. "You did well today. I will mark it in my report." Just because the lad was an inferior, didn't mean he shouldn't be supportive.

Kirkadite turned to his tent and stopped as Arch-Seeker Varsath, the leader of the Purification of the entire Westlands, approached. Saluting with fist to chest, Kirkadite knelt. "It is an honor, Arch-Seeker, to be in your presence."

"Stand, young man," the older man replied. "How did it go today?"

Kirkadite did as ordered, holding himself erect and keeping his eyes straight ahead. "Seventy-five simpletons Purified, and forty-eight Purged—sixteen of those during the assault."

"You are doing great work here," Arch-Seeker Varsath said. "Grand-Seeker Torq placed great faith in you, and you do not let us down. But you should not refer to these good people as *simpletons*. They are lost souls in great need of saving."

Kirkadite bowed with a fist to his chest, internally flailing himself for his hubris. "Yes, Arch-Seeker."

"When we found you here, lost in this land of dissidents, you were filled with zeal. I am happy that light has not diminished, and grown brighter. You are meant for great things, I think. You have a true passion for finding the wicked." The Arch-Seeker tilted his head. "Did you find any still under the influence of Chaos?"

"No, Arch-Seeker, only heretics and the guilty."

"Good, that is five of the last six villages. The influence of

Edis fades fast."

The Head Militant-Seeker approached and saluted. "Arch-Seeker Varsath, the villagers said a large group of Travelers left here this morning, heading south."

Varsath scowled. "Take a company and hunt them down."

"It would be my pleasure," Kirkadite said, barely holding in his excitement.

Varsath shook his head. "No, Truth-Seeker Kirkadite, I've another mission for you ... we'll discuss it later. Send your Militants, with your Pursuant in command. This will be a good experience for him. We've no need of proof of their guilt—they are Travelers, after all. Just have them hunted down and purged, every one of them."

Kirkadite saluted with a bow, his face hard as fury seethed in his chest. "Yes, Arch-Seeker."

"You have a particular disgust for Travelers, Truth-Seeker Kirkadite," Varsath said. "Why is that?"

"They are the very symbol of the lie of Edis, everything that was supposedly good about Chaos. They are his spawn and need to die."

"What you say is true, but why the vehemence?"

"I grew up in the village of Fars Glen, a week's ride from the Cunning River," Kirkadite explained. "The village was burned to the ground by a priest in search of a group of Travelers who'd just visited—Concord's Grand Traveling Show. The priest tortured and burned nearly everyone to find out where the Travelers went."

Kirkadite then bowed. "If you will excuse me, Arch-Seeker, I need to inform my men of the mission, and then eat and rest."

Varsath inclined his head. "I will talk with you in the morning."

Kirkadite went to the camp of his Militants, seething. He didn't tell the Arch-Seeker the entire truth, something for which he would need to Purify himself later. The thing he held back, the thing he'd never admitted to anyone, was he'd loved those Travelers. He'd even dreamt of joining them, to his great shame. Because of Concord, all his friends and family died. To know that even one Traveler survived when his loved ones didn't ...

They all deserved death.

Evan eyed the dust cloud behind them and cursed. That kind of thing was never good, especially with word of roving armies of insane Ukase worshipers about. He flicked his reins and heeled his horse, urging it to the front of the troupe.

"Zimmer." he called out. "Dust behind us. Most likely a lot of horses coming our way."

The animal trainer and now leader of the troupe flicked his own reins. "Pass the word. We press hard. Perhaps they're just a caravan headed in the same direction, but I'll not chance it. It's times like these we need Ellis to know for sure."

The scout nodded and laughed. "And here we thought the fall of Chaos would make things better."

As Evan came abreast with the hedge mage, he passed the word, but Whisp's blue eyes appeared distant. "Whisp," Evan cried out. "Did you hear me? What's wrong with you?"

The old man shook his head. "We need to stop."

"What? Have you gone mad?"

"No," Whisp replied. "In fact, I've never seen everything clearer. Do as I say. Tell Master Zimmer to stop and get everyone in a tight group. I'll make an illusion to send them off in the wrong direction. There's no way we can outrun men on horseback, but we can confuse them."

"You mean, like we did in the South all those years ago?" Evan had his doubts. "If you recall, that only worked because Cord and the others sacrificed themselves."

"This is different," the gray-haired wizard replied. "It will be an optical illusion. I'll mask us and have them running off after the wrong group. But they must be within sight of us to take the bait."

"You *have* lost your mind," Evan said. The old man only did parlor tricks—sleight of hand, moving small objects, twinkling lights. He would get them all killed. "Sorry, old friend, but I don't think that would work. Pardon me for saying so, but you're not *that* good."

Scowling, Whisp flicked his wrist. A shimmering mist formed next to Evan, and with a flash, it formed into an exact replica of him, horse and all. The copy smiled and then made a gesture, telling Evan where he could shove his opinion.

Evan laughed. "Since when could you do this? Why haven't you used it in your shows?"

"Because Bylum only now revealed herself to me," Whisp said. "And with the God of Light now in my heart, I can do this. And a great deal more." He closed his eyes, smiling. "Edis was never this glorious."

Nodding, Evan spurred his horse forward. He told Master Zimmer, who agreed and reined in his team. The pulled into a tight bunch, but did not circle. The plan was to move out at a slow pace, so it would be easier for the wizard—or now former wizard having found his new god—to create a screen for them as they made their escape.

"This is risky, Whisp," Zimmer said. "If we wait until they come into view, they may see what you're doing."

"They have to be close enough to see the illusion," Whisp replied. "But don't worry, they should be far enough away that they won't notice the switch."

Time crept by as the dust cloud approached. The rest of the troupe whispered and muttered, fear painting their faces. Evan shared their fear, for if the plan didn't work, they would all likely die. Even with the old gods' return, Evan chose to follow none of them, feeling it made little difference in a normal man's life. But desperate times called for desperate measures. "Please, Great Mother, let this work."

When the soldiers came into view, Whisp closed his eyes and murmured, waving his hands and making odd gestures with his fingers. A wavering curtain formed in front of the troupe, while at the same time, a mist grew next to them. The mist formed into a replica of the entire troupe, and sped away at a right angle.

"It's even kicking up dust," Evan said.

The troops, seven of them, all dressed in red, veered off after the illusion, and the troupe sent up a cheer.

"Quiet," Whisp said through clenched teeth. "It's only visual. If we're too loud, they will still hear us. Okay, Zimmer, let's head out. I'll need to be in the rear, and I'll need someone to drive for me." Sweat formed on his forehead. "This is harder than I thought it would be."

They started out at a walk, and Evan rode next to Whisp, who sat at the back of his wagon. The gray-haired man's face was pale, and his hands shook. Evan hoped he could keep it up long enough.

The troops were roughly three-hundred yards from the illusion when the troupe stared down a slope into a large, wooded area—a perfect place for them to hide. Evan's heart sank, though, as one of the troops pulled up, shouting and pointing in their direction.

"They've seen through it somehow," Evan shouted. "Quickly, we must make for the woods, it's our only hope!"

"I'm sorry," Whisp said, his voice rough. "It was just too far away. I couldn't hold it. If we make it to the woods, I can cloak us." The old man looked ready to pass out.

"I hope you're right," Evan said.

Fifty feet from the tree line, the soldiers topped the hill. Three pulled up and raised crossbows as the rest raced on. Two of the bolts struck Whisp's wagon with a thump. The other slammed into Evan's shoulder. He toppled from his horse, his shoulder flaring in blinding pain as the ground shoved the bolt deeper and to the side. Evan came to a stop. He tried to stand, wanting to die on his feet, but his right leg refused.

Broken, he thought. *So, this is how it ends. We spend our lives running from Chaos, only to die at the hands of Order.*

He watched, nearly numb as the four men barreled down, their swords held at their sides, ready to strike down the first they rode past. His pain started to subside and his vision closed in on the edges. He knew he was dying, but his only regret was not being able to help the others.

He thought his eyes were playing tricks on him when the tall grass around the soldiers flailed and thrashed. The horses screamed as the grass entangled them, sending their riders tumbling to the ground. The ones atop the hill raised their bows for another shot, but a brilliant wall of light flashed through them. Men and horses alike tumbled to the ground in pieces, as though the light had cut them in half.

"I'm going mad," Evan mumbled.

When the four soldiers regained their feet, a large, black mass rose up out of the grass next to them. It was a wolf. It tore into the first man's throat, throwing him aside, and then dove at the second. The two remaining raised their blades to strike the wolf, but the ground erupted with flames and earth, sending them flying.

"Am I dreaming?" Evan asked.

"No, my old friend," a woman's voice replied next to him.

Evan turned, and his mouth gaped. Kneeling at his side was a beautiful woman, her long, brown hair waving in the wind. Her eyes shone like burnished, golden orbs, and she glowed, as though light came from within her skin. "Daylin? Is that really you? What happened to you?"

"Hush now," she said. "I will explain once Veil has finished with those men."

"Who's Veil?" Evan asked.

The two soldiers, bleeding from various cuts, regained their feet and put their hands to their heads. The wolf was gone, and in its place stood a tall man with coal-black hair and bronze skin. He wore black pants and boots, with a snow-white shirt beneath a long, black coat.

"Return to your masters and you will not be harmed further," the stranger said, his voice strong and ominous.

"By Ukase," the soldier on the left shouted, charging forward and hacking at the stranger with his sword. But the blade stopped short, as though it struck a wall. The soldier raised his blade for another attack. With a brilliant flash, the soldier exploded. Blood and gore sprayed in all directions, but none of it touched the stranger in black. The remaining solder ran, sprinting up the hill away from his impending death.

Daylin's eyes glittered as they turned from the stranger, back to Evan. "Now, let's see to you."

Warmth spread throughout him, and his pain disappeared. When Daylin removed the bolt, he felt nothing, but when she placed her hand on the wound, it grew hot. The heat faded, and she removed her hand. The wound was gone. She placed a hand on his leg, and that too was healed.

She helped him to his feet. "All better now."

His eyes wide, Evan's mouth gaped once again. "By the Mother."

"Quite true, my good man," the stranger said as he approached.

Evan tilted his head. "I know that voice. But I don't know

your face."

"This is Veil," Daylin said. "You knew him as Betal."

"That name is gone," Veil said. "I chose the one my wolf-mother gave me to honor her memory."

It was all too much for Evan. He shook his head. "But, you were the embodiment of Chaos?"

Veil laughed. "That's what they thought. And in a way, what I wanted them to think. My original name was Gabriel."

Someone gasped behind Evan. Turning, Evan saw the rest of the troupe approach, with Whisp at the lead.

"Gabriel?" Whisp said. "But, that is the name of the Arbiter, the hand of the Council of the Gods."

Daylin grinned. "Hello, you old fart."

The troupe gathered about, tears of joy and cries of happiness escaping them. They all hugged Daylin, everyone asking her what had happened and what was going on.

"That's quite a belly you've got yourself," Whisp said.

Evan gasped. "You are with child?"

Smiling, she placed a hand on her tummy. "Yes. It shouldn't be much longer now. It's a girl. Here name will be Victoria."

She then told them of her adventures in the Lands of the Dead, about the ghostly apparitions of former soldiers stuck out of time, and the massive lake so big it took days to cross. She regaled them of the sights of Durgia, its bounty and beauty. Then her face turned sad. "Ellis is gone," she said, "killed by a paladin of Chaos." As the others cried, she smiled. "But do not mourn him long, for he did as he was meant to, and returned to his rightful place among the gods."

"*Her* rightful place," Veil said.

Daylin laughed. "Quite right, my love. You see, Ellis was like Veil, a god brought forth to life as a mortal. Her true name is Artuse, and she is Veil's sister. Well, in a manner of speaking. They were both born of the Mother at the beginning of creation. But regardless of all that, *he* will always remain Ellis in my memory and heart."

"It seems we have new tales for the people," Whisp said.

"And tell them you should," Daylin said. "I will regale you as we guide you north, across the river, out of these dangerous lands. It will take some time, as the tales of the gods are many.

But there is one thing of utmost importance, a warning that everyone must hear."

She explained what happened at the Chamber of the Champions. She told them of the end of the Great Games of the Gods, about how they would never come again, and about Twitch. "He has been twisted by Dekriot—the Abomination, the eldest demon of the Void. Dekriot is on the rise and his influence spreads. He has but one goal, the utter destruction of everything."

"How is that possible?" Master Zimmer asked.

Veil stepped forward. "Dekriot was brought into being at the Creation. It is something he resents. He sees existence as nothing but pain and torment, so he yearns to end it, to kill the Mother and creation itself."

"But, why do we have to leave the Westlands?" Evan asked, his mind reeling from it all. "With what I just saw, can't you get rid of them? Or, at least, convince Ukase's followers to leave us alone?"

"I am forbidden," Veil said. "It is part of the bargain I made with Aelaz, the God of Life. I cannot interfere in the affairs of mortals. There are people out there who hate and fear change. They despise what they don't understand." His face turned dark. "Like those who killed my father. For that crime, I might let you all die."

Daylin put a hand on his cheek. "My love, we talked about this."

"Yes, and I still hate those who killed him. It is because of what happened to my father that I am allowed this one thing: to aid Daylin in her protection of you Travelers. For you are the givers of joy and knowledge, something this world desperately needs."

Veil's eyes drifted over the troupe. "But, my primary task is to protect the moral plain from the enemies beyond, like Dekriot. He is vile and devious." He moved into the crowd. "His whispers can be enticing to those who wish to hear ..." He stopped in front of Alex, Master Zimmer's young son. "But some have no choice. Show me your arm, son."

Alex shied away, grasping his forearm. "No."

"Leave the boy alone," Strong Tom said.

Veil pointed at the strongman. "I'll deal with you next." A

shimmering light encased Tom's body. Tom struggled, his head thrashing, but his body remained still. Veil then pointed at Lem and Hoak. "You two, as well."

The two horse handlers were also encased.

"What's going on?" Master Zimmer asked. "What's wrong with my boy?"

Veil reached down and gently picked up Alex's arm. He pointed at a pink, four-pointed star in the boy's arm. "This is the mark of a succubus, a minion of Dekriot. It devours part of your soul, giving it to the Abomination and sealing you to it."

"You lie," Alex screamed, trying to yank his arm away. He kicked at Veil until the shimmering sheathed him as well.

Tears flowed in the eyes of many of the troupe, including Evan. He remembered the day Alex was born. "Can anything be done?"

"Yes," Veil said. He then turned back to Alex. "I am sorry, child. This must be done. I will sever the connection to the Abomination, but it will be painful, and your body will remain weakened for months, possibly years. As for your soul, it can only be replenished once it returns to The Stone. I am sorry."

Veil closed his eyes, and Alex arched his back, screaming and thrashing until he passed out. After a few moments, the pink mark faded and disappeared in a trail of smoke.

"He will be all right in time," Veil said. Alex levitated into Master Zimmer's arms. "For now, he needs rest and food. I will now tend to the others."

Tom, Hoak, and Lem each shrieked and convulsed as Veil made his way to them. Veil repeated the process, and had them sent to rest afterward.

Madam Dominica, the fortuneteller, cried openly. "What about the rest of us?" she asked.

"Always be on your guard," Veil said. "And keep an eye out for that mark. There is nothing else, unfortunately."

Realization struck Evan. "Wait, where's Dirge? Why isn't he with you?"

Daylin sighed. "He has returned to the fold, back to the followers of his god, Ukase. His path is one of hardship, I fear. In some ways it will be as bad as Mangin's." She then grinned. "But do not grow too concerned. I gave Dirge a token: Ellis' bronze sun pendant. If ever he should need me, I will be there for him. There's no way we would abandon that stubborn, old fool."

"I have told you, my love," Veil said, "he is beyond my aid, as he is no longer with the Travelers."

Daylin rolled her eyes. "Yes, as you've said more times that I'd care to hear. And as I have told you, I will not forsake Dirge."

"Know this, my wife." Veil stood taller, taking on the air of authority. "If Dirge calls for aid, you will see to him alone."

Daylin's face darkened and she turned her back. "So be it."

Chapter 7

Decisions

In Cross Corners, men of all ages celebrated a day of hard work before heading home. The aroma of fresh bread and roasted meat, mixed with the stink of sweat and stale beer, filled the tavern, along with the raucous laughter and conversation. Serving maids traipsed through the throng like a dance, dishing out food and drink.

The revelry was a buzz to Dirge, something barely noticed as he stared into his mug. His back ached following a long day of sword and horse practice with Estonia, and his arms were sore from chopping wood. Mangin kept telling him to let Barret do it, but Dirge liked the calm repetition of swinging the ax. Barret, his wife, Amelia, and their two children lived in the outbuilding—a modest sized home—and worked the land, growing crops and tending the animals. Even after all that time living in that cavernous mansion, Dirge felt more like an appendage than a landowner.

Still, he was proud of everything they had accomplished in only a year's time. Thanks to God's influence, people created a proper society, destroying totems of the wicked past, and building appropriate worship halls, roads, and homes. With their army of Righteous, they consolidated all the lands east of the river and spread into the Westlands. The entirety of the Reach would soon become Ardentia, the country of the peoples of Ukase.

A maid glided up to him, her protruding belly suggesting she was with child. "Would you care for a refill, My Lord?"

Dirge paused. "No, I think not. Thank you. I'd best be heading home."

The maid's belly reminded Dirge of a conversation he had with Lynette on that last, fateful night: she'd told him she was pregnant. The pain was sharp, even after all those years. *What would it be like to be a father?* he wondered as her last words to him floated through his mind. Raising the mug to his lips, he murmured a reply that echoed hers, "Until tonight."

"Well, aren't you a fresh one," the maid said with a smile. She looked him up and down in his tight, black pants and white shirt, paying special attention to his black surcoat. "You seem to be a good man of God, and you're quite handsome, but as you can see, I have a husband ... though I thank you for the compliment."

Shocked, Dirge held up a hand. "No, I'm sorry, you misunderstood. It's something I say when I take my final drink. It's to my wife."

Her laugh was musical. "Then why not just say it to her when you get home?"

He looked away with a frown.

She gasped. "Oh, My Lord, I'm so sorry. You know, my mum always said a kiss, if offered with a pure heart, could always sooth an ache." She leaned over him, her bosom, though contained in a proper blouse and vest, hovered near his face as she kissed the top of his head. "I hope that helps ease the pain. A good evening to you, My Lord." She took two paces and stopped, turning back with a grin. "A good man always needs tending by a good woman. If you're interested, I do have a cousin, just come of age. She's a lovely lass who remembers her place, but who's also been taught how to please a husband. I made sure of that myself." With a giggle, she hurried off.

Trying not to growl, Dirge closed his eyes. It wasn't the first time someone suggested he remarry. Nor was it the tenth, for that matter, often with someone particular in mind.

A man at the next table said something that caught Dirge's attention.

"Whilst tending the field last week, I eyed a small band of Travelers heading down the road," the man said, scratching the dark stubble on his neck. "I felt a tingle run up my spine and that's when a saw *them*, right at the wood's edge ... the Maiden and the Wolf—her, glowing all in white with the giant, black wolf at her side. They was watching the Travelers, too. Nearly scared me out of my britches. But when she looked *my* way ..." He shook his head. "I can't rightly explain it. It was calming, like being bathed in a warm embrace. 'Tis a good omen, I tell you."

"It's not!" the man across the table cried, his curly, red hair waggling. "They are harbingers of doom for any who see them. They protect the Travelers—those spawn of Chaos. You must seek out the Veridical for protection." He took a gulp from a small bottle, most likely eska from the looks of the brownish liquid dribbling from the corners of his mouth.

Dirge closed his eyes; he'd heard that kind of talk before. How many people really knew the truth? He was one of the few, of that he was sure. But the truth was also heretical, especially those days.

"It has nothing to do with God," the stubble-neck said.

"Ukase is everything!" The red-haired man pulled open his shirt, revealing God's sigil embossed in the center of his chest. "There are no other gods but the Lord. I tell you, the Maiden is a she-demon of Chaos out to tempt the weak. She feeds them to the Wolf, who devours their souls."

Dirge put down his cup. "Her name is Daylin," he said, his voice low but hard. "And the Wolf is Veil." An image of Daylin popped into his mind—slim, beautiful, and glowing even before she became a god. He pursed his lips. The only god he should contemplate was Ukase.

The red-haired man sneered at Dirge. "What do I care what the demons' names are? They are vile."

Dirge squeezed the mug, his hand shaking. "Watch your

tongue."

"You don't like my talking about your bitch demon?" the red-haired man asked. "Are you a Chaos worshiper? I'll set the Seekers on you. The Lord will cast that demon bitch and her wolf into the void, and you with them."

The mug shattered in Dirge's hand. He stood, placed his hand upon his sword hilt, and spoke through clenched teeth, "You will not speak of Daylin that way. Do you understand me? Or by Ukase, they will be your last words."

The red-haired man's eyes went wide, and his mouth hung open as he stared at Dirge's surcoat, the star of Ukase emblazoned on the front, obviously seeing it for the first time. "M-My apologies, Righteous Warrior, I did not mean to offend."

"Lies are sins," Dirge said. "Watch yourself, or I'll set the Seekers on *you.*"

The two men knelt, but Dirge ignored them and approached the bar. He fished out a gold piece from his pouch and presented it to the tavern owner. "For the cup. I am truly sorry."

"The cup cost only a pittance, My Lord." The owner ran his hands down his crisp, white apron that hung to his knees. "I could accept a copper, but what you offer is far too much."

"No matter." Dirge placed the coin on the bar. "I wish to help out in whatever way I can. You've a fine establishment. It reminds me of one from my youth."

"Thank you, Lord Malik. You honor me." He picked up the coin. "This will go a good way to finish my restorations. Why, I lost nearly all my good tables and chairs in that freak flood after the Lord returned."

The man then cleared his throat and glanced away. "Is it true, what they say, Righteous Captain? That Ukase sent all that water down the Cunning to clean out the remnants of Chaos?"

Dirge paused. The Cunning River ran at near flood levels for a month after the initial burst that swamped the embankment from Gate Hall, to the Corners, and on south. Even until that day it was still several feet over its bank. He thought about his travels in the Lands of the Dead with Daylin, Ellis, Veil, and Mangin. He considered the mammoth lake they had crossed, and the rivers flowing in and out of it. Dirge reasoned that when the Chaos-infused prison fell, time returned there. That meant the water would once again flow. He regarded the tavern owner, trying to decide what to say. Was it truly all God's will?

He shrugged. "I'm not sure, to be honest." Turning, Dirge marched out.

In front of the God's Glory, men were lighting the street lanterns, installed a few months before to help keep down trouble, and then headed down the street to light the rest. Dirge shook to try to calm himself, turned south, and headed home—with the tavern at the southern edge of Cross Corners, it took only half an hour by foot. He often chose to walk cross-country to the Corners, as it was too close to take Striker, his gelded, black charger. Striker needed much longer rides; otherwise, the animal grew too frisky.

When the two-story mansion came into view through the trees—it was shorter to go through the forest, rather than take the lengthy manor lane—he stopped. The setting sun bathed its front, making the red and brown brick sparkle and shine. The smell of hay and horses drifted on the breeze, mixed with those of the flower garden between the mansion and Barret's house several hundred paces beyond.

"Lynette would have loved this." He felt her absence every day, but for some reason, it had grown more acute since moving into the estate.

Estonia rode up on Justice, his bay courser. The horse skipped and gamboled when Estonia pulled him to a stop. "Good evening, sir."

"You need to exercise him more," Dirge said.

"Yes, sir." The squire saluted. "But then, we've not gone more than five miles beyond the estate in months."

Dirge shook his head. "If you're in such a hurry to spread the faith, why stay with me?" The young man nearly clung to his side whenever possible.

"I couldn't do that, sir. You still need me. You don't read the scriptures nearly as much as you should, with or without me holding mass in the manor's chapel. Without my prodding, I doubt you'd ever pick it up." The squire laughed. "So, when are we going afield? I swear to you, I'm ready."

"You're ready, when I say you are." Dirge scratched his chin. "What if I chose to stay in retirement? What would you do?"

"I'd stay with you, sir. It's where I belong. You'll never

lose me, or my services, *that* I swear."

A shiver ran down Dirge's back as thoughts of Lynette, Daylin, and Ellis flashed through his mind. "In time, I lose everyone. Why would you be any different?"

Estonia grinned. "Because I am different, sir." The smile faltered. "You could rid yourself of that miserable woman, though."

"Mangin is my responsibility, not yours. Leave worrying about her to me."

"But, she does nothing, not really; just stays locked away in her rooms with those books. The house is covered in grime. Even Frey complains." He puffed out his cheeks, and imitated the cook's somewhat garbled voice, "By the Lord, I could almost swear I taste dust in the stew."

"I'll talk with her." Dirge paused, eyeing Estonia. With the lad's black hair and blue eyes, he made a striking figure. "When are you going to get yourself a wife?"

The squire laughed again. "I've no time for that. I'm going to go curry Justice." When he rode away, he had a tightness in his eyes.

Dirge entered the manor—making sure to scrape his boots first—then marched up to the second floor, down to Mangin's room, and knocked. "I would have words with you."

A muffled curse came from inside, followed shortly by the thumping of feet. Mangin threw open the door and stood with a hand on one hip, but rather than looking upset, a smile played on her lips. Her hair was in disarray and she wore only a short slip—her bosom straining the material—and a pair of stockings. She licked a finger. "Care to give me a hand with something?"

A sweet, earthy scent drifted to Dirge, causing heat to course through him, both out of ardor, and anger. "What if I wasn't alone?"

"Oh, I think your darling squire would enjoy the sight."

He shook in anger, biting off each word in reply, "What if I had someone from town, from the sanctum?" He paused, letting it sink in, and then continued, "Do you want a Seeker to come here?"

Her smile gone, Mangin shrunk in on herself, trying cover her nether region. "I'm sorry. You're right." Her face then firmed, and she stood tall. "What do you want?"

"Get dressed, fix your hair, and come see me in the parlor. We need to talk."

Sighing, she rolled her eyes. "Fine." She slammed the door closed.

Dirge took a deep breath, trying to calm himself. The part of him that hated her had waned over the months, replaced with pity. However, with the abhorrence gone, a different fire seemed to have replaced it, especially when she flaunted herself. He hated himself for it. Lynette's memory deserved better than simple lust for a woman. It also made him recall his past, back to a time when he debased himself with women of the night in order to forget the pain.

And before that, the beguiling priestess with the green eyes who had bewitched him …

He slammed his fist into his thigh and snarled, "Never again." With another deep breath, he went to await Mangin in the parlor.

They sat across from each other, Dirge in his large, over-stuffed chair by the fire, Mangin on the fainting couch. She wore a proper maid's dress—black, covering from ankle, to wrist, to neck—with her fire-red hair in a bun. A feather duster lay on the small, round tea table between them. Dirge pointed at it. "It wouldn't hurt you to use that more."

She pursed her lips, like she'd bit into sour fruit. "I'm not so sure about that."

"I'm trying to protect you, as I promised Daylin." He touched the bronze sun pendant beneath his shirt. "But you must do your part as well."

"You don't understand. I lost everything that made me, me. And I must find that again. Betal told me—"

"His name is Gabriel."

Mangin grinned. "Actually, I believe he goes by Veil now. Anyway, he told me to not give up hope. He said there was another way to use my gift than … the *old* way. I must find out how. It's in my books, I'm sure of it." Her eyes turned haunted as she seemed to look inward. "If I don't, I'll die."

"I remember the emptiness of my soul all those years after I lost the touch of God," Dirge said. "I understand your feelings. Though I'm not sure I agree with them. The things you did with people's minds was … unnatural." He held up a hand when she tried to argue. "I'm not saying you must stop looking. Just curtail it a bit. If you're to stay here as a maid, you must, at the very least, do more work. One of these days, Estonia will complain about you where the wrong person will hear, and that will raise questions—ones neither of us can afford."

She put on a pout. "But your High Priest said I was absolved."

"*The Magnus* absolved you, yes. But if you're to live in a world of Order, you must maintain decorum. According to Estonia, the Consul's have a place for women they deem *unruly*. It's called the Chastenary. There, the Immaculate—women who've given themselves over to God—will judge and castigate you. And if you are still *unruly*, they will deem you a heretic and make you a slave."

Mangin glowered. "And if I refuse to be a slave?"

"They will *purge* you by removing your head."

Her eyebrows raising, she shuddered. "How can you people be so brutal? You run around cutting off heads with such fervor you'd think ... Well, to be honest, I don't know what you people think."

Dirge's mouth hung open, flabbergasted. "*We're* brutal? Were you blind to what happened under the rule of Chaos?"

"Of course not." She huffed. "But we at least gave people their freedoms."

"*Freedoms*? Your people were butchers. They—"

A knock at the door cut him off.

Dirge motioned Mangin to pick up the duster. Once she did and started on the furniture, he called out, "Enter."

Estonia opened the door and strode up to Dirge. "Veridical Barnhold has just arrived. He wishes to speak with you."

With a quick glance at Mangin, Dirge told Estonia to bring in the Veridical.

Moments later, Veridical Barnhold strolled in, his robes—white with a black Star of Ukase outlined in red on the chest—were crisp and clean. "Good evening, young man. I hope you don't mind my arrival so late in the day."

"I am hardly young, Veridical Barnhold. I'm nearing forty," Dirge said. "And no, it's not too late. What can I do for you?"

Barnhold looked at Mangin as she glided about the room. "Has your maid come to accept her new position in the world? I trust she's worshiping in your chapel under Estonia's tutelage, but there are those who call for her to go the sanctum with the other adherents."

Dirge eyed Mangin, who froze a moment, and then rushed deeper in the room, dusting the bookcases. He pursed his lips. "I see. This is something the Immaculate have spoken of?" When the Veridical nodded, Dirge sighed. "I suppose it would help her learn the ways of the Lord even more. I'll have her go with Barret and Amelia. Was there anything else, or would you like a seat?"

The Veridical nodded and took the chair to Dirge's right. "It is good that you come to the Corners and share your wealth. But, Dirge, I believe you left Edmond a bit frazzled."

"Edmond?"

The Veridical laughed. "The owner of God's Glory. You've been going there for a year; I'm surprised you didn't know his name."

Dirge grunted. "I guess it never came up." He hadn't wanted to get too familiar with the place, especially the owner. It sent his mind dwelling on a past, one filled with regrets. "What upset him?"

"Your casting doubt on the Great Flood."

With a shake of the head, Dirge sighed. "I don't think it's that simple. There are huge lakes in Durgia. When the prison fell, the water started flowing again, like a burst dam."

"The water didn't come from Ukase directly," Barnhold said. "But it did come because the Lord freed the Lands of the Dead. Chaos fell, and the waters came to clean the foulness of Edis away. We must have the people know God's influence in the world. And if they wish to think He sent the waters directly, we should not deny it."

Barnhold then paused. "There is another thing. I understand there was an ... altercation as well. There were whispers of blasphemy."

"I merely had a disagreement with a man about Travelers."

"There was a mention of the Maiden and the Wolf," the Veridical said. "Some would call that heretical."

"Veil was formerly Gabriel, Arbiter of the High Council of Taneer. And Daylin ..." Dirge hesitated. "Daylin is now an offshoot of Aelaz and a God of Life."

Barnhold held up a finger. "Ah, but therein lies the problem. Veil and Daylin are Principles, like Aelaz and Aza'zel, divine servants of Ukase. They do the Lord's bidding."

Dirge was taken aback by the radical new dogma created during his ... convalescence. *What else are they twisting?* he wondered.

The Veridical continued, "The *Maiden* and the *Wolf*, however, are heretical." He tilted his head. "There was talk of calling for a Seeker."

Dirge frowned. "I am under the glory of God, I've no fear of them. The truth is, I'm concerned about their ..." He scratched his head. "What was the word she used?" he muttered, trying to recall what Mangin had said. "Fervor. I worry about the fervor of the Seekers, as of late."

"Yes, they do have a true passion when it comes to finding the wicked."

"We've spread the influence of the Lord throughout most of the Westlands," Dirge said, "across to the Talendor Mountains, and even somewhat into the former Lands of the Dead. This is good. But Veridical, Nardo Torq has them—"

The Veridical held up a hand. "Grand-Seeker Torq."

"Yes," Dirge said, his voice flat, and then continued, "The man has them tearing apart entire villages. And not just to seek out those poisoned by Chaos. He has been ... purging people if they worship any of the other gods. The man is leaving a bloody path in his *fervor*."

Veridical Barnhold spread his hands. "You must understand that with the failing health of the Magnus, the Grand-Seeker has chosen to be more vigorous in the pursuit of heretics."

"That's just it. When Gabriel banished Chaos, he also returned all the other gods, not just Ukase. Even God bows to the will of the Council of Gods and The Mother."

Barnhold held up a finger. "But, not the other gods and demons. Dirge, these are troubled times. The world needs Order to come back from the rampant destruction under Chaos. These people are merely lost, and we are helping them find the true way."

"Yes," Dirge said. "That or be put to the sword."

"It is as God prescribes." Barnhold then reached into his robes and pulled out a palm-sized pendant of Ukase. The bronze was warped and lumpy, with several scorch marks, as though it had been pulled from a fire. "What do you make of this?"

Taking it, Dirge frowned. The thing made him itch from wrongness, but he wasn't sure why. Then God's heat filled him, revealing the truth. "This was touched by Chaos."

Barnhold nodded in agreement. "I formally require your assistance in the matter."

"If there's any chance of running into Chaos, I may need a Rod of Divinity. Are there any in the Sanctum?"

"No. They are no longer made by man and blessed. You will make it yourself."

Dirge shook his head. "I don't know metalworking."

Barnhold let out a laugh. "No, my son. You merely hold out your hand, make the proper prayer to God, and focus his will on your open palm. Minor ones will come quickly, but the major ones take more time and effort. They are quite draining, so keep that in mind."

Dirge nodded. "I will talk with Estonia regarding the prayer. I've still so much to learn."

"You'll not be going alone, either. Righteous Warrior Kent—your would-be successor—needs command experience. All he's learned thus far is how to root out and purify villagers." Pulling out a letter from his robes, Barnhold handed it to Dirge. "I have corresponded with the Arch-Righteous, and he agrees with me. The Arch-Righteous demands you escort Righteous Warrior Kent. Let the young man lead but give him corrections when they are needed."

Dirge accepted the letter with a frown. "Purifying villagers? Where was Kent before this?"

"His first command was under Grand-Seeker Nardo Torq, in the Westlands."

Dirge's frown deepened. "Torq is a butcher."

Barnhold Waved his hand. "Grand-Seeker Torq may well be in the camp of those who believe Ukase is the only god, but he does as Ukase prescribes." He then took hold of Dirge's shoulder. "Understand, we are not completely recalling you from your furlough. It's a simple assignment, though a vital one. We must find out what is happening out there, and how Chaos has circumvented the Arbiter's ruling."

The weight of the letter was insubstantial, yet to Dirge, it felt as heavy as a stone. He might not be versed in politics, but he understood the nuance of the message. Was Veil somehow involved in the return of Chaos?

Chapter 8

Hunting Chaos

Many things had changed on the road to Cool Winds since Dirge last took this trip. The trees that once edged the road—now twice its former width—had been clear-cut over a hundred feet. Also, there were four locations, cleared and leveled, used as layovers at the quarter marks from Cross Corners to Cool Winds.

At the second layover, Dirge knelt in the low grass next to the well in the camp's center. A light breeze filled with the scent of pine tugged his cloak. He fingered a charred portion of missing brick from the sidewall, roughly the size of a man's head. He then examined the waist-high berm and ten-foot-wide dry mote at the camp's perimeter. "How was the caravan ambushed? These defenses are sufficient to stop a bull rush, and the tree line is out of bow-shot."

"They must have been too lax in their watch," Righteous Warrior Kent said, his square jaw set.

Dirge gestured to the well. "And what would cause this? It certainly wasn't Chaos."

The tall, pale, Righteous Warrior grunted. "Chaos is gone, Ukase saw to that. It's most likely poor workmanship. Someone laid their torch against it and left it overnight."

Dirge had his doubts. "Edis is gone, yet Chaos somehow remains." Standing, he put his gauntlets back on. "What is our next move?"

"We'll learn nothing here," Kent said. "The attack is over a month old. I say we push on to the latest site, beyond Cool Winds."

Dirge crossed the open grass to where Kent and his Militants waited by the road with Estonia. The squad sat stock still, their heads facing forward, all but Smythe. The Head Righteous-Militant eyed Dirge with stern eyes and a twist in his mouth as though he'd tasted something bitter. The entire trip, Kent's men hadn't said a word to Dirge or Estonia, keeping themselves separate. Dirge thought they were simply being proper, but Smythe's expression wasn't one of respect.

Turning his attention back to Kent, Dirge mounted Striker. "You have the lead, Righteous Warrior."

Riding next to Kent, Dirge pondered the expression on Smythe's face, and the hostility that burned behind it. Then Dirge thought about whom Kent served under last. "I understand you were part of our expansion in the Westlands."

Kent kept his eyes on the road ahead. "I was. It was quite glorious—we showed them the truth."

"They were accepting of the Lord Ukase?"

Kent snorted. "Hardly. It was filled with heathens."

"Truly?" Dirge frowned. "I spent a great deal of time there, and a vast majority were not followers of Chaos. I was born in the South; I know the look of people under the sway of Edis."

"I do not speak of Chaos," Kent replied. "Every town resisted. False gods filled most of their hearts and needed purifying by Truth-Seeker Kirkadite."

"I don't believe I've heard of him."

"He grew up there, and was hand-chosen by Grand-Seeker Torq."

Dirge cringed inside, as that didn't bode well for those poor people. "I understand Purification can be quite painful."

"Indeed." Kent turned to Dirge with a smile. "I would say at least one in eight failed and met the Lord's last embrace to face

His justice."

Dirge was aghast. Torq was out of his mind. One in eight? There were a couple of hundred towns and villages dotting the Westlands, each one packed together for protection against roaming bandits. That meant thousands were slaughtered for simply believing in something other than the Lord Ukase. What was Torq thinking? Ukase was the righteous god who called to Dirge's soul, and the followers of Chaos deserved to die, but Ukase wasn't the *only* god. Gabriel returned the others to the mortal realm, and people had a right to worship them. He then frowned. *Don't they?*

As the evening sun dipped, they broke the tree line and Cool Winds came into view. Dirge could hardly believe it was the same village. A fifteen-foot-high wooden wall now surrounded the town. And judging from the wall's circumference, Cool Winds was at least three times its former size. The forest north of the village was now a lake of waving grain.

"These people have been busy," Dirge murmured, eyeing the stone gatehouse.

"They have indeed," Kent replied. "The people of Cool Winds have embraced the Lord, and He has blessed them. They are the pride of the East."

"It makes sense that these highways are being attacked," Estonia said. "Both villages, Tapers Pointe to the north and Hill Top to the south, ship their goods here before they are sent on the Corners."

"Not to mention those from the slave camps and mines in the Talendor mountains," Dirge added. "Isn't there a town south of Hill Top?"

"Not anymore," Kent said. "And they aren't all slaves; only those whose patriarchs were idolaters, refusing to embrace Ukase as the one true god. Most are penitent Offenders, doing what they must to pay for their crimes against God."

Once the guards waved them through, Dirge spotted a man he recognized in the garb of a Head Adherent-Militant—the leader of the town-guard. Dirge nodded toward the Sanctum in the center of the town, surrounded by a wide, paved road with a bastion on its north side. "Righteous Warrior Kent, please inform the Veridical of our arrival. I will find a place for the men to bed down for the night."

As Kent saluted and rode away, Dirge dismounted and approached the guard leader. "Erin Cruchfield. It is good to see you again. You are doing well, I see."

Cruchfield put on a snide smile, but still saluted with a fist to the chest, an *H* brand adorning the back of his hand. "Yes, we are *all* doing quite well. It would appear the Beast didn't care what happened to his *father*."

Dirge nodded to the brand. "It would seem the Seekers did care." He ignored the man's snarl and continued, "We need a place for the night, preferably on the east edge of town. Do you know of anything?"

"Try the Eastgate Inn. They should have room—the mountain caravan isn't due for another few days. Take the south branch of the road around the sanctum. That's the merchant sector. The north is reserved for residential, and we keep the traffic there at a minimum."

Dirge mounted, but before leaving he asked, "You have a son, Cobb, don't you? Is he manning the other gate? I don't see him here."

Erin Cruchfield's face hardened. "I have no sons." He spun on his heel and marched into the guardhouse.

"I wonder what happened to Cobb," Dirge said to Estonia.

"Perhaps the Seekers purified him."

"Perhaps." Dirge nudged Striker forward.

They rode around a now brick-walled pond, and entered a large, paved square, filled with carts and shops. Estonia spoke up, "I'm surprised they just didn't leave the land salted."

Dirge cocked his head. "What do you mean?"

"Isn't this where the old temple was?"

The lad was right, nothing remained of the old temple to Edis, not even the grass-covered Green that used to front it. "I guess they didn't want to waste the space."

After squaring everyone away at the inn, Dirge took dinner in the common room. He and Estonia shared a table. Kent and Smythe refused to join them, taking seats with the rest of the squad. Smythe sneered at Dirge from across the room the entire time while the rest refused to even meet his eye.

Dirge grunted and dug into his mutton stew. Filled with pearl onions, carrots, and chunks of potato, it was spiced just the way Dirge liked—salted, with only a hint of hot spices.

"They are fools, all of them," Estonia said, then took a pull from his ale.

"Who?"

"The squad ... especially Smythe. I talked to him when you were getting the rooms. They resent your presence but won't come out and say it. Smythe and a pair of others I understand, but not the rest."

"Why do you understand them?"

"There are converts, the Consecrated devotees of God. Smythe used to be a guard at the Citadel. The day of the Lord's return, he fell on his knees before the Magnus and pledged himself to Ukase. He was branded within an hour. You'll not find any more faithful than those who have undergone Consecration."

Dirge glanced at the other table. "But why do they resent me?"

"They think you are tainted by the Travelers."

Anger boiled up in Dirge, but he tamped it down. Part of him understood where they were coming from. "They know only what they've been told. Most of them are from Gate Hall, or villages east of the Cunning. Travelers rarely came to this area. They were loved by Edis, so they must be Chaos incarnate."

Still, Dirge had to wonder if part of Smythe's condemnation was true. He lived with, and cherished people whose ways were antithetical to the teachings of God. They lived as they wished and loved who they loved, regardless of their gender. It disgusted him, but he cared for them, nonetheless. The hard truth was, if Ellis had lived to see the glorious ending to Chaos, God would demand Ellis be purged for lying with other men.

He shook his head. "It doesn't matter what Smythe and the others think, so long as they follow orders." When Estonia started to interject, Dirge cut him off, "That's enough, now. I'm going to my room. We've much to do tomorrow."

Before heading upstairs, Dirge approached the inn's proprietor, a short man with thinning, sandy hair. "Pardon me. It's been some time since I was here last. What happened to Erin Cruchfield's son, Cobb?"

The inn keeper's face flushed and he looked down. "He fled. When the Seekers came and corrected those who did the homicide to the— To our old *friends*, he ran off rather then

accept the brand, the lashes, and the seven weeks in the mines."
He lifted his head, face stern. "They were my friends: John
Simmons, Adam Killings, the rest. It was wrong what happened
to them. In my mind, Erin and the rest deserve worse than a few
licks and a brand." The heat went out of his eyes and he bowed.
"I humbly beg your pardon. It is not my place to speak on
doctrine of Ukase. I do all that is asked of me by the True."

"Unfortunately, not all get what they deserve," Dirge
replied with a frown. When the inn keeper went pale, Dirge
patted the man on the shoulder. "I do not speak of you, do not
fear. You are a good man. It is plain in the eyes of God. I will
speak to the other Righteous back in the Corners and recommend
your establishment. Your food is wonderful." He then went up to
his room.

Dirge lay in bed, and thoughts of the Travelers floated up
from his memories, especially Daylin—her smile, her laugh, the
way she loved people for who they were. He would do anything
for her. Even suffer and succor a wanton witch who deserved to
die, regardless of how comely she was. Or how sweet she
smelled.

He rolled over with a frown, trying to clear his mind, but
Mangin still plagued him. It took a great deal of time before
sleep finally came.

They set out the next morning. Dirge ignored the snarls
from Smythe. After passing through the eastern gate, they
approached an oncoming caravan of stone from the work camps
at the edge of the Talendor Mountains. Kent appeared to ignore
them, but Dirge hailed their lead guardsman.

"Were there signs of any trouble on your way here?" Dirge
asked as Kent pulled up his mount and looked back, annoyance
plain on the man's face.

The guardsman's leather armor squeaked as he saluted
Dirge. "None, Righteous-Warrior. We saw nothing out of the
ordinary."

"What do you know of the caravan that was attacked
recently?"

"Nothing, Righteous-Warrior. Only that it happened at the
waystation."

"Did you know their guard leader?" Dirge went on. "Was he the type to be lax at camp?"

The man's face darkened. "My best friend, Camron, led them. He, along with myself and two other friends, were assigned our duty by High-Consul Leyte himself. Camron was the best of us. He would never shirk his duties in anyway."

"I did not mean to offend," Dirge said. "I simply needed to know. We are hunting the rogues, and any information you can give will be of great aid."

"I wish I could help, but as I said, there's been nothing out of the ordinary." The guardsman then frowned, looking down to his right.

Dirge smiled, hoping he looked encouraging. "Tell me your thoughts."

"Nothing really, sir. It's just ... The eyes, they play tricks on you on the long hauls."

"What kind of tricks?"

The guardsman shrugged. "Trees that are there one minute and gone the next. Rustling in the night, but nothing's there." He paused. "A feel in the air, a sense of wrongness that reminded me of the time before God's return. I'm sure it's just my imagination—I grew up in Gate Hall, in the heart of Edis."

The hair on Dirge's neck bristled. "You felt Chaos?"

The guardsman shrugged. "As I said, the mind plays tricks. With all the attacks, paranoia sets in; especially after Camron died. I meant what I said. There was never a better man. The four of us were being groomed to be Adherent-Militants at the Corners. But High-Consul Leyte said we needed seasoning first. Camron was to be Head Adherent-Militant."

After thanking the man, Dirge returned to Kent. His mind went back to the waystation to Cross corners, to its defenses and layout. *I'm missing something,* Dirge thought.

"Tell me you're not taking that man seriously about the Adversary," Kent said.

"Should I not?"

Kent sighed. "I told you, Chaos is gone. The man was simply reliving nightmares. Every God-fearing man has them."

"He may be sensitive to the spiritual realm, feeling things most do not."

"The High-Consul was preparing him to be an Adherent,

not a member of the militants or Seekers. He lacks vision and knowledge of the world Ukase has given us. All lesser men are susceptible to the whims of the demons released by the Fallen One."

Dirge cocked and eyebrow. "The Fallen One?"

"Yes. Gabriel, the former Arbiter to the Council of Edis."

"You mean the Council of Taneer, set forth by the Mother."

"Your squire needs to do a better job. You are behind in your scriptures," the Righteous Warrior said with a laugh. "The Council was created by Edis to aid Him in taming the spiritual plain, not some imaginary tree. Everything and everyone has its place. The demons need to be reminded of that."

"I spoke to Veridical Barnhold about this very subject. He agrees that even God bows to the will of the Council of Taneer and to The Mother."

Kent's eyebrows furrowed and his face darkened. "I'll not hear of such blasphemy. It would appear Veridical Barnhold needs to be reported to High-Consul Leyte for reeducation."

It took a moment for Dirge to realize Kent was not joking.

As he opened him mouth to reply, Estonia spoke up, "Righteous-Captain Dirge, may I have a word with you?" When Dirge pulled his horse back to ride next to his squire, Estonia continued in a hushed tone, "I advise against responding to Righteous-Warrior Kent, sir."

"What are you talking about?" Dirge asked, then glanced at Kent and lowered his voice. "I was there. I was in the presence of gods. I felt the truth in their words."

"Be that as it may, Righteous-Warrior Kent is correct. According to updated scriptures I received from High-Consul Leyte, the True changed its stance on the matter, less than a month ago. The doctrine now states that Ukase is the only god, and all the others—The Mother, the Council, all of them—are beneath him. They are now called *angyal*, attendants to God."

Dirge's mind reeled. It made no sense. The hierarchy of the True of Ukase, the Magnus and all those under him were positing something that wasn't … true. How could that be? He stayed at Estonia's side, contemplating the incongruity of it all.

Chapter 9

A Shadow in the Dark

Near midday, while riding through a stretch of dense evergreens, the squad approached a clearing on the side of the road many caravans used for a break station. Something ahead unnerved Dirge, like an itch he couldn't scratch. Its source was in the clearing, not yet visible.

"I don't like this," Dirge said. "Do you feel anything, Righteous-Warrior?"

Kent nodded. "Yes. Do you know what it is?"

The itch increased, and Dirge loosened his sword in its scabbard. "It's familiar. But I don't know what …" Realization struck Dirge like a blow to the head. The last time he felt it was years ago, during his time with the Prophet. "It's Chaos." After the Prophet Isaac died, Dirge had lost his connection with Ukase, and along with it, his heightened senses to those not of his god.

"Again with that nonsense?" Kent ground his teeth. "How many times do I have—"

Light flashed ahead of them. Smoke started to rise above the tree line in the location of the campsite. A man and a woman, each garbed in their black, sanctum clothes, ran into the road, their arms flailing. Behind them, a man with long, grizzly hair, wearing tattered leather armor chased them.

Righteous-Warrior Kent drew his blade and shouted, "We caught them in the act. Charge!"

Dirge hesitated. Something was wrong. The squad's horses whinnied in excitement as they sprinted to the peasant's aid. The wind picked up, gusting through the pines with whooshes and creaks. But the farm-folk made no sound at all.

Eyes widening, Dirge raised his arm. "Stop! Kent, stop the attack. It's a trap!"

The squad ignored him, racing ahead as more villagers stumbled into the road, chased by a dozen ragged brigands. Kent slashed at the first highwayman as he rode by. The blade sailed through the assailant as though the man didn't exist. The attacks by the rest of the squad proved equally ineffectual.

Anger burrowing in his stomach, Dirge urged his horse into a cantor, keeping his eyes on the trees. "Stay tight," he told Estonia. "This is an illusionist's work."

He prayed to his god, "Protect me, Ukase."

The power of God rushed into him, and Dirge summoned a cylindrical shield of force encompassing both him and his squire. When he reached the clearing the rest of the squad was in disarray. Meandering about, still slashing at the phantom brigands filling the area as crossbow bolts whizzed at them from the trees and slammed into their steel plate armor. The men shouted in pain, several already down with bolts protruding from their bodies.

"What's wrong with them?" Estonia asked. "It's as if they've lost their minds."

"In a way they have," Dirge replied. "The illusion is powered by Chaos. Before you say anything, I know it shouldn't be possible, yet the evidence lies before us. The Chaos has infected their minds because they did not guard against it. Kent is a fool." Dirge then scowled. "Forgive me. I should not have said that."

"What is there to forgive? It's true."

"Nevertheless, I should not speak that way of a fellow Righteous-Warrior." Closing his eyes, he clenched an empty fist. "Be quiet now and keep a watch out for the locations of the archers."

Crossbow bolts ricocheted off his shield as Dirge once again called out to his Lord, "Ukase, grant me the power to purify this land."

The will of Ukase flowed into his fist. It grew heavier and heavier as a Rod of Divinity formed from the pure might of the Lord of Order. Looking to be made of black iron, it was seven feet tall with the sigil of Ukase capping each end. Four more sigils jutted out of the center, one for each major direction of the compass.

"By the will of Ukase," Dirge bellowed, and slammed the rod into the earth.

A shockwave blasted away in all directions, sounding like the ringing of an enormous bell. The wave swept through the illusion, shattering and scattering it like dust motes before a gale. Kent and the rest of the squad shook themselves, as though coming out of a haze.

"Squad assemble," Kent bellowed. "Strike formation!"

An arc of light flashed from the trees to Dirge's left, at the middle of the tree line, followed by a thunderous boom. The bolt of lightning struck Kent, throwing him off his horse.

Dirge's shield was immobile, so he dropped it and charged the location with his blade before him. Another lightning blast lashed out at Dirge, but it struck his blade and arced to the ground to his left. The lightning had no effect on his blade— Death's Tongue had been a gift from his father.

Dirge caught sight of the light-wielder at the edge of the trees and knew immediately the man was a Chaos user by the hazy, wild aura whirling about him. And by the looks of his silvery, scale mail armor, Dirge guessed he was likely a former paladin. Tall and lanky, wild, black hair framed the man's gaunt face.

He's using gifts from the God of Light, but it's powered by Chaos, Dirge thought. *How is that possible?*

As he reached the tree line, Dirge bounded off his horse and gave chase into the forest, crashing through the thick underbrush which slowed him. Dirge knew the former paladin would outdistance him soon.

Dirge stopped. "Great God Ukase, I beseech you to surround us with your will."

A cylindrical wall of force surrounded Dirge for over a hundred feet, encircling the paladin as well. The paladin slammed into the wall and fell to the ground with a curse. The man stood, wiped blood from his nose, and faced Dirge with a snarl, drawing the rapier at his side.

Dirge advanced, holding his father's sword before him. His plate armor would protect him against the man's narrow, thin blade. But he would still need to be careful. Rapiers were fast and sharp and could find the gaps in Dirge's armor. So long as he didn't overextend himself, Dirge thought he'd be fine.

The paladin stepped forward into an opening in the trees and held up his left hand, loosing another bolt of lightning. It raced at Dirge, but his father's sword again deflected it to the ground. Dirge continued his approach, slow and steady. The best way to defeat Chaos was a disciplined, relentless attack.

Twenty feet away, the paladin lifted his hand once more, so Dirge raised his sword. But instead of lightning, a solid, thin beam of light struck Dirge in the chest a hand-width below his heart. It melted a hole in the steel plate, and pain flared in Dirge's chest. He shoved his blade over to intersect the light, but the damage was done. A hole, three-fingers wide now gaped in Dirge's armor. Smoke rose from the hole. His padded undercoat was smoldering, threatening to catch fire.

The paladin was down on one knee, panting. The attack had obviously taken a lot out of him. Dirge took the reprieve to draw his dirk with his left hand and shove the hilt into the hole to stifle any embers that might ignite. He gritted his teeth to keep from screaming, but he still groaned. He then pulled the dirk out and clutched it over the hole—with its long, slim blade, dirks were ideal for parrying and piercing mail armor. Dirge shuffle-stepped toward the paladin who had regained his feet.

"You've no idea how I've looked forward to this." The paladin's voice was soft and wispy. "I knew the attacks would bring you ... the man who had betrayed his own god to protect Travelers, the Great Lord's favorites."

Dirge ignored the remarks and continued to advance.

"I remember you from Gate Hall," the paladin continued, "how you leered at Betal's woman as she danced. Is that why you betrayed your god, for the lust of a woman? Like she would ever choose you when she was already bedding the Hand of God."

"Betal was not the embodiment of Chaos," Dirge said, hoping to distract the man. "He was the one who ended Edis' reign. He cast down your god."

The paladin laughed, shifting to his left, his rapier extended. "Oh, I've heard the lies. We all have."

Stepping forward, the paladin stabbed at the opening in Dirge's armor, but Dirge knocked it away and slashed. The paladin leapt out of reach.

"Is it true Daylin is now a god?" the paladin asked. "Yes, that part makes sense. She was touched by the Mother and made a god. That's why you forsook Ukase. That's why you took in Mangin and bed her every night." He feigned left and stepped back.

Dirge probed the paladin's right, but the man swatted his stroke to the side.

The paladin circled to the left. "She's quite fun. I've had her myself. When you see her, ask her about Lasan. I gave it to her like none other. But I warn you, Mangin has a way to twist your mind if you let her. You should have seen the way she wrapped Kenja around her fingers. That man would do anything to have her."

Dirge mirrored the paladin's footwork. The man was highly skilled, patiently waiting for Dirge to make a mistake. This paladin was quite unusual for one of his ilk.

Lasan grinned. "I bet *she's* the one who turned you from Ukase."

Dirge shuffled forward and stabbed at the paladin, but Lasan spun out of the way.

"Or did Daylin turn you herself? A woman you've lusted over for years who is now a god. You would do anything for her, wouldn't you? Even promise to protect a priest of Chaos."

Dirge stepped, stunned. How did the man know about his promise?

"So, it's true. You now worship another god."

Snarling, Dirge slashed at the paladin's legs.

Lasan jumped back and flicked his wrist.

Light blinded Dirge. It came from every direction, but unlike the earlier flash, this time it didn't dissipate. It remained. Dirge stepped back and raised his right arm over the slits in his helm, both to ward off the brilliance and for protection from a strike he wouldn't see coming.

"You're all so predictable," the paladin said as he jabbed at the slight gaps Dirge's plate. "The master will be quite pleased with me."

A strike slid under Dirge's armpit. Only the undercoat prevented it from going deeper than a slice.

"With your death I will grow even stronger," the paladin said. "I didn't get a chance to claim your friend's soul, but the master will enjoy feasting on yours."

Dirge pulled in on himself, trying to minimize his armor gaps.

The prodding sword poking at Dirge's right. "When I see Mangin at the next meeting I'll tell her you died like a dog," the paladin said. "She'll like that."

Dirge started to turn in the direction of the prodding and voice to protect his back but stopped. Why was the man taunting him? With his eyes shut tight, Dirge saw only black. Why would the paladin give away his position? Dirge realized he saw something more, a silhouette of pitch that radiated wrongness sliding to his left.

When the shadow closed in on his flank, Dirge struck with his dirk, slamming it into the center of the blackness with a thunk. He then swung and hacked at a downward angle with his sword. Dirge felt the sword's impact through the hilt.

The light winked out as the paladin's lifeless body gurgled and slid off Dirge's blades to the forest floor.

When his vision cleared, Dirge knelt next to the body, cringing from the pain. Hanging from a chain about the paladin's neck, a crystal pendant the size of Dirge's palm was lying halfway into the wound from Dirge's strike. Covered in blood, Chaos flickered from the pendant, but so did something else. The wrongness he sensed earlier came off the crystal in waves, each pulse growing slightly stronger than the one before. When Dirge pulled the pendant from the paladin's body, the pulse stopped, but the wrongness remained.

With sweat trickling down his face, Dirge hunched over in pain as he grabbed the paladin's corpse and dragged it into the center of the clearing. He dropped it and closed his eyes, concentrating, trying to deaden the pain. His eyes snapped open when Smythe addressed him.

"Is it true?" Smythe asked.

"Is what true?" Dirge replied, his voice weary. He counted the remaining, upright members of the squad as they gathered the marauders who still lived. Only two of the squad were down, one of which was Kent, whose body still lay where he'd fallen.

"I followed you into the forest but couldn't get through your shield to aid you. I heard what he said." Smythe's eyes narrowed, his hand sliding to his hilt. "Is it true you now follow the demon Daylin?"

"Daylin is not a demon."

"Then what about the witch? The two were obviously conspiring." Smythe clasped his hilt. "Are you part of their cabal?"

Dirge's voice turned hard a steel. "If you draw that blade, I will have your head for insurrection."

The clearing was quiet, everyone still, their attention on Dirge and Smythe. The faces of half the squad still held contempt, but the remaining stared at Dirge with adoration.

Smythe licked his lips and pulled his hand away, his eyes going to Righteous-Militants. "I apologize for my indiscretion, Righteous-Captain." He bowed. "I submit myself for punishment."

"We will see to that when we get home," Dirge said. "As for what the paladin said, you should know better than listen to the words of a Chaos wielder. He was trying to distract me. Nothing more."

Smythe's eyes narrowed slightly, but he made another bow. "Yes, sir. As you say."

Dirge nodded. "Bind and tether the prisoners—with them walking it will make it slow going, but they must meet justice— and then see to the wounded. Gather the heads of the dead thieves, we'll need them for identification. Any Militant who can't ride will be placed in a stretcher drawn by their horse until we reach Cool Winds. Also, place Righteous-Warrior Kent's body across his horse. I will bind him in place. He will return home in honor."

Upon returning to the Corners, Dirge decided that Smythe was to be raised to Righteous-Warrior as soon as Arch-Righteous Agadonday returned from Gate Hall. Dirge had put in the recommendation with the clerk at the bastion. Then he gave Smythe seven strikes of the rod for insubordination. Dirge felt Smythe deserved the promotion regardless of the man's momentary flare-up. Besides, it was what Kent would have wanted.

Sitting in his favorite short-backed chair, the warmth from the study's hearth-fire soaked into Dirge's skin through his cotton shirt. He set down his wineglass and fingered the spot where the paladin had burned him, now a pink scar. He marveled at how quickly the wound had healed after Immaculate Clara laid her hands on it. It reminded him of the day he was anointed a Righteous-Warrior. Heat gushed from her touch, so strong he thought he'd catch fire. It flowed through him like a massive river, aligning his body and spirit, and then stopped. She had then healed the rest of the squad.

Mangin lazily dusted the small bookshelf across from the study window. Dirge had no idea what information the four-dozen books held—nor did he care—but it was appropriate for a man of his stature to have a library, regardless of its size. She then moved behind his chair to dust something. To his shock, she pressed herself into the back of his head, and reached toward his drink in the side table.

"Would my Lord care for another?" she purred.

He snapped his finger and pointed at the lounger to his right. "Sit."

She stiffened against his head and quietly asked, "Am I nothing more than a dog now?"

"Mangin, please take a seat. There are things we must discuss."

The swishing of her dress as she strolled to the lounger was the only sound in the room other than the pops of the fireplace. She sat stiffly and refused to meet his eye. "What?"

He decided not to correct her lack of decorum. "The man leading the brigands was a former Chaos paladin. He claimed to know you." He went on to describe the man. "He said his name was Lasan."

"And?"

"Did you know him?"

"He doesn't sound familiar."

"He somehow knew I'd made a promise to Daylin, to protect you." He narrowed his gaze. "How did he know?"

Mangin finally looked his way. "He knew, or he *said* he knew?"

Dirge wiped the scowl from his face. "He claimed to have met you recently."

"He lied." She flicked her wrist. "Honestly, Dirge, you know better than to listen to some brigand who claimed to have been a paladin."

"It was more than a claim. He held Chaos while also wielding magics with light."

She narrowed her gaze. "How do you know he used ... Chaos?"

He pulled the crystal amulet from his vest. "He had this. It holds Chaos, though not nearly as much as it used to."

Her lips compressed, trembling slightly, and her back stiffened as she stared at the amulet. "How is this possible?"

"I was hoping you would tell me."

She seemed to snap out of a haze. "Again, how would I know? If I had access to something like that, do you think I'd still be hanging around here?"

"He said he was meeting with you. Perhaps he was planning on giving you one in the future."

Her face darkened and she turned her head. "Please put that away. I never thought you a cruel man, so please do not tempt me with something I will never know again." After he put it away, she straightened her dress. "As for the man, I told you, I don't know him."

"He claimed you two had ... congress together. How can you not recall that?"

She gave him a wilting look. "Congress? Really, that's what you're going with?"

"He said you two have been meeting with someone named Kenja."

"Kenja Badell? Last I saw him was ... Well, that doesn't

matter. I'm sure he's dead. He was too weak willed to have survived the loss of … his former god."

Eyes narrowing, Dirge knew she was trying to be evasive. "Kenja lived here in the Corners, didn't he?"

Mangin sighed. "Yes. I've known him since I was young, when Father first sent me to learn under that sniveling moron Dithiyar in Cool Winds."

"You've not seen him around, or Lasan?"

Throwing her arms wide, she snarled, "How would I meet anyone when I'm stuck in here all the time?"

Dirge relented, knowing she told the truth. She rarely left the building, and when she did, she was chaperoned. Besides, he would have recognized Lasan if the man had been near the manor. Dirge decided to ask Barnhold, just in case. Perhaps the Veridical would know something about Kenja. One couldn't be too careful regarding Chaos.

Mangin continued, "Kenja was the first person I has sex with. But truth be told, he wasn't very good. All grunting and trying to show dominance. How childish." She grinned wickedly, looking him up and down. "Unlike some men, men who ooze supremacy without even trying." She then tapped her lip. "I can't help but wonder, do you know what happened to your father?"

Anger and shame smashed Dirge. Springing from his chair, he marched out, Mangin's light giggles taunting his retreat.

Chapter 10

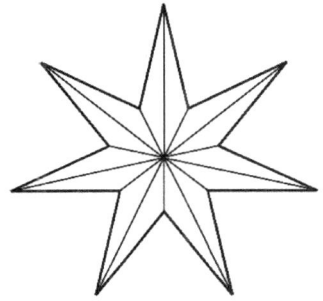

Desires and Devices

Laughter and conversation washed over Kenja. He sat with his back against the common room's wall, opposite the front window. The place smelled of sour beer mixed with baked bread and stew from the kitchen. Enjoying his ale, he kept his wide-brimmed hat pulled low over his eyes as he watched the street traffic. Follett's map told him to wait in the River Rest Inn for G'kaals—a bald man with the tshoma-pulled wagon who would lead him to Moira in the heart of the Great Waste.

Kenja figured G'kaals would be easy to spot. Tshomas were rare up north. The lizard-like creatures were often used as a beast of burden, but mostly in the southern desert region. Tshomas were roughly the size of an ox, but possessed short legs, making them stand only around four feet at the back. They had thick, leathery hide covered in small scales. Truth be told, Kenja was surprised G'kaals used one. It would stand out for those on the run, but it would attract the eyes of others as well. But then, the city of Kindermark was the largest river port on the southern edge of the Reach. A half dozen hamlets and mining towns spread to the east and south, not to mention the dozens on the southern end of the Westlands across the river. If anyplace would possess tshomas, it would be there.

Sitting next to Kenja was Dammers, a plump, former priest of Chaos. Wearing dark, commoner's clothes, Dammers clutched his ale tight—most likely to keep his pale hand from shaking. He bounced his right leg incessantly under the table.

Kenja had recognized Dammers when he first arrived at the inn. They had studied together in Gate Hall. Kenja didn't know where Dammers got his information about Moira, but he doubted it was from Follett. It must have been from a person or group funneling priests out of the Reach, and the hands of the stinking followers of Ukase. The question was, who would do such an organized thing for minions of Chaos?

"How much longer do we have to wait?" Dammers quietly asked. "I don't know about you, but I'm running low on coin." He took a swig, then wiped his mouth with the back of his hand. "Any one of these people could be agents for the Seekers."

Kenja doubted it. The cronies of Ukase had not yet spread to Kindermark, but the cursed god's influence was prevalent. The common-room tables were set up in a six-by-six grid, each table holding four chairs. It allowed enough room in between for the serving girls to weave in and out without jostling patrons. Or, just as likely, to limit their molestation by the drunken rabble.

Truth be told, the River Rest was just the kind of place Kenja liked: cheap, but not a dump, with only a small, central chandelier and a pair of lanterns at the bar for lighting. Kenja enjoyed the dimness, especially after his new allegiance.

He tapped the boundless well of power behind his third-eye, his connection to Dekriot. As his master burned into his soul, he wanted to scream in agony mingled with ecstasy. It took only a flash. His eyes turned ice-blue while he chilled his ale and then released the power. He didn't want anyone to notice the feeling of a hole of emptiness, one that threatened to swallow everything.

"What does it matter if there are agents?" Kenja said. "If they caught you, you'd no longer have to worry about being on the run."

Dammers shot him an angry look. "If they caught *me*? We're in this together. Don't forget."

"They won't catch me," Kenja replied. "I can take care of myself."

"Did you suddenly learn how to wield a blade when I wasn't looking?"

Kenja tickled the blackness in his soul but didn't embrace it. "You'll find out once we reach Moira."

A bar wench, likely in her mid-teens, glided up to their table. "Would you like something from the kitchen today?"

He eyed the auburn-haired young woman with a twist of his lips. Her off-blue skirt was too long, hanging just to the tops of her sandals, hiding her legs. And her tan blouse was far too puffy. Kenja couldn't decide if her chest was slim as a boy's or more like Mangin's.

The thought of his former lover brought a smile to his face. He would have her again, one day. His master had promised it. Only this time, she would be his to dominate, to take when he pleased or lend to others for favors. He wouldn't give her away, though. No, she would belong to him forever.

The appealing barmaid took a step back, uncertainty in her eyes. "Is everything all right, sir? Is there anything I can get you?"

Returning his attention to the maid, Kenja smiled, trying to make it warm. "What is your name, my dear? My friend and I have been here nearly a week and I never found out. How rude of me."

She took another step back. "My name's Anette."

"Anette," Kenja leaned forward, "I confess I *am* rather hungry." He looked her up and down again, taking his time doing so. "Why do you dress this way? The other girls at least show some thigh or breast. This isn't the Reach, my sweet. You can still dress as you please, do as you please. Why don't you show me what you're hiding under all that fabric?"

The barmaid's cheeks turned red and she lowered her head.

Kenja continued, "If you're too modest, we can go up to my room. Your face is lovely, and I'm betting your body is made for pleasure. I relish breaking women in and would pay you handsomely. No promises, but I think you'll enjoy it nearly as much as I will."

With trembling lips, she spun, and fled to the bar where she talked with the bartender. The tall, broad-shouldered man glared their way as the girl talked. He patted her on the shoulder, and she fled to the kitchen.

"What are you doing?" Dammers hissed. "You'll get us thrown out."

"Over some harmless flirtation?"

"I believe she's the man's daughter."

"So?" Kenja shrugged. "A smart man would charge me double for that."

When the bartender started their way, Kenja smirked. "Looks like you may be right. How silly. These people truly have lost their way."

Standing half a head taller than Kenja, the barkeep approached and crossed his arms. "I would appreciate if you would not treat my child that way. My barmaids are all honest women. If it's night-women you're after, there are several establishments down by the docks."

Taken aback, Kenja twisted his head. "Honest women? What does that even mean? I'm not asking if she—or any of them for that matter—are trustworthy. I simply want to fuck her for a few minutes, not keep her."

"Watch your tongue," the barkeep growled, his face hardening and mouth drawn in a line.

A smile spread across Kenja's mouth. "Or what?"

"That's it. Out, the both of you." He shouted over his shoulder to two muscle-bound men at the bar. "Don, Kek, escort these two to their room to get their belongings, and then see them to the door. They are henceforth barred from my inn."

Kenja snatched his newfound power and funneled it through his soul. It threatened to tear him apart, dragging across his soul like a rough saw on leather, before putting him back together. His eyes turned ice-blue and fog flowed from his mouth and nose as though he breathed in the harshest of winters. "I decide when I leave. Not you."

The innkeeper and the surrounding patrons drew back with fear in their eyes. Kenja was sure they felt the dread he emitted, his link to Dekriot.

Motion from beyond the inn's large windows drew Kenja's attention. A bald, dark-skinned man in simple workman clothes led a lizard-like creature, pulling a small wagon. A diminutive woman in a tan cloak sat in the passenger side of the driver's bench. The man stopped and turned to the inn a moment, then went about checking the beast's harness, while the woman jumped down and moved toward the center of town.

Who is she? Kenja wondered. *Could that be Moira?*

He shrugged and released his power. "Some other time," he said to the innkeeper, then looked over his shoulder. "Come along, Dammers."

"But I need my things," the former priest said.

"As you wish." Kenja shrugged. "I'm sure the good tavern owner's men will help carry your bags. I already have everything I need." He then stared at the innkeeper. "For the moment." He marched to the front door, considering all the things he could do to the innkeeper and his daughter.

The street traffic was modest for mid-day, at least on the north eastern side of town. Only a couple of dozen people walked the street in rustic tunics and pants, all of them wearing the same type of wide-brimmed hat Kenja sported. There were no trader wagons. Those clustered mostly at the warehouse district at the center of town, near the break where the land sloped to the river's edge. A warm breeze filled with scents from the river whisked away the stench of human and animal waste, but it did little for the cacophony. Kenja enjoyed it. It reminded him of his former home in at the Corners.

He strolled up to G'kaals and stopped a few feet away, showing him the signal to let the man know who he was: both arms low in front, his left arm grasping the right wrist with the right hand held open as though holding something. He then gave an appropriate phrase, "Good afternoon, my good man. Don't you just love a day with a crystal-clear sky?" The exact phrase didn't matter, so long as the word *crystal* was in there.

The man turned to Kenja, the thumb on his right hand clenched in his fist, and spoke with a slight lisp, "A clear day is always preferred, but I fear clouds may be on the way."

The man's reply indicated everything was good for them to go, but there might be trouble in the future.

"That always seem to be the case in the troubled world we now live in. My name's Kenja."

The man gave a sight bow of the head. "I am G'kaals."

"Who was the woman?" Kenja asked.

G'kaals shot a glance at a pair of men in colorful silk shirts walking past. "She is a friend of mine. Her name's Sashel. But let me save you the trouble. She has a man and isn't looking for another. Now, if you don't mind, I have much to do."

Kenja's back stiffened. "But—"

G'kaals interrupted him, "Perhaps I will see you on the road one day. Until then." He then went back to checking the tshoma's harness.

Turning, Kenja went up to Dammers who was just leaving the inn, lugging a pair of packs. "Come on, let's go," Kenja said. "We don't have all day."

Dammers stopped short, his eyes going to G'kaals and then back to Kenja. "What's going on?"

"We're leaving, that's what's going on." Kenja headed down the road toward the eastern road, not caring if Dammers followed.

Dammers caught up, his packs bouncing on his back. "I don't understand."

Kenja replied, his voice low, "He inferred he would pick us up on the road. It makes sense. People might start noticing if he was constantly ferrying strangers into the woods. Once we're a good way into the forest, we'll step off the road and keep an eye out for him."

After walking for an hour, Kenja chose to stop and strode a half-dozen paces into the woods. The town was well out of sight and there was virtually no chance anyone was spying on them. He had a good view of the road, and the underbrush should keep them hid from prying eyes. Not that he expected any. The branch they took had very little sign of traffic.

Dammers crouched, panting. "I don't know how much more I can take of this." He let his lumpy bag slide off his shoulder to land with a thump.

With a shake of the head, Kenja chuckled. "How did you even get this far south?"

"I took a boat. I'm not made for life on the road."

Kenja pointed at Dammers' bag. "What in the Great Lord are you carrying that's got you puffing like that?"

The former priest didn't look up. "My books."

"Books?" Kenja stared, incongruity on his face. "Are you

telling me you've been lugging those things all the way from Gate Hall?"

"Yes. I couldn't leave them. It's a life's worth of research."

"I always heard you were a fool, but I didn't know you were stupid," Kenja said with a laugh. "What if one of those thrice-damned Ukasers demanded to look in your bag? The Seekers have a way of winnowing out the truth, but with you they'd have no need. You might as well be carrying a sign pronouncing your allegiance to the Great Lord." Kenja glanced between Dammers and his pack. "What kind of research?"

"I've been examining the connection between the Mother, and the gods of Life and Death. How connected they are. I'm also seeing how they interact with the Soul Stone. Is it all separate, or are they all linked beyond the obvious?"

Kenja's cold, black center, his connection to Dekriot, pulsed. It seemed his master had interest in the connection as well.

He was about to ask another question when the jingle of harness and the creak of an axle came from the road. Kenja looked up. "It seems our ride is here."

They sat in the back of the small wagon opposite one another surrounded by two dozen sacks. As the wagon rocked to and fro, Kenja eyed Dammer's pack, contemplating the potential wonders therein.

Instead of pressing Dammers, Kenja turned to Sashel in the driver's seat. "What's in the sacks?"

She turned toward him, her dark hair spilling over her shoulders and framing a pale face. "Food, mostly. We can't exactly farm out there. Others contain minerals to help purify the crystals we mine from beneath the Waste."

"People aren't suspicious you're buying food this close to God's Wonder?"

"They think we're from the mountains beyond, just a couple of miners with no time to farm."

"Where do you get your meat?" Dammers asked.

Sashel laughed. "We don't. There's no game left here with all the grunkin about."

Shaking, Dammers stiffened. "There are grunkin around here?"

"Many dozens," G'kaals replied. "But you needn't worry. I

will protect you as best I can here in the forest."

Kenja cocked his head. "And just how will you do that?"

G'kaals shivered. His scalp and clothing slid off like sand, revealing a large head and slim body. G'kaals' skin was shiny and jet-black but covered with yellow splotches. Hanging over the wagon seat was a long, whip-like tail. "I am a Plaz," he said. "It is a gift from the Mother. I can mask my appearance and scent at will. Although, it does cause me considerable strain when I do the same to my surroundings."

"Fascinating," Dammers said. "In all my research on the Mother, I've never come across your people. Do you also go to the Great Soul Stone when you die?"

"Of course we do," G'kaals snapped. "We have souls, like any other—we are not imps or demons." Grunting, he flicked the reins, but the tshoma did not increase its speed.

"By 'surroundings,' do you mean you can do the same with us?" Kenja asked.

"Yes," G'kaals replied. "It is why Ms. Moira summoned me. When grunkin approach in the forest, I simply mask us all until it leaves. Although, the illusions do not work well in the Waste."

Sashel smirked. "That's why I'm here."

As if summoned, a high-pitched wail, like that of a trumpet, came from the right.

G'kaals pulled the wagon to a stop. "Stay quiet and don't move."

The air around them shimmered. All of them—wagon and tshoma alike—seemed to melt like ice over a roaring fire. In their place was a large shrub.

Kenja worried. It was an obvious disguise. Though grass sprouted between the often-used wagon tracks of the road, it had not been so unused that a shrub of this size should be there. Grunkin might not possess much intelligence, knowing only to kill anything they saw, but they were still clever.

Cracking twigs announced its approach, moving through the trees at a trot. The size of a bear, it looked like a massive porcupine with six legs, and a short, snake-like nose. Its three large, yellow eyes scanned the road until it stopped ten feet away. Lifting its stubby, trunk-like nose it sniffed several times. Its quills stood on-edge, quivering and rattling like a dozen vipers, as the grunkin puffed up, raising its haunches. It opened its mouth, revealing multiple rows of needle-like teeth, and drool poured onto the ground.

The stench of rotten meat, as though left in the sun for days, hammered Kenja. He knew it was about to pounce. He reached into the blackness of his soul and grasped his master's power.

The grunkin stopped its shaking and twisted its head like a quizzical dog. With a grunt, it spun and raced back the way it came.

After several minutes passed, the illusion about the wagon fell.

"Why did it do that?" Dammers asked. "Did it smell us?"

"No," G'kaals replied. "I masked our scent as well."

Sashel shook her head. "This is not the first time one has acted queer. Ever since Edis' touch left the world, the remaining grunkin have lost some of their frenzy. They no longer attack each other."

"This is true," G'kaals said. "They roam and hunt like normal predators—enraged predators."

Sashel turned to Kenja and Dammers. "That, of course, does not mean they aren't a threat. But they will not approach Moira's compound. We will be safe there." Lowering her gaze, she chewed her lip. "But is any place safe with the minions of Ukase choking the world until it succumbs to their god's will?"

As the surrounding trees thinned and became stunted, Kenja contemplated on how to bed Sashel—it had been far too long, and the interaction with the bar wench had him randy. Plus, there was something about the young woman that reminded him of Mangin.

Yes, he thought. *You will learn to love my touch, just at Mangin will.*

The breeze shifted, carrying a stink, a mixture of rot and burned ozone. Kenja's skin tingled.

"By the Great Lord," Dammers said, his eyes wide with wonder. "I can feel it, the Lord's Breath."

Kenja realized he also sensed a thin miasma of Chaos all about them, but it held no call to him. Kenja's new master was all.

G'kaals pointed ahead to the oncoming forest's edge. "We have reached the Waste."

Brown, wilted grass dotted the ground for a half-mile. Beyond, lay a two-mile-wide shimmering lake of solidified Chaos, looking like massive plates of shattered, multi-hued glass. The residual Chaos caused the air to waver.

Dammers smiled at Sashel. "It must be glorious to once again be always surrounded by the Lord's Breath. How do you stand it, losing His touch every time you go into town?"

"Chaos has to call to me," she replied. "I bow to the will of another, now."

Kenja cocked an eyebrow, intrigued at how close her statement mirrored his. He scanned her exposed skin for the sign of the incubus' kiss but found none. "Sashel, have you ever met Follette Dinar?"

"From the Citadel? Of course. She's a bore." Sashel paused. "But she was right. And those of us who paid attention, had a leg up. Those who didn't ..." She glanced at Dammers. "That's why we're here, risking our lives. I hope you appreciate that."

Dammers bobbed his head. "I do, believe me. Thank you."

Stopping short of the Waste, G'kaals hopped down and slipped canvas bags onto the tshoma's feet. "The surface is corrosive. These—along with the wheels—are warded to nullify the effect." He hopped back onto the driver's seat and shook the reins, urging the tshoma into the Waste.

The glass-like crust of Chaos popped and snapped beneath the wagon's wheels. "We leave an obvious trail," Kenja said. "If some Ukase-lover sees this, it may draw the Seekers."

"There are no worries there." Sashel then pointed ahead to an unbroken surface. "We took this same route to town only a few hours ago. It may not look it, but the residual Chaos is still fluid, acting much like dried tree sap."

There was no smell in the air, as though the breeze dared not enter the plain. Kenja reveled in it, reminded of the brief moment he was in the presence of Dekriot.

Out of the wavering haze, a building stood as though it had sprouted from the molten surface. It was shockingly untouched.

"Why is it untouched?" Kenja asked.

"Moira said she found it like this. We're not sure why. I've always thought it had something to do with Heartless."

Dammers joined their conversation. "But he created the Waste. Why save one townhouse?"

"Because, this was *his* house," Sashel replied.

Four stories high, the white stucco walls and gray-tiled roof blended with the background. It had four windows abreast on each floor except the first where a single door was centered. On the building's right side, an arched entrance with a pair of doors meeting at the center pierced a ten-foot high wall. Kenja presumed it was for a drive leading to the back of the building. He'd seen many townhouses from bygone days in Gate Hall. This one likely had an open yard in the back as well. It was said that Heartless came from a wealthy family, so he expected the yard to be quite large.

G'kaals pulled to a stop at the front door. "You will enter here. I must take the cart around back."

Kenja jumped out next to Dammers, who shook his head and said, "This truly is holy ground."

Kenja eyed Dammers' bag as the man passed into the house. Kenja was unable to keep a grin from his face. He then turned to Sashel who approached him. "You said you would protect us in the Waste. How?"

Sashel kicked off her sandals. With a smile, she pointed into the Waste, just off the track they took. The surface cracked, and five-feet-tall spikes of stone jutted up. Their sharp tips sparkled in the sun. "That is what I do. I also create the crystal shards— there is a large deposit beneath the entire Waste, but Moira used up all she could gather within the safety of the house. I make the shards, and Moira imbues them with Chaos. We then give them to those who need them." She spread her arms wide. "And it is all thanks to Amurru who found me in my deepest point of despair."

"The God of Earth and Stone?" Kenja had to reassess the young woman. Her story might be a lie to cover her connection to Dekriot. But again, it might not. In which case, Sashel would need to be eliminated once his job here was done.

"Why are you helping Moira?"

"I feel sorry for my former brothers and sisters." She cocked her head. "Like you. You are all lost. We are simply helping you get by until you escape the region to find your own path in the world." With that, she turned in entered building.

Chapter 11

Fruitless Search

Mangin's head throbbed as sweat trickled down the alabaster skin of her cheek. With only the light of her single lantern Dirge limited her to, her eyes strained. She wanted to scream in rage at both his stubbornness, and her lack of success. Thus far, she found no secrets hiding in her books. No mysteries to manipulating the mind without Chaos. She worried that they might have been in the volumes she lost, but she doubted it. Betal said she still had power within her, but began to wonder if he was wrong. Her entire life had revolved around Chaos, and without it, she was nothing, leaving her feeling hollow and blind. The world was now empty, a massive void without the constant caress of the Lord's Breath. It was not a life worth living.

She slammed the book closed and sighed. That type of thinking didn't help. It led to anguish and melancholy, two things that sapped her strength, and she needed every bit. Mangin refused to give up. The answer had to be in there somewhere, but she wasn't going to find it tonight—just as she hadn't found it the night before ... or the one before that.

Standing, she stretched, stifling a yawn. It was late, hours past sundown, and she had to get up early. Dirge had left her day-to-day supervision to Estonia because he said, "It would do you both some good ..." Whatever in the hells that meant. The squire was a taskmaster with limitless energy. Aside from his own workout regimen and training he did with Dirge, the heartless young man had Mangin up before dawn, scrubbing floors, cleaning out fireplaces, dusting, and a half-dozen other things.

"At least he hasn't stuck me in the kitchen yet," she said with a yawn, pulling off her nightshirt. She was supposed to sleep with it on, according to Barret's wife—the woman was teaching her how to behave as a *proper* woman in the eyes of Ukase. But Mangin refused to wear the thing. She loved the feel of the sheets against her bare skin, even the ones she now had, though they were of a far worse quality than she was used to.

Mangin turned down the lamp and crawled into bed. Her hands played across her body, and her mind drifted to better times. She thought of Betal, of the first time she finally tasted him and felt his power and manhood within her. Her fingers tweaked her nipples and caressed her womanhood as she thought of Daylin. Mangin remembered the amazement at how voracious the woman was in her lovemaking. Mangin still felt chagrin over all the opportunities she'd missed due to her misguided jealousy.

But mostly, she thought of her darling, Adel. How the young woman smelled, her touch, her taste, how she felt in Mangin's arms as they made love, and the warm glow they shared afterward. Mangin rocked and shook, groaning in climax.

Panting, sweat soaked her skin as she came down from her bliss. She wondered where Adel—the love of her life—was at that moment, and if she returned Mangin's adoration. Regardless, wherever Adel was, it was safer there than with Mangin.

"Take care of her, Worm," Mangin whispered.

Closing her eyes tight, she reached out with her will, hoping the new god and Hand of the Mother in the world would hear her. "Please, Daylin, if you can hear me, look out for my Adel. She needs your protection; something I can no longer offer her."

She drifted off to sleep, hoping to find success in her search the next evening.

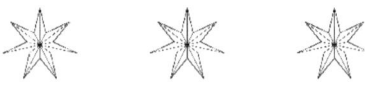

Dust motes filled the air, illuminated by the light streaming through the parlor windows. Heat from the fireplace pummeled Mangin as she shoveled ash into the steel ash-bucket. Once finished, she stood, rubbed her aching back, and whipped sweat from her brow. Filth clogged her nails, and her hair was a tangled mess. Cuts and abrasions covered her hands from all the scrubbing and cleaning. The least Dirge could do was let her wear decent clothes; her black dress fit like a sack and hid all her wonderful attributes. *How dare the man! I should clock him upside the head for what he's done to me!*

Sighing, she shook her head, annoyed with herself, rather than Dirge—she'd be dead if not for him. She'd found nothing in her reading, no hidden truth between the words. Her power was gone and nothing would bring it back. It was time to given up.

"Why are you standing there pouting?" Estonia asked behind her.

Mangin jumped. "Don't frighten me like that!"

He strode forward and loomed over her. "Watch your tone."

Mangin was not a short woman, but Estonia stood a good head taller. Looking away, she shrunk in on herself and muttered, "I'm sorry."

"You're sorry, what?"

She ground her teeth. "I'm sorry, My Lord."

"I am not your Lord. That is Dirge. You will address me as Squire Estonia." After Mangin nodded, he continued, "Go dump those ashes, and then tend to the fire in *Your Lord's* chambers. The last I saw the hearth it was choking in ash. When's the last time you cleaned it?"

"I don't remember. He doesn't like—"

"I told you to address me properly!" The young man nearly shook and his eyes burned with hate. "Go dump that bucket and tend his hearth, now!"

She dropped a slight curtsy—another thing she hated

doing—and murmured, "Yes, Squire Estonia."

Mangin shuffled off, making sure not to spill the ash bucket. Once out of the room, she quivered with her own anger. Oh, how she hated that man. At least Dirge treated her with a modicum of respect and was kind to her—even if it was out of pity. She wanted to throw the bucket at Estonia, but that would only gain her a caning from the squire.

After dumping the bucket into the ash pit—to later be spread on the fields—she returned the bucket and went upstairs to Dirge's suite. Her hand hesitated before opening the door. Dirge told her not to go into his rooms, but she knew Estonia would beat her if she didn't. She'd wanted to see his rooms for some time, and this was her opportunity. Dirge would be upset, but it was his stinking squire's fault. Besides, the worst Dirge would dole out would be a stern scolding.

A smile spread across her face. She finally, after what seemed like a lifetime, got the chance to do what she wanted. Even small victories were something.

Mangin entered and stopped short. "This place is a mess." Dust covered the tables and furniture. Ash choked the fireplace, and the bucket was overflowing. The fire in the hearth was nearly dead, and a chill filled the room. "How does he stand it?"

She filled the hearth bucket three times before she was able to re-stoke the fire. Then, she went about dusting. After finishing the sitting room, she entered the bedroom and stopped. He had a massive, four-post bed, two lounge chairs, two wardrobes, and a stand for his shining steel-plate armor. However, it was his sword that drew her. He rarely wore it, but when he did, it was like a part of him. But here, alone on its stand, the sword both frightened and enthralled her. It looked no different from any other blade, yet it gave off a sense of foreboding, like a snake ready to strike, only controlled.

Dirge's voice boomed behind her, "Don't touch it."

Mangin jumped, a lump in her throat and heart hammering. She was surprised at her closeness to the blade—within arm's reach. She didn't remember crossing the room. Mangin spun around. "Don't scare me like that!"

He strode up to her with the grace of a wild cat. "What are you doing in here?"

She swallowed the lump. "Your squire ordered me to clean

your room, and I didn't feel like telling him no and getting a beating for it."

Dirge's eyes went wide. "When did he lay hands on you?"

She wanted to lie, to tell him Estonia did it all the time, but thought better of it. "It was several weeks ago. In retrospect, I probably shouldn't have slapped him. But he deserved it. He said you should have taken Adel to the Truth-Seekers, that if she were still under the influence of Chaos, she deserved purifying."

Dirge growled. "I will have words with him." He then regained his usual stony expression. "In the meantime, I want you to leave."

She pursed her lips. "In a moment."

His eyebrows furrowed. "What?"

"There's been something I've wanted to ask you for some time, but up until now, I've not had the chance." She paused, trying to decide the best tact. "You should have died when you fought Hogar. But you didn't. In fact, you were a marvel, both beautiful and terrifying." She paused again. "You were like *death*, come to life."

"I did what I had to do." He motioned toward the door. "Now, if you please?"

But Mangin refused to give in. "Hogar had said something, but it didn't strike me until just now. He called your sword *Death's Tongue*, the blade of the High Slayer." Gliding forward, she ran a finger down his cheek, and her skin tingled. "That's the Brotherhood of Assassins, isn't it?" When he didn't reply, she went further, running her fingers through his curly, black hair. "Your father is the head of the Brotherhood. Tell me I'm wrong."

He took a deep breath. "You are not wrong."

More things tumbled into place. Pressing her body into his, she felt afire, wanting him so badly. Yet dared not press too much, like a horse trainer breaking in a new stallion. "And you were a member once yourself."

Lust burned in his eyes as he breathed deep, but then he blinked and shook his head. Grasping her arms gently, he pushed her away. "Everything you said is true. But that was a long time ago. Now, if you would please, leave my room and do not come back."

She wanted to scream in frustration, her body aching to be

touched. Lowering her head, she nodded. "As you wish, My Lord."

When she reached the outer door, Dirge spoke up. "I will talk to Estonia. He'll never lay hands on you again. And I'll send to the Corners for another maid to help you. This house is too big for only yourself. I see how much it's taking out of you."

"Yes, My Lord. Thank you."

"Also, don't forget you are to attend service tomorrow with Barret and his wife. Amelia is a good woman, she'll look out for you."

Worry ate at Mangin. She had not taken Ukase into her heart—nor would she. What would happen when she stepped into that hall? "Yes, My Lord. Thank you." Mangin closed the door behind her and shivered.

Chapter 12

The Light of God

The sun glittered off the Cunning River, and the morning breeze drifting through the carriage window carried the scent of lilac and pine. Colorful birds flitted about, their chirps light and cheerful. It was as if the world mocked Mangin.

She tugged at the collar of her dress. It was so constricting she was sure the thing was made to choke her. Though tight at the neck and wrists, the rest of the black, ruffled dress was so loose it felt like a sack. And with a hem going an inch below her feet, she needed to lift it to keep it out of the dirt and not trip. The only part of the ensemble she liked was her thigh-high, black stockings and slippers accentuated her pale legs, but with her ridiculous dress, no one would ever see it. She scowled and pulled at her collar again.

"Try not to fuss at it," Amelia said, wearing the same garb as Mangin, except for a hint of white lace at the top of the collar. She sat next to her husband, Barret, on the seat opposite

Mangin's. "You look quite lovely."

Mangin's mouth quirked. "How can you tell?" Amelia made her wear a deep, black bonnet that completely covered her red hair and face. It was like looking at the world from a tunnel. Oddly, the only thing not black was her snow-white gloves. "Does everyone have to dress like this?"

"It is proper attire for a woman." Amelia then pointed to her husband. "And men dress thusly." Barret's black coat was buttoned to the neck, with only the collar and cuffs of his white shirt visible. His pants and shoes were also black, but he wore no gloves, as he held his wide-brimmed white hat in his lap.

"Why does everything have to be so somber?" Mangin asked. "It's like yo—" She cleared her throat to choke out the word. "It's like Ukase doesn't believe in color."

"One does not question the word of God," Amelia said. "That kind of talk will see you into the Chastenary. Please, young miss. Do be more careful. We are members of Lord Dirge's household. We do not want to bring shame to him or his house."

Mangin looked away and muttered, "The only shame is I didn't bed him."

Amelia gasped. "Please, Miss Mangin, you must watch what you say. It's not proper, especially in public."

Mangin went back to staring out the window. They entered the bazaar, right in front of the town hall, which was formerly the temple to Chaos. There had been much discussion over whether or not to tear it down, but it was decided that since it predated the reign of Chaos and was the seat to the Council of Merchants it would remain. They turned east down the main road into what used to be the East Warren, which had been cleared away for the sanctum and the Chastenary, along with organized and sturdy housing.

Amelia spoke again, her voice hesitant, "Are you saying … How do I put this? Do you … *wish* to be his wife?"

Mangin's head snapped around. "Wife? Of course not. No. I just— I want …"

Closing her eyes, she lowered her head. She wanted her freedom, to be able to do as she pleased, to take Dirge to bed and ravish him. She was certain Dirge would be as good as his father. Mangin wanted other things as well.

She grinned and glanced up at Amelia. There was something about the short, plump woman Mangin found enticing. Amelia's face was round and rather plain, but her gray eyes held care and warmth. And though currently tucked away in that silly bonnet, her long, sandy-blonde hair had shimmered in the candlelight when helping Mangin prepare the night before. Oh yes, Mangin wanted to show the "godly" woman true ecstasy—if only as a repayment for the kindness she'd showed.

The throttling collar of Mangin's dress—as though Ukase was threatening to choke out her life—brought reality crashing down. Her smile faded, and she sunk in on herself. "It doesn't matter what I want. I'm now forced to take what comes to me."

"That's right," Amelia said. "And it is a good thing. Ukase has a plan for you—for us all. We need only to obey, and we will bask in His glory in the hereafter, cradled in His loving arms forever."

"Forever?" Mangin tilted her head. "That doesn't make sense. We don't go to the god's realm when we die. We go to the Soul Stone and are then reborn."

Barret glared at Mangin, then grumbled and shifted away, looking out the window. "You should not say such things."

Amelia patted her husband's thigh. "Hush now, my love. It is my place to guide her. Remember?" After Barret apologized, Amelia turned back to Mangin. "You must not blaspheme. The ancient myths and superstitions are to be forgotten. Ukase has returned, and he will show us the way to glory."

Mangin couldn't believe what she heard. *Superstitions*? She had gazed into the Stone herself, albeit briefly, and had been in the presence of Aelaz, the God of Life. What were the Veridicals teaching these people? Mangin was about to retort when the carriage came to a stop.

It appeared she was about to find out.

The coach jostled when Barret's two boys jumped down from the driver's seat. The eldest, Jon, opened the left door for Barret, while the younger, Ben, opened the other for Mangin and Amelia. Both boys were tall and slim, like their father, and wore clothes to match.

People milled about in front of the temple to Ukase. The women gathered on the left, chatting with their girls at their sides, while the men and boys stood solemnly on the right.

Beyond them, the white walls of the rectangular sanctum seemed to glow. Etched in the round window near the roof was the symbol of Ukase—a glowing, seven-pointed star, looking like seven diamonds radiating from a central point, with a line bisecting each one from center to tip.

As they made their way to the women's side, Mangin roasted in the mid-morning heat, her sack-dress feeling like she wore a thick wool blanket before a raging fire. Her only relief was the breeze off the river funneling to her face. She itched to rip off her bonnet and bask in the wind's cool caress.

A woman closer to the sanctum—her wrinkled face barely visible—waved at Amelia. "Goodly-wife Kentson," the woman said. "How are you this fine day?"

"Who is Kentson?" Mangin asked as the woman approached.

"It's the family name Barret took upon accepting Ukase into his heart," Amelia said. "He didn't have one originally, so like most others, he used his father's, adding son to the end as an honorific. As his wife, I of course took Kentson as well, supplanting my previous family name."

"You had a second name already. That's rather rare."

"Yes." Amelia kept glancing over to the waving woman. "My father was on the merchant's council. My family is an old one. We've lived here going back hundreds of years." She sighed. "Father was not happy I left the business to be with Barret. A couple of years later, my father was almost apoplectic when my sister moved to one of the eastern villages. He wound up with no children left to take over for him."

A tingling started at the base of Mangin's neck as a memory popped up, one about a sister. "What was—" Mangin had to clear her throat. "What was your family name?"

"Floweret," Amelia said, and then turned to the newcomer.

"Amelia, my dear," the woman said, "how wonderful to see you. Did you hear about—" She glanced at Mangin and put her arm around Amelia. "Let's go over here. I have some unfortunate news."

Mangin barely paid attention as her head spun and the world seemed to tilt. Amelia was Adel's sister. How? Was it all some kind of sick retribution for her past life as a priest of Edis? But more importantly, had Dirge known all along?

She felt like throwing up.

"Are you all right, my child?" a woman asked behind her, then took hold of Mangin's elbow. The tall, slim woman of middling years came in front of Mangin. She looked familiar, in a pure white dress with a black Star of Ukase outlined in red on each shoulder, and her salt and pepper hair in a tight bun.

"Do I—" Mangin tried to get a hold of herself but failed as her head still felt light. "Do I know you? Have we met?"

"Of course we have, silly girl," the woman replied in short clips. "I am Immaculate Clara. I head the Chastenary." Clara's face was one of pure serenity, yet there was a tightness in her eyes that worried Mangin.

A bell tolled from the sanctum, and Clara nodded to Mangin. "I must take my place. Ukase be with you." She then glided into the temple.

Sweat stared to trickle down Mangin's lower back. The last thing she needed was to run afoul of such an odious woman.

Amelia returned, frowning and her eyes saddened. "Maddie said a good friend of ours, Zama, was sent to the Chastenary. Apparently, she ..." Amelia chewed at her lip. "She lusted after Barret. I've known Zama for years. How could she do such a thing? And what else has she been hiding?" Amelia shook herself. "Best not to dwell on it."

She then placed a hand on Mangin's back. "We must wait for the men to enter and take their seats. We will follow after and sit on his outside. You needn't worry about finding him in a timely matter, as we always sit in the same place—halfway up, right on the outside aisle."

The closer Mangin looked at Amelia, the more she saw Adel. They had the same nose, the same eyes—albeit a different color—and the same lips. Mangin wondered if they had other things in common as well. It hadn't taken much tweaking to improve Adel's intellect—the young woman's mind was already sharp, and all Mangin had to do was streamline a few things. Was Amelia the same? Mangin had a feeling Amelia led Barret round by the nose without even letting the man know it. Mangin smiled. That meant they had other things in common as well. The moment Mangin had delved Adel's mind, she knew the lovely blonde was attracted to women as well as men. What would it take to test the theory now that she no longer had access to Chaos? Betal had said Mangin still had the ability to touch minds. The question was, how?

"You know, you've quite a lovely smile," Amelia said. "I can see why Lord Dirge has taken a shine to you."

Mangin's smile grew. "Did he say as much?"

"Not in words, but I've seen the way he looks at you. Now, I know you said you do not seek to rise above your station, and become his wife, but if you should change your mind ..." She shrugged and then placed a hand on Mangin's back, gesturing toward the sanctum. "The men are all inside. We must enter now."

Mangin jumped, her head snapped to the building. Her eyes focused on the symbol of Ukase radiating in the window. The light filled her with fear and dread, as though it pierced her mind and heart, judging her. She swallowed. "I don't even know what to do."

"I will guide you as it goes," Amelia said. "Just do as I indicate and say not a word."

The women filed in two at a time. Mangin suppressed a shudder when entering. It interior was dim. The only light came from candles ensconced on the walls between tall, arch-topped windows that ran down the sides of the sanctum. The farthest window was even with the foremost row of benches. There were six columns of the simple wooden benches, three on either side of a central aisle wide enough for four men to walk abreast. Aisles ran the length at the outsides as well, but only wide enough for two people at best.

Amelia guided Mangin down the outer aisle—which apparently was intended for the women as none used the center, not even those who sat next to their husband. Once Mangin settled in at the outermost portion of the bench, she started to scan the room, but Amelia nudged her with an elbow. Adel's sister shook her head, and then lowered it with her hands in her lap.

This is ridiculous, Mangin thought as she followed suit. A few moments later, Veridical Barnhold's voice boomed from the front of the congregation, causing Mangin to start.

"You may lift your eyes, adherents," Barnhold said. Light from above the doorway bathed the Veridical.

Mangin found the sermon odd. For the men, it entailed lots

of sitting and standing while muttering prayers. But whenever the men stood, the women had to kneel with their heads down in *silent reverence*. It was ridiculous. And, it got worse. Amelia took hold of Mangin's elbow to guide her when to kneel. And every time she did, Mangin shuddered as thoughts of Adel flashed through her, filling her with both sorrow and desire.

Mangin muttered under her breath, "I don't know how much longer I can take this."

Amelia grasped Mangin's thigh, sending a jolt shot straight to her privates—she bit her lip to keep from moaning. The farmer's wife put a finger to her lips, making a shushing motion. She pointed at Mangin, then herself, and then at her lips. For a brief moment, Mangin thought her mind was slipping, thinking the woman asked for a kiss until Amelia went on to shake her head, and with her hand, mimicked a closed mouth.

Mangin remembered what Amelia had said about not talking and realized what she really meant. "You can't be serious," she whispered.

Amelia's eyes were wide, her head rapidly bobbing in tiny nods.

Mangin's eyes went back to the Veridical. As he spoke, an aura pulsed off him in waves, making Mangin squirm, much like the sanctum's widow had. Only worse. The pulse pushed at her, slamming down as though to shove her face through the floorboards. She knew the light was the spirit of Ukase trying to force Mangin to his will, to drive her into submission until nothing of her remained. In the eyes of this god and his Veridicals, and Seekers, and Righteous Warriors, Mangin was nothing but a lowly woman, a possession to be seen, but only when they wished it.

Anger flared in Mangin. How dare this man and his oppressive god try to force her to be less? "I will not submit," she mumbled. She clutched her dress with trembling hands.

A hand fell on her shoulder.

Clara loomed over Mangin's shoulder, her eyes hard. She motioned for Mangin to stand and follow.

Mangin stared at Clara and seethed. Whatever the woman wanted, it didn't bode well for Mangin. She took a deep, calming breath and opened her mouth to apologize. Clara grabbed Mangin's arm, yanking her to her feet. The woman's bony fingers were like a vise as she towed Mangin down the aisle.

Mangin stumbled. "Slow down." She hopped she didn't fall, because there was no doubt the enraged woman would drag her regardless. A pair of gray-haired women in dresses matching Clara's followed them outside.

Once they were outside, Mangin asked, "Where are you taking me?"

"You are guilt of delinquency in the eyes of God," Clara said. "Thus, I am taking you to where all women go to be judged: the Chastenary."

Chapter 13

The Chastenary

The words rang in Mangin's ears: the Chastenary. People called it "the house of pain," spoken either in fearful hushed tones or with veneration. The sight of it in the distance twisted Mangin's stomach. Constructed in the shape of the Star of Ukase, the two-story high building was roughly twice the size of the bazaar. Windows ran along the top of its white walls, right under the broad eaves, and there was only one entrance: a pair of blood-red doors at the end of the southernmost point.

"Please don't," Mangin said. "I'm sorry. I won't do it aga—" She stopped short and yelped as the woman on Mangin's right nearly yanked her arm out of place.

"The guilty do not speak unless bidden to," the woman said in a low, sharp tone.

"Immaculate Mara is correct," Clara said without breaking stride. She stopped at a stone path of black-slate, two-hundred feet from the doors. "You must now remove your shoes. The path or correction must be met with reverence and humility."

When Mangin lifted her dress to remove her slippers, Clara hissed, "Decorum, young woman! Do not bare your flesh in public."

"I wasn't—" Mangin cut herself short and changed her tact. "How am I supposed to remove my slippers if I don't lift my hem, Immaculate Clara?"

Clara sighed, shook her head, and replied as though to a child, "By kneeling, and placing your hands under it, of course."

Mangin wanted to slap the insufferable woman but knew it would make everything much worse. She knelt and removed her slippers, one at a time, and stood with her head high.

Clara continued their march to the Chastenary. The heat from the black slate walk made Mangin fidget. She thought if it were mid-day, rather than late morning, it might actually raise blisters. She did her best not to think of it until she saw the slate ended fifty feet from the red doors. There, the path turned to jagged gravel. *What is with these people?*

As though reading Mangin's thoughts, Clara spoke up. "This last portion is as a reminder to tread lightly in the eyes of God."

The Immaculates flanking Mangin tightened their grips on her arms and marched forward. As Mangin gingerly set her right foot—already smarting from the hot slate—on the jagged path she yelped and nearly collapsed. The Immaculates kept her from falling, but they didn't stop moving forward either. Mangin scrambled to keep her feet, clenching her teeth to keep from shouting—she didn't want to give them anymore satisfaction than they already had at her expenses. She took each step with caution, surprised the women slowed to her pace instead of simply dragging her. The rocks weren't sharp enough to actually cut, as she'd first thought, but they were still painful, especially to one who hadn't made a habit of running around barefoot like some kind of animal.

When Clara stopped, Mangin gave a start at seeing the set of red doors right in front of her. She'd been concentrating so hard, she'd not realized they were there.

Clara spoke, her back rigid and head high, "Once we are inside, I will show you what happens to the wicked. Most have come from across the river—those here already know what is proper in the eyes of God. All though, there are the occasional Delinquents—such as yourself—and even some Offenders, but most of the Corrupted come from the Westlands.

"What—" Mangin started to ask, but Mara once again yanked hard on her arm.

Clara held up a hand. "It is all right, Mara. She may speak."

Mangin glanced at the hateful woman on her right and then back to Clara. "What is the difference between them?"

Smiling, Clara pushed open the doors. "Let me show you."

Screams—along with muffled crying and chanting—echoed down the dim corridor. The only light came from a glowing, seven-pointed star window at the far end of the hall. The odor of sweet incense mingling with sweat and urine twisted Mangin's stomach, and each new shriek made her jump. The hallway was wide enough for four people to walk abreast, yet it still seemed to press in on her, as though they'd crush her at any moment.

Clara stopped at the first door, roughly a third of the way down, and addressed Mangin, "I will show you seven examples of correction today, before we see to your own." She entered the room. Mangin's handlers bracketed her front and back, ushering her in after Clara.

In the center of the room, a dark-haired woman—wearing only a white slip and a wide, lace choker—trembled as a pair of Immaculates strapped her, chest-first, to a rack in the shape of the star of Ukase. Light poured down on her from the obligatory star-shaped window in the ceiling as she wept.

At the back of the room, seven girls in white robes and red-leather bands about their necks chanted in unison, "Ukase is truth. He knows all. He sees all. He is the light filling the darkness. Ukase leads all down the path of righteousness. Only through Him will you know life. All else, is death."

Clara motioned to Mangin to come closer, then pointed to the woman on the rack. "This is goodly-wife Zama. She admitted to the Veridical to lusting after another's husband, and asked to be turned over to us. Coveting is a crime of Delinquency, and is thus punished by seven strikes."

One of the Immaculates handed a whip to Clara who then unfurled it and set her feet. "Ukase is truth," she said and struck Zama across the lower back, the whip making a loud crack.

"He knows all."

Crack!

"He sees all."

Crack!

"He is the light filling the darkness ..."

Clara spoke each of the lines the young girls chanted, followed by a strike to Zama's back. Zama cried out with each stroke, her blood soaking through her slip in a pair of locations.

Mangin shuddered, her stomach twisting with each pop of the whip.

Once Clara administered the final stroke, the Immaculates removed Zama's straps and helped her turn to face Clara. Tears streamed down Zama's lovely face. "Thank you, Immaculate Clara. I will not stray from the path again."

"This is good, goodly-wife Zama." Clara then nodded to the Immaculates holding the young woman. "See that she gets rest and that her wounds do not fester."

Clara's gaze locked onto Mangin, her face a picture of serenity. "I see questions in your eyes."

Mangin was aghast. "How could she thank you after that?"

"Fortitude, young miss," Clara said. "One must have fortitude to serve Ukase. Pain must be tolerated, endured. To do otherwise is weak." Clara left the room, and Mangin was forced to follow.

Clara strode farther down the hall. "The weak pull us all down in the eyes of God. Weakness can be tolerated, but only for a short time. If one cannot grow strong, they cannot be allowed to infect the rest." She stopped and turned, her face calm, but hatred burned in her eyes. "And thus, they must be culled."

Mangin refused to look away. *This woman in insane.*

Clara spun. "We haven't time to dawdle." She marched to the nearest door, opening it, and pointed to an elderly woman— her skin looking like spotted parchment—being strapped to another rack. "This one couldn't pay her tithe. Everyone who produces or earns a wage must give twenty percent of their goods or proceeds, and this one was several coppers short. To make up for that, she will serve seven months at one of the labor camps. But she must be whipped first as a reminder."

"What if ..." Mangin licked her lips, wanting to make sure she used the right words. "What if a person doesn't produce goods or make a wage?"

A grin spread across Clara's face. "You have never paid your tithe."

When Mangin started to explain she'd not known, Clara overrode her. "You need not worry. This is known. Your wage is room and board with Righteous Warrior Dirge Malik. Thus, your tithe is included in that of his estate. It is how all indentured servants are handled."

The crack of a whip and a shriek made Mangin jump—she'd been so focused on Clara she had forgotten the poor old woman.

"On to the next," Clara said, heading farther down the hall.

Room by room, Clara showed women being tortured. They removed a woman's hand for stealing bread. Another was fitted with a red-leather slave collar—the same collars the chanters wore—and branded with an A on the forehead for laying with a man not her husband. It didn't matter that she'd been raped. They removed the tongue of another and branded her forehead as a heretic for denying Ukase. In another room, a woman and her two small children cried as slave collars were fitted around their necks—Clara said the woman's beheaded husband had worshiped another god.

"Have you learned anything yet?" Clara asked as she strode.

"Yes," Mangin said. She fought the fury roiling in her belly. These people had berated her and the ways of Chaos, claiming themselves as superior moral beings. They were hypocrites, displaying torment and piousness as virtue and purity.

"What have you learned?" Clara asked.

"I'd rather not say."

"I see." The head Immaculate's face somehow grew even harder. She then smiled, but it didn't reach her eyes. "Follow me. I've one more thing to show you."

They traversed two more corridors, and Mangin worried about Clara's reaction. *I didn't even think the witch knew how to smile*, she thought. What could make the vile woman look at Mangin like that—something so terrible she would get joy out of Mangin squirming at just seeing it?

Clara opened another door. Shrieks and cries buffeted Mangin as she entered. The latest torture room held not one, but two bruised and bloody women, each on their knees and tied with arms outstretched to a pair of posts, instead of the obligatory star-shaped rack. The one on the left had long, brown hair and a round face, while the other had short-cropped, sandy hair, and a heart-shaped face. Their shifts were tattered and stained with blood.

"Why are they doing this, Nomnan?" the brunette shouted.

"Hush, Yadomino," Nomnan, the sandy-haired one said, then shouted at Clara, "We only came here for trade. You've no right to do this."

"We're sorry if we did something wrong," Yadomino sobbed. "Please, let us go and we'll just leave. You can keep our goods."

"To take your belongings would be theft," Clara stated. "As for why we do this …" She looked to Mangin as she continued, "You two were caught in bed together having sexual congress. It is an abomination unto God to lie with someone of your own gender." Clara's attention returned to the battered women. "And there is only one punishment for your crime." She then nodded to a pair of Immaculates who stood behind the women.

The Immaculate behind Yadomino grasped the bawling woman's head, making sure it was pointed at Nomnan. The other Immaculate hefted a forearm-length rod with a looped cord at its center. She placed the cord around Nomnan's head and affixed it to her neck under the chin. "Ukase is truth," the Immaculate said, and twisted the rod until the cord grew taught.

"No," Yadomino shrieked.

"He knows all," the Immaculate intoned, and twisted the rod again.

Nomnan gurgled and thrashed, her short, sandy hair flailing as the cord dug into her throat.

"He sees all," the Immaculate said and twisted the rod again, her face calm and smooth as though she were doing laundry, rather than strangling a woman to death.

"Stop," Yadomino cried. "Please, don't do this! Nomnan, I love you! Don't leave me!" She looked to Clara. "Please, stop this. I will do whatever you want."

Clara held up a hand. "Hold and loosen the cord."

The Immaculate stopped, untwisting the cord until Nomnan took in a ragged breath.

Clara glided over to Yadomino. "Will you give your soul to Ukase?"

"Yes, I swear it."

"Immaculate Sedona," Clara nodded to the one with the cord, "fetch a Veridical. Tell him we have need of a Consecration."

After the woman hurried out, Mangin spoke, trying to keep her voice calm, "Immaculate Clara, what is a *Consecration*?"

"This young woman has agreed to be blessed by our Lord God, Ukase, and to be welcomed into his fold." She turned to Mangin. "It is a glorious thing. You shall see."

Sweat trickled down Mangin's back as she stared at the door. Whatever they planned to do to Yadomino it would apparently get them to spare Nomnan. But if that were so, they why was Mangin so anxious? Why did she have the feeling that what would happen next would be horrible?

A steady tap of feet echoed from the door, rowing louder. A placid, gray-haired Veridical entered the room, followed by the returning Immaculate, holding a black, forearm-length, iron rod. The rod was—not surprisingly—capped with the symbol for Ukase.

"Don't do this, Yadomino," Nomnan croaked, and was quickly slapped in the face by the Immaculate behind her.

The Immaculate behind Yadomino removed the girl's restraints and helped her stand, as the Veridical took a position in front. The aged man held the black rod vertically in front of him, its symbol level with his eyes. "Do you submit to the will of Ukase, the one true god?" the Veridical asked.

"Y-Yes," Yadomino stammered.

The Veridical fixed his eyes on the bloodied girl. "There can be no doubt in your mind. You must be resolute in this, or I will not continue." He took a deep breath and repeated his question.

"Yes."

"Do you forsake all other false gods?" The symbol of Ukase in the Veridical's hands turned a dark cherry.

"I do." Yadomino stared at the rod as though nothing else existed.

A sense of dread came over Mangin in waves.

The Veridical spoke again, "Will you adhere to His laws?" The symbol was now bright red.

"I will."

"Do you take Him into your heart?"

"Yes, without reservation." The girls voice was growing stronger.

"Do you agree to this of your own free will?" The tip of the Veridical's rod was white hot, so much so that Mangin felt it from several feet away.

Yadomino trembled. "Yes!"

The Veridical pressed the glowing symbol into the center of Yadomino's chest. Her skin hissed. She shrieked and quaked, and then collapsed into the arms of the Immaculate who said, "Be at ease. Feel the hand of God through me as He takes away your pain."

"Yadomino, are you all right?" Nomnan asked.

The girl's eyes fluttered open. "What?" They fixed on her friend. "Oh, yes. I am wonderful. You must repent our sin and join me. It is glorious, Nomnan."

"What did they do to you? Look at me, Nomnan, me, the woman you love."

Yadomino sneered. "Do not speak of such blasphemous filth."

Nomnan glared at Clara. "What have you done to her?"

Clara tilted her head, spreading her arms. "You saw what happened. She is now one with Ukase." Clara then stepped closer. "Will you accept God into your heart as well?"

Nomnan spat at the hateful Immaculate.

Immaculate Sedona once again placed the cord Nomnan's throat. "Ukase is truth." She twisted the rod once more.

"Only through Him will you know life." The Immaculate twisted again, the cord digging deeper.

Bile crept up Mangin's throat.

The woman's eyes bulged, and her tongue protruded from her mouth. Her face turned red, then purple, then blue as blood dripped from her neck.

Yadomino stared at the scene smiling, a glint of frenzy in her eyes.

Mangin quaked with every turn of that terrible rod. Her stomach roiled. The horrific scene changed before her eyes. Nomnan faded away, and Mangin felt the cord around her own neck instead. It bit deep, digging into her flesh, cutting off her breath and the flow of blood to her brain. She felt her as though her life was slipping away as the Immaculate throttled her.

Suddenly, Yadomino turned into Adel. Adel shouted, saying Mangin had forced her into a life of sin, echoing Yadomino's words. It sparked anger in Mangin. A sin? The very idea was ridiculous. If two people desired each other—be it out of love or lust—why should someone else care, let alone a god? It was preposterous! These people and their sickening laws were insane. If a person chose to follow a god and its rules, so be it. But why force others to do likewise? Who did these people think they—

The loud snap and crunch of Nomnan's neck breaking brought Mangin back to reality. She stared, eyes wide at the still form that used to be Nomnan, a woman who died only because she loved another woman.

The Immaculate finished her discourse. "All else, is death." She then untwisted the rod, digging the cord out of Nomnan's neck with a hook.

With a sneer, Yadomino spat at Nomnan's corps. "It's what you deserve."

Mangin vomited.

"Is everything all right?" Clara asked her.

Wiping her mouth with the back of her hand, Mangin stared at Clara. "Why are you doing this?"

Clara cocked an eyebrow. "Because it is God's law. Do you mean why we do it in this manner? The answer is simple. This is how a woman is purged. You see, men get the luxury of the ax. It's honorable and simple—just like they are. Only women know the true pain of bringing forth life. Thusly, they must also know it in death." She spun on her heels and motioned to Mangin's escorts. "Come along now. Your tour is over and I've not all day."

Mangin shuddered and she swallowed her remaining bile. "Where are we going now?"

Without turning, Clara said over her shoulder, "Now, we see to *your* punishment."

The cool, evening wind pouring through the carriage window—carrying the smell of flowers and trees, along with the stink of the city—made Mangin's skin pimple as she shivered.

Birdsong and cheerful conversation filled the countryside, creating a cacophonous mixture of false joy. Mangin's buttocks, back, and legs were afire from Immaculate Clara's whip. Seven strokes for speaking out at the service.

They had taken her to a room with the star-rack, stripped to her shift, and then *corrected* through the lashes. Afterward, they lead her to an infirmary to rest for an hour before bringing her back and giving her seven more for refusing to go with Clara in the first place.

The two Immaculates who had hauled Mangin around all day sat on the opposite bench. Backs rigid, they peered straight ahead, oblivious to everything. Clara explained that as Mangin was in the service of a Righteous Captain, the two were giving her the *honor* of escorting her home. Common women, on the other hand, had to see themselves out, no matter their condition.

When the carriage stopped in front of the manor, Mangin was surprised to see Dirge out front with Estonia and Barret. She climbed out of the carriage on shaky legs, which nearly buckled when she turned to walk up the steps. Barret rushed forward and took her right arm to keep her from falling.

"Estonia," Dirge barked, "help her."

Steadying herself, Mangin held her head high. "No, that's all right. I'm fine. Thank you." Keeping her face smooth, she took short, gingerly steps to and up the stairs. She stopped and addressed Dirge, "My Lord, I am surprised to see you awaiting me."

"I was wor—" He swallowed. "It is the proper thing to do." He held out his arm. "I will help you to your room." He then turned to the two men. "You are both dismissed. Barret, give your goodly-wife my best. And Estonia, you will go chop a quarter of a cord for not rushing to the aid of a woman."

The squire opened his mouth as though to retort, but closed it, nodded, and ran off.

Concern and piousness warred on Dirge's normally stoic face as he helped her into the house and up the stairs. Mangin had never seen so much open emotion from him. She didn't know whether to laugh or cry. Though why she would want to cry was beyond her.

At the door to her room, Dirge cleared his throat and

nodded. "Do not worry about your duties for the rest of the day, as well as tomorrow. You may read your books and rest. I give you leave to do as you will."

Mangin cocked an eyebrow. *Do as I will?*

What she wanted was to take him into her bed. The feel of his strength and heat at her side made her ache. But then an image of a red-hot brand pressed to her head flashed through her mind. She swallowed and forced down her fear. Regardless of what she'd seen at the Chastenary, Mangin still wanted him, to feel the ferocity that burned behind his eyes—and, of course, finally see if he would be equal to his father.

Sternness and hate returned to his eyes. He must have read her expression.

Her thoughts of lust evaporated like a drop of water on a hot skillet. Dirge loathed her, still. His previous appearance of courtesy was obviously only a show for the men. Dirge would rather die than bed her.

Everything crumbled down on her at that moment. She saw the truth of her world for what it was. With Ukase ruling the land, she would never find another lover—not after what happened at the Chastenary. The next person who would touch her would be the man the True forced on her. That was if anyone would even have her—a former *witch* of Edis, forever tainted, whatever the Magnus had said.

The walls closed. Adel was gone. Betal was gone. Her *power* was gone. Mangin was alone and always would be—a pathetic wretch no one wanted. A slave in all but name, with no chance of reprieve. The hall started to spin, shrinking and growing dark. Shuddering, she looked inward and found nothing. No anger, no frustration. Only cold. Only emptiness. A hollow husk without dreams or ambitions until they day she died.

Face sagging, she slouched, turned, and opened her bedroom door.

Dirge spoke up, "When was the last time you read one of your books?"

Mangin hesitated, unable to think. "I don't remember, my Lord." She then sighed. "And the truth is it doesn't matter." She closed the door behind her and crawled into her cold, lonely bed.

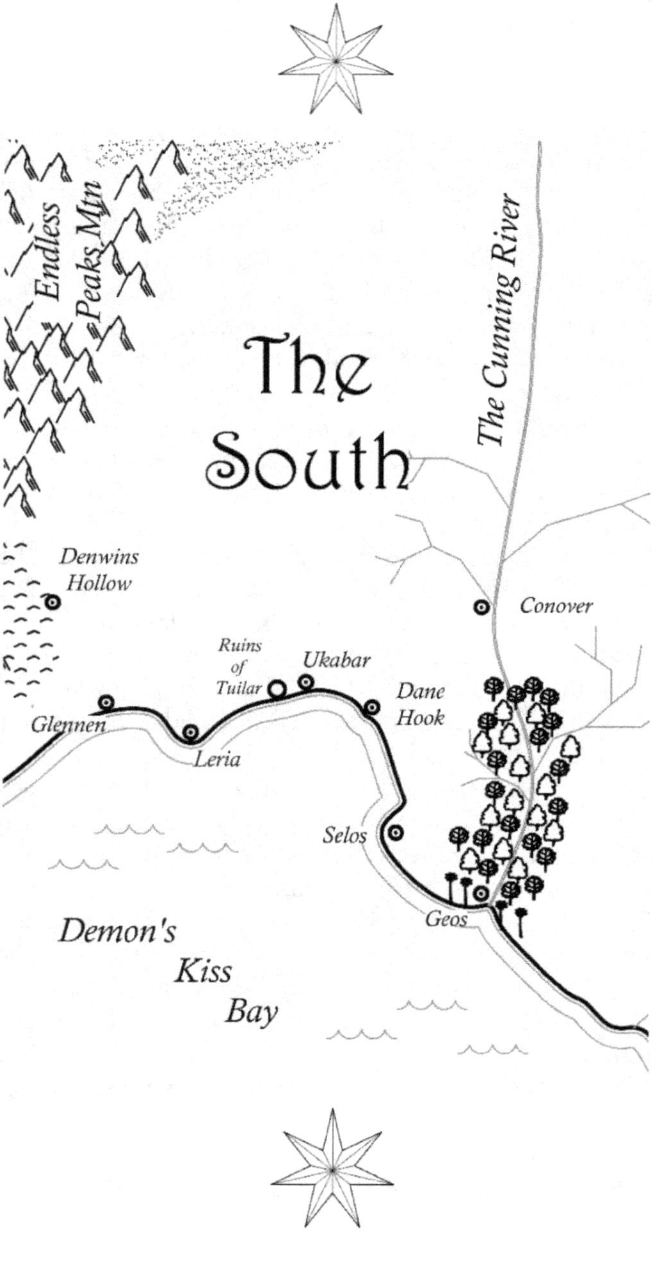

The
South

Endless
Peaks Mtn

The Cunning River

Denwins
Hollow

Conover

Ruins
of
Tuilar

Ukabar

Dane
Hook

Glennen

Leria

Selos

Geos

Demon's
Kiss
Bay

Chapter 14

A Very Long Memory

Frank checked the back-trail. As head of the rearguard, it was his responsibility to make sure the caravan from Dane Hook to Conover wasn't attacked from behind. The rest of the squad of five rode ahead of him, their eyes on the heavy underbrush skirting the road. With thick forest on either side, it was a prime opportunity for an ambush by bandits.

"The Pinch is in sight, sir," his sergeant said.

"Keep a sharp eye out," Frank replied.

The North Road was the main thoroughfare from the southern, coastal cities, to Conover on the Cunning River. The road was broad enough for caravans to run both ways with room left over for foot and horse traffic. But it was also a target.

Located between two large hills the road wrapped around, The Pinch was a favorite for attackers, since the front of the caravan was well out of sight from the back. Brigands could strike the front or back without alerting the rest if the caravan was too spread out.

Frank's horse snorted and whinnied, then began to hobble. "What's wrong, Champ?" He patted its flank and looked down. The horse was favoring its front-right.

Pulling to a stop, he waved to the rest. "You keep on. I need to check Champ."

He dismounted and found large clump of mud with a sharp stone had lodged itself under the hoof. Pulling out he dagger, he popped it loose and checked for bruising, but found none. "There you go, boy. You should be fine." To make sure, he checked the other hooves, needing to clean one.

A shriek from ahead snapped his head up. Most of the caravan was past The Pinch, but drivers were sawing at reins. The rest of the van raced forward as more screams erupted, followed by the snapping of wood as the underbrush exploded outward at the rear of the caravan. Two huge forms from either side of the road smashed into the mounted men, sending them flying. Blood sprayed, and horses screamed while hulking beasts tore into them with twisted, fang-filled mouths and claws.

As Frank put his foot in the stirrup, a stench of rotten meat mixed with moldy fur and fish hit him. Champ reared, throwing Frank to the ground. With a scream, the horse bolted down the road, back toward Dane Hook. Frank rolled over onto his stomach and started to stand when his back exploded in pain, and what looked like a massive crab's claw burst out his chest.

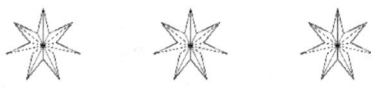

"They're a week past due, sir," the secretary said.

Kellen glanced up from his ledgers. "Thank you, Miss Beamish." His office smelled of pipe smoke, paper, and ink— something he took great pride in. As the Master of the Coin for the city of Selos, he wanted the office to be inviting, yet remain as a reminder that it was a place of business.

"That's the third one in the past four months," she added.

"Yes, I know," he said, his voice deep and strong as he waved her toward the door to his office.

The plump, brown-haired woman paused before leaving. "Do you think it's them?"

Kellen wanted to grind his teeth. Not at his secretary. She was prompt, precise, and had a nose for troublemakers—just the thing a man like Kellen needed to keep his shipping empire running at full steam. His frustration was over the caravans. The first two that went missing were never heard of or seen from again, but the odd thing was that the goods they carried disappeared, too. The usual brigand would try and sell what they stole. And with Kellen's network of eyes and ears, he would have heard of some of the more exotic item hitting the black-market. But there was nothing.

The third was different. Remnants were discovered by a long-range patrol out of Dane Hook. The only remaining wagon had been destroyed, shredded to pieces. They also found a handful of body parts. Some were torn to bits by something with large claws, while others looked to have chopped up, the cuts as clean as though done with massive shears. That meant only one thing.

"Miss Beamish, send word to the bastion in Ukabar," Kellen said. "Ask them to send a Veridical. Tell them we need help against grunkins."

Over the dark skin of his stapled fingers, Kellen eyed Consul Falmer. "I must admit, I am honored. I'd expected a Veridical of Ukase to come from Dane Hook, not one of the city's leaders."

"You are an honorable man, Mister Kellen, one of great renowned, and one who is very generous to the True, the disciples of Ukase." The man's brown eyes weighed Kellen. His crisp and clean priestly robes, and smooth shaved face added with the man's eminence, as did his salt and pepper hair. "Besides, I've been meaning to come to Selos for some time. And from what I've seen, your people have great need of the Truth of Ukase."

Kellen frowned. "I don't understand. There's a bastion of the True only three blocks from here?"

"Yes, but it's small. And as I understand. There are some here who've been reluctant to allow it to grow larger."

"This is not Ardentia," Kellen said. "Some on the City Council are worshipers of other gods, and they fear your Seekers might … expunge them if the True grew too large in number."

He leaned back in his chair. "What do you ask of me in return for you aid with the grunkin?"

Consul Falmer smiled. "A straightforward man. I like that. Few here in the South possess the strength of will and purpose you do. Ukase shines on you, my son. What I ask is you convince the others on the council to enlarge our presence here. We require a training ground for our Militants as well as a sanctuary for the Seekers within the city walls."

"You ask for a great deal."

The Consul spread his arms. "I am a man of God and I ask for what is needed. The South is rampant with heathens, and the remnants of Chaos. If we are to help you, our presence must be strong."

Kellen didn't reply. He eyed the Consul for a few moments, waiting to see if the man would continue, or try a different tact, but he didn't. The man knew his own weight, as well as the depth of Kellen's predicament. Softening his expression, Kellen sat forward. "It's my belief that no specific religion is good for business. But that said, there is no commerce without order. So long as The True don't interfere in the daily goings on of our affairs, I see no problem for your presence to expand."

Kellen was no fool. He knew that with increased Order there would be increased interference. He didn't want his people of newly rediscovered faiths to be put at risk. But sometimes, compromises had to be made. Besides, this would aid him in a task he'd long sought.

He opened his desk and pulled out two pieces of paper. They weren't originals, having been copied so many times of the years as he distributed them. He also didn't look at them, knowing their contents by rote. "I would ask you for one more thing." He slid the sheet across is desk. "I'm looking for two men who wronged me some years ago, and I thought you might be able to help. I think your Seekers would like to talk to them as they were last seen with a priestess of Chaos. One light of skin and the other dark; their descriptions are there along with the names they used—though they were likely false."

Consul Falmer picked up the sheets. "How long have you been searching for them, if I may ask?"

"Nearly twenty years now."

The Consul's eyebrows rose. "So long? Are you sure they even live?"

"The truth is, I don't know. My eyes and ears are many, and they were spotted several times early on. I've not hears news on the blond one for some time, but last I heart, the dark one was up north somewhere." Kellen frowned, his voice growing harsh. "As to why I still seek them? I hired them as guards, and they turned out to be murdering thieves. They killed all the others in the caravan and thought I wouldn't mind." He leaned forward even more. "I have a long memory and a long reach. That is something I want everyone to remember."

The Consul's eyes went back to the paper, and then they went wide. "Dirge?"

"You've heard of him?"

"I'm not certain, but the description and name match. If it is the same man, I can't help you."

Anger burned in Kellen. "Why not?"

"Dirge—if it is indeed the same man—is a Righteous-Captain. More than that, he is a legend. He helped bring about the end of Chaos and the return of God." Falmer slid Dirge's sheet back across the desk and held up the other. "I will give this to our Seekers. If this Jacob still lives, we will find him and bring him to you." He then stood. "As we are in accordance regarding our other agreement, I will be leaving you. As soon as we receive word of your aid, well will bring forth the might of God and destroy those monsters. Good day, to you." With a bow of the head, he left.

Kellen seethed. *A Righteous-Captain? How is it possible?* "Miss Beamish, come here, please."

"Yes, Mister Kellen?"

"Send word to Geos, to the Angelic Inn. I wish to speak with a member of The Brotherhood."

Chapter 15

A Rightful Claim

Something didn't feel right to Dirge. Several days before, he suddenly felt chilled, like a hearth-fire flickering and going out, leaving a room cold and empty. But a short time later the flame burst forth once more, a fire so hot it threatened to crack the bricks, yet at the same time cold and hard.

He needed to put it out of his mind.

He'd been doing sword practice with Estonia, working the boy to his wit's end ever since the lad struck Mangin. Dirge worked himself as well for nearly giving in to his lust for her that day. Another sword practice might clear his thoughts, but Estonia had not yet returned from town. So, he went out back to chop firewood.

Stripping off his shirt, he picked up the ax. Daylin's bronze sun pendant, hanging about his neck, glittered in the sunlight. The muscles beneath his dark skin rippled as he chopped. But the scene with Mangin played through his mind all the same: her touch upon his cheek like the lick of a flame, her fingers running through his hair, making his brain burn with desire, wanting to take her in his arms, and throw her onto his bed. She was the second most beautiful woman he'd ever met. And the look in her eyes was one of desire and need, a look that said she wanted him. Not just anybody, but him.

He hacked at the wood even harder, each chop a cut into himself.

No, Mangin was an abhorrent woman. Immaculate Clara had been right to take her to the Chastenary. He was a fool for feeling sorry for Mangin when she came home, looking lost and filled with sorrow. To the witch, it was all a game.

Again, his mind went back to their altercation in his room. It was her eyes that brought him around—smoldering green pools of desire, like those of the temptress from his past. It had been years since Dahlia ensnared him, and she still haunted his nightmares. And Mangin was no different. She had tangled countless people into her bed, including Daylin, the woman he—

"Stop it, you fool." Snarling, Dirge threw the ax away in disgust. Daylin was in his past. Ukase was all that mattered.

Taking a deep breath, he stacked the wood, put his shirt back on, and picked up the ax, placing it in the woodshed. He went inside, the clump of his boots echoing down the hall, and headed up to his room to wash up. The same room in which he found Mangin, where she didn't belong. When he closed his eyes, he could have sworn her scent still lingered: lilac, mixed with earth and musk.

Throwing off of his shirt, he dipped his hands into the wash basin and scrubbed his face and torso—he'd take a full bath that evening. After pulling on a new, snow-white shirt, he tucked it into his pants, then left his suite and headed for the kitchen for a bite. There, Mangin was cleaning out the ashes from the oven.

She glanced up as he entered, but quickly looked away. "Good afternoon, my Lord." Standing, she held the ash bucket in both hands, and addressed him with her head held high. "I hope you are well this day. Is there something I could—" The smile that had started to creep across her face was replaced with a frown. She dropped her head, turning slightly. "I'm sorry, my Lord. I still have to clean out the hearths upstairs. Good day to you." She gave a slight curtsy and shuffled out the back door.

Dirge shook his head. Even after all that time, the words 'my Lord' didn't sound right coming from her, as though she were an equal rather than as a subordinate.

What was he to do with her? She'd changed since her visit to the Chastenary, walking with eyes downcast and shoulders slumped. Whenever they crossed paths, Mangin would linger a moment, but at a distance. As though he were a roaring fire and she wanted to stay close for the heat but without getting burned. Had the Chastenary truly changed her, or was it all a ruse to get him to lower his guard?

Frey, the cook, stepped up next to Dirge, rolling pin in her plump fist. "I do beg your pardon if I overstep myself, my Lord, but I must admit she's a far sight better at her job than when she started. Though she still leaves a lot to be desired." Frey adjusted her apron, centering it on her large form, and then touched her hair as though to make sure it was still in a tight bun. "I mean, just look at the mess she left. Didn't sweep up after or anything."

Dirge continued to stare at the door Mangin left by. "Do you wish me to replace her?"

Frey waved a dismissive hand. "Oh no, my Lord. She's fallen far in the world. I believe it will just take some more time. I'll be sure to keep on her. A good lord must have something pretty about the house to look at when he doesn't have a wife. I understand that. Even if she is too scrawny. A good woman should have a bit of meat on her, otherwise people will start thinking something's wrong with her.

"Now that I think about it," she put a finger to her lip, "ever since the Immaculates brought her back, she seems gaunter that usual—her cheeks a bit hollow. Must have seen something to throw her off her appetite. Don't you worry about it, though, my Lord, I'll make sure she's well fed. Can't have her falling over from hunger, now, can we?"

"No, we can't," Dirge said.

Just what did happen to her there? he wondered, then shook off the thought. Why should he care what they did? The Immaculates do as Ukase prescribes.

"Oh, and thank you, my Lord," the cook added.

He cocked an eyebrow. "For what?"

"For asking my thoughts on the situation. There's some

who wouldn't do that—they's a bit too stuffy. You're a good man, my Lord. If'n you don't mind my saying." She then strode back to her board and slapped the rolling pin into the dough.

Dirge went to the parlor, taking his favorite chair before the fire, to think on what the cook said. Was he a good man? His past was littered with dreadful deeds and mistakes, lives and loves lost … among other things. He promised to take care of Mangin, a woman who should have been purged because of her terrible deeds. The promise was made to a woman he loved. No, not loved, cared about, someone he'd help raise since childhood. But Daylin was now a god. And Dirge could serve only one. Shaking his head, he took a deep breath. No, he'd promised Daylin, the woman, not the god. So, there was no problem there. Of course not.

As for Mangin, she just needed a reminder of her true place in the world. She was a maid, nothing more. And if she didn't improve her work, he'd be forced to replace her, expel her into a world ruled by Ukase … a world she was ill fitted for … where many wanted her purged.

The cook's voice echoed from the kitchen. "Now, young miss, I want you to sweep up the mess you made with the ashes. After that, you can head to your room for a while."

Mangin murmured a reply, but Dirge couldn't make it out over the pop and hiss of the fire.

After a short time, the sound of slippers came down the hall. They slowed approaching the parlor but hastened again, and Mangin's red hair flashed in the doorway as she rushed past.

Dirge wondered if she had initially intended on entering but changed her mind. He wouldn't have cared if she had. Frey had given her leave to take a break. Mangin knew she was welcome to relax in the parlor so long as they didn't have company. He would have left if she came in, but that was irrelevant. There were always things that needed doing elsewhere. Just not at that moment.

Time passed. His back itched and legs refused to remain still. He had to do something to release his pent-up energy. Bounding out of the chair, he went to foyer, intending on heading out the front to visit Barret, but paused at the stairs, glancing up. "I'll just remind her of her place," he muttered, mounting the staircase. It wasn't as though he missed her company.

He was at the top of the landing when Estonia burst in the front door. "Sir," the squire shouted. "Magnus Malik has died. Donavan is now Magnus. And Truth-Seeker Evram Kirkadite is on his way here with a squad of Militant-Seekers."

With a deep breath, Dirge descended the stairs. "So, that's what it was," he murmured. No wonder he felt cold. His father-in-law had passed, and with it went the warmth of family. Another reminder of his beloved wife was lost to him.

"Until tonight," whispered through his mind, and it was as though Lynette touched his cheek one more time.

"Fitting that it would be Kirkadite." Dirge approached Estonia. "He's one of Nardo Torq's favorites. How soon 'til they get here?"

"Any moment. They were coming down the lane behind me. I was at the Sanctum when I heard the news, and they were already on their way. I raced Justice here, only passing them when they made the turn toward the estate."

"When they get here, I'll deal with them. Go talk to Barret, tell him to do whatever the Seekers want and not to interfere—"

The front door reverberated as someone banged on the outside. Dirge readied himself, straightening his shirt. "Answer it. Then do as I said."

Bowing with a fist to his chest, Estonia spun and opened the door. "Who calls upon Righteous Captain Dirge?"

A gaunt man with tan skin and a sword at his hip entered. "Step aside, squire." He marched up to Dirge. The man's tight, red pants and coat with a white Star of Ukase outlined in black spoke of a fastidious man—as did his expression. "I'm here for the witch."

Kirkadite then turned to the eight men who followed him in—all with swords, and in uniforms of Seekers that matched Kirkadite's. "Go find her."

The Head Militant-Seeker saluted and gestured to both his left and right. The rest of the squad spread out, in search of Mangin while he stayed at Kirkadite's side.

Rage burned deep within Dirge, but he held it down. "Do as I said, Estonia." After the squire saluted and left, Dirge turned to Kirkadite. "It's been a long time, Evram. When did you return for the Westlands?"

"A month ago, when it became evident Malik would return to God."

"I'm surprised Torq could spare you, with all the work you've been doing in the west."

"Grand-Seeker Torq," Kirkadite replied, biting off each word, "personally called me back." He then flipped his hand. "The Westlands are well in hand. He needs me for our next move to the north, where Chaos thrives."

"Those lands were ruled by Kala," Dirge said. "I doubt the God of Time and his Timekeepers would appreciate an invasion."

Kirkadite smiled, one that didn't reach his eyes. "By your own description, most of the Timekeepers are mad. The ancient empire of Durgia is in a state of bedlam. The people will accept us as liberators."

Dirge very much doubted that, but he knew it would do no good to rebuff the Truth-Seeker. He pointed to the door. "Then go do it, and stop harassing good, God serving people."

"I do what needs doing in the name of God." Kirkadite tilted his head. "Unlike some. Tell me, Dirge. Are you enjoying your time rotting in this tomb?"

A woman's scream bellowed from upstairs. The second-floor hall door banged open, with two Militant-Seekers dragging Mangin between them. She kicked and thrashed, her hair flailing. "Who are you? Let me go!"

"Shut up, witch." The militant on her left slapped her across the face.

Mangin's head rocked back and she nearly collapsed.

With a snarl, Dirge stabbed a tight-fisted finger at the militant. "Strike her again and I'll have your hand."

The Head Militant stepped forward, drawing his sword, and pointed it at Dirge. "You dare threaten a Seeker?"

With a flick of his wrist, Dirge knocked the blade aside by the flat, stepped forward, and slammed his fist into the Head Militant-Seeker's face. As the man yelled, Dirge hacked down with an open hand onto the Head-Militant's wrist, grabbed the sword, and stepped back, holding the blade at his side.

The rest of the Militant-Seekers rushed back into the foyer, hands on their blades, but Kirkadite held up his hand and shouted, "Hold!"

He then turned to Dirge. "My apologies for my Head Militant. He will be punished for his indiscretion." As the men got Mangin down the stairs, Kirkadite bowed his head and saluted Dirge. "We will now be leaving."

"You have no right to seize Mangin," Dirge said, his voice like iron. "The Magnus absolved her of her past crimes."

Kirkadite's hard, brown eyes turned back to Dirge. "I will be the judge of that. Following my questions, she will reveal her true self. Then we will see—"

"Do you presume to know more than God?" Dirge bellowed. "You can plainly see, as do I, that she was forgiven in His eyes."

Kirkadite sneered. "Then you are blind, for she has lust in her heart. She is a wanton woman. And once she confesses, the Immaculate will see to her redemption … or purging."

Dirge wanted to rebuff the man as they made their way to the door, but he knew Kirkadite was right, knew it in his soul. Mangin was a woman of lust. She had not—nor would she ever—take the Lord into her heart. Yet, he had to protect her, even if she deserved to be corrected again, to be whipped for lusting after men. For lusting after Dirge. He remembered the gleam of desire in her eyes, the touch of her hand on his skin …

She hung limp between the two men who dragged her to the door, but she stared at Dirge with a mixture of terror and resignation. Mangin knew she was going to die and could do nothing about it.

Dirge's heart hammered in his chest and he shook. Mangin was a former priest of Chaos, but she was also a woman, one who needed his protection. And he was honor-bound to do so.

He had made a promise.

"Hold!" He held up his hand.

The Truth-Seeker stopped short and slowly turned. "What?"

"I said hold. You will not take her."

Kirkadite puffed up his chest. "You dare to impede a Truth-Seeker in the performance of God's will?"

"I do, in accordance with God's law." Dirge held himself erect. "I, Dirge Malik, claim this woman as my own, to be my wife."

Mangin gasped.

The seeker drew back with a sneer. "You claim a *witch*?"

"It is my right," Dirge said, his eyes on a bewildered Mangin.

The Truth-Seeker's eyes burned in anger. "And it is my right to see minions of Chaos brought to justice!"

"I am a Captain of the Warriors of the Righteous, and my word supersedes yours. This woman has repented—as is the right of all people—and was dubbed clean of all crimes by the Magnus. I now claim her as my wife. Her life is mine to hold and judge, not yours."

Kirkadite trembled, snarling in rage. He then closed his eyes and took hold of himself. "Release her. We are done here." The Militant-Seekers dropped Mangin to the floor and walked out after their leader.

Dirge knelt to Mangin and helped her to her feet. "Are you all right?"

As Mangin stood, Estonia ran up, concern on his face. "Is everything all right? Why didn't they take her?"

"Because they have no right to her," Dirge said. "Now, I want you to go fetch Veridical Barnhold. Tell him I'm taking him up on his offer."

Perplexed, the squire saluted and ran for his horse.

"Why?" Mangin asked, tears streaming down her pale cheeks. "Why would you say such a thing? Why do this? You find me disgusting, I know it." A gleam of hope twinkled in her eye.

"Because, I meant what I said." He brushed hair out of her face, and then pulled his hand back as though burned. "And because I promised to protect you. With the passing of Magnus Malik, the best way to do that is to make you my wife."

"You want to protect me," she said, the light going out of her eye as she looked down with a frown. "Not because you want me, but because you have to keep your word to Daylin." She took a deep breath. "So be it." She then held her head up. "Thank you for your protection. I assume I have no say in all this?" When Dirge shook his head, she sighed. Then a wicked grin spread across her face and she bit her lip. "Well, at least I finally get to know if I was right."

Dirge stood at the front of the sanctum, God's light shining on him from the seven-pointed prism over the front door. The pews were packed. The entire congregation came to witness the union of the most prestigious man in the region. Estonia sat at the front, his eyes cold. Dirge couldn't understand why seeing his squire pained him, but he brushed it off.

Veridical Barnhold stood to Dirge's right atop the shorter, secondary dais. Memories bombard Dirge: standing with next to the Prophet with Lynette's parents and family looking on.

Mangin marched down the central isle in a long, billowing gray dress, and a large piece of snow-white lace covering her head and shoulders. Lynette had worn white.

Immaculate Clara strode at Mangin's side, slightly in front. Her face was stern as ever, but for some reason, there was a hint of pride in her eyes when she glanced at Dirge, like a matron proud of her favorite pupil. She looked so familiar, but he didn't understand why.

When the two reached the front, the Immaculate stepped back and pressed down on Mangin's shoulder, then stepping behind her. Mangin knelt at Dirge's feet, head hanging low in what he knew to be mimicked reverence and servitude. Lynette's devotion had been sincere.

Barnhold held out a strip of white lace, embroidered with Dirge's name with the seven-pointed star of Ukase before and after. "Do you claim this woman?"

Dirge took the lace. "I do claim her." He held it up and intoned, "With this collar, this woman is made holy, bound to me until the Lord takes my life. I will protect and support her to the best of my ability. I will father her children in the glory of God." With Lynette he had only a simple cord with an Ukase pendant.

Mangin, hands trembling, gathered up her veil and held it under her chin, exposing her neck.

Bending slightly, Dirge placed the lace about her neck snugly, attaching it in the back with tiny pearl buttons. He straightened and stared down at Mangin. "From this day forth, you will do as I wish, raise my children, and serve me in every way. From this day forth, you are mine. You are my wife." The power of God pulsed in him, sealing their union.

He bent again and lifted the front of Mangin's veil, resting it on her head, and held out his hand. Her eyes were filled with loss and sadness. With a slight scowl, she took his hand, smoothed her features, and stood to his side, one step back. Dirge faced the congregation, gaze drawn to the glowing star, bathed in the Lord's light.

With Lynette, the ceremony had been glorious, filled with love. This time he knew only regret and resignation. But he did what was right.

Chapter 16

Leaving a Message

Doing his best to keep frustration from his face, Kenja stood at the door of Moira's dark, cluttered room. She sat with her back to him at her black hardwood desk, scribbling something in a notebook with a gold quill. A single dark-brass lamp illuminated her curly, gray hair, making it look like the edge of a storm cloud as it drifted in front of the sun. Much of the furniture—four-post bed, chairs, wardrobe, and the like—matched the antique desk. Plush, burgundy rugs littered the floor. And the room, like the rest of the house, smelled of mold, dust, and body odor.

Moira put the quill back in the ink-well and poured herself two fingers of brandy from the crystal decanter at the desk's edge. "Would you care for some? I know how much you like it."

"No, thank you. But I must say, Lord Heartless had fine taste judging by his wine and brandy."

"Come now, Kenja." She put the glass down and turned her chair to face him. "We've no need for honorifics with that man."

"The Great Lord may be lost to us, but Heartless was still His champion."

"Not anymore. And I find Twitch to be a much more fitting name now for Heartless." She rested her wrinkled chin on steepled fingers. "I heard the tale of his fall from grace from many lips—many of whom heard it directly from the source."

Kenja snarled. "You believe the words of that Ukase lover?"

"If Dirge said it, I must believe it. I've kept track of him since his youth. He believes lying to be disrespectful."

Kenja's brows rose. "You've met Dirge?"

"Of course not." Moira waved her hand dismissively. "Don't be silly. He's never come here. And I hardly had time to run off to view a troupe of Travelers with my research. No. I heard about him through letters from Ruddick's paramour, Celeste. She harbored an obsession with Dirge, though she never told me why."

"Who are Ruddick and Celeste? Should I have heard of them?"

"Perhaps, perhaps not. They were prominent priests in the South, both politically and with their power of the Lord. Ruddick had the wild idea of linking mundanes to Edis. According to Celeste, and others, he actually succeeded with one child; a girl who garnered the ability to speak with animals." Moira chuckled. "Much good it did him. The child wound up killing him because of his success."

The hair on the back of Kenja's hair stood on end. "You're talking about Daylin."

"Yes, I am." Moira tilted her head. "I'm surprised you've heard of her. I only knew the child's name from Celeste."

A near panic griped Kenja. He'd heard of Daylin from the darkest of sources, Dekriot. His master was obsessed with the woman turned god. He covered his shock with a smile. "How could I not know of her. She was at Dirge's side at all times."

Moira's jaw dropped. "The same Daylin. Are you sure? It's a rather common name along the coast."

Cursing himself inside, he shrugged. "I didn't know it was a popular name. You're right, they must be different people. Ruddick's child likely died long ago."

"No, she's not dead. I understand she's rather off—

something to do with the poppy—but she's still alive."

Kenja lifted an eyebrow. "Poppy?"

Waving a hand, Moira shook her head. "I thought you were referring to— Never mind. You meant Daylin. No, I believe you may be right. It makes sense with Dirge's story. Ruddick inadvertently connected Daylin with the Mother. It stands to reason the girl would be involved in the downfall of the Lord of Chaos. Dirge claimed she is now a god of some kind. I wonder if she still has a connection with Edis?"

Dekriot stirred in the back of Kenja's mind. He needed to get Moira to change topics. "How much longer until G'kaals returns?"

Moira's eyes focused, obviously pulled out of her thoughts. "What? Oh, yes. Soon. Why, have you finally decided it's time to leave us?"

"No, I don't mean that—" Kenja started but Moira overrode him.

"It's well past time." She turned back to her book. "Your friend left months ago. And we've over a dozen more come and go in that time. Yet here you stay. Don't get me wrong, you have been a help, but it's time for you to go. You've likely used half your crystal already. You'll need all you can before you get out of the Order's range of influence."

"Yes." A small smile touched Kenja's lips. "I believe you're right. I'll ask G'kaals to take me to the edge of the Waste when he returns. Thank you for all you've done for me." He left, not caring about her response. He had work to do.

Knowing he had time, he went to the pantry and gathered a little food for the trip: bread, dried meats, and some hard cheese. Then, he hurried to the basement where Moira stored the excess Chaos shards. He opened the chest, and fished out the black stone given to him by Follett, touching it to the top shard. Kenja grew cold as blackness seeped into the crystal. He relished the feel of his master's essence passing from the stone to the crystal. He'd done the same thing to every shard given out to those passing through. As each former priest used the Chaos, a portion of Dekriot would bleed into them, allowing his master to devour small portions of their soul with each use. Soon after, they would beg the master for life, which he would grant for a price.

After fouling the thirty or so shards, leaving one untouched, he gathered them all into a satchel and took them to his room. There, he collected his clothes and pulled the bundle of books he'd hidden under his bed. Dammers would sooner die than give them up. Or so he claimed when Kenja caught up to him in the forest after G'kaals dropped the man off. Kenja often wondered how many coyotes, foxes, and bears found comfort the bits of Dammers spread about the forest.

Slipping out the back door, and then the drive gate, he headed due west so as not to come across G'kaals and Sashel as they returned from town. His footsteps hissed and popped as they sank slightly into the hardened Chaos, leaving charred footprints. He didn't care. If someone followed, he would deal with them. Wrapped in his master's power, he used it to feed his arctic center, making his eyes glow ice blue. The solidified Chaos could not touch him.

As Kenja reached the edge of the Waste, a trumpeting wail echoed from the distant tree line, the same sound as the grunkin that approached them on his way into the Waste. He stopped and grasped hold of his dark power, ready to unleash it on the beast.

The grunkin lumbered out of the trees, like a bear-sized porcupine with six legs. It came to a halt and sniffed the air with its elongated snout, then turned and peered back into the wood. A man walked out of the forest. At least Kenja *thought* it was a man, but from its lack of genitals it may well have been a woman. Its skin was a mass of black crust, crisscrossed with slashes of red as though someone had roasted him on a spit.

To Kenja's surprise, the charred person halted next to the grunkin and put one hand on the thing's back while the other hand motioned to Kenja to join them.

Kindermark's main street was choked with traffic. Kenja didn't care. If anything, it would make his job all the easier. But where should he do it?

An inn door opened a short distance away, raucous laughter and merriment billowing out. A tanned-skinned man stepped into the street on unsteady legs and staggered toward the wharf district. The name over the inn brought a smile to Kenja's face: The *River Rest Inn.*

Pulling out the unadulterated crystal shard, he strode to the inn.

People packed the place, all stomping and hammering their tables in time with a minstrel playing his lute. The man wore yellow pantaloons and a red-satin shirt. A long, multihued feather jutted out the top of his blue turban. The entire get-up screamed Traveler.

"This is perfect," Kenja murmured, scanning the crowd for the one he sought.

It didn't take long to find her. The auburn-haired young woman wove through the tables, empty mugs in hand.

What is her name again? Kenja mused. *Ah, yes.* He stepped in front of her as she walked past. "Anette. How lovely to see you again."

She jumped back. "I'm sorry, good sir. But I'm quite busy. Just take a seat and someone will see you shortly."

She tried to get around him, but he again blocked her way. "But I don't want just somebody. I want you."

"Please, sir. I'm very busy."

Grabbing her arm, he yanked her close. "I never got the chance to see you alone. I believe it's time to rectify that."

The mugs fell from her hands and crashed to the floor, sending pottery flying. She yelled and flailed her arms, trying to fight him off as he dragged her toward the back. Patrons jumped up to intercept him, but he channeled Chaos through the crystal in his other hand and flung them back.

The girl's father rushed from behind the bar with an ax handle in both hands. "Let her go, or by all the gods I will brain you."

Kenja grinned. "Will you now?" He pointed the crystal—making sure it was plainly visible—and funneled pure Chaos into the girl's father. The man didn't even have time to scream as he melted into a pool of bubbling ooze.

The bar erupted. Shouting patrons fled, fighting each other in an attempt to flee the inn. Kenja sent more bolts into the crowd, killing several, and blasted large holes in the wall by the front door. People jumped through the new opening, as well as the front window, in their escape.

Anette trembled, her face white as she stared at the pool that used to be her father. "Papa?"

Kenja asked her, "That should be enough to draw the

Seekers, don't you think?"

"How is this?" She trembled, staring at Kenja in horror. "This isn't possible. You're gone. You're all supposed to be gone. We're free of you."

"Assumptions are dangerous." He dragged her to the back door. "In the meantime, we'll have to complete our business elsewhere."

She struggled, throwing back her head as she thrashed and at kicked him. So Kenja wrapped her in a cocoon of force and lifted her into the air. But he left her mouth uncovered. "I do love it when they scream. Mangin was always full-throated while in her throes of passion."

As he walked out the back and headed for the tree line, he sniffed deep. "Ah. There's something invigorating about sex outdoors. Mangin always thought so."

When he drew her close for a kiss, she bit at him.

Grasping her chin until she squeaked in pain, he stared into her eyes. "Don't fight me, or I'll hurt you." He threw his head back and laughed. "What am I saying? Of cours I'll hurt you. It wouldn't be fun, otherwise."

Kenja left Kindermark to meet up with his new guide with his prize in tow. Kenja was content. He'd sent his message to the Seekers. Moira was no longer of any use to his master.

Chapter 17

Charred Men

Kellen scowled as he went over his ledgers. Several months had passed, and his deal with Consul Fulmer was costing him a fortune. After not receiving the full consensus from the other members of the City Council, he'd been forced to give up many of his land holdings in the city to keep his promise to the Consul. Furthermore, it put him at odds with Chancellor Haddock. Something he hoped to remedy soon.

After a knock, Miss Beamish stuck her head in. "Mister Kellen, Chancellor Haddock is here to see you."

Kellen cocked a brow. He was supposed to go see the man the next day at the chancellor's office. Why would Haddock come to him? "Wonderful," Kellen said. "Send him in." Closing the book, he straightened up his desk, and ran a hand down his vest.

The chancellor entered with the slight nod of a man who knew his weight. Tall and slim, the man's gold and red coat fit perfectly, and the peppered gray in his jet-black hair added to his regal presence. "Good afternoon, Coin Master. I was on this side of the city and I thought I'd drop by. Is this a good time?" His deep brown eyes held a hint of amusement.

The bastard is trying to put me on edge, Kellen thought. "Of course, Chancellor." He stood and extended a hand to the chair across his desk. "If you please? Thank you for seeing me." The man took the seat, seeming to lounge, but Kellen knew better. Haddock was a viper, lulling the unexpected until he was ready to strike. "How are you this day?"

"Busy," Haddock replied.

Kellen nodded. "I wish so speak with you regarding the Word of Order—"

The chancellor cut him off. "I'm well aware of Ukase's book of rules. Most are common sense—don't murder, don't steal, and so forth. But it's the others that trouble me." He pulled a piece of paper from his coat and read, "Thou shall not worship another god? Come now, Chaos is over and the other gods have returned. Who are we to withhold them from the people? And then there are these. Shall not lie with own sex, break the Sabbath, wear the clothes of another sex?" He stabbed at the sheet. "Speak back to one's parents? All of which are death sentences. It's ridiculous. Cutting out the tongue for disrespecting a member of the clergy? *Whipped* for coveting another man's goods? You of all people should find this ridiculous. Without coveting there is no commerce."

Kellen squirmed a bit. "Be that as it may, Ukase is good for the people after wallowing under Chaos."

"You mean it's good for you."

Kellen cleared his throat. "Be that as it may—"

The chancellor sat forward. "For someone who has so embraced Ukase, you don't quite follow all his tenets, do you?"

Scowling, Kellen pressed on. "I do as best I can, just as any man could."

"I happen to know you still run several smuggling operations," the chancellor said. "True, they are in Geos and Selos, so you break no laws here. But I think your fellows in your sanctum would take this information poorly."

"Is that a threat?" Kellen trembled. *The nerve of the man!* He knew of at least three smuggling ships the chancellor owned sitting dockside.

"Not at all, Coin Master," the chancellor said. "I don't care what you do outside of your wonderful city. I'm merely pointing out your hypocrisy. If you truly believe so much in Ukase, you should do a better job at following his rules, that's all." His eyes darkened. "I uphold the laws in Dane Hook, the laws we of the council deemed best for all the people. Not for a few religious fanatics."

He then stood. "Now, if you don't mind, I've better things to do. Good day to you, Coin Master Kellen." With a nod, he left.

Kellen took a deep breath to calm himself. "That could have gone better."

Reopening his register, he shook his head at the amount of food the bastion needed, let alone their iron requirements. He'd have to find a way to spread the influence of The Truth to the other members of the City Council otherwise it would bankrupt him. "What do they need so much iron for, anyway? Are they planning on going to war?"

The creaking of the wagon's wheels washed over Righteous-Captain Yolden as he rode at the head of the caravan. His gray eyes searched the wood-line, occasionally checking the vanguard twenty yards ahead. However, he primarily used his sensory gift for God, expanding his awareness of all things alien within a hundred years. He could extend it farther, but it required greater concentration and effort, and he didn't want to overstrain himself if the grunkin showed themselves.

"Why are we acting like common caravan guards?" Yolden's squire asked. "It's beneath us."

"Because," Yolden said, "Consul Falmer made an agreement with Coin Master Kellen to hunt down the grunkin."

"But, you are the Righteous-Captain of the entire South," the squire said. "And they have twenty guards with them, and only four of us mounted. If they attack, the guards will be killed. Why hide our forces?"

"Grunkin are mindless, but if they see too many, there is a small chance they'll pick another target. Now, that's enough questions. Pay attention to your surroundings." He pointed ahead to the curving road. "We're closing in on the Pinch. It's where the last attack happened, according to the Consul."

The caravan rounded the turn without incident. The road ahead was clear for miles, but Yolden didn't like it. "Something's wrong. If they were going to attack, that was the best place."

"Perhaps they killed each other," the squire said.

"You may be right," Yolden replied. "But more than one caravan was lost."

Something flickered at the edge of his perception to his right, a twisting malignancy of all things natural. "Ready yourselves," he said louder so the men could hear. "Ahead and right. Pass the word to the—"

At the back of the caravan, dozens of thumps erupted from the trees, followed by pained screams of men and horses. Yolden spun his mount about. Drivers and guards were on the ground, along with one of the Warriors of the Righteous. More thumps came, this time at the caravan's middle, and more crossbow bolts struck horses and wagons.

"Brigands!" Yolden bellowed. "Return fire!"

The wagons' canvas tops were thrown back, and his men sat up, crossbows in hand. Twenty-eight bows fired as one into the woods, but no screams came from the tree line.

His perception flared from a dozen places on either side of the road, both up and down. Like twisting, stinking maggots, they sped through his senses on their approach. He'd linked his senses to his Righteous Warriors, so they knew where the attack came from, but he couldn't help the caravan guards.

Three grunkin slammed into the Vanguard, their twisted maws filled with razor-like teeth sinking into human, and horseflesh, as claws, pincers, and spikes ripped them apart. Five of his men turned and fired, their Ukase-blessed bolts sinking into stinking grunkin flesh. The beasts screamed as they died.

Three more beasts came at Yolden from the side through the trees. His reloaded and fired. Yolden's eyes went wide as the grunkin stopped short and dove behind the trees for cover. He drew his sword as Righteous-Warrior Kelts rode up next to him, ready to take on the beasts. Yolden and Kelts guided their horses aside as the beasts slammed into the wagons. The two of them slicing and hacking into two of the monsters' flesh, their blessed blades killing the monsters, while the third turned and ran off. Farther down the caravan, two more ducked and dodged the arrow fire. One went down, but the other spun and returned to the safety of the forest.

"Captain Yolden," Kelts said, his words quick and clipped, "what's going on? They are acting as though they understand death, as though they had thought."

Panic seized his squire's eyes. "How can this be, sir? It makes no—" Two black bolts slammed into his head, and another sank into his chest.

Two more struck Yolden's horse. As his mount dropped dead, he rolled to safety. Kelts' horse lay dead on the ground as well, but there was no sign of the Righteous-Warrior.

Up and down the road, men sprinted out of the trees like things out of a nightmare. Wielding swords, maces, and clubs, each one was naked, burned black from head to toe—the skin in between the charred flesh was red and seeped pus. Yolden hacked and slashed at them. Each one died under his blade, but none of them screamed in pain. Their eyes, solid orbs of black, held only hate.

Something slammed into his back, and pain exploded in his legs. He tumbled to the ground and rolled under a wagon as the grunkin that attacked him continued on down the line. His ears rung, and his vision blurred. The charred men hacked and slashed, the grunkin fighting at their sides. His men fell under the onslaught, as did those of the caravan. There was only one thing he could do.

Yolden crawled out from under the wagon, his legs screaming in pain. Dragging himself up onto the side of a wagon, he clenched his fist, focusing all his will into one point. He pulled on his power from God, willing his last and greatest weapon into existence. A grunkin spun and charged, but Yolden ignored it. It didn't matter, only Ukase did.

A glowing rod sprung to life in his upheld hand, a rod tipped with the seven-pointed star of Ukase—a Rod of Divinity. "In the name of Ukase," he bellowed, and slammed it into the earth.

A pure sound filled his ears, like the ringing of God's own bell as a blast wave hurtled through the air, a hemisphere of the very will of God. It struck the grunkin, turning it to ash and dissipating it in God's holy wake. The essence of Ukase purified whatever it didn't destroy as it grew. The charred men writhed and clawed at their burnt skin, tearing away chunks of flesh as they died.

Yolden fell to the ground and the world went black.

What was left of the caravan reached Conover. Yolden lay in a litter, his mangled legs covered in bandages. "I will tell the Magnus of your courage," he told Kelts. "You did your people proud."

Silver hair stuck out from out of the bandages around Kelts' head. His purple eyes shone with pride. "I was the first of the Ulawun to see the glory of Ukase, but I will not be the last. Though we are somber, my people will come around." He saluted Yolden and bowed.

Yolden did not know what to think of the strange, yellow-green skinned people when he first met Kelts, but he had a feeling the man was right. "Return to the Sanctuary, inform Consul Falmer of what happened. But take no chances. I've informed the City Master here of what happened, and he will send you with a company of the city guard." He handed over the Rod of Divinity. "I've realigned this one. Activated it if needs be on the road, though I've a feeling you won't need to. We dealt them a terrible blow, but I know many survived. Go now, Eric Kelts, Righteous-Warrior of Ukase. I will not return, but rest assured, a regiment will come in my stead."

The sprawling, two-story manor house sat in the middle of the forest, all but forgotten by the outside world. Thickly packed oak, maple, and brushwood hid its existence from the outside world. The miles-long lane heading south was overgrown with shrubs and tall grass. Which was for the best, as it kept prying eyes from her experiments.

Her green eyes hard, she scowled at the two-dozen charred men cowering before her—she'd already sent her few returning pets to their pens. "It would seem your excursion didn't go well."

"We are sorry, Great Mistress," the charred leader croaked. "But this is all we could recover." He indicated the half-dozen crates behind them.

A young woman appeared at the doorway of the manor. Frail and wan, her ski-blue silk robe hung open to the waist, exposing a skeletal chest. Sickly and muted, her heart-shaped face, brilliant green eyes, and golden hair shining in the sun hinted at her original beauty. "Mother?" she said, her voice soft and weak. "Did they get any leaf or poppy? I need to make more."

Celeste's long, dark hair twirled as she turned to the manor. "I'm not sure yet, my sweet. We shall see soon enough."

She turned back to the charred men, her eyes boring into them. "Two of you, go through those crates and see if they have what my daughter requires, then take the rest to the basement. The rest will go out with more of my pets. Go to the village of Catspaw to the southwest, a mile off the main road. They will have what my daughter needs. Bring back all they have, as well as those who survive. I need to replenish your numbers. Fetch their livestock as well; I need to make more pets, too."

She'd lost nearly half of her grunkin in that attack. It was unacceptable. Ukase and his stinking men of Order were growing stronger in number, becoming more than the simple nuisance they'd started as. And yet, she couldn't help smiling. With each creation, her grunkin were stronger and more easily controlled than those that came before.

Spinning, Celeste returned to the manor and hugged her sweet daughter. "Come, Dahlia. You need some rest."

Chapter 18

God's Need

Glowering, Mangin blew her hair out of her face. "And here I thought it'd get better with time," she muttered.

"What did you say?" Dirge asked as he rolled onto his side of the bed.

"You barely give me time to enjoy it," she replied, scooting to the edge, and sitting up.

"You seemed to be enjoying it from all that … moaning."

She threw up her arms. "Yes, I moan. I love sex. Lots of people do. We're not all emotionless rocks who'd die before sharing an intimate moment or thought."

He crossed his arms. "I'm not emotionless."

Getting out of bed, she faced him. "Do you find me disgusting? Do you still hate me after all this time?"

He stared at the ceiling. "You are my wife."

"Look at me." She ground her teeth. "I said, look at me!"

His head turned toward her, his eyes impassive. "Yes,

wife?"

Screaming in frustration, she pulled on her robe. "I don't get you. You're this cold thing, but when we have sex I swear … I swear that—"

"What?"

With a sigh, she shook her head, hand playing with the too-tight marriage band about her neck. "Nothing." She headed for the door.

"Where are you going?"

"To the privy. Why, do you want to join me?" When he made a face of disgust, she laughed. "I thought not. Though if you did, you might actually learn a bit more about the female body."

She padded down the hall, still thanking whichever god who was listening that the privy was inside, and not an outhouse. "What is wrong with that man?" she whispered, not wanting to wake Estonia. The cook and maid—she kept forgetting their names—slept on the first floor, so she'd no worries there. But the stinking squire was a different manner. The young man's room was but two doors down, and the last thing she needed was his smart lip.

Her thoughts went back to Dirge. "I swear, it's like that man is doing it on purpose." Right before she could reach sexual bliss, the man would finish, his eyes filled with both lust and disgust. Well, that wasn't quite true. His eyes never changed, but she knew how he felt.

After emptying herself, she went to her study for her herbs—the last thing she needed was to get pregnant. Opening her dresser, she pulled out the small jar, and opened it. Only one dose remained. And it was small, possibly too small. She checked her other jars and found them empty.

"Oh no." She forgot she'd finished that one. "This is all I need." Popping the mixture of crushed herbs and powders, she chased it with a sip of wine.

Returning to bed, she found Dirge snoring. "How does he not rattle the windows?" She curled up in bed and tried to sleep.

In the morning, Mangin told the housekeeper to fetch Barret with the carriage. When Mangin stepped out of the manor house, she ran her hands down the front of her favorite dress. Although it covered her from neck-top to wrists, with a hem that dragged the ground if not held up, the black dress was embroidered with small, black flowers. Just because it had to be black, didn't mean she couldn't still look pretty. Even if the flowers were only noticeable from up close.

The sky was clear, the sun warmed her face, and birdsong filled the air along the scent of wildflowers. It did not improve her disposition. She adjusted her baby blue bonnet with disgust. It was ridiculous. *Why shouldn't a woman be able to let her hair down?* She loved the way the wind caressed her scalp.

But Amelia had been adamant. "*We must remain humble, in the eyes of the Lord,*" she had said. "*And we mustn't be a distraction to godly men.*"

Mangin wanted to thrash the world for the ridiculousness of it all. She strode down the steps, and Barret opened the carriage door. "The apothecary," she said, climbing in.

The apothecary was on the north end of Cross Corners. Once there, she entered and wrinkled her nose. The dim, cramped place always stank of poultices, deep earth, and sharp spice.

She approached the proprietor—a plump man with a bald pate. "Good morning, sir. I require some items." She handed him the list.

After perusing the paper, he frowned and returned it. "I am sorry, Lady Malik, but I cannot."

Mangin's jaw dropped. "What? Why is that?"

"I am sorry, but the Grand-Consul has deemed many of these to be illicit. He said ..." The man lowered his gaze and clenched his smock. "You see, apparently, some women have used these to ... well, prevented themselves from getting with child." He held up his hands. "Now I am not implying that with you, my good Lady, certainly not. But some of the lower born and women of the ..." He cleared his throat. "Anyway, some have been known to use them for that purpose. I'm sure they're just for tonics for your Lord, to keep him in good health. But, I'm sorry. I cannot."

Mangin wanted to box the man's oversized ears. "Can you get me any of them?"

"Yes, Lady Malik. I will get what I can. But you must understand, I cannot get them all." Rushing off, he returned a short time later with several pouches.

Her face like ice, she handed over the required coins, which he took as though she would bite him. Something she was considering.

Out on the street, she held in a scream. What she had wouldn't work, not by themselves. She needed the others. But where to get them? Barret's wife certainly wouldn't know, not the way she went on and on about her five children and wanting more. And she certainly couldn't ask any random woman. They might be able to help, but they were more likely to talk to an immaculate about it.

"Where can I go to find someone I might trust not to..." Smiling, she hopped into the carriage. "Barret, please take me to the Over Reach Inn."

"All right," she muttered, staring at the closed sign on the door to the Over Reach. "What do I do now?" She'd thought if anyone could help her, it would be the Brotherhood of Assassins. As worshipers of Death, surely, they could point her in the right direction. Worry ate at her while she slogged down the steps.

As she reached for the door to her carriage, a woman spoke behind her, "Mangin, is that you?"

Mangin turned and her eyes went wide. "Jandal?" She glanced up to see if Barret was close enough to hear, but the man was gone. "What are you doing here? This place isn't safe for— It isn't safe for disciples of the Great Lord."

Jandal approached, the tall, slim woman swaying, her black eyes locked on Mangin's. "Yes, I know. But you needn't worry. There are other ways. I could show you, if you like?"

Mangin pulled back. "What are you talking about?"

"There are other powers than Edis; than Ukase. I can take you to one who knows, who can show you a greater way. You miss the power, I know you do. You sit in that big house, thinking yourself safe. But you know you're not."

Mangin's back pressed against the carriage as the former priestess of Chaos closed in. "What do you mean? How do you know where I live?"

"They will come for you," Jandal said, running a hand up Mangin's arm. "The Seekers will come for you. You know they will. Your soul is black to them. They will take you, torture you with their touch, make you talk. They know you do not follow Ukase and they hate you for it." The woman's finger went under Mangin's chin. "But there is another way."

Terror filled Mangin. Jandal was right. One day the stinking Seekers would come, and her life would end in agony. "What way?" Her voice trembled.

"Come with me," Jandal said, her voice like a caress. "I will take you to Follett. She will show you the way to true power. Only then will you be safe. Only then will you once again be the master of your world, one where you can do whatever you want."

Clasping Mangin's hand, Jandal pulled her away from the carriage. "Come, my friend," Jandal cooed. "I will show you—"

Jandal's eyes went wide as she stared over Mangin's shoulder. Snarling, the woman cursed and sprinted away, turning a corner leading deeper into the city.

"Who was that?" a man's voice inquired behind Mangin.

She spun, her heart in her throat. "Veridical Barnhold!" She shook in terror.

"It was someone you knew from before, wasn't it?" He tsked. "You mustn't let them tempt you. You are clean now, but you must remain strong and resist your past."

Swallowing, Mangin lowered her gaze. "Yes, Veridical. If … If I may ask, what are you doing here?"

"I got word from a goodly-woman that you went to the apothecary to acquire certain herbs. She was worried for you. And then good-man Barret found me, saying you wanted to come here … Well, I knew you needed help. So, I came."

Her eyes went wide, and Jandal's words echoed in her head, *"They will come for you."* Frantic and shaking, Mangin looked all about for an escape. "I-I just— I was—"

"Hush, child," Barnhold soothed. "I'm not here to punish you or send for Immaculate Clara. This is a trying time for you, and I'm here to help. I assume you were at the apothecary to purchase herbs regarding your … well, your cycle and your potential motherhood. I will help you."

"Y-You will?"

"Yes." Veridical Barnhold put an arm on her back, guiding her down the road. "There is a midwife's hold, not far from here. They will help you with whatever you need. As followers of

Aelaz, the Principle of Life—"

"Principle?" Mangin interrupted. "I thought she was the God of Life?"

The Veridical smiled. "There is but one God. Life and Death are a part of the Mother, who created the world for Ukase. Life and Death are not gods, but Principles of Creation, the natural order of things."

Mangin wanted to correct the kindly old man. She met Aelaz, who was most certainly a god. But to try and correct any ardent follower of Ukase was foolish. Instead, she nodded. "Thank you for understanding."

"Not at all. We shall wait for Barret to return—I sent him to alert the midwife of your coming. Barret will take us there, and afterward, return you home. You've much preparation to do. Great things are ahead for your husband. God has called upon him once again, and he will need you at his side."

"What do you mean?" she asked.

"Righteous-Captain Malik will explain it when you get home."

Dirge and Estonia glided back and forth in front of the stables like a dance, their dulled practice swords clanging with each strike. Sweat coated Dirge's brow as he parried a strike from Estonia.

Either I'm getting old, or he's getting good, Dirge thought.

The young man's expression was one of eager concentration, his handsome eyes watching Dirge's every move. Estonia's body was made for swordplay: lithe and strong, he possessed both strength and quickness.

Frowning, Dirge cursed himself. *You're teaching him to kill, not impress women.* Dirge pressed forward, each strike near to flesh, causing Estonia to retreat.

Yet the young man seemed to accept the attack, countering Dirge blow for blow until his eyes went wide. Raising his hand for a reprieve, he stepped back. Lowering his sword, Estonia pointed behind Dirge. "Sir, Arch-Righteous Agadonday approaches." Estonia then wiped the sweat from his brow. "Were you expecting him?"

The Arch-Righteous, his steel armor glinting in the sun, rode a pure white stallion. Behind him was his squire, carrying Agadonday's banner—the sign of God on a black field with his knots of rank along the top—and a contingent of a half-score men. A carriage donning the High-Consul banner followed a short way behind.

Dirge sheathed his sword. "Go fetch our coats and towels. We must be presentable."

Once Estonia retrieved the items, Dirge wiped his face and donned his black coat as the party pulled to a stop by the stables. Placing a hand on his sword as a sign of respect, Dirge saluted with a bow. "Good day, Arch-Righteous. What brings you to Malik Estates?"

Agadonday dismounted and returned the salute. "Good day to you, Righteous-Captain Malik. May I call you Dirge?"

"Of course, sir."

Agadonday nodded to Estonia. "And how are you this day, Squire?"

"I am well, Arch-Righteous," Estonia replied, bowing until his torso was parallel to the ground.

A bad feeling rumbled in Dirge's belly. It was at thought he felt God stir. "What brings you here today?"

"One moment," Agadonday said. "Let us wait until the High-Consul joins us."

As the elderly minister slowly exited his coach, Barret rounded the corner and started up the lane.

Dirge's stomach clenched. *Please, Lord*, he thought, *please let her be on good behavior today.* When Barret pulled to a stop in front of the manor, Dirge was doubly surprised when Veridical Barnhold exited with Mangin. The Veridical said something to her and then he headed in the direction of the other men. Dirge was curious as to the look of bewilderment on Mangin's face as she went into the house. He then shook his head. *Why should I care? At least she went in and didn't do anything stupid—like talk to a superior before being addressed first.*

The High-Consul shuffled up to the men and slightly bowed his head. "Good day, Arch-Righteous Agadonday. Good day,

Righteous-Captain Malik." He then turned to the approaching Veridical. "And good day to you, Veridical Barnhold."

Barnhold joined them and retuned the honorifics. "It is such a glorious day for this auspicious occasion."

Dirge didn't like the sound of that. He turned to his squire. "Estonia, please have the housekeeper get refreshments for our guests."

After young Estonia trotted off, the Arch-Righteous turned to Dirge. "He will make a fine Righteous-Captain one day. He'll need to find himself a wife, and soon. We need more Warriors like him."

Dirge frowned, not liking the bold statement, but he didn't understand why. "Yes, Arch-Righteous, he is a perfect squire."

Agadonday glanced at Dirge. "So, when can we expect a progeny from you?"

Dirge blinked repeatedly while trying to think of an answer.

"As it just so happens," Veridical Barnhold interjected, "I just took Lady Malik to the midwives to aid that."

Dirge clamped his jaw shut to keep it from falling open.

"Well then, the Lord willing, we'll have that child soon." Agadonday patted Dirge on the back. "On to the matter at hand. Dirge, I know you've been in emeritus, but God has need of you."

"In what way?" Dirge asked.

"Deep in the South, a Righteous-Captain was severely wounded and all but one of his men killed by a pack of grunkin and something he called 'charred men.' We know very little of these men, but it is the grunkin that concern me. He said they acted with intelligence, and as a group."

The hackles on Dirge's neck stood on end. "How is that possible?"

"We don't know. That is why we are sending a contingent of Warriors and Seekers to investigate. As this will be a military expedition, you will have ultimate authority."

"As you command, Arch-Righteous. I will stop this before it spreads." Dirge felt like his head was spinning as past failures assailed him. "I … I don't know that I should be in charge, sir."

"Nonsense," Agadonday said. "You've plenty of experience. The men respect and trust you."

Memories drifted up from a place Dirge thought he had

locked away: men of Tuilar who looked to him with hope and pride screaming as they died, grunkin slaughtering on mass, the Prophet's platform exploding. The sight of Lynette, just before the bolts of black lightning tore her to pieces.

He swallowed hard. "The last time I led an army, I failed ... they all died because of me."

Agadonday clasped his shoulder. "Son, those were different times. And besides, not everyone died. Some of those men escaped. They told the tales of your heroism, of how you led them against terrible odds on a mission no one could have accomplished." The man squared up with Dirge and looked him in the eyes. "You were destined to lose that battle. But in so doing, you won the war. You escaped and saved a boy who went on the awaken a Principle of God. If not for you, Chaos would still reign. Do you understand me? On top of that, those who survived knew there was a chance that Chaos was coming to an end, and when it did, they would know how to fight back."

"Until tonight," floated through Dirge's head. He shook it away, surprised to hear others had survived his debacle. With a deep breath, he stood tall. "As you command, Arch-Righteous Agadonday. When do we move out?"

"Everything should be ready in a week. It will be a small unit, as you'll need to move quickly. You will lead a company of seven Righteous-Warriors, each with a full squad under them, as well as a Truth-Seeker and his men. Keep the camp-followers to a minimum—cooks, horse-handlers, armorers, and the sort. Wives will be the only family allowed to join." He grinned. "We need you to start producing right away, after all."

An image of Mangin lying naked beneath him popped into his head, filling him with both lust and revulsion. He blinked repeatedly. "Um, yes, sir."

Chapter 19

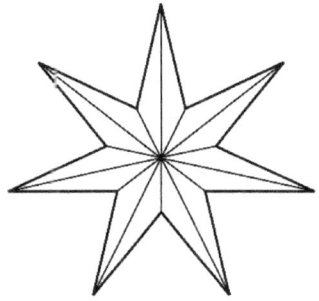

Unshed Tears

Gulls cried as Dirge made his way down the creaking gangplank. The wind flowing through his hair—his full helm stowed with the rest of his gear—caused the ship's rigging to jangle. Estonia marched behind him. The town of Kindermark had but one dock large enough for their ships, so it would take the rest of the day for the company's four ships to disembark. But much like the Corners, Kindermark's wharf stank of fish and mire. On their way south, the Arch-Righteous ordered Dirge to "take care of" the Great Waste, a desolated area that was once the ancient city of Ravenwood before the War of the Gods.

Dirge eyed Evram Kirkadite's ship waiting to dock next. He was not happy upon learning Kirkadite would lead the Seekers on the expedition.

Pausing on the wharf, Dirge addressed his second in command as the man came abreast, "Righteous-Warrior Parkinson, scout out an area outside of town for us to camp.

Restrict the men to camp; we've no time for leave at this moment. If all goes well at the Waste, I'll let them enjoy themselves on the way back for an evening. If the rest of the trip south is as rough as what we just experienced, they'll need it."

Parkinson saluted, clenched fist to chest. "Yes, sir." He nodded to his own second—who trotted off down the dock with the rest of his squad in tow—and then headed back to the ship to coordinate the debarkation.

The Cunning River had its name for good reason. Unexpected rapids, sandbars, and whirlpools plagued the river. Dirge's stomach was still a tad queasy. His only other extended trip onboard ship had been when they crossed the massive lake in the former Lands of the Dead. That ride had been much smoother, motion wise. Emotionally it was much worse, with tensions high between the two groups. It all seemed so strange to Dirge. Then, Betal and Mangin were the hated enemy. Now, one was a god, protecting the mortal world, and the other was his wife.

"Who could have imagined," he muttered.

"What was that, sir?" Estonia asked.

Dirge shook his head. "Nothing—idle thought. Tell Parkinson we're heading into town. I need a decent inn where the command staff can rest and gather information. Then, I want you to come back, and pass on the orders to my third so he can inform the rest of the company. Afterward, you will escort my wife to the inn—she should have disembarked by then."

Estonia glowered. "Yes, sir."

"Don't give me that look," Dirge said. "She's put off being the only woman on our ship, and not being allowed out of our cabin the entire trip." He mused, "How it is that I'm the only married man in my staff? It still baffles me."

He started toward shore but stopped and turned back. "And be *polite* to her. Understand? I'm the one who has to deal with her when she's prickly. Not you. I know you enjoy raising her ire. But I'll have none of it."

Dirge headed into town through a lingering stench of dung. "Do these people not clean up after their horses?" After a few feet into town, he realized they did. Rotting garbage littered some of the allies, the odorous runoff flowing into the gutters and down to the river. Such practices were outlawed in the

Corners and Gate Hall. "Clean streets make clean hearts."

"They'll learn better once our control spread here," Estonia said behind him.

Dirge hadn't heard the lad catch him up. "That was quick."

"I didn't want to lose sight of you, sir."

The town was prosperous. Traffic filled the streets, and hawkers cried out their wares. Most wore clean clothes of simple fashion—tan pants and shirts for the men, and colorful dresses for the ladies.

Near the far side of Kindermark, Dirge picked a three-story inn with a tidy porch, and the scent of fresh food wafting out. He poked his head in.

Of the two-dozen common-room tables, half were occupied. The aprons on the serving maids and bartender were crisp and white. And the bottles of spirits—likely ranging from eska to brandy—were aligned behind the bar in a neat row. The only one who looked rough was a man leaning against the wall next to the bar in unkempt shirt, vest, and pants. Dark hair partially obscured his hard, wary eyes as he surveyed the room with a scowl, his hand playing with the cudgel at his belt.

There was something about the bouncer that seemed familiar to Dirge. Keeping it in the back of his mind, he turned to Estonia. "This will work. Go fetch the Lady Malik. We'll sup here."

As Dirge entered, all of the patrons' heads turned, their eyes following him as he crossed the room. Dirge didn't blame them. They were common folk. He doubted many armed and armored men came to their town, let alone a Righteous-Captain. Dirge took a table at the far end, so he could survey his surroundings. Most of the patrons eyed him with fear and uncertainty, but the bouncer's face held contempt.

In short order, the people went back to their business. Dirge enjoyed the atmosphere. The place almost felt like home. Smiling serving maids glided from table to table, their arms filed with food and drink. The floors and tables were washed, and the food smelled delicious. It reminded him of the Angelic.

A plump maid approached. "What may I get you, Great Lord?"

"Ale and bread for now," Dirge replied. "My wife will be joining me soon. When she does, we'll need a meal."

Once the maid returned with his ale, Dirge took a short pull. His mind drifted back to simpler times, working with the other Angelic bouncers to ensure the peace while listening to conversation as Jacob—Dirge's best friend—sang to the crowd. Dirge eyed the bouncer again. The man may be angry with his lot in life, but part of Dirge would have been happy if he'd stayed a bouncer. It was simple and rewarding.

A frown crept over his face. Life was never simple. The bouncers in his youth were actually members of the Brotherhood of Assassins, the inn was blessed by Aza'zel. Jacob wound up resenting him. Then Dirge ran a blade through his back.

No, his live was far from simple.

When Mangin and Estonia entered the inn, Dirge muttered, "And there's proof of it."

His wife wore a full-length, ruffled, dark burgundy dress with lace at the wrists and neck, just below her marriage-lace. It was elegant, if not a bit extravagant. It also hugged her body, accentuating every curve, yet remaining perfectly proper. Her red hair hung in curls down her back, and her fiery green eyes searched the establishment until they landed on him. Smiling, she sashayed his way, her hips swinging with each step.

Lust flared in Dirge, and he cursed himself for it. "Good day, my wife," he said upon standing. "That's hardly a dress for going into the field. And you're not wearing your bonnet?"

"I tried telling her that," Estonia said, but a glare from Dirge left whatever else he had to say in his head.

"It is a bit much, I know, and I'll change for the morning's ride, of course," Mangin said, bowing her head to Dirge, waiting for the squire to pull back her seat. "As for the bonnet, I wanted to feel the wind in my hair—especially after being bottled in that cabin for so long." She sat at his right, with her back straight and head held high. "Besides, I wanted to look pretty for you. Do I look pretty?" Her gaze bore into his eyes as her lips curled into a seductive smile.

Dirge swallowed a lump in his throat, the room seeming to grow hotter. "Yes, wife, you look quite pretty."

Estonia took the seat on his left. Dirge felt like an apple between two horses, each wanting to claim him as their own. Though why he felt that way to his squire was beyond him.

Mangin scanned the crowd, then gasped. "Oh, my." Her

face paled as she stared with eyes wide at the bar.

"What is it?" he asked.

The bouncer glared at Mangin with murder in his eyes. He yanked the cudgel out of his belt, drew a small dagger from his vest, and started slowly forward.

"It looks like he knows you," Estonia said to Mangin with a chuckle.

Dirge stood in front of Mangin, resting his hand on the pommel of his sword. Jerking to a stop, the bouncer scowled. He gripped his weapons so tight his knuckles whitened. Dirge had a feeling the man was considering attacking anyway but turned and rushed into the kitchen.

"That man is filled with hate. Who is he?" Dirge asked as he retook his seat, but made sure his blade would be easy to draw.

Mangin fussed with her dress, not meeting his eyes. "No one of importance."

Dirge bristled. "*Who* is he?"

"Someone from my past ... who's obviously fallen far in life." Smoothing her face, she turned to him with a grin. "I'm surprised you don't recognize him. That's Cobb." When he lifted an eyebrow, she chuckled. "Cruchfield? From Cool Winds? He was with my retinue when we first met."

Dirge nodded. "Oh, yes."

Estonia sneered. "The one who abandoned the faith. I'm surprised he didn't flee farther south." He then glared at Mangin. "What did you do to him?"

Mangin's expression turned cool. "I told him to go, that I'd outgrown him."

"What did you do to his mind?" Estonia growled.

"That's enough," Dirge snapped.

The maid returned to their table. "I hope I'm not being too forward, my Lord, but your wife is the most beautiful woman I've ever seen. You're a very lucky man."

"Yes, he is, isn't he," Mangin cooed. "What foods do you have? It smells divine."

"We have a lovely peppered stew; spicy but not overwhelming," the maid said. "We also have roast chicken, mutton, and steaks—both pork and beef."

"Do you have any wine or cheese?" Mangin asked.

"Yes, my Lady, we do," the maid said. "We've a fine selection of white and yellow cheeses, as well as two types of red and white wine."

Dirge ordered the stew, while Mangin selected the chicken, with white cheese and wine. Estonia ordered the beef steak with a cup of the red.

Dirge cocked an eyebrow at his squire's choice of drink. "Really?"

Estonia laughed. "Yes. I grew tired of ale some time ago. The wine shops at the Corners converted me." The young man's smile was practically glowing.

Momentarily admiring the young man's glowing smile, Dirge shook himself and cleared his throat. "Yes, well I never took a liking to the stuff. Not sure why. It's just too … winey, I guess."

Mangin laughed. "Yes, dear. That's why they call it wine."

When the food came, they dug in. Mangin ate daintily, wiping her fingers and mouth on the cloths supplied by the maid. To Dirge's surprise, Estonia was also rather reserved in his eating. Dirge shrugged and dug into his stew. The maid was right, the pepper, while sharp, didn't overwhelm, allowing the taste of the beef and vegetables to come through.

They were nearly finished when Evram Kirkadite entered the tavern with his Pursuant at his heels. Kirkadite looked about the room, and then approached Dirge. "Righteous-Captain, my men are in camp." He surveyed the common room again. "It would appear you've actually found a respectable establishment in this mud-hole. My compliments." He shot a glance at Mangin. "One would say it is almost perfect. How is the food?"

"Wonderful, Truth-Seeker." Mangin took a sip of her wine and frowned. "Though, it does seem to have soured a bit at the moment." She shrugged and popped a piece of cheese into her mouth.

"Yes," Dirge said, hoping to hold off any sparks between the two. "The food is excellent. Have your man inform the Warriors. They deserve a good meal before we head out."

The Truth-Seeker's face darkened. "As you command, Righteous-Captain." He bowed and nodded to his Pursuant. As his trainee ran out of the inn, Kirkadite crossed to the other side of the room and took a table.

Dirge grunted. "Of all the Truth-Seekers, why did Agadonday saddle me with him? You'd think Torq would want the man at his side for the push north."

"Perhaps Grand-Seeker Torq want's Truth-Seeker Kirkadite more seasoned in battle first?" Estonia suggested.

"Perhaps," Dirge replied. He then turned to Mangin. "What do you think?"

Fork halfway to her mouth, Mangin froze, and then looked at Dirge, her eyes wide.

"Why are you asking her?" Estonia said. "She's only a woman. And a formerly wicked one, at that."

Dirge's brows furrowed and he turned back to his squire. "*Respect*, Estonia." He paused before continuing. "I want her opinion, because she's intelligent."

"Devious, you mean," Estonia muttered under his breath.

Dirge growled. "Must I remind you every time? Or do you want to run laps around the town?"

The squire lowered his eyes. "My apologies, Righteous-Captain."

Dirge nodded to Mangin. "Apologize to my wife, she's the one you insulted."

Estonia sat erect and turned to Mangin. "I humbly apologize, Lady Malik."

Mangin's eyes flitted between the two men and she licked her lips. "Thank you, Estonia."

"This will not be a short excursion," Dirge said. "I will need both of you to remain civil toward one another." He then nodded. "Now, I want my wife's opinion because she knows how people think. She's trained in the way of politics— something I'm sorely lacking in. And, as I said, she's intelligent."

Mangin stared at Dirge and smirked. "I do believe that's the first time you've ever complimented me."

Dirge stiffened. "I'm not playing games. I was speaking the—"

She interrupted him. "Thank you." Her eyes softened. "I mean that I didn't mean it as a quip and I'm sorry it came out that way. Some habits are hard to break. You've no idea how much what you said means to me. Thank you." Holding her head high, she continued, "I believe the reason Kirkadite is here is twofold. First, I believe Estonia is right about the Truth-Seeker needing seasoning. It will be an uphill battle for you—" She cleared her throat. "For us to gain control in Durgia. From what we saw, those lands will be a difficult conquest. True, much, if not all, of their army is gone. Or it was as of over a year ago. However, their population is huge. If their ruling class remained strong through the upheaval, it won't take them long to regain some military strength. This will be no simple purification like the Westlands. Kirkadite will need to know what a real fight looks like."

She took a sip of wine. "And we are headed into one. If the reports are correct, we are up against controlled grunkin, and soldiers who feel no pain. It's going to be ugly and brutal. You'll need more than discipline to survive this. So be bold, but also wary. Don't run in headstrong without thinking it out first." She paused and gazed into Dirge's eyes. "I can't afford to lose you."

Estonia then asked, his voice sharp, "What's the other reason?"

"*I* am the second reason Kirkadite is here." She glanced toward the Truth-Seeker. "He is the type of man who holds a grudge. He resents Dirge for protecting me." She glanced at Dirge. "Let's face it, we all know you didn't take me for a wife out of love. Kirkadite is sure to know this as well. He'll be looking for a reason to take me and … purge me. This puts you in a difficult position, my husband."

Dirge cocked an eyebrow. "What do you mean?"

"He could use me to take you down. You don't like Grand-Seeker Torq. You've told me—and *anyone* who would listen—that you think Torq's methods are unnecessarily brutal. Magnus Malik was a kind man at heart. I don't think the same can be said for Magnus Donavan. Would you agree?"

Dirge nodded. "Donavan is a hard man. I felt when Lynette's father passed, and Magnus Donavan replaced him as the voice of God. My connection to Ukase turned cold."

"Magnus Donavan could have let you stay in retirement," Mangin continued, "but he didn't. He's sending you to the land of your birth, against monsters that shouldn't exist. He's testing you. You stuck your neck out to protect me—a former priestess of the god you all despise—instead of letting Kirkadite kill me. I think the Magnus wants to know where your true loyalty lies."

Estonia's face grew dark. "His loyalty lies with God. No one is as true as Dirge. Without him, we wouldn't even be here. He is the truest man I've—"

Dirge held up a hand, cutting the squire off. "She speaks the truth. And it makes sense."

Doubt rose in Dirge. A true man of God would never have stopped a Truth-Seeker in his job. Yet Dirge did, because he promised Daylin, who was now also a god—regardless of what the new dogma said. What did that say about him? His hand went to the bronze sun pendant under his shirt without thinking. He pulled it away. His promise mattered because Ukase demanded one stand up to follow through with all vows they make.

"We must be careful and vigilant," Dirge continued. "We must be true to Ukase, but we must also be true to ourselves and to those around us. No one is perfect. Not even me, Estonia."

Mangin then said, "What I really want to know is why are we *here*?"

Estonia's eyes grew hard. "We are here to destroy the remnants of Chaos, a filth that needs to be scrubbed away."

"But why now?" she asked. "This could have been done long before this. Why now? Why has it become so important?"

"Because of these." Dirge pulled the once Chaos imbued crystal shard from his pouch. "Do you remember this?"

Mangin swallowed and averted her eyes. "Of course. Would you please put it away?"

"You've no need to worry, wife. It's perfectly safe. The High-Consul dispersed the Chaos it once held." Dirge held it up, twisting it. Light from the surrounding lamps danced within its depths. "A few months back, a man came to Kindermark and left with people who claimed to be miners beyond the Waste. When the man returned, he carried one of these. At an inn not far from here, he made off with the proprietor's daughter. But not before killing her father, along with several others in the common room with Chaos."

Mangin shook her head. "But why?"

"Because he obviously got it in the Waste," Estonia growled. "Someone out there is making these foul things, and we must put it to an end."

Sighing, Mangin rolled her eyes. "Yes, I understand that.

But why did he kill these people with Chaos, where everyone could see?"

Estonia sneered. "Fetid devotees of Edis will do anything."

"Perhaps," Dirge said. "You've given me much to think on, wife. I thank you and will take it to heart."

Mangin's cheeks grew rosy. She tilted her head, eyes glistening with unshed tears. "Thank you, my darling husband."

Wiping his mouth, Dirge stood. "It's time we make for camp. We've a long road ahead of us, and it starts with the Great Waste."

Nearing the edge of the forest on their way to the Great Waste, Mangin's nethers tingled as she reminisced about the night before leaving Kindermark. Dirge was aggressive, taking her with near animalistic passion. She'd grabbed him by the head and wrapped her legs around him, loving every moment. It was the best sex they'd ever had. Yet loathing mixed with the lust-filled fire in his eyes, a hatred so strong it was nearly palpable. He seemed to hate himself for enjoying it—much more than his distaste for her. Mangin didn't understand it. If he still reviled her, why did he compliment and treat her with respect at dinner?

They didn't have sex the following night. Dirge said he wanted to retain his strength for the fight to come. It was a lie, of course. She saw it in his eyes when she ran her fingers through his tightly curled hair. But when she warned him to test the surface of the Chaos for its destructive potency, he thanked her for the idea. For a man who worshiped the God of Order, Dirge was an enigma.

Chapter 20

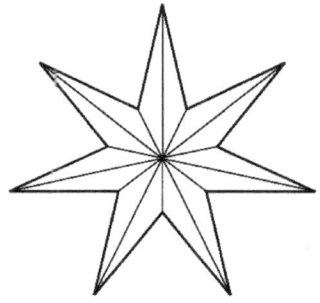

The Great Waste

Dirge's skin tingled as they wound their way among the stunted trees, the air stinking with a mixture of rot and burned ozone. He hadn't sent out a squad to scout the route for fear of grunkin overwhelming them. Luckily, they'd not run into any. But Dirge didn't need scouts for directions. After some questions, he found a cartographer in town who had maps for sale. Over the years, many a brave fool sought to find riches in the ruins of Ravenwood. Few ever returned.

Through the slots of his helm, Dirge spied an opening in the forest. Breaking into the clear, he wanted to vomit. Withered grass spread for a half-mile before it met a lake of shimmering, multi-hued glass. At least Dirge thought it was glass, the way it glinted in the sun. The air above it seemed to warp and wave, as though the surface gave off a rainbow of fumes. The two-mile wide surface wasn't flat. It contained lumps and bulges, divots and valleys, as it sloped to the south.

"By the Lord," Estonia said at his side. "It's disgusting."

"Yes, it is." Dirge peered over the Great Waste. "And with the way the air twists, anything could be hiding in there."

He gestured to his left and right. "I want two squads on either side. The rest, I want formed up in a defensive position, with my wife at the center, to protect her and our retreat." He turned to his second. "Parkinson, her life is in your hands. Keep her safe. Oh, and if she has any ideas, listen to her. She knows more about this stuff than anyone else here. It's why I brought her along." He looked to Mangin and worry ate at his gut.

Her eyes were tight from strain. She smiled. "Worry not, my Lord husband, I will be safe."

Dirge then looked to Kirkadite. "Truth-Seeker Kirkadite, you will remain as well." When the man opened his mouth to argue, Dirge overrode him, "You and your men are vulnerable. You do not possess our God-given protections. Stay vigilant, though. There may be people here as well."

Mangin's mouth tightened and she seemed to quiver.

I am sorry, he thought, *but I just can't trust you, not around this.* He knew Chaos filled the air. It hammered the aura of God surrounding him. He also knew she'd be tempted to use the Chaos. With the Truth-Seeker there, however, she'd resist the urge. At least, he hoped she would.

"Righteous-Warriors," Dirge shouted, "forward at a walk.

A vapor of Chaos slipped past Mangin. She opened her third eye and wanted to cry. Waves of the Lord's Breath filled the air. The essence of the God of Chaos swirled about, tickling her senses to nearly orgasmic proportions.

She'd seen the Great Waste from above, miles away when they climbed the mountain with Gabriel to Vale of Sa' Gula, and even at that distance, she felt it. Now, she stood at the edge of that lake of solidified Chaos. It was as though her Lord hadn't been banished, only muted. All she had to do was reach out and grab it, and she could return to what she'd once been. People would fear and respect her. She could seek out Adel, and they'd spend the rest of their lives together, free of the cursed Ukase.

She didn't dare touch it. Looking over her shoulder, the Truth-Seeker stared at her with a knowing smile. She shuddered and turned back.

Dirge's men moved out into the Waste, each of the four Warriors clutching the Rod of Divinity he'd created for them the night before. But for this, Dirge would need a big one for himself. Unlike the small Rods, which popped into his hands as solid iron, his larger Rod would be a conduit to God, a thing of Holy fire that would dissipate upon activation.

"When we reach the center, I want you to take up four corners, one-hundred-fifty feet from my position. When I plant my Rod, you will plant yours when the wave reaches you."

His Warriors called out in unison, "Righteous-Militants, ready crossbows!"

Normal bolts would be useless against grunkin, but the militants were blessed by God, the head of each possessing seven blades forming the seven-pointed star of Ukase. Anything touched by Chaos would fall to them.

As Dirge approached the edge of the mutated surface, he pulled out a silver piece and tossed it onto the color-swirled surface. It clinked and bounced, then came to a rest, but nothing else happened.

He turned to his squire. "Estonia, grab a stick—one not too close to the edge—and throw it as far as you can into the Waste."

The young man galloped off and quickly returned with a branch roughly the size of his arm. He hurled it into the cursed land where it slid to a stop. Within a few moments, smoke rose from the branch and it turned black.

Mangin was right, Dirge thought. It acted like an acid, much like Hogar's blade when Dirge fought the Chaos paladin at the Tower of Time.

"Dismount. Cut off a piece of your surcoat and tie it over your horse's hooves." Dirge said. "The Lord's blessing upon the fabric should protect them."

After doing so himself, Dirge urged Striker onto the color-swirled surface. It belied its glass-like appearance, depressing slightly where Striker stepped, but was also viscous, adhering to the cloth, so Dirge went at a slower pace than he'd initially planned for stability.

A hundred yards into the cursed land, and the forest behind them was obscured by the haze. There was no wind, as though it didn't want to be there. Sweat sprung up on Dirge's face. The air was heavy, muffling sound as though a wall of cotton surrounded them. His men began to mutter.

"Focus," Dirge barked. "We're not alone out here." Normally, he would be able to feel the wrongness of a Chaos beast as it neared, but the Waste overwhelmed his senses.

Farther and farther they crept into the eye-twisting miasma. And still, nothing.

Dirge's eyes strained for a glimpse of the enemy; his throat was parched, and nostrils stinging. He shrugged his shoulders to ward off tightness the lingering stress brought on. How much longer? *Were the grunkin even here? Did they also fear this place?* It was an unnerving thought.

A grunting bark shattered the stillness, emanating from somewhere out front. It was difficult to judge the distance. Snarls and whines followed suit from their sides. The glittering surface of the Waste heaved and cracked a hundred feet away. Grunkin burst forth from beneath by the dozen, their maws or beaks screaming. The size of small horses, each was a twisted mishmash, possessing hooves, claws, or pincers. Some were covered in greasy hides, while others had scales or quills. One even had gnarled caricatures of wings. But the thing would never fly. Flight took precision and beauty, of which grunkin possessed none. They raced toward Dirge and his men, their feet crushing the surface in their haste.

Crossbows thumped. The closest monsters screamed and thrashed, and then went silent. Yet others kept coming. The steady clack and thump of bows riddled the beasts, but more came on.

Knowing there were too many, Dirge dismounted, not wanting to risk Striker. He took up position twenty feet forward. "Estonia, cover our mounts. I'll draw them to me."

"Why are you doing this, sir?" The squire leapt from his

horse. "Why not create a shield to hold them out?"

Dirge drew upon the Lord until he glowed. "I need to reserve my strength."

The grunkin all turned toward Dirge, bringing death.

When the first reached Dirge, he drew his sword in an arc to meet the lunging beast, cutting it in half. He spun and stabbed, dancing into the mass of beasts. Whatever his sword cut died. Death's Tongue, the blade of the High Slayer, the sword of his father was as light as a feather in his hands. He cut a swath into the grunkin until none remained.

Panting, he pulled a cloth from his belt, and wiped the blade clean, then returned it to its sheath. The enemy's attack somehow cleared the air—they were less than halfway into the Waste.

"Remount," he told Estonia. "We're losing time."

More grunkin attacked as they neared the Waste's center. Each monster died, but they slowed Dirge's advance, which worried him. The cloth covering Striker's hooves started to smoke, and Dirge didn't know how much longer until the fabric's protection would give out. He urged Striker to move faster.

Then, out of the gloom, a tall, brick building came into view near the center of the Waste, like out of a dream. The ground shook near the building, rippling away through the slimy Chaos-infused surface. A swirling mass the size of a horse's head arched from the building's top. It hurtled over the heads of Dirge's group, landing behind them.

Someone unseen shouted from townhouse, "You do not belong here! Return now and I will let you go in peace. If you persist, I *will* kill you."

Dirge urged Striker forward.

The ground shook again, and a large bubble formed in the Chaos to their right. The bubble burst, splashing everyone near. Men shouted in pain, and horses screamed and reared. Then, a jagged shaft of black rock, sharpened point at the end and as large as a man at the base, thrust out of the ground. It stabbed into the belly of a Militant's horse and up through the man himself, killing both.

"Warriors," Dirge shouted, "gather your militants. Shield them and move into position!" He concentrated, creating a shimmering sphere of pure force to encompass both him and

Estonia. His Righteous-Warriors did the same, only theirs had to be bigger to enclose their squads.

More rock shafts jutted up, slamming into the sides of the spheres and shattering. With defenses up, the Warriors' progress slowed, having to lower the shield to move, and then bring it up when attacked. Occasionally, they were too slow, the rock piercing man or horse. Regardless, the might of God protected his Warriors.

"This is where it gets hard," Dirge said.

While maintaining his shield, he clenched his fist and drew more upon the Lord. "Ukase, grant me the power to purify this land." He dragged the might of God from his own soul and focused it into his fist. Light burst forth from his gauntlet, and Dirge pulled even more. Shafts of stone hammered at his shield, and Dirge shook from the strain.

Whoever was attacking, must have known what Dirge was going to do. The shafts concentrated on him, dozens hammering his sphere. The ground shook and roiled, coating the shield in semi-molten Chaos.

The force sphere thinned, and Dirge shook, pain wracking his brain. He seared in agony as his vision swam. Finally, the Greater Rod of Divinity formed in Dirge's hand. It shimmered and pulsed, glowing with the true might of Ukase.

His shield shattered. Dirge grunted as rock spears slammed into his chest-plate where they broke, sending ragged chunks up into his helm, scoring his face.

Dirge held the Rod high. "By Ukase, I hereby banish you!" He slammed the Rod into the ground, which rang like a massive bell. The perfect tone filled the air as the blast wave rocketed away. The surge turned the jagged rock to dust, ate away the layer of Chaos, dissipated the miasma. It struck the building, obliterating it. The blast then sailed past his Warriors who enacted their own Rods, multiplying the effect. The might of God spread throughout the land, purifying it until no trace of Chaos remained.

The Rod in Dirge's hand winked out, and he fell from his horse.

At the time, Mangin had wanted to laugh when Dirge told the others to *protect her*. She couldn't see his eyes through his helmet but knew what he was thinking. She appreciated his asking the man to listen to her, but she also knew the truth. The desire to grasp the Lord's Breath was nearly overwhelming, but she kept it smashed it down.

Fear gripping her, she searched to forest for signs of any former priests. They'd likely try to kill her before anyone else. She now lived in a world where everyone hated her and sought her life. She'd never felt so alone. Despite that, she smiled. He had heeded her advice to check the land before riding into it. *Small victories*, she thought.

The cries and snarls of grunkin made her jump. She searched their surroundings, before realizing the calls came from deep within the Waste. She urged her horse closer to Parkinson for protection, even though she hated herself for doing so.

"What's wrong, witch?" Kirkadite said with a sneer. "Are you afraid of your pets? I'm surprised. What do you have to fear? All you need do is reach out and take your god's power—we both know it's all around us." He turned his head away. "Why, I bet you could strike us all down in the blink of an eye."

"Watch your tongue, Truth-Seeker," Parkinson said. "You speak to the wife of the Righteous-Captain. She was pardoned for her past crimes by the Magnus, and Righteous-Captain Dirge took her in. He wouldn't do so if she were still wicked."

"Malik pardoned her, not Magnus Donavan," Kirkadite said.

Parkinson's voice firmed. "Do you question the judgement of Magnus Malik when he was the voice of God?"

"Not at all." Kirkadite's eyes narrowed. "However, I do question Captain Dirge."

The remaining Righteous-Warriors bristled, and Parkinson rode up to the Truth-Seeker. "You are insubordinate, questioning your superior officer. You are now on report. I will inform the Arch-Seeker of your sin."

"Do as you feel you must," Kirkadite said. "But you must admit that *Righteous-Captain* Dirge is a man out of his time and element. While we trained and awaited the coming of God, he wallowed with Travelers, riding among the worst that was

Chaos." Kirkadite's voice also grew hard. "It is because of him that my—"

Kirkadite cut himself off. "It matters not. Mark my words. Something is wrong with *Righteous-Captain* Dirge. He will show his true self one day, and I hope to be there when he does." He reined his horse and dropped to the back of the group.

Parkinson returned to Mangin's side, keeping a keen eye on the surroundings. "You've nothing to fear, Lady Malik. The Righteous-Captain is a godly man, one of the best. He will not abandon you."

Mangin stilled her face, not realizing her emotions were showing. She turned back to the Waste, straining her eyes in hopes of seeing Dirge. *Be safe, you hardheaded lummox.*

The grunkins had been quiet for a time when shouts and screams erupted from deep in the haze. The sounds of cracking and rumbling stone followed, as though a rock slide hit the Waste. It continued for some time.

Mangin tried to will her eyes to see through the wavering air, to no avail. *Don't you dare die on me.*

"Do you know what will happen to you if he dies?" Kirkadite's voice was like a velvet-covered anvil; soft, but unyielding.

She jerked, startled at his closeness—she'd not heard him approach.

"Yes, I see you do," he continued. "Good."

"That is enough, Truth-Seeker," Parkinson barked.

Mangin urged her horse forward. *He may need my hel—*

A brilliant light flashed within the Waste, and the ground quaked. The horses jerked and snorted. Then, a dust-filled wall raced toward them out of the Chaos infused lands. When the wave passed over, a ringing filled the air.

"The Lord is triumphant," Parkinson shouted. "Glory be to God!" The rest of the men cheered with him.

But Mangin heard none of it. She hugged herself, wanting to cry. Chaos was gone, once again leaving her world bleak. She could almost feel Kirkadite's smile as he stared at her back.

Chapter 21

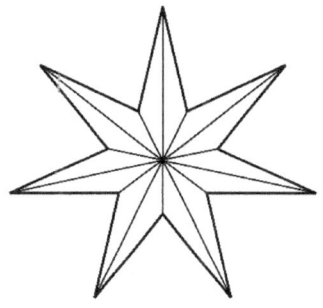

Things Change

It took three days to return to Kindermark. First, to Mangin's dismay, they had to have a proper funeral pyre for the fallen Militant-Warriors. Organized memorials to the dead were something Mangin still didn't understand. Everyone grieved in their own way. What was the need to do so together?

The second reason it took so long was Dirge could hardly stay upright on his horse. He had suffered three broken ribs and several lacerations to his chest and face. But the stubborn fool refused to be carried in a litter. He claimed it wasn't becoming of an officer, not when there were real wounded who needed them.

Once they were back at the main camp on the outskirts of Kindermark, Dirge allowed his wounds to be tended to. He sat bare chested and stiff in his tent on his favorite stool as the medic stitched him up. Blood-crusted bandages lay on the ground around him. His gashes were red and angry, but there didn't appear to be any pus or atrophy.

Mangin sat next to him on the edge of their cramped travel bed in her full-length, deep navy-blue dress. "The scars will make you more rugged."

"And here I thought my face couldn't get uglier," Dirge replied, grimacing with each suture.

She swatted at his shoulder. "Nonsense. You're not ugly. You're not pretty, though—you never were. You've a face like a rock. Do you even smile? Never mind, where was I? Oh, yes. But that doesn't make you ugly. Far from it. You've the face of a warrior, one that frightens men and excites women." She glided behind his stool and ran her fingers through his hair. "You excite me."

"This is hardly the time, wife. Not with broken ribs."

She whispered into his ear, "I'll be gentle with you."

"Not now." Shooing away the medic, he stood and took a moment to gather himself. "I need to check on the men." He then exited the tent.

She stood there, quivering after he left. Her mind raced. He had said, "not now," but she knew he wanted to. His lust made her skin tingle. Then his hatred boiled over, making him flee. She knew it. But how? She was behind him the entire time, not once seeing his eyes. It was as if she read his—

"No!" She shook her head in disgust, refusing to accept that train of thought.

"I'm sorry, my Lady?" the medic asked as he packed his things.

"It was nothing. I must be going." She dashed out into the evening, the sun just disappearing behind the trees.

Rubbing her arms, she wandered, aimlessly. There was no way she could have read his thoughts. She had no power, not anymore. Chaos was gone, and Ukase certainly hadn't entered her heart. She had no god to power her abilities. "It was my imagination. Yes, that it. I've been with him so long I must have read his body language." She needed a drink.

The True Heart's Rest was subdued, having only a third of the tables taken. Dirge had deemed the inn *for officers only*, so the other Militant soldiers caroused more lively establishments. With the night on its way, lamps filled the common room with a soft glow as a troubadour played his harp low for ambiance.

Righteous-Warrior Parkinson, sitting at a table near the door, talking quietly to his Head Righteous-Militant, bowed his head as she passed.

Mangin took a seat at the back. After the maid brought red wine and cheese, Mangin stared into her glass, nibbling the delicious chunk of white. *What happened back there?* she thought. *Am I going mad?* It was not a pleasant prospect. She remembered rumors from her time at the Citadel, talk of people who were somehow cut off from the Lord of Chaos and going mad because of it. She didn't believe it at the time. Now, she wasn't so sure.

"May I join you?" a man asked.

Looking up, Mangin shuddered. It was Evram Kirkadite. She'd been so engrossed with her morbid thoughts that she'd not noticed the Seeker entering.

Wiping the smirk from her face, she tried to replace it with a pleasant smile. "Of course." She didn't want to incite the man any more than necessary.

The man pulled back a chair and sat stiff backed. "You seem to be enjoying yourself."

"Why shouldn't I? My Lord Husband did well out there."

"The Lord Ukase triumphed. Righteous-Captain Malik was merely a conduit of God's will. One day soon, the truth of Ukase with spread to every corner, wiping out heretics where they are found. All will fall beneath the Righteous Hand of God." His cruel brown eyes bore into Mangin. "Everyone else with be purged."

Trying not to shake, Mangin stood. "The hour is late, and I must return to my Lord husband. Good evening."

With the slight nod, she strode to the front door. Part of her wanted to run, but Mangin wouldn't give the spiteful man the pleasure. Out on the street, she kept glancing back toward the inn as she made her way out of town. She did not pay close enough attention to what lie ahead.

A man stepped out of an alley, cutting Mangin off; she had to jump back to not slam into him. As she stared into his angry eyes, the color drained from her face. "Cobb?"

Grabbing her neck and clasping a hand over her mouth, Cobb dragged her into the alley. "Keep your mouth shut, witch."

Terror gripped her as she fought and kicked, biting his hand.

He pulled it back with a yelp, so she took a deep breath to scream for help. Cobb's clenched fist slammed into her stomach, turning Mangin's shout into a grunt as her breath fled. She doubled over in pain, so Cobb grabbed her by the midsection and carried her into a back-alley behind the buildings.

Cobb shoved her back against her wall and covered her mouth once more. "Bite me again and I'll slit your throat. Do you understand?" After she gave a trembling nod, he continued, "Where is she?"

"Who?" she mumbled between his fingers.

Cobb full-armed slapped her across the face.

Stars danced before her eyes, her head swimming. Once Mangin regained her faculties, she asked, "Do you mean Adel?"

Cobb's hand wrapped around her throat and squeezed. "Don't you dare say her name," he growled.

Gurgling, Mangin clawed at his hands to pry them away, but his grip was too tight. Part of her, the part not terrified, wanted laugh at the irony. Back in Cool Winds, she used to have Cobb choke her during their rougher sex-play. In her youth, his physical prowess thrilled her, and she loved to be taken roughly. But, back then, she was the one in control, his mind a plaything at her will. Now, she knew only terror.

"Don't you ever say her name." Cobb squeezed her neck even tighter, his fingers digging into Mangin's skin.

The edges of Mangin's vision thinned and her struggle weakened. She knew she was about to die. She grabbed his head weakly to shake some sense into it. How could she answer if he killed her? He needed to stop!

"You don't *ever*—" Cobb cut himself off and pulled back, rapidly blinking his eyes.

A brick exploded from the opposite building and clipped the side of Cobb's head. He staggered into the middle of the alley, blood matting his hair. Another brick flew, this one from Mangin's right, smashing Cobb in the face with a crunch. He dropped to his knees, blood pouring from his mouth and nose, then fell forward and went still.

Mangin took a ragged breath, gingerly touching her throat. *What just happened?* She searched the dark back-alley and jumped when a cloaked figure stepped from the shadows of the side-alley.

"Are you all right?" the stranger asked in a high, soft woman's voice. She lowered her tan hood. Dark, shoulder-length, wavy hair framed a lovely pale face. "Did he hurt you badly?"

The last time Mangin saw the woman was in the Citadel. The young acolyte had animated marble statues in an attempt to kill Mangin on her arrival. "Sashel?"

The former Chaos priest took Mangin by the hand and drew her toward the side-alley. "We need to get out of here. He may not be dead. And if he is, there's sure to be trouble with all the Ukase people about. Come on, my place is not far. We can have a drink and talk."

In a cramped, second floor apartment, Mangin sat on a rickety chair next to Sashel's bed. The room smelled of incense as well as deep earth, for some reason. The former priest stepped bare foot into a shallow box of dirt and sat down on her narrow bed. She then poured them each a cup of wine, placing the bottle on her nightstand next to a bowl of red-brown pellets. "You can spend the night," Sashel said. "And in the morning, I'll book you on the next boat south. I don't have enough coin to get you far, but I'll do what I can."

Mangin took a sip and did her best to hide a grimace—it was so bad she wasn't sure if the cup held wine or vinegar. Setting the cup down, she asked, "What's that in the bowl? And what's with the dirt ... do you enjoy being filthy?"

"The bowl contains iron," Sashel replied. "As for the box," she scrunched her toes in the soil, "I don't like to be too far from the ground."

"I don't ..." Mangin shook her head. "It doesn't matter. You shouldn't be here. If Kirkadite finds you, he'll kill you."

"Kirkadite?"

"The head Seeker with us. Why are you even this close to the Reach? It's dangerous."

Sashel laughed. "Yes, I know. I came here to help our former brothers and sisters—just as they told you. We gave each a crystal containing a small portion of Chaos to get them to safety, where they would have to find their own way in the new world. The process went well until Kenja showed up and ruined it."

Mangin was about to ask who *they* were but stopped, eyes widening. "Kenja? He's the one who killed those people and took that girl?"

Sashel nodded. "That arrogant bastard. If he'd just slipped away like everyone else, none of this would have happened." With a sigh, she leaned her back against the wall. "First I tried to scrounge up enough coin to book passage south—G'kaals took his tshoma and went east toward the mountains after dropping me off at the edge of the Waste."

Mangin was about to ask who G'kaals was but decided it didn't matter.

Sashel continued, "That's when Annella showed up. She was the only person at the Citadel I was close enough to, to call a friend. And since Moira had refused to take anyone else in, I had to do something. I gave Annella what coin I had at the time and sent her south. Then another came, and another. I guess the network hadn't heard about Moira shutting her doors. Why else would they send you?"

"I don't know who *they* are. I came with—" Lowering her eyes, she bit her lip. "I came with the battalion of Righteous and that stinking Kirkadite."

Sashel's jaw dropped, her cup falling to the floor, spilling its contents. The woman didn't seem to notice. "What?"

Mangin told her story brokenly, filling in the detail only when prodded. She didn't trust Sashel enough to tell the entire truth, let alone her true feelings.

After Mangin finished, Sashel took a deep breath and sighed. "I guess I understand." She burrowed her feet deeper into the soil. "We each must do what we can to survive."

She then grinned. "So, what's married life like?"

"It's … complicated." Mangin laughed. "My entire life I thirsted to sample everything, to experience every touch, taste, and smell. And now…" Her smile faded. "Dirge is a good man. He takes care of me." She added under her breath, "Even if he hates me."

Sashel reached out and clasped Mangin's hand. "The world has changed, and we must follow suit or die. I'm no longer who I once was as well. The day I attacked you, I was a lost soul. I knew only darkness and strife. When Chaos was cut off, I thought all was lost. Then Amurru found me." Her smile beamed, wiggling her feet in the dirt-filled box.

Mangin pulled her head back. "The God of Stone and Earth?"

"Yes." Sashel sat on the edge of her bed. "Think about it. We all had special abilities; mine was the manipulation of stone. Amurru showed me the truth of my soul. I didn't realize the darkness that had resided in me due to Chaos. I belonged to Amurru, and she showed me a world rich with life. I now know peace and stability."

Mangin nodded. "Yes, it does make sense. Some loved cold, while others did wonders with wind or light. It was their true god's calling." Tightness gripped her chest. "But what does that say about me? There is no God of the mind." She shook her head. "Who is my true god? What am I?"

The door to Sashel's apartment crashed open, and Evram Kirkadite entered, his head held high. "You are heretics. And it is time you were both put to the question." He waved his hand and Militant-Seekers rushed into the room in leather armor and steel pot-helms, their boots hammering the floorboards.

Sashel grabbed a handful of the pellets and flung them at the approaching soldiers. The iron nuggets flew far faster than Sashel's toss. They pierced the chest armor of the two men up front who dropped. The next man in line dove at Sashel, slamming her in the side of the head with his gauntleted fist. Sashel collapsed.

Mangin jumped out of her chair shouting, "What do you think—"

Kirkadite backhanded her across the face. "Shut up!"

Mangin fell back in her chair, her head ringing.

The Truth-Seeker then pointed at Sashel. "Bind her feet and hands in bags and carry her—don't let her touch the ground." He pointed at his men. "You two, see to these men. The rest, follow me."

One of the militants grabbed Mangin whose vision was still blurred from the blow, while another took control of Sashel. Despite the pain, Mangin struggled. She'd just survived Cobb and wasn't about to go quietly this time. "Release me!"

The militant grabbed her by the hair and yanked. "Shut your witch mouth!"

Yelping, Mangin leaned forward for fear the man would rip the hair out of her head. Trying to put on a meek face, she nodded, letting the Militant-Seeker herd her out of the room by her shoulder. Another Militant hoisted Sashel over his shoulder, and they all went down the stairs, and out of the building.

When they reached the nearly empty street, Kirkadite said over his shoulder, "I look forward to purging you both. There is only one God, and you will meet His justice."

Desperate, Mangin tried another tact. "You are making a mistake, Truth-Seeker Kirkadite. You do not have the right to hold the wife of a superior officer."

Kirkadite replied, "Militant-Seeker, if she speaks again, shut her up."

Rage and frustration boiled up in Mangin. As did fear. Desperate, she reached out and grabbed the man holding her by the jaw. "I said, you've no right to do this and will let me go."

The man stuttered to a stop and released her shoulder, his eyes going foggy. But he quickly shook it off and snatched her by the throat, his eyes burning with a zealous fire. "You were warned." He drew his other fist back to strike her.

A gauntleted hand reached in and grabbed the wrist holding Mangin's throat. The armored fist clenched, and the Militant-Seeker's wrist snapped. Screaming, he released Mangin and staggered back, cradling his arm.

Dirge spoke as he came abreast of Mangin, "I warned you about laying hands on my wife." He smashed the militant in the face. The man's nose exploded in blood and he flopped to the dirt.

Kirkadite spun about. "She was consorting with a heretic," Kirkadite snapped. "This woman," he pointed at Sashel, who groaned, "is a worshiper of Amurru. The two of them were talking blasphemies and it is my right to question them."

"We did what we came here to do," Dirge said. "The Great Waste is no more. Our job is not to purify and purge on the way. At this time, this land is not of the Lord Ukase."

"All land is of the Lord!"

"Not yet," Dirge said. Then turned to Estonia. "Take the young woman to a healer of some sort. Then get some rest. We leave at first light." Dirge turned back to the Truth-Seeker. "When the time comes, these people will be under our jurisdiction. But, until that time, they are free to do as they please."

Kirkadite quivered in rage. "You blaspheme."

"I speak the truth. Remember, Evram, this is an expedition of War, *not* Purification." He looked at the Militant-Seeker holding Sashel. "Release the woman. She is free to go. The rest of you, get out. We leave at first light."

As soon as Estonia got Sashel standing on her bare feet, the woman shook herself, coming to her senses. When Estonia tried to urge her forward, she shook him off, holding out one hand defensively. "I'll be fine." She spied the disposition of the situation and licked her lips. "What just happened?"

Mangin spoke up. "Sashel, I want to introduce you to my husband, Lord Malik, Righteous-Captain of the True of Ukase." She wanted to be precise so as not to give Kirkadite any more ammunition.

Sashel grinned. "You were right, Mangin. He's quite lovely." She turned and bowed her head to Dirge. "I … thank you, Lord Malik, for the aid."

"I apologize for your treatment," Dirge replied. "Our ways are not for everyone. But the world is changing. In time, we will all have to choose sides."

Sashel seem to drink in his words. "I suppose you're right. And, perhaps I can return your fair treatment of me in kind, one day." With her head held high, she walked back into her building.

Mangin watched Sashel go and thought, *Be careful.*

The Truth-Seeker eyed Sashel as well with a sneer. "It matters not. She *will* be corrected, if not today then soon." With the jerk of his head toward his men, he marched toward camp.

Dirge place a hand on her shoulder. "Don't worry. I'll have Estonia see she gets enough coin to take ship. This will not be a safe place for her from here on, I fear." He then took Mangin by the hand. "Come, my wife. I've need of you in our tent."

With a smile, she reached up and touched his face. Somehow, she sensed feelings of tenderness and respect, mixed with a good deal of lust pouring out of him. The hatred was still there, but it was muted behind acceptance. "What's going on?" she asked, her mind a whirl.

"Things change," he said softly, and kissed her hand.

Chapter 22

Containing the Void

The tightly packed tavern stank of sweat and piss, its clamor washing over Calidos Flint as he wallowed in his sour ale. He considered ordering an eska. Derived from fermented corn or grain, the light-brown spirit was widely known for its kick, and he enjoyed the burn as it went down. But his head still ached from the amount he'd consumed the night before.

Shouts, along with the crashing of mugs and chairs, erupted from the far end of the bar, signaling yet another fight. The three bouncers trudged their way to the ruckus. Calidos guessed it was easier for the bouncers to let the drunks wear themselves out first—even if it was hard on the furniture.

He'd been holed up in the slums of Dane Hook for months, spending much of the time in varying states of inebriation. Reaching into his coin purse to order another mug, he found it empty. He'd forgotten he spent his last on the empty cup before him.

The good thing about living on the coast in the South was it was usually hot. He didn't need a proper room, just something over his head to fend off the rain—of which there was a lot—so bungalow rooms were aplenty and cheap. That left more coin for drink. Only his purse was now empty, which meant he would also have to spend the night on the street.

Raaz squatted in the next chair, his forked tongue tasting the air. Calidos had originally feared traveling with the imp. They were far from common. And with the new spread of Ukase, he would draw their attention. But, for some strange reason, very few ever seemed to take notice of the little, scaled monstrosity.

"How long are you going to ss-sulk?" Raaz asked. "I'm hungry, but even I wouldn't eat here the way these people poison themselves-ss."

Calidos' own stomach gnawed at him. "Are you reading my thoughts now?"

"Hardly. Come, Calidos-ss, let us find a more reputable establishment."

Pursing his lips, Calidos fingered the sleeve of his loose, stained, red shirt. He missed his multi-colored robes, but only a great fool went about advertising they used to be a priest of Chaos. "Fine." He pushed his mug away and rose. "The stink is starting to get to me anyway."

Outside, Calidos blinked, letting his eyes adjust to the sun after the dim of the tavern. The heavy, salt air made him think of his old home city of Leria, which seemed several lifetimes ago. They started down Incense Lane, heading out of the Squalor. The name often brought a grin to his face—he doubted the denizens understood the meaning. Unfortunately, he was too hungry and hungover to feel like smiling.

They entered the Que district. It didn't stink of shit as much as the Squalor, and the inn's food was more digestible, but it was hardly posh. "I know a place with good food not far from here "

Raaz walked up to a man haggling with a booth owner displaying cheap baubles. The imp took hold of the man's purse, cutting its strings with a sharp claw. He then delivered the purse to Calidos who counted out the silver and copper coins. "This will be more than enough for food and several mugs of good wine."

Raaz smirked. "More food and less wine, this time. You're

getting gaunt."

Calidos, ignoring the imp's statement, frowned at the people of the Que. The seedy parts of Dane Hook always appealed to Calidos, but with the way the city was going, even the less rundown locales, like the Que, were becoming too orderly and strict. The influence of Ukase had spread throughout the city. The City Masters hadn't yet given free rein to the True—a title the Ukase worshipers preferred—but Calidos thought it only a matter of time before the True would have complete control.

They entered a large city square lined with people. Entertainers filled the open center, twirling hoops, juggling balls, and flipping batons. Others rolled about the ground doing cartwheels and handstands. They left hats and baskets for whatever the crowd desired to give them. It wasn't quite begging, but Calidos saw little difference. It reminded him of Travelers, those roving performers beloved by the Lord of Chaos. Calidos had loved Travelers when he was a child. Now he hated them. His lip curled into a snarl. The world would be right if not for that stinking Ellis Concord; the one child he failed to Cleanse. If not for that, Edis would not be lost to him. If Concord appeared before him, Calidos would throttle the stinking man out of spite. He yearned to seek the Traveler out and fulfill his revenge, but what good would it do? Besides, the man could be anywhere. And Calidos was powerless to do anything.

A man strode into the center of the open square grasping a torch. Holding it before his lips, he sprayed fire into the air to great applause.

"I miss fire," Calidos muttered, eyeing the firebreather with envy.

"There are other ways," Raaz said, handing Calidos a full purse the imp had gotten somewhere.

Calidos snapped up the coins. "I'm *not* groveling to Tohil. The Fire God means nothing to me. How any times do I have to tell you?"

Raaz shrugged. "One does not have to worship Tohil to use his gift."

"What do you mean?" Calidos gave the imp a sideways glance.

"You did so before, did you not?" Raaz handed over a fresh,

red apple. "You need only use something other than Chaos to manipulate it."

"Watch what you say," Calidos hissed, his eyes darting about. "Someone might call for a Seeker. Word is they pay bounties nowadays."

"Like him?" Raaz pointed across the plaza to a man in a bright red uniform with the white star of Ukase, staring at the entertainers with disdain.

A lump formed in Calidos' throat and his skin pimpled, seeking for an avenue of escape.

Raaz continued, "I suppose you're right. It would be best if we went elsewhere. Don't you think?"

Cursing, Calidos hurried down the nearest street to escape the Militant-Seeker but stopped short with a curse. A pair of Righteous-Warriors in their shining steel marched toward them one block away. Calidos' guts churned and he seethed at his own fear. "What now?"

"In here." Raaz went to the first door on the right and entered.

Calidos darted through and slammed the door behind him, his heart thumping in his chest. He hated the feel of missing the Great Lord's power coursing through him, it was like being only half alive. But it was better than being dead.

"What are you doing in my home?" a man's voice asked behind him.

Calidos spun about.

A short man with black hair, his tan tunic and breeches having seen better days, entered from a back room. He held a mutton leg as though brandishing a club. "Get out or I'll drub you."

Raaz sprinted across the room and leapt at the man, sending them both toppling to the floor. Raaz then clasped his scaled hand over the man's mouth. "Hush now. Death should be quiet at times-ss such as these."

The man's eyes bulged as he thrashed, but his muffled screams barely reached Calidos at the end of the hall. The shouts turned guttural as blackness spread from the man's mouth and down his body until he went limp.

Grabbing the mutton, Raaz tossed it to Calidos. "To sate your hunger while we wait. I smell more food in the back." The little thing grinned, flashing white teeth. "This one shall fill me well."

"What then?" Calidos asked.

"We wait a day or so and make for the wall. From there, you should be able to steal a horse or catch a wagon train north." Raaz bit into the dead man's neck. Bones snapped, and blood oozed from the corner of the half-demon's mouth.

Flint's stomached knotted watching Raaz gorge himself. "Why north? Why not Geos?"

Raaz lifted his head, bits of flesh hanging from the gaps in his needle-like teeth. "Because Geos fell to Ukase months ago. You would have known, but you were too busy wallowing in self-pity. Now, go and eat and leave me to my feast. Human flesh should be eaten fresh after death." He licked the gore away. "It tastes best when they still live, but I couldn't risk his raising an alarm, now could I?"

Calidos nearly retched as he made his way to the back of the townhouse, wondering yet again why he still let Raaz stay near him.

Two days north of Dane Hook, atop a stolen horse, Calidos didn't like how things were proceeding. Their journey had been slow, needing to parallel the road through thick forest and underbrush. He feared being spotted by Dane Hook patrols or caravans. Originally, Calidos wanted to head west to either Leria or Glennen, but Raaz had told him Ukase had his own city of Ukabar, next to the ruins of Tuilar. Their warriors guarded those roads with vigor.

"When did that damned god get his own city?" Calidos raged as he brushed hanging moss from his face.

Raaz scampered alongside of Calidos' horse. He was surprisingly fast and didn't need a horse of his own to keep up— not that one would let him atop. "Over a year ago. But, again, you were acting too pathetic to notice."

"Everything is changing too fast."

Raaz's laugh sounded like a rasp dragged across rusted steel. "You worshiped Chaos and now you complain of change? You humans never cease to amaze me."

Calidos opened his mouth to reply but stopped. The acrid

stench of rot mixed with scorched flesh tickled his nose. Then, a miasma brushed by, causing the hair on his arms stood on end. He opened his third eye and found traces of Chaos drifting through the woods. "What is this? How can this be?"

The half-demon seemed to be smiling, but with him, it was often hard to tell.

"What aren't you telling me?" Calidos asked.

His horse jerked and screamed. Rearing, it threw him to the ground, and dashed off. However, it only made it a few yards before a grunkin smashed into its side. The beast sank razor-sharp teeth and pincers into the horse's neck, and tore its head off. The grunkin then gorged on the flesh.

Calidos froze, eyes wide. "They never eat."

"Of course it eats." a woman said behind him. "They grow hungry otherwise."

He turned, and his jaw dropped. "How…"

A stunning woman with long, jet-black hair sat atop an equally black horse. Her green eyes held a sparkle of delight. "Calidos Flint. And here I thought you long dead."

"Celeste?" he croaked. "How is any of this possible?"

"Let us discus that over dinner."

Chapter 23

Eyes of Jade

Memories, both glorious and damning, slammed into Dirge as he led the company through the gates of Dane Hook. Eric Kelts, a local Righteous-Warrior, rode at Dirge's side as a guide. Just like the coastal city of Tuilar where Dirge was born, salt was heavy in the air. As was the fetid stink of so many people and animals crammed together within its walls. It was odd how he'd never really noticed the smells growing up. Only having spent so long in the Reach, did he realize the aroma was missing from his life. The cacophony was reminiscent as well: the creaks of axles, the whinny of horses, and above all, the murmur and laughter of the city's residents. Vendors shouted from their stalls as Dirge and his men passed. They promised things, not only what the newcomers wanted, but what they needed, and of how low their life was without the traders' wares.

It all made Dirge's heart ache. Though the city was different, the similarities to Tuilar were too strong. The people wandering about their daily lives might as well be ghosts to Dirge. He didn't see them. He only saw those he remembered.

A blonde woman with a flirtatious smile became one of the barmaids he'd known from the Angelic Inn. Another with dark-red hair haggling with a fishmonger became Caitlin, the Angelic's owner. The young man strolling by with his harp became Jacob. That apparition stung Dirge so hard he winced. A square-jawed man strolling past with a cudgel at his hip made Dirge think of one of the bouncers from the Angelic, who, like the rest, had actually been a member of the Brotherhood. The man's hair was gray instead of black though. But the eyes were the same. As was the smile ...

Dirge's jaw dropped open, and he pulled his mount to a stop. "Cal, is that you?"

Cal turned and his smile fell. "Hello, Dirge. I'd heard you were coming. You look well." He glanced at Dirge's company and added, "Considering your circumstances."

When Dirge started to dismount, Cal held up a hand. "No. I've not the time, and I suspect you don't either."

"Certainly, you've the time to—"

Cal cut him off. "A clean break. Remember? You turned your back on us, and that's how it must stay. I wish you luck in your future." He paused. "Have a care, Dirge. Your past is catching up to you." Turning sharply, he disappeared into the crowd.

"Who was that man?" Kelts asked.

Tearing his gaze off the throng, Dirge shook the reins to urge Striker forward. "Someone from my past." He refused to look at the people of Dane Hook for the rest of the ride.

The Bastion of the Righteous took up four city blocks of what Dirge expected to be prime real estate—adjacent to the thoroughfare that sloped down to the wharf. Its ten-foot high wall was manned by Righteous-Militants, their steel helms glinting in the sun as they walked the battlements. Dirge passed through the gatehouse and into a courtyard large enough to fill two hundred men. Two buildings filled the rest of the space. The larger was five floors of thick, white stone with windows lining only the top two floors—each floor cantilevered over the one below it to make it more difficult for someone to try and climb the wall to gain entrance. Arrow loops ran along the second and third floors. The second building was only two floors of the same white stone, but its roof led directly to the wall by a pair of stairs. Dirge took it as a garrison house.

"Impressive defenses," Dirge said.

"Though smaller than those up north in Ardentia, our bastion is formidable," Kelts said, his words short and quick. "We don't have the luxury of space like you do up north. Righteous-Captain Yolden requested more land, but this is all the city's government would allow us."

"I'm surprised they gave us this much," Dirge said as he dismounted, handing over the reins to a stableman. "Why doesn't it have seven faces to honor God?"

"We did not construct it," Kelts replied. "It was gifted to us by Magistrate Bachman, the city's Master of Defense—a recent convert. When the city is truly the Lord's, we shall rectify that."

A short, slim man dressed in black with gray at the temples approached Dirge and bowed. "I am the steward, Reginald. I will show you and your goodly wife to your suite while the valets see that your men are properly quartered according to rank. The primary residence is designated for the Company Commander and his men. I will house the Seekers in the blockhouse."

Reginald took them to the top floor, to a double door just down the hall from the stairs. Entering, he stepped aside and bowed. "Your bedroom with attached privy is through the door on the left, and your library is on the right—your predecessor used it for private meetings. Is there anything you desire from me at this time?"

Mangin crossed the room, gliding between a pair of heavy chairs—one padded and one not—to the central of the three windows beyond. "Husband, would you please ask the steward to bring some wine, along with some meat and cheese?" She pushed open the heavy wooden shutter and breathed in the ocean breeze that flowed in.

"Please do as my goodly wife asked," Dirge said to the steward. "And send word to Righteous-Warriors Kelts and Parkinson that I will be down shortly."

"Right away, your Lordship." Reginald bowed and exited, closing the doors behind him.

Dirge joined Mangin at the window overlooking the

courtyard. The city spread out below, gently sloped down to the bay beyond. Gulls circled and cried above the wharf. The last time he was this high above a coastal city was when he stood atop the walls of Tuilar, inspecting the Army of the Righteous before their ill-fated crusade, with Lynette at his side.

Again, her voice echoed in his mind, *"Until tonight ..."*

He cleared his throat. "Will this suffice, wife?"

Rolling her eyes, she said, "We're alone now. No need to be so stuffy." She then went to the coal-gray, padded chair facing the window, testing its comfort with a hand. Upon sitting, she examined the bare stone walls. "It's so stark in here. Needs color. I'll go buy some lovely tapestries and dressing blinds. I hope the bedroom isn't this bland."

Dirge gazed out the window. Dozens of boats skimmed in and out of the harbor, while the deep rolling waves of the bay stretched to the horizon. "I rather like it," he murmured.

Mangin laughed. "What a surprise."

He turned his back on the panorama. "I'm sure Reginald can find decorations for the room—they must have something in storage."

"No. I'll do it myself. If I'm going to be living here, I want it to have my own touch."

"Be sure to take an escort."

"I can handle—"

Dirge interrupted her, "This is not the Corners. The streets are not safe. Trust me, I know what these cities are like." When she rolled her eyes, he sighed. "Think of it this way. The southern citystates are much like Gate Hall from the time before. Only now ..."

Blushing, she turned away. "Only now I'm helpless." Straightening, she looked him in the eye. "Fine. I will take an escort. You're right, I don't know the city. And until I do, I need to be careful."

Dirge knew her version of careful was different than his. Once she felt comfortable with the city, she'd ditch the guards the first chance she got.

As though reading his mind, she laughed. "You know me too well, don't you? All right. I'll keep my minders as close as possible." Her face softened. She stood with the grace of a dancer and stepped close, caressing his cheek. "Thank you, my husband, for wanting to keep me safe."

Dirge wanted to push his concern, but she forestalled him by changing the subject.

"What are your thoughts on Kelts?" She strolled to the open bedroom door. "I've never seen anyone with such striking features—silver hair, purple eyes, skin like a lime." She then entered, not waiting for his response.

Annoyed, he followed after. "Righteous-Warrior Kelts is an Ulawun, a tribe of seafaring folk from the Torq Isles, beyond the bay. He preformed exemplary according to his former superior, Righteous-Captain Yolden. I expect him to do the same with me."

Mangin ran a finger along the footboard of the large, hardwood bed, and then went to the window, opening the shutters. "He doesn't like you." She took a deep breath and expelled with a sound of contentment.

Growing even more frustrated, Dirge went to her back. "Where did you hear this? What game are you playing at?"

She spun about. "I heard it from no one—it'll likely take weeks for anyone here to speak with me outside of the housing staff. No, I saw it in his face and mannerisms. They were the same as many of Kirkadite's men." She then smirked, a glint of mischief in her eyes. "As for my game ..."

She nudged him, causing him to take a step back. "What makes you think I'm playing one?"

Dirge didn't like being pushed, but he reined in his temper.

She prodded him another step back. "I'm a contrite convert."

When Dirge's boots hit the side of the bed, she gave one more push, toppling him onto the bad. As she crawled onto his lap, his breath quickened. His heart pounded.

Mangin leaned over him, running a finger down Dirge's cheek. "I just want to spend some time with my husband."

Member firming, Dirge couldn't look away from her smoldering eyes. They ensnared his thoughts. Only once had Dirge seen eyes that shade of green, like shimmering pools of jade. So captivating. So wanton.

The image of a blonde woman flashed in his head. A woman with jade eyes.

Dahlia.

Dirge tossed Mangin to the side and jumped out of bed, shaking.

Mangin squealed. "Yes. Take me!" It turned into a squawk when he walked away. "Hey, where are you going?" she asked, dripping with indignation and hurt.

Staring out the window, Dirge refused to look her in the eye. "There's no time for that." He cleared his throat and straightened the rumples in his shirt. "I must meet with my second. I want to find out exactly what's going on before we go on patrol."

Dahlia's face haunted Dirge as he exited the suite. How had he not noticed the similarity between Dahlia and Mangin before?

The voice of a long-dead friend replied in his head. *"Because you never had the guts to look her in the eye before."*

Though the voice wasn't really Jacob's it was still right. He hadn't looked past the façade he'd given Mangin since taking her into his care: an amalgam of Lynette and Daylin. He'd no choice at the time. She was just a thing thrust upon him, a disgusting creature of Chaos who had bewitched Daylin. After accepting the burden, Dirge needed to see Mangin as something he didn't loathe. If he were to protect Mangin, she needed to be someone else, a person whose life mattered more than his honor.

Yet, ever since Kindermark, something changed between them. The animosity and distrust had faded. Mangin was no longer a burden. She was a person he could count on. Albeit not completely—her nature was still too wild—but she was worth trusting.

At least, he hoped so.

A Righteous-Militant saluted him. "Righteous-Captain."

Dirge snapped out of his reverie. The high sun shining in his eyes, he stood between two soldiers guarding the entrance to the bastion. He was so wrapped in his thoughts he hadn't noticed descending the stairs, let alone exiting. "Yes, um, where is the command room?"

"You just passed it, sir. First door on your left."

"Yes, good." Dirge shook his head to clear unwanted thoughts. "Assemble my squad and Righteous-Warrior Kelts. Have them meet me there."

The militant saluted again and then nodded to his compatriot. But Dirge barely noticed reentering the keep. The jade eyes haunting him refused to leave, and a part of him didn't want to let them go—they'd become a part of him. The problem was he couldn't even tell if they were Mangin's eyes or Dahlia's. What bothered him the most was it didn't matter.

Chapter 24

Reconnaissance

They'd patrolled the road to Conover and back twice with no sight of any grunkin or charred men. So, Dirge decided to head to Geos where the Cunning met the bay. He'd received several reports of small villages being ransacked along the river. The attacks themselves weren't a surprise, pirates had always plagued the Cunning. The odd thing was, in many instances, entire populations had disappeared.

"It doesn't make sense," Dirge said to Kelts riding on his right. "If it were grunkin and these charred men, there would be bodies. Yet the scouts reported minimal signs of bloodshed."

Kelts replied, "If you say so, sir." The Righteous-Warrior's hard eyes stayed on the wide, hard-packed road ahead—heavy trees lined both sides. Kelts rarely looked Dirge in the eye, and only when they were off horse when Dirge asked him something.

Righteous-Warrior Parkinson spoke up from Dirge's left, "Perhaps it was slavers?"

Dirge shook his head. "Unlikely. If they were slavers, they wouldn't take all the people, only those with real value. Too much hassle otherwise."

The road ahead started up a long hill and a large caravan was headed their way. Dirge guided his horse to the right, shaded side of the road. "It's getting late. We'll bed down for the night at Highpoint ahead. I presume it's still a favorite for caravanners?"

Kelts only nodded.

"How did you know about that?" Estonia asked behind Dirge, the standard of Ukase snapping in the breeze atop the squire's flagstaff.

Dirge didn't reply. He was trying to block out memories. It hadn't been a problem on their trips to Conover, and the road was a new to him—the river-side city had grown over the last twenty years, from a small fishing town to a major transportation hub. That wasn't the case with the coastal roads. Dirge knew them well. Every village they traveled through, every escarpment layover they passed, every time the tree line broke exposing the grand vista of Demon's Kiss Bay brought back memories. They tore open old wounds, exposing the painful truth hidden beneath. The shameful truth.

Dirge urged Striker for more speed. Perhaps Highpoint had changed enough to smother his haunted past.

The trees cleared and the village came into view. It was indeed bigger than he remembered, at least twice its former size. The entire top of the hill had been cleared to make room for more buildings. Some of the area was even being farmed: people scuttling about tending crops, chickens, and pigs. Highpoint had changed, but not enough to quell the ghosts.

Sighing, Dirge nudged his horse to the largest, foremost building. People milled about, coming and going through the front door. A sign hung above. One panel depicted a laughing man, dancing and drinking. The other panel showed him lying abed.

"Reveler's Rest," Dirge muttered. "Kelts, see that the horses are properly tended. Parkinson, see to the men's lodging." He headed for the doors. "I'm getting a drink."

It was like stepping into the past. The staff and customers were different, yet they looked the same. Warm light bathed the room. The smell of food mixing with candle and pipe smoke gave it a comforting feeling, as did the chatter of the crowd. Or, at least, it should have. At the room's far end, a young man in motley stood atop a small dais, strumming his lute and singing some pleasant song. For the barest moment, Dirge thought it was Jacob.

"May I get you something, Righteous?"

Dirge jerked his eyes to the plump, petit, young woman at his side. "Yes," he barked, but quickly shook his head. "I apologize. I would like an ale." He unbuckled his sword belt and sat at the empty table next to him, staring at the singer. "And an eska."

Estonia took the opposite chair. "Eska, sir? It's a little strong, isn't it?"

"I'm fine," Dirge replied. It wasn't that he wanted to forget. He was just tired and sore, and the spirt would help.

The rest of the patrol was uneventful. They didn't even enter Selos—Dirge decided it wasn't necessary—and camped outside of the walls. They forewent the inns on the return trip as well. Dirge said he didn't want the men to get too used to their comfort. It had nothing to do with the inns' musicians.

As he laid out under the stars at the campsite, he stared at the dancing shadows the fire cast on the roadside escarpment. The popping of the firewood blended with the insects and the animals hidden in the trees. Dirge only heard the screams of the caravan guards he and Jacob had murdered years before.

Back home, in the comfort of his own bed, sweat covered Dirge and his breathing slowed as he glared at the ceiling. The scent of sex filled the air as Mangin's hand played through his hair.

"You are getting so much better, my husband." She giggled and played with the pendant nestled in his sparse, tightly curled chest hair. "It's almost like you no longer hate doing this."

Closing his eyes, he hammered down memories. "I don't

know what you mean."

Mangin let out a low growl and got out of bed.

Dirge asked, "You're going to take more of those herbs, aren't you?"

"Why, I don't know what you mean," she replied, stopping at the bureau holding the wash basin and a pitch of water. Opening the drawer, she pulled out a small pouch, emptying the contents into a cup she then filled with water. "I simply have a headache." She downed the concoction.

He wanted to grind his teeth. "Is there a reason you don't want to carry my child?"

She signed. "Again, husband, I have no idea what you're talking ab—"

"Please, Mangin, all I ask for is the truth. Is … is there a reason you don't want to carry my child?"

She twisted her lips. "You want to play truths? Fine, answer me first. Why do you hate having sex with me so much? I'm no longer a woman of power or prestige. I have no connection to …" she twisted her lips and lowered her voice, "to my former god. So why do I see so much revulsion in your mi— in your eyes when we have sex?"

He wanted to say it wasn't true but couldn't. He sighed. "I don't hate you. I hate myself for enjoying it."

She threw up her arms. "That's ridiculous."

"It's not. To enjoy it would be disrespectful to the memory of Lynette." When she tried to interrupt, he held up a hand. "You asked, so I'm telling you. It's disrespectful because I took a vow to be faithful to her."

"But she's gone, long gone."

He scowled. "I know. I talked about it with the Veridical and he said my promise to her was until her death, and that God demands we live on. I understand what he meant, but in my heart, the vow was until *my* death."

She sat next to him on the bed, replying softly, "That is admirable. But the … I can't believe I'm going to say this, but the Veridical was right. You must live on. I am your wife, and according to your book," she grinned, "you must lie with me. So, you are breaking no promises by having sex with your wife."

"You are not the first woman I've lain with since Lynette passed."

Mangin's jaw dropped, and she grinned again. "Why, Dirge, you rake. Who was she?"

Closing his eyes, he tried to burn away the memory. "Her name was Dahlia. Jacob brought her to our room one night and she became obsessed with me. She got a barmaid to seduce me into taking her to my bed, but when I declined at the last moment, Dahlia was waiting in the hall." No matter how hard he tried not to, he saw it all again. "She bewitched me and used foul smoke and drink."

She cocked an eyebrow. "*Bewitched* you? As in …"

"Yes. I realized the next day that she was a priestess and had manipulated my mind." He shook with disgust. "I debased myself with a woman who was the epitome of everything I ever stood against."

Mangin ran a hand through his hair again. "And you think of her every time you look at me. You always have." She let out a small laugh. "It makes sense now."

"Yes. Well, no. Not all the time, only sometimes. But there's more."

He told her of his time with Jacob, of how his former friend manipulated him into theft and murder. "Every whore I bedded made me think of that woman. I even forced them to look at me the entire time in case …"

"In case she changed into Dahlia."

Dirge nodded. "I wallowed in self-hatred, believing I had to listen and follow Jacob."

"Why would you do that?"

"Because I owed him."

"How did you owe him? For a man like you, theft and murder is … well, a lot."

Dirge turned his head away. "Because I killed his family."

Mangin's eyes went wide. "His family?"

"Yes. There was a contract and Aza'zel demanded I do it. Anyway, it wasn't until I met the Travelers and Ellis that I finally saw the light."

"So you hate laying with me because of a past vow and because I remind you of a woman who twisted your mind."

Taking a deep breath, he looked into her eyes. "Not entirely. I hate myself when we have sex because I enjoy it. A great deal."

"A great deal?" She bit the corner of her lip and chuckled.

"I thank you for that. And there's nothing wrong with enjoying sex," she replied, running a finger over his chest. "Well, it's good to know I'm appreciated at least. I do try, after all. I didn't used to. Before we met, I cared for only two other people, and I could only lie with one of them. It wasn't until I met your wonderful troupe that I learned to give as a lover. Your Travelers are an amazing people. I see why you stayed with them."

She tilted her head. "Whatever happened to your friend, Jacob?"

"I killed him. He wanted to rob the troupe, and Ellis interrupted us. When Jacob tried to kill Ellis, I rammed my sword into Jacob's back." He saw it again in his mind—the blood, the shock in Jacob's eyes ... the look of betrayal.

"Dirge, your friend wanted to kill a child. One, who if you recall, took us all to the Tower. If not for that, Betal would still be Betal—a man in constant search for himself." She grabbed him gently by the hair. "Betal ended the time of Edis. I should hate him for that, but I don't. I will always love that man, even if he is a god. So, I understand feeling at odds with yourself." She got up and headed for the privy, the bounce of her heart-shaped rear drawing his eyes.

Dirge pushed aside his growing desire. "You never answered my question. I have no children, and I don't know if I want any. But why do you not want to carry mine?"

She spun about. "I don't want to carry anybody's child." The threw her arms wide. "I'm not *mother* material. I'm too selfish."

"According to the word of God, a woman is to bear her husband's children," Dirge said.

"Your god does not define me." She stabbed a finger at him. "You do not define me. I am not an extension of you. I may be your wife, but I am still my own woman." She strode into the privy, slamming the door behind her. "And I always will be."

Dirge reached for his nightstand, picking up the half-empty flask of eska which he purchased at the bazaar a few days before. The brown liquid burned as he gulped it down.

Chapter 25

Out of Order
and Chaos

Calidos' feet were sore by the time the trail reached a portion of the thick forest strewn with stunted, charred trees. The burn looked fresh, yet there was no smell of smoke. Through the blackened trunks, a two-story, sprawling manor covered in white stucco came into view. Six fluted columns centered the structure's doorway, running from the elevated front porch to the tiled roof. Windows littered the façade without apparent rhyme or reason on both floors, and black vines, some as thick as Calidos' leg, crisscrossed the manor. But what really fascinated Calidos was the residues of the Lord's Breath encircling the entire glade.

Raaz's tongue lolled out. "I like it here."

"I remember this place," Calidos said. "Ruddick lives here.

He had me over for diner to show off some parlor trick."

"Yes." Celeste sighed. "I took it after he passed."

Calidos frowned. "I didn't know he'd died." He'd thought the old man a complete fool but decided it was best not to remind Celeste of his opinion. "I'm sorry."

"I'm not," she said. "I'd wanted this place for years. But enough of that for now. We need to get you freshened up. Again, I'm sorry for making you walk the entire way. My men are using the wagon for supplies."

A beautiful, young woman in a short, white dress that hugged her curvy body exited the mansion. Tall, with tan skin and gray eyes, she danced down the steps. Her long, curly, black hair flowed behind her as she spun about. "You're home. It's like you've been gone for days."

Calidos stared at the newcomer with hunger. It had been some time since he'd lain with a woman. He would have to find a way to take this one.

"That's because it has been days, silly girl," Celeste said with a laugh. She turned to Calidos. "This is Glory." She turned to the girl. "Glory, this is a dear old friend, Calidos Flint."

The girl shrugged. "Who's the demon?"

"This is Raaz," Calidos said.

The girl frowned and scrunched her nose. She then shrugged again and dashed around the side of the manor, giggling.

"She's amazing," Calidos said, eyeing the girl's luscious rear as she fled.

"Yes, she is," Celeste replied. "And if you touch her, you will pray for death."

Calidos felt worlds better as he languished in his bath on the mansion's second floor. A pair of young, beautiful women—one with tan hair and the other with blonde—tended to his every need. With each brush it was as though miles of road dirt and fatigue fluffed away, clinging to the sudsy flotsam, and then adhering to the side of the tub. The crackle and pop of the fire heating both the room and the water further eased him, as did the incense smoldering all about the room.

"I can't recall the last time I felt this good." His hands played across the supple, naked bodies of the women as they scrubbed him. "I can't recall being this hungry either."

Jumping from the bath, he grabbed the blonde by the arm, and flung her face-first against the wall. He took her roughly from behind, relishing her screams and moans. Before long, he was sated and limp. As he stepped back, the blonde gathered his clothes as though nothing happened.

They took him to a large bedroom and showed him a wardrobe filled with men's clothes. "These are for you," the tar-haired one said.

"How do I know if they'll even fit me?" he asked.

"They were tailored to your precise dimensions."

"How is that possible?"

They left without answering.

Dubious, he tried on a pair of black pants and was shocked to find they fit perfectly. It was the same with the sky-blue shirt that followed. After slipping on his boots, he headed downstairs where Celeste awaited him in a low-cut, skin-tight, black dress.

"How was your bath?" Celeste asked.

"Wonderful," he replied while descending. "How did you know my size?"

"Don't be silly, man. We did have sex, remember."

He stopped in front to her, cocking his head. "But, that was years ago."

She ran a finger along his cheek. "I know every inch of your body. And I have a very good … memory." She slinked away. "Come along, Calidos. Dinner awaits."

They entered a large dining hall. Paintings and sculptures lined the walls in between the large windows, and three chandeliers hung from the ceiling. They joined two others already at the table; Celeste sat at the head and pointed Calidos to the seat next to hers. At the foot of the table was a familiar looking pale fellow with dark hair, his nut-brown eyes following Calidos with an air of anticipation as his hand toyed with the dagger at his belt. Across from Calidos, a gaunt woman, with long, golden hair and green eyes stared listlessly at her empty plate. With high cheekbones and a slim nose, she had the looks of a woman who was once quite beautiful but had grown sick with age.

Celeste gestured to the ailing woman. "This is my daughter, Dahlia. You can talk to her if you like, but she'll likely not answer."

Calidos tried to quell his distaste. "Is she all right?" Whatever the woman had, he hoped it wasn't catching.

Celeste didn't answer, instead picking up and ringing a bell.

Three young women—different from the two who tended to his bath—glided into the room. Each bore a different bottle of wine. They poured whichever was asked of them, then set the bottle on the table and retreated to the other room.

Calidos sipped his red and smiled. "Exquisite." He looked to the dark-haired man. "And who might you be?"

"I obviously didn't make much of an impact during your trip to the Corners." The man nodded his head. "I am Kenja Badell."

"That's right, You're the one who took me to see that fool, Rendell Morgan."

Kenja smiled. "And you were the last to see the High Priest alive, absconding with his aid."

"I hardly ..." Calidos scanned the room with a frown. "Where *is* Raaz?"

Celeste replied, "Your friend declined dinner. And thank you for the compliment on the wine. The locals have wonderful vineyards and they give handsomely." She grinned.

The women returned with steaming platters of beef and pork, along with a myriad of vegetables. They moved in and out, gliding with ease as though dancing.

Calidos accepted heaping helping of each and dug in. "I must say, Celeste, you look amazing," he said to Celeste around a piece of beef. "You haven't aged a day."

"Thank you. I do try to eat healthy." She took a sip of white. "It's so good to see you, Calidos."

He nodded. "My pleasure." He took a drink. "So, how did Ruddick die, anyway?"

"He was done in by his own success."

Calidos cocked an eyebrow. "What do you mean?"

"As you recall, he was experimenting on children—trying to connect them to the Lord. Well, he succeeded. One child changed and survived. You remember her. She was at one of Ruddick's last dinners."

Calidos' eyes went wide. "That scrawny thing? I was sure it was a joke at our behest." The girl had been prodded into claiming she could talk to a rabbit.

Celeste shrugged. "It was no joke. He not only connected her to the Lord, but to the Mother as well."

"Amazing."

"Yes, quite," Celeste said. "The problem was, she escaped, killing him in the process."

Closing his eyes, Calidos shook his head. "How could a child kill a priest of the Lord?"

Celeste giggled. "I misspoke. She didn't kill him, per se. It was actually a wolf she'd befriended; one Ruddick had acquired only weeks before."

Calidos sat up, a tingle running up his spine. "Wolf? What did the girl look like, again? I didn't pay enough attention at the time."

"Oh, a darling child ... pale, slim, with such lovely brown hair. However, it was her eyes that I loved most. Thanks to the Great Lord, they changed color, constantly."

His jaw dropped. "Daylin."

Celeste waved her hand. "She didn't have a name."

"Yes, she does. It's Daylin. I'm sure it's her. She was with that bastard, Ellis, constantly at his side. Along with some dark-skinned swordsman named Dirge. Apparently, they found her wandering the wilds with a wolf."

Celeste's daughter snapped out of her stupor and stared at Calidos. "Dirge? My Dirge?" She spun to Celeste. "Did you hear, Mother, he knows my Dirge. Oh, he was so beautiful, so special." Her eyes glazed over again. "He was so beautiful, so special." Putting a hand to her midsection, she gazed off into nothing. "And I was right."

Celeste patted her daughter's hand. "It's all right, my dear. I told you, I'm working on that. Give it time." She then asked Calidos, her voice cool, "You're sure of this?"

Calidos told her about the Travelers, and his search for them. "It's because of them we lost the Lord." He couldn't keep the anger out of his voice.

"Fascinating," she replied. "What are the odds they'd end up together?" She then added under her breath, "I will have to consult him about this."

When he asked what she meant, she didn't reply, but stared at him with a hint of a predatory smile. He took a drink, deciding to change the subject. "Where's Glory?"

Celeste took a bite of pork. "With Raaz."

"Are you sure that's safe? Raaz is—"

"Half Void dragon, I know." Celeste chuckled when his eyebrows shot up. "You didn't know? Oh, this is too funny. You've been traipsing around the countryside with one of the most dangerous creatures in existence, thinking it nothing but an imp." Waving her hand, she took a sip. "You needn't worry. Glory can take care of herself. She's showing Raaz her pets."

As if bidden, Glory ran in. "The void-men have returned!"

"Wonderful." Celeste wiped her mouth and stood.

"Void-men?" Calidos asked.

"You should come see," Celeste said. "It's quite fascinating."

Downing his wine, Calidos stood. "Are you coming, Kenja?"

"I've seen it," Kenja replied. "I'd rather finish my meal."

In front of the mansion, six men, black as char, stood behind five people—two woman and three men—all dressed in simple village clothes. The men were bruised and beaten, one cradling his arm, and another walked with a severe limp. The women were both young and quite lovely—one red-haired and the other with brown—though their eyes were red from crying. Next to them was a large wagon filled with foodstuffs and livestock— four small pigs, two cows, and a goat.

Calidos grinned. "Donations from the locals?"

"Yes, something like that," Celeste said. She then turned to Glory. "Would you please ease the young women's minds? We have need of a scullery maid and another handmaiden. I do believe our dear friend Mister Flint here has done us the good favor of impregnating little Ashly. She will be laid up for a while."

"It was only the once," Calidos muttered.

"That's all it takes, my dear," Celeste said. "Especially after they've been sweetened."

Pulling a crystal shard from her pouch, Glory placed it around her neck and then approached the red-haired woman. "Yes, these are often quite fun in bed." She then grabbed the woman by the head with both hands.

The redhead gurgled, and her arms and legs went stiff as she shook. When the convulsions ended, her face went slack, her eyes hollow.

Glory let go. "Go upstairs and seek out Ashly. She will tell you your new duties, and how best to serve your new master."

The woman blinked several times, and her face grew placid. "Yes, Mistress." With distant eyes, she walked into the mansion.

Glory then went to the next woman, who shied away. "What did you do to Alice?" When Glory grabbed the woman by the arm, she pulled away. "No. Stay away from me. No!"

Glory jumped forward and clasped her head. "Shut up, cow."

The woman screamed and then went stiff.

Glory snarled. "Don't fight me!"

The woman thrashed, hissing through clenched teeth, and then went slack, her eyes dull. When Glory asked the woman if she'd do as she was told, the woman only grunted.

Celeste tsked. "Honestly, girl, you must curb your temper. You've made her an imbecile. She's no good for the scullery now." She sighed. "We'll see if she can at least muck out the stables. If not, we'll feed her to the grunkin." Celeste then looked at the black-skinned men. "Bring them."

As the black men passed with their prisoners, Calidos followed them inside, getting a good look at the dark men. He realized they didn't have black skin—they were severely burned over their entire body, their skin charred and flaking off, revealing more burned skin beneath.

The charred men pushed the three village men after Celeste and up the main stairs. On the second floor, she turned the opposite direction from Calidos' room. At the end of the hallway, they entered a large bedroom. A four-post, black wood bed sat against one wall. Several brass lamps hung from all four red-paneled walls, a multitude of small tables lining them. All the furniture appeared to be cut from the same dark-red wood as did the door trim. And the ceiling was painted to look like a blue sky with a smattering of multicolored clouds.

Celeste looked to Calidos. "What you are about to see, my dear friend, few others have." She grinned. "Well, except for my void-men."

She walked to the far wall opposite a large window and ran her hands along the brick wall. A brick depressed, and a portion of the wall popped outward. Behind lay a twisted door. Celeste opened the door and entered, with the charred men shoving the villagers right behind her.

The room's interior was of no particular shape, having many odd-angled walls made of black stone with a dull sheen. Nooks and crevices covered the walls, catching and reflecting some of the light of the thirteen torches scattered about the room. Other areas held nothing but darkness.

It barely registered with Calidos. His eyes were on the center of the room, where a black, fluted pedestal jutted up from the floor. Sitting atop the pedestal—within a thick nest of thin metal rods—was a globe about double the size of an adult's fist. Within the globe, Chaos swirled—a multicolored ball of the essence of the God of Chaos.

"Come to me," a feather soft whisper echoed in Calidos' mind.

He yearned to touch the orb, to grasp the Lord's Breath and once again feel his inner fire burn with splendor. He reached out, sweat popping out on this brow, and he licked his lips. The power of God was so close it made him shiver.

Celeste stepped in front of him and said in a low voice, "It is not yours to touch."

He blinked repeatedly. "What? But I must. It's been so long." His soul ached.

"You would not like that which lies within. Not yet. You are not ready." She grinned. "But I will let you see what happens to those who do touch it."

Celeste turned to the villagers. "You needn't worry about your women, nor yourselves. You will not be harmed. In fact, you will soon be revered, gods among men. All you need do is touch the orb and the truth will be revealed to you. Just give yourselves to it, and the world will be yours."

The villagers shuffled forward, their eyes wary. Their hands hovered near the orb and then snapped to it, as though sucked in against their will. The men shrieked and thrashed, but their hands remained attached to the globe. They shook, and their hair smoked, their skin started to char and blacken. Their clothes burst in flames and fell away. The stink of burnt flesh and hair filled the room as the men's screams faded away and ended. Only then did they take their hands from the orb and turn toward

Celeste. Their eyes were dead black, and their skin was charred and cracked. Just like the men who brought them.

Celeste turned to Calidos Flint. "They have just given their souls to Dekriot, the great demon of the Void. That is why I call them void-men. For they no longer have souls. Thus, they no longer know pain or fear. They will do whatever I wish. Aren't they marvelous?"

Calidos' mouth was dry, and he quivered. "But that is the Lord's Breath. How can a connection to the Great Lord do such a thing?"

"It is not a Chaos orb, like the one used to create the Lands of the Dead. No, it's a simple containment orb, created for Ruddick by Moira."

Celeste went into the bedroom, beckoning the rest to follow. "My darling Ruddick encountered a Chaos Storm one day. He cast the orb into the storm and captured it. But that room is a shrine to Dekriot. So he also touched the orb, allowing some of his essence to reside within."

She turned to her void-men. "You are to go and gather more. A war is coming, and we will need more of you and more of Glory's pets. Oh, and get another woman … better make it two. I still need that scullery maid, and Glory has a tendency to lash out if they don't behave."

Calidos' eyes were drawn back into the chamber as she spoke. The orb swirled and pulsed, but unlike before, he was a shadow there, a blackness that called to him.

"You still want it, don't you?" Celeste asked him.

He tore his eyes away and lied, "No."

Her laughter was like a chime. "Do not feel so bad. Even I dare not touch it." She pulled a foot-long, fluted rod from her sleeve. "But I can still channel the power within with one of these."

"When did you make the room?" Calidos asked.

"I didn't It turned out Ruddick also worshiped Dekriot, along with the Lord of Chaos." She scoffed. "The man always was indecisive."

Celeste described how she discovered the room. She had escaped Geos after the Fall of Chaos with Dahlia and Glory, along with Henrick, another former priest. Safe in the secluded mansion, Celeste had consoled the others. "I had to take control of the situation or I would have lost my own mind as well.

"One evening, we felt a pull upstairs, to this very room. A voice whispered to me, telling me the secret to entering the temple beyond. We stared at the orb, much like you did. Henrick rushed in ahead and grabbed the orb. He was always too greedy. He was the first turned, the first charred man."

"Where did the rod come from?"

"It fell from the pedestal as Henrick changed and rolled across the floor. The same voice that told me of the room said the rods were safe to handle." Her eyes grew distant. "It was like a warm embrace, the first time I channeled from the orb. Dekriot came to me, freeing me of worry and fear. He showed me what true power was.

Blinking, she waved to Calidos. "Come. Let me show you Glory's pets. It's time to make more."

Bile rose from Calidos' stomach. He still wanted to touch the orb, to feel power once more, even after seeing what it did. He shook himself. "What kind of pets are we talking about?"

"You'll see," she replied.

She descended the stairs, went through a hallway, and out the back of the manor. The raucous noise of livestock filled a penned area taking up half the length of the mansion's back. Next to it were a half-dozen iron cages, large enough to hold a bull. Three held animals: a cow, a pig, and a goat. Raaz and Glory stood next to the goat, talking.

"Having fun, Raaz?" Calidos asked.

"Oh, yes-ss. Did I not tell you, you would find something here, something that would call to you?"

Calidos ignored the question. "What are you two doing?"

"We're waiting for Celeste to make more pets," Glory said. "I have to be here to make them do as they're told."

"That's right," Celeste said. "Would you like to see a miracle, Calidos?"

She pulled out the rod, and it flared to life, the Lord's Breath funneled into Celeste, as did a miasma of darkness. She pointed it at the goat, and a bolt of black lightning burst from the tip of the rod, stabbing into the animal. The goat shrieked. Its hide bubbled and roiled, and three more legs burst through, each one black and segmented with a sharpened prong for a foot like that of a massive spider. The goat's head expanded, puffing up like an inflated bladder. Fangs sprouted from its mouth and a forked tongue slithered out as it screeched.

Heart hammering in his chest, Calidos stared in disbelief. "You can make grunkin? Is this what Ruddick was really working on all those years ago?"

"Of course not," Celeste said. "He was very open about his experiments. No, this is something I came to on my own. Though I must admit, it was by accident. I was merely testing the destructive ability of the rod at the time."

"You're right." Calidos nodded. "It is a marvel. To make the ultimate gift of the Lord to let loose on the world is wonderful."

She laughed. "Oh, no, my friend. This is not the miracle." She pointed to Glory. "This is."

To Calidos' horror, the young woman approached the cage. The grunkin thrashed and snarled, stabbing at her through the bars. But the tipped feet stopped short of stabbing Glory, as though it struck an invisible wall. The tanned girl held up a hand, her eyes focused on the grunkin. The beast froze and hissed. It rammed its head into the bars and screeched, but then stopped. It huffed and wheezed but remained still.

The girl unlatched the gate. "Now, go to Celeste. Do as she tells you."

The grunkin skittered out of the cage and went to Celeste. To Calidos' amazement, it then bowed.

"Controlled grunkin," he said in awe. "She controls them. But how?"

"Glory has the remarkable ability to conquer minds, bend it to do as she wills. You see, these grunkin are special thanks to Dekriot. They possess more intelligence than normal ones. Thus, they need to eat and rest."

Celeste repeated the process on the next two animals. The cow grew two more heads and five limbs, each resembling those of a bear. The pig wound up with only one head that appeared much like a man's, while the body looked like that of a gorilla.

Glory approached the gorilla grunkin, the thing hissing and spitting. It smashed into the bars, reaching for her with three of his seven arms. When Glory concentrated on it, the thing howled and gnashed its teeth, shaking its head repeatedly.

Glory bared her teeth. "You *will* do as I say!"

It roared and hammered on the bars, throwing itself back and forth. The cage rattled and bent. The door burst open, and the grunkin started to scramble out.

Glory screamed in rage, and shoved her hands together as though crushing something between them. The door slammed shut, and the bars bent inward, popping and snapping as they curled around the gorilla-grunkin. The bars wrapped around it, piercing its hide, and then the grunkin screamed as it, too, started to compress. Blood popped to the surface and oozed around the outside, but nothing escaped the invisible crushing ball. Glory screamed again, her eyes blazing with fury, and she slammed her hands together. The ball collapsed inward. Blood and gore spewed out the back, spraying fifty feet into the woods. What remained—hide, guts, and iron—dropped to the ground with a crunch.

Calidos shook, eyeing the young woman with uncertainty as he took several steps back.

"Are you quite through, young woman?" Celeste asked.

Glory closed her eyes and took a deep breath as she gathered herself. When she opened them, calm serenity remained. "I am sorry, Celeste. I won't let it happen again."

Celeste laughed. "You say that every time. Well, so long as my guest wasn't hurt, everything is fine. I'm expecting more animals soon, as I need more pets. So next time, try harder to control them and you won't be forced to destroy them."

Glory looked to Calidos and smiled, tilting her head. "You're quite handsome. How did I miss that before?" With a shrug, she went inside.

"An amaz-zing creature, isn't she?" Raaz said.

Calidos jumped, having not heard the half-demon approach. "Um, yes."

"Let us finish our dinner," Celeste said, and headed back inside.

"You want the girl, don't you?" Raaz asked quietly.

Calidos shook his head. Though beautiful, Glory held a rage that terrified him, one that could snap at any moment. And with Calidos no longer having powers, he'd be as helpless as the grunkin.

Raaz's laugh sounded like a snake on fire, hissing and popping. "Yes, she is dangerous. But therein lies the fun. Just think of how it would feel to dominate such a creature. It would be easy. All you need do is accept Dekriot, and then nothing could stop you."

Without answering, Calidos went back inside to finish his meal.

Two days passed, and Calidos lay in bed next to a sleeping handmaiden, the one with the sandy-brown hair. He'd had sex with both several time. For some reason, Celeste wanted them to be with child. Calidos didn't care, so long as he could continue to bed them.

Glory had mentioned on several occasions that she wanted to bed him as well, but Calidos refused. He remembered the lock in Celeste's eyes. If the girl didn't snap and kill him in the throes of passion, Celeste would certainly do so afterward.

Celeste's daughter, Dahlia, approached him once as well, but it didn't go far. She was smoking from a pipe, her eyes glazed, and asked him if he thought she was pretty. Before he could come up with a discrete answer, she went on about the dark-skinned man, Dirge. She called him handsome and special. Calidos remembered him. Tall and stoic, with a face like an iron. Calidos heard many stories about the man when he crisscrossed the Westlands in search for Ellis Concord. Dirge had a self-possession that bordered on the extreme. It was almost as though the man were touched by—

Calidos sat up. "Order. The man was touched by Order, and he was with Concord." He jumped out of bed, got dressed, and headed downstairs.

Celeste met him in the main hall. "You're up early."

"I must be going," Calidos said.

"Why?" Raaz asked from behind him.

Calidos jumped and spun. "Stop sneaking up on me!"

The half-demon grinned. "Why would you wish-shsh to leave such a wonderful place?"

"I must find Ellis Concord and undo whatever it is he did." He turned to Celeste. "I appreciate what you've done for me, but I must do this."

She laughed. "For someone so true to the Lord of Chaos, you were always too single-minded." She spread her arms. "I will aid you. I will give you a horse, food, and coin."

Calidos nodded to her. "Thank you. I don't know how long it will take, but I will find him."

"I can take you right to him," Raaz said.

Calidos turned back to the half-demon, scowling. "You know where he is? Are you saying you've known all this time?"

"Of course-ss." Raaz's toothy grin split his face. "But I don't think you'll like what you find."

Lying in the fainting chair, Dahlia took another puff from her pipe, her eyes glazing over as she breathed out the acrid smoke—a combination of coca leaf and poppy. "But, Mother, why did you let him go? He knew my Dirge. I miss my special man so much. I must have him again. Everything would be all right if I had my Dirge, just one more time."

Standing behind the chair, Celeste ran her fingers through her daughter's hair. "Hush, my child. All will be well. I know far more about your darling, dark-skinned man than Calidos ever could."

For instance, she knew he had arrived recently at the head of a large contingent of Ukase warriors. It brought a smile to her face. With the aid of Dekriot, Glory could be more powerful then both of them. But Celeste had to be sure.

Her aging spells worked wonders, keeping her young while also aging others. The children fathered by Calidos would come to term soon, and she would age them to adulthood in the matter of weeks. Many times, their mental aptitude left a lot to be desired, but she was successful on one occasion thus far, so she could do it again. If a coupling could produce someone as powerful as Glory ... "Imagine how powerful a child would be with me?"

Dahlia gazed up. "What, Mother?"

"Nothing, my dear." She caressed Dahlia's hair. "Take another draw and enjoy yourself. I'm watching over you." Thanks to her powers from Dekriot, she'd been able to keep the lethal effects of the drugs from harming her daughter, though it still took a toll.

"I need to find a way to lure the man here without bringing his entire force," Celeste mused.

Dekriot whispered into her mind.

She smiled. "Yes. How could I have forgotten? He's gotten very protective of her, hasn't he? Yes, I need only let the right word slip into the right ears ... He'll come running. And if things go very well, we could have her as well." She licked her lips. "I wonder if she's as good as her mother."

Chapter 26

To End Pain

Perspiration soaked Evram Kirkadite's snow-white shirt as he sourly sipped his orange juice in the primary building's rooftop patio. Reserved for officers and dignitaries, a half-dozen tables scattered about the area covered by a vine-choked roof of horizontal slats, allowing the afternoon air to circulate. Despite the breeze, heat still saturated the shaded area. Kirkadite refused to remove his coat, though. To be out of uniform was unsightly. He took another sip of juice, enjoying the local staple—the water was not to be trusted. Considered a luxury up north, he refused the juice in the past, thinking it too extravagant, and thus immoral. But the fruit grew everywhere along the coast, falling from practically every third tree, so it was no longer a vice.

Staring over the front gate at the city beyond, he was growing to resent the bastion. Dane Hook was a squalid pit of degenerates in dire need of the Lord with no concept of honor, with most not knowing their place in the eyes of God. At least the Westlands had been somewhat orderly from the start.

His thoughts went back to Dirge. "How can the man not see what's all around him?"

As though summoned, Dirge entered the lounge, and after a pause, approached. "Would you mind if I shared your table?"

Kirkadite nodded, wondering what the man was up to. "I saw your return. Still no luck with the boogeymen in the jungle?"

"Mock it all you like. They are out there."

"I still think Yolden killed them all."

"So you've said." Dirge waved over the steward. "A strong ale; chilled, if possible." He then turned back to Kirkadite. "I understand you are chafing in your role as of late."

"Chafing? You mean stifling. When will you allow me to do as God demands and cleanse this place?"

Dirge held up a finger, his eyes cold. "Do *not* use that term." When his drink arrived, the man gulped half of it down, and then sighed. "You want to bring the righteousness of God to these people. Why aren't you doing it?"

Trembling, Kirkadite replied, "Because you will not let me."

"What are you talking about? Since when do I have to tell you to do your job? Go, spread the true word of Ukase."

"I am not a Veridical. I do not preach the gospel."

"Then do what you do." He took another long pull. "But no purging."

Kirkadite pulled back as though slapped. "What? You dare to—"

"I mean it," Dirge interrupted, his face hardening. "This is not an invasion. Not yet. We are here to solidify our footing and ready the people for what is to come. Until then, these people will believe what they will without molestation."

"Your words border on heresy."

"Hardly." Dirge ordered another ale. "Think it through, Evram. If you push the populous and their rulers too far, too fast, they will not stand for it. We don't have the manpower to fight an entire city, let alone the region." His drink arrived and he took another long pull. "If you doubt me, you can send word to Gate Hall."

"I would never think of ignoring the chain of command." Kirkadite sneered. "What kind of man do you take me for?"

Dirge chuckled. "I think we both know the answer to that." Finishing the ale, he sighed. "Speak with Kelts. He knows this city, these people. He will back up my assessment."

Kirkadite remembered the peculiar looking man from their entering the city. "He's not even human. How he stands so high in the eyes of the Lord is beyond me. That thing should be mucking out the stalls and latrines. He's just another reason to question the thoughts of the former Righteous-Captain."

"Must you always be such an ass?" Shaking his head, Dirge stood and left.

Two days later, back in his office, Kirkadite pondered Dirge's words, seeing the potential opportunities in them. He noted the thoughts in his journal when a knock came to his door. He closed the notebook and set it aside, carefully cleaning the tip of the pen. Then, he spoke up, "Enter."

Kelts entered, his unhuman complexion and facial features looking out of place in his surcoat of a Righteous-Warrior. He approached and bowed. "You summoned me, Truth-Seeker?"

Kirkadite pointed to the opposite chair. "Yes, Righteous-Warrior. We've not been formally introduced."

"I apologize, but Righteous-Captain Dirge has had me on constant patrol." He saluted, fist to chest, with a slight bow. "Righteous-Warrior Eric Kelts, at your service."

"I must be frank," Kirkadite said. "I've just come from a foray into the city, and very little has been done to spread the might of God. Heretics and blasphemers were everywhere." It enraged Kirkadite seeing the rabble wallowing in a broiling soup of sweat, excess, and debauchery.

"There is much work yet to be done," Kelts replied. "But it is only a matter of time before they see the truth, and bow to the will of God. Our presence in Geos is quite strong, and Ukabar is only a few miles to the west. It's magnificent; an entire city modeled in the glorious might of Ukase. Have you been there yet?"

Kirkadite shook his head. "No, unfortunately I've been stuck in this ... chamber pot of a city." Kirkadite kept his disgust from his face. He didn't trust Kelts. Despite his being clean in the eyes of God, Kelts didn't deserve to wear the uniform. He was subhuman.

"Our biggest problem from the beginning has been Dane Hook's chief legislator, Chancellor Haddock," Kelts said.

"I've heard. How can a man who claims to uphold the rule of law be so malleable, bending to the desires of the people?"

"It makes no sense. But we've made great strides, thanks to Magistrate Falmer. He is a True man of God. Before he took his post, few here even heard God's name. It was he who got Magistrate Bachman to convert and gift us the bastion."

"Be that as it may, this city is still in dire need of God's will," Kirkadite said. "And right now, *Righteous-Captain* Dirge refuses to let me do as I must."

The Righteous-Warrior looked down and away, unease plain on this face.

"I do not question the Lord's judgement in placing Dirge at the head of our expedition. However, we should see to the purification of this city first before we worry about what lies outside its walls."

"As you say, Truth-Seeker Kirkadite." Kelts nodded. "But according to Righteous-Warrior Parkinson, the Righteous-Captain was ordered to investigate the threat from the wild and deal with it. I was with Righteous-Captain Yolden when the scorched men and grunkins attacked. Their peril is real."

"So I gathered." Kirkadite paused. "What is your opinion of the Righteous-Captain?"

Kelts frowned, seeming to search for the right words. "I will not speak ill of my commander, but he is not what I expected. From the stories from his youth, one would think Order sprouted from every step he takes. He's just a man. Also, they say he spent years in the company of Chaos-loving Travelers. I don't understand?"

The unasked query lingered. Kelts did not want to question the will of God.

Kirkadite leaned forward. "And how is he in the field?"

"Correct in all ways …"

"Go on."

Kelts again looked uncomfortable. "The Righteous-Captain is deeply troubled by something. He does not say so, but I read it in his face and manner."

Kirkadite laughed. "Troubled. He should be. The man may be Righteous in the eyes of God, but the company he keeps is disgusting."

"What do you mean?"

"His wife, Mangin, is a witch—a Chaos priestess of some renown before the coming of the Lord."

Kelts' eyes went wide. "You cannot be serious."

"I am. Her father was as well; a High Priest who oversaw the Lands of the Dead."

"How could Captain Dirge do such a thing? He followed the Prophet and led God's army in revolt against Chaos. He was the first man anointed Righteous-Captain in over five-hundred years. How could he take a witch into his bed?"

"That is something I ask myself often."

"Why hasn't the Magnus—" Again, Kelts ended the dangerous line of thought.

"Magnus Malik exonerated her," Kirkadite said with a sneer. "However, when he died, Magnus Donavan wanted proof Mangin denounced her past. Dirge blocked me."

"How?" Kelts tilted his head. "And why?"

"Righteous-Captain Dirge thwarted my inquisition and claimed her for his wife."

"As is the right of any man," Kelts said with half a heart, then paused, his eyes narrowing. "It's said they came out of the Lands of the Dead together. Is that correct?" When Kirkadite nodded, Kelts continued, "Perhaps she bewitched his mind in there before Chaos fell?"

Kirkadite pursed his lips. "I hadn't considered that. It could be he doesn't even realize her control over him."

"Someone here might remember Dirge for something other than his Righteous past," Kelts said. "With your leave, I will ask around. Righteous-Captain Yolden was … is the best man I've ever known, and I can't, in all good conscience, let Dirge remain Righteous-Captain if he has been compromised."

Kirkadite smiled. "You are wiser than I first gave you credit, Kelts. Your race must be the highest of all sub-humans."

Kelts lowered his gaze. "I think you for the compliment. One day I hope the rest of my people see the truth as I do."

"As do I." Kirkadite nodded. "Chaos is still the greatest threat the world has ever known. And must never forget that. We can't let his followers continue carrying on his evil mission. They must all be purged."

Chancellor Haddock, annoyed at the interruption of his work, shook the stranger's hand. "Good day, Mister …"

"Ormond Cantor," the tall, slim man replied.

"Ah, yes. It's good to meet you. Magistrate Yates speaks quite highly of you." Haddock sat in his plush leather chair, the litany of things still needing to be done that day running through is mind. "He claimed you were a scholar, is that right? Selos is in great need of learned people these days."

Cantor brushed his long, curly gray hair from his eyes. "Thank you. It is nice to know some are willing to talk with a man with my past. Unlike up north." He took the seat across from the chancellor.

Fishing out his pipe, Haddock cocked an eyebrow. "What do you mean?"

"I thought the Magistrate Yates told you," Cantor said. "Just so we have everything out in the open. Other than my scholarly duties, I used to be a priest of Edis."

Haddock waved his hand. "Yes, well, what's past is past. Those of Ukase would not be pleased to know I'm meeting you, but I'm the law in this city, not Ukase."

"That is wonderful to know." Cantor scratched behind his ear.

The chancellor held up a finger. "But that doesn't mean I can ignore them. They're a thorn in my side. Most of the people are happy to see Chaos gone, myself included, but Edis' followers are not outlawed. If anything, they are to be pitied."

Cantor spread his arms. "That is understandable. Thank you. However, I did not come here to speak of Edis."

"Then what can I do for you?"

"I have something that will garner you even greater power, prestige, and knowledge than you already possess."

Haddock frowned. He'd heard such talk before, often from fools. "I've no time for idol boasts, Mister Cantor."

"Please, call me Ormond."

Haddock sighed, annoyed at the wasted time. "Ormond, then. As I said, I've no time for wild boasts. Many have said they hold all the answers but were actually trying to sell something. We need teachers and academics, not people pedaling arcane foolishness." Standing, he pointed at his open office door. "Now, if you don't mind, I'm a busy man."

Cantor remained seated. "I'm quite serious, Chancellor. What I offer is priceless. And with this knowledge, and with the help of my master, you will have complete control over the city. Perhaps the entire coast."

Chancellor Haddock scowled. "Will I have to call my guards?"

"I think not. Not until they are brought under the fold as well." The gray-haired man raised his hand and a black mist formed around it. He flicked his wrist, and the door slammed shut without making a sound.

Cursing, Haddock sprinted around his desk, headed for the door, but slammed into an invisible wall. He staggered back, his hand going for the dagger at his belt.

Cantor smiled. "I think it's time you met my friend." The air next to Cantor wavered, and a woman with long, black hair appeared.

Haddock yanked his dagger out and lunged for Cantor, but the woman grabbed his arm. He screamed as she squeezed, nearly breaking his wrist. He dropped the dagger and stepped back. "Who are you?" he shouted. "How dare you—"

Her eyes pulsed and glowed. "Come now, Chancellor. There's no need for this."

Haddock blinked, and his head throbbed. "What ... what are ..." He stared at her eyes, unable to look away.

She moved to him, a tubular tongue slithering out of her mouth. It snaked about the back of his head and his mind exploded in agony. His skull reverberated and pulsed. It felt like she was boring a hole into his head. While painful, it was also euphoric. Never in his life had he known such bliss. Unfortunately, the ecstasy faded, replaced by more pain. He felt cold, so cold he thought his bones should shatter.

Then a voice spoke, one distant and crumbling. It told him the truth. The only truth he ever knew. For the pain to end, all of it, the world had to burn, all of creation must come to an end. Only then would the anguish end.

Chapter 27

Where to Place a Kiss

The morning breeze caressed Mangin's face as she relaxed on a chaise lounge in the library. She sipped her fruit juice, enjoying the sweet, tangy flavor. If it had only been chilled. She pulled up the hem of her lose, full-length, white dress, wanting the wind on the rest of her body. In her youth, she loved the feel of the breeze upon her naked flesh, but that seemed ages ago.

"Put that back down," Dirge said, sifting through papers at the table. "What would the steward think if he came in seeing you like that?"

She hiked it more. "He would think of how wonderful it would be to ravish me."

He put the papers down and glared.

"I didn't say he'd do it, just think about it. He'd likely blush and stammer the entire time, then go back to his room and pleasure himself, riddled with shame." She laid her head back, fingers grazing her now exposed thigh. "I doubt he's ever ravished a woman—or a man for that matter."

"Watch your tongue!" Dirge rushed to the library door and checked the outer room, then strode to Mangin, hands on hips. "You don't think such a thing, let alone say it. Not here. And stop touching yourself like that."

"Then I can think it somewhere else?"

With a sigh, he rolled his eyes and returned to the table.

"I'm serious." Mangin sat up, putting her skirt back in place. "Take me on one of your patrols."

"No."

"It would be just like that time with the Travelers. The cool air. The night sky filled with stars. We would make love to a chorus of peepers and cheepers."

"The men would hear us." Dirge pulled out his flask, took a drink, and set it on the table.

A grin crept across her face. "Yes, they would. They'd stare with envy, even consider joining us."

Dirge seemed to look inward, as though remembering something. Grimacing, he squeezed his eyes shut and lowered his head to the table. "Please, stop."

Concerned, Mangin went to him, stroking his back and then running her fingers through his hair. "I'm sorry."

He trembled slightly beneath her fingers.

She'd grown to read his body language, knowing what her touch did to him, but there was something more this time. "There's nothing shameful about enjoying the touch of your wife. I thought you'd learned that by now. What's wrong? You've been even more tense than usual. Last night you were like a rock. In more ways than one."

"I'm fine." Rising, he took a step back, as though gathering himself, then took her hand. "And your touch does not shame me." He kissed the back of her hand. "But you must guard your words at *all* times if you're to remain safe."

Dirge picked up his papers and flask, then headed for the door. "As for the patrol, no women are allowed. It is both unseemly and unsafe."

Mangin followed after. "But I'm so bored, stuck in here day

and night."

"I thought you were going to get furnishings?"

She couldn't keep the scowl off her face. "Any time I step out of this suite, there's someone in the hall. They don't stare, but it's obvious they're spying on me. Watching my every move."

Dirge's brows furrowed. "Kirkadite. I'll have a word with him. You are not a prisoner—you may come and go as you like. Just remember to take an escort." He headed for the door.

"You're leaving again, aren't you?"

"Yes, we must find and deal with the threat. Their attacks are growing, and we're always too late to help. I don't know how long we'll be." When he opened the door, he paused, mouth open as though to say something, but turned and left without another word.

Before exiting the apothecary, Mangin tugged at her collar. The black dress was fine for wearing up north, even if it was too prudish, but in the South, it was stifling. She carried a parasol to protect her light skin from the sun, but it wasn't enough to ward off the oppressive heat. Opening her pouch, she examined the herbs. Unlike Cross Corners, the proper ones were readily available—the reason she had her escort, Righteous-Militant Aubrey, wait outside. She considered herself lucky the earlier makeshift concoction had worked thus far. But how long would the proper herbs still be available?

The city was rapidly falling under the overbearing sway of Ukase, and the general populous whispered of better days. Those with means fled farther down the coast or across the ocean waves to distant shores. Brothels were boarded up. Establishments catering to those who sought intoxication from forms other than alcohol were forced to move to the poorest part of town. With the time of Chaos over, the oceans were safer to travel. Blessed by the God of the Sea, deep hulled vessels came and went every day with exotic cargo, only to have much of it confiscated and burned by Veridicals and Seekers. With each passing day, fewer and fewer of those strange ships came to port. People who openly enjoyed couplings other than what the True found acceptable were whisked away to the Chastenary outside of Ukabar.

The memory made Mangin shudder.

She shook it off and stepped outside. "I'm finished, Aubrey, we can head back ..." Her voice trailed off and looked about. The man was gone.

Worry ate at her stomach. When Aubrey had wanted to come in with her, she asked him not to as it would be embarrassing—she was, after all, purchasing "womanly things." Mangin remembered he looked none-too-pleased. What if he'd gone to fetch a Seeker? Dirge was a day gone ...

Swallowing, Mangin stared up the road. The walk wasn't too far, and as hot as it was, she'd insisted on not taking a carriage, which were downright boiling in the afternoon sun. After a time, her feet slowed, and she chewed her lip. She was alone. Why even go home? It was nothing but a military bunker where every moment was like measured torture—death by a thousand cuts. The women there turned up their noses, and whispered accusations. The Veridicals talked down to her, saying she needed to give herself to the Lord. The Seekers eyed her with suspicion and disgust. Only the Warriors accepted her presence, and that was just because of Dirge. Home? She actually found herself missing the estates at the Corners. At least there she did, more or less, as she pleased.

Music from a nearby inn pulled at her. Memories of the Travelers, their artistry, skill, and passion. She missed them so. Betal as well, of course. But the person she missed most, whom she longed to see and touch just one more time was Adel. Mangin searched the crowd, hoping to catch Adel's face, and then chastised herself for doing so. Adel was safe ... away from Mangin.

A woman spoke up behind Mangin, "You look lost."

Mangin knew that voice. She spun around as a medium-height woman approached. Mangin's jaw dropped open. "Follett? Follett Dinar?"

In a sheer, tight, black dress with a plunging neckline, Follett took hold of Mangin's hand. "It's wonderful to see you again." Follett then guided Mangin to the side of the road, out of traffic, and near an alley. "How have you been? It's been so long."

"What are you doing here?" Mangin hissed as she looked about. Spotting the back of a Righteous Warrior surcoat, she pulled Follett into the alley. "Do you have any idea how dangerous it is here?"

Follett's smile didn't touch her brown eyes. "Aren't you tired of hiding?"

"I'm not hiding." Mangin held her head high, trying to seem calm. "I've no need to."

Follett cocked an eyebrow. "Don't you? True, you are allowed to walk about like a pet on a leash, but you're still leashed."

"I don't know what you're talking about," Mangin lied. "I'm a woman of standing."

"You are a *pet*, Mangin. And a good one at that. You do as you're told, wear what they want you to wear, say what they want to hear." Follett pulled her long, black hair over her shoulder. "You are a perfect, proper wife."

Mangin seethed, hating the truth. "You shouldn't be here. Go now. Go to Geos, from there you can take ship and be free of them."

Follett ran a finger down Mangin's arm. "Imagine what you could do with the Lord's Breath within you once more."

Pulling away, Mangin muttered, "Dreaming the impossible only leads to heartbreak."

"But it's not impossible," Follett said, her eyes seeming to glow with zeal. "To the north, not far, there lies a hidden mansion. And within it, an orb." She stepped closer, her eyes pulsing. "Within the orb, the Lord's Breath pumps and flows."

Mangin's lids fluttered. "O-Orb?"

"It is in the hands of Celeste. Her lover was a man named Ruddick. You know that name, I think."

Trying to step back, Mangin's head swam. "What … what are you talking about?" Her back bumped into the building.

"You miss doing as you please, don't you?" Follett asked, her voice echoing as though coming from a tunnel.

Mangin tried to turn away, but she couldn't move. She wanted to deny what the former priestess said, but no sound came out.

"Dirge doesn't love you," Follett said, her eyes pulsing with light. "He only uses you to sate his lust. He loves another, a woman who is now a god. However, he hides from his own past as well. He's a man haunted by secret desires. It truly is a tangled web you've found yourself in, my darling Mangin."

Follett smiled, flashing fangs Mangin had never seen before. "Do you want to know what real love is? I will show you love." She opened her mouth and a long, tubular tongue snaked out. The tip split and opened like the pedals of a black star-shaped flower and retracted.

"I will kiss you and drink a portion of your soul. I will give it to my master. You will become his slave and adore him. But where should I kiss you? Not your forehead, as much as it would please me to mark you for all the other slaves to see. But that would alert your husband, and we can't have that. I could put it under the lace at our neck? That has a certain appeal. Or how about your lips? No, again, your brand must not show." Her laugh came as a hiss. "I know. I'll kiss your other lips so that every time you lay with another you will remember to whom you belong. You'll writhe like a worm because the kiss of Dekriot is one of agony and emptiness."

"Worm," Mangin echoed softly. She stared in horror as Follett opened her mouth and the tongue reemerged. It flicked back and forth, as Follett knelt. The words of the succubus burned in Mangin's head, and she was powerless to stop it. Tears streamed down her face as she squeaked out what she was about to become. "Worm."

Steel flashed in front of her face, quickly followed by an ear-piercing screech. The hypnotic spell broke, and Mangin stumbled sideways, her eyes going to Follett. The succubus sat on the ground with a hand to its mouth, black blood pouring down its chin. It rolled away and dashed deeper into the alley.

"Are you all right, Mangin?" a man asked, his voice deep. "Please tell me it didn't touch you."

Mangin focused on the man, now kneeling at her side. Concentrating on his stern, gray eyes set deep in a beautiful, dark skinned face, one filled with worry, she said, "Dirge?"

He gently ran his hands over her face. "Did it touch you?" He reached for the hem of her dress but stopped. "Not here. I'll check when we get home." Scooping her up in his arms, he carried her out into the street.

Her head still spun as she clung to his shoulder. "What are you doing here?"

"We found evidence of an attack a day's ride from here. A caravan. Looks like one of the guards lopped off the arm of one of those burned people. Unfortunately, the caravan was wiped out, so we've no witnesses. I brought the arm to show to the Veridical. Perhaps he can glean something from it."

Mangin shook her head at the deluge. "But how did you find me?"

"Righteous-Militant Aubrey was talking to the steward when I arrived. I overheard his disapproval and told them I would tend to you."

"Tend to me," she mumbled, still too weak to let her real ire at the term come out.

He trotted down the street, ducking and dodging traffic as he went. "I'll make sure you're well before I head out again. We finally have something, but your health comes first."

"Thank you." Her lips quivered as she caressed his head. "So, you don't hate me?"

"No, of course I don't hate you." He paused. "In fact, I don't know what I'd do without you. And you may not like me for it, but I can't let anything happen to you. I have to know you're safe, while I'm gone."

Tears streamed down her face because she knew he spoke the truth. She felt it somehow. He didn't hate or feel burdened by her. He cared for her. It wasn't quite love, but it was good enough. "I'm safe ... thanks to you, my sweet husband." She blurted out a laugh. "Just don't try and treat me like a pet. Remember, this cat scratches."

Chapter 28

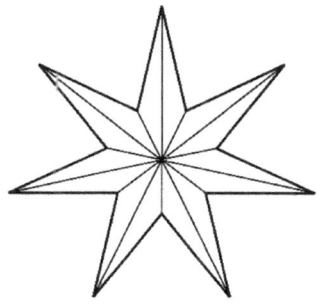

Right of Trial

Boots echoing down the corridor, Kellen hurried to his office. The impromptu City Council meeting went longer than he expected. First, the chancellor was late, and then he set down edicts that were the exact opposite of what he said he'd do only half a year before. It was bad enough the man was placing more restriction on the True of Ukase—something that would only make his job that much more difficult—but he eased restrictions on the import on poppy and the dens. He also loosened the restrictions on the import of exotic animals. He called for an increase in military spending, claiming Selos privateers were raiding their shipping; something Kellen had heard nothing of through his network. He said as much at the meeting, and the chancellor shouted him down.

"What has gotten into that arrogant ass?"

He mounted the broad stairs, taking two at a time, his black eyes searching the faces of those in the Ministry of Coin for anyone he didn't recognize. There had been whispers of other people of prominence acting strange as well, and if bewitched.

He shook his head. "Now you're sounding paranoid."

As he marched through his agency, staff members bowed their heads, and he acknowledged them with a nod or simple word. These people were his backbone, and he needed to keep them happy.

Entering his outer office, Miss Beamish, sitting at her desk, her gray eyes holding a twinkle of excitement, jumped up. "Minister Kellen. High-Seeker Evram Kirkadite is in your office. He is asking for aid. I do hope it's all right that I sent him in rather than making him wait outside." She lowered her gaze. "Many of the staff are intimidated by the Seekers and I didn't want to upset them."

"No, you did well," Kellen replied, waving a hand.

She grinned. "I do hope he has good news."

"As do I." Tugging his red and black coat, Kellen entered his office.

In the chair in front of his desk sat a tall, gaunt man in the blood-red livery of the Seekers of Ukase. The man's hard, brown eyes measured Kellen as he rounded the desk and took his seat. "Good afternoon, High-Seeker." Kellen nodded with respect. "What is the honor of your visit?"

"I am seeking information," the High-Seekers said. "I understand you've been doing business in this region for many years. Caravanners are often people with extensive information networks."

"True. I've been in shipping for going on twenty years now." Kellen ran a hand through his taut, black hair. "Though some days it feels like longer. How can I help the True?"

"I understand Righteous-Captain Dirge was born in the South. Do you have any information about him?"

Eyeing the High-Seeker, Kellen wondered if it was some kind of trick. "What kind of information are you looking or?"

"I will be blunt," The High-Seeker said. "Some things have come up of a ... delicate nature. What can you tell me of his past? In particular, anything following the failed revolution."

Kellen tried to hold in his excitement. The moment he saw Dirge entering the city several weeks before, Kellen knew it was the same man, the same murdering thief from twenty years ago—the man's face was older, harder, but the eyes were the same. His meeting with a member of the Brotherhood of Assassins had not gone well, and he was loath to travel to Geos to meet their head; the absence would take too much of a toll on his business.

"To be honest," Kellen said, "I'm surprised you are willing to hear me out. When last I spoke to Magistrate Falmer regarding Dirge, he said the True would not help me."

Evram Kirkadite's eyes remained cold, and a compressed smile spread on his face. "The Ecclesiastical arm of God is not the same as the Seekers. They govern and see to the people's daily needs. We, on the other hand, seek the truth. We strive to rid the world of heretics and blasphemers wherever and *whomever* they are."

"That's good to hear." Kellen pulled his pipe out of his desk's top drawer in an attempt to hide his elation. "I must admit, at first, I thought my deal with the True had turned rather one-sided. The members of Ukase have taken much more control of this city than I originally expected. But with Order, my business thrives."

He leaned forward, pointing the butt of his pipe at the Seeker. "The short answer is yes, I know Dirge, I know him well. And if you are willing to bring me his head, I'd swear my allegiance to Ukase and offer whatever the True require. I will finally know that Ukase is the true god of vengeance and the righter of wrongs."

The High-Seeker's smile broadened. "That would be fortuitous for us both. With your influence, we will spread the Word of God to the entire southern coast and beyond." His smile then faded. "What information do you have on *Captain* Dirge?"

Kellen told him about hiring Dirge and Jacob as a caravan guards, of how they turned and murdered the other caravanners, and then stole the goods. "There have been no sightings of Jacob. I've a feeling he met his end long ago … probably at the hand of Dirge. But truthfully, Jacob doesn't matter to me. It's Dirge I want. He's the one I hired as a guard, and he's the one who broke that covenant."

The eyes of the Seeker smoldered with zealous fire. "Truly, this is the first I've heard of your request. Do you have anything else?"

Kellen reached into his desk and pulled out a sheet of paper. "I came across this information only a short time ago." He gave the Veridical the page. "It seems both Dirge and Jacob had dealings with a Chaos Priestess named Dahlia."

The Seeker leaned forward, his eyes keen on the sheet. "What kind of dealings?"

Kellen spread his hands. "Apparently, she bedded them both before they went on their murdering spree. The priestess was seen going into their room on two different nights. The second night, she went in when Jacob wasn't there, and she took a barmaid with her. The body of the barmaid was later found with her belly ripped open."

Glee spread across the Seeker's face. "I am indebted to you, sir."

Mangin paced back and forth in the sitting room, chewing her lip, and idly playing with the small dagger on her belt. She'd never felt so alone. Dirge left for Conover the day following her rescue, and in the ensuing week she'd yet to leave the apartment.

That first day, she had demanded an inspection of the entire house staff, looking for a pink, four-pointed star. She remembered seeing one on the wrist of Jandal, Follette's lackey, and assumed that was the mark the incubus was referring to.

When the steward balked at her demand, Mangin went to the Veridical for aid. The man was skeptical, at first. However, when she showed him the end of Follette's tongue that Dirge has retrieved at the scene, the Veridical's doubt turned to horror. He took the tongue to his superiors, who then ordered a search of every member in the bastion. They found thirteen people with the mark somewhere on their body. They were immediately questioned and purged.

What Mangin didn't understand was how the tainted staff went unnoticed. Dirge told her that all the members of the True, directly connected to Ukase, could see the guilty. It was what had Mangin in a constant state of unease. Yet, those marked by Follette were hidden.

Sitting in front of the fire, Mangin sipped a cup of tea. It was called oolong, a type newly acquired from the Isle of Tork beyond Demon's Kiss Bay. She enjoyed its sweet, floral taste while staring at the dancing flames, thinking about her husband. "Stay safe, you muscled oaf."

Mangin set the tea down and picked up one of her few remaining books. One of them contained a section on demonic mental possession, but she'd yet to find it. She hoped it wasn't in one of the volumes she lost years before. Mangin needed to know how strong a succubus' control of its victim was. As it involved the Abomination, Mangin was willing to bet it was quite a lot.

Someone knocked on the apartment door. When she asked who it was, the head maid stuck her head in. "The High-Seeker would like to see you—"

She squawked as someone shoved into the room. A half-dozen Militant-Seekers marched in, with Evram Kirkadite on their heels.

Furious, Mangin slammed the book down on her footstool and stood. "What is the meaning of this? You've no right to barge into our apartment, Seeker."

Kirkadite turned to his Head-Militant. "Search it."

The men spread out, ransacking the apartment, as Kirkadite approached Mangin. "We are here under the auspices of God, Lady Malik. I go where I must." He picked up and flipped through the book's pages. "This isn't a book of the Lord. What are you doing with it?"

Crossing her arm, she held her head high. "That is none of your affair."

"Lady Malik, everything is the affair of the Seeker of Truth. Ukase is all, and anything not of him is heresy and blasphemy." He turned cold, hard eyes on her. "I would have thought you knew that by now?" With a smirk, he tilted his head. "Or have you yet to lose your old ways?"

One of his henchmen came out of the bedroom with Mangin's herb pouch. Her heart sank as the Seeker went to his man and took the pouch.

He opened it, going through its contents with his finger. "These are not prescribed by the midwives, are they?" When Mangin remained silent, he chuckled. "No, I thought not. My man questioned the apothecary. What have you to say?"

"I have nothing to say to until my husband returns."

He pointed at one of his men. "Bring her with us for questioning."

When the man grabbed her arm, panic flared in her mind. She grasped his hair and yelled, "No! Unhand me!" Shocked, Mangin realized she knew the militant's conscious thoughts, she felt his disdain and disgust for her. In desperation, she delved into his mind, forcing her consciousness into his. "I said, unhand me."

The militant stopped short and let her go, his eyes blinking.

Mangin shook in disbelief. "How?"

Kirkadite took a step back and smiled. "Witch." He then punched Mangin upside the head.

She crumpled to the floor.

"You did well today, Estonia," Dirge said as they rode toward the city.

"But we failed to find them again," the squire replied.

"Patience. We will find them. Have faith.

"Yes, Righteous-Captain. Next time they shall fall to your might." The young man's blue eyes gleamed and adoration flowed from his almost-too-handsome face.

Frowning, Dirge turned away. "Yes, well, we will see about that. When we reach the bastion, I want you to get some food and rest. You've earned it."

He stared at the crowd as they passed through the city gates. Again, seemingly familiar faces from his past sprung up. As they neared the city's central square, Dirge slowed his horse. It was in Tuilar's central plaza were he first saw Lynette. She stood with her father and brother on that fateful day when the Cleansing was announced. It wasn't the proclamation he recalled most. That blended together with the rest of the night, one of blood and misery. The night he became the *Guardian of the Angelic*. The thing he recalled every time he entered a city plaza was Lynette's eyes, shimmering blue orbs that pierced his soul. Her eyes would haunt him until the day he died.

"What's the matter, sir?"

Dirge jerked at Estonia's question—he'd not noticed the squire come abreast. "Nothing." He shook Striker's reins, urging the horse to go faster.

He tried to put it out of his mind, but Lynette kept creeping back: her scent—a mixture of rose and lilac—the way she ran her fingers through his hair and then caressed his cheek, her last words, *"Until tonight."*

In a sour mood, Dirge rode into the stables, dismounted, and knuckled his back. He handed his reins to the stable boy with instructions and headed into the bastion. Not wanting to bring his poor attitude home, he decided to take Mangin to dinner at the Tea Garden, an establishment catering to the wealthy. He'd been away far too often and knew she was feeling trapped. "I owe her that much, at least."

Trotting up to the top floor, he entered their apartment and froze. Tables were overturned, the bookshelves were empty, and debris lay everywhere. The hair on the back of his neck rose.

"Mangin?"

When she didn't answer, he raced to the bedroom and found it in a similar state. Returning to the main room, the housekeeper entered, wringing her hands. "Where's my wife?" he asked.

"My Lord," the housekeeper said with a shaky voice while bowing. "High-Seeker Kirkadite has taken Lady Malik."

"When?" he barked.

"Three days ago, My Lord. We were ordered by the High-Seeker to leave everything as it was." She shook her head. "I don't understand it, My Lord. He wouldn't tell us why they took her or why we were to leave your apartment in such a state."

Dirge's fists shook as he spoke through clenched teeth, "It's a message to me." He slammed a gauntleted fist onto the wall table, breaking it in half. "It's all a message to me! I knew nothing good would come of that stinking man gaining High-Seeker.

With a deep breath, he took hold of his temper. "Please, clean this up. And whatever happens, whatever you hear, just do as you're told. Nothing will happen to you."

He stormed down the stairs and out to the courtyard, his boots hammering on the flagstones and his armor jingling. At the

Seeker's blockhouse, he addressed the acolyte assigned to the foyer, "Tell High-Seeker Kirkadite Righteous-Captain Malik demands his presence."

The acolyte bowed. "Of course, Righteous-Captain." He hurried off.

Standing with his arms crossed, Dirge waited, making his face firm so as not to show his agitation. Even so, several Militant-Seekers walked past, first looking smug, but their expressions turned defensive at Dirge's hard stare.

Many minutes passed before Kirkadite finally showed his odious face. He sauntered up to Dirge, smirking. "What do I owe the honor of your illustrious presence, Righteous-Captain?" he asked.

"Where is my wife?" Dirge snapped.

"In the cells," the Seeker replied with a sniff. "She's been charged with witchcraft."

"You will release her at once."

Kirkadite's eyes turned cold. "I think not." He snapped his fingers, and two dozen Militant-Seekers rushed in. "I have spoken with his Lordship, Coin Master Kellen of Selos. He told me some tales of your doings in the time before the Return," Kirkadite snarled, approaching Dirge. "He tells me of a time when you did theft of his merchandise and murdered his men. Is this true?"

Dirge took a deep breath. "I do not deny the truth of the past." He knew it would haunt him; he just didn't expect it to take down those he cared for as well.

"And just where were you during the dark days of Chaos?" Dirge asked. "Where were you during the time of murder and monsters? Were you so clean?"

"My past does not matter," Kirkadite replied. "All godly men were cleansed upon His resurrection." He pointed at Dirge. "But you, you were already anointed, a man who pledged himself to the Lord. You cast Him off and debased yourself. Do you deny it?"

Dirge thought of his early days of debauchery. His worst sin during that hellish time, after his Righteous army was decimated, after the Prophet died, after Lynette ... "I thought it was all a trick of Chaos. I lost my faith." Shoulders slumping, he lowered his head.

Kirkadite's smile never reached his eyes. "Then I hereby accuse you of heresy and murder. You and the witch will be taken to the cells where you will be put to the question and then purged."

Dirge raised his head high. "I demand a trial before the Grand-Righteous and the Magnus. I also demand a trial for my wife, as she is a noble woman in the eyes of the Lord."

"What?" Spittle flew from Kirkadite's lips. "How dare you—"

"It is my right," Dirge roared. His hands shook from a desire to throttle Kirkadite. He took a deep, calming breath. "All were absolved of their crimes before His return. If God wanted me dead, he would have done it Himself when He spoke to me that day."

Kirkadite snarled, "More heresy."

"I know my rights, High-Seeker. As well should you. Or do you think yourself above the Lord?"

"Get him out of here!"

Dirge sat on the edge of a thick, wide, straw-stuffed pallet with his back against the wall of the cell. He felt empty, hollow inside. Mangin lay curled up next to him, her head in his lap. The Seekers had taken his weapons and armor, but left him his surcoat out of respect—which was covering his wife. That wasn't the only luxury. As Dirge had temporarily abdicated his position—losing his connection to the Lord in the process—Kelts had taken the mantle of acting Captain. He had demanded Dirge be treated with the respect he'd earned. Dirge and Mangin were allowed to share a cell. They were fed regularly and given several candles in order to read the Book of the Lord. But he didn't feel much like reading without the Lord's touch. He took a drink of watered wine, placed the clay mug on the table next to him, and laughed.

Mangin glared up at him. "You find this funny?"

He ran his fingers through her hair. "No. I just thought if it wasn't for the must and stink, this would almost be romantic."

She scoffed. "You, romantic? I didn't think you knew the meaning of the word."

"I do, I assure you." He placed a hand under her chin. "In

fact, I had planned to take you out tonight. Some wine under the moon, on a balcony overlooking the sea."

Mangin looked at him as though he'd grown horns. "Who are you and what have you done with my husband?"

"I mean it. I've not been the best to you, and for that, I apologize."

Sitting up, she pulled the surcoat closer to cover the rags they'd replaced her dress with. "Are you all right?" She patted the side of his head. "How hard did they hit you before tossing you in here?"

"The High-Seeker will do much worse before this is all over," a menacing voice said from the iron-strapped door. A dark face appeared at the bars atop the top of the door. "I've waited a long time for this, thief."

Dirge's eyes went wide. Though older, with gray at the temples, he knew that face. "Kellen?"

"So, you do remember me." Kellen laughed. "I'm surprised someone like you would care."

"It's hard to say what a man who forsakes God cares for," the High-Seeker said from the hallway.

"When can we get this over with?" Kellen asked. "I'm busy, and I want his head over my mantle by nightfall."

Mangin groaned and pressed herself harder into Dirge.

"I'm sorry, but it will have to wait," Kirkadite said.

Kellen pulled away from the window, his voice holding an edge. "Do you plan to cheat me?"

"Watch your words," Kirkadite said with equal menace. "You speak to a High-Seeker of the True." He paused. "Dirge has demanded a trial before the Magnus, as is his right. In compensation for the delay, I will give you this."

"A sword?" The disdain in Kellen's voice dripped.

"The blade used to belong to the condemned."

Rage boiled in Dirge's gut. "You've no right to give away my property. The Grand-Seeker will hear of this theft."

Kirkadite's face appeared at the window. "It is not theft to take from a dead man. Just be glad I let you lie with your stinking witch until your transport back north."

"What's to become of her?" Dirge asked.

"She will go with you. After witnessing your death, she will go to the Chastenary to face Immaculate Clara's judgment."

Mangin whimpered and clung even harder as Kirkadite left, the fading sound of his boots echoing from the hall.

Kellen's face reappeared. "Regardless of how precious you think this blade is, it's poor recompense." A grin crept across his face. "Though it would look nice on my desk. I think I'll mount your head atop it."

"Have a care, Kellen. That blade belongs to another, and he will exact a heavy toll upon its retrieval."

"You stole this as well?" Kellen laughed. "Did you take it from Jacob's corpse?"

Guilt washed over Dirge, but he refused to look away.

"I thought as much," Kellen said, and then left.

Dirge took a deep, calming breath and sat back. "I'll see Kirkadite dead before this it done," he caressed her hair, "for what they've done to you."

"The Chastenary," Mangin muttered. She then looked about the cell. "I just can't help but wonder if Follett will find us here. There's nothing to stop her from killing you and finishing what she wanted to do to me."

"First, she'd have to get through all the Seekers."

Tears formed in her eyes. "You can't underestimate her; she's a demon, a succubus for Dekriot. The Abomination is tricksome as well as powerful." She clung to Dirge once more. "And for some reason, he wants me."

"I'll protect you."

She barked a laugh. "I thank you for the sentiment." She chewed at her lower lip. "Is it true, what Follett said? Did you love this Dahlia?"

He laughed. "You just said Follett is a tricksome demon and then asked that?" His face firmed. "No, she bewitched me. I felt nothing but loathing for her ... Well, that's not entirely true To my eternal shame, I did lust after her."

"She had green eyes, didn't she?" Mangin asked. When he nodded, she sighed. "Another reason you hate me."

"I don't hate you. I ..." He paused, uncertain. Her clinging, trembling arms brought forth a desire to protect her. As well as feelings he could not yet face. "You're nothing like Dahlia. not anymore."

"But I used to be." Sitting up, she wiped at her tears. "At the time, it didn't seem wrong, forcing those to please me. How could it? Under Chaos, there was no such thing at wrong. But now … The Travelers taught me to give and accept what was given. As did women at the Corners. Miss Barret told me of how she was treated before, about all the things men did to her against her will."

Dirge smiled. "Without the influence of Chaos, you now see the truth."

"No." She shook her head. "Chaos didn't work that way. We are who we are, what our upbringing and situations taught us to be. I was a spoiled girl. Betal and Daylin taught me to be a better person just by watching them. Besides, there are many things the True believe in that are just plain wrong. My feelings for Adel are the most honest thing I've ever known."

Dirge sighed, not even sure what the truth was anymore. During his time with Ellis, many in the troupe laid with whomever they wanted, regardless of sex. The love they showed each other was real. He couldn't deny that. And without his connection to the Lord to guide him, he found no way to justify his past prejudices.

"Do you think there's any way Veil or Daylin could help us out of here?" Mangin asked.

"No. Even if there was, I would not ask. Ukase is my god, and my faith is in Him. I cannot call upon another." As empty as he felt, he knew it to be the truth.

After several moments of silence, Mangin asked, "Who is Celeste?"

"Who?"

"Celeste. The one Follett mentioned."

"I'm not sure." His jaw clenched. "But I remember Daylin mentioning the name before, about the days of her slavery as a child. If what the succubus said was true, I'll kill this Celeste for what she and Ruddick did to Daylin."

Mangin laid her head on his shoulder. "And just how are you going to do that, my dear husband?"

"I don't know." He clenched his fists, knuckles cracking. "But I swear by it."

Yet, his oath rang hollow in his own ears; he had no way of fulfilling it. Without God, his life had been nothing but heartache, tragedy, and debasement. The truth was, he had no power to do anything. The emptiness of his soul without Ukase threatened to drown him.

Chapter 29

What Should Not Be

Fifty-six grim Militants accompanied the open wagon headed to Conover. Two Righteous-Warriors rode at the column's front with their Head-Militants and footmen. Estonia, promoted to Righteous-Warrior, rode at the rear with his own Head-Militant behind him, his soldiers marching in formation on either side. The four mounted Truth-Seekers surrounded the wagon, with two on either side, along with their own flunkies. Kirkadite and his men rode directly behind the wagon, his eyes burning with hate as he stared at the prisoners.

Mangin did her best to ignore the man.

The way the footmen marched unnerved Mangin, each stride lockstep with the rest, their boots crunching in the dirt in unison as though following a drumbeat, only no instrument was needed. The men were also of the same general height and build, something that perplexed Mangin. She remembered when the men were assigned to Dirge before they left the Corners. Their size was as random as any other group. It was as if Ukase had molded the men over time, turning them into models of his vision of perfection.

The thought was fleeting as she silently suffered her misery. The wagon's rocking back and forth didn't bother her—she rather enjoyed it—but the sudden drops and bumps left her posterior battered and bruised. Her wrists ached and her fingers kept wanting to cramp from the wire-caged manacles. The unrelenting sun beat down, making her face tingle and burn, while sweat matted her hair and tattered, full-length dress to her skin and caked dust to her face like cracked plaster.

"This is going to destroy my complexion," she said. "My skin is burning off at this very moment. I think I actually preferred sitting in that stinking cell for two months." Mangin hoped her muted tirade sounded pithy. In truth, she was terrified. All her worst nightmares were coming to pass, but she didn't want to give the Seekers the satisfaction in knowing it.

"I swear to you, they will pay for your treatment," Dirge said next to her on the floor of the wagon.

Cocking an eyebrow, she held up her manacled hands. "Again, how are you going to do that?"

The wagon dropped and then slammed into her falling bottom as it rose again. Her jaw snapped shut and she groaned. "I don't know how much more of this I can take."

"Stay strong," Dirge said. "Resilience comes through hardship."

Mangin chuckled. "So, by the end of this I'll be as stone-like as you? Thank you, but no. I'd be no fun in bed like that."

She chewed her lip, her thoughts lingering on the future. "The Chastenary. I'll be worked to the bone under the thumb of that sour, old woman—who I doubt knows the meaning of enjoyment—and then be killed anyway."

A Militant-Seeker riding next to the wagon slapped Mangin on the head with a riding crop. "Shut your blasphemous mouth, witch."

Dirge spun to the man, his eyes like iron. "Don't strike her again."

The man raised the crop but stopped, fear creeping into his eyes as he stared at Dirge.

Estonia, steel armor shining under his new surcoat, rode up on the other side of the militant. "Knock it off and keep your eyes on the road."

The man snarled, likely at his own hesitation, and sawed at his horse's reins, dropping back behind the wagon.

Dirge nodded to Estonia. "You'll make an honorable Righteous-Warrior. I'm proud of you."

"Thank you, Righteous-Captain," Estonia replied. "Though it still doesn't feel right, my replacing you." He then looked to Mangin. "I don't think you need worry, Lady Malik. I see no guilt in you."

Kirkadite rode up to the back of the wagon and addressed Estonia, "Your emotions color your vision, Righteous-Warrior Den. Leave finding the guilty to the Seekers." He pointed to the head of the procession. "And you also need to keep watch on the road. Take your men to the front, we approach The Pinch."

Estonia nodded. "Yes, High-Seeker." He flicked the reins, and Justice trotted forward, his men marching after.

Kirkadite then eyed Mangin with a sneer. "What will happen to you when they find you guilty, witch? I will personally purge you. My touch will sear your heathen soul with the might of God until you can take no more."

Dirge sat forward "That's enough, High-Seeker. You're out of line. Women go to the Immaculates, and you know it."

Kirkadite ignored the comment, his gaze boring into Mangin. "And when you can take no more, I will push further until you scream out your crimes. You will beg for death, which I will, eventually, oblige."

Dirge climbed to his feet. "I said that's enough, Kirkadite! She's clean, and you know it."

The man smiled. "How would you know? The Arch-Righteous cut you off from the Lord."

Dirge held his head high. "He will reinstate me when my innocence is proved."

The wagon still rocked and bounced, but Dirge remained standing, bending his legs, and swaying his hips with each movement.

Mangin didn't know how the man did it, but it put a smile

on her face. *All I have to do is teach him a little more and he'd be more than a match for his father.* Her smile slipped, and she muttered under her breath, "If they allow me to lie with anyone ever again."

"What was that, witch?" Kirkadite asked. "Do you wish to confess something? No, I thought not. Contemplate your crimes. If you are honest with the Lord, he may spare your life as a slave in the Chastenary. If you've been pure, that is." Laughing, he urged his mount to the front of the caravan.

Dirge sat next to her once more. "You are innocent, my wife. You've no need to worry." He paused. "Though this may well be a good time to truly take the Lord into your heart."

Mangin saw the doubt in his eyes before he looked away.

With a sigh, she stared at the passing underbrush without really looking. Trees of all types slid by: pines, oaks, and palms. Some were little more than man-sized, scorched trunks.

Dirge spoke up once more, "What *did* you say back there, anyway? I know that look."

"Nothing." She forced a grin. "I just hope we have some privacy on the ship. I still can't believe you denied me all that time we spent in the cell. It can be fun knowing people are listening."

Affront filled Dirge's eyes. "That's the kind of thing ..." His frown melted, and he let out a chuckle. "You almost got me." Lowering he voice, he leaned close with a grin. "I assure you, the next time we're alone, I'll make sure you're satisfied."

Laughing in true amusement, she laid her hand on his shoulder. "I'm sure you will." She kissed his cheek. "Thank you, my fiery husband."

They passed another patch of burned trunks intermingled with healthy trees. Something about them seemed wrong. "What kind of fire burns only a handful of trees?"

The Righteous-Warrior at the head of the column shouted, "Militants, alert! Grunkin closing—all directions!"

Dirge jerked upright. "Let me help!"

Kirkadite ignored him as Militants setup a tight perimeter defense around the wagon and team leaving a five-foot gap. They wove amongst each other like a dance as they set up, with swordsmen out front and crossbowmen behind them.

Minutes passed and nothing happened. No screaming

attackers. No grunkins crashing through the foliage. The only movement was the gentle swaying of the burned tree trunks in the motionless forest.

Mangin's eyes went wide in realization; those weren't burned trunks. "Charred men!"

Thumps came from the tree line on both sides of the road. Dozens of bolts flew at the militants, most ricocheting off shields and armor, but some found flesh. Men screamed and fell with crossbow bolts protruding from necks and faces, but the rest flowed into position to cover the gaps. The lightly armored horses fared far worse though. Those that didn't die reared and shrieked, striking nearby Militants.

Dirge tried to cover Mangin with his body. "Stay down!"

But she had to watch, as though compelled by the chance of carnage. Terrified, she peeked over the wagon-wall as dozens of men poured from the trees. Charred black as though freshly scorched and wielding swords, maces, and spears, they smashed into the line encircling the wagon. They uttered no noise when charging. They didn't scream as the militants' blades hacked and slashed their bare, blackened flesh. It was as if the charred were mechanical, not caring what happened to them so long as they achieved their goal.

More bolts flew from the forest, this time focused at one point near the front of the wagon, right behind the horse team. The charred men attacked the same spot, pressing and piercing the wall of Righteous-Militants and Militant-Seekers. A grunkin burst from the forest and sped through the gap. It struck between the horses and the wagon, smashing the hitch, and shredding the now screaming horses. The wagon spun sideways, slamming Mangin into the sidewall and sending Dirge tumbling away.

Please, don't let me die, she prayed to whatever god would listen. *Where are you, Betal? I need you.*

"Don't let them through," Estonia yelled. "Stay in line, stay focused."

One of the Righteous-Warriors up front held his hand high. "Hold them while I made a Rod!"

Shrieking squawks ripped from the sky. Mangin's jaw dropped. A thing looking like an eagle covered with fur, with a twenty-foot wingspan flapped toward them. It had two heads on long, snake-like necks. One head looked like a bird's, but the other was nothing but fangs. It had four legs, two of an eagle and two that were only tentacles.

"A flying grunkin," she muttered.

Dirge crawled to her. "What?"

She pointed as the thing, now only a hundred feet away.

"That can't be," Dirge said. "Ukase, protect us."

It swooped down, clasping the Righteous-Warrior's hand as its beak slammed into the man's throat. As the Warrior fell, Militants fired their bows. Bolts pierced the grunkin's side, and with a shriek, it crashed to the ground, dead.

A screech came from behind Mangin. Something feathered hammered into her, sending her sliding across the floor. Another flying grunkin, exactly like the first, grabbed Dirge with its tentacles and talons. The closed, fanged maw banged the top of Dirge's head. His eyes rolled up into the back of his head and his body went limp.

Mangin scrambled up, wrapping her arms around Dirge's legs, but without the use of her hands, he slipped away as the thing launched skyward, taking to the air with Dirge in its grasp. "No," she screamed.

A grunkin, this one a cross between a massive boar and a scorpion crashed into the wagon, knocking her off her feet. Using pincers, the thing tore at the wagon's wall, crushing it. Splintering wood flew as the grunkin reached for her, the dagger-like fangs in its pig head snapping at her foot as it tried to climb in. She scrambled backwards out of its reach. With a hiss, it backed off and spun, smashing the wheels on that side. Mangin screamed as the wagon tipped, sending her skittering toward the grunkin's gaping maw.

Estonia rode up and sank his blade hilt deep into the grunkin's leathery hide. The monster shrieked, snapping at the blade with its pincers. Estonia, gripping his blade, leapt off his horse with the rest of the sword lodged in the monster. It sliced through the leathery hide with crunches and snaps. Nearly cut in half, the grunkin shuddered and went still.

Covered in gore, Estonia stood and went to Mangin. "Are you all right?"

"It took Dirge," she shouted, pointing skyward.

"I saw." Estonia helped her to her feet and pointed to a pair of Righteous-Militants nearby. "Johnson, Hempstead, help me tip this the rest of the way over. Mangin, get under the wagon, they will guard you."

Once tipped over, she crawled through the opening in the wall and huddled in the center as the clamor of monsters and men slaughtered one another. Tears streamed down her face as she huddled and shook, hands over her ears to drive out the cacophony. Never before had she felt so worthless. This was how her life would end, a once proud priestess of Chaos who could kill with a thought, reduced to a quivering wretch.

The screams of men died, replaced by moans and panting breath. An argument broke out, two men shouting, but she couldn't understand them from under the wagon. Someone shouted in pain, and then silence returned.

Estonia appeared at the hole and reached to her. "You can come out. They've fled."

Crawling out and standing on shaky legs, Mangin surveyed the scene. Militants moved about the bloody road, tending to the wounded and dying, while others searched among the charred men.

"Did you kill them all?" she asked.

"No," Estonia replied. "After one final push at the wagon, they fled. We must have killed fifty of them, along with four grunkin."

A tingling crept up her spine. "Was that all the grunkin?"

He shook his head. "No, there were more, but they retreated as well." Worry filled his eyes.

"They were controlled," she said. "Grunkin used in a coordinated attack. How is it possible? And some that can fly? This is madness."

"This may be the first time I've ever agreed with you."

A Head Righteous-Militant approached Estonia and saluted. "Sir, Righteous-Warriors Beechum and Craig are dead, along with two Truth-Seekers. High-Seeker Kirkadite was struck in the head and is unconscious. We lost eight Militants, but the Seekers lost two dozen."

Estonia returned the salute. "Thank you, Head Righteous. Inform the others we are going after Captain Dirge as soon as we straighten out this mess."

After the Head Righteous saluted and left, a Truth-Seeker approached Estonia. "We are taking High-Seeker Kirkadite on to

Conover, along with the witch."

To Mangin's surprise, Estonia stepped in front of her. "Lady Malik stays."

The Truth-Seeker frowned. "The witch is coming with us. High-Seeker Kirkadite is still in charge, and his orders were to take her to trial."

Estonia drew his sword, as did Johnson and Hempstead. "If you wish to flee like cowards, be my guest," Estonia said. "But we are going after the Righteous-Captain, and she is coming with us."

The Righteous-Militants stood next to Estonia, making a wall between Mangin and the Seekers.

The Seeker quivered, his eyes burning with rage. "The traitor Dirge is dead. If you wish to go off on this fool's errand, so be it. But Righteous-Captain Kelts and Arch-Righteous Agadonday will hear of this insubordination and will punish you accordingly ... if you survive." Spinning, he marched off, shouting orders.

Estonia produced a key and removed Mangin's manacles.

"Where did you get that?" she asked.

"Him." Estonia pointed to a Militant-Seeker staring at them with hate, clutching his arm to his chest, the same one who struck her with the crop. "After I had a word with him, he thought it a good idea for me to have it."

"Why?" she asked, rubbing her wrists. "Why take them off?"

"Because we need you. Captain Dirge said you can reach into minds." He pointed to a charred man tied up to a tree—his arms and legs jutted at odd angles, as though they were all broken. "That is one of the few who still live. We tried to make him talk, to tell us where they took the captain, but these things seem to feel no pain. Captain Dirge said that when you were a priestess, you made people do what you wanted. And from what I gathered from the Seekers, you still can."

She shook her head. "I don't know. I did it to the Seeker without thinking. I'm not sure how."

Placing an arm about her back, he eased her toward the charred man. "You can do this. You reacted out of instinct. Just think back to then and repeat it."

She followed, feet dragging. "I don't know. I'm nothing

without—" She looked away, cheeks reddening. "I'm nothing without … my powers."

"You can do this," Estonia repeated. "I believe in you. And it's the only chance we have at getting Dirge back."

When she knelt next to the charred man, he hissed and bit at her like a wild beast. "Hold him," she said.

Jamming a strip of leather into his mouth, three men held the charred man's thrashing head to the tree.

Mangin clasped his head between both hands, but felt nothing other than scorched flesh, still damp and oozing like an ever-open wound. She pulled back. "I'm getting nothing."

"Don't give up," Estonia said. "Think of Dirge and try again."

Taking a deep breath, she clasped his head once more and stared into his eyes like empty black pools. Only, they weren't empty. She gazed deeper, sinking into their darkness, until, at last, she made contact.

His anger assailed her, a seething ocean of hatred for everything living. He felt no physical pain because his soul was on fire, a never-ending agony that swallowed everything. Beyond that lay something, a dark, malignant presence as big as the world, as big as all existence. She'd felt it before; back when she pulled it from the mind of the lovely Traveler, Angharad.

Squeaking, Mangin jumped back, cutting herself off before it could make a connection.

"What's wrong?" Estonia asked. "You can do this."

"Hush," she snapped. "You can't rush this. Something else is in this man's mind."

"What is it?"

She was afraid to answer. Grasping the charred man's head again, she snarled and shoved her will into his head. She avoided the sucking void—though it pulled at her, threatening to drag her into its bottomless depths—and concentrated on the individual. Little existed of what was once a man, but he was still human. She delved the mind, seeking recent memories. Through dim and shadowed thoughts, she saw the direction the men and grunkin came from, the days it took for them to reach their destination. And their intent.

Her eyes snapped open. "Celeste told them to take me, too."

"Who?"

"A former priestess of Chaos. She's given herself over to the Abomination."

"Do you know where they came from?" Estonia asked.

Mangin nodded. "Several days to the south. There's a mansion in the woods, that's where they took Dirge."

"Excellent. We lost a lot of horses, but we should still make good time."

Mangin bit her lip again. "They'll know were coming."

"How?" Estonia asked.

She pointed at the charred man. "The Abomination is in him. He's in all of them. And what one knows, Dekriot knows." She furrowed her brow. "And now Celeste does as well."

The dense forest forced them to walk the few horses they brought, and after most of the day slogging through the underbrush, Mangin fretted over losing their way. Trying to remember the memories of a dark and twisted mind became a nightmare of doubt and second-guessing. "It has to be here somewhere."

Something landed on her neck, and she swatted at it. "I swear these things are going to drain all the blood out of me. That, or carry me away." She thought of Dirge and bit her lip out of worry.

"You need rest," Estonia said at her side. "You're looking deathly pale. But then, you always have."

Mangin grinned. "Was that a joke? Well done, sir."

"How much farther to the trail?" he asked.

"I don't know. It seems like we should have come to it by now. But with all this," she swatted at a leaf-heavy limb, "foliage, it's easy to get turned around."

Hempstead stepped forward and pushed a large fern out of her way. "Lady Malik."

Surprised and pleased, Mangin tilted her head. "How noble of you. Thank you. I shall have to ..." She trailed off and stopped, face sagging and eyes going wide.

"What is it?" Estonia asked.

Mangin raised a wavering hand. Through her third eye, a wisp of the Lord's Breath wafted past from her right, almost like a dream. "Is it real?" she murmured.

"Do you remember something?" Estonia then growled,

"Damn it, woman, answer me."

Mangin turned in the direction the power came from, her heartbeat increasing as she pushed through the greenery. She wanted to breathe the power in and wrap it about herself like a warm blanket, though an exceedingly thin one.

"If you are playing some kind of game, I'll strap your hide," Estonia said.

"I feel Chaos in the air. It's weak, barely even there, but it's coming from this direction."

Estonia scowled. "Are you ..." His voice trailed off. "I see it, the corruption of Edis in the trees. You're right. It's faint, but it's there."

A few minutes later, they came across a small, two-track running in the same general direction. "This is it," she said. "This will lead us to the mansion."

"You're sure?"

"Yes. From here it only took them a day to reach the ambush point, but they rarely stopped to rest. It will take us several more."

"With the added rations from those we lost, we'll have enough for over a week," Estonia said. "More than enough to get there and back."

Mangin rubbed her arms. "It's not the rations I'm worried about."

Chapter 30

Progeny

The sky was the color of blood and the background little more than a dark-gray mist. Dirge knew the place, regardless. He wanted to run, but his feet were held in place as though nailed. He tried to scream for it to stop, but no sound came. The dream refused to go away.

"She must stay," the Prophet Isaac said, staring down from his dais at the rear of the Army of the Righteous, his eyes glowing red. "You must go and see to your condemned men. She cannot go with you. Everyone has their place, Dirge. Hers is to die with me. Go now and be soiled. Ukase will judge you in time."

Dirge thrashed. He didn't want to see her again. It would make it all too real. Yet, she appeared anyway, pale skin aglow from an inner light. Long, brown hair framed her perfect face as she gazed at him, her eyes the blue of a deep forest pond. She flowed to him as though made of mist and they kissed.

"Until we dine tonight, my love," Dirge said.

"Until tonight," Lynette replied, giving his shoulder one last squeeze, then evaporating.

Dirge jolted awake, his head throbbing as the dream faded. He hated that dream—it came every night. However, there had been something sinister this time, like his memory was tainted. He tried to put his hands to his head, but they didn't move. He couldn't move at all.

Shocked, his eyes snapped open.

He lay on a fainting couch in the center of a room. Books lined one wall, and sunlight shone through tall windows on the other side. It smelled of beeswax and dust. Sitting in a chair at the foot of the couch was a petite, blonde woman of middling age, her green silk robe hanging open to the waist, exposing a skeletal chest with pallid, sallow skin. Dark circles hung beneath green, dull eyes. They hadn't always been dull. The last he saw her, those eyes were brilliant, hypnotic, the kind that ensnared a man simply in passing.

"Dahlia," he muttered. "What hellish nightmare is this?"

She replied, her voice slightly slurred, "I finally have you, my darling. I've waited a lifetime, and I finally get to make you mine."

"What is this?" Dirge shouted, trying to thrash but it was as though iron straps covered him from the neck down. A sense of panic crept in. *Ukase, help me!* But God did not reply.

A beautiful woman with long, jet-black hair strode into view, placing delicate, slim fingers on the back of Dahlia's chair. "This is a reunion," the newcomer said. She caressed Dahlia's hair. "When my daughter brought you to my attention all those years ago, I had to find you. A minion of Ukase? It shouldn't have been possible. You had all died when Hannibal's army and Storm crushed you. Yet, you somehow survived. I had to know how Ukase's touch had affected your Life-spark. How would it differ from the rest of us?"

She pulled up a chair next to her daughter, perching on the edge. "I created a network of sorts, people to report your whereabouts. It wasn't until Ruddick died and I took his home that I made any real progress. Ruddick had resources I never knew about. I used that, and finally found you, and who you …

traveled with."

Dirge didn't like where she was headed. "Who are you?"

The woman ignored his question. "After that it was easy, but you were too far away. In a world under Chaos, it's nearly impossible to get what you want when dealing with great distances. In a way, I need to thank you. If not for my search for you, I would never have found my master. I would have been lost once the Great Lord's influence fell. Thanks to my master, my reach increased."

"Ukase will destroy you," Dirge spat.

She burst out laughing, then dried her eyes with a sigh. "Ukase brought you to me, where you belong. The True are fools, easy to predict and manipulate when you have the right pieces in place."

The woman caressed Dahlia's cheek. "My poor child was a wreck over you. Your absence left a hole in her soul, one she was desperate to fill. She went through many reluctant lovers, trying to find a replacement. To no avail. It nearly broke her. The fall of Edis made things even worse. You truly are one of a kind, Dirge." She turned to him and smiled. "Glory is proof of that."

As she spoke, he had been examining the room, trying to find a way to escape. But that smile sent a chill ran up his spine. "Who *are* you?"

"My name is Celeste."

"Celeste?" Rage burned away Dirge's fear and uncertainty. "You're the one who hurt Daylin," he said through clenched teeth. "You tortured and raped her. I'll kill you for that!" He thrashed even harder, yearning to put his hands around the woman's throat and snap it like a stick, but the invisible bindings kept him lashed in place.

Celeste flicked her hand as though to swap away a fly. "Ruddick took the girl, not I. No, I merely observed and obliquely tested her connection to Spirit."

"You're no different than he is!"

She continued, "It's remarkable, really. Daylin, once a mortal, and now a god. I think Ruddick would have been pleased at the results he'd commenced. I understand she's quite fond of you … I wonder how much?" She shook her head. "For another time. We have more pressing matters at hand. That being you and my daughter."

"Yes," Dahlia slurred. "My room is all set for us. I have enough smoke to last us days. It will be just like the first time. I could even get one of Mother's maids. I did love watching you take the bar wench." She looked up at Celeste. "Could I, Mother?"

Dirge cringed, trying to beat down the memories that refused to leave. Disgust twisted his stomach.

"Anything you like, my darling," Celeste replied, gazing at Dahlia with adoration. "But first we need to introduce him to Glory."

He had to get out. He would *not* relive that moment. Dirge knew his mind would break from the guilt.

Celeste's eyes then returned to Dirge, eyes as green and radiant as her daughter's used to be. Without looking away, she held out a hand. "Come, Glory. Come meet your father."

He stopped thrashing. "What? No." A cold wave washed over his body. "It can't be."

A young woman came into view and took Celeste's hand. When she turned to Dirge, he wanted to scream. She was tall and slim, with skin like caramel. Long, black, curly hair framed her face. However, it was her eyes that tore at him, gray as slate, searing his soul in damnation. They were his mother's eyes.

Dahlia reached out to Glory. "Isn't she wonderful? I knew we would have an amazing child."

"This can't be," Dirge mumbled. "It just can't."

"He's pretty," Glory said, tilting her head. "But he's not happy."

"Dirge, I know you are upset," Celeste said. "You

needn't be. Very soon, you'll feel quite differently about all this. I promise you."

Glory pulled a crystal shard amulet from the neck of her dress. It was just like the one Dirge took off the body of the paladin up north. The young woman smiled as though reading his mind.

Chapter 31

Dead Wood

On the third day of their march to find Dirge, the underbrush grew dark and stunted as though something poisoned the soil. Some of the trees were blackened and withered as well. They had made good time, with Johnson and Hempstead at Mangin's sides, hands on hilts, but there were no signs of either charred men or grunkin. The group had refilled water skins from passing creeks and switched off on riding the horses to keep the men as fresh as possible. But even so, four horse for eighteen people made slow going.

With each passing day, Mangin wanted to scream out of frustration. The Lord's Breath grew stronger and stronger. It wasn't enough to do anything substantial, but she wanted to embrace it, nonetheless. Yet, she dared not let Estonia take notice. Each day had been a struggle not to grasp the tantalizing power of Edis. At that moment, she had an understanding with Estonia: to get Dirge back at all costs. Regardless, she knew the young man still hated her. If she took in the Chaos, it would be a damning crime in the eyes of Ukase. Estonia would use it against her the moment they returned.

"I don't like the feel of this place, Righteous-Warrior Den," Hempstead said.

"As well you shouldn't." Estonia stared straight ahead, worry plain on his face. "This place is tainted."

Mangin studied Estonia's face. He was no mere follower of Order and advocate for Dirge, walking in the footsteps of his mentor. Estonia revered Dirge. To the former squire, his master was infallible. The look in Estonia's eyes was one of worry and fear, like he would never again see his—

Mangin's eyes went wide in astonishment. Estonia was in love? Yes, it all made sense. The squire had always acted like a jilted lover whenever Mangin was around. But how was it possible? Lying with one's own sex was a crime to them, and those with the power of Ukase would see it. Or couldn't they? Mangin had never lost her own desires, yet Dirge maintained her purity in the eyes of Ukase was intact. She had thought Dirge was blinded to her proclivities by the promise of protection to Daylin. And yet, Estonia himself said she was clean, "in the eyes of God."

It must be about deeds, not desires, Mangin thought.

It was all conjecture and supposition, but she needed to know, if only for her own ease of mind. The question was, how to ask without causing offense and alerting the others to her intimation? She needed to tread lightly.

As she opened her mouth, he turned to her, radiating authority and anger. "How much farther?" he asked.

She swallowed her question. "Do you see that white through the trees? That should be it. See how much of the forest is all burned out? That's caused by the Abomination." She pointed to a stubbed, charred tree next to a healthy one. "We'll have to be watchful; the charred will easily hide in—"

Eyes popped open in a nearby tree.

Mangin gasped. "Charred men."

They raced from all directions with clubs and spears, stabbing at the Righteous-Militants and slamming their spiked-clubs against shields and armor, doing little damage. Estonia danced about, lopping off arms and heads, while the rest of the men's blades sank deep into charred flesh. But there were simply too many of the Abomination's men. They overwhelmed many of the men of Ukase, pinning them to the ground and stabbing their spears through the slots of the helmets.

Mangin's heart hammered and she panted as she crouched between Hampstead and Johnson. But both men were pulled away, Johnson slumping to the ground with an arrow to the eye. Turning to flee, Mangin stumbled over Johnson and fell on her rear. A charred man ran at her, club held high, but stopped, as though uncertain what to do. Desperate, Mangin sucked in the tenuous Lord's Breath and lunged at the charred man, grasping his head. She spun the Chaos into a web of enslavement and sank it deep into his mind.

As she did so, the blackness of the Abomination rushed forth. It latched onto her, and she fought back, trying to force it away. It didn't go. The Abomination oozed past her defenses like oil on water and seeped into her mind. Screaming, her body grew cold. She was dying. Yet, that didn't matter. Dekriot didn't want her body, it wanted her soul.

The outside world disappeared, and she dropped into a vast pit of nothingness. She had no body, sensed nothing, yet still she fell. A crackling chuckle echoed from everywhere as she plummeted, hammering her consciousness. It wanted her to wail and gnash, to wither in anguish until it devoured her soul over what would seem like an eternity. During that time, it would use her body to do its bidding, turning her into a marionette. The Abomination wanted her consciousness to remain, to hear and see everything while writhing in pain as it supped on her essence. She would be at the mercy of something that had none.

White-hot rage flared in Mangin. She was no one's puppet. Mangin grasped her fury, the emotion that connected her to her mind, and she stopped falling. As the blackness faded, she grasped it, squeezing it into a ball, and pushing it down into a tiny speck. But no matter how hard she pressed she couldn't get rid of it completely.

Gasping for breath, Mangin opened her eyes and leaned against a tree. It felt as though a lifetime had passed, but it had only been moments.

The charred man she'd enslaved raised his club and smashed it down on his nearest fellow with a crunch. Blood and brains flew. Mangin's slave then spun and attacked another charred man, crushing him upside the head with similar results. It laid into his fellows, killing two who had Estonia pinned to the ground, helmet askew. Estonia didn't move after the attackers were dealt with.

A dark man then sprinted past Mangin from behind, up to her mind slave, and hacked off its head. Sword gleaming in the scattered sunlight, the man spun to Mangin.

She gasped. "Dirge!"

His eyes stern, he marched up, clasped her wrist, and dragged her away from the melee toward an opening in the forest.

Mangin slid through a dense layer of fallen leaves. "I worried you were dead, but we came to find you." Her bottom thumped across a knobby branch. "Ouch! Okay, you can let me go. I do know how to walk."

Dirge didn't let up.

"I said you can let me go." She feared he would dislocate her shoulder and tried to pull away, but he clamped down even more. "Not so hard, that hurts."

Ignoring her, he continued away from the battle.

"What are you doing? They need your help. Stop," she shouted, digging her heels.

Twisting rivulets of Chaos flew past her and into the fight. It struck the still standing Militants and flowed through the gaps in their armor. The militants shrieked as the Chaos melted their flesh and bones. All Mangin could do was gasp in horror.

"That's quite enough," a woman said.

The drag ended, but Dirge did not let go. A tall, beautiful woman, with long, black hair and deep-green eyes strode up to Mangin from beyond Dirge. She held a black, fluted rod pulsing with Chaos ... and something else. It was a dark, malignant power that made Mangin think of rot, decay, and ash, a blackness straight out of the endless depths of the Void. The woman pulsed with the power of Dekriot.

"We finally meet, Miss Karados," the woman said, a smile playing across her ruby lips. "I am Celeste. Welcome to my home." She turned to Dirge. "Take her to the house. Be gentle; she has promise."

Panic swelled in Mangin as Dirge swept her up into his

arms. She struggled. "What's going on? Dirge, stop this. You have to help them!"

"He doesn't want to, dear," Celeste said. "Can't you see that?" She then turned toward the charred men. "I'll have my men bring those who still live. It's always fun to watch them writhe as they die."

Head spinning, Mangin kicked and screamed in Dirge's steel-like arms as they entered the shadowed, vine-encrusted manor house.

Chapter 32

Tempted

Nightmares tormented Mangin. She lived out the day's events, over and over, only worse. The charred men were thick as flies on a midden heap. Estonia and the Righteous wallowed in agony as grunkin by the hundreds devoured them. Dirge was made of stone, his eyes vacant as he dragged Mangin by the hair toward the mansion. The building was silhouetted in black, its doorway an open maw to the Abomination's pit. Mangin shrieked as she fell. Dekriot reached out to her, its hand and arm coated in black, crunchy, scaly flesh. The Abomination caressed her naked skin. She writhed in torment from its touch, for along with the pain, there was also pleasure.

Mangin jolted awake.

A beautiful, dark-haired young woman sat next to her on the bed, wearing not a stitch. She gently caressed Mangin's naked breasts with a genteel smile on her face.

Mangin jerked away. "Who are you? Don't touch me."

She remembered how the day had actually ended. Dirge took her to a second-floor bedroom and tossed her on the bed as though she were only laundry. As he left, closing the door behind him, she had jumped up and raced to the door. It was locked from the outside. No amount of pounding and screaming had elicited a response. After what seemed like hours, Mangin passed out on the bed, curled into a ball, shuddering but refusing to cry. Without the power of the Great Lord, she felt a pathetic, worthless mess.

The young woman again reached out. "I just want to bring you pleasure, Mistress."

"No one touches me unless I wish it."

"Yes, Mistress," the young woman replied, sitting back on her haunches.

"What's your name?" Mangin covered herself with the sheet—she did not remember undressing.

"I am Ahlil, Mistress. How may I please you?"

"You can please me by getting me out of here."

"I am sorry, Mistress, but I cannot do that," Ahlil said, still wearing a pleasant smile.

"Then you can't very well please me, can you?"

"Does Mistress not find me appealing?" Ahlil ran a hand over her small breasts as the other hand went between her legs. "I wish only to bring you pleasure, to ease your distress in every way I can."

Mangin considered Ahlil, taking in her slim, supple form, and soulful eyes. She looked delicious. It has been so long since she's felt the touch of another woman, to taste what was now deemed illicit. "Where is Dirge?"

"I am sorry, Mistress. I do not know." Ahlil raised her hand slowly, leaned forward, and caressed Mangin's cheek. "Please. let me help you in a way that I can."

Closing her eyes, Mangin relented, luxuriating in Ahlil's soft touch. Mangin thrilled as it moved down her neck and circled her left breast. When the finger reached the nipple, Mangin gasped. It was like an electric shock raced through her body. The hand moved on, below her chest and across her belly with quivered in anticipation. The moment Ahlil's hand reached

Mangin's mound a groan burst from her lips.

It had been so long.

Opening her eyes, Mangin grabbed Ahlil by the neck and pulled her in for a fierce kiss. They moaned in unison, taking in each other's breath as Ahlil's fingers delved deep. Ahlil broke the kiss, her lips following the trail blazed by her finger. Mangin's head swam, her body rocking with pleasure.

Ahlil stare from between Mangin's legs was one of joy and lust.

Mangin clasped Ahlil's head with both hands, pulling her in tighter. Her mind opened, wanting to experience the lovely, dark-haired woman even more. She delved Ahlil's mind, thrilling at the hunger therein. The desire to please her mistress. To please Celeste.

"What?" Mangin mumbled.

She delved deeper, without quite knowing how she did it, and found the mind buried deep within. Buried behind a construct of false emotion and personality was a brain shrieking in terror at the inability to stop what she was doing to Mangin and filled with disgust at having to do it.

"Stop," Mangin shouted, and pushed Ahlil away.

"But I just wish to please you."

"No, you don't," Mangin said. "What have they done to you?"

But she already knew the answer. It was the same thing she'd done to numerous others in her youth. Never before had she witnessed what the host mind really felt during enslavement. She hadn't cared. Ahlil brought it all home like an avalanche.

Mangin took Ahlil's hand. "I can fix this. I know how."

She attempted to delve Ahli's mind, but nothing happened. With a shake, she concentrated harder, trying to will herself inside, but again failed. What she did so easily moments before, just as she had with the charred man, was beyond her. Before she'd plumbed their minds without even thinking. So why not now? It was like slamming her head into a wall.

Failing to help Ahlil, Mangin couldn't stop thinking, memories of all the times she enslaved others to please her in every way imaginable. Was this some kind of divine punishment, a glimpse into her past to remind her of the damage she'd done?

She wanted to vomit.

The door opened and Celeste stepped in. "That's enough for now, Ahlil. It's time for lunch. To the kitchen with you." She smiled as Ahlil jumped off the bed and sped past without bothering to cover herself.

Celeste's gaze turned to Mangin. "Lunch will be ready soon. If you wish to wash and dress, there's soap and water on the cupboard and several lovely dresses in the wardrobe."

Mangin opened her mouth to demand to know where Dirge was, but Celeste exited, pulling the door shut behind her.

"Bitch!" Mangin leapt off the bed and yanked the handle, but again it was locked. Slamming her palm against the door, she strode toward the cupboard, waving her stinging hand. She splashed water on her face from the basin to cool off. "Who does that stinking woman think she is?"

"I am your host." Celeste leaned against the frame of the now opened door wearing a sly smile.

With a growl, Mangin raced to the door, but Celeste waved her hand, and Chaos poured into her. She enveloped Mangin with it, lifting her a foot off the floor. "I expected a person as refined as you to be more civil," Celeste said. "Why the ferocity?"

Mangin thrashed, but she knew it was useless. "Because I am *no one's* plaything to be kept in a box."

"Aren't you?" Celeste tilted her head. "It seems that since the fall of Chaos, that is all you have been. Coddled by a man who by all rights should hate you. Yet, he doesn't." She flicked her wrist. "Oh, you were a scullery maid before he took you for a wife, but that hardly counts. Think of how the countless others like us were treated. You are a pretty bird, kept in a golden cage and played with at your master's whim."

Tired of the woman's sanctimony, Mangin concentrated on the Lord's Breath flowing into Celeste. If Mangin survived, she would deal with the ire of the Seekers later. She reached out to grab the Chaos, but hit a barrier encasing the flow. Gritting her teeth, she tried again and again, flailing at the encasement until she saw stars from the exertion. Her head sagged.

Celeste approached, her gait slow, hips swaying. "You cannot touch it." She lifted Mangin's chin with a finger. "Not yet. Not until I know you're ready.

"Now," she set Mangin down but did not release her hold, "I want you to freshen up. As I said, slips and dresses are in the wardrobe and pants are shirts are in the dresser. Choose whatever you like. You will find all your choices to be quite flattering. You should be comfortable. I want you at ease during lunch. We've much to discuss." She released Mangin and strode to the door. "Someone will come and get you shortly."

Anger flooded through Mangin and she stood tall. "*What* do we have to discuss?"

Celeste smiled. "Your future."

Chapter 33

At the Bottom Of a Well

A variety of breads, meats, and cheeses, along with fresh fruit and steamed vegetables, covered the dining table—currently sitting six with room to spare. A large serving bowl of barley soup sat at the center, filling the room with its fragrance. Ahlil ladled soup into a saucer in front of Mangin sitting next to the foot of the table. "What delicacies would my mistress like as well?" Ahlil asked.

Mangin's stomach growled. She considered not eating, but what would that accomplish other than making her go hungry? "Ham and flatbread," she replied, doing her best not to fidget as she stared at her setting. "Along with some grapes and a piece of blue goat cheese."

Celeste spoke from the head of the table, "I do hope you

like it, there isn't much left—it came from a village not far from here."

Mangin took a bite of the strong, salty cheese, enjoying the flavor. "If you're running out, just get more." She tried to keep her tone light.

"Well," Celeste tilted her head slightly, "my people were a bit ... overzealous there. There's no one left to make any. It's a pity, really. I've yet to find anything else like it. How is the wine?"

Taking up her glass, Mangin sipped the sweet white. "Lovely."

Kenja spoke from the table's foot. "I prefer the red." He radiated cold like a loose window in the dead of winter, and his smile reminded Mangin of a hungry wolf. He bit into a piece of rare, roast beef. "But then I've always liked things that are red."

Taking another sip, Mangin did not reply. She had been quite surprised to see Kenja when she entered the dining room but had yet to acknowledge him. He had presumed too much of their couplings when she was younger back in Cross Corners, acting as though he had a claim on her. She thought he had learned better the day she arrived there with Betal, but it was obvious Kenja didn't understand his place.

Mangin tried to focus on her food, but her gaze slid to the seat across from her like iron filing to a loadstone. Dirge sat next to a pallid woman with lanky, blonde hair. They held hands and smiled at one another like sycophantic lovers. The expression on Dirge's face baffled Mangin. He looked like a different person. The hard jaw and stern eyes were soft, relaxed even, and he spoke to the woman with gentle, glowing tones. He'd yet to even look at Mangin, as though she didn't exist.

The lovely, caramel-colored young woman to Mangin's left spoke up, "Does it hurt?"

Mangin's attention snapped to the woman. "What?"

The young woman toyed with a crystal amulet about her neck. It leaked Chaos as candlelight danced on its surface. "You are sad. Does his happiness make you so?"

Wiping her mouth with a napkin, Mangin looked away. "I don't know what you're talking about."

"Of course you do. He is happy with my mother and that causes you distress because he wasn't happy with you." The young woman rolled her eyes. "You're very easy to read, like most simpletons."

Mangin's head snapped to the left, eyes smoldering. "Watch your tongue."

"No need to be offended," the young woman replied. "All common people's minds are easy to read. You are no different."

Rage boiled up in Mangin, but she reined it in for fear of lashing out. The young woman was obviously a reader. Angry, Mangin forced her out.

"In fact, I'd say ..." The young woman trailed off, her eyes widening. "How did you do that?" She turned to Celeste. "Grandmother, she shut me out." She turned back to Mangin, eyes narrowing. "How long can you do it?" Chaos poured from her crystal amulet.

Pressure slammed into Mangin's mind like her head was in a vice. Sweat popped up on her brow, but Mangin refused to let in. Even without Chaos, she was still the master of her own consciousness. The moments that passed felt like days and her head started to throb.

"That's enough for now, dear," Celeste said, placing a hand on the girl's shoulder.

"But I can break her."

"I said stop, Glory."

Anger flashed in Glory's eyes. "Fine!"

The probe vanished, and Mangin's head sagged. With a deep breath she sat taller, putting on an air of defiance. The last thing she needed was to let them know how close it came to folding. She then looked to Celeste. "Is this why you brought me here, to test me?"

"Of course not." Celeste's tone was light, and she wore a mischievous smile, but her eyes were cold. "As amusing as it is to see you fret over Dahlia and Dirge, I simply wanted to offer you a fine meal and some entertainment." She stood, wine glass in hand. "Speaking of which, it's time to retire to the library."

As they left the dining room, Kenja took up position next to Mangin. A chill prickled her skin and she shivered.

Seven chairs were arrayed in a slight arc at one end of the library while the other end was obscured in a shimmering curtain of haze. Celeste took the center chair, between Glory and Dahlia, with Dirge next to the wan woman. Mangin was shown to the next and farthest by Ahlil. Kenja was visibly put out having to sit on the opposite end next to the empty seat.

Mangin turned slightly to Dirge and asked in a low voice, "What is going on?" But he still had eyes only for Dahlia.

Celeste spoke up, "I'd hoped Calidos would be here for this, but it would seem Razz couldn't talk him into returning. Pity that. So, for your viewing please, let us get on with the show." She drew from the rod on her lap and flicked her wrist.

The haze disappeared on one end. Hempstead sat in thick, wooden chairs, straps around his arms, legs, and chest. Next to Hempstead stood a charred man holding a cudgel—a smoldering brazier with iron rods, tongs, and shears sticking out was on the other side.

"Release me," Hempstead bellowed. "By Ukase, you will all die! You ..." His eyes focused on Dirge. "Righteous-Captain?" Fury burned in his eyes and his face reddened. "What have you witches done to him? Lady Malik, flee! Get hel—"

The charred man slammed Hempstead upside the head with the cudgel. Hempstead's eyes crossed and his head sagged.

"Not so hard," Celeste snapped. "He needs to feel everything." Sighing, she turned to Mangin. "Now we will have to wait until he gathers himself."

Mangin seethed but didn't respond.

Celeste raised an eyebrow. "Truly? You pity this man because he was nice to you for a few days?" She tsked. "How far you have fallen. Not that long ago you would have relished seeing this. They all hate you. He was polite because he was only following orders; it's what they do. They've no will of their own. If ordered he would have sliced your throat."

The truth of the words struck harder than Mangin thought they would as her cheeks reddened. Celeste was right. They all hated her. Yet, she couldn't help but wonder if there was a better way.

"Perhaps you're right," Celeste then said. "Maybe he was being nice because he somehow liked and respected you. But if that were so, he is a fool. As disgusting as Ukase and his sycophants are, they do share a belief with Edis: might makes right, only the strong survive. It is the paradox of opposites. Fire will burn you, but so will cold. Too much light will blind you, sending you into complete darkness."

"Lady Malik," Hempstead muttered, "you must get out. Get help."

Sitting taller, Celeste smiled. "Ah, he's back." She nodded to the charred man. "You may begin."

The charred pulled out the arm-length sheers, its tip glowing red, and cut off two of Hempstead's fingers. The militant threw his head back and screamed as the shears also cauterized the wound, filling the room with the stench of burned flesh.

With a frown, Celeste shook her head. "Well, that's disappointing. I expected it to take much longer than that from one of you."

A warbled voice came from beyond the still curtained side of the room, "Militant, hold. We will not give her the pleasure."

Hempstead stopped screaming and stiffened. He stared straight ahead but his eyes still bulged from the pain.

Celeste tapped her lower lip. "Fascinating."

"Who is that?" Mangin asked, sweating. She knew the answer but hoped to be wrong.

Celeste turned to Mangin with a wicked glint in her eye. "Yes, I believe it's time to expand our game." She then snapped her fingers.

The other curtain faded away, and Mangin's stomach clenched. Estonia stood strapped to a large, heavy wooden X, his arms and legs splayed—another charred man stood behind him with a blank expression. Blood matted Estonia's hair on the left side of his head, and that eye was swollen and bloodshot. He wore not a stitch. Despite herself, Mangin enjoyed his slim, muscular form.

"Quite delicious, isn't he?" Celeste said, mirroring Mangin's thoughts. "I may even have some fun with him before putting him down." She nodded to the charred. "Proceed."

Over the next hour, the hot irons, pincers, and shears were used on Hempstead. They snipped off his fingers and toes, slowly sliced off his scalp with a flaying knife, and burned out his left eye. But Hempstead never made a sound. His head and body remained rigid, his breath steady. He didn't even move when they scorched off his genitals.

Mangin gagged several times from the scene and the stench of burned flesh. Never the wilting violet, it still disgusted her, reminding her of the Chastenary. At the time, Mangin thought them the most horrible people in the world. In the time of Chaos, they—

Mangin had been a fool. Though boring, life growing up in Cool Winds was idyllic, insulated from the realities of the world. Chaos and Order were no different in the end, reveling in cruelty for cruelty's sake.

Not wanting to think of it longer, Mangin's eyes flitted to Estonia and went wide. He shook. Not seemingly from rage, though she was sure there was a good deal of that, but from what appeared to be exertion. Sweat soaked his forehead and his jaw was clenched so tight Mangin thought he may well have broken some teeth from the effort.

"He's using his own will to make Hempstead remain still," she muttered.

"What was that?" Celeste asked. Standing, she glided toward Estonia. "I think you're right. I was enjoying the show so much I didn't even notice. I thought he was merely upset. This must be how they keep their men in line. Glory, dear, put the pretty one to sleep for a moment. Just a quick nod, I want to test something."

Glory squinted, and Estonia's head bobbed to his chest and popped back up, his eyes blinking.

That was all it took. The moment Estonia's head fell, Hempstead shrieked and thrashed. The man bellowed as though the world died. He quickly followed suit.

"No," Estonia shouted, thrashing at his restraints. "Damn you, no!" He glared at Dirge. "Why don't you do something!"

Through the entire ordeal, Dirge and Dahlia held hands and gazed into each other's eyes as though nothing else existed.

"My Lord, please, you have to snap out of it," Estonia screamed. "Don't let the witch consume you!"

Celeste took a step back. "Look at the hurt in his eyes. Like those of a betrayed lover. I wonder." She turned to Glory again. "Search his mind. How deep are his feeling toward Dirge?"

Glory concentrated. "He's stubborn, but I can still read him. Yes … Yes, he loves Father."

Eyes wide, Mangin's head snapped to Glory. "Father?" she whispered.

Celeste laughed. "Wonderful, isn't it. His past came back in the most *glorious* way." She let out a chuckle at her pun and then tilted her head. "You've known, haven't you, that the young man has feelings toward Dirge?"

"I surmised, recently," Mangin said with a scowl.

Shaking her head, Celeste said, "What is this, jealousy?" She tsked and turned back to Glory. "How much does he love your father?"

"A great deal, Grandmother," Glory said. "He has never loved another and believes he never will."

"How wonderful." Celeste laughed and clasped her hands. "Does Dirge feel in kind?"

"I will have to break through some of my construct." Glory crossed her arms with a petulant face. "It wasn't easy *reminding* him how much he loved Mother."

"It's all right, dear. You can rebuild it."

Rolling her eyes, Glory got behind Dirge's chair and ran her hand through his hair. "This will hurt a bit, Father." She then clasped his head, and Dirge sucked air through clenched teeth.

Dahlia gasped. "Why are you hurting him? Stop it. I said, stop it!"

"Calm yourself, Mother," Glory said through slightly clenched teeth. "Soon enough you'll both go back to sucking on your pipe and be numb again. Now, let me work." Glory's brows furrowed as her fingers dug into Dirge's kinky hair. "I'm through. Now I just have to … Oh, yes. There it is. He does care for the young man. A great deal more than he will let himself admit."

"Does he love the young man?" Celeste asked.

"He does, Grandmother," Glory said. "Though, he doesn't know why. He has never had sexual feelings toward another man. He finds them disgusting."

Celeste's laugh was like a chime. "You and your mother's smoke have cured him of that misnomer."

"You freaks! You monsters!" Estonia bellowed.

"Don't worry, my lovely," Celeste said. "If you play nice, I just may let you live out your wildest dreams."

"Never!"

Her eyes on Estonia, Celeste pulled power from her rod and waved a hand at him as though trying to coax a flame to burn higher. His head pulled back as though in pain.

"There has to be more here," Celeste said. When she placed

an index finger to his forehead, he sucked in air through a clenched jaw and his eyes rolled back into his head. Celeste tilted her head as though hearing something. "Yes, there it is. The impression left by Aelaz is far greater than it should be. She paid extra attention with this one."

"You stinking whore," Estonia spat. "Ukase will end you all." He then gave a weak grin. "Except for the girl. I see a hint of an aura of Ukase about her. Once the Immaculates are done with her, she will gladly embrace God."

Eyes going narrow, Celeste turned back to Estonia. "Are you trying to anger me? Let me guess, you want me to lash out with Chaos and end your miserable life." She laughed. "No, my young man. I'm not that stupid. You know that if I kill you with Chaos, Ukase will know it. He doesn't care what hurts you. But if I ended you with Chaos his eyes would find us. Besides, I've plans for a great deal of one-on-one time with you."

Glory spoke up, "Who is Aelaz, Grandmother?"

Walking back to Glory, Celeste said, "The God of Life. She pulls souls from the Stone and sends them on to mortals awaiting birth. This smells of the Mother's handiwork. Put him to sleep, would you, dear?"

Estonia's eyes rolled back again, and his body went limp.

Celeste nodded to the two charred men. "Take him below. Put him on the examination table and secure him."

Mangin shuddered at the implication.

"I'm going to fix Father now," Glory said, and placed her hands on Dirge's lolling head.

Mangin needed to do something. She had to know what Glory was doing to Dirge if there was any chance of reversing it. When a hint of Chaos wafted past, she sucked it in ever so softly and directed it to her third eye. She watched Glory at work, how Glory looped threads of Chaos with something invisible and sent them into Dirge's mind. It worried Mangin. Without knowing what the other thread was she—

Ahlil stepped up from the back of the room and slapped Mangin's cheek and ear. Mangin's head rocked to the side, stars danced before her eyes, and her ear filled with a warbling sound. When her vision cleared, Celeste stood in front of her, arms crossed.

"None of that now," Celeste said. "You'll not use your

Lord's Breath unless I say so. I let you have a taste to lure you here, to get you to tap one of my men, at my master's bequest. Dekriot got a latch on you, but obviously not as strong of one as he'd hoped." She tapped her lip. "Which reminds me. I need to shut off the leak. I don't want to lead some fool here against my wishes. No matter how much fun it would be."

Kenja stood, ignoring Glory and Dirge. "As fun as this has been, Celeste, you made me a promise."

"I did, didn't I?" Celeste turned to Glory. "Are you finished with your father yet?"

"Hurry," Dahlia urged. "I want to get back to my room."

"It takes what it takes," Glory snapped. "You want me to rush and melt his brain?" A grin spread across her face. "I should shred his mind just to teach you a lesson."

Celeste frowned. "You'll do no such thing."

"And why not? When they're not sleeping, they're in a stupor from her pipe." Glory's eyes softened as she looked at Dirge. "He deserves better."

"Why do you say that?" Celeste asked.

"Because I know the truth. I've seen his life, the few precious moments he's been happy, mixed in with silly self-doubt and guilt he constantly wallows in. It's not right that his god should make him feel this way."

"Then what you've been doing for your father is a gift." The softness in Celeste's voice did not touch her hard, cold eyes.

"This isn't about him. Do you think I'm stupid? This is to keep Mother happy, which makes you happy."

"What would make *you* happy?" Celeste asked.

Glory's eyes flitted to Mangin then went to Estonia. "For starters, I want some time with him before you ruin him with your experiments. He doesn't like women. I want to teach him what he's been missing."

Celeste laughed. "Is that all? Oh, my sweet dear. Of course, you can have some time with the young man. We're in no rush, after all. But first, you must finish with your father—"

"I already did," Glory interrupted. "Some time ago."

"You do love to play games. All right then, wake your father so Dahlia can have him back, then I need you to see to this one." Celeste motioned to Mangin. "Kenja is right. I promised to give her to him."

"Make her love me," Kenja said. "I want to toy with her the way she toyed with me."

"Toyed?" Mangin snapped. "Have you lost your mind? We had fun and that was all. I made you no promises. I never even intimated such things."

Kenja puffed up. "I had plans—"

Mangin laughed. "We all had plans. But Edis knows there's no such thing as certainties."

Kenja continued, "Then you brought *him* to town, parading him about like a prized stallion. You loved him, didn't you? 'The Hand of God, Himself,' you proclaimed. And where did that get us? Edis is gone because of Betal. If you hadn't hindered the master's plans, none of us would be here."

Celeste stepped forward. "That's enough, Kenja." Her eyes bore down on him until he wilted. She then said, "Glory, please do as I instructed. Then we will see to the young man."

Desperate, Mangin sprang from her chair to run. She knew was about to happen—the same as she'd done to countless others. Something grabbed her body, holding her in place. Mangin tried to flail, to scream, but could do nothing. Glory was already in her mind. Mangin dug deep and pushed Glory's mental touch to her periphery.

Glory leapt and grasped Mangin's head. "You *are* a strong one. I like that." Her fingers dug into Mangin's scalp.

Power surged into Mangin's mind; the same matrix used on Dirge. She tried to latch on the Chaos portion of the web, but the other part was pushing her away, almost as though Glory somehow wielded the power of Ukase along with Edis. But that was impossible. According to Dirge, that power came directly from the Magnus.

"How?" she muttered, dropping to one knee, barely holding Glory out.

"Ukase is not the only form of Order in the multiverse," Glory said, kneeling next to Mangin. "You've so much to learn. Let me show you."

The web spun and sliced through Mangin's defenses. It slithered into her mind, engulfing her consciousness. The ball squeezed, pushing her down. The world around her dimmed and funneled, as though she were in the bottom of a well.

"That's better," Glory's thoughts echoed down. "Relax.

You needn't worry. I'm not going to wipe you like I did the others. They're pathetic. No, you're special, like my father. I wouldn't dare destroy something so precious."

Mangin slammed her will at the ball, but the web may as well have been made of steel.

"But," Glory continued, "Grandmother made a deal with the cold, creepy one. So, I must do this."

Glory then constructed a false consciousness, gleaned from Mangin's memories. It wasn't complex, like the one Mangin had made for Worm. No, it was more like a puppet—simple and stiff, yet also pliable and easy to manipulate. The false mind created a haze of sorts. Somehow, Mangin thought she might appreciate that in time. Finally, a glowing weave spun through the construct and attached to Mangin's mental cell, making her writhe in momentary pain.

"That last bit is for me," Glory said with a laugh.

"Is it done?" Kenja asked, his words coming in like an echo.

"It is," Glory replied. "She will do whatever you want."

Kenja came into view. "She no longer rejects her love for me?"

Glory laughed. "She is whatever you want her to be."

"Good, good." Kenja clasped Mangin's chin. "Come, my love. It's time I gave you what you've been missing all this time." With a sneer, he ripped off her marriage lace and threw it away.

"Anything you wish," Mangin's mouth replied.

Inside, she screamed and hammered at her mental prison as Kenja led her upstairs.

Chapter 34

Interlude

Monotony. Arduous, terrifying monotony. Mangin had no idea how much time passed in her shadowed, peephole cocoon. Thanks to the construct Glory created, Mangin felt nothing that happened to her body, but she couldn't shut out the view or stop up the sound. The eyelet was always there whenever her body was awake. Every snarl, every grimace, every rapturous smile on Kenja's repugnant face while he grunted atop her body was there for Mangin to abhor. But what really horrified Mangin was the sound of her own voice moaning and egging him on. Every time he asked if she loved him, her voice said yes, flowering him with sycophantic blather and praise. She prayed for death; anything to end the nightmare.

Days blurred into the next. Weeks passed into months. She lost count.

As Mangin's body knelt before Kenja in his room, pampering his feet—which stunk like rotten cheese—she tried not to dwell on her past, about the things she'd put others through. Those kinds of thoughts didn't help. They came, nonetheless.

Was this how Cobb felt when she twisted his mind to lust for her, trapped and unable to control himself? What about the countless others she had manipulated into her bed or forced to do her bidding? No. She decided it wasn't the same. She never completely enslaved a mind to do whatever she wished …

Except for Worm.

No! No, what she did to Worm was different. Jason Connor tried to stab her in the back. Besides, the man who was there before no longer existed. Mangin had completely reconstructed his mind. There was nothing left behind to wallow in misery.

Was there? *Had* she missed something, some scrap of consciousness that was still Jason? Was that how she'd been able to construct the false Jason?

It didn't matter. His job was to protect Adel, the only thing, the only person who really mattered in the world. Worm was where he needed to be. She refused to feel guilty over that.

Her musings were interrupted when someone entered. Kenja looked up and asked, "Is dinner ready?"

"I'm not one of the servants," Glory replied.

Mangin mentally jumped. The only time she'd seen or heard Glory since that day was at the occasional meal. Why was she here now?

Glory continued, "Though you might as well go get something to eat. This will take some time."

"What will take time?" Kenja's face darkened. "What are you playing at now?"

"I merely wish to spend some quality time with her."

"No. She's mine. *That* was the bargain."

"I'm not taking her away from you," Glory said with a giggle. "Her mind will still belong to you once I've finished. The young man proved disappointing. Whereas Mangin's appetites are well known."

A sneer crept across Kenja's face. "Fine. But I will join in."

Glory barked a laugh. "Hardly. You're disgusting."

Kenja jumped to his feet, knocking over Mangin in the process. Her head bounced on the floor, causing her tunneled vision to swim for a moment, but she could still make them both out.

He stabbed a finger at the door. "Get out! Or I'll—" He stopped short and shook, eyes blinking rapidly.

"You'll what?" Glory strode forward, her long, blue, silk dress swirling about her bare feet. She then laughed. "No, the master will not be upset. He doesn't care about little things like this, and you know it. If you cannot protect yourself, then you are too weak to do him service."

Her face grew stern. "Now, as I said, go get something to eat." Her eyes went to Mangin. "And perhaps a pipe afterwards. I intend to enjoy myself."

Mangin trembled in her prison at the implications. Then, angry at herself, she slammed against the prison, searching for any crack she might have missed. Anything, to wipe the smirk off the little monster's face. But there was nothing.

Kenja gasped, wobbling on uneasy feet. Once he'd gathered himself, he stood taller. "Fine. I'll return with one of the maids. The one who looks like you. It won't be the same, but it will be close enough."

"I'm sure it won't be the first time." Glory then stepped aside and pointed to the door. "If I'm not down in an hour … wait another hour."

Kenja stormed out, slamming the door behind him.

Glory knelt next to Mangin, caressing her cheek. "Not too hurt, I see—how fortunate for him. Get up, my dear. Sit on the edge of the bed."

"What do wish of me, Mistress?" Mangin's mouth asked as her body heeded. "Shall I undress?"

"No." Glory shook her head. "Not like this." Glory then reached into Mangin's mind.

Mangin's consciousness stiffened. Was this the time? Would Glory destroy her mind completely just to spite Kenja? Part of her looked forward to it. At least then it would be over.

Glory created a small mind weave and traversed it down the silver cord she'd attached to Mangin's cage. The cord pulsed and quivered as the spell ran along it. When it reached the attachment point, the construct opened, and Mangin raced through the opening.

Mangin's consciousness flooded into her body. Head aching from where it hit the floor, her stomach rumbled with hunger—

Kenja fed her sparingly, saying he liked her rail-thin. The room swam for a moment and she blinked to clear it. She slowly lifted her hand before her face. The hand shook, but she controlled it. "What game is this?" She couldn't keep the quiver out of her voice.

"No game," Glory replied.

"Then, I'm free?"

Glory grinned. "No, this is only temporary. As I said to that buffoon, I merely want to spend some quality time with you."

"You didn't have to let me out for that."

"True. But what's the fun in that? You've so much strength, more than you know. And your mind might be the most beautiful I've ever seen." Glory gently sat next to Mangin, her head slightly tilted. "Sex is to be enjoyed. It's about the give *and* the take. You learned that firsthand."

Mangin was surprised at the stab of guilt she felt at the observation. "And if I said no?"

Glory shrugged. "Then I put you back in your cage. And I leave disappointed, just like I did with Estonia. That poor boy is so twisted by his faith. He's convinced that sex should only be between a man and a woman who are *married*, of all things. Don't get me wrong. I meant it when I said he loves my father. But he won't even allow his conscious mind to admit he wants Father to take him." Her face twisted. "In oddly specific ways."

Mangin glanced about the room, hoping for a way to escape. "What way is that?"

"He wants to be taken like a woman." Glory glanced at Mangin and her face darkened. "Don't."

Calming her features, Mangin shrugged. "Can you blame me?"

Tilting her head, Glory laughed. "You're right. I can't." She leaned in as though for a kiss but stopped. "So, what is your decision?"

Mangin licked her lips and pursed them. "I'm not sure, with everything he's done to me."

"Are you sure?" Glory took hold of the string knotted at the neck of her own dress and pulled. The knot unraveled, and the dress slid off her caramel shoulders, revealing she wore nothing else. "Do you not find me appealing? You've enjoyed my father. And though I could only read your surface thought—your mind does flit about quite a lot, giving things away—Father is an open book. He's under the impression you had sex with *his* father as well. Is it true?"

Mangin couldn't stop her grin. "It is."

"How was he?"

"Amazing."

Glory reached up and thumbed Mangin's chin. "Then you can't tell me you're not curious."

The young woman was right. She was gorgeous and seemed to know what she was about. Still, Mangin hesitated. "I'm still a slave."

"For now." Glory's lips brushed Mangin's. "Convince me otherwise."

Mangin clasped Glory's head and pulled her tight, crushing their lips together in a passionate kiss. With the intimate contact, Mangin saw into the outermost of Glory's mind, reveling in the passion and hunger therein. Glory wasn't lying, she wanted Mangin and nothing more. Mangin didn't dare push further, though. She was no match for the young woman's power. Besides, she wanted this, too. She wanted to *take* Glory, to be in charge for once. It might well be her only chance.

They rolled into the center of the bed, Mangin flinging off the black nightgown Kenja always kept her in, as Glory shimmied the rest of the way out of her dress. They pressed their bodies together as they kissed hungrily. Fingers and tongues explored, reveling in the exquisite textures and tastes.

Afterward, Mangin laughed. "You do live up to your name." They kissed once more. "You are glorious." As she came down from her high, tears streamed down her cheeks and her lips trembled.

Glory wiped away the tears. "What's wrong, my dear?"

"I'm still a slave."

"Not for long."

A blinding flash struck Mangin and she reeled. The room spun and her ears rang, then it faded away. "What happened?" She placed a hand to her head.

"We are done, for now," Glory replied. "You were by far one of the most wonderful lovers I've ever enjoyed." She sighed. "But, I'm afraid it's time to put you back. I did promise Kenja, after all."

Mangin tensed, but for some reason, she wasn't terrified. She merely nodded with acceptance, and a hint of ... anticipation? Glory pressed into her mind, weaving a cage once more. Only this time, it wasn't as deep once finished. The mesh was far thinner with larger gaps in the warp and woof. Mangin wondered why Glory would be so sloppy. But it gave her hope.

Glory stood and went to the door, but upon reaching it, she turned back to Mangin and smiled. "Stay strong. You can do this." Glory's voice was only muffled, as though she'd spoken from beyond the closed door, rather than coming from the bottom of a deep well. And as Glory left, the sound of the door closing was far more cogent.

Mangin tested her cell, but to her disappointment, found it just as strong. Yet, unlike before, Mangin had a vague sense of touch, like a tingling limb recovering from being constricted, only without the pins and needles. Mangin pressed on the construct, straining with all her might, and ever so slowly, some of her consciousness seeped through. The tingling in her face faded. She tried to blink her eyes.

They closed and opened of her own volition.

Elation flooded Mangin, but so did fatigue. She lost contact with her body and snapped back, then everything went fuzzy. Floating in a haze of unawareness, she had no idea how much time passed. But she at least had some control.

Hearing returned first. When she realized Kenja had indeed returned with the maid who resembled Glory, she wished it hadn't. Mangin barely felt a thing, it was as though she were completely covered in a thick comforter. Thankfully.

Mangin tried to fight him, to gain a modicum of control over her body, but was still too exhausted. She screamed in frustration, but her throat emitted only the tiniest whimper. Mangin fell back from the wall of her cage and again entered the haze. When senses started returning, far too quickly, she tried to swim back into that fog. It worked. She floated in that gray, thanking Glory for the modifications to her prison. Mangin was still a slave, but she had hope, now.

Chapter 35

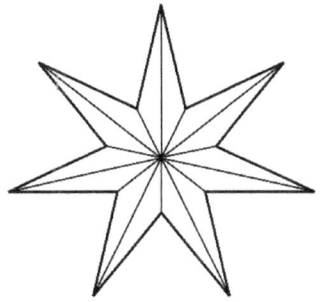

Mixed Feelings

Over the next few days, Mangin honed her touch on the construct, testing her limits and pushing them. Kenja took her down for every dinner now. Apparently, Glory didn't like seeing Mangin so skinny, so she forced Kenja's hand.

Celeste was absent, but this was the first time Dirge and Dahlia joined in the meal. Mangin was appalled at seeing him. His face was gaunt, with large circles under his eyes. His shirt was rumpled and stained, and he sported several days of growth on his face. He wasn't as bad as Dahlia. Stains covered her rumpled yellow dress, the low neckline showing ribs beneath Dirge's bronze sun pendant. But her appearance often waxed and waned. According to an off comment from Kenja, Celeste cast a rejuvenating spell on her daughter from time to time to keep her from wasting away.

The enslaved serving girls brought out plates of roast lamb and roots. Dahlia was listless, picking at her plate, but Dirge dug in as though he'd not eaten in days. Which might well be the case.

When a plate was placed before Mangin, the sweet and sharp spice wafting up enthralled her. She wanted to dig in but held herself in check. Her hands wouldn't have cooperated anyway, but they might twitch from her effort, and she wanted the others to remain unaware.

Taking a bite, Glory moaned. "It's so wonderful. The cook has outdone himself." She then glanced at Mangin and grinned. "It's the best thing I've tasted for several days." Her eyes traveled to Kenja, and she added, "I may have to have seconds."

Kenja snarled and hacked at his meal with knife and fork.

Glory looked back at Mangin. "Eat, my love."

"Yes, Mistress," Mangin's mouth replied.

Kenja held out a hand. "Not too—" He stopped short when Glory glared at him. He lowered his hand and went back to his meal.

Mangin cut off a slice of meat and took a bite. The taste was a rich as the smell. She pressed herself against her cage to enjoy as much as she could. The sweet and tangy sauce made from some kind of peppers was so delightful Mangin wanted to close her eyes to enjoy it.

Her lids started to close.

Panicked, she pulled back and her lids snapped back open, her mouth going back to its task woodenly. Had they noticed? What else had she done that might give herself away? Did Glory see? Mangin doubted the young woman was monitoring her thoughts or she would have felt the pressure on the cage.

"That's it, my sweet," Glory said, her gaze alone seeming to pierce Mangin. "Eat up. You need to keep your appetite up if you're to stay strong."

Mangin retreated into the fog.

Several more days passed, but Mangin remained at the edge of her cage during meals. She decided what she gleaned from there was enough to satisfy her. Sometimes Dirge was there with Dahlia, sometimes not. Celeste's presence was hit and miss as well. Mangin wondered what kept the woman away. And she also dreaded the likely answer.

She'd not seen or heard anything new about Estonia since

the day Glory re-locked Mangin's mental prison. How was he? Was he even alive? Part of her found it funny she even cared. The man had done nothing but harass her for years. Until Celeste took Dirge. It was the one thing that united them. If Estonia died, she would truly be alone.

One particular evening, the dinner was only Celeste, Kenja, and herself. *Where is Glory?* Mangin wondered. The young woman had not been to dinner for three straight days. It worried Mangin, because with her gone, Kenja might revert to his previous treatment. But she also felt a growing anxiety, like the sense of anticipation before something momentous. With Glory gone, Mangin had more opportunity to test her limits.

Kenja looked around, beansprouts dangling from his lips. "Where's Glory?" he asked, mirroring Mangin's thoughts.

"She went for a little excursion," Celeste replied, poking at her plate of greens. "The poor dear is at the age where she wants to know everything." She paused. "Though usually not for this long. I'll have to get some of my pets to do look for her." A scowl spread across her face.

"From that look, it appears you're going to rein her in."

Celeste's head popped up. "What? Oh, no. Glory can do as she likes. I just want to make sure she doesn't bring the wrong kind of attention. No, the problem is I can't wrap my head around that boy."

Kenja popped a chunk of chicken into his mouth. "What *I* don't understand is why he's still alive."

"If you're asking why I haven't killed him, it's because I'm not done with him. He possesses an exceedingly strong will. Spirit probes are quite painful. Most don't survive for long. What vexes me is I still haven't found out why the touch from Aelaz is so strong in him. And there's something about his soul as well, as though it has tw—"

A zeal blossomed in her eyes and she jumped up. "Yes. That might be it." Without another word, she rushed out.

As Mangin's hand brought a piece of bread to her mouth, Kenja slapped it away. "I said I don't want you getting too fat," he snapped.

"Yes, Master," her mouth replied, even though Mangin wanted to spit at him.

Kenja grabbed her hand and jumped up, yanking her to her

feet. "It's time we work that fat off you. Besides, you'll never give me a child stuffing your face."

Mangin panicked. He *wanted* her pregnant? She tried to stop, but it only caused her feet to stutter step and she nearly fell as they reached the broad central stair.

"Clumsy bitch. If you can't run, I'll drag you." He started quickly up the stair. "What did that brat do to you last time? It's like your body isn't working right lately."

He knows, she thought. *I've got to get out of here!* But her earlier attempt had drained her.

They reached the landing and headed to his room. "If she damaged you, I'll kill her."

Relief flooded Mangin, allowing her to catch her mental breath. She couldn't help but laugh at his false bravado. Glory would flay his mind if he even honestly thought he could get away with harming her. Just the thought buoyed her spirits and strengthened her resolve.

Entering his room, he flung Mangin on the bed and pounced atop her. "Now, my sweet, tell me you love me."

Mangin flung herself against her cage, willing her mouth to remain silent.

Kenja's face grew dark, and his hands clamped down on her shoulders. "Are you truly broken?"

"No, Master."

"Then tell me how you really feel," he shouted, spittle falling from his lips.

How could she ever have felt anything for such a pathetic pig? What had she ever seen in him? He'd always been spoiled and entitled, acting as though he was so much better. The few times she remembered him as eager and optimistic about the future had obviously been stripped away by the Abomination. He was nothing but a pathetic husk now.

Kenja shook her shoulders. "Tell me!"

Her lips parted, and Mangin spoke through them. "I hate you."

Kenja's jaw dropped and his head snapped back as though slapped. "What?" He trembled and shouted, "What did you say to me?" His hands clamped about her throat. "This is that bitch's doing, isn't it? Well if I can't have you, neither can she." His fingers squeezed.

Inside of her cocoon, Mangin laughed. Even if he killed her, he would know her true feelings.

Her vision dimmed

Not that it mattered, she had won. He would never get the child he'd always wanted.

The whooshing in her ears began to fade.

Glory's last words drifted through her head. But the truth was, they didn't matter. She didn't *want* to die. It just wasn't her choice. What good would staying strong do now? She was powerless. It wasn't like she could just reach out and grasp the Lord's—

Something pulsed on her chest, as though mocking her. As the beating of her heart weakened, it grew stronger …

Something she'd wished for, for so many years …

All she had to do was reach out and …

Chaos flooded into her soul, her body, her mind. Mangin touched it to her cage, to the exact place Glory had left her silver thread, and her prison melted. With her remaining strength, she grabbed Kenja's head and funneled Chaos into his mind. Synapses snapped like burned threads, and blood vessels popped like bubbles atop a mineral spring as she whirled the Chaos about, shredding his gray matter into pulp.

Kenja twitched and collapsed atop her.

She rolled him off and gasped for breath, dragging sweet air into her lungs until she could see once more. Mangin lay there for several minutes, reveling in her body once more, and the power flowing through her. Only, something else was there, attached to the Chaos like a shadow. That's when Glory's words rushed back to her:

"I'm still a slave," Mangin said, crying.

Glory smiled. "Not for long."

"What do you mean?"

"I have plans of my own," Glory said. "I'm sick of being cooped up in this tomb, this twisted forest. I used to go out from time to time on horseback. But Grandmother was always there with me in one way or another.

She clasped Mangin's hands and squeezed them. "Then I saw the world through Father's eyes. There's an entire world out there full of life and diversity. I must see it for myself."

Glory then frowned. "I don't like what Grandmother has become since we came here, since Dekriot took hold of her. She thinks he's in me, too, and I let her think it. But I can hold him out."

Mangin's eyes went wide. "How?"

"With great difficulty," Glory said with a laugh. "He's not really a demon, you know that, right?"

"What is he then?"

"He is a god. The God of Desolation and Destruction, created when the Mother made reality. In order to have one, you must have its opposite, else all would be imbalanced."

"Why are you telling me this; why are you helping me?"

A wicked grin spread on Glory's face. "I need you as a distraction. There will come a time when she notices I'm gone. That's when you'll free yourself."

Before Mangin could talk, Glory continued, "Once you're free, I want you to also free my Father. I don't want him to turn into a pathetic addict like my mother. He deserves better."

"How am I supposed to do all this? Your cage is too strong." Mangin hated admitting that. "And I have no power at all now that Celeste has shut off her leak."

Grinning, Glory pulled a delicate silver chain holding a crystal shard from her purse—one similar but smaller to the one about her own neck. It pulsed with the Lord's Breath.

Mangin shook from wanting to grab it and suck the power in, but she stilled her mind and hands, lest Glory discover her desire.

Glory placed the chain about Mangin's neck.

Mangin's mouth gaped. "Why?"

"This is for later." Glory waved her hands as though burying something in sand.

The necklace sank beneath Mangin's skin, chain and all.

Glory nodded. "There. Now you won't have to worry about it bouncing around or being seen. When the time is right, use the chaos in the shard to open your cage." She held up a finger. "But, be careful how much you use it. Unlike mine, it is connected to Dekriot. The more you use it, the stronger his touch will be. Plus, there is a limited amount of Chaos in it. It won't last forever."

She paused. "Perhaps you should forget all this for a while."

Mangin's mind came back to the present. "The manipulative bitch." She couldn't hold back a smile. "I swear, if I didn't hate her so much, I'd be in love."

She sprung to her feet and went about searching Kenja's room. If Mangin were going to free Dirge without using too much of the shard, she'd need a weapon. Kenja's body lay sprawled on the bed, blood oozing out his ears and pooling on the sheets, but for some reason he wasn't wearing his own shard.

It wasn't on or in the dresser, so she pulled open his wardrobe. She smiled at Kenja's belt draped on a hook on the inside of the door. At the bottom of the belt hung his favorite, black leather grip dagger, pommel shining in the lamp light. "Yes, I think I can do something with this."

Chapter 36

Empty Chamber

The floor was smooth beneath Mangin's bare feet as she slipped down the hall, dagger in her palm with the blade up her loose sleeve. Her clothes were not in his room, and she felt exposed in only a nightgown. How could they escape with her dressed like this? Even if she were able to free Dirge, she needed to find something more appropriate to wear—at least a good pair of shoes. If not, he would have to carry her through the forest. And Mangin was tired of being at others' mercy. But then, she was at the mercy of the fates at that moment. If Celeste found her roaming about untethered, the loathsome woman would have none for Mangin. With Glory gone, Celeste might well just kill Mangin.

As she neared the main stair, she jerked a little when Ahlil entered the central hall and started up the stairs. Mangin stilled her breathing, trying to remain calm. *You are brain dead*, she thought to herself. *You have no will of your own.*

"Where are you going?" Ahlil asked.

Mangin tried to keep her voice neutral as she replied, "My master bade me to get him some food."

"There is no time for that. Mistress Celeste needs him at the stables. You are to stay in his room."

"But my master said—"

Ahlil overrode her, "His desires do not matter. You are to follow me to his room." She then strode down the hall.

Mangin did her best to turn smoothly and follow. If she did anything to give herself away, Ahlil wouldn't hesitate to turn her in. Which is exactly what would happen the moment she saw Kenja's body.

Glancing about to see if anyone else were around, she eased the dagger from her sleeve as Ahlil opened the door to Kenja's room. Mangin shoved her inside and quickly followed, slamming the door behind her.

Ahlil stumbled to a halt, her eyes on Kenja's body. She then spun and attacked Mangin, teeth bared, trying to get past.

Mangin attempted to fight her off with one hand. The real Ahlil was still in there, and Mangin didn't want to kill her. She kept the dagger at arm's length behind herself while trying to grab the woman's head. If she could get through, she might at least be able to detain Ahlil. But if the woman got ahold of the weapon … No, Mangin couldn't allow that.

As Mangin's hand slid up the side of Ahlil's face, the woman bit Mangin's fingers. Mangin yanked her hand back with a yelp.

Ahlil shoved Mangin aside and made for the door.

Mangin regained her bearing and grabbed Ahlil's hair, slamming her face into the door. "Hold still. I can free you," Mangin grunted.

She breathed in a trickle of the Lord's Breath from her shard and launched into Ahlil's mind. She fumbled with the woman's construct, trying to find the back door like Glory had made with her own. But, there was none. The prison was complete. To make matters worse, the matrix was covered in a layer of darkness. There was no way in, no way to stop Ahlil from running out, screaming for Celeste.

The blackness in Ahlil's mind pulsed and oozed. Ahlil spun about, snarling. Her eyes were dead black. When she spoke, it was the voice from the Void, dry and crackling, "This one is mine. Just as you will be."

The blackness latched onto Mangin's probe and pulsed. The darkness swirling about in the Lord's Breath Mangin wielded throbbed in time with the one in Ahlil's head. It dove at Mangin.

Screaming, Mangin plunged the dagger up Ahlil's chin and into her brain, severing the connection. Mangin jumped back, and Ahlil's body dropped with the dagger still in her head.

Mangin's heart hammered and she shook. She heaved raged breaths and backed into the room. The blackness still inside of her fluttered and faded, but it did not go away completely. Taking a deep, calming breath, Mangin eased back to Ahlil, making sure not to step in the blood pooling about her body. She yanked out the dagger and pulled Ahlil's corpse away from the door.

She paused, placing her foot next to Ahlil's. "Close enough."

When she reached for Ahlil's green slippers, she cursed. Her hands were bathed in blood. The few spots that got on her nightgown would not be noticeable, but her hands would.

Hurrying to the washbasin, she quickly scrubbed away what she could. When Kenja didn't show up in a reasonable time, Celeste would likely come get him herself. The hourglass had been turned, and the sands were falling.

After putting on her new shoes—which were a tad tight—she cracked open the door. The hall was empty. Palming the dagger once again, she quickly crept down the hall, head swiveling all about, to Dahlia's door.

She hesitated to open it. What if the construct around Dirge's mind was just like Ahlil's? She wouldn't kill him. Probably couldn't. "Please, Great Lord. Let his be different."

She opened the door.

The stench assaulted Mangin, a mixture of acrid smoke, sweat, and sex. Only a single lantern lit the room, keeping most of it in gloom. But she saw enough. Dirge sat naked, with his back against the backboard, and his chin resting on his chest. Dahlia lay on the far side, head facing the wall. She wasn't moving.

"Go fetch Mistress Celeste," Dirge muttered. "Dahlia hasn't roused in over a day."

Mangin crept closer. "Is she dead?"

Dirge's brows furrowed. "You are not right. Maid," he shouted.

"I don't have time for this." Mangin dove onto the bed and latched onto Dirge's head. She pulled Chaos and sent it into his mind.

"Only my love may touch me." Dirge grabbed her wrists and squeezed, trying to yank them away.

Mangin pulled more Chaos, anchoring her hands to his head. When he squeezed harder, she feared he'd crush her forearms. She changed the grapple, moving it off her hands and onto his, forcing them to stay put. She then focused the probe, sliding it along the surface of Dirge's construct, hoping to find the keyhole. With each passing moment, the touch of Dekriot grew stronger, slithering up the Chaos weave and into Mangin.

Her stomach roiled and panic rose. How much would it take for him to have her? How much longer until she was lost? There might be no keyhole. It could have all been a rouse, Glory playing one of her cruel games, all to allow Dekriot to gain control of Mangin's soul. It might already be too—

There it was, a glimmering jewel at the back of his construct. Mangin pushed inside, deep into the thick layers of false ideas and beliefs until she touched his actual mind. The cage dissipated, unraveling layer by layer like a hedge doctor removing gauze from a wound until nothing remained.

Dirge blinked repeatedly and focused on her eyes. "Mangin? What's going on? Where am I? I've had the worst nightmares." His eyes narrowed. "Why can't I move my hands?"

Mangin banished the Chaos and pulled back a little. "You've been a prisoner, a mind slave to—"

"Celeste," he said, putting a hand to his head. "I thought it was all a dream. A black nightmare I couldn't wake from."

"How much do you remember?"

His gaze traveled to Dahlia. "Enough. Not all of it. Something tells me I was shielded from the worst, but I remember enough."

He looked back to Mangin. "Where is my ..." his face hardened, "my daughter?"

"Gone. Just like we should be." She then filled him in on what Glory told her. "Plus, Celeste just summoned Kenja to the stables. My guess is to help look for her."

"Where is he now?" Turning to the side of the bed, he winced. "I feel like I've been pummeled for days."

"I killed him," she replied with a grim smile. "Along with the one sent to get him."

Mangin went to the nearest wardrobe and found Dirge's clothes. "Oh, sure, they kept yours. What the hells did they do with mine?"

"What?"

"Nothing. It just seems I'll have to go about like this for now."

"Check the other wardrobe. If this is her room, she'll likely have something proper enough for you."

She tilted her head. "Proper? That's the first place you go? Let me tell you, you've been far from proper—"

"No," Dirge interrupted. "Please, not now."

She saw the look in his eyes. He truly remembered at least some of what they did to him. "I'm sorry. Here, put these on and I'll check what she has."

Dresses of every shade and style filled the other wardrobe. And Mangin discovered several were in different sizes. "They're a bit small for me, but here's to hoping." Mangin selected the largest she could find, a short-sleeved burgundy dress that laced up the sides. The laces were unnecessary as it was still a tight fit. As hard as it was to fathom, she actually looked forward to her own dresses, even if they did cover her from wrist to neck.

She was about to close the door when something caught her eye. Hanging on a hook on the back of the door was a necklace with a bronze sun pendant. She took it and handed it to Dirge. "I believe this is yours."

Dirge took it with a shaky hand. "Yes, thank you." He then rose on unsteady legs, stomped his feet to properly seat his boots, and settled his cloak about his shoulders.

Mangin smiled. "You're still sallow, and you needed a proper shave, but you look worlds better."

"Pants are a bit loose," he replied. "Are you ready to go?"

"I am." She went to him, handing over the dagger. "Here, you'll have better use of this than me."

"No," a croak came from behind them. Dahlia tumbled out of bed, landing with a thump. She staggered to her feet, wild, dingy-blonde hair covering her face. "You can't go. You are mine."

"Not any longer," Dirge said.

The woman bent over and pulled something from what appeared to be under the mattress. It was a long, fluted black rod, a twin to Celeste's. "Mother said this one was mine, but I was always afraid to use it."

Chaos, mingled with the power of the Abomination, made the room grow cold.

"You're not taking him." A sense of dread filled the air along with static, which lifted and separated Dahlia's hair, making it a wild mane. "He's mine, and always will be."

Dirge's knuckles whitened on the dagger and he took a step forward. "Let's end this then."

But Mangin had a feeling it wouldn't make a difference. The power flowing into the woman from the rod was enough to destroy the room. Perhaps the entire manor. Frantic, Mangin pulled Chaos from her shard, hoping to somehow shield them, but knew it was too late.

Dahlia lifted her arm as smoke rose from her body, her skin and eyes darkening. She gasped … and dropped to the floor.

The feeling of dread vanished, so Mangin crept to the other side of the bed. Dahlia lay on her back, eyes open, staring at nothing. Mangin shook her head. "It was too much and killed her."

"It doesn't matter," Dirge said. "We have to find Estonia."

"What?"

"I don't remember much, but I do remember the torture room—what she did to him and Hampstead."

Mangin was about to argue that they didn't have time. But he was right. They couldn't leave Estonia behind. "You're right." She smirked. "What *have* you done to me, my darling husband? But if we get caught, I'll not be a slave again."

Dirge glanced to the far side of the room. "She'll likely kill us both for that."

Mangin gestured to the door. "You first, my Lord."

Dirge's head throbbed. As they made their way down the stairs and through the mansion he ran on mostly adrenaline. He doubted it would last. His stomach gnawed at him and mouth tasted like he'd been sucking used boots for days. What was in that concoction she had forced on him? His memories were even more fractured during those times, to his relief. The things he could recall were bad enough.

Mangin pointed the way through the dining room, practically clinging to his back. "The kitchen is this way. It's where Celeste always went when she said she would work on Estonia. She said something about a lower lab when they took him away, so I'm guessing it's past there."

The dagger in his right hand, Dirge pushed open the door with his left—Mangin shook against his back as he poked his head in. Light flooded the room from a row of windows, glinting off pans on the walls and cutlery dangling above a central table where a plump man hammered and kneaded dough. The man didn't look up from his work. When Dirge stepped in, the cook stopped and plodded to a cupboard. Dirge eased into the room, dagger low and ready to strike. When the cook spun around, he held a plate heaped with meats and cheeses, placed it on the table, and then went back to his work.

"He's one, too, isn't he?" Dirge asked.

"Yes," Mangin replied. "Take up the plate or he'll think something's wrong."

Dirge grabbed it, placed it in the hand holding the dagger, and stuffed a piece of hard sausage into his mouth as they made their way to the back. The more he ate the hungrier he got. "Did the damnable woman not even feed me?"

"Not from what I saw." When they pushed through the kitchen's back door and into a well-lit hall, Mangin pulled him to a stop. "I've never been back here. So be careful."

Placing the rest of the meat and the hard cheese into his pouch, Dirge set the plate on the floor and advanced down the short hall to where it split. Ahead of then, the hall entered yet another room. The one to the left went about ten paces ending at a door. Next to it was a bench and several hooks on the opposite wall.

"That must go outside," Dirge said, and continued forward.

The room was ten by fifteen and completely empty. At the far end was another short hall, one far less lit, smelling dank and of mildew, with stairs going down at the end.

"That must be it," Mangin whispered.

A lantern lit a landing where the stairs turned 180 degrees and continued down. They reached the bottom and entered a vaulted basement. To their right, next to a blazing fireplace, lay a naked man atop a table. Several long rods and needles pierced his chest, which barely moved.

It was Estonia.

A lump formed in Dirge's throat as he approached, feelings of affection—which he didn't want to face—welling up in his chest. He handed the dagger to Mangin and cupped Estonia's head. "We're here. We'll get you out."

Estonia opened his blue eyes and gazed at Dirge. "It's all right," he croaked. "It doesn't matter. I finally got to see you again, to love you again. That's all that matters. I will always love you, my sweet."

Dirge's lips trembled. "I-I'm here for you."

Estonia reached up, clasped Dirge's neck, and gave it a squeeze. "Until tonight, my loving husband." His hand fell, lifeless.

Dirge staggered back. "What? What did you say?" He stared into those dead, blue eyes. He'd known them from so long ago. Another time. Another life.

His heart shattered.

Dirge grabbed Estonia's shoulders. "No. It can't be. No. No!" He shook the corpse, tears running down his face. "Don't leave me again! Lynette, please don't leave me! I love you." He put his forehead to Estonia's and whispered, "Please, don't do this to me again. I love you. I will always love you."

His sobs echoed in the empty chamber.

Chapter 37

Abomination's Return

Dirge moved woodenly as they eased the rods and pins from Estonia's body, then covered him with Dirge's cloak. Throat ragged and eyes blurry, Dirge was numb, mind empty and body hollow, as though a part of him died all over again. Just like the first time he lost … her.

Mangin stood at his side, trembling. She reached out to Estonia but pulled back, looking haunted. She then glanced to Dirge, her eyes like moist emerald pools. "I'm sorry. I really am. He was a good man; a good … person. We didn't always get along—and I guess I understand why now—but we had a sort of détente. We agreed to do anything it took to find you. And he saved my life more than once in the process." She reached out and took hold of Dirge's forearm, squeezing it.

What game are you playing? Dirge wondered. *Are you part of all this, or a true victim of it?* He stared at her, hard, but she refused to look away or wilt. *If she's not behind it ... she has more courage than I.*

"We should get going," she said. "We've not much time."

Dirge handed her the dagger. "Here. It's too bad you didn't get the sheath." Then he picked up Estonia's body. "What's the best way out?"

Mangin twisted her mouth. "I wasn't exactly worrying about sheaths at the time. I was a little preoccupied."

"Which way?"

"If you like, we could go up to his room and get it."

"Mangin, which way is out?"

She shrugged. "I don't know. You dragged me in by the front door. We could use that, but I'd advise against it."

"Would you be serious?"

"I am serious. I really don't know. We could try the one at the top of the stairs. You said yourself it looked like one that led outside."

Anger rising, Dirge took a deep, calming breath. Moments ago, he was dead inside, never wanting to ever feel again. Now, he was filled with aggravation and annoyance. And appreciation. *She doesn't want me wallowing.*

He nodded toward the stairs. "Lead on. And thank you."

She edged toward the stairs. "For what?"

"Caring."

"I'm your wife. I'm supposed to care." Her grin was apparent even in the gloom as she cast her gaze about. "And you're welcome."

"Just don't care too much."

Mangin stopped short and turned, her face quizzical.

"People who care for me are still dying *because* of me. Keep that in mind."

She eased up to him and caressed his cheek. "I'll keep that in mind." She then lightly smacked it. "And I'll care as much as I like. I told you, you don't own me." She spun and stalked toward the stairs.

It took everything he had to not grin as he followed.

With still no one in sight, they made it to the first floor and to the door down the other hallway. Mangin eased the door open and peeked out, only to yank her head away and quietly close it again.

"She's there," she hissed, nodding to the door. "That's the stable yard. What now?"

"That leaves only one option."

Scowling, she eased past him and headed toward the kitchen.

Before they reached the door, a woman shouted from farther in the manor, "Alarm! Mistress, alarm! He's been killed!"

Mangin spun, shaking. "What do we do?"

Dirge paused for inspiration from the Lord. But, of course, there was nothing. How had he lived and led so long without God's guidance and support? The truth was, he hadn't. He'd done nothing but followed others: first Jacob and then Ellis. He hadn't even led the troupe while Ellis was young. Not really. He had asked others to put forth ideas and then waited for a consensus before *making the decision*. Now Mangin looked to him to make the right decision, her feet shifting and gaze flitting about.

Finally, he nodded toward the way they came. "To the basement. We've no choice."

They quietly rushed back downstairs, Mangin's breath quick and stunted behind him. Reaching the bottom of the stairs, Dirge closed his eyes and turned away from the fireplace. After a moment, he opened them, waiting for his eyes to adjust to the dim. Large cages and barrels lined the walls, the floor littered with moldy straw, so there had to be another way in and out.

Mangin stuck close to his back. "How long before they come searching down here?"

Ignoring the question, he tried to picture the layout of the first floor. The fireplace was located at the end where Mangin said held the stables. So he went the other direction.

"Where are you going?" Mangin asked.

"There must be a ramp along the back wall. There's no way they got those cages down the steps." A glimmer of light shone halfway down the wall near the ceiling. "There. That's got to be it."

They found a shallow ramp and made their way up to the double-hinged cellar door. Mangin slowly lifted one door and peeked out with one eye. "Nothing that way." She did the same with the other. "Nothing," she squeaked in obvious excitement and pushed one open. Mangin held it for Dirge and softly closed it behind him.

Dusk was upon them as they crept from the house, but not enough to obscure them. Dirge searched the ground for anything that might trip them up or give them away, all the while trying to keep an eye on the corner of the manor where the stables lay. Estonia's body dragged his arms down and his legs felt watery. He'd lost much strength while enslaved to Dahlia. Maybe too much. His back ached and eyes hurt from looking in so many directions. Mangin kept to his side, panting from either exhaustion or panic. Grunts, snarls, and squawks echoed from the stable yard, bouncing around, making it sound like some came from the forest ahead. If a grunkin truly were in those dark trees he could do little about it but die. Still, they crept closer and closer to escape.

They were at the edge of the woods, when a woman's voice came from the stable yard behind them, "I am impressed, Mangin."

Staggering to a stop, they slowly turned.

Celeste, face serene, strode around the corner of the vine-choked mansion, flanked by a pair of grunkin. "You *actually* figured a way to get out of Glory's mind-cell. Master was right, you have so much promise."

Taking a deep breath, Dirge moved to the side and gently put down Estonia. He picked up a thick, dead branch, breaking off all but the thickest end to the length of his arm, and set his feet, assuming a balanced stance. For whatever good it would do. Without God or his Father's sword he knew he had no chance against the Chaos monsters.

Mangin stiffened, knuckles whitening on the dagger. "I'm not going back. I'll die first."

"Who said anything about you going back?" Celeste replied, holding aloft her fluted rod. "No, my dear. The master wants you. And you will want him." She waved the rod gently, and a sense of dread rose, just like it had with Dahlia. "With this you can have as much of your Lord's Breath as you want."

A soft, swirling wind flowed in front of Celeste and headed toward them, picking up leaves and making them dance in the air. It washed over Dirge, draining him even further. His eyes grew heavy, his body cold. The trepidation in that wind drained his spirit as well as his body.

Mangin was unsure of what lie within the power-wave flowing toward them—it somehow looked simple, yet infinitely complex. She drew power from her shard, readying a counterattack.

The wave hit Dirge and he slumped as though teetering on the edge of collapse. She drew in Chaos to shield her mind form the apparent sleep spell. When the flow hit her, though, there was no spell to deflect. It was only power; Chaos mingled with something far stronger, a matrix of energy so pure and clean she wanted to cry. She drew it into her lunges, her grip loosening on the dagger. Even in her height, when The Lord's Breath bathed the world, she had never known a thing so beautiful. And with it, she could do anything.

"It's … it's so glorious," she muttered, eyes fluttering.

Never again would she know fear. The world would weep at her coming.

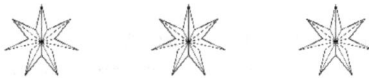

Dirge struggled to remain standing as Celeste moved slowly forward, still twirling the rod. "And, Dirge," she said. "You know you want to be with me again. You want to put a child in me just as you did Dahlia. It will be even greater than Glory, and we will raise it to its fullest."

Memories flitted through his head, crazed, hedonistic dreams of smoke and sex with mother and daughter both separate and together. It disgusted him. And aroused him. He yearned to obey his mistress. To do as she bid and dominate them both with his prowess. He ground his teeth to hold his yearnings at bay.

Celeste continued cooing, "I am sorry about your squire. Or should I say," she paused, smiling, "your wife. But you belong to my daughter, not some ghost from the past. You know that. You will forget, and never have to feel that pain again."

"No." Rage flared in Dirge, snapping him out of his stupor. "No! You will *not* take her away from me. She … *he* may have died, but I will *always* have the memory of my Lynette."

"I don't think so." Celeste glanced at the grunkin on her left.

The smaller beast bounded away on all fours; an amalgam of a hairless dog and insect, it raced toward Dirge. Mangin snapped out of her own trance and danced back, her face white with fear. The grunkin slid to a stop, only feet from Dirge, and snapped at him with its fanged mouth centered on its chest, beneath a head that held a multitude of eyes. The thing's clawed arms and pincers snapped and tore up the ground. Dirge held his club before him, ready to try and knock away any strike.

"That's a good boy," Celeste shouted. "Keep him there." Her eyes went to Mangin. "Now to deal with you."

Mangin finally realized what suffused the Chaos from Celeste. It was the essence of Dekriot. Dragging her mind out of its malaise, she snarled and threw the dagger. Celeste smiled contemptuously. The vile woman's smile slipped at Mangin guided the dagger with Chaos, causing it to zig and zag to Celeste's obvious surprise. Celeste threw up her hands, and globs of multihued Chaos flew at the blade, but Mangin twisted it around them. Just as the dagger reached Celeste, the woman created a shimmering, jagged shield, knocking the blade aside. Mangin used momentum of the deflection and drove it into the mouth of the grunkin next to Celeste—if she couldn't kill the bitch, she would at least take away one of her pets. The grunkin staggered from the impact and howled as Mangin spun the blade in the thing's guts. The beast shuddered and dropped dead.

Celeste shook and bellowed, "Do you have any idea how hard they are to make?"

Snarling, Mangin scrambled to the forest's edge a dozen feet away. "He can't have me!"

"Yes, he will." Celeste strode forward.

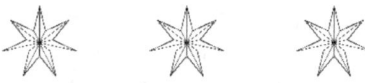

The dread rose until Dirge's stomach roiled. He swatted and stabbed at the beast in front of him with his stick. Needing to protect to Mangin, he dashed to cover her back. When he did, the thing dove for Estonia's body.

"No!" Dirge spun and slammed his shoulder into its side, knocking it away. The grunkin rolled with the blow and pounced, clawing Dirge's chest, and bowling him over. Dirge shoved his club into the beast's mouth, pushing it away. The beast bit the club in two. He grabbed it by the eyestalk and a foreleg. "Please, Great Ukase, help me."

But, he felt nothing; no fire of Truth; no Righteous strength. God had completely turned his back on him again.

Celeste continued her saunter toward Mangin. "You know you want this. Kenja's Chaos shard will only last you so long. You want more than that. You know it."

Mangin slowed her retreat. "No, please no, I don't want it," she said, voice wavering.

Dirge knew she was about to either be turned or die. They were both going to die when Celeste discovered her daughter's corpse. Ruin had come again, and Dirge was powerless to stop it. Not without the Lord Ukase in him. What else was there? Dirge closed his eyes and did the only thing he could think of; something he swore to himself to never do.

He prayed to a different god.

"Please, Daylin. If you can hear me, we need you. *I* need you!"

The sun pendant on this chest grew warm, and the gloom around them faded. The surrounding dead trees cracked, and new, green limbs sprouted forth. Lilac scent filled the air along with roses fresh in bloom. Daylin glided out of the forest as though walking on air, her diaphanous white dress glowing. The grunkin spun to her, but thick vines burst from the ground, wrapping around the monster, and keeping it at bay.

"What have you gotten yourself into now, my sweet

Dirge?" Daylin asked, halfway between him and the house. Her pure golden eyes glowing, she turned to Celeste. "Stop pestering my friends."

Vines burst forth about Celeste, only to wither and die. Celeste smiled. "At last." She lifted her other hand and dozens of glittering crystals shot toward Daylin.

Thick shrubs and creepers grew in front of Daylin in an instant, but some of the crystals made their way through, slicing her in several places.

"That wasn't very nice," Daylin said through gritted teeth. "For that I'll—" Her eyes shot toward Dirge, or more precisely, behind him. "I've got this."

A deep, hollow grunt came from the forest just as the grunkin broke free from its entanglement and lunged at Dirge. The crack of an enormous whip split the air, and a black, limbless tree, half as think as Dirge, plummeted end first from the sky, smashing through the grunkin with a sickening squelch.

Instead of falling over, the tree became sinuous, like an enormous snake's tail, glittering with scales. Terror filled Dirge as his eyes followed the tail, dreading the grunkin attached to it. The thing grew larger, bending and twisting toward the forest, broadening to a scale-covered torso low to the ground and nearly as big as the manor. The thing sported two rear legs tipped with claws the length of Dirge's forearm. Its forelegs were the same, connected to the body with leathery wings like that of a bat. A long neck thicker than two horses was topped with a huge horned head, its mouth filled with dozens of spiked teeth. Golden eyes, filled with a terrorizing intelligence, stared at Celeste.

Celeste stepped back, shaking, and waved her arm to those in the stable yard. Six more grunkin swept from the side of the house, along with dozens of charred men wielding swords and axes. They charged, the grunkin trumpeting and howling.

The massive creature behind Dirge seemed to smile. It opened its mouth, and a guttural, fluttering sound came forth, like the world's largest blacksmith billows drawing in air. The inside of the mouth glowed, and the beast roared, belching out fire hotter than a hundred smithies.

Celeste threw up a shimmering dark shield about herself as the flames rolled along the ground and enveloped her and her host. When the fire abated, only Celeste remained. The rest was nothing but blackened ash. Smoldering, Celeste screamed and raised her rod. Black lightning crackled out the end, stabbing at the monster. The beast fell back into the forest and disappeared.

Celeste shouted in triumph, stabbing her fists into the air. But her smile quickly faded.

Veil strode out of the forest where the monster had disappeared. Garbed in black and face hard as though carved from rock, he walked past Dirge, one hand raised. A beam of light shot from his palm. Dirge had to shy away from the intense brilliance and heat. The beam slammed into Celeste's shield. She shrieked and staggered back, her skin blackening.

"He's taking her," Mangin shouted as she ran up to Dirge. "I can feel it. The Abomination is entering Celeste."

Veil took a step forward, raising his other hand to join the first. Palms cupped, the light increased, now pulsing with bolts amongst the beam. Celeste's shield fell, but she did not. A dark aura grew around her with each pulse of white, and she laughed, the malevolence sending a chill through his bones.

The laughter ended as though hacked by an axe and was replaced by a scream. It reverberated within the dread making Dirge want to shrivel. Black lighting crackled from her rod. Much was dispersed by Veil's white pulsing attack. But some got past. It tore at the ground, running a straight line toward Mangin.

Dirge thew Mangin to the ground and covered her body. He could do nothing to stop Celeste, but he could at least offer some protection to his wife, even if it cost him his life.

Mangin felt the presence of the Abomination flair within Celeste when Veil's attack hit her. She also sensed Celeste's mind dwindle, replaced by a charred blackness that wanted to end everything.

She sprinted up to Dirge, shouting, "He's taking her. I can feel it. The Abomination is entering Celeste."

This isn't good, she thought as Veil increased his attack. It was not going to be enough against Dekriot who grew more and more within Celeste. And thanks to the amount of raw power concentrated about one spot, reality was thinning. Mangin felt Dekriot dig at the membrane between them and the void, striving to rip the world asunder as it had during the Great War centuries before. It seemed Veil did not notice for some reason.

Mangin had to do something, anything to distract Celeste. Pulling even more from the shard, she tried to bore through Celeste's shield to reach her mind, but her attacks were rebuffed. Every attempt slipped away, deflected by Dekriot's presence. She knew what she had to do but was loathed to do so. It was what the demon wanted. There was no choice.

She delved deep into the shard, seeking the black filaments within, the power of Dekriot, and plucked at them. Each touch, no matter how gentle or quick, left their mark on her soul. The Abomination seeped into her, strand by strand as she spun the demon's power into her probe. When ready, Mangin stabbed it at Celeste's shield. It bored through and Mangin made contact.

"What is this?" Celeste said with her mind. "You think you can dominate me? The Master protects me! When I am done, I will give you to my daughter as another plaything. I know you genuinely care about Dirge; it will be glorious when you watch him grovel and beg for Dahlia's attention."

"The dead don't care about attention," Mangin replied.

"Don't try to play me for a fool."

Mangin opened her mind, showing Celeste the memory of Dahlia's blackened corpse on the floor of her bedroom. "As I said, the dead do not care."

Celeste screamed in rage, her force shield growing erratic from the lack of concentration as she lashed out with black lightning. Mangin had her opening. Now all she had to do was break Celeste's mind and it would be over.

Dirge tackled her, driving her to the ground and smothering her body. She couldn't breathe as Celeste's lightning drove toward them. In the back of her mind, she hears the distant chuckle of Dekriot and shivers, feeling soiled

Dirge rolled them away and the bolts tore the earth where they had been. He had saved her, but for now long? Prone, they were not easy targets.

More lianas and trees grew up and wrapped around Celeste only to wither and burn. Then, one thick, black vine the size of Dirge's leg detached from the house. It wavered a moment, as though waiting for something, and then slammed into the back of Celeste's skull. She shuddered and let loose an unearthly shriek as black fungus and lichen burst from her eyes and ears. She puffed up as though being filled with air. Creepers snapped out of her arms, hands, and chest. Celeste's corpse dropped to the ground, a smoldering ruin.

Chapter 38

Guardian

Daylin glared at Veil. "See? I told you I could handle it."

Veil took a deep breath and shook himself as though dispersing rainwater. "With simple people, yes, my love, you can. But you had no good strategy with the likes of her. The Abomination's presence was too strong. She might have killed you." He stepped close and caressed her frowning face. "Aelaz gave you the domain of life. You needn't sully yourself with killing. We've talked about this."

"*You* keep talking about it. All I'm saying is I'm not some helpless little girl. I can do this." When Veil reached for the cut on her neck, she pulled away. "It's nothing. I'm fine." The wound closed. "Honestly, I don't even know why you came after all your, 'you will go to his aid alone' talk."

"Not with the Abomination involved." Veil glanced at Dirge. "Though I fear they my yet be repercussions."

Mangin elbowed Dirge. "Get off me, oaf." She stood and

brushed off her dress. "Unless your plan was to have sex. If that is case, I'm not against having spectators." She grinned at Daylin and Veil. "Especially if it's these two."

Dirge jumped to his feet and puffed his chest. "I was not—" He cut short when she laughed. Rolling his eyes, he bowed to the two gods. "I thank you. I am in your debt."

Daylin waved her hand. "Oh, pish posh."

"Besides," Veil added, "I think Ukase might take offense to that thought." He twisted his mouth. "He's always been an overly officious ass."

Swallowing with a nod, Dirge asked Veil, "What was that … creature you showed up as? I'll admit I wanted to soil myself I was so afraid."

Veil's face firmed. "It was the form of a beast that has returned to the world. With Chaos gone and the Elementals returning, they have awoken from their slumber. Tread lightly with them—I mimicked a small one."

"What are they called?"

Veil paused. "Dragons."

Mangin swatted at Dirge. "Don't worry, I read all about them at the Citadel. I'll fill you in when we get home."

Dirge shook from the memory of the tremendous beast, trying to contemplate them ravaging the world in large numbers. He shook himself and replied to Mangin, "We're not going home. We're going to The Seat of Truth in Gate Hall. I must present myself to the Magnus."

"What are you talking about?" Mangin asked. "You still want to go through with this trial by combat?"

"What I want is irrelevant. God demands it of me."

"You two are adorable." Daylin's laugh filled the air with joy, and nearby songbirds joined in. "Congratulations on your nuptials. I hope your first night was everything you'd hoped for."

Chuckling, Mangin replied, "Well, he did try his best. But he's getting better every time."

Dirge's cheeks heated and he couldn't meet anyone's eyes. "Must you be so crass in public?"

Mangin rolled her eyes. "This is hardly public. Besides, they're practically family. Or a good sight better, considering what we just went through."

Dirge wanted to retort but couldn't. Mangin was right, his

family life was hardly enviable. At the age of four, Dirge had discovered his mother's body in an alley. His father, who helped raise him, only admitted so well after Dirge had grown and after the debacle that was Dirge's failed religious revolution. Even then Talic only did so via a letter, not to his face. And worst of all, his daughter was a manipulative, mind-twisting monster who thought only of herself. In the end, Dirge had only one reply, "Mangin is a … dutiful wife."

Mangin huffed. "Dutiful?" She then swatted him on the shoulder.

Daylin smirked at Veil. "I told you they'd make a fun couple."

Her face then darkened, and she turned to the manor house. "As for this place …" She shook, her voice filled with rage. "I never wanted to see it again." Her glare moved to Celeste's ravaged carcass. "She killed Jasper, the only friend I ever had here. She doesn't deserve rebirth."

"The Soul Stone will cleanse her spirit," Veil said. "What remains of it. I fear Dekriot consumed most of her."

Celeste's body twitched. It shook and roiled, as more fungus, mold, and lichen grew and consumed the remains.

"There," Daylin said, "put to use in one good way, at least. Now, for the house."

The ground shook as trees, moss, and earth-covered vines grew and surrounded the house until they enveloped it. Windows shattered and beams cracked as the mass of vegetation clamped down. Then the earth split open, swallowing the entire mass. When it was done, nothing remained but a grass-covered glade.

Daylin glared at Veil as though part of that was his doing. He shrugged. "Don't be angry. It seems fitting this way, it's now a place for growth and beauty."

Laughing, Daylin kissed him hard. "Have I told you lately how much I love you?"

Mangin eased forward. "Any chance I can join in?"

Dirge spun to her. "Mangin!"

"What?" Mangin shrugged. "I miss them, and it was fun." She peered at him mischievously. "If you ask nicely enough, they might let you join, too."

Anger and disgust—mixed with a modicum of shame—filled Dirge as he glowered at his wife.

His wife …

Hoping beyond hope, he went and gingerly picked up Estonia's body, holding it out to Daylin. "You are an extension of Aelaz. Is there any chance to bring her— *him* back?"

Gliding over, Daylin placed a hand on Estonia's forehead. She frowned. "I'm sorry, Dirge. The soul has gone." She closed her eyes and tilted her head as though listening, and then smiled. "But Aza'zel says it will wait for you. You can enter the Stone together. Some souls are bound. They dance in the Stone together until they are reborn. Always with a chance of being together again in life." She cupped Dirge's cheek. "You *will* see your wife again, one day."

While Dirge tried to comprehend and compartmentalize what she told him, Veil pulled Mangin aside.

"I have something for you, if you would take it." He placed a gold ring in her palm, thin and twisted as though made of a single strand of hair. "I am not omnipotent. Plus, I have restraints placed upon me by Aelaz. I am to protect his world from all outside forces. I cannot interfere in mortal lives except where the Abomination is involved. Dekriot is very difficult to detect. That is where you, and others like you, come in. With this ring, I can monitor the world around you. It also contains a small tap into my power."

She put it on and closed her eyes with a blissful smile.

"It is for peril only," Veil cautioned. "Do *not* abuse it."

Her grin turned mischievous. "I wouldn't think of it."

"You are now a Guardian, a protector of the world."

"You are not alone in this," Daylin said. "There are others. Nalan, for instance."

Veil rolled his eyes. "Let's not give out all the others, shall we? No need for them to go and seek each other out. It would only go to their heads." He turned back to Dirge and Mangin. "I will take you to the outskirts of Conover. I believe the Seekers are waiting there for you."

"How do you know that?" Mangin asked. "You said you weren't all knowing."

Veil smiled.

When the shimmering, spherical gateway closed, Raaz poked his head around the bole of a long dead tree across the glade, further blackened by Veil's dragon-breath. The flames had not touched him being half Void-dragon. He scampered over and gathered up the shards Celeste had flung at his master's greatest prize, noting the small chips missing from some of them. He took them to a wagon hidden deep in the woods, not far from the only road to what used to be the manor house. Jumping in the back of the wagon, he opened one of three crates. A three-inch layer of Void-blessed padding lined the crate to hide its contents: Chaos shards. Nearly a hundred filled the crate with little room to spare. The other two were packed full.

Raaz then hopped up next to the driver, who had a pink star on the side of their neck. "Time to go north," Raaz said. "There are many there who have need of our master's touch." He hissed a laugh. "Even if they don't know it."

Chapter 39

A Pondering Gaze

Stepping out of the gateway, Dirge's boots crunched on dry grass and dirt of a forest clearing roughly a hundred paces across. He felt like he'd been there before. Only this time his burden was physical as well as spiritual. Estonia's body felt like the weight of the world, yet Dirge's own heart felt heavier.

Mangin stepped out next to him, holding the odd stretcher of vines and limbs made by Daylin. Other than the usual side supports, it had four rear-facing bowed branches, each twice the thickness of Dirge's thumbs. When Mangin put it on the ground, the litter's bed sat nearly waist high.

Dirge laid Estonia on the stretcher, gently tying him in place, and turned to Mangin. "You don't have to follow me. Thanks to the legs, I can drag it myself."

"I'm coming with you."

"They will judge you." Dirge stroked her cheek. "I," his eyes flashed to Estonia's body, "care about you. I cannot shield you from their zeal. You know what will happen."

Mangin playfully bit at his hand. "I'm pretty fierce myself, you know." She then went to the back of the stretcher. "You're not scaring me off that easily. Besides, who else is going to look after you? All right now, get off your lazy ass and to the other end of this thing. I'm not pushing him all the way there."

He couldn't help but admire Mangin's courage. "You've a warrior's heart."

"Quit trying to flatter me. I know you only want me for my body. Go on, pick it up. I want to get there before sundown. I'm starving."

They crossed the opening toward the road traffic visible from a short trail on the far side. The scent of fresh water and fish mixed with subtropical birdsong from the canopy. Dirge decided the space must be used by caravans that wouldn't make it to Conover before they closed its gates at sunset.

It took less than an hour to reach the city, for which Dirge was thankful—his arms ached. He set his end down and approached the nearest gate-guard in hard leather armor and holding a poleaxe. "I am Righteous-Captain Dirge Malik. Please inform the Seekers I am here with my wife and the body of Righteous-Warrior Estonia Den. We require an escort."

The guard looked them over for a moment, then clicked his heels and nodded toward the gatehouse where a young man in livery dashed off into the city. The guard then addressed Dirge, "You can rest at the gatehouse; there's water."

Reaching the gate, Dirge accepted a tin cup from the rain barrel and gulped half of it down. It seemed like days since his last, and the water soothed his parched throat. Handing the cup to Mangin, who accepted it with a grimace, he then pulled out a piece of hard sausage from his pouch and held it out to her.

She eyed him, then his pouch. "No, thank you. I prefer my food not taste of sweaty leather."

"You'd better get used to it if you want to join me on a campaign."

"What are you talking about?"

"Before we left the Corners, Kirkadite mentioned a move into the former Lands of the Dead. I'm willing to bet they'll want me along after I prove my innocence before the Magnus."

"But …" She compressed her lips and glanced at the men in

the guardhouse. "Foregoing *my* probable future, you said women weren't allowed on campaigns."

"I said you weren't allowed on patrol. This will be completely different. If it's anything like my time with the Prophet, women will act as camp followers and messengers. You'll act as my aid. And when we're not in battle," he glanced at Estonia, anger roiling his gut, "I'll make sure you'll always be at my side where it's safe."

She took another sip. "You do have a point. Someone needs to keep you safe."

The guards guffawed.

Kirkadite arrived a short time later with a full squad of Militants in tow along with the local Righteous-Warrior and took them into custody. The High-Seeker's head was bound in wrapping and his left arm was in a sling. They headed for the bastion with Dirge in manacles at their center next to the Warrior. Mangin was somewhere in back.

"Why hasn't Kirkadite sought healing?" Dirge asked the Righteous-Warrior.

"We've no immaculates on Conover. And he didn't want to wait for one to arrive from Dane Hook."

Once in the bastion, Dirge and Mangin were taken to a cell while the ship bound for the Corners was loaded with provisions. They were there only an hour when Kirkadite came with Militants who took Mangin.

High-Seeker confronted Dirge, "Before I put her to the question, I will have the truth from you. What happened?"

Dirge told him about being taken to the mansion. About Celeste, Dahlia, and Glory. "I don't remember much after that. Not clearly. I was caged in my own mind. It was like a shadowed nightmare."

Kirkadite smiled. "You have a daughter begotten by a priestess of Chaos. I think the Magnus will find that quite interesting." He paused, tilting his head. "Have you nothing to say?"

"I will speak of it at my trial before the Magnus."

"Of course, of course. In the meantime, you will come with me. I want you to be there when I put your wife to the question."

Dirge stood, shaking from his desire to throttle the pompous ass as the remaining Militants took position around him.

They took Dirge to a brightly lit room with only a single chair in the middle, then through a doorway on the left covered in a beaded curtain. The room was dark with a row of seven chairs at the back, three of which were taken: one by a Truth-Seeker, one by the local Veridical, and the centermost by the Consul Falmer, head of the ecclesiastical branch in the South.

Dirge put a fist to his chest and bowed his head. "Consul Falmer."

"Dirge," the man intoned. "You will sit next to me. Once Chancellor Haddock arrives, we will send for the Lady Malik."

Dirge sat, back rigid, awaiting whatever happened. He worried about Mangin. She had not told him much about what happened to her, aside from killing the two corrupted. And knowing Mangin, he had much to worry about.

Several minutes passed before a gaunt, stooped man with salt and pepper hair shuffled in. "My apologies, Consul. I was irrevocably detained."

The consul nodded and then addressed the acolyte by the door, "Bring in the accused."

Mangin glided in, head high like a queen. It was enough to make Dirge wince. But once she took her seat facing the beaded doorway, she lowered her head in proper humility. He couldn't decide if it was any better. She was far from modest, but she had been humbled some over the past few years.

Kirkadite marched through the door and stood over her, his head high and sneering. She looked up at him—with his tufts of black hair sticking out in several places—and was obviously fighting not to smile.

"Do you find something funny, goodly-wife Malik?"

Her face cleared. "I find nothing about this funny, High-Seeker Kirkadite."

"What happened after the grunkin attacked the caravan and Righteous-Warrior Den absconded with you?"

"Absconded?"

"You were under our custody and he took you. If he had survived, he would have been flogged and Purified!"

"He did what he thought was right to save Dirge!"

A sneer crept across Kirkadite's face. "Is that contempt I hear? Disrespect of a member of the clergy is punished by seven months in the work camps, *after* you've been properly branded and had your tongue removed."

She held her head high. "I have no less respect for you now than the day we met, High-Seeker. I'm merely saying that Righteous-Warrior Estonia Den did what he thought was right to save my husband, a man who is still Righteous-Captain, even though he has been stripped of his power pending trial. When he is found innocent, all his rights and privileges will be returned. Am I right, High-Seeker?"

Kirkadite trembled. "That is—" He visibly took hold of himself. "I ask you again, goodly-wife Malik, what happened after the battle and the caravan?"

She told a story of heroism, of Estonia fighting his way through scores of charred only to succumb in the end. Dirge wanted to flail himself when she got to his arrival, of how she thought he was saving them, but instead dragged her away to bondage.

"His mind had been enslaved by a young woman named Glory, the granddaughter of a former priest of Chaos who resided there. Glory's powers of the mind are unmatched. She did the same to me a short time later. I don't remember much after that."

"A priestess of Chaos, you say? What does that matter now that the devil Edis is gone?"

"I don't know for sure. It may have something to do with Dekriot. She was in league with the Abomination. They all were."

Kirkadite rolled his eyes. "Dekriot is a myth."

Mangin leaned forward, eyes fervent. "He is real."

"There has been no proof of his existence."

"If you cannot believe your senses, then I cannot help you."

Sneering, Kirkadite asked, "How did you escape?"

"Glory released me. She said she wanted to escape herself and used us as a distraction."

"What happened then?"

She told him all of it, about finding Estonia in the basement and escaping through the cellar door into the woods. About Daylin and Veil saving them; two gods killing Celeste and banishing the Abomination within her.

"Two Principles of Ukase arrive just in the nick of time. That's quite a tale." Kirkadite stepped forward. "But you are holding back. I will find the truth. If you will not tell me, then I will scour your soul for it."

Dirge knew she was holding back. She had freed him from his mind-cage but didn't say how. What else was she hiding? The Searching Touch was exceedingly painful, it raked the mind and soul, seeking what was hidden. Some failed to live through it. He sent out a silent prayer that she not suffer.

The High-Seeker grabbed Mangin's head with his good hand and he concentrated. And nothing happened. No reeling, no seething, not even a twitch. He stepped back, eyes wide. "What witchery is this? What did you do, Edis lover?"

"I see no guilt." The consul stood and walked into the room. "If the touch cannot find anything, she must be innocent."

As Kirkadite stepped back, obviously baffled, Consul Fulmer continued, "There can be no doubt depravity took place there, but perhaps as she was made a *mind-slave*, as she puts it, she consciously broke no law against God? It is something I will have to confer with the High-Consul about. It will likely go before the Magnus."

"I-I see your point," Kirkadite replied, visibly shaken. "Yes, that must be it. That means there must be sinners amongst us who are innocent, yet still doing evil deeds because they are puppets of evil. And we are somehow blind to it." He shuddered. "What a terrifying thought."

The consul nodded. "But, as she let it happen in the first place, she is guilty of Disobedience in the eyes of God. She will go to the Chastenary when we reach Cross Corners. I'm sure the Immaculates will agree. The delinquent crime will be apparent by all once the Magnus rules."

Dirge was aghast. It had to be true, they were blind to Dekriot. And yet, the succubus, Follett, Dirge felt her. It was how he saved Mangin in time. He would bring it up with the Magnus at his trial.

Fulmer paused and stepped forward. "What is that ring. It possesses power, I can feel it."

She placed a hand on the ring. "Veil gave it to me. His mandate is to find and destroy the Abomination. I am to help him."

The consul's eyes went wide. "A gift from a Principle of Ukase. You are truly blessed, goodly-wife Malik. You are doing

God's work. He will help see you though." He bowed his head to Mangin.

At that moment, Dirge knew his life just grew far more complicated.

Mangin lay in the small bunk, Dirge curled up next to her with his arm draped across her stomach snoring lightly. The gentle swaying of the ship tried to lull her to sleep. It didn't work. Like their trip south, their cabin was befitting someone of Dirge's stature; in this case little more than a cell: small, cramped, and windowless. The truth was, she expected something far smaller. She was surprised to be alive at all.

During the entire inquisition by Kirkadite, she'd been petrified, certain he sensed the truth, that she has wielding Chaos, and would condemn her to death. She had force herself to stillness, lest she would have broken down and cried, if not to flee, all together. A warrior's heart, indeed. What Mangin couldn't understand was how none of them could see she'd used the Lord's Breath of her own volition—let along having sex with Glory. She had kept him out of her mind, letting him see what she wanted. But how?

She fingered the gold ring from Veil on her right index finger. As it came from Him, a *Principle of Ukase*—which Mangin nearly laughed out loud when hearing—she was now doing the Lord Ukase's work. Was the ring shielding her? Or was it something else?

She touched her chest, just above her breasts. The crystal was still there, but even she couldn't feel it.

Her hand moved to her belly. She had asked Dirge to make love to her the first night aboard, and every night since. She had no conceptive concoction. *Will it quicken?* she wondered. *Will I become with child?*

Her gaze went to the ceiling of the cabin.

Or was I already?

Chapter 40

Returning Home

The trip to Gate Hall took three times longer than the one going south. To Dirge, it seemed to take even longer. They treated him with respect, yet the only person who would talk to him was Mangin, and after a while that became arduous. Halfway home she grew ill, sicking up every morning and then off and on throughout the day. Dirge grew concerned when she didn't get better. She had difficulty keeping down food, when she even ate at all, sometimes reaching for the bucket upon just smelling food. Her mood grew as foul as her stomach, but thankfully she only vented her rage on him, keeping a tight lip when anyone came with food, or drink, or to exchange their chamber pot and Mangin's bucket. Thankfully, her illness abated shortly after they passed Cross Corners. Unfortunately, her mood swings didn't fade with it.

Upon reaching Gate Hall, Kirkadite opened their door with a pair of militants behind him holding shackles. "The time of your judgement is at hand," he said, the hint of a sneer on his lips. Hatred filled his eyes when they went to Mangin. "If only you both received the same sentence." He then turned to the militants. "Shackle them and do it quickly. We need to get to the Axiom with all haste."

"What is the Axiom?" Dirge asked, holding out his wrists for the manacles.

"It is where the magnus took up residence. The initial plan by Magnus Donavan was to demolish it for something more fitting. But the keep, outer walls and all, seemed to … How did the Grand-Seeker put it? Resist. Yes, he said the building resisted demolition. Magnus Donavan determined that God had put forth his presence on the structure."

Dirge felt a pang of doubt. The building must have already been ensconced with spells and wards. How else could it have survived over five-hundred years of Chaos? With a scowl, he crushed his momentary skepticism.

Upon reached the deck, Dirge shivered. The wind had teeth, its bitter cold biting deep, yet the ground was free of snow. Had he really grown so used to the ever-present heat of the South? He shrugged off the thought as well as the cold. Neither mattered. The one hundred-foot tall, gray-stone walls of the Axiom loomed only a few hundred paces away. They marched Dirge and Mangin through the open gates and into the courtyard. Construction workers and stone blocks took up half the space, with ramps to the top of the massive keep.

"Are they making repairs?" Dirge asked.

Kirkadite kept his head forward, a measured stride ahead of Dirge. "They are constructing the Axiom-Suprema to honor God, a top floor that will be the permanent residence for the magnus, to raise him above the mundane and closer to God."

A dozen paces from the keep, the thick, iron-bound double doors opened, and Immaculate Clara stepped out, her more-gray-than-black hair in its ever-present bun. Kirkadite spoke to her, "Ah, good. Immaculate, I relinquish the Lady Malik into your custody."

Clara nodded to Kirkadite, then looked to the militant escorting Mangin. "You may remove the restraints. She is only Delinquent in the eyes of God."

As the militant removed Mangin's manacles, the immaculate turned to Dirge. "Have strength, Righteous-Captain. So long as your faith has not faltered, I know you will prevail."

Kirkadite bristled. "You speak above your station. You cannot know the will of God."

"I have faith," Clara replied, not taking her eyes off Dirge. She then smiled softly, like a mother to a chastised child. "I have known Righteous-Captain Dirge for a very long time."

"How is that possible?" Dirge asked. And yet, there was always something familiar about her. "When did we ..." Memories popped in his head as though bubbling up from the mental chamber he had been trapped in. "You came to see the Troupe perform here. You passed by me while I guarded the entry fee box."

"Yes, there was that. It had been so long since I'd seen you last. Magnus Malik said I could not interact with you for fear of somehow altering the Lord's plan, but he allowed me a look, to see the young man who'd saved my life, now grown into a man."

"Tuilar. You came with the magnus from Tuilar." Dirge shook his head. "I hardly saved you. The Prophet did that when he bade Magnus Malik to come here."

"That's not when I was saved." A hint of sadness and pain glinted in her eyes. "I was friends with your mother; we were alike in *many* ways. I was a lost soul for quite a while. Then, one evening, you came rushing into Hoke's smoke hall all dressed in black and out to kill."

Dirge's mind rushed back, back to the night he had fulfilled the contract on Jacob's family ...

"You could have killed me that night for interfering in your hunt. But you didn't."

... an emaciated, naked woman with lanky black hair stepping into the hall. Her lips and fingers stained black, she begged him for coin, saying she'd do anything ...

Immaculate Clara smiled with a sigh, obviously seeing the recognition in Dirge's eyes. "I felt it in you then, a power that touched my soul. At first, I thought you a devil spat up from the abyss. I was so afraid I didn't touch the poppy for months. But, as always, it pulls you back. Then the Prophet arrived, and I saw you standing at his side. I knew what I had to do. I pledged myself to God. The Prophet told me that God would forgive my sins, but I had to forsake all Earthly pleasures and relations. It was an easy choice."

Mangin spoke up, her voice filled with shock, "You were a ..." She faltered and lowered her gaze.

"I was a whore," the immaculate replied. "But the Lord forgives all who take Him into their hearts. Things change. As well you know." She glanced at Mangin's midsection. "How far along are you?"

Dirge stared at Mangin, his world reeling as she touched her stomach, replying, "At least two months."

"We will furlough you sentence then until after you have the child. We don't want to take the chance of anything harming it." She took Mangin gently by the arm. "Come along now. Do not worry about your Lord Husband. The Lord will wash him of any sins and return him to us, a True Righteous man of God."

Dirge watched them go, his mind abuzz. He was going to be a father ... again. Only this time, it would be raised in the protective arms of God. He thought back to the night Lynette told him she was with child. The pain once again flared to life, but it quickly abated. It was as though she reached out from Aza'zel's realm and caressed his soul, telling him it would be okay.

Kirkadite broke the reprieve. "The immaculate's faith in you is ill placed, and ill deserved. I have faith that God will smite you for your past, your unredeemable sins."

Standing tall, Dirge replied, "We shall see. Lead on, my wife and child will have need of me."

Their boots echoed down the halls as they zig-zagged their way to the center of the Axiom. People bustled about, men of all three branches of the True along with common servants going about their daily lives. Lamps, hanging every ten feet down the fifteen-foot wide, twelve-foot high hall shone off the white marble walls making it as bright as day. The smell of incense and lamp oil filled the air. But it all rolled off Dirge without notice, his mind still reeling from the immaculate's words.

They stopped before a pair of blood-red doors leading to what used to be the library, and to the private quarters of the magnus beyond. Kirkadite intoned, "I bring forth one who requires correction or purging from the Grand-Seeker."

Dirge was about to demand to be brought to the magnus but held his tongue. It made sense. He was, after all, demanding the truth be known. That fell on the Truth-Seekers.

The door opened and they took him to the left, the seeker half of the circular chamber surrounding the magnus' residence. In the center of the space, Grand-Seeker Torq stood upon a raised dais. Head shaved, all except a ring of hair just above the ears, Torq's hard, unfeeling eyes regarded the newcomers. His heavy jowls and blotchy complexion were offset by a large, flat nose jutting out of his face like a stone monument. In short, Nardo Torq was nothing like what Dirge had expected. Especially since even on the raised platform the man was still stood several inches below Dirge.

"The accused will approach," the man said, his voice quick and crisp as a whip. "Now kneel and know the True touch of God."

Dirge marched up to the Grand-Seeker, meeting him eye-to-eye. Then lowered his head in reverence to the position and knelt. "I seek justice and judgement."

When Torq laid hands on Dirge's shoulders, fire seared his mind and spirit. It dug out every truth, every lamented sin Dirge had ever performed. The murders demanded by Jacob. The fornication with women of the night. Debasing himself with a priestess of Chaos. Doubting the will of the Lord.

The crimes were mountainous, climbing higher and higher until he feared to be crushed from existence. And then the sins faded away like a petal in a gale. All but the worst. He had doubted his faith in God. That truth scoured his being. He shrieked and thrashed in the Truth-Seeker's grasp, knowing his soul was being consumed by the fires of God. His shirt started to smolder on his chest, just below the shoulders. It burst into flames and flashed out, leaving only ash. The brands of Ukase glowed red as though they were hot irons fresh from the forge.

Dirge opened his eyes, cleansed of his sins. The words God had spoken to him nearly two years before echoed in his head, *"YOU HAVE MUCH MORE WORK TO DO."*

Epilogue

In the Dark

Kellen entered the inn. It was quite pleasant if a bit tame. Half the tables were full, there was no screaming, a minstrel played at the back, and the smell of good food permeated the place. It was not what he'd expected.

An older woman with wiry, red hair approached. "Welcome to the Angelic. My name is Katlyn, the owner. How may I help you?"

He eyed his surrounding, felling exposed with only a sword and no bodyguards. Was this all a trap of some kind? It couldn't be this simple. "I … I've been told to ask for a man named Talic."

"Certainly. If you would follow me." She headed to stairs between the kitchen and the bar without looking back.

Kellen's anxiety stepped up a notch. He followed her up and to a door on the second floor, where she stopped and knocked.

"Talic, someone to see you." Katlyn nodded to Kellen and left.

Kellen watched her go, then jumped when a voice spoke behind him.

"I am Talic. How may I be of assistance?" The man was tall and dark skinned, with a strong jaw and deep brown eyes.

There was something familiar about the assassin, but Kellen couldn't put a finger in it. "My name is Kellen. I was told to come to you for things that need … removing."

"Euphemisms, Mister Kellen? They are a bit lowly for someone of your economic and political stature. Don't you think?" He stepped aside and swung his arm, indicating Kellen should enter.

Kellen entered but stopped next to the door. "I am here about a contract."

"People like you usually are. I'm impressed you came here yourself. You usually send lackeys."

Kellen's brows burrowed. "I'm tired of being told no."

The corner of Talic's mouth tweaked. "And you expect to hear different from my face?"

"I do." After several moments passed, Kellen grew angry. "As I said, I'm here about a—"

Talic cut him off, "You have something that belongs to me."

Kellen pulled his head back. "What are you talking about?"

Talic pointed to the blade as Kellen's hip. "You hold what does not belong to you."

"This is mine!" Kellen's hand grasped the hilt of his prize. "This and what comes with it."

"That is the sword of the High Slayer," Talic said. "Are you he?"

"The what?" Kellen's jaw dropped and his mind whirled. "Then how did a scum like Dirge get his hands on it?"

"That is not of your concern."

Rage flooded Kellen; after years of being thwarted he would not be denied. Calming himself, he eased the sword and scabbard from his belt. "As a sign of good faith, I now return to you what was yours."

"I thank you." Talic drew the bade and gazed at Kellen.

A coldness filled the room along with an odd smell, like that of a freshly opened tomb. "What are you doing?" Kellen asked. "Has the God of Death demanded my head now?"

"If Aza'zel wished your soul to return to the Stone you would not see me coming."

"Then what are you doing?"

"This is about Dirge."

Kellen stiffened his back "It is. But you and your God rejected my contract multiple times in the past. Is this some kind of ultimate no?"

Talic's eyes burrowed into Kellen. "Are you still seeking Dirge's life?"

"Of course I am. He's a thief and murderer—both him and his friend."

"Jacob embraced Death long ago. It was Dirge that sent him to my master."

Kellen scoffed "Figures. Murdering thieves often do each other in. Just more proof that Dirge needs to die."

"Would it change your opinion if you knew he killed Jacob to save the life of a child?"

"His motives don't matter to me. He's a murderer and deserves death. So, do you now accept my contract?" He stared at Talic, practically daring the man to deny him. That's when it hit him. The man's mouth, the structure of the head, the way he held himself, even the shape of the eyes looked like and older version of Dirge. Kellen suppressed the urge to swallow.

Talic waited several moments before replying. "You are such a petty man, Mister Kellen. The reign of Chaos was a time of death and destruction. And now Ukase wishes to continue that. It's a sad world in which we live."

"Is that a n—"

Talic sheathed the blade and bowed. "My master, Aza'zel, will now accept the contract, Mister Kellen. And he has charged me to fulfill it as I wish. A life will be taken from this. Just know, Mister Kellen, that your time will come as well one day. Pray that the person who wishes it has less malice."

Dahlia sat cross-legged on the floor of the temple to Dekriot, her eyes glowing in the blackness. When she had pulled power through the orb, Dekriot burned away the toxins in her brain, leaving holes behind. Safe underground, she had time to read Celeste's books and enjoy herself with the animated corpses left behind—Dekriot didn't want her to be alone. She felt comfortable there, with food and drink and all the entertainment one could wish for.

Lightning crackled between her fingers and the chaos orb as she caressed it in her lap, illuminating the charred cracks crisscrossing her face. She thought of Dirge and smiled. When the time was right, she would take back what was hers.

To be continued in
Madness in a Land Out of Time

Glossary

Adel Floweret {a-Dell} – The former lover of Mangin Karados

Amurru – The God of the Earth.

Ardentia – The new country of the followers of Ukase.

Aza'zel {a-Za-Zeel} – The God of Death. /Brother to Aelaz.

Aelaz {A-Laz} – The God of Life. Sister to Aza'zel.

Axiom, the – The seat of the Magnus in Gate Hall; formerly called the Citadel.

Bastion – A fortified encampments for the missionaries for Ukase.

Betal {Be-Tal} – A former priest of Chaos, now going by the name **Veil**.

Brotherhood of Assassins – Assassins and worshipers of Aza'zel.

Calidos Flint – Priest of Chaos from the Southern Region.

Celeste – A former Chaos priest and mother to Dahlia.

Channeling – To manipulate the power/essence of one's god.

Charred, the (Void men) – People who have touched Dekriot and had their souls devoured. Their skin is charred black and cracked, with red, pus filled flesh in the cracks. Their eyes are dead-black, including the sclera.

Chastenary, the – A religious reserve to Ukase run by the Immaculate. They take in "unruly women" for correction, contemplation, and purification.

Council of Taneer – Godlike individuals who oversee the city of Taneer and The Great Games.

Dahlia – A former priest of Chaos who bedded Dirge years before. Daughter of Celeste and Ruddick.

Daylin Dragonvein {Day-lyn} – Former animal telepath, empath, and dog trainer for the Travelers.

Dekriot {Dek-rIot} (AKA The Abomination) – God of the Abyss, Desolation, and Destruction.

Dirge Malik – Sword master, former Travelers lead guardsman, and Righteous-Captain of Ukase.

Durgia – Large empire from before the War of the Gods; formerly known as the Lands of the Dead.

Edis – the Lord God of Chaos.

Ellis Concord – Late head of Concord's Grand Traveling show.

Erin Cruchfield – Cool Winds Head of militia and commander of the caravan to Gate Hall.

Estonia Den – Dirge's fawning squire.

Evram Kirkadite – A Truth-Seeker a fast riser in the Seekers for showing his tenacity in the name of God.

Follett Dinar – A former priest of Chaos.

Great Soul Stone, the – The crystal latus where all souls derive before life and return to after death; nestled in the roots of The True Tree.

Grunkin (AKA Chaos Beast) – A creature mutated by the Lord of Chaos.

Gunther Karados {Gun-ther Care-a-dose} – Mangin's father. Head Priest at Gate Hall.

Heartless, Lord (AKA Twitch) – The Champion of the Lord of Chaos and master of the world during the reign of the God of Chaos.

Immaculate – Un-wed women who give themselves over to Ukase.

Kellen – The Master of Coin for the city of Selos and owner of a large trading conglomerate.

Life-spark – The essence of life.

Lord's Breath, the – The essence of the Lord of Chaos.

Lynette Malik – The late wife of Dirge.

Magnus – Head of the Truth of Ukase, the Right Hand of God, and His Voice in the world.

Magnus Malik (Duncan) – Lynette's father, Dirge's Father-in-law, Magnus of the Truth of Ukase.

Mangin Karados {Man-jin Care-a-dose} – Chaos priest. Life-long friend of Betal. Friend and one-time lover to Daylin Dragonvein.

Mother, the – The first. The creator of life and the multiverse. The creator of the Great Soul Stone.

Raaz – Half Demon lackey of Dekriot.

Reach, the – A region in the central part of the content of Bindane, just south of the Lands of the Dead.

Ruddick {Roodick} – Chaos priest who experimented on Dalyn when she was a child.

Sanctum – The temple to Ukase.

South, the – A region in the southern-central portion of the content of Bindane.

Talic Sern – High Slayer of The Brotherhood of Assassins and Dirge's father.

Taneer (the Eternal City) – The city at the center of, and yet outside of, the matrix of the multiverse.

Travelers – A traveling group of entertainers.

The True/Truth – Faithful members of the church of Ukase.

True Tree, the – See Mother, The.

Ukase {oo-case} – The Lord God of Order.

Veil – Shape-shifting god and protector of the mortal world. Formerly known as **Betal**, and before that, **Gabriel**, Arbiter and Champion of the Council of Taneer.

Veridical – A local pastor to the True.

War of the Gods (the Great Game) – A clash between the champions of the gods. The winning god rules the world for 500 years.

Hierarchy of the Truth
(The church of Ukase)

Magnus: The head of the Truth and the only one to commune with Ukase. (Wears pure white robes trimmed in black and red, with a tall, diamond-shaped hat, also trimmed in black and red)

- **Grand-Consul Legate**: The representative and Head Grand-Consul to the Magnus. (Dress in white robes, with a black Star of Ukase, outlined in red)
  - The **Immaculate**: Women who've given themselves to God and run the Chastenary. (Same dress)

- **Grand-Righteous Legate**: The representative and Head Grand-Righteous to the Magnus) (Dress in black surcoats over shining steel armor, with a red Star of Ukase, outlined in white)

- **Grand-Seeker Legate**: The representative and Head Grand-Seeker to the Magnus) (Dress in red uniforms, with a white Star of Ukase, outlined in black)

Ecclesiastical: Governing branch.
(Dress in white robes, with a black Star outlined in red)
- **Grand-Consul:** Head priest of a continent
  - **High-Consul**: Head priest of a country
    - **Consul**: Head priest of a region
      - **Veridical:** Local priest
        - **Acolyte**: Veridical in training
          - **Head Adherent-Militant**: local leader of town/city guard
            - **Adherent-Militant**: town/city guard

Militant: Military branch.

(Dress in black surcoats over shining steel armor, with a red Star outlined in white)

- **Grand-Righteous**: Head militant-priest of a continent
  - ○ **Arch-Righteous**: Head militant-priest of a country
    (Star on each upper chest & below throat)
    - ▪ **Righteous-Captain**: Head militant-priest of a region (Star on each upper chest)
      - • **Righteous-Warrior**: Militant-priest (Star on left upper chest)
        - ○ **Squire**: Militant-priest in training-to Righteous-Captains
          - ▪ **Head Righteous-Militant**: Squad Leader
            - • **Righteous-Militant**: soldiers

Seeker: Purifying branch. (Dress in red uniforms, with a white Star outlined in black)

- **Grand-Seeker**: Head of the inquisition
  - ○ **Arch-Seeker**: Head Seeker of a country
    - ▪ **High-Seeker**: Head Seeker of a region
      - • **Truth-Seeker**:
        - ○ **Pursuant** (Truth-Seeker in training)
          - ▪ **Head Militant-Seeker** (Squad Leader)
            - • **Militant-Seeker** (soldiers)

Acknowledgments

I wish to thank everyone at the Writing at the Ledges group; Randy, Colleen, Rosalie, Lori, and well, the list goes on and on. Thank you all.

I wish to thank my many friends at the Meet up - Lansing Writers & Readers Guild for their help in the proofreading.

I wish to thank those who helped me created the audio book versions: Charles Brock, Sherolyn Smith, Margaret Hauck, Colleen and Morgan Nye, Laurie Westby, Chris Bilinski, Kevin Tomczyk, Stacy Kucharek, and Eric Kelts.

I also wish to thank my folks, Jerry and Barb for your years of love and support.

A special thank you to Angharad for the use of your name. We'll never forget your talent and heart. We miss you, and will keep you in our hearts, always.

I especially want to thank my wife Sarah. I couldn't have done it without you, my loving Angel Eyes.

About the author:

G. S. Scott enjoys writing all types of fantasy stories and poetry. He is active in local writing groups and is an avid gamer, enjoying local theater with his playwright wife. They share their home with their sweet and cuddly cat and hyperactive dog.

Also, by G. S. Scott:

True Tree Chronicles:
The Chaos Trilogy
Book one: *Cleansed*
Book two: *Chaos Reigns Vol 1: The Hand of God*
Book three: *Chaos Reigns Vol 2: The Tower of Time*

Restoration Trilogy
Book one: *The Tyranny of Gods and Men*

~~~~~~~~~~

Sorrow's Heart
(A True Tree Chronicles Origins Story)

~~~~~~~~~~

DONALD L. BRAKE & SHELLY BEACH

LEBANON

DAMASCUS

N

GAMALA

W   E

CAPERNIUM

S

TIBERIUS

NAZARETH

IN THE
SHADOW
OF HIS
HAND

JORDAN RIVER

DEAD
SEA

"Dr. Brake has done it again weaving Holy Scripture and historical culture into *In the Shadow of His Hand*. You will find yourself running to keep up with the beautifully crafted scenes. Dr. Brake has taken you on an incredible journey with the Apostle Paul."

~Ysavel Medina, Executive Pastor, The Ridge Church

"As fictional characters interact with Paul, we eavesdrop on his conversations and get a front-row seat on his movement from a rigid legalist to a Christ-following, liberty-celebrating believer."

~Dr. Art McNeese, Author of *Making Space for Grace*

"Brake's *In the Shadow of His Hand* is steeped in historical detail as well as the New Testament writings of Paul, this fascinating novel draws the reader into the life of the first century church."

~Dr. Diana Severance, Director, Dunham Bible Museum, Author of *The Living Word*

"Brake and Beach have produced a highly readable story of the Apostle Paul and the early church. *In the Shadow of His Hand* brings readers into Paul's world and they become eyewitnesses to crucial first-century events."

~Michael Kuykendall, Professor, Gateway Seminary

"*In the Shadow of His Hand* is one of the most fascinating novels I have ever read. Dr. Brake masterfully weaves the biblical narrative with a riveting tale to tell this amazing story. It is a must read."

~Carl Johnson, President, International Society of Bible Collectors

IN THE SHADOW
OF HIS HAND

A Novel

Donald L. Brake

and

Shelly Beach

Published in the United States of America by Credo House Publishers,
a division of Credo Communications LLC, Grand Rapids, Michigan
credohousepublishers.com

Previously published by Bold Vision Books, Friendswood, Texas

ISBN 978-1-62586-302-7

Cover art by Ken Wiegand
Cover design by Barefaced Creative Media
Interior design by Kae Creative Solutions
Editing by Cynthia Ruchti

Printed in the United States of America
Second Edition

DEDICATION

DON

In loving memory of my brother Gary Brake

SHELLY

To my dear former teacher Edith, who taught me
to love the Word.

CLASH OF CULTURES
BACKGROUND

The first-century *Anno Domini* world was a welter of competing cultures. The combination of social and religious forces bound in one political system provided the backdrop for a Shakespearian-like drama. Three great cultures set the scene. Judaism provided the roots of Christianity. Roman imperialism offered *Pax Romana* for western expansion. And Hellenism—with Greek language, culture, and intellectual thought—united to expedite worldwide communication. The success of the Jewish Maccabees a century earlier had fueled dreams of Jewish pride and independence. The result was a deeply ingrained warrior's mentality and a legalistic drive for preserving Jewish God-given Mosaic Law.

It was inevitable that Roman justice, Jewish nationalism, and Greek culture would clash. Into this raging world order, a child was born that touched each of the cultures of the new millennium.

No bright stars illuminated *that* night. No "wise men" came seeking the fulfillment of prophecy. No shepherds rushed to see this newborn baby, and no announcement recorded his birth. Yet a child slipped quietly into the world during one of history's most turbulent eras.

This young boy, Gaius Julius Paulus of Tarsus, entered this crazed world, with an echo from the words of Prophet Isaiah, "Before I was born the Lord called me. … he hid me *in the shadow of His hand*." The birth of this Hellenistic Jew and freeborn Roman citizen began a struggle that would make him a vital catalyst in vaulting a little-known, local Jewish sect into worldwide Christianity.

Authors' Note: This is a creative retelling that leans heavily on historical and biblical records, culture and customs of the times, what we know from Scripture, and the blanks of what we don't or cannot know, researched and filled in with informed imagination. No one can know the conversations in Paul's life when he was a child. But we can imagine.

TABLE OF CONTENTS

CHAPTER 1

CHOSEN

TARSUS, AD 5/6

Benjamin's steady left hand tapped hammer to awl as he punched holes in the black goat hide he was preparing to be sewn into panels and stitched into tents, blankets, and clothing. Sweat rolled from his left eyebrow and dripped onto his workbench. He reached for a rag that hung from a shelf on a nail and blotted the moisture.

As he replaced the rag that would no doubt be needed again, he took note of the other awls placed diagonally on the shelf in front of him, from small to large. Beside them lay knives for scraping fat and hair from sheep and goat skins. As every expert tanner should, he cleaned, sharpened, and oiled his tools after every use to prevent rust. Beneath his workbench, large tongs for gripping and knives for slaughter were carefully stored in wood cabinets that rested on the stone floor.

Pride swelled in Benjamin's chest as he observed his tools and workshop. Like his grandfather before him, he was as meticulous about organization and maintenance as he was about the quality of his work. He could provide well for his family by selling well-made tents to the caravans, nomads, and Roman military that frequented Tarsus.

Smiling in contentment, Benjamin ran his hand along a smooth goatskin. He enjoyed laboring in his well-furnished shop. He had invested years of work to procure each tool and hone the skills needed by a quality craftsman.

And very soon he would add the only accomplishment that could surpass his previous life successes.

Earlier that morning, he had risen and sent their servant girl to the well to fetch water before the women gathered to cook for Sarah. Benjamin stepped outside for a moment of solitude. In the distance, the sun burst over the horizon as dawn swept away the darkness. He rubbed his arms. The air was chilly, invigorating. Autumn was approaching, painting regal colors that heralded the change of seasons. Patches of snow glistened atop the distant Tarsus Mountains.

The sound of bleating drew Benjamin's gaze through an open window to the loading chute in front of the house. It held the goats going to slaughter. A merciful death. Tenderly dressed. His father had taught him to make use of all parts of the animal—meat for food for the family and sold at the market, fur and hides for clothes and leather products. As honorable and profitable as Benjamin could make his business.

A cry from deep inside the house startled him.

"Come quickly, Benjamin. It's time!"

Time? His heart raced, a mix of fear and exhilaration. He turned from the window and ran toward the cry, his thoughts racing.

"I am coming, Sarah!"

No! The child is not yet due, the baby will be too small to survive. Please, dear Yahweh, protect my wife. Bring our child safely into the world. We have lost too many. Sarah has endured so much—she cannot endure another stillbirth. Please, most gracious Av, extend Your mercy to my wife and child. Help me comfort her and help her, for I am worn out with grief.

Benjamin composed his face before he pulled the goatskin curtain from their bedroom doorway and stepped inside. The room glowed with soft candlelight. Sarah lay on a pallet of blankets atop a bolster of plaited goat's hair. A soft blue mantle covered her, and

Abigail, the midwife, stood near her head, feeding her dittany leaves and root of *vervain* to help ease her intense pain. Sonja, their servant girl, stood a few steps behind.

One glance told Benjamin that Sarah was ready, but the baby was not. He forced himself to mask his escalating concern. Slowly, he bent and kissed her brow, then sat beside her and clasped her hand tightly in his.

My precious Sarah. Av, have we sinned against You and caused these tragedies for our unborn children? If I have done something, please hold it against me, Av, and not my child. Extend Your loving mercy to us.

Benjamin remained beside his wife in the flickering light as morning turned to midday, then dusk, then night. He relived the difficulties of this pregnancy—continual sickness, swelling in Sarah's legs, occasional bleeding. Sonja had faithfully served Sarah during those long months. According to Jewish custom, Sarah had rested in bed for days to "preserve the seed," and Sonja had treated Sarah's pregnancy symptoms with a diet of eggs and rice and had massaged her mistress's feet daily with olive oil.

Abigail had immediately tried to banish Benjamin from the room when he'd entered, but he refused to leave his wife's side. He sat near Sarah's head, stroking her hair and wiping sweat from her face with a soft cloth. After what seemed to Benjamin like an eternity, Sarah whispered that it was time, and her body shook with an intensity that frightened him. Abigail cried out that the child was coming and hastily draped his wife's lower body as Sarah gripped his hand tightly and began to push. Then push again and again as Abigail directed her.

Suddenly, a child's cry, piercing and persistent, broke the silence, and all tension dissipated.

"You have a son," Abigail announced as she swept the child away to clean and swaddle.

"No!" Sarah raised herself on one elbow and reached for her child. "We have waited for our son for too long. His father needs to see him, and I must hold him. Now!"

Benjamin looked into his wife's eyes and saw the fear that resonated in his own heart. He had glimpsed their tiny son. Born too soon. It would be a miracle if he lived a month, and he and Sarah both knew it.

Abigail reluctantly laid the tiny babe in Sarah's arms. Together, Benjamin and Sarah looked upon their newborn son with love and trepidation. His tiny legs were crooked, his head misshapen, and his bright, deep-set eyes trembled in an unnatural manner. But an indescribable quality overshadowed his unusual features. Sarah cupped her son's head and moved it toward her breast. Instantly, the child began to root for his first nourishment, and Benjamin felt a rush of relief. He caressed Sarah's hair as he lifted his face toward heaven.

"Yahweh, I thank You for Your mercy in bringing our son safely into the world. Thank You for protecting Sarah. I ask for You to watch over our boy. We dedicate his life to You and will bring him up in the ways of Torah. And when he reaches majority, we will once again give him to You as a young man."

The baby suckled until he tired and dozed off. Sarah returned him to the midwife's care and moments later slipped into a deep sleep. Benjamin remained at her side, lying on the floor near her until morning.

Over the following few days, Benjamin and Sarah discussed their mutual confidence that Yahweh would preserve their son's life through the first precarious weeks of life. Prayerfully, they agreed to honor tradition and wait eight days before naming their baby. They had him circumcised and gave him his Latin name, Gaius Julius Paulus of Tarsus, a Cilician. In Hebrew, he would be known as Saul ben Benjamin. To family and friends, he would be known as "Pauli," meaning "tiny."

Pauli's grandfather and great grandfather had served in the Roman military years before, which brought Benjamin great pride. This gave Pauli the unique opportunity to be issued a *bulla,* a document that identified him as freeborn. Rome gave special attention to non-Romans who were born with a *bulla.*

Yet even with a *bulla,* after Pauli's circumcision Benjamin continued to fear for his son.

What does the future hold for Pauli? Can he possibly survive childhood with his physical problems? How will his abnormalities affect his life? Will his intellect be normal? Will he follow our faith, or will he reject Yahweh? I must dedicate myself to assuring that our son grows up both strong in the Jewish faith and strong as a man.

The more he pondered, the more Benjamin began to fear his inabilities and deficits.

Do I know how to raise a son with physical limits? Will I know how to answer his questions about life, truth, living righteously, and caring for others? But most of all, do I know how to raise my boy to become a good servant of Yahweh? Do I have the wisdom to do this well?

"Nothing matters more to me than loving and protecting my wife and child and nurturing them in the Law of Moses," Benjamin whispered. *But am I a good servant of Yahweh? Will my life be an example of all I teach my son? Will I be enough?*

The question followed Benjamin to bed as Sarah rocked their son to sleep in her arms.

CHAPTER 2

THE VOW

TARSUS, ANATOLIA, AD 16

Pauli raced toward the temple, his legs cramping with pain as he struggled to keep up with Reuben. His friend reached the stone wall first and clambered to the top. Panting, Pauli willed his aching limbs to carry him the final distance. He collapsed against the temple wall, his chest heaving. Reuben reached down and pulled him to the top of the narrow ledge.

"Take slow, deep breaths," Reuben encouraged him. "We made it this far. Now all we must do is crawl down to the courtyard where we can watch the ceremony without being seen or heard."

Pauli closed his eyes and struggled to slow his breathing.

What am I doing here? Why did I allow Reuben to talk me into this? I should be at beit sefer, not sneaking around a pagan temple so we can spy on their secret ceremony! I must stop listening to him. Abba can never find out about this. Ever.

Pauli pushed away thoughts of Abba's reaction and Ima's heartbreak if they ever found out. Abba would boil with anger, dishonor, and indignity at Pauli's outright defiance. For a moment he thought of jumping to the ground and running back to *beit sefer*.

"Today's celebration honors the Roman god Mithras," Reuben whispered as he poked Pauli in the arm and signaled him to creep down the ledge behind him. "This secret cult celebrates friendship and loyalty." He raised a hand to stop the argument Pauli was already forming. "Yes, we Jews are forbidden to watch pagan ceremonies. But this one celebrates friendship, so it cannot be bad. You'll see."

Pauli blinked.

Celebrates friendship? That's not bad. Jews are taught to be loyal friends, so perhaps Reuben is right. If the ceremony celebrates friendship, I might learn something good from it.

The churning in Pauli's stomach eased as Reuben babbled on in a whisper and inched forward on his hands and knees. "I've been told that *Votaries,* the followers who worship Mithras, often build temples in caves hidden from the public. They don't share their secrets with outsiders."

Raising a hand to his lips, Reuben suddenly motioned Pauli. Several gnarled sycamore branches ahead of him overhung the courtyard wall and hid the boys from view. Reuben pointed down into a large open courtyard.

Pauli's eyes widened. His heart raced like a gazelle fleeing a jackal. In the courtyard below, a thin girl with dark, blood-matted hair lay writhing on the floor beside a stone altar. Her hands were tied behind her back. Her eyes silently screamed in terror.

Pauli muffled a gasp.

"Isn't that Cassia, the sister of Sonja, your slave girl?" Reuben whispered. He whirled to face Pauli, fear blanching his skin. "What is Cassia doing here?"

"She's been beaten!" Pauli whispered. "Why are they ... why ..." His words stuck in his throat.

Reuben remained wide-eyed and silent as a man dressed in ceremonial priestly garments stepped forward.

"We come today to appease almighty Mithras. We bring this girl, who was brought to us to serve as a faithful and loyal slave. She has proven to be a traitor. In her service, she overheard plans for a surprise attack against pirates that would strip them of their weapons and cripple their strength. In an act of disloyalty to her master, she revealed the plot to this young man, her friend, who was one of the pirates. In retaliation, the pirates set a trap for the Roman attack and brutally butchered the Roman regiment. The soldiers were not members of the *Numeri*, the barbarian mercenaries from outside the Roman Empire who fight alongside our regular forces. They were soldiers from our town and our men of Tarsus."

Beside him, Reuben shook like an olive branch in a storm.

"Our temple priests have therefore declared that the traitor be sacrificed to appease the anger of Mithras. The slave girl known by the name Cassia has violated sacred rules of 'loyalty.' The Votaries order this sacrifice to be carried out here in secret in opposition to Roman laws, to regain the favor of the gods." The priest stepped toward the altar.

Pauli froze, bile rising in his throat. Then he tried to inch backwards on the ledge because it was too narrow to turn around.

Below, a rumble of anticipation rolled through the crowd gathered in the courtyard. Pauli could not escape the scene nor change its outcome. He swallowed hard, but his effort did not ease his heaving stomach.

The priest motioned for two men in similar robes to lift Cassia onto the roughly constructed altar made of earth, blood-stained rocks, and smaller stones. Beneath the structure was a shallow pit for burning remains.

Pauli's mouth went dry as the reality of the scene before him thundered through his mind. He wanted to scream, but his body and mind had gone numb.

Thrashing and screaming, Cassia was lifted from the ground and placed on the altar before the priest, then lashed down. Pauli pressed his hands to his ears to silence her cries, but his effort was futile. The priest's lifeless gaze fixed on Cassia's neck as he quickly pulled a knife from beneath the altar and drew it across her throat, her blood splaying out upon those holding her suddenly-still body.

Pauli stared into Cassia's face as blood spouted from the gruesome gash in her throat. His last glimpse of her was her face melting into death.

Pauli squeezed his eyes shut so tightly that lights glimmered against a field of black. The crowd below shouted in anticipation as the snapping and crackling of the altar fire grew hot, then their final cheers rose as thirsty flames consumed her lifeless body. As the crowd roared, Pauli's soul absorbed the reality of what Reuben and he had witnessed.

The sickening stench of evil choked his throat as he held his breath against the rancid odor of burning flesh.

A voice inside him told him to run, which was impossible. Pauli tried to turn around, but the ledge was too narrow. Feeling his way, he backed down the ledge, then jumped. Reuben followed close behind. They raced to a cluster of bushes and retched up their stomach contents, tears dripping into the putrid puddles at their feet. Ashamed and horrified by what they'd witnessed, they made their way home through the dusty streets.

Guilt had already clawed deep into Pauli's soul with the life-changing knowledge that his decision to spy on the scene had been far more than foolish. He had unwittingly shaken his fist in the face of God by defying Jewish laws and willfully defying his parents.

Sick with guilt, Pauli vowed he would never do such evil again.

But even as he prayed, his heart told him his vow and remorse were not enough. The guilt of his willful sin required atonement for the remainder of his life. And would even that be sufficient?

Could one *ever* be certain that their atonement was enough?

CHAPTER 3

THE WEIGHT OF SHAME

Over the next few months, Pauli often wandered off by himself to be alone, trying to erase the haunting memories of the incident at the temple. But no matter how hard he attempted to push away the picture of Cassia's pleading eyes as the knife swept over her throat, the image returned. Questions about Yahweh, who required animal sacrifice, and the Roman god Mithras, who required human sacrifice, obsessed his thoughts.

Had not Yahweh asked Abraham to sacrifice his son Isaac? Did Yahweh, too, demand ultimate loyalty—even to the point of sacrificial death? Isaac had been spared. What did that mean? But how could the blood of an animal atone for the sins of a man or woman?

Day and night, questions tore at Pauli's mind as he felt himself slowly slipping into a black hole of despair. Answers eluded him, and he could not sleep or eat.

Abba came to him with questions, obviously concerned about Pauli's health, as well as his mind and spirit. But each time Abba asked, Pauli responded with vague answers and silence.

The simple truth was that he was afraid to tell Abba and Ima about his terrible choice—missing school to go to a pagan temple. Abba would certainly be angry—a level of anger that Pauli did not want to contemplate. His mind raced contemplating the discipline that would await him if Abba found out. Denial and avoidance seemed the best course of action. Evasion, at least, delayed the inevitable moment when he would face Ima and Abba's shock and disappointment, perhaps even their disgust.

Pauli had never shamed his parents before. The thought of causing them disgrace crushed his heart with guilt.

After days of anxiety and sleepless nights, Pauli despairingly approached Rabbi Aharon's home late one bleak afternoon. With rain saturating his cloak, Pauli quickly made his way through the streets in an effort not to be seen. He soon arrived at Rabbi Aharon's door and knocked, as was the Roman custom, rather than yelling like an uncultured Spartan. From inside, he heard the bright, musical voice of the rabbi.

"Why, *Erev tov*, my young man, is that you, Pauli ben Benjamin?"

"Yes, most honorable rabbi, it is I."

The door creaked open, and the rabbi pulled Pauli inside. The room's stone walls were aglow with candles tucked inside strategically spaced niches.

"May I offer you a cup of goat's milk?"

"No *toda*, I came to ask you a question."

"Of course, young one. Speak." The rabbi settled on a wooden bench covered with brightly colored pillows and motioned Pauli to a chair with an ornately carved back. Pauli sat at the edge and took a deep breath.

"Rabbi, I came to ask a difficult question, but can you *not* tell Abba or Ima we talked?" A prayer began to form in Pauli's mind, but he could not find the words to finish.

Forgive me, Yahweh.

The rabbi crossed his arms. "I must wait until I hear your

question and then decide. You must promise to trust my judgment. Certain ... circumstances obligate me to consult your parents, Pauli. If you have committed gross sin or misconduct, I may be required to reveal your secret. Of course, you understand that I cannot help you hide sin or disobedience from your parents."

Rabbi Aharon's final words were a statement, not a question. And his eyes were not smiling.

Pauli's chin dropped to his chest as he pondered his plight.

If I don't tell the rabbi, he will tell Abba and Ima that I came to him to confess a transgression, and they will make me tell them what it is. And if I don't confess to someone, my dishonorable actions will torment me forever. I am forced to face the consequences, and it appears that the moment has arrived.

Pauli looked Rabbi Aharon in the eyes. He could no longer endure the turmoil inside. "I did a terrible thing. My friend Reuben and I did not go to beit sefer one day. Instead, though we knew it was forbidden, we secretly watched a pagan ceremony to the god Mithras at a temple Reuben discovered. We didn't know what the Romans were going to do ... but they ... they offered a slave girl as a sacrifice. We had crawled up on a ledge where we couldn't be seen, and the ceremony happened before we could turn around and get down.

"I can't get it out of my mind. I knew the girl, Cassia. We were on the far side of the courtyard and hidden by tree branches, but it seemed she stared into my eyes as she was dying ...." Pauli's voice faded away, and for a moment he couldn't speak. "It was horrible. Every time I close my eyes, I see her face and the knife at her throat and the blood when they ... slit her throat."

Rabbi Aharon's lips thinned. His jaw tightened.

Pauli pounded his hands against his legs. "I can't sleep. I can't eat. I feel like evil crawled into my head, and I don't know what to do. I can't tell my parents because I have shamed them by doing such a horrible thing."

Pauli dropped his head. Spent. More ashamed than ever. He could hear Rabbi Aharon's huffed breathing. *How can I ever look at Rabbi Aharon or anyone again? How can I go home? I cannot go home!* Pauli stared at the floor, unable to look up.

"My son, you deliberately sinned, and, yes, you shamed your parents. But more importantly, you shamed and disobeyed Yahweh, the true God, when you chose to entertain yourself in a pagan temple." The rabbi's jaw tightened again as if he chewed a bitter root. "You must tell your parents what you have done. As soon as you leave. You owe them at least your honest confession."

The rabbi's words echoed off the walls of the small gathering room, and Pauli quaked. His offenses were not minor, and he had followed Reuben willingly. He had broken Yahweh's law. In his willfulness, he had unwittingly participated in the murder of a friend—the bloody sacrifice of Cassia to a pagan god. For a moment the room disappeared in a burst of flaming orange, and Pauli felt as if his legs might give way.

"Pauli?"

He swallowed hard and forced himself to sit up straight. "Yes, most honorable rabbi. I will tell my parents as soon as I go home. And I will ask their forgiveness for my shameful choice."

"It will be forgiven, Pauli, by Yahweh, but expect consequences. Now what was the question you wanted to ask?" The rabbi patted Pauli's shoulder.

Pauli cleared his throat, relieved to change the subject. "What does the Torah say about the sacrifice of people? Why does Yahweh require animals to be butchered to pay for the sins of men and women? How can an animal sacrifice be enough for human sin? Do animals have a capacity for sin? And can God not forgive people who do wrong because they are sorry for what they have done? I have spent much time trying to find answers."

The rabbi sat back, a dumbfounded look on his face. "You are but a child. Why do you ask such questions? The Torah says Yahweh requires blood sacrifices to atone for human sin, to pay the price."

Pauli cut him off. "Why animal sacrifice for human sin when the animal is innocent? Is *human* sacrifice forbidden? If so, why?"

Rabbi Aharon tapped his foot nervously and flashed a strained smile in Pauli's direction.

"The Torah strictly forbids human sacrifice, Pauli. The subject is mentioned throughout the Torah. 'Any Israelite or any foreigner residing in Israel who sacrifices any of his children to Molech is to be put to death. The members of the community are to stone him.' The gods of other nations require human sacrifice. Yahweh asks for atonement through animal sacrifice."

Pauli's heart lifted by a feather's weight only.

"As for the question of blood sacrifice, the Torah says, 'For the life of a creature is in the blood, and I have given it to you to make atonement for yourselves on the altar; it is the blood that makes atonement for one's life.' Sacrifices provide the blood that satisfies the demands of Yahweh."

Rabbi Aharon continued.

"Pauli, since Adam and Eve disobeyed Yahweh in the Garden of Eden, the sin of their disobedience has been passed down through man's blood. You, Abba, and I have the blood that came from Adam and Eve—as did Abraham, Isaac, Jacob, and Moses. You have the same blood. That is why you are tempted to sin."

Pauli consider what was being told him and worked through it methodically.

"So that is why Yahweh made provision for us to have forgiveness for Adam's failures, as well as our sins." Pauli summarized his conclusions carefully. "He wants us to live 'holy lives' in obedience to Yahweh's commandments and the Law of Moses. We must offer the blood of sheep and goats to maintain holiness and purity before the Lord."

Aharon leaned back on his cushioned bench, his eyes smiling in satisfaction.

Pauli tilted his head. "But if Yahweh requires a blood sacrifice for the forgiveness of sins, why does he require animals in payment for human sin? Should He not require human blood for human sins?"

Cassia's blood-covered face once again flashed through Pauli's memory. *But how could Yahweh ever require such slaughter?*

Rabbi Aharon's smile turned to a scowl. "Why do you still question? As I have told you, the Law forbids human sacrifice, and offenders face dire consequences. Only animals are used in Temple rituals. This has been the practice for centuries."

Rabbi Aharon exhaled deeply, as if he was releasing the shock of the question.

"Pauli, the Torah is Yahweh's absolute authority on all matters. And Torah says, 'There shall not be found among you anyone who burns his son or his daughter as an offering. You shall not give any of your children to offer them to Molech, and so profane the name of Adonai: *I am Yahweh*.'"

Pauli still wrestled to understand. He *wanted* to understand, but his mind could make no sense of the rabbi's words. "If human sacrifice is forbidden, then why did Yahweh, through the words of Moses, ask our father Abraham to offer his only son Isaac, whom he loved, on the very mount where our Temple now stands?"

Pauli hesitated and then added, "Our Prophets also say,

'Jephthah made a vow to the LORD: If you give the Ammonites into my hands, whatever comes out of the door of my house to meet me when I return in triumph from the Ammonites will be the LORD's, and I will sacrifice it as a burnt offering.'"

At the rabbi's nod, Pauli said, "My rabbi, did not Jephthah after a period of time offer his daughter?"

Aharon hesitated as a look of frustration flashed across his face and then answered: "Ah ... well ... Pauli, Abraham did *not* offer his son. When our *Av* saw Abraham was willing to obey Yahweh at any cost, Yahweh provided a lamb to be sacrificed and burned."

Pauli thought for a moment and retorted, "But it seems that God was approving the possibility of human sacrifice for sins."

"Yes, I understand your thinking process, Pauli, but the story of Abraham happened hundreds of years before Moses gave the Law at Mount Sinai." Rabbi Aharon touched his fingertips together.

"So, God changes His requirements, depending on the time or the circumstances?"

Shaking his head vehemently, Rabbi Aharon continued. "We must always believe and adhere strictly to the precise words of Torah, for they are Yahweh's words. We never doubt them, nor do we accept arguments that disagree with Torah." The rabbi crushed a straw he had been chewing, and with an air of finality threw it to the floor.

Pauli crossed his arms but looked at the floor respectfully. Nevertheless, he told himself to be satisfied—for the moment—with Rabbi Aharon's words.

Cassia should not have been sacrificed to Roman gods. I will never accept human sacrifice as a form of atonement for sin and will fight to the end of my life to defend the Torah's authority. And someday, after further study, I will more fully understand Jephthah's story.

With little comfort from Rabbi Aharon's words, Pauli departed for home. It was at least reassuring to know that Yahweh did not require human blood sacrifice for sin. The thought was repulsive.

His conversation with Abba and Ima was long and heart-wrenching. Ima cried, which twisted Pauli's heart with remorse. Abba beat a fist against his chest in anger and shock as he paced in tight circles. He too cried over what his son had witnessed. Neither Ima nor Abba embraced Pauli, but that was more than he had dared hope. Although Abba granted forgiveness, Pauli knew it cost him dearly to extend it. Exhausted, heartbroken, and humbled, Pauli went to bed early, but his sleep was again shattered by visions of the pleading eyes of a slave girl as a knife sliced through her throat.

CHAPTER 4

HOME AND HEARTH

Pauli sat motionless on a couch in the courtyard of the Benjamin family home. His knees were pulled to his chest, and his arms coiled around his thin legs. His chin rested atop his knees as he fought back angry tears.

The courtyard was partially covered by a canvas awning that extended from one wall to a series of pillars that supported it and gave the space a measure of protection from the heat. An open area against the wall featured a low porch where a couch offered a place for sitting or reclining during the day and sleeping at night. Or escaping Abba's gaze. Small palm and olive trees marked the center of the courtyard.

Along an adjacent wall, stone stairs led to the upper story of the house. The rooftop, made of mortar and mud brick, provided space for drying fruits, preparing foods, or sewing.

Pauli rose from the couch and headed toward the stairs to the open rooftop, his destination for reprieve.

Maybe, for once, Abba won't look for me. He's never satisfied with anything I do. No matter how hard I study, it's not enough. If I make the slightest mistake quoting Torah, he makes me repeat the passage over and over. When I prepare goatskins in the shop, he points out every defect and makes me correct my work until it's perfect. Well, I am tired of trying to be perfect, and I'm NOT perfect.

I dread coming home after beit sefer, knowing Abba will ask about what I haven't done well and ignore all the studies where I excelled.

I think Abba cares about Sonja more than he cares about me, even though she is Ima's house helper, and she needs a slave. But he didn't have to agree with Sonja's father that if she served six years, she would be free. It has been longer than six years, and she is still here! Abba acts like she is a member of our family. Teaching her to read and giving her our family name?

No wonder she continues to work willingly for our family although her debt is paid.

Pauli settled himself in a canopy-shaded corner strewn with brightly colored pillows and kicked the toe of his sandal against the woven mat floor.

As soon as I finish beit sefer and celebrate my Bagrut, I will go to Jerusalem to complete my advanced studies. When I am there, I will obey the Law with every fiber of my being. I will not tolerate any deviation from Yahweh's commandments and will devote myself fully as a talmid, a disciple of a rabbi. I will finally prove to Abba that I am worthy to be his son and see the light of approval in his eyes.

With that solemn vow burning in his heart, Pauli fell asleep in the evening shadows under the open sky.

ↅ

Sonja stood next to Sarah at the synagogue door, greeting guests and directing them to tables piled high with food. Sarah had spent weeks preparing the most lavish spread the family could afford. Specific foods had been chosen to remind guests of God's provision.

Sonja was familiar with the *Bagrut* celebration that pronounced a youth to be of a mature accountable age and had helped many other proud Jewish mothers prepare for the event. Somehow, Pauli's celebration felt different, although Sonja did not understand why. For years, the only son of the household had treated her as if he despised her. She could think of nothing she had done to bring about his ill feelings. Both his ima and abba had always expressed appreciation for her service. Sonja glanced out the door to try to estimate the number of guests they who would still need to be seated. The room was nearly filled, but only a few more guests were in sight. She sighed and returned to her ruminating.

The boy's attitude could hardly be based in arrogance. Pauli could not be considered attractive in anyone's opinion, although his angular chin and dimpled cheeks somewhat redeemed his odd eyes, short stature, and weak legs. His articulate and well-spoken manner, his unusually vibrant voice, along with his confidence and mysterious demeanor attracted many people to him. Sonja had heard that even as a child, Pauli exuded confidence. People often said that no one really knew what he was thinking, except that he was a "passionate Jew" who was zealous for the letter of the Law.

She shook her head and tried to push away hurtful memories. Early in her service, Pauli had shown signs of friendship, but he'd soon grown indifferent, almost angry. Then around the time of her sister Cassia's disappearance, he had become distant and sometimes harsh with her. Why had she wasted thoughts that he could one day become a friend, when she was a slave?

Sonja led a guest to a table and returned to Sarah's side.

Of course, Benjamin encouraged his son to make trustworthy friends. Reuben, the son of Hiram, seemed to be a good choice because Hiram and Benjamin were friends. Hiram's family was close-knit, well-positioned, and respected in the Tarsus synagogue. And, of course, Reuben wasn't female.

Reuben's academic acumen was a match for Pauli, and Reuben also walked with a slight limp. But unlike Pauli, Reuben was tall and slender, with silky black hair that hung to his shoulders. His dark honey-colored eyes complimented his unblemished olive complexion. He was animated and often spoke and acted without thinking and spoke with a slight lisp. But he was a faithful friend and admired Pauli without envy, and Sonja was happy for Pauli's friendship with Reuben.

Sonja knew Pauli was a diligent student of the *Tanakh*. She had often heard him practicing his recitations as she went about her daily tasks and had come to enjoy the sound of his voice as she worked. Now the day had arrived for Pauli to show his commitment to the Law of Moses. She hoped he was proud of his accomplishments.

On the first Shabbat after a boy turned thirteen, a celebration of *Bagrut* was held among many conservative Jewish families to honor the passage of their son into adulthood. The Bagrut announced his change in status, as a former child became accountable for his own actions and for his education in the ways of Torah and the commandments.

Among these observant Jews, it was customary for the father to pronounce a blessing praising God for relieving him of complete responsibility for his son's conduct, who now had the help of the community. The highlight came when the newly "blessed" Bagrut gave a recitation on one of Torah commandments.

Sonja had heard many recitations at many Bagrut celebrations. But never had she anticipated hearing one as she did Pauli's.

Sarah had prepared fresh lentil stew for the feast. Early that morning, Sonja had risen to help Sarah add bits of lamb from the neighbor's recent butcher. Some of Sarah's friends had also come to the house early to join in the preparations by providing bread, wine, and olive oil that represented the three main crops of the Jewish agricultural calendar—wheat, grapes, and olives. Long wooden tables had been carried to the synagogue and laden with goat's milk, assorted fruits and vegetables, fish, eggs, and generous amounts of goat meat and mutton. The ceremony would take place after the guests had eaten.

Guests crowded into the room, expressing their respect to Sarah, Benjamin, and Pauli at the door, then followed Sarah to their seats. Sonja overheard many people express kind thoughts about Pauli's character, spiritual insight, and passion for Torah beyond his years. She watched Benjamin struggle not to smile, to suppress pride as positive comments about his son poured from people's lips. Pauli's abba obviously did not know how to respond to the outpouring of praise for his son.

Sonja's eyes flew to Pauli's face. His father's quiet deflection must have pained him like disapproval.

Pauli stared at the floor, his face frozen in a polite half-smile. He had spent much time preparing for his Bagrut recitation: studying, memorizing, and preparing the Scripture lesson he would present to the guests. Yet his face told Sonja he was struggling with resentment as his father awkwardly diminished his accomplishments.

Rabbi Aharon broke into the painful scene and spoke quietly to his patrons standing nearby. "Pauli has been a wonderful student in beit sefer and a model citizen in the community. His youth is masked by his mature behavior and dedication to the Torah. He once came to me with an incredibly deep theological question, and even I struggled to give him an adequate answer."

Those within hearing chuckled, and one aged sage commented, "That sounds just like Pauli."

Sonja inhaled deeply and silently gave thanks for Rabbi Aharon's insight as she walked several more celebrants to remaining open seats.

Does Sarah notice her husband's awkwardness with his son? How difficult that must be.

When all the guests had gathered, Rabbi Aharon introduced Benjamin. As the candidate's father, he held the privilege of offering prayer for his son.

Sonja noted the spark of pride in Benjamin's eyes as he glanced toward the calm and confident Pauli and reverently raised his hands to offer his blessing.

"Yahweh, we thank and praise You for entrusting us with the privilege of raising Saul ben Benjamin, of bringing him to this memorable time of his life, and of educating him in the ways of Torah and Your demands…"

Benjamin's voice grew stronger as he thanked family and friends for joining them to celebrate this milestone in his son's life. Drawing a deep breath, he paused, and Sonja noted a tremor in his chin as his eyes moistened. Benjamin looked toward Sarah, her face buried in her shawl and her shoulders heaving. He closed his eyes again and swallowed, concluding the prayer.

"Blessed is he who brings forth bread from the earth."

With his final words, the feast began.

Pauli was seated as the guest of honor with his family surrounding him. He was now a Jew equal in the community with his abba. The sound of voices and laughter rose and fell, filling the room. Sonja slipped back into the role of servant, filling platters, wine glasses, and removing dirty dishes. The buzz of conversation punctuated by laughter eventually died down as the feast concluded.

The time had come for Pauli to address the guests, and Sonja's heart fluttered with anticipation. She had heard the speech many times as he had practiced, whispering the words with him. She walked toward the table where Sarah and Benjamin were seated and refilled their drinking vessels. Then she sat on a bench near the door as Benjamin rose and invited Pauli to present the brief reading he had selected. Sonja watched the faces of the guests, who were waiting for Pauli to announce that he had chosen to speak on a commandment that highlighted his commitment to be faithful to the Law. This is what candidates almost always chose to do.

But not Pauli.

"I have deviated from the normal practice of selecting a commandment and, instead, been led to a passage from Exodus in the Torah: 'Make an altar of earth for me and sacrifice on it your burnt offerings and fellowship offerings, your sheep and goats and your cattle. Wherever I cause my name to be honored, I will come to you and bless you.'" His voice was assertive, and his eyes swept the crowd with the confidence of a rabbi.

Sonja watched as eyes widened, heads turned, and whispers flew among the crowd. She smiled.

Pauli continued self-assuredly and rolled through the panels of the community scroll of the Torah and continued with a second text from Exodus: "Sacrifice a bull each day as a sin offering to make atonement."

Then he paused, looked up from the scroll and scanned the audience.

Benjamin turned to Sarah, and Sonja inclined her head so she could hear their whispers.

"Using only the words of Torah, Pauli has gained total attention of his listeners. He shows no evidence of awkwardness and commands his topic. His speech is clear and his grammar flawless. Every eye is upon him and waiting for his next word. I could not have wished for more from my son."

Sonja saw Sarah coil her fingers into Benjamin's and sigh as she nodded in agreement.

Pauli continued his lesson, and Sonja noted a passion she had not observed with other young scholars. "Abba taught me the importance of the Day of Atonement for the forgiveness of sin. Yahweh calls us to obey every commandment, but when we stumble and fall short, we must atone for our sin. This pleases our Heavenly Av."

The guests turned to one another and whispered their approval. They seemed stunned at Pauli's command of The Law and the wisdom with which he spoke—far beyond that of a thirteen-year-old.

One guest quietly commented, "He will one day be a great rabbi."

Sonja tucked away all that she was observing to tell Pauli later—to be sure he recognized that he was a gifted teacher. Of all the times she had helped serve tables at Bagrut celebrations, she had never heard seen a celebrant capture the heart of his audience in such a powerful way. Certainly, Av was going to use him in a powerful way, and he needed to prepare.

Pauli turned the scroll to yet another passage in the third book of the Torah. This was a bold move for a scholar so young. Yet Sonja recognized the passage as one that had occupied Pauli's continual study.

"Because I sometimes have trouble seeing the words of the text, I have memorized this passage. I want to refer to this extended passage, for you to observe it as I observe it."

Then with a calm and commanding voice, Pauli quoted the entire section of the Hebrew Bible concerning the order of worship and the rituals observed on the Day of Atonement. When he finished, he paused to catch his breath.

A *zaqen* with a long white beard and furrowed brows stroked his prized beard as he whispered to his seatmate, "This young man is too uneducated to instruct us on details of the Atonement. Bagrut is a festive celebration, and this reading is inappropriate." He huffed as a parting statement of disapproval, and Sonja glanced down at the floor to hide the response she knew was written on her face.

The *zaqen* barely finished speaking when Pauli cleared his throat and continued. "This is Yahweh's word to all men, women, and children." He wet his lips from the small Roman wine jug on the table next to the lectern and continued quoting the Law's requirements for participation.

> "… a lasting ordinance for you…. On the tenth day of the seventh month … deny yourselves and not … work—whether native-born or a foreigner … atonement will be made for you …. [B]efore the LORD, you will be clean from all your sins. It is a day of sabbath rest, and you must deny yourselves ….
>
> "This is to be a lasting ordinance …. Atonement is to be made once a year for all the sins of the Israelites."

The congregation sat in silence. They had gathered for a lighthearted celebration of a child becoming "bagrut." They had not expected to be schooled in Scripture by a thirteen-year-old who still ate from his mother's table.

Stillness hung in the air like a gathering storm. Then, one by one, Sonja watched as people began to clap, and clapping transformed into the singing of psalms and spirited dancing. Soon, everyone in the room was praising Yahweh for the special gift He had given Pauli, shared with God's people for the first time in an extraordinary Bagrut celebration.

Benjamin rushed to his son, love and pride flowing from his eyes and streaming into his thick beard. "Pauli, you have spoken a message far beyond what I had dreamed. Your Ima and I are so proud of you." He pulled Pauli into his arms as Sarah joined them and a crowd gathered around the family.

Sonja had stood, along with the rest of the crowd, and tears flowed as she watched the partial fulfillment of her prayers: Pauli drinking in

41

his Abba's approval like a thirsty child. She would continue praying that Pauli would recognize the deeper, driving thirst within him that so often cannot be slaked until we see our total hopelessness and our Only Hope in our coming Messiah.

CHAPTER 5

BEIT MIDRASH

Pauli's satisfaction lasted far into the evening of his Bagrut celebration. At home, the family rehearsed details of the remarkable day. Pauli basked in Abba's continued glances of approval and Ima's gentle strokes on his back. The time was right to finally ask the question he had longed to ask for many months. He waited until the evening meal was over and the family gathered on the roof in the cool of the evening to relax and talk.

From his favorite long, cushioned chair, Pauli sat up and fingered a tasseled pillow and spoke into a lull in conversation between Abba and Ima.

"Abba, I know 'Pauli' is a beloved family name. I have always been smaller than other boys my age, but I am now thirteen and growing into adulthood, and I would like my name to reflect my maturity. I'm asking if I may now be called by my Hebrew given name after King Saul of Tarsus."

Abba's brow furrowed for a moment, and finally a warm smile crept across his face. "I understand, my son. Certainly, today you demonstrated your maturity and command of teaching. Yes, we will call you by your Hebrew name to honor your entry to manhood. Be blessed in recognition of your maturity and accomplishments, Saul of Tarsus."

At last, perhaps, Abba will now view me as a worthy son, and I can cease striving.

But even as the thought passed through Pauli's mind, a second followed, whispering ever so softly that even Saul of Tarsus would never be worthy, never be enough.

℅

Saul was no longer a child. His highly successful academic career in beit sefer had secured him a seat in advanced beit midrash—his boyhood dream. Like most Jewish boys, almost all of Saul's friends planned to enter the adult world and learn their father's trade when they completed beit sefer. But if a young man showed promise in becoming a rabbi or priest, he was given the opportunity to enter the prestigious beit midrash. This had been Saul's dream from the time he was young.

He could barely contain his excitement on his first day of studies in Rabbi Akiva's home. He raced past the bowl of warm *kashi* of grains and dried fruit Ima had set on the table for him, out the door, and full speed through the courtyard to the street. The satchel that carried his goatskin writing panels and corked ink jar slapped against Saul's bony thigh as he ran. He stumbled several times on the uneven path as he dashed past the Cydnus stream, sending the waterfowl squawking and fluttering to flight. By the time he reached the main street where the beit midrash was located, he was panting.

This day will change my world. It is the beginning of my journey to becoming a rabbi.

Saul's surroundings passed unnoticed. His mind tried to grasp one consuming thought: he was starting the journey to become a rabbi. Yahweh's servant. The reality exceeded his comprehension.

Saul slowed to a walk as he approached Rabbi Akiva's home. Apparently, he had arrived early. Six other students were sitting on the stone wall that marked the boundary of the rabbi's courtyard. Saul smiled faintly and took a seat near the other boys. Minutes ticked by without conversation. The waiting was torture. The prestige of entering beit midrash was so elite that, while the privilege brought pride to families, it instilled fear in students who were selected.

Finally, an elderly male servant with unkempt hair poked his head out the door.

"*Boker tov*, young scholars. Come in. Rabbi Akiva is expecting you." Without observing queue protocol, the boys tumbled through the door and took their places at several oak tables arranged in the middle of the room. Each "scholar" jostled for a seat closest to Rabbi Akiva's large throne-like chair with inlaid cedar carvings. Saul managed to scramble into one of the two-person desks just two places away from the rabbi.

All students stood as Rabbi Akiva entered the room and took his place in his "seat of authority." The room was bare and the walls burnished gold stone blocks and plain, which showed the students that the room was a serious venue for study. Saul sensed the tension, trepidation, and anticipation among the boys and silently thanked Av that he was familiar with the rabbi's teaching approach.

Saul had learned all he could about Akiva's simple instructional method. He followed traditional Jewish educational philosophy and curriculum. Writing, reading, and oral recitation were practiced through repetition. Jewish rabbis believed that young scholars required trained, disciplined, and retentive memories and so strived to develop those qualities.

Saul was also aware of Rabbi Akiva's reputation as a stern, disciplined teacher. When he became upset with a student's performance, he repeated his foundational philosophy: "The teacher must strive to make the lesson agreeable to his pupils through clear reasons, as well as frequent repetitions, until they thoroughly understand the matter and are able to recite it with ease and fluency."

At the rabbi's direction, the students sat and waited for their instructions. Several of the boys laughed when Akiva buried his head in his prayer shawl as he fumbled with his Torah scroll. Quickly, he lifted his head and stared into the culprits' eyes until they cracked, and their gaze dropped to the floor. Then Akiva boldly spoke in a monotone. "Students, take out your scroll panels, styli, and ink goblets and prepare for Leviticus, the section beginning with the words, 'There are six days....'"

Students fumbled as they hastened to get their writing utensils on their desks and their styli inked before the rabbi gave them the next direction.

Akiva boomed, "Don't write the letters, draw them. This is Yahweh's holy word. Treat it that way."

The boys stopped, and Saul saw puzzled looks all around him.

Draw the letters? And how does one do that? This is obviously going to be a long day.

Akiva dictated slowly as the students carefully drew the letters of the text.

"There are six days … when you may work … but the seventh day… is a day of sabbath rest … a day of sacred assembly. …You are not to do any work … wherever you live … it is a sabbath to *YaHWeH*."

When the students came to the word YHWH, they marched together to the water basins sitting on the benches lining the walls and washed their hands so they were ceremonially clean enough to pen the name of *Yahweh*. Then, they returned to their seats and wrote YHWH.

"Good." Akiva barked in a voice that sounded like a bullfrog crying for its mate. "Good. You must *never* copy the name of YHWH without purifying your hands. Now exchange your scroll panels with your neighbor, and I'll read the passage again so you can check the accuracy of the copyist.

After tirelessly working on a few passages, Akiva announced, "It is the sixth hour (approximately noon) and time for your daily meal. Go to the basins and purify your hands, sit, say your blessing, and eat. We will begin again when you hear the ringing of the bell."

Saul made his way to the hand basin. Earlier he had learned his seatmate was Asher of Adana. The two began discussing their backgrounds and the day's experiences to that point in beit sefer. Soon, they were laughing and talking as if they had known each other since childhood.

When the meal was over, the boys returned to their seats for the afternoon session.

After the students had filled their panels, the Rabbi spoke. "By tomorrow you will have put to heart today's lesson, and I will hear your recitations. But now it is time for ritual bathing."

The students folded their writing sheets and headed for the *mikvah*. Saul had been told each beit midrash had a mikvah nearby so students could be trained in proper ritual bathing, or ablution. *Tevilah* was a full body immersion in a mikveh, and *netilat yadayim* was the washing of hands with a cup.

Rabbi Akiva addressed the young scholars. "While the usual practice of tevilah is for those unclean through touching or encountering death, there are other instances for immersion: on the day prior to Yom Kippur, before the three pilgrimage festivals, and before Rosh Hashanah. In some cases, pious Jews additionally immerse themselves before a Shabbat and before morning prayers."

As the students began to disrobe, the rabbi continued, "But for you who are training to be teachers, rabbis, and priests, we will practice ablution in tevilah every day to be sure we are ceremonially pure when writing and studying Moses' Law."

With those words, the boys draped themselves with white linen togas that had been placed on a bench and entered the mikvah one by one until all had immersed themselves in the waters of purification. Saul emerged from the mikvah sobered by his newly discovered responsibilities to Yahweh. He continued to ponder all he would need to learn as he dressed and began his walk home. *Will I ever truly understand God's Holy Scriptures? And have certainty about my faith?* Questions tumbled through his thoughts as he made his way through the city toward home.

The Cilicia Prima, the center of the civil and religious metropolis, was still bustling with activity as Saul ambled pensively toward home. The day had been long and tiring, but his heart was overflowing with praise.

Great Heavenly Av, I cannot comprehend why You chose me to serve You, but I do so with joy and humility. Guide my steps as I prepare to represent You and guard Your Law. Make me worthy of the task You have set before me.

Days of instruction passed, with many challenges. Saul's studies proved to be more difficult than he had envisioned. Daytime classes were spent in rigorous debate, while evenings were spent memorizing texts copied from Rabbi Akiva during class sessions. Line by line, phrase by phrase, Saul mastered the nuances of Torah.

When he produced less than perfection, he returned home and retreated to the roof, where he scourged himself with self-hatred in the darkness and made jagged vows for the next day. And the next.

And vowed that no one would ever see the scars upon his heart. Or know the price he was paying to give his all to his religion while watching his faith slip away.

CHAPTER 6

SCHOOL OF HILLEL

Benjamin leaned against the east wall of the house, gazing at the morning sun cresting the treetops in shimmering spectacle. He breathed deeply, trying to push away unspoken worries.

In the past months he had observed Sarah's growing fears in her furrowed brow and clipped responses. They both had noted Saul's growing pharisaical fervor, and his growing zeal troubled them.

Passion is good, and passion for Yahweh is admirable. I have taught my son this, but what other influences are shaping his fervor for the minutiae of the Law? Where are Saul's passions and dreams taking him? What is feeding his heart? What purpose lies behind his extreme zeal for the Law?

Benjamin chewed rigorously on a piece of straw he'd found in his workshop.

From the time of his studies in beit midrash, Saul had exhibited extraordinary enthusiasm for Judaism. Some people in the community even accused him of possessing a fanatical passion. It was obvious to Benjamin that Saul had learned all he could in Tarsus, where the Yeshiva was influenced by Hellenistic culture, philosophy, and social sciences. But the Yeshiva offered little that could advance Saul as a God-fearing rabbi. He needed guidance from more moderate teachers.

Only Jerusalem could provide appropriate teaching for neophyte rabbis. Saul's precocious mind needed the best education possible, which meant the School of Hillel in Jerusalem. Besides, the method of teaching in Jerusalem was discussion and debate—a method of learning where Saul excelled.

Jewish fathers around the world sent their "promising sons" to Jerusalem for advanced rabbinic studies. Rabban ha-zaqen Gamaliel, who had earned the title *Rabban*, which was conferred only on presidents of the highest religious council, had founded a large school in Jerusalem. He was also President of the Great Sanhedrin Council in Jerusalem and the people's spiritual leader. Benjamin had considered the advantage this would offer someone like Saul. In addition to theology, students' education included Greek philosophy and other secular studies so that pupils could interact in an educated manner with provincial governors.

Benjamin tossed the piece of straw to the ground and headed toward the rooftop, where he could sit beneath the awning and rest while he pondered.

He realized that Saul's pious rabbis in Tarsus avoided the excessive influence of Greek philosophy taught in the local university, even though many people considered education better at the school in Tarsus than at the great seats of learning in Athens, Greece, and Alexandria, Egypt. But observant Jews discouraged secular education for budding Jewish theologians.

However, his son's insatiable desire for knowledge had led Benjamin to discuss the tenets of stoicism with local university students. He was Saul's Abba, and he needed to know what his son might battle someday. This Greek philosophy applied cynicism to the choices of living a rational and virtuous life. Basically, stoicism taught self-control and inner fortitude as a means of overcoming destructive emotions—which appealed to Saul. Benjamin had observed his son's struggle with self-condemning emotions for a long time—ever since he had visited the pagan temple with Reuben.

Benjamin turned away from the view of the sunrise. He knew

what he had to do. Either he and Sarah needed to send Saul to boarding school in Jerusalem or move the family to the city. Amira, Saul's younger sister by six years, would see the move as an adventure and make friends quickly. Tentmaking in Tarsus had given him sufficient funds to pay for relocation and time to establish himself as a tentmaker in a thriving city like Jerusalem. And after Saul completed his education, the family could decide whether to remain in Jerusalem or return to Tarsus. The transition to Jerusalem would be easy.

Except for Sarah.

The move would be hardest on her. His wife would dearly miss her friends, but Sarah had always been willing to do what was best for her children. And Saul was their eldest and would reach majority all too soon. Who knew how long they would have Saul with them or where Yahweh might lead him?

A picture of Saul with satchels packed, leaving their home, flashed through Benjamin's mind. But he quickly pushed it away. The boy turning man needed to prepare for his future, and now seemed to be the time to take a leap.

&

Thanks to Sarah's excellent planning, Benjamin's physical strength, and Saul and Amira's tireless help, the move progressed seamlessly—from Benjamin's point of view. He'd found a home for them in an observant Jewish community near *Nebi Samwil,* about seven Roman *mille passus* from the Temple in Jerusalem. Saul could easily travel to and from the Temple Mount school when he had days off or when school was not in session. Other than those times, he would board at the Yeshiva.

The day they arrived, Sarah turned to him, a smile lighting her face as she beheld their new home in the distance. Benjamin sighed with relief.

"How did you find such a perfect house, my husband? The incline gives us access to the upper level from the street above and the bottom level from the lower. Such a convenience!" Sarah clapped her hands with joy, and Benjamin's heart swelled.

"I have been told that the interior walls are constructed of trimmed stones covered with high-quality plaster," he responded. "And I am pleased with the large square-cut stone ashlars on the exterior, doorpost and lintels."

The building faced an inner courtyard surrounded by other family homes. Rock-cut cisterns provided the families' water supply. Benjamin was pleased. The reports he had been given on the community had been accurate. Most of all, Sarah would be content here.

Almost on cue, Sarah announced, "I'm pleased we have close neighbors, Benjamin. This means fellowship for us and friends for Amira. And the fortification will provide safety."

Benjamin smiled. All factors he had considered in his choice. In the years they had been married, he'd learned that Sarah enjoyed the company of women while he worked in his shop. And she was constantly aware of safety risks and schooled herself in the best home remedies for himself and the children. Her skills in creating poultices, salves, and teas would certainly be welcomed in the community.

As the family settled in, Sarah and Amira busied themselves finding furnishings for their new home while Joseph introduced himself to men in the neighborhood and set up his tools in an abandoned barn within the compound. Saul, of course, launched into his studies.

As Benjamin set about establishing his work, men from the community dropped by the barn to investigate what new craft or service he would be bringing. As expected, they also inquired about his family.

Of course, Benjamin bragged about his beautiful Sarah and

Amira. Then he paused. *Here it comes—either slaps on the back, congratulations, and support for my work, or thinly veiled derision, a hasty exit, and cold nods when we pass.*

"And my son Saul has just entered the school of Gamaliel."

Nearly every Jewish man was aware of the two schools of thought that separated Jewish matters of ritual, practice, ethics, and interpretation of scripture or theology that shaped oral law. These two schools were Beit Shammai and Beit Hillel, and the two schools of thought fiercely competed for supremacy among Jewish followers. Rabbi Gamaliel was a staunch believer in the school of Hillel. Judaism was being confronted by a contemporary and dominant Gentile world view. Gamaliel sought to maintain peace amidst the new situation by offering social relief to Gentiles. He drew up the *halakha,* the totality of laws and ordinances that regulate religious observances and daily life to encourage Gentiles to adhere to Jewish laws.

Change had brought great controversy among the Jews and two divergent schools of thought. Beit Hillel sought to expand the law in a wider context, making it easier to interpret the Law in a tolerant spirit. His new interpretation of the Law also improved the position of women. Under Hillel's interpretation, if a husband divorced his wife, he had no right to refuse her marital intentions in another court. Hillel's interpretation also made it easier for a woman to remarry if her spouse died.

This was the moment Benjamin would discover if he had truly found a haven for his family.

An older man with eyebrows like thistle who'd introduced himself as Abner pounded Benjamin on the back fiercely. "Our own student of Gamaliel—finally!"

Later that night, Benjamin settled on a mat beneath a woven rush awning behind the house and pondered the events of the day as he munched on dried figs and roasted barley.

Placing Saul under Hillel's teaching still concerns me. Yes, Saul was a shining star in his previous schools, but will the frailties of his health be too much for the most intense theological education available in Israel? And how will he fare against other students in a classroom structured totally on debate and rational argument?

More importantly, where is zealous passion for Torah leading him, and where will Gamaliel's discipleship and education lead my son?

CHAPTER 7

THE CANOPY QUESTION

Sarah tore a large chunk from a crusty loaf of bread. Nothing pleased Saul more than warm bread. If she hoped to draw her son's thoughts from his stubborn head, she would need plenty of help. She grabbed a handful of figs and nuts from a bowl on the table behind her and headed toward the sturdy wood front door.

Saul's studies were going well, but Sarah had been concerned for months about more important matters. Her son was showing no interest in marriage. None. He studied day and night, only taking time off occasionally to spend time with fellow students.

A Jewish young man must marry to fulfill Yahweh's commandments, have children, and provide an example to the community. His studies are important, but they cannot overshadow other expectations. It is time for a wife and children. What am I to say to the women who ask me when my son plans to give me grandchildren?

Streaks of orange signaled the approach of the setting sun on the western horizon as Sarah walked across the courtyard and joined Saul, who leaned against a date palm.

"Good evening, Ima," Saul greeted her with a smile. "The setting sun tonight enhances your beauty. Everyone who has met you knows why Abba is so devoted to you. You radiate from within. And your hands are as delicate as those of Aphrodite, although I doubt Aphrodite spoiled her hands making bread."

Saul reached out and accepted the fragrant piece of bread Ima extended to him. She laughed, her voice mixing with the melodies of songbirds amid the rustling tree leaves.

"*Erev tov*, my son."

"Erev tov."

"*Mah Koreh*?" echoed Saul.

"Nothing really," Sarah replied casually. "I finished my evening chores and wanted to talk to you."

She opened her mouth to speak, but nothing came.

My Saul is getting older, and his eyes, legs, and problems from birth still hinder him. His limitations are my fault. Something was wrong with my body. I lost so many babies before his birth. Even before he was born, I knew something was wrong.

He has the countenance of an angel, but young women will not see him as his Ima does. Will he ever find a bride? Does he believe women find him unattractive? How can I ask him these things? But I must know his heart.

Sarah watched her son eat the bread he so loved, then the fruit and nuts. She couldn't prevent his infirmities or protect him from insult or abuse, but she could feed him. And always pray.

Saul makes light of his deformities, calling them "a thorn in the flesh." His bowed legs, his eyebrows bushy and as one, his hair oily and thin and his nose crooked and weak eyes. But he is not ugly. He has strong oratory skills and uses them to hide his perceived inadequacies. I fear he sees himself as limited or inferior as a maturing "man of the commandments."

She laid her hand gently on Saul's arm. "My son, I must speak to you as a man. You are almost eighteen, the age to 'come under the canopy.' Have you given any thought to marriage? Jerusalem will be the perfect place to find a mate. Abba and I have been talking about searching for a suitable bride for you. But—we don't want to hurry such an important decision. But we want to know if you have anyone in mind who has tugged at your heart." Sarah glanced sideways at her son's face.

Saul's eyes grew wide like a child, as if he was bewildered by the question. "I have never given thought to marriage, Ima. It does make sense that you would ask, since I am at an age when most young men consider taking a wife. And I am certain you would like grandchildren."

He paused before he continued, drew a deep breath, and straightened to his full height.

"Ima, I have given my life to Yahweh, and I am privileged to study without family responsibilities. Yahweh has called me to this place at this time in my life, and I believe one should persist in the situation Yahweh calls them to unless He calls them to something else."

Sarah could not argue, but still… She turned toward her son, and Saul reached out and took her hand.

"Ima, you know that as a rabbi, I am not under any compulsion to marry, although I must remain pure. If Av calls me to enter the canopy, then I am free to enjoy the delights of matrimony."

Oh, but son— Thoughts ran through her head, but she remained silent.

"Don't worry about me, Ima. I am content. Yahweh will guide my life, and I will follow Him at all costs, whether it be to the canopy or whether it be to death."

To death?

Sarah sat frozen as images horrible beyond description flashed through her mind. Waves of fear and grief washed over her unlike anything she had felt since the loss of her unborn children.

Where do these frightening images come from, my Av? Are You trying to show me something?

She squeezed Saul's hands and inhaled deeply as she tried to wash the pictures from her mind. "Saul, your Abba and I are so proud of your accomplishments, character, and dedication to Yahweh and Judaism, His true religion. We trust you to listen to Yahweh and will faithfully pray for you as we have always done. I will not press further about this."

Saul's eyes held hers, but she could not read the odd expression on his face. Unsettled, she turned toward the last glow of the setting sun on the horizon. She drew her hands away from his as they both wordlessly drank in the beauty of the evening. Closing her eyes, Sarah gathered the last rays of twilight in her memory to soothe her disquieted spirit.

I do not have words, but I am afraid. Av, please protect him and give him wisdom. Be with him where we can no longer be.

"*Layla Tov*, Saul," Ima spoke softly as she pivoted and walked toward the house.

"Layla Tov, Ima."

Sarah watched from the doorway of the house as Saul stood in the falling darkness. Then she entered the house, gathered her prayer shawl, and headed to the rooftop.

CHAPTER 8

RABBAN GAMALIEL

Saul wolfed down wheat bread and goat's milk before bolting out the door of the yeshiva gathering room where he had slept the night before. He'd studied late into the night and felt ready for the day's challenges—until, as he heaved open the oak door into his classroom, he noticed his two goatskin writing sheets had slipped out of place and were visible, hanging lower than his prayer shawl—a violation everyone could see. Saul, like all students, wore an off-white outer garment the color of unwashed fleece, covered by a traditional prayer shawl.

The classroom building was in the *xystus* complex, the former gymnasium, and the council house stood adjacent to the Temple wall. Classrooms, a kitchen, bathhouse, and mikvah surrounded a central open-air courtyard. The instructional rooms were small, with stone floors and pale yellow stone walls occasionally marked by lesson charts. Small tables with benches provided desk space for three students per table. A special chair for the rabbi and a lectern that held the Torah were placed at the front of each classroom. Stone benches lined the outer walls for occasional visitors who desired to observe the lessons.

As a young Pharisee, Saul had set his eyes on becoming a member of the Sanhedrin, or the Sadducees. But he had never dared to hope that he would one day study under Rabban Gamaliel in the most prestigious school of all of Judaism. He still could barely put words to this privilege beyond his wildest dreams.

Gamaliel's large, ornate carved oak chair stood empty at the front of the room, so Saul took a seat on the front row and attempted to recall the lesson he had studied late into the night. The moment the rabbi entered the room, he and the other students would be required to stand as a sign of respect until they were given permission to sit from Gamaliel.

The remaining students drifted into the room one at a time. Several who had observed Saul race into the classroom scowled imperiously as they passed him. Unintimidated, he smiled in return and saw flashes of frustration—even anger—on several faces.

One young man with a broad grin and dark curls that tumbled to his shoulders slid into the seat next to Saul.

"Joseph of Cyprus," he whispered as he lowered his head. "I hope you like to study. I plan to become a Levitical priest."

Before Saul had a chance to answer, Gamaliel swept through the door. The students rose and repeated the *Shema* in unison: "Hear, O Israel: the LORD is our God, the LORD is One." Then at Gamaliel's direction, they sat again. As Saul anxiously awaited the first question, Gamaliel asked each student their name and about their family, town, and interest in rabbinical studies. Saul's legs bounced in anticipation as he awaited the first question. The rabbi's expectations were high, and setting himself apart on the first day was important. Too often he had been misjudged and set aside, based on his appearance.

Saul knew that Gamaliel did not consider anyone a scholar who could not set forth a well-argued presentation. The rabbi was known for asking probing questions that challenged students' assumptions. He designed his forum for open-ended inquiry, where both learner and teacher used analytical questions to develop a deeper understanding of selected scriptural subjects. Students often found their teacher leading them out on a limb and then cutting it off behind them.

Gamaliel smiled. Saul sensed his pleasure in launching into the day's teaching.

We are fortunate that our rabbi likes to make learning enjoyable. His pleasant personality is already evident. But I must be prepared every moment. He is known to be demanding, and my studies will be difficult, at best.

The rabbi began.

"An elderly man stumbled through a wheat field on his way to synagogue. Having overslept, he'd ignored his morning breakfast and needed nourishment. He stopped momentarily and pulled off a few grains of wheat and ate them. Did he violate the commandment to keep the Sabbath holy?" He crossed his arms and surveyed the students, a smile teasing the corners of his mouth.

Saul had already analyzed the question. At Gamaliel's request, he and the other students had copied that portion of the Torah the night before in preparation for class. After copying it, Saul had anticipated the question and started crafting his argument. Gamaliel didn't like superficial, rote answers. Instead, he wanted responses that thoughtfully and comprehensively applied other texts that had been committed to memory. In fact, he was known for saying, "I don't want the Torah's text to go from the written page to your scrolls without first dancing through your brain."

The student named Uziel shot up his hand, his arm waving like a flag in a storm. "I know! I know!"

The young man reminded Saul of students he'd observed in the past who longed to be the first to answer, but whose answers seldom showed depth of thought or analysis of additional texts.

"Yes, Uziel, I see your hand," Gamaliel replied patiently.

"He violated the command that says we cannot work on the Sabbath." The young man smiled proudly.

"Does your answer come from the written law or oral law?" Gamaliel challenged.

"The oral law. We follow the wisdom of the Elders to be holy and observe the law to the letter." But Uziel's confident tone faded away like an apology.

"Did you consider the man's health and circumstances? What if his health was in danger? Was he a poor elderly man seeking food to sustain him? Or was he taking the opportunity to relieve the owner of his rightful crop? Perhaps others, to use the law to cling to their shekels, refused to give him alms. Would that make a difference in your interpretation?"

"I did not think about these things, Rabban," Uziel responded.

A smile washed across Gamaliel's face. "In these cases, the Law might side with you."

Saul, disappointed in Rabban's answer, raised his hand.

"Yes, Saul. Can you enlighten us on this matter?"

Saul hesitated for a moment. A wrong or incomplete answer would bring Rabban's criticism. He spoke reverently. "I would like to bring up *Pikuach nefesh* (saving a human life takes priority). It states that if a medical emergency is known or suspected that warrants eating on *Shabbat, Yom Tov,* or even *Yom Kippur,* that a person is permitted to eat—but only what is required, not all he desires. Only when we assess the entire situation can we accurately reflect the wisdom of Yahweh."

Rabban Gamaliel's eyes brightened. "Saul, you are right. You may be seated."

Saul remained standing. He heard several students sucking in their breath. The Rabban held his gaze, curiosity in his eyes. "Saul, do you have more to say on this matter?"

"No, Honored Rabban. I have another inquiry."

"Please state it."

"Not long ago, I passed by the prison on Mt. Zion and saw a member of the Essene community who lives in the southern section of our city. The Essenes have many heretical views. They forbid sacrificing animals as atonement, encourage communal ownership, and forbid eating meat. Additionally, they teach that the one called The Teacher of Righteousness is believed to be the Messiah who will return after death, overthrow Rome, and establish a new kingdom that He will rule in righteousness. Some even suggest that the writings of their sages at Qumran insist that two Messiahs are coming: one from the kingly line of David, and one from the priestly line of Aaron."

Saul turned to the other students, trying to assess their reactions. "How do we refute this heresy? And more importantly, how do we stamp out this wayward teaching?"

Rabban stroked his long beard. His face showed satisfaction with the question, but he remained silent. Saul assumed that the rabbi did not think it appropriate to overly praise his students and was pondering a moderate response.

"Israel has no Messiah, and we have already experienced the greatest opportunity for a messianic age in the days of Hezekiah, whose reign rebuilt Jewish religious society. There is no individual Messiah who will bring in a perfect world. Instead, the Messiah will be a future world in which human efforts will usher in a utopian age."

Rabban launched into a deep river of rabbinical thought.

"Many rabbis match violent images from prophecy with historical periods. They often interpret messianic passages to point out that the generation immediately preceding the coming of the Messiah will be characterized by a decrease in Torah learning. A righteous generation will be replaced by an unholy generation--even an evil one." Gamaliel nodded his head to emphasize his point.

"But Rabban," Saul interjected, "how are we to regard these anti-Jewish teachings, as well as those who spread them?"

Rabban turned to the class. "What advice would you give young Saul?"

The student named Chanoch, after his father, answered quickly without being recognized. "I would force them to abandon their heresy. They have no place in Yahweh's community and will undermine our faith."

Saul stood, his frustration rising for Chanoch's simplistic answer, as he waited for Gamaliel to grant him permission to respond to his classmate.

"Saul, set your feelings aside. Don't let them cloud your judgment and the exercise of wisdom. When you show your feelings, you also reveal your thoughts." Gamaliel's tone was firm, yet assuring. "You now speak as a member of the Sanhedrin Sadducees, who often comment without toleration. However, we can disagree with certain religious groups, yet grant them the freedom to co-exist."

Students suddenly turned toward one another, and in hushed tones they exchanged ideas and critique of what they had heard. Saul and Chanoch remained standing as the classroom buzzed with response to the rabbi's comment.

Ethan ben Simon, a student from rebel-infested Galilee, stood to be recognized. Saul wondered if this "Bagrut" had relatives or friends who were secret supporters of the Galilean Zealots. If so, Ethan would be aware that his family and friends in Galilee were in danger, and he would not want to suggest that he was sympathetic with the Zealots. Saul scrutinized his fellow student, who was standing to his left.

Ethan's brow was dripping with sweat, and his eyes darted around the room as he breathed heavily. Perhaps it was because the room was warm, Saul speculated. Or perhaps he was fearful. After an awkward silence, Ethan spoke, his words halting as he stuttered.

"I have a case to p-present. A friend of mine shared with me the teaching of Shammai ha-Zaken who b-believes Israel should rise and forcibly take b-back the land Yahweh b-bequeathed our forefathers."

Rabban Gamaliel rubbed his beard as he tilted his head. "Class, what does Torah say about *Mar* Ethan's case? Is ha-Zaken Shammai correct, or are we going to be his instructors?"

Silence hung in the room as Rabban Gamaliel waited.

From a rear desk, Jonathan of Gamla finally slowly rose for permission but did not speak.

"We are from the same city in Northern Israel are we not?" Rabban remarked.

Saul crossed his arms and leaned back. *Gamaliel is using a rhetorical question to calm Jonathan's nerves and put him at ease to give him time to gather his thoughts and present the best answer. I have heard that the rabbi does this to assist his students, but how interesting to watch him so automatically use such instructional strategies. If I am alert, I will learn so much more from Gamaliel than content.*

"Yes, Rabban," Jonathan responded. Saul observed his pitted chin and hairless face deformed from childhood. He, too, would have endured the same torment Saul had known growing up. But Saul had also heard of Jonathan's academic acumen and top rhetorical performance throughout his school years.

"Our area of Galilee and Batanea has had its share of rebel activity," Jonathan answered Gamaliel. "In fact, many of my relatives have suffered greatly from the cruelty of occupiers. I have often seen bodies hanging from Roman crosses. My mother witnessed her family nailed to these punishing methods of torture."

Jonathan turned toward the other students. "Yahweh gave this land to us, and we have Scripture's permission to take it back by any means available to us—which may mean the shedding of our nation's blood." With a smile of satisfaction, Jonathan sat down with a plop.

Gamaliel's nostrils flared slightly. "Mar Jonathan, your case reeks of personal experience and emotion, rather than Torah's instruction." His voice was commanding.

"Is our plight any worse than we experienced as captives in Egypt or Babylon? How many trained soldiers do we control as Jews, and with what military training? How many soldiers does Rome command? What is their reputation for defeating their enemies? At Alesia, Julius Caesar wiped out the Gaulish force. And what about the Battle of Silva Arsia, or the Battle of Carthage? Is your case simply that if we want something, we can take it, whether we have a military?"

Saul glanced around the room. Students clung to Rabban Gamaliel's every word, respect glowing from their faces.

Rabban Gamaliel leaned toward Jonathan. "Now tell me, my bold hero Jonathan, how will Israel—with no trained military—stand against such fierce opponent as Rome?"

Jonathan looked down. "I hadn't considered those things, Rabban."

"Jonathan," Gamaliel's voice softened, "you *must* think of those things. And others, before you render judgment. As a Pharisee, your word is law."

Saul struggled to read Rabban's thoughts.

What is he seeking? Does he agree with Rabbi Shammai? Is he waiting for us to discover his interpretation? Or does he prefer we show independent thought?

Saul suddenly shot his hand into the air.

"Yes Saul, do you wish to contribute?"

"Honorable Gamaliel, you told us that we are to seek our logic and arguments from Tanakh. However, your answer to Jonathan is a diversion from the Creator's words. The point you argue is that our plight now is no worse than what our ancestors experienced as captives in Egypt or Babylon."

Saul spoke confidently, as he threaded together scriptural truth with logic and argument.

"I present a middle case," Saul said. "I was born a freeman in the free city of Tarsus. I am a child of Rome. Yet I am a Jew and follower of Yahweh and hold no hatred toward Rome. I am an obedient observer of the Torah, and it does instruct us not to 'kill.' Nevertheless, Moses intended the commandment to forbid permission for wanton murder for personal gain. We are given examples of times when Yahweh permitted our forefathers to raise the sword to protect our people, and it was not a violation of the commandment."

He drew an unneeded breath. Passion propelled his words. "If we put our thoughts in context, we will find our example of slavery in Egypt and captivity in Babylon instructive. We were not overthrowing occupiers with violence. We were in a foreign land, not ours."

Saul's mind was speeding like a deer eluding a hyena. A wave of dizziness rolled through him, and he took a sip of the diluted wine placed on students' desks for maintaining hydration and moistening the mouth.

He continued. "Is it not true that Yahweh used warfare? Did He use an army to overthrow Pharaoh? Our ancestors were freed from Egyptian bondage by the overpowering miracles of Yahweh though our lawgiver, Moses. Pharaoh and his Egyptian henchmen lay at the bottom of the Red Sea as a reminder that Yahweh rules His people's destiny, not a self-crowned militia leader who believes he is a god."

Rabban stood and cut Saul off. "Good, Saul, good. I see your logic. The Babylonian captivity called for measures controlled *only* by Yahweh. Yahweh stirred Cyrus, king of Persia, to proclaim in writing that all captives of Israel could return home. The prophet Daniel showed him Jeremiah's prophecy about Babylon's fall and Israel's seventy-year captivity."

Students had stood, ready to contribute to the discussion. A tall student, Tamari, courageously contributed, despite his broken speech. "Ezra, the priest, and scribe, wanted to teach the Torah and its regulations to the people who had come to Jerusalem in the first Aliyah. With letters from the new Persian king, Artaxerxes, Ezra led a second wave of Jews back to the Promised Land."

Joseph of Cyprus' voice rose over the students clamoring to show Rabban their knowledge of the prophets and the Torah.

"A cupbearer in the Persian summer court at Shushan was saddened because Nehemiah received news that Jerusalem's walls and gates remained in ruins. Strengthened by prayer, the cupbearer spoke to the king and was granted permission to go to Israel to assess their condition."

During the discussion, Gamaliel's hands had raised toward the class. "Yes, yes, you have done well, and we have exhausted this debate. Your logic and arguments have been sound. Most importantly, you all engaged in the discussion." Rabban lowered his hands and returned to his chair.

"We are free to worship the one True El." Gamaliel's voice was thick with emotion. "This land is still ours, as the Abrahamic Covenant states. Although Jews do not exercise total control, we have Yahweh's promise that one day we will reign over the House of David as the prophet Samuel promised us."

Saul sat silent. The discussion had invigorated him. Would class be like this every day—like a gymnasium for the mind?

But why did Rabban mention the reign of the Davidic house and its future? I must learn more about that and its importance to the future of our people.

Days and months passed in a whirlwind of learning, deepening friendships, exploring the city, and observing the interplay of rabbis, Pharisees, and other religious leaders within Judaism. Increasingly, Saul's family time diminished as his studies became more difficult and bonds of friendship increased. When his classes were completed, he signed up for the required apprenticeship that would fulfill the final requirement in his theological studies and preparation for serving Yahweh.

And yet, Saul wondered, was there more? Had his education filled the gnawing void in his belly when his mind was not occupied with tasks? Would priesthood let him rest in the satisfaction that he had done enough, was worthy enough, had sacrificed enough?

Why, after years studying with the greatest mentor in Jerusalem and preparing to teach others about life with Yahweh, was he still searching for peace and purpose?

CHAPTER 9

BEIT DIN

Saul's white woolen tunic and *tzitzit* billowed around him as he solemnly hurried across the stone floor of the immense Xystus. A clutter of benches slowed his pace through the massive room where large assemblies were held. Thrusting a bench aside, he abruptly turned a corner into the arched stone hallway that led to his classroom.

He stopped, bent forward, and inhaled deeply. It seemed that no matter how hard he tried, his short, weak legs could never keep up with Joseph's long limbs. His best friend was well ahead of him.

"Joseph! Joseph, wait for me!" Saul called out. He dared not hurry more, which would be undignified.

Joseph paused and turned. "Boker tov, Saul," Joseph's smile revealed beautiful straight teeth that complemented his thick hair and dense beard. "I'm sorry I left before you and didn't wait."

Panting, Saul continued. "I couldn't sleep last night. I kept thinking about the choice we face. Have you decided?"

Joseph shook his head. "I, too, tossed and turned all night. I do not excel at debate and rhetoric as you do and have longed to learn more about Temple procedures. As a Levite, I desire to become a ranking priest. When I was a boy, a cousin of mine from Galilee introduced me to a carpenter from Nazareth and his son who were visiting the Temple during Yom Kippur, and I joined them. Since then, I have longed to know more about Temple procedures.

"As an intern, I would like to assist the Temple Guard and perhaps one day be appointed to join them."

Saul and Joseph discussed internship possibilities further as they slowly made their way to their last day of class with Rabban Gamaliel. Saul mulled over his dream of continuing an internship that would lead to becoming a judge and a Pharisee, one of the highest appointments in Judaism.

The day when he would finally fulfill his father's hopes for him … and see the light of approval in Abba's eyes.

❧

After five years of dedicated study about Jewish law and life while sacrificing their private lives under relentless pressure, Saul and his classmates completed their course work. Eight of the fifteen young men who began studies with Gamaliel did not finish. They were assigned as teachers in beit sefer and beit midrash schools in towns and villages throughout the land.

Successful graduates of Beit Gamaliel were awarded a uniquely designed *tallit*—the symbol of communal solidarity and devotion to Yahweh. The Beit Gamaliel tallit was made of pure white wool and did not include traditional blue stripes. The purity of the all-white tallit was considered more "holy" than the blue and white of an ordinary tallit. White signified a tallit so perfect and flawless as to be beyond reproach.

The tzitzit was colored in pure blue green (turquoise) dye from the rare *Hillazon* snail, and wool threads flowed from the four corners of the tallit. The tzitzit was tied with the finest pure wool that contained eight individual threads (when doubled over) that were tied with five sets of knots, making a total of 613. Observant Jews immediately identified the distinctive, superior-quality garments worn by Beit Gamaliel graduates.

Saul contemplated the path that lay before him and the other graduates. Internships after graduation, followed by ordination. They would then qualify to teach in synagogues and schools throughout Judea, Samaria, and Transjordan, or to work as judging assistants in Jerusalem under the supervision of Temple priests.

While Saul enjoyed the challenges of teaching, his desires lay with the judiciary. Enthusiastically, he announced his decision to intern with the "law court," *beit din*, and rested in satisfaction that he was one step closer to Abba's dream for him.

❦

A breeze tinged with the scent of budding spring flowers greet Saul with the morning dawn, but his head and eyes pounded as he hastened toward his assigned seat at the entrance of the Temple Mount. The memory of relentless studies had receded like the waves of the Gennesaret. His love for Jewish law and passion for justice had driven him to this day when he would begin assisting Temple priests in executing legal matters.

The priestly judge was waiting and greeted Saul at the gate.

"Boker tov, Dayan Zadok. I am Saul from Beit Gamaliel."

Dayan Zadok nodded dismissively and directed Saul to his position behind a small wooden table where a copy of the Torah had been laid.

"Boker tov, Saul. I know who you are, and I look forward to training you in honest and open judgment—applied with Torah wisdom and fairness." The priest addressed Saul matter-of-factly, without eye contact, as they took their positions behind the all-important Torah.

And I have heard of you, Zadok, a Levitical Dayan who is known to interpret the law in its strictest sense. Your lack of eye contact with me comes as no surprise. Those who know you describe you as impersonal,

73

aloof, and often arrogant. Saul had already started pondering how best to deal with those qualities in a superior.

Saul knew that the well-organized Jewish court system of which he was now a member, had well-defined channels of authority. When matters presented to the central court were clearly addressed in the codification of the *halakha*, members of the court heard the ruling, and judgment was pronounced without opportunity for appeal.

Freedom to follow the established code pleased Saul. He could express his judgment, but if he felt a problem needed further clarification or appeal, he could refer it to a higher court with more experience judges who would evaluate the issue and pass judgment.

Over the next several days, Saul observed as Zadok tirelessly listened to cases, clarifying halakha precedents, and pronouncing judgments—with no evidence of sympathy or compassion. Saul sat quietly, absorbing and learning, hoping to be asked to help make a judgment in matters that involved areas of his knowledge. However, his superior consistently made rulings without emotion and empathy. So consistently and with such callousness that Saul's frustration grew. Would he ever be offered an opportunity to insert himself into Zadok's judgment process?

One particularly slow day, a drizzle of cold rain slapped and spattered on the makeshift covering that protected the judges' desk. Only a few brave souls dared fight the elements to present their cases.

But early in the afternoon, a young couple appeared before Dayan Zadok.

The young husband, dripping and cold from the long journey, spoke, his voice shaking. "Sir, we are a Jewish husband and wife from the tribe of Benjamin in Bethlehem. We have not been blessed with children, but we love each other dearly. I have tried to bring brightness into our lives, but the crushing emptiness of our home has proven unbearable. After ten years of trying to have children, we now come before you, O righteousness Dayan, seeking a divorce."

Zadok gaze did not focus on the couple—the troubled husband and the grave-faced woman by his side. Instead, he drew his robes tighter, hunched his shoulders against the chilled and damp air, and offered only a monotone pronouncement. "I have heard your tale of woe. Here is my decision: A divorce will be best, and I hereby grant your request. Put this sadness behind you and move on."

Saul's anger flared as he listened to Zadok's counsel. *How dare this man exercise his authority as a judge of Israel in such a thoughtless, unscriptural, and ruthless manner?* Saul reined in his ire and forced himself not to speak the words pressing his lips. *I must conduct myself wisely and not incite Zadok's ever-ready pride.*

"Dayan Zadok, permit me to offer advice to this troubled couple," Paul suggested, his tone sedate.

"The student speaks," Dayan retorted sarcastically as he stood and strode toward a nearby portico for better shelter from the rain. Saul took his departure as permission, although not stated.

"You must understand that your problem is not unique," he said to the now shivering man and woman. "Many couples struggle to have children, as my mother and father did. But you have the most important ingredient for a successful marriage: intense love for each other. I can see the pain in your eyes as you wrestle with this. Let me tell you a story."

Saul rubbed his forehead with his index finger as he gathered his thoughts and then began.

"A pious couple responded to advice similar to what Dayan Zadok gave you."

Saul was careful not to undermine Dayan Zadok as a duly appointed judge under whose authority he sat.

"The couple heeded the advice and received permission for divorce and returned home. The family prepared a fitting feast for the last day of their marriage."

At his words, the couple glanced at each other as if wondering how they would endure a celebration of dissolution.

"At the meal, the wise woman poured cup after cup of wine for her husband. As he drank, his mood gradually lifted and he said to her: 'My dear, look around our house. Is there any precious item here that you would like? Please choose a keepsake and take it with you to your father's home, where you will soon be living.'"

The wife stood silently before Saul, the moisture on her face a mix of rain and tears.

"She waited until her husband fell into a deep sleep," Saul said. "Then, 'Quick,' she ordered her servants. 'Load him onto a litter and take him to my father's house!'"

The man's chin lifted slightly at Saul's words.

"At midnight, the husband woke sober. He yelled out in the darkness, 'Where am I?'"

"'You are in my father's house,'" his wife answered.

"'What am I doing here?'"

"'Did I not do exactly what you told me?' said she. 'You instructed me to take my most valued possession from your house back with me to my parents' home. You, my sweet, are my greatest treasure.'"

The man in front of Saul unclasped his hands and slowly reached for his wife's.

"Realizing that they were meant to be together, the couple once again approached their Rabbi, who prayed for them, and they were blessed with children."

Saul looked into the couple's eyes.

"Yahweh may grant you children as you ask Him in prayer, but the decision is His. And if you never have children, you will be able to say to each other: I desire nothing in the world more than *you*."

The husband moved his wife to lay her head against his chest. After a long embrace, they walked away with his arm around her.

The following day again held few cases to be heard. Saul and Zadok passed the time discussing recent judgments. As they talked, three men engaged in a heated, contentious argument approached Saul and Zadok. Zadok muttered something about needing to relieve himself as he strode away, leaving Saul to deal with the situation.

Inwardly, Saul was pleased, despite the challenge. He did not mind difficult cases. To the contrary, he found them interesting. They gave him opportunity to practice his profession and apply the law and common sense in the application of fair judgment. He inwardly thanked Yahweh that Zadok had stepped away. The case was a simple matter of hearing each man's argument, then showing them where each view was strong, and each view was weak. After hearing Saul's advice, the men left, having reached a mutual and amicable agreement.

Paul returned home that evening infused with new passion to execute the law and rise to the highest position of power Yahweh would grant him to bring righteous judgment to his people.

Day after day, the pattern continued. Saul and Dayan Zadok passed judgment on cases large and small that came before them. Late one morning after the rainy stretch had passed, a distraught young widow approached Zadok's bench with a stirring story.

"Last Shabbat, my dim-witted neighbor stabbed a man who had stolen his prize sheep. My neighbor fled to my house to hide from the Roman soldiers. I hid him for more than two days before he left to take refuge in the Judean hills. But my friend has told me I could be charged with aiding and abetting a murderer and face the wrath of Roman justice. Is this true?" The woman trembled as she waited. Saul's heart was moved.

Dayan Zadok spoke in his usual emotionless way.

"Did you know when you hid the man that he was a fugitive from the law? Did you ask him…?"

Saul dared to interrupt, brushing aside Zadok's irritated expression. "Dayan Zadok, remember that as a lower court we cannot judge or even hear a crime potentially connected with a murder case. This case must go before the Sanhedrin High Court."

Red-faced, Zadok turned to the woman. With jaw tight, he said, "My colleague is correct. Unfortunately, you must take your case to the Sanhedrin."

Word spread about Saul's even-handed judgment, and those who came before their table increasingly appealed to *his* judgment. Zadok's pride was slighted, and it was noted in both his posture, his coldness toward Saul, and his attitude toward those seeking judgment. Zadok grew increasingly rude and rigid—so much so that those seeking legal counsel in their court became obvious in their attempts to avoid him in favor of Saul.

The changing culture presented constant opportunities to test Saul's mettle and his interpretations of the law. Many in and around Jerusalem had accepted the practice of destroying unwanted pregnancies. One searing afternoon, a young woman approached Zadok, her body bent forward, and her expression tight and angry.

"In the late evening, I was heading toward Gihon Spring for our family's daily water," she began. Saul could hear despair in her voice. "As I made my way through the groves on the Mount of Olives, suddenly a hooded man attacked and raped me. Now I'm in danger of being pregnant and that my husband might take revenge because he is outraged with thoughts that I was unfaithful or was raped. I see the hatred in his eyes every time he looks at me. I fear what he might do. Does the law permit me to prove I have not been unfaithful to my husband and if pregnant rid my body of the bastard growing inside me?" she spit out.

Dayan Zadok deliberated a few moments, consulting the Torah in the middle of the table, and then responded.

"The Law doesn't speak directly to this subject. But the Torah allows for a *sotah,* which permits a husband, when he suspects his wife has been unfaithful and will thereby give birth to a child who is not his, such an option. I suggest you use an abortifacient by drinking the 'ordeal of bitter water,' which will help prove your story. If you have told the truth about the rape and drink the water of bitterness, you will survive the ordeal even though you may become very sick. And if you are pregnant, it is likely you will lose your child."

Saul had seen this response in Zadoc before. He was hoping to dismiss the issue with as little compassion and time as possible. "The Scripture also gives you permission by way of example from *Shemot.*"

He cleared his throat, as if for emphasis. "If men fight, and hurt an *isha harah* (pregnant woman), so that she gives birth prematurely but not with any injury; he shall be surely punished, according as the *ba'al haisha* will assess a fine upon him; and he shall pay as the judges determine. And if any *ason* (harm, fatality) follow, then thou shalt take *nefesh for nefesh,*

Ayin for ayin, shen for shen, yad for yad, regel for regel."

Saul bit his tongue as Zadok continued. "Notice the impact of the saying. If the harm to the unborn spoke only of miscarriage, the teaching would then support the life of an unborn child with only a fine, and only if the mother later died, would *her* death require taking the criminal's life. So, my judgment is for you to drink the abortifactant to be certain you will not give birth to a bastard."

Zadok leaned back in his chair, locked his fingers, and smiled thinly.

"Before you proceed down this path," Saul interjected, no longer caring if he offended Zadok, "there is no reason to assume from the Torah that the woman was unfaithful and impure or pregnant. The final proof of her guilt of unfaithfulness would be pregnancy." Drinking the abortifactant demonstrates in a practical way the innocence or guilt of the woman with a miscarriage or the swelling of the abdomen."

Saul took a deep breath, as he often did when he knew he would be challenged. "Let's look at this in a more meaningful way. Remember, dear ones, an unborn child is a human life and as such is a valuable creation of our Heavenly AV. While a child may seem like a burden now, the baby is God's gift to you, and the infant will bless others. Our father David wrote of the precious value of human life."

Zadok closed his eyes in disrespect as Saul continued. "God clearly specifies that a human baby is formed in a mother's womb in a manor fitting His glory and plan. Our heavenly Father forms each baby and ordains the existence of every infant."

As Paul's conviction grew, his voice strengthened. "Our prophet Jeremiah also says, 'Before I formed you in the womb I knew you, before you were born I set you apart; I appointed you as a prophet to the nations.' Job also speaks of the humanity of the unborn. 'Did not he who made me in the womb make them? Did not the same one form us both within our mothers?'"

Saul rushed on before Zadok, who was now clearly angry, could deter him.

"If the unborn child is a human created by the Holy One, then is that unborn child not a life worth preserving—and destroying the child not an act of murder?"

Saul knew Torah scholars varied in their opinions, and he did not hesitate to disagree with elder sages. Especially Zadok Dayan, who often ruled out of tradition or pride.

Dayan shook his head in frustration. After a long pause, he

leaned back in his chair and snipped, "You are free to choose between our judgments. Go with our blessing." Then he dismissed the young woman with his hand. She quickly draped her head with a shawl and hurried away.

Frustrated, Saul turned to his superior. "Note the intricacies of the story, Dayan. If a pregnant woman gives birth prematurely but there is no serious injury, the offender must be fined whatever the woman's husband demands and the court allows. But if there is serious injury to the child or mother, a life is to be taken for a life. Therefore, the passage imposes only a fine on the criminal who *accidentally* causes a premature birth, but the punishment is life for life if the baby dies."

The debate ended with Saul and Dayan disagreeing, and Saul certain that once again his desire for a fair interpretation of the Law had stirred Dayan Zadok's ire against him. No matter, Saul conviction to refuse to compromise the teaching of scripture deepened.

The day ended without further disagreement, but concerns still troubled Saul. *The people are talking about my court rulings and view me as a fair judge, but Zadok sees me as an upstart Pharisee who threatens his leadership. I'm certain he is drawing Temple priests to his side and filling them with reports that are inciting fear and anger toward me.*

What life have I chosen? What enemies are forming against me in Judaism, my first love and my call, and what battles may lie ahead for me?

❧

Saul walked slowly toward the Xystus, where the graduates would form a line. His one-year Beit Gamaliel internship was complete. The time had passed as quickly as a star falls from the heavens, and the day for *semicha*—ordination and laying on of hands—had arrived. A shiver of anxiety ran through his body. Every student who had completed their formal studies and internship faced oral examination by the presiding rabbi. Those who passed their oral examination would be ordained. And those who did not?

Saul could not allow himself to think of the humiliation.

Semicha ensured that each student was a worthy link in the Mosaic Law tradition and authorized to judge cases involving punishment. Young sages would receive the title "rabbi."

Saul stepped into the line of candidates preparing to file into the Xystus. The building's highly polished floors and partial roof supported by fluted pillars created an imposing entry. The entire structure was walled, and outside, marketplace patrons passed through as they entered the Temple area.

To his surprise, Saul had no difficulty answering the oral examination questions. His eyes searched the crowd of family members, friends, dignitaries from the Sanhedrin, and Roman-appointed dignitaries that included Caiaphas and the high priest Annas. Abba had not come. Saul's younger self still felt reverberations of anger. And, of course, Ima would not have come without Abba.

I will never be enough for him. The words echoed through Saul's head, overshadowing the joy of the day.

He watched as the dignitaries were seated on backed benches under the shade of the roofed portion of the Xystus. The high priest Annas, respected by Jews throughout the land, slowly rose and spoke in short wisps of breath that betrayed his age and addressed the candidates.

"Young men, Moses placed his hands upon worthy sages and commanded them, in accordance with what the Lord had spoken, to take their ordination seriously. Torah tells us that Moses ordained seventy judges. Likewise, Joshua and the seventy elders ordained others, and they in turn gave *semicha* to their disciples. One day you will be called upon to ordain others to come behind you—be faithful in your duties."

Annas haltingly took his seat and Rabban Gamaliel rose to speak.

Rabban Gamaliel, the title reserved for the patriarchate, stood erect before the distinguished guests. "This occasion is the formal recognition of your outstanding accomplishments while studying in Beit Hillel. You represent the great traditions of our sacred Torah. Serve your office with piety and holiness. Judge honestly, fairly, and impartially. Your decisions must be based on Torah, applied with wisdom and logic."

Saul felt a surge of pride as he rose with the candidates and filed to the center of the open area, where the sages formed a circle around them and placed their hands upon the graduates' heads. In solemn tones, Caiaphas offered a parting challenge and prayer of dedication.

At his final words, the candidates turned to each other with congratulations, embraces, and words of parting.

Paul scanned the crowd one final time.

Strangers. Peers. Pharisees.

He is old, and it is to be expected, no matter what I achieve. It will never change, and I must lay it aside.

If I only knew how.

☙

With ordination over, Saul set his eyes upon his future. He continued studying in beit din and lecturing in the Hall of Hewn Stones, where he quickly became a prominent force in intellectual debates between Pharisee and Sadducee scholars.

With new-found leadership and the respect of Temple insiders, Saul of Tarsus quickly rose in the ranks of elite Pharisaical Judaism. At the same time, a growing self-loathing and deep anger stoked the fires of his blind zeal for the letter of Jewish law. And hatred for all else.

CHAPTER 10
SAUL MEETS JESUS

With his first awareness of morning, Saul was greeted by the pain in his head that had kept him awake far into the preceding night. He forced his aching legs to move and threw off his wool blanket. Pain or no pain, he had to get up. The morning sun had warmed his stark room, but he dared not tarry. Passover had arrived, and he was late for predawn worship.

As a boy, he'd tried to envision his future. Saul had never been drawn to Abba's tentmaking craft. But he'd also never envisioned himself rising for a rabbi's daily prayer and study.

As Saul washed up, he remembered it was the Passover Feast's Sabbath day. He would not be required to provide judging services because laws that legislated Sabbath behavior would limit the day's routine.

Dawn was rising and warming his family's home. Since returning to the Nebi Samwil district after completing Beit Hillel, Saul's morning began each day in the comfortable private living space Abba had built for him on the side of their house. Saul was now on his own and expected to find his own niche in the sacred world.

After completing his years of study, Rabbi Saul had finally attained the ability to earn a living, his income funded by taxes paid to the Temple, from *Machatzit Hashekel* ("half-shekel"), an annual tax/donation of a half-shekel paid by every Jewish man over the age of twenty. This special tax provided funds for maintaining the Temple.

as well as judges' salaries. The taxes his father often complained about were now providing Saul's income.

He also received a portion of communal funds collected specifically for rabbis, whether rich or poor, who taught Jewish youth. It was customary for every individual to pay tuition for their child if they could afford it. This allowed a steady income for Saul. If a person lacked the ability to pay, the community was required to pay on their behalf. The system, of which he was now was a key part, had developed from years of careful adherence to the law and respect for the hierarchy of leadership. He would do everything in his power to uphold the tradition.

Saul spent his day in the Temple and surrounding area ministering to worshippers who had faithfully come from all over the country—as they did according to the requirement three times a year—for the Passover Feast.

But as the day wore on, Saul joined a group of Pharisees walking along the rugged ravine of the Tyropoeon Valley that separated Mount Moriah (Temple Mount) from where Mount Zion emptied into the Hinnom Valley. As they strolled, they discussed the day's activities and their experiences with various worshippers.

The lead Pharisee spoke of his self-avowed accomplishments. "I caught a group from Samaria traveling on the Sabbath more than the stipulated two thousand cubits." His chest puffed with pride. "I gladly assessed a tax for their oversight."

The story brought chucks from some in the group. Not all Pharisees were dedicated to the service of their God. It was an honorable occupation with rewards of power, authority, and a handsome income.

Saul glanced at the other Pharisees, but no one acknowledged the overt display of hubris.

Is this the essence of guarding the Law and teaching its fulfillment?

"I found a camel driver," one of the newly ordained Pharisees stated proudly, "tying a knot forbidden on the Sabbath in the 'descendant works of the Law.' He tried to justify the task by saying that he was tying a necessary knot on a broken sandal strap so he could get to the Temple."

"What punishment did you apply?" inquired a Pharisee, who had been straining to hear.

The first priest huffed. "I'm sure he thought his 'reason' would gain my mercy and I would let him off. For his arrogance, I doubled his penance."

Stories of petty infractions and rigid punishments flowed like freshly drawn blood as the group continued their walk. Saul remained silent but noted every detail.

Earlier in the day he'd caught wind of an acutely curious and intriguing rumor that had warranted growing attention around Jerusalem, Judea, and Galilee. Supposedly, a religious teacher called *Jesus of Nazareth* was stirring up the masses performing what was claimed to be miracles and teaching contrary to the doctrines of the religious leaders.

A guest traveling to Jerusalem claimed he saw the man called Jesus turn drinking water into wine at a wedding feast. While such rumors were often summarily dismissed, the stories about Jesus were different. For some time, reports had been circulating that the mysterious Nazarene had the power to heal and even forgive sins.

How could such things be possible? Unless …

As they walked, Saul kept his eyes fixed on the path. "Are you hearing reports about the one called Jesus from Nazareth?" He kept his tone indifferent.

The tall pharisee with the peculiar voice snickered. "I've heard that he has conscripted followers to spread heresy against our beloved elders and the Torah. They say he can perform miracles, unlike soothsayers and magicians—which I doubt.

"He is simply another clever magician pulling childish tricks on the gullible. The ignorant peasants in Galilee fall for every swindle that comes along."

Another pharisee chimed in. "He arrogantly claims to be of royal blood and seeks to take our land for a kingdom."

The quick-tempered Pharisee bully shook his fist. "He recently tried to convert one of our sages to become his follower by telling him he must be born a second time. This comes after the Nazarene claimed to be able to forgive sins. Heresy!"

A pharisee named Levi joined in with the sneers. "That is disgusting. How can one climb back into his mother's womb again? I don't imagine his ima would favor that."

The men laughed as more joined in the ridicule.

The tall pharisee prodded the group. "I heard the fable that this Jesus came to the temple as a child and preached to the Sanhedrin, claiming that they didn't understand the Law. According to the story, our master teacher, Gamaliel was there listening to his foolery."

Laughing, he continued. "He must have torn his tunic to shreds to hear such blasphemy."

Saul couldn't remain silent no longer. Shading his eyes from the sun's glare, he turned toward his fellow pharisees.

"You dismiss this man far too lightly. Our leaders are beyond concerned. While they instruct us to ignore him as a charlatan, they privately fear his growing influence among the Jews—and their alarm increases with every new believer."

Saul hoped his sharp tone caused the men to take note. "As guardians of the Truth, we must be vigilant against all attempts to suppress, destroy, or undermine our sacred law—to the point of confrontation and punishment!"

The men fell silent, then, quietly meandered away, talking in whispers among themselves. As they approached the Sheep Gate, Rabbi Akiva, their former beit Midrash teacher, joined them.

Recognizing an opportunity, Levi stepped into pace beside Akiva. "Have you heard that the heretic, Jesus of Nazareth accuses us of being overly zealous regarding outward, ritual observances and keeping the minutiae of the law? And he even condemns us for appearing pious in public?" His tone dripped with sarcasm.

Saul observed Akiva's hesitation, as if to be sure his comments were limited to only the other pharisees. "His teaching in his home country of Galilee is becoming a blight upon our order. I know you are keeping the law and enforcing it, but this Jesus is corrupting all we have taught for generations."

Unlike the others, did Akiva know of widespread fear? The look on his face told Saul the rabbi knew more than he was telling.

"I just returned from Galilee where religious rebellion is festering and turning multitudes astray. I have just spent two days with the Sanhedrin discussing what to do about Jesus and his heretical teaching."

"What did you decide?" Saul quickly interjected.

Akiva stopped, reached down, picked up a hand full of dust and let it sift through his hands. "We have issued orders to keep a strict watch on him." His tone was ominous. "Our sages seek to trap him into breaking the Law, and we will be done with him. But we must be cautious, for his followers are growing in numbers daily, and we do not want to incite their suspicion."

Seth, the youngest of the pharisees, had been following slightly behind to hear the discussion. "He told a merchant I do business with that the leaders of Judaism teach the law but do not practice the most important parts of the law—justice, mercy, and faithfulness to God. He insists we only obey the minutiae, such as tithing spices, but not the weightier matters."

Saul had heard enough, and he forced himself to remain in control. "Will this Jesus come to Jerusalem, stir up the masses, and flaunt our authority?" Pain pulsed through his eyes, but he continued. "This false teacher is a threat to all we believe and must be stopped. The only question is whether we trick him into blasphemy or gather evidence of his heresy. I vow to do everything within my power to thwart this imposter's teaching—to death if need be."

Whispered comments faded to silence as the men slowly continued their walk, veiled in somber contemplation.

Soon they approached the Sheep's Gate and the Pool of Bethesda, the well-known pool that drew multitudes for healing when an angel of the Lord stirred the waters. Just beyond the gate, a commotion roared, and Saul was pulled from deep thought as the pharisees sought the source of the noise. Saul noticed the crowd parting, and a man coming toward him carrying a pallet and dancing as he made his way toward the gate. But his way was blocked by the crowd that surrounded him, laughing, clapping, and praising God.

The Pharisees burst out in rage—for the clamor and the violation of the Sabbath, but also because their path was obstructed.

Saul bellowed over the noise of the crowd. "What is going on, and why are you violating the Sabbath? You—you!" He pointed toward the dirty, disheveled man. "Carrying your pallet is a violation of the commandment to keep the Sabbath holy. What is your name?"

Waiting, Saul expected the lawbreaker to hesitate, apologize, or beg for mercy. Was the violator too weak of mind to know he had been confronted by a powerful Pharisee who was backed by the witness of other Pharisees? Did he not know he stood in grave danger?

But the man lifted his arms and held his mat over his head as if in victory, his face alternating wonder, joy, and confusion. He did not cower, apologize, or beg for mercy.

"My name is Abner, and for thirty-eight years I have suffered as a paralytic. Today a man who passed by said to me, 'Pick up your mat and walk.' My crooked legs straightened, but I experienced no pain. The crowd saw my legs become new again. At first I was afraid, but I stood, and my feet and legs were strong. The stranger healed me! He healed me!" Tears coursed down the man's face.

Levi the Pharisee opened his mouth to speak, but Abner quickly raised his voice. "I was sure I would fall. As I attempted to stand, I leaned on the arm of the friend who had brought me to this pool again and again. Suddenly, I realized I needed no assistance! For thirty-eight years my legs refused to move. Now I can jump and dance!"

He fixed his gaze at the Pharisees as he leaped into the air. Then again. And again. Paul's pulse thundered in his neck. How dare this man defy their authority in such a brazen way?

"Rabbi, I need to carry my pallet. Would Yahweh expect me to leave my mat behind, my only possession, on a day when I can now carry it and praise His name for healing me?"

Saul heard ripples of laughter drift throughout the crowd. The shame of childhood derision shot through him like the sear of a branding iron. Anger flamed into rage. A retort formed, but caught in his throat.

From the corner of his eye, Saul saw the Pharisees trading glances. He sensed their tension and saw their jaws tighten and brows furrow. They were waiting for him to reveal the trickery of what the crowd had seen and to respond with righteous anger and commensurate punishment.

Paul seethed. *This troublemaker Abner is trying to make us look like fools, and I must make sure that he pays.*

But what happened today? Everyone in the community knows this paralytic by name. He has sat beside the pool so long that we expect to see him there. I myself have seen the healing effects of these waters for many years, but never anything as profound as this—a known paralytic who could instantly walk again.

How can this miracle be explained? Only witchcraft could accomplish such a thing. Or perhaps … Could this be Jesus from Nazareth … But Saul could not allow himself to entertain such a thought.

"Who is this man who told you to pick up your mat and walk?" Saul challenged, his voice harsh.

"I don't know who he is." Abner rubbed his thighs, as if exploring the wonders of his newly functional limbs. "When I looked up after I stood, he had disappeared."

Why the hesitation? Maybe he'd been overwhelmed, which would make sense. Or perhaps he was trying to protect the person who healed him. If it was the Nazarene, perhaps he was practicing witchcraft, which would explain his power. and increase the need for the Sanhedrin to lay their trap. Evidence was clear that harassment and threats would not stop Jesus or his followers. The Sanhedrin needed to lay their trap with haste!

"You know we have means to force you to tell the truth, don't you?" Saul stepped forward as he spoke, his voice hissing with rage.

How dare this man lie to me? If, indeed, he was healed, he would certainly know who did it and why, and if it was the work of the Nazarene.

"Your healing is a ruse," Saul spit out. "You are a fraud and are now trying to evade punishment for carrying your mat on the Sabbath."

Abner swallowed and sweat broke out on his forehead as the joy drained from his face.

"I did hear someone in the crowd mention that the Prophet from Galilee was among us," He is known for miracles and healings. Maybe he healed me as he passed." But his demeanor shifted as he straightened his shoulders and said, "You can ask others who were at the pool if I am correct. I am going to the Temple to give thanks, and I will find the *medicus* if he is there and point him out to you if you follow."

Saul turned to the other Pharisees who were intently listening. With his brows raised, he snorted. "Can anything good come out of rebel-infested Galilee, home of despicable zealots and Sicarii, among the most skilled assassins in the world? If your medicus is here in Jerusalem, he is recruiting rebels to overthrow the Romans and establish a Jewish kingdom. He is a traitor, and we seek to arrest him."

Saul turned again to the accused and unfurled his scorn. "Go to the Temple and offer sacrifices to make amends for your indiscretion. If we hear that you are spreading lies about your healing, we will take the fullest measures justice offers. Be waiting for us when we get to the Temple. Now get out of here and find Jesus of Nazareth!"

Turning quickly, Abner ran in the direction of the Temple without the merest sight of a limp. As the crowd watched him speed away, new ire rose in Saul. The man's very existence was testimony of healing, whether he spoke a word or not.

As whispers drifted on a soft breeze, the crowd began to disperse, and the Pharisees turned toward the Temple in clusters marked by animated conversation. Saul remained behind and questioned onlookers for confirmation of the presence of the so-called Prophet from Galilee.

But he had already learned what he needed to know. Jesus of Nazareth was a real and rising threat to Judaism. His overriding goal as a Pharisee had become clear—to seek out and destroy not only the Nazarene, but also his message.

CHAPTER 11

TEMPLE CHAOS

Abner stood in the shade of a Temple portico, out of view. Saul and other Pharisees had arrived and were wandering the square, observing the comings and goings of worshippers who might be committing Sabbath infractions while they also searched for him. He could not hide in the shadows much longer. He would have to reveal himself to the Pharisees who had refused to believe his healing was a God-given miracle.

Suddenly, Abner felt the weight of a hand rest gently on his shoulder. He gasped, forcing himself not to scream. As he turned, he found himself looking into the gentlest eyes he had ever seen—loamy brown and flecked with gold. The *medicus* spoke softly in a Galilean Aramaic accent.

"I *chose* to make you whole again, Abner. I came because you needed me. Your sin separates you from God. Repent and turn from your sinful ways. I offer you more than new legs today. I offer you new life."

Sin? Does the Nazarene who healed me also call me a sinner for carrying my mat? Did he heal me, only to leave me to be stoned when I get up and walk after thirty-eight years?

"Stop sinning? By carrying my mat after you heal me? I've been a paralytic all my life. Tell me, how did I sin when I could not even move?" Abner retorted.

He pushed Jesus' hand from his shoulder and fled across the Temple square in Saul's direction.

I'm better off telling the Pharisee that the Prophet from Galilee healed me and is here and beg for mercy. All my life I have been told that I could not walk because of my sin or my parents' sin. My legs were paralyzed at birth, so maybe the sin was the fault of my Ima. I want to be forgiven and free from condemnation before I die, but perhaps this is never possible!

As Abner's newly strengthened legs carried him toward the Pharisees, the words of the medicus pounded through his mind. *I chose to make you whole, Abner. I offer you new life.*

How had the prophet known his name? And what "new life" did he speak of?

Approaching the Pharisee who had questioned him at the pool, Abner stopped.

"The Prophet from Galilee who healed me is there." He turned and pointed to his medicus, who had stepped out of the shadows into full view.

Saul dismissed Abner with a flip of his hand. "We know he is here. You may go, but you are never to speak about him to anyone. We will deal with him."

Like a bug flicked from the Pharisee's robe, Abner was dismissed. He turned away and stepped behind a nearby pillar where he was out of view and listened. The group of Pharisees had gathered and were plotting their next move against the Prophet from Galilee. A young Pharisee spoke first.

"We have been looking for charges worthy of a death warrant. The Nazarene has violated the Sabbath, so we can have him stoned."

A Pharisee wearing a colorful *migbalah* around his head interrupted. "He is not only guilty of breaking the Sabbath, but he also makes himself equal with Yahweh. He claims to forgive sins and breaks any commandments he chooses. Pharisees in Galilee have told us he claims to forgive sins—the ultimate blasphemy and something only Yahweh can do."

A senior Pharisee new to the conversation stepped up. "We have been watching this rebel for months. His ministry had been confined to cities around the Sea of Galilee. But his following is now gaining momentum, and he is recruiting many disciples. He is the devil's sorcerer, a threat to our authority, and a danger to our relationship with Roman prefect, Pilate."

Abner's stomach roiled. Was the Nazarene a healer or a heretic?

Saul scratched his chin. "I knew he was preaching in Galilee. But until now, I thought he was preaching a reform of Judaism, rather than an actual threat to our authority and existence. I will be watching him carefully and will ask Joseph, my friend in the Temple Guard, to keep his eye on him while Jesus is in Jerusalem. We may need Joseph's assistance later when we arrest this menace."

A short distance from the Pharisees, the Prophet from Galilee had started speaking to a small crowd of worshippers. Abner could hear bits of his message. "… my Father is always at His work to this very day, and I, too, am working."

Would the Pharisees notice him? Abner held his breath. Ah. They had looked his way. All Pharisee eyes shifted to the scene and the Nazarene's words. "My Father is always at His work…"

Swallowing, Abner marveled. *Jesus never paused or glanced their way. Obviously, no Pharisee can intimidate the medicus or stop His message.*

Who is this man? Where does he get the authority to stand up to the leaders of Judaism?

If the Nazarene continues to test the limits of the Law, the Pharisees will prosecute him as a blasphemous Sabbath-breaker, which will mean certain death. Why is he willing to risk death for his message?

As he watched the rabbi from Galilee interact with the crowd, Abner made a vow. He would follow this teacher, learn more about him, and decide for himself. After sitting at the roadside his entire life, he was ready to find a purpose for living.

ᴇↄ

Saul slowly paced the wooden platform, arms folded behind his waist, until he reached the end, pivoted, and walked in the opposite direction. Again. Again. His eyes scanned the crowd at Anna's Bazaar. The shopping area in the Temple courtyard buzzed with activity, providing services and goods to the many Passover worshippers.

As a neophyte Pharisee, Saul had been assigned to keep order between worshippers and Temple merchants during the feast. Disputes often turned violent when priests and rabbis falsely declared worshippers' sacrifices unworthy. For this reason, Saul had requested that a raised dais be constructed to give him a better view of the crowd.

In the distance, he spotted a familiar face and smiled. He quickly made his way down the stairs from the platform and pushed his way through the throng of men and women. Two money changers had set up makeshift shops in booths with goatskin awnings for protection from the sun. Both merchants were busy exchanging foreign money into local shekels to be used for Temple taxes.

Saul's former classmate, Uziel, was entering one of the money-changing booths. Saul called out, hoping to be heard above the clamor of bleating sheep, hawking cries of vendors, and vociferous bartering for doves.

"*Shalom Aleichem*, Uziel."

"Aleichem shalom," Saul's friend shouted back, and raised a hand in greeting. "I have not seen you in a long time. Have you been well?"

Saul pushed through the crowd to the moneychanger's booth, stepped inside, and greeted him. "Yes, thanks be to Adonai, I am fine. My duties keep me occupied, and I am enjoying my assignment. Have you heard word of any of our friends from Beit Hillel?"

"Yes, Saul, I have. Have you heard about Joseph of Cyprus?"

On the far side of the courtyard Saul could hear voices rising, but he ignored the clamor and focused on Uziel's words.

"No, but you know Joseph was my closest friend in Beit Hillel. I have seen him on occasion when I need a favor from the Temple Guard but know little more. What have you heard?"

Uziel stroked his beard. "Joseph is being influenced by the Nazarene, and certain priests are concerned about his loyalties. He still works with the Temple Guard, but I have heard rumors that he is unhappy and is planning to leave."

Planning to leave the Temple Guard? Impossible. No Pharisee would walk away from such a position of honor. He would be walking away from all he has ever known and worked for. And for what?

"I find this hard to believe. The Nazarene is a diabolical deceiver who is leading many astray. I am sorry to hear Joseph is listening to that charlatan. My friend had a promising career." Saul paused for a breath. "But he always seemed to be seeking more from the scriptures than just the Torah law. Looking for the messiah. I can see how Joseph would be a gullible candidate for the false claims of a self-proclaimed messiah."

Oh, Joseph, my friend. How could you have been so deceived?

Saul had barely absorbed the disturbing news about Joseph when a man in a nearby inspection booth began yelling at the rabbi in charge about declaring lambs unsuitable for sacrifice. Saul excused himself from conversation with Uziel and hurried in the direction of the commotion.

A distressed man in shepherd's clothing stood stroking a white lamb led by a rope. "This lamb is pure and spotless. I am Elias ben Kenon from Galilee, and I have raised this lamb from birth to a yearling. My family and my father before me are known for respectfully caring for our animals like Yahweh's own, and we have always raised pristine, pure sheep who have never been rejected. Never. In generations. You may ask anyone in Galilee and regions beyond."

Elias glared at the rabbi, his hands now on his hips.

A voice rose from the crowd. "All of Galilee knows Elias' reputation. He raises the finest sacrificial lambs and is an honest man. The Passover inspectors know this."

A murmur spread like spilled water among those gathered.

"We've also heard," the voice continued, "that you are an inspector who cheats worshippers to put money in your own pockets."

The murmuring grew, and Saul felt a measure of fear in the voices. However, the anonymous speaker continued. "If you reject this yearling, Elias will be forced to sell it below market value and buy a new yearling, and the kickback money will come to you, will it not?"

The inspecting rabbi crossed his arms, his face flushed with rage. "One more word of accusation against me, and I will have the Temple Guard haul the lot of you away!"

The crowd quieted as Saul's eyes bored into Elias. The law must be upheld.

"Your yearling is rejected. Leave and bring back a spotless lamb instead of this filthy, speckled one."

"You are a thief and a crook hiding beneath the robes of a rabbi. May your mother be a leper!"

"Stand down, Elias!" Saul interjected. "Do not force me to call the Temple Guard and have you removed. The inspector's determination stands. No exceptions, no appeals. Now take your yearling sheep and go."

"I will go as you say," Elias stated loudly, pulling himself to his full height, "after I make my case. Before you I bring an unblemished prize yearling that I must now sell for table scraps. I am now forced to buy a replacement lamb from Temple priests for an inflated price. I refuse to give you the satisfaction of cheating me. I will take my lamb home and let *Elohim mishpat*, the God of Justice, judge you for your cheating."

"Do as you like," Saul replied coldly as he walked away to oversee other vendors and worshippers. But within a few steps, he paused as he passed a table filled with an assortment of aromatic, freshly baked bread.

At that moment, a cacophony erupted at the far end of the market. Loud thuds, one after the other, as if the booths, tables, and verandas were collapsing. Among the din, he heard dove wings beating against cages, bleating sheep scrambling, goats ramming through the crowd. But nothing more shocking than the rush of worshippers, trampling over each other to flee the Temple courtyard, careening straight toward him.

The Passover Feast bazaar transformed to mayhem.

Saul reached out and caught the mantle of a young man trying to scramble through the crowd. "What's going on?" he demanded.

"The Nazarene ... turning over the money changers' tables, and the seats of the merchants selling doves!"

Saul clutched his robe as he glanced in the direction of the chaos.

"He is saying," the young man panted, "that the Temple is God's house of prayer and the priests and rabbis have made it into a den of thieves. People are yelling, arguing, and some are frightened."

The young man jerked his arm and broke away from Saul's hold, then melted into the river of people headed toward the street.

Saul rushed toward the guard house, stumbling past terrified men and women, young and old, and uncaged animals, to summon the Temple Guard to attend to the disruption. But the guard station was empty.

One glance at the Temple courtyard told Saul that the Nazarene was gone. Vanished into the fleeing crowd.

In the aftermath, amid the cursing, accusations, and frantic plans to put to behind them what Jesus had so publicly upended, Jewish authorities gathered to determine how to destroy Jesus of Nazareth. But they soon discovered that growing numbers of worshippers and curious followers applauded his message, even his approach.

Based on this newfound knowledge, the Sanhedrin and Pharisees prepared to manage riots that seemed to be simmering beneath the surface at public gatherings. Since the incident at the Temple. Jesus' name was a topic of hot debate among the people.

And hatred for the Galilean who threatened to extinguish his beloved faith gnawed more deeply into Saul's soul. And with the growing hatred, growing anger—not only toward Jesus—but, strangely, for the boy inside him who silently watched as a knife drew the blood of an innocent slave girl.

CHAPTER 12

THE WAY

So much had changed so quickly that even the air felt different atop the Mount of Olives. How had his life changed so quickly? From the rough life of a fisherman to chosen disciple of the greatest of the Messiah, the Son of God. How could this be true? Nothing in the past weeks had prepared Peter for the wonders and the horrors. Nothing was the same as it had been before Jesus. And now—after today—nothing would ever be the same again.

Peter shaded his eyes as he gazed, transfixed, into the translucent Judean sky. He blinked as he searched the azure expanse. His mind told him that what he had witnessed was impossible, but his heart shouted that it was true.

Moments before, Jesus had lifted from the ground before his eyes, then slowly risen through the air and disappeared behind a cluster of puffy clouds.

Gone. My Lord is gone.

He rehearsed the surreal events of the past few years.

Like a hammer on a blacksmith's anvil, Jesus' first words to him rang through Peter's memory.

"Come, follow me."

He had followed, obeyed, and breathed in every word, even walking on tumbling sea waves to follow his Lord.

And then, the denial had so easily slipped from his lips.

Denial that had been forgiven by the one who'd been taken from them, returned to them from the dead, and now had risen in the clouds.

Peter fell to his knees in the stony soil of the Mount of Olives. His fingers bit into the dirt as he rocked back and forth, his chest heaving.

Why? Why did the Lord choose **me**? *I'm not a teacher or a rabbi or even the best fisherman. I talk when I should listen and rush to judgment. I'm stubborn and selfish. So why did He choose me to witness His miracle walk on the sea? Why did He choose me when He knew I would deny Him in a flash of fear? And if He ever loved me, how could He possibly still love me? And yet, He does. He does. He's enlisted me—ME!—to spread His message.*

Peter pressed his hands to his face to hide his tears.

Lord, I cannot change the wrongs of my past, but because of You, I am forgiven. You promise to use me despite my many failures. I am unworthy, but cleansed through Your blood and chosen by You. I offer my life to You. Work in me through Your power and make me a worthy servant for whatever lies ahead.

Peter wiped his face, then stood and glanced around. Other disciples had come to the Mount of Olives to see Jesus. They, too, had witnessed His ascent and were scattered, kneeling or standing with hands lifted to the skies. He saw fear and despair on some of their faces, and he understood.

How could his friends who had also followed Jesus, make sense of this conclusion to the last years? They had seen the lame walk, the wind and waves obey, demons flee, the dead rise to new life—all at Jesus' command.

And now He was gone. They were alone. But He'd left them with a promise. A comforter, He'd said. But what did that mean?

Peter turned to face the valley. He needed time to think. He plucked a pebble from the sparse grass and hurled it.

Then he drew his prayer shawl over his head, asking God to soothe the aching pain in his heart.

☙

The aroma of herb-crusted lamb filled the upper room, and Peter inhaled deeply. Mary had busied herself for days preparing food for the gathering.

"May it help take her mind off the departure of her son." Peter thought, as he glanced around the room Jesus and the disciples had shared for their last Passover meal. Caleb, leader of the God-fearing Essenes who lived near Qumran and the Dead Sea, had traveled to Jerusalem to meet with the disciples and had generously offered them use of his business space. Peter and the other disciples had thanked him, then notified Jesus' mother, and a few other women who'd followed Him, when to join them in the room in the Essene quarter.

When everyone arrived, they settled on pillows around a low central table where the women set out Z'roa (roasted shank bones); bitter maror; charoset made with figs, dates, walnuts and wine; salt water, and boiled potatoes. A quick look around the room told Peter that everyone was anxious to discuss plans and pray for the promised coming of the Holy Spirit. While they all weren't sure what that meant, Jesus had commanded them to wait in Jerusalem.

And so, here they had gathered, obedient and expectant.

Peter took a sip of wine and led the group in prayer. Jesus had placed the role of leadership upon his shoulders, and he had humbly accepted it. He still carried the weight of publicly denying his Master. Yet Jesus had reassured him that His death atoned for all sin. Peter's sin no longer existed. As a forgiven child of God, he no longer lived under condemnation.

The other disciples and Jesus' followers were looking to him for direction. He took a deep breath. "Before Jesus ascended into the clouds, He gave us a profound exhortation: 'Do not leave Jerusalem, but wait for the gift my Av promised, which you have heard Me speak about.' Therefore, we are here to discuss how we move forward and to pray. But first I would like to discuss a practical matter with you."

He paused and looked around the table. The time had come to discuss a question he knew weighed on the minds of many present. "Our Lord gave us the command to go into all the world to preach the gospel, but He did not tell us what to do about our families. I have a wife, Abigail, and two sons. While I followed Jesus these past three years, I entrusted my family to my mother-in-law. But what do husbands like me do now if we are called to travel to distant locations like Greece and Rome?"

Philip motioned first to speak, and a sense of calm flooded through Peter. He could count on Philip for sound counsel, and the other disciples loved him deeply. Always eager to encourage those around him, Philip's words were life-giving. "I appreciate the kind and generous spirit of my wife and her love and care for our children. Sarah willingly sacrificed to enable me to follow Jesus and do his work. She has told me she will continue to do so for as long as I follow the call of Jesus. And our oldest son Elijah is now in an apprenticeship for his trade. He can help."

Next, Bo John, brother of James, son of Zebedee, and one of the sons of thunder, told the group that he believed the Lord had called him to remain single to better serve Him. Matthew the tax collector stated that his wife would stay at her parents' estate with other family members to enable him to follow his calling.

Peter scanned the room, his heart glowing with gratitude for his friends and companions in the gospel. "Your commitment to our Lord blesses me as I see your faith. We do not know what lies ahead, but we will continue to trust Av to help us protect and raise our families as we fulfill His mission."

Didymus Thomas had been trying to gain his attention, and now he raised a hand. Peter sighed inwardly. Like himself, Thomas had a reputation for impetuous speaking, as well as deep-seated skepticism. He typically asked more questions than everyone else at a gathering combined, before his mind could settle on a matter.

Thomas stared at the floor. "I would like to say one thing. I will be quick. I know you all sigh when I ask to speak, and I do not blame you." He smiled wryly. "It's obviously that I have difficulty trusting. I did not trust that Jesus would rise from the dead after He was crucified. My doubts pounded in my head like a cartwheel on stone pavement. But now I struggle with sorrow and regret that I did not trust Him sooner."

Thomas had barely spoken the words when Bartholomew cut in.

"I also regret that I hesitated to believe Jesus would come forth from the dead."

Peter tried to maintain an impassive expression as his brothers in Jesus admitted doubt.

Thomas slid an arm around Peter's slumping shoulders in a gesture of comfort. His friend waited for him to respond, but Peter could not find words. Finally, Thomas spoke.

"Will Jesus's message die with us? No, this is not His plan. Is Jesus the Son of God? We, of all people, know this most certainly. We can trust the message and mission He gave us. Peter, you are our leader, so lead us, and we will follow. Strengthen our faith and encourage our obedience."

Peter turned toward Thomas. "You have already encouraged us, Thomas. In our pride, we have called you The Doubter. You are right, we must stop feeling sorry for ourselves and step out in faith."

With those words, the disciples and followers of Jesus stood, offered prayers of thanks, then quietly moved toward the door and their mission.

❧

Peter's eyes moved to and from as he surveyed the crowd that had gathered at the bottom of the stairs below the upper room. Fortunately, Judas was not among the throng. The time had come to replace the apostle who had betrayed their Lord—and to do it as quickly as possible.

More than a hundred believers stood before him, crowding into the street in the Essene quarter. Peter raised his hands to quiet the crowd. The power his Master had conferred upon him stirred his spirit, and Peter stood tall as he prayed for wisdom.

He briefly summarized Judas' role not only in their ministry, but also in guiding Jesus' enemies to arrest Him. Peter suggested that they quickly replace Judas with someone who had been with Jesus from the beginning of His ministry and witnessed His resurrection.

The crowd murmured and nodded in assent.

Strengthened by their support, Peter quoted from the *Tehillim* (Psalms) in the *Ketuvim* (Writings). "'May his place be deserted; let there be another one to dwell in it.'" Then he added, "'May another take his place of leadership.'"

Peter motioned to James, Jesus' brother. It was no wonder he was highly respected. He'd so quickly risen to a position of leadership among the believers. With a ring of authority in his voice, James spoke. "I suggest Joseph, also called Barsabbas, and Matthias to meet the requirements. They are men who have proved themselves worthy of trust."

Those in attendance nodded their assent. Mary, Jesus' mother led a group of women to a quiet spot away from the crowd, where they could pray without distraction. The men continued in passionate discussion that seemed it might never end. Peter finally determined he could not let the disagreement dissolve into disharmony. Decision made. God would choose through lots. By lot, the decision fell to Matthias.

After the crowd dispersed, Barsabbas confided his disappointment to Peter but assured him all was well. "Nothing can lessen my love for my Lord, and only He knows where and how I can serve best. Who am I to think that my way is better than His? He has a plan for me, and I must patiently await its unveiling."

Peter silently thanked both Av and Jesus for peace among the men.

With the first major shift navigated, his uncertainties about his leadership faded. The disciples appeared enthused about their new roles and confident of their calling. But more importantly, their faith in Jesus' divine power and authority had been reaffirmed. They were stepping into their future with anticipation and joy that were tempered by realistic questions about the unknown.

But for Peter, a burning question remained: Could this diverse group of minimally trained followers preserve Jesus' live-saving message? Would the difficulty of their task destroy the integrity of their commitment—to one another, and to Jesus Himself? The Son of God inimitably communicated the truths of His Father. Could a ragtag group of men and women do justice to His cause?

And most importantly, would the gospel continue to spread throughout the world, or would the message of the cross flicker and die?

∾

For Andrew, the days before The Feast of *Shavuot* (Pentecost/ Weeks) had crept by. Stirred by His questions about the future, he rose before sunrise and made his way to the Temple, anticipating fulfillment of the promise Jesus had given before leaving Jerusalem.

What will that fulfillment look like? Who or What was the Holy Spirit? Would it look like an angel or appear as bright, shining lights, or will we feel an internal infusion of power?

Andrew's robes swirled around his legs as he hurried. He rounded the final corner, then stopped, shocked by what he saw in the dim light of early dawn.

Many disciples, in fervent anticipation, had already arrived. The faithful from all over the empire had gathered on the southern steps of the Temple to celebrate the Feast of Weeks, which was required of all male Jews and Gentile converts.

Andrew joined the crowd standing patiently outside the Temple Mount. As he looked for friends among the throng, a tall, white-bearded man with a shepherd's staff turned and inquired, "Is it true what they say—that the Nazarene who was crucified has defied the confines of the tomb and come out of the grave?"

Before he could stop himself, words tumbled from Andrew's mouth.

"I was there! I saw with my own eyes Jesus' resurrection and His ascent into heaven. Today you will see for yourself the fulfillment of His promise to send His Holy Spirit to be our comforter and guide."

The bearded man's eyes grew wide—Andrew could not tell whether in amazement, fear, or mockery. Enemies of *The Way* lurked around every corner. He had been hasty and unwise in speaking so quickly! Was this man a spy, watching for an opportunity to round up believers and sentence them to a death as tortured as the one Jesus faced?

A sudden jab in his back sent Andrew reeling, and he struggled to maintain his balance. The crowd on the steps to the Temple had grown restless, pushing and shoving. As he scanned the faces of those around him, he recognized believers, unbelievers, Temple priests, and Pharisees among the throng. The typical Feast of Weeks crowd.

But his eyes stopped when he noticed a familiar face.

The prominent Pharisee Saul of Tarsus was watching every move of a cluster of members of *The Way* and listening to their conversations. He must have been lapping up Andrew's comments like a hungry jackal. He smirked at Andrew and leaned his direction.

"Some time ago, I was in the Hall of Hewn Stone, and I heard a rabbi from Nazareth in Galilee debating the elders about God's Kingdom. Many of the sages disagreed with the rabbi and threatened to have him removed from the hall. Could this be the man you are now proclaiming has resurrected?"

Anything Andrew said would be twisted to bring charges not only against himself, but against any believer in Jesus. The truth was embodied in Jesus, not people like this Saul. Andrew returned Saul's gaze unflinchingly. "You are obviously here today to discover something. Observe for yourself and draw your own conclusions."

With those words, Andrew shoved his way through the growing crowd—praying Saul of Tarsus would not pursue him.

☙

Standing less than a stone's throw from Andrew, Peter had observed the brief confrontation between Saul and his friend. He shouted above the tumult, his voice carrying to the farthest edge of the crowd. Years of making his voice loud enough to be heard by his fishing crew over the sound of the wind and the waves had strengthened his voice.

"Men of Israel, Jesus of Nazareth was accredited to you by God through miracles, wonders, and signs. God gave Him to you according to His foreknowledge to fulfill His set purpose and plan for your people. And you … put Jesus of Nazareth to death by crucifying Him on a cross, hoping to kill Him. But you failed, for God raised Him from the dead."

Peter fixed his eyes on Saul, who was slithering through the crowd in pursuit of Andrew. Upon hearing Peter's defiant words, Saul turned, as Peter had hoped, and Andrew disappeared among the press of the growing throng.

Scanning the faces in front of him, Peter strained to make sense of the words and phrases—Greek, Hebrew, and Aramaic, as well as other languages he could not identify. Hopefully, interpreters could assist those in the audience who could not understand him. Interestingly, he thought, the further the message of Christ spread in the world, the more frustrating it would become for the apostles to be understood without translators—and who among them could translate? No one.

Saul of Tarsus had pushed further toward him, and Peter sighed inwardly as he continued to preach. The crowd had shoved forward, and more people had moved out of the street and into the Temple precincts. As excited listeners surged inside to hear, Peter suddenly felt the ground beneath his feet tremble like a woman travailing in birth, the movement swelling and heaving until the stone slabs threatened to crack. People were falling to the ground, clutching one another in terror as they fell.

A mighty wind suddenly swept through, knocking bodies to the block tiled precinct floor. Peter miraculously managed to remain standing and glanced toward the sky. No storm clouds were present. The roar of the wind quickly faded into a sound like the lapping of waves on the shore, and flames of fire descended from heaven and settled on the heads of each of the apostles.

Peter stood transfixed at the scene before him. Flames hovered low above the heads of the disciples and other members of *The Way,* yet not one hair was singed. Warmth emanated from the flames and radiated through his body. He searched for a word to describe the sensation.

Glow? Ember? Spirit? Presence?

He watched in silence from where he stood on a low wall as fire descended on people around him as they began speaking in languages unknown to them. The energized crowd broke up as confused people began searching for someone else who spoke the language that flowed from their mouths. Overcome with awe and worship, Peter slipped his prayer shawl over his head and closed his eyes.

Is this Your plan, Yahweh? Is this how You are providing for us to carry the good news of Your Son to the world? Is this how You will strengthen us through the power of Your Spirit for what lies ahead—whatever that will be?

A profound sense of peace settled over Peter.

"I will never leave You or forsake you, Peter. Feed my lambs."

Peter pulled back his shawl and considered the crowd before him.

Staring back at him was the wolf plotting to devour those lambs.

Saul of Tarsus.

❧

Joseph of Cyprus, eyes focused forward, his face devoid of expression, stood before Saul of Tarsus in the inner court of the Temple Guard and awaited his orders. As Captain of the Temple Guard, he had mastered self-control, automatic obedience, and unquestioning loyalty. One harsh word from a Temple official could mean his death or send him to the farthest corner of the world.

Saul of Tarsus screamed, the veins in his neck bulging and his face nearly purple with rage. "We have been made fools of! The followers of *The Way* created a public spectacle and a mockery of a holy day, and they must pay for it! Their disciples have divided thousands of new believers into groups and dispersed throughout Jerusalem to private ritual baths, cisterns, and the springs of Gihon, Siloam, and the Virgin Pool, we believe, to perform mass baptisms. You must stop them!"

Joseph refused to flinch, on the outside.

"Throughout the city," Saul continued, "people claim the disciples are healing the sick and the blind. We must stop this heresy!"

Joseph maintained his unemotional gaze, but the irony did not escape him. *The sick and blind are being healed, and we must do something to stop it? If people are being miraculously healed, how can this not be through the power of God?*

"My orders, honored Saul of Tarsus?" Joseph inquired, his tone intentionally deferential.

Saul's voice filled the air. "Gather the guard in full and pursue these heretics. Their teaching is a threat to historic Judaism and the traditions of our people.

"Joseph, your orders are to find both the leaders and the followers of *The Way* and anyone who professes to follow the teachings of Jesus of Nazareth…and exterminate them. All of them!"

CHAPTER 13

DESTRUCTION INTENDED

The blistering afternoon sun beat down on the stone slab where Eli had sat for the past fourteen years near the city gate called Beautiful. The frail palm leaf awning above him provided but a patch of shade.

Eli pulled himself as far under the covering as possible while remaining on his pallet. This position made it harder for him to gain the attention of passersby from whom he could beg, but his withered legs could not bear the searing midday sun.

His friend, Nathanael, carried Eli's pallet to the gate every day. He'd brought Eli a jug of water with a bit of wine, but Eli had eaten nothing since his morning crust of bread with honey. His stomach rumbled, and he took a sip from the jug.

Av, You alone know my needs. You are my provider. Please, just a few coins to take home to Miriam today to buy food.

The prayer was interrupted by the sound of men's voices in the distance. Then the sound of quiet singing—a familiar psalm. How long had it been since he had heard a song of praise offered to Yahweh? Eli's heart lifted. Drawing himself forward with his hands, he scooted to the front of his pallet at the sound of familiar voices.

These are men who served Jesus from Nazareth before his execution— the one called Peter and the other, John.

"Sirs," Eli called out, holding out his hands in supplication, "I have been crippled from birth and place myself at your mercy, begging for my daily bread, as I implore Yahweh daily for my healing."

Eli heard footsteps stop, then approach him. "What is your name?"

Beneath the words, Eli heard tenderness, concern, and interest. "Eli, sir."

Footsteps crunched closer. "Eli, my name is Peter. Neither my friend John nor I have a mite to offer you. We are sorry." Peter gently touched Eli's shoulder, and he recoiled.

"You pious Jews are filled with yourselves. You are hypocrites who lie and won't give a crippled man even a widow's mite," he retorted in anger.

People passing by turned toward them, but Eli didn't care. The men didn't appear impoverished. The one called Peter was obviously lying.

Peter smiled and spoke again. "Eli, I have spoken honestly to you. Silver or gold I do not have, but what I have I will give to you." Peter bowed his head for a moment.

Eli was shocked. He had heard rumors about Peter: a brash, arrogant defender of Jesus in the Garden of Gethsemane and the disciple who reportedly denied knowing his arrested Master. What kind of a disciple had he proved to be? All of Jerusalem knew he was a coward and a liar.

"Eli," Peter spoke with power and confidence, "in the name of Jesus Christ of Nazareth, get up and walk."

His words were even less unexpected than the rush of warmth flashing through Eli's legs. The feeling mystified him. For the first time in his life, he felt sensation in his legs. He wiggled his toes and marveled at the response of movement. Tentatively, he shifted his weight and knelt as he stared at a knee that now bent and supported him. Then he slowly rose to his feet. His legs pulsed with life beneath him: strong, steady, taunting him with the urge to run. He wiggled his toes again, and a laugh erupted from his throat.

Eli adjusted to the dizzying feeling of balancing on two feet. Moments later, he struck out walking, wandering around the area of the Beautiful Gate, then dancing, yelling about the miracle of his healing, and singing at the top of his voice.

After the shock wore off, Eli returned to his pallet and attempted to thank the apostles for not only healing his legs, but giving him a new life. Tears streamed from his eyes as he bent down and picked up his pallet and mat. The act infused Eli with such overpowering gratitude to Av that he was rendered speechless.

People who had passed by Eli for years erupted in expressions of amazement and joy. Some had heard about the works of the Nazarene and were certain they had just witnessed Jesus' disciples repeating His wonders.

Peter stepped forward and began to preach. Eli listened respectfully as Peter condemned the people of Israel for their actions and praised his Lord in a short, powerful message.

"You handed Jesus over to be killed and disowned Him before Pilate, although he let Jesus go."

Eli watched Peter's blazing eyes dart through the crowd, making eye contact with the multitudes as he continued to proclaim his message in a clear voice.

"You acted in ignorance, as did your leaders. Repent, then, and turn to God, so that your sins may be wiped out, that times of refreshing may come from the Lord, and that He may send the Christ. He must remain in heaven until the time comes for God to restore everything He promised long ago through His holy prophets."

Eli could have left the scene, propelled by his own now-strong legs. But he was riveted to Peter's words and the crowd's response.

"Because you have done this in ignorance," Peter assured them, "you can receive pardon by repenting and turning to God so that your sins might be forgiven."

Three words captured Eli's attention: "Turn to God."

Eli pushed through the crowd as he made his way toward Peter. He wasn't sure what it meant to turn to God, but he wanted to know more about the God who cared enough about him to heal him.

☙

Saul stood atop the stairs that led into the Temple. He'd seen more than enough from the Nazarene charlatan and his band of followers. The commotion caused by the cripple claiming to be healed by Jesus' disciples had inflamed his anger as never before. He bellowed out a warning.

"Followers of the Nazarene will pay a high price for their heresy and denial of the faith of our fathers. We cannot allow them to continue to proclaim this message. This is not a new *Way*, but a message as pagan as heathen worship of Egypt's false gods. True Jews worship only one God, Yahweh, as revealed in the Torah."

As Saul began to speak, the Temple Guard and a contingent of Sadducees moved forward and infiltrated the crowd, then paused for further instructions.

An unidentified man dressed in beggar's clothes yelled out from the crowd, "Who are we to believe? The Pharisee Saul or the disciples of Jesus of Nazareth?"

A Temple Guard tried to shout a response above the noise of the mob—but Saul interrupted with an answer.

"This man Peter is preaching a false interpretation of Judaism.

He is seeking a revolution. We know for certain one thing about the false prophet from Nazareth—He's dead. How can His followers proclaim that He has come back from the dead? Because they took His body and hid it. The Sadducees are right in this matter—there is no reincarnation. Once we are dead, we are always dead. This so-called '*Way*' needs to be silenced."

The repulsive idea of human sacrifice had long troubled Saul. His childhood experience in Tarsus had frightened him to the core of his being, and his loyalty to Temple sacrifices was immovable.

He remembered his school days when the subject was debated. *I argued for the possibility of human sacrifice—but only to see if my rabbi could give me scriptural justification for his views.* Pushing the thought from his mind, Saul fired off words of skepticism.

"How can this man Jesus, a simple carpenter, die as a human sacrifice for the sins of humankind? Who dies for his sin? The Scriptures forbid human sacrifice. Yahweh seeks the sacrifice of animals for sin—not human sacrifice. Torah specifies sacrifice of goats' blood sprinkled on the temple altar, not a man who hung on a cross as a criminal and was buried with sinners."

Saul's comments and rhetoric were obviously making inroads into the thinking of those already unsympathetic to the apostles' message. He watched a mix of fear and soberness wash across those gathered. Incensed by the rhetoric of Jesus' followers, he raised an arm and shouted to the Temple Guard. "We must make an example of these imposters. We won't tolerate this evil speech! Seize them! Take them to prison. Let's be done with them."

Immediately, the guards seized Peter and John and dragged them to the central jail on Mount Zion.

Saul turned to the nearly five thousand onlookers and shouted in utter scorn, "Let this be a lesson to you who follow this anti-Jewish radical! He holds no power equal to Yahweh, our God. Be it known that the name of Jesus the heretic will be purged from the earth."

Peter and John settled compliantly into their cells. Considering their ominous future, Peter suggested they focus their time praying to the God who controlled their future and possessed the power of heaven and earth to move on their behalf. They prayed, sang psalms, and praised God for spiritual and physical blessings despite their circumstances.

The evening and night passed quickly as Peter and John even prayed for their guards and their families, Roman authorities, as well as their fellow believers, their families and loved ones, and that the Good News would reach the farthest corners of the world.

Word traveled from cell to cell through taps and signals. But Peter and John made no effort to keep their faith expressions quiet. Soon every guard and prisoner in the jail was aware of the prayer and praise pouring heavenward from Peter and John's cell.

A sliver of dawn slipped through a high slit in the wall of their cell, bringing welcome light to the otherwise dark room. Their bleak circumstances did not deter Peter's enthusiasm for a new day.

Sometime later, a guard entered Peter's cell, grabbed his arm, and jerked him to his feet. Man-handling Peter was not an easy task. Years of work at sea had toughened him and built thick muscles on his tall frame. When the guard grabbed him, Peter did not resist, but he stumbled as the guard pulled him through the narrow cell opening, out of the prison, and marched him to the home of the high priest, Caiaphas.

Peter calmly established a humble stance before the high priest as he anticipated the worst—perhaps an extended prison term or even execution. Members of the Sanhedrin sat behind Caiaphas, bearing their most intimidating expressions. One look at Caiaphas told Peter that the high priest was still raging in the aftermath of Pentecost and didn't hide the fact that he was in no mood to deal with fanatical followers of the Galilean he'd condemned to death as a blasphemer. Caiaphas sat motionless on his "throne," staring at Peter, who assumed from the man's posture and expression that the high priest was attempting to contain an angry outburst.

"By whose authority did you heal this crippled man?" Caiaphas bellowed. Peter noted a vein pulsating in the priest's forehead.

He inhaled deeply before answering. When Peter followed Jesus into the high priest's house the night of Jesus' trial, he had barely avoided an encounter with Caiaphas. But now, Peter stood before the high priest with strengthened boldness.

"It is by the name of Jesus Christ of Nazareth, whom you crucified, but who God raised from the dead, that the cripple was healed." Peter boldly took a step forward. "Our message and power are given to us by God himself. They are not our own."

Peter knew that denying the miracle was impossible—and it would be untrue. The healed man had been brought into the room and now stood before them. Denying the evidence was impossible—unless Caiaphas charged that the healing had been done by Satan's power or a sorcerer's trick.

The Sanhedrin withdrew to confer about what should be done and returned sooner than Peter expected. He looked Caiaphas in the eyes as the priest read the decision.

"As protection against rioting among the masses and incurring the wrath of Pilate for public disturbance, followers of Jesus are hereby forbidden to perform healings."

Peter expelled his breath in a burst as he forced himself not to laugh. The ruling officially validated the disciples' *power* to heal while simultaneously banning them from helping people in need. Yet their freedom to preach was not mentioned. The ruling was an unofficial decree that Christians could continue to spread the Good News about Jesus.

This freedom will be short-lived. We will not be allowed to preach openly for long. Saul of Tarsus has become our nemesis and cannot be trusted. His fury will fall on us soon.

And it will fall hard.

CHAPTER 14

WISE COUNSEL

News of Caiaphas' retaliation had spread rapidly throughout the prison through the loose lips of guards who continually gossiped about the actions of the high priest. Before five days had passed, Peter heard that Caiaphas' concerns about the growing influence of *The Way* had convinced him to send out spies to report on the apostles' activities. As the high priest suspected, they were continuing to preach and perform miracles, but moved by Peter's bold defense, Caiaphas instructed Jewish authorities to respond to followers of Jesus with threats only.

Peter had further learned, that despite Caiaphas' harsh threats, the apostles continued their ministry undeterred, committed to serving God and not man.

The news did not surprise Peter. In fact, it was what he had expected to hear. He understood his brothers' faith and strong commitment to Jesus. So, it did not surprise Peter when, a few days later, outraged Sadducees attempted to squelch him and his believing brothers again. Once again, they were arrested as Jesus' followers.

But this time, in the middle of the night, an angel had interrupted Peter's sleep. The Angel of the Lord flung open the jail doors and told him, "Go and stand in the Temple courts and tell the people the full message of new life in Christ."

The next morning, their empty jail cell bore witness that God's message could not be silenced.

According to prison gossip, the news had first enraged, then troubled Caiaphas and the chief priests. Caiaphas and the chief priests had reportedly met to discuss a plan to guarantee that interest in Jesus' message be ended. They seemed especially disturbed that even jailing the top leaders was not stopping spread of the faith.

Caiaphas, the Sanhedrin's high priest, once again called Peter to give an account of the apostles' actions. Peter stood quiet and unmoving as Caiaphas angrily poked a finger in his face. "We gave you strict orders not to teach in Jesus' name, yet you have filled Jerusalem with your teaching and are determined to proclaim us guilty of the Nazarene's blood!"

Unflinching, Peter bore the harsh words and prepared a retort. But to his surprise, Saul's mentor, Rabban Gamaliel, stepped forward.

"Men of Israel, consider carefully what you intend to do to these men. Allow me to recount an incident. A man named Theudas appeared one day, claiming to be an important person. He had a charismatic personality and had assembled about four hundred followers. He was killed, and his followers dispersed. After him, Judas from Gamla in Gaulanitis, led a revolt against paying tribute to Caesar. The rebellion was crushed, Judas killed, and his followers dispersed. However, his cause took root. He was viewed as a martyr, and his influence continues among zealots today."

Gamaliel leaned forward to emphasize his point. "I propose we leave these men alone! Let them go! If their purpose or activity is of human origin, it will fail. But if it is from God, you will not be able to stop them; you will find yourselves fighting against Yahweh Himself and will forever regret it."

Peter could not believe his ears. The revered Gamaliel had spoken on *their* behalf, words that carried power to solicit a reprieve from imprisonment or death—if only temporary—for the disciples and their followers. Every day, every message preached would carry the gospel further into the world, like ripples in a pond.

Out of the corner of his eye, Peter noticed Gamaliel watching Saul of Tarsus whispering complaints to a group of Pharisees, supposedly about Gamaliel's opinion to allow the religious movement to continue. From his body language and gestures, Peter gathered that Saul was doing his best to diminish the weight of Gamaliel's wisdom.

Peter swallowed. *Those who follow Jesus must use every opportunity to share their faith and not waste a minute. Time is short, and Saul is intent on slamming the door.*

CHAPTER 15

MARTYRDOM

Joseph of Cyprus, Captain of the Temple Guard, shifted his weight. "We did not want to make martyrs out of these fanatics," most honored Caiaphas. We thought if we left them alone, their zeal would fade after they found the body of their dead leader."

He watched from lowered eyes as the high priest paced, his soft-soled sandals barely brushing the mosaic floor of the Council Chamber. His chin rested on his chest and his eyes stared at the floor as he walked, then turned, walked, then turned, while muttering hatefully against the Nazarene who tormented him—still.

Caiaphas suddenly whirled toward those in the court, his white robes billowing around him, then falling flat. "I am Rome's appointed Jewish High Priest! Who does this worm think he is to publicly defy me and dishonor my authority!" he screamed as he rubbed his temples. "Find him! I *will* end the memory of this filthy Galilean sorcerer and his followers once and for all."

Caiaphas plopped into an ornately carved chair and dropped his head into his hands.

"Someone bring me wine. I am not well. I do not understand how this has become *my* problem."

A member of the Temple Guard who had been standing near the back of the Council Chamber fled from the room, seemingly to find wine.

You!" He pointed at the Sanhedrin. "You are supposedly responsible for enforcing laws regulating Jewish worship and daily affairs, maintaining law and order, and preventing dissidents from congregating. With Levites keeping guard at each of the five gates of the Temple Mount, how is it that we cannot find this reprobate Jesus? And why the followers of Nazarene have become my problem?" Caiaphas' voice rose until it echoed from the vaulted ceiling.

Joseph lifted his head slightly. In all his years serving with the Temple Guard, he had never seen Caiaphas overcome with such rage. But the high priest seemed to be feeding off the terror he created in the room.

The question hung in the air.

The soldier from the Temple Guard strode back into the room with a bottle of wine and a glass and quickly handed them to Caiaphas. Joseph noted the priest's smile when he saw the young man's trembling hands.

"You *will* deal with these followers of *The Way* once and for all. Do you understand?" Caiaphas barked. Joseph nodded and kept his eyes glued on the floor.

"And what actions have you taken to prevent his disciples from proclaiming the reincarnation of their leader?" Caiaphas pointed a finger. "Don't dare tell me you threatened and jailed them ... because you released them again so they could continue their defiance!" His voice rose to a roar. "They have gone so far as to use our mikvahs to baptize their converts. Blasphemy!"

Joseph of Cyprus, Captain of the Temple Guard, struggled for words. "Followers of *The Way* multiply like thistle weed and share a faith like no other sect we have seen. Trying to eradicate them will be like trying to rid all Judea of fleas."

Caiaphas leaned back, eyebrows raised. For several long moments he said nothing. "Your answer is so idiotic as to be unworthy of a response." Then, slowly, he leaned forward again and hissed, "You dare offer such a stupid excuse—the Captain of the Temple Guard? Where is his body? You are telling me that the entire Temple Guard is unable to find one dead body? Have you gone insane? Or do you think me so ignorant to believe such rubbish?" Caiaphas nearly knocked over his wine glass with the flailing of his body.

"And you stand with your head bowed like a sycophant. What do you have to say? Why should I not throw you in the deepest bowels of the prison?" The priest took a long drink of wine.

Joseph straightened his stance. "I did give this investigation my best effort, and I have valuable information about *The Way*. Their most faithful followers are Jews. They observe Shabbat, the annual feasts, go to Temple, pray, and eat clean foods. But they worship Jesus as the Son of God and spread his message of forgiveness of sins through his crucifixion, which they insist is a sacrifice to remove the sin of the world. A new leader named Stephen bar Yacov has recently brought new followers."

Caiaphas shook his fists. "I am concerned, Joseph, that their message is spreading so quickly that it could find a foothold among people outside Judea. And I fear it is already finding acceptance among our own priests, who are changing our religion into something new, misinterpreted, and dangerous.

"But I will infiltrate *The Way* if need be. I have an association that could make that possible, but I also have another idea."

"Whatever you must do."

"My lord, I know of a young Pharisee who has is a zealot for our faith and has no fear about the dangers of associating with Nazarenes. He has shown his loathing for *The Way* in no uncertain terms."

"I will not accept failure again," Caiaphas warned. "I require results and will not tolerate excuses. Who is the man? Talk to him!

But I am holding *you* personally responsible for the solution to this problem, Joseph. Do you understand?"

Joseph returned Caiaphas' threatening gaze. He refused to be intimidated. "I understand. I will share my plan with a Pharisee. Rabbi Saul of Tarsus."

Caiaphas nodded and clasped his hands as if the matter was settled. "Oh, yes, I know the man. His hatred for followers of *The Way* exceeds passion and nears insanity."

Joseph felt the tension in the room dissipate as if storm winds were abating. "Yes, whatever it is that drives Rabbi Saul will serve our purposes quite nicely."

The moment Caiaphas released him, Joseph began to craft a plan. Jesus and his friends would not escape this time. Joseph had to make sure of it.

❧

Joseph glanced toward the door of his favorite neighborhood drinking establishment. He sipped a glass of weak wine and drummed his fingers. Peleg always made him wait, which meant Joseph was always irritated before he got the first word out of his mouth. He'd never liked working with the man, but Peleg faithfully carried out Caiaphas' wishes when Joseph didn't have the stomach to get his hands dirty.

Little had he known as a student under the great Gamaliel the jobs that would one day be required of him as Captain of the Temple Guard. What would his revered rabbi think of his actions? Did he know about the many secrets hidden inside the Temple and the precincts of Judaism?

The job hadn't required much from him. After several cups of strong wine, Joseph convinced Peleg to falsely confess that he had heard Stephen speak blasphemy against God and Moses. Joseph even went so far as to tell his hireling what to say. "You're to claim, 'As I stood at worship in the Temple, I heard Stephen speak words of blasphemy against God and Moses.' You may choose the specific blasphemy. If you swear to do this," Joseph mustered up his most intimidating leer, "and if you convince the religious leaders that what you say is true, I promise you double the money you are receiving now."

To seal his plan, several days later, Joseph mentioned to Saul that he'd heard rumors that Stephen had spoken blasphemy. He urged Saul to take Stephen before Pilate, governor of the Roman province of Judaea. After numerous sleepless nights, Joseph devised a scheme that would deflect Caiaphas' rage away from him and onto Stephen. Certainly, the Prefect would take swift steps to arrest the culprit and his friends. They would be rushed off to prison before the masses had an opportunity to secret Stephen away.

Joseph clung to his plan as he walked into the Council Chamber in response to a summons from his childhood friend, Saul. In moments, Joseph found a way to cunningly pass along his poisonous lie and watch Saul purse his lips in disdain.

"Pilate will do nothing about this. He is so afraid an uprising will bring the ire of Rome that he will pass the matter on to Caiaphas," Saul said with a huff. "He will regard our action as going over his head and will be furious. We don't want to deal with that. Pilate did not find the charges against the Nazarene credible. To further complicate the matter, his wife Percula warned him not to get involved with the man she called 'the Christ.' No, we must take Stephen to the high priest."

Joseph called for Stephen, and, with Saul, marched the accused to face the Sanhedrin.

❧

On the other side of the stone wall, Caiaphas heard the pounding of the bailiff's gavel. "Quiet, quiet. This court is in session!"

Always the waiting. Ceremony is an important aspect of power.

He could envision the Great Hall of Hewn Stone on the other side. The chamber's fresco walls covered with long scarlet drapes. Intricate mosaic stone tiles in opus sectils design covered the floors and porticoes. Students and religious authorities would be seated opposite the elders of the Great Sanhedrin, who were now decorously shuffling into the hall one by one, uniformly dressed in black robes layered with blue-on-white striped prayer shawls and scarlet stoles. Their black linen head-dress added an air of authority and reverence. They would be seated on three-tiered stone benches in a semi-circle that faced the accused and visitors.

The crowd of students and religious authorities hushed, Caiaphas' cue. He entered the room dressed in ceremonial robes. His long, white robe covered with a blue tunic that hung to his feet. Alternating decorative tassels crafted as golden bells and pomegranates hung below his garments. Atop his attire he wore an embroidered cape adorned in bands of gold, purple, scarlet, and blue tied around his waist with a girdle. But he took special pride in the breastplate that covered his chest. He forced himself not to glance down at it—a breastplate of pure gold inset with twelve precious stones, each representing one of the tribes of Israel. His head was swathed in a length of blue cloth. He paused briefly before stepping up and taking his seat on a raised, throne-like chair that faced onlookers.

Caiaphas raised his hand, and the bailiff called out, "Bring in the prisoner!"

Two Temple guards entered the room, each clutching one of Stephen's arms. They dragged him to a designated spot in front of the high priest as onlookers laughed and jeered. Stephen's shoulders slumped beneath a stained and ragged cloak. Around his neck was a soiled linen scarf.

One of the elders, a Sadducee sitting in the front row, turned to the man next to him. "He has the face of an angel. Who is he?"

"Silence!" Caiaphas bellowed, fighting the urge to have the elder thrown into the dungeon for his impertinence.

Caiaphas sternly stated the charges: "Stephen ben Yacov, you have been charged with serious crimes. Do you understand that if found guilty, you will receive capital punishment?"

Stephen held his head high as he looked back at the high priest.

Caiaphas waited. *Why will the man not answer? Does he not understand that I hold the power of life and death?* Suddenly uncomfortable, Caiaphas looked away from Stephen's serene gaze. "Would the people's advocate come forward?"

Saul moved forward with quick, confident steps.

"Saul of Tarsus, please state Torah's words on the charges and the consequences placed on the violation."

Saul muttered under his breath as he fumbled to find the ruling, then straightened his back as he read from the Torah.

> "'If thy brother, or thy son, or thy daughter, or the wife of thy bosom, or thy friend, entice thee secretly, saying, Let us go and serve other gods, which thou hast not known, thou, nor thy fathers. But thou shalt surely kill him; thine hand shall be first upon him to put him to death, and afterwards the hand of all the people. And thou shalt stone him with stones, that he dies; because he hath sought to thrust thee away from the Lord thy God, which brought thee out of the land of Egypt, from the house of bondage.'"

Caiaphas smiled in satisfaction.

Stoning. Yes.

"Call the first witness."

The court bailiff called for Peleg. The long-haired Cyrenian's face was etched with fear as he entered the courtroom.

"Yes, My Lord, I … I am here to testify against this … evil man," he whimpered apologetically.

"Speak up!" Caiaphas bellowed. "What can you tell us about this heretic's actions?"

Peleg looked at the floor. "This man continually speaks against the Temple and against the Law. He has been overheard worshipping the Nazarene as Adonai."

As the witness was led from the room following his statement, the room filled with buzzing.

Accusations intensified when three other frightened witnesses gave their depositions. Through each testimony, Stephen stood tall and locked his gaze on Caiaphas.

Because capital punishment was considered vile among the Jews, standards of evidence for a guilty judgment were extremely high, as well as qualifications for witnesses. Two adult, pious Jewish witnesses who were knowledgeable in both written and oral law were required. Witnesses must have seen each other at the time of the crime. They had to be able to speak clearly, without a speech impediment or hearing deficit, and they could not be related to one another or the accused.

The beit din was required to examine each witness separately, and if even one point of evidence was found to be contradictory—even a minor point—the evidence was dismissed.

After hearing the charges, a self-satisfied Caiaphas turned to Stephen again. "Are these charges true?" His tone dripped with accusation.

Stephen took a step forward, then positioned himself to address both Caiaphas and onlookers. Caiaphas saw his deep brown eyes narrow in determination.

If this man Stephen had something to say—it was going to be more than a statement of innocence or guilt.

Far more.

CHAPTER 16

THE SERMON

Stephen paused before responding to Caiaphas. The room went silent as all eyes fixed on him.

Time slowed as he gazed at bloodthirsty faces. His last flicker of hope had long ago trembled and died ... but a vision of indescribable glory burst to life before his eyes.

Stephen.

The voice shimmered like summer rain.

You were born for this moment—a destiny God has reserved solely for you. He is here and has already given you more than you need.

Stephen drew a breath, then spoke boldly, surprising even himself. He immediately recognized the power beneath his words as the work of the Holy Spirit, who had flooded his life and the lives of all of Jesus' followers on the day of Pentecost.

"Sons of Abraham, listen to me. Our glorious Yahweh appeared to our ancestor Abraham in Mesopotamia and told him, 'Leave your native land and your relatives, and come into the land that I will show you.'" Stephen could hear his voice resonating throughout the room.

He watched Saul lean over to the rabbi sitting next to him and snidely remark, "Is he going to lecture us on the Torah's history as if we were ignorant Galileans?"

Stephen ignored the comment and continued. "But God gave him no inheritance here, not even one hectare. However, God promised that eventually the whole land would belong to Abraham and his descendants—although he had no children yet. God also told him that his descendants would live in a foreign land, where they would be oppressed as slaves for 400 years. 'But I will punish the nation that enslaves them,' God said, 'and in the end they will come out and worship me here in this place.'"

Stephen scanned the crowd. No one appeared disturbed or ready to stop him.

"God also gave Abraham the covenant of circumcision, so when Abraham fathered Isaac, he circumcised his son on the eighth day. The practice continued when Isaac fathered Jacob, and when Jacob fathered the twelve patriarchs of the Israelite nation."

Stephen continued, eloquently relating stories of Abraham, Isaac, and Jacob, citing the history of the Jews, who continually rebelled against leaders chosen by God to fulfill His promises.

Saul was growing visibly agitated, no doubt angry that a follower of *The Way* was reciting an elementary beit sefer history lesson to elders, rabbis, and priests, not to mention Caiaphas himself. Stephen surmised that Saul was infuriated because no one had objected, and everyone in the room appeared to be fully engaged in his speech.

Saul's face was the color of ripe pomegranates.

Stephen's heartbeat calmed. *If my arguments persuade the council and I win my freedom, Caiaphas will blame Saul. Of course, he's furious. Truly the Spirit of God is at work in our midst!* Stephen lifted his hands toward heaven as he continued.

"Moses himself told our ancestors that God would raise up a prophet from among our people and would speak to us from Mount Sinai where Moses received life-giving words to pass on to us. But our ancestors refused to listen. They rejected Moses and wanted to return to Egypt ...."

Saul's eyebrows were now drawn together, and the veins in his neck bulged as he gritted his teeth. But Stephen calmly continued as nearly everyone in the room fixed their eyes on him. High above the crowd, near the back of the hall, he heard a rustle. Then a sweet scent unlike any flower or perfume he had ever smelled filled his lungs.

Stephen pointed heavenward as words poured from his lips in a voice like thunder.

"You stubborn people! You are heathen at heart and deaf to the truth. Must you forever resist the instruction of your God? Yahweh sent prophet after prophet because of your rebellion, and your ancestors persecuted them! They also killed the prophets who predicted the coming of the Righteous One—the Messiah you betrayed and murdered."

Stephen's voice rang out like an angel from heaven. "You arrogantly disobeyed God's law when He sent it to you by angels, and you blindly rejected His love when He sent His own Son."

The expressions on faces in the room told Stephen his words were piercing guilty consciences. The crowded room suddenly erupted into shouting as rabbis, priests, Saul, and Caiaphas himself demand his blood. Their anger fomented into rage. Voices cried out, "...common ... unlearned ... blasphemy."

Stephen glanced at Saul. His eyes were drinking in the sight of the incensed crowd, a leer etching his face.

Stephen caught another waft of heavenly fragrance as more cries erupted.

"This man has condemned himself with his own words."

"This heretic must be silenced, or his message will spread like fire in dry fields."

Caiaphas pounded the floor with his scepter in a vain effort to calm the pandemonium. "Silence! It is time to hear the elders' judgment. How do you find the accused—guilty or not guilty?"

Stephen closed his eyes.

Caiaphas' question was barely out of his mouth before members of the Sanhedrin called out their answers.

"Guilty. Guilty."

Stephen breathed slowly and steadily. The sweet scent enveloped him. He tilted his head back, and a brush of air fanned his face.

"Guilty. Guilty."

The word rang with hatred each time it was spoken.

He opened his eyes and calmly proclaimed, "I see heaven open and the Son of Man standing on the right hand of God."

The crowd began tearing their clothes and screaming, "Blasphemy! Blasphemy!"

Distant and faint, Stephen heard members of the Sanhedrin order that he be taken to the garden outside the Damascus gate north of the city wall to be executed.

He fixed his eyes heavenward as his body was jostled and dragged through the streets to the designated location. He was pulled, pushed, kicked, stomped, and spit upon, but his surroundings had faded. Captivated, he fixed his gaze on countless joy-filled beings dancing and darting about him, their translucent wings stirring the air with heavenly fragrance as they wafted peace into his soul.

Saul called out to Stephen's accusers, "The Torah commands, 'You who accuse him may have the privilege of casting the first execution stones.'"

Saul stepped forward and picked up a sizable rock. Officials and the public, including children, would join in the stoning until he was dead.

But other voices whispered, beckoning from above as Stephen stood in the middle of the growing mob with his hands tied behind his back. He was helpless to protect himself from the blows of the stones, surrounded by executioners who'd laid their outside garments at Saul's feet to free them to throw their rocks more forcefully.

The first stones were hurled to jubilant shouts. Two struck Stephen in the head, and one fell wide. Saul joined in the spectacle, his stone striking a glancing blow to Stephen's shoulder. Within moments, the Sanhedrin joined the stoning, then the growing crowd with mob-like fervor.

Stephen released himself to the heavenly fragrance as he looked into the gentle eyes of the winged creature before him.

He sent me for you, Stephen. You finished well. It's time.

Stephen's knees collapsed beneath the weight of his broken, bloody body as a rock cracked against his shin.

"Lord Jesus, receive my spirit. Do not hold this sin against them." Stephen's voice rang out with Spirit-filled power and hung over the crowd as they hurled rocks until he lay immobile, blood pouring from his wounds.

When they had slaked their thirst, the people soundlessly dispersed, and Saul returned to the Temple, an unsettling disquiet plaguing him. He would not sleep that night nor for weeks to come.

CHAPTER 17

ARREST WARRANTS

A cock crowed, beckoning the sun in the predawn darkness, and Peter stirred. He rubbed his eyes as he slowly stood and gazed over the rooftops of the sleeping village of Bethany. James and John remained dozing on their mats. From the time he'd been a child, Peter had enjoyed sleeping in the open air on the rooftop, where he could watch the stars and listen to the sounds of the city dance through the air.

But last night he'd listened for more than the night sounds of Bethany as he'd pulled his mantle around him on his sleeping mat. Thankfully, John, James, and he had found refuge in the home of friends. The three of them had barely eluded Temple Guards patrolling Jerusalem and surrounding villages, rounding up members of *The Way*. His vigilant mind had not allowed him to sleep and prodded him to keep watch all night.

Peter turned, picked up a sandal, and playfully tossed it at James' head, hoping to cut short his wheezy snore that had plagued him all night. The sandal thudded against his friend's skull, and he jumped to his feet, hands flailing at his face as he hollered unintelligibly in his sleep-fogged state. Peter laughed and prepared to pitch the second sandal at James when John rose on an elbow and hissed, "Be quiet, you two, or you'll wake up everyone from here to the Temple."

Someone cleared his throat behind Peter, and he turned.

Lazarus stood at the top of the stairs built on an exterior wall of the house, leading to the ground level near the kitchen door. He was munching his morning *kasha*.

"A little early for men to be rollicking like boys, I think, but the past days have been hard, and perhaps laughter is what you need," he observed.

Lazarus stepped closer. Peter inhaled the grainy richness of kasha.

"Ima said to tell you she made your porridge from wheat bread, figs, dates, and red wine, and it's ready and waiting for you. You'll make her very happy if you hurry down and eat two bowls each," Lazarus smiled.

Peter quickly pulled on his sandals. Lazarus knew the details of their past several days—running, hiding, grieving Stephen's death, but little time for eating or rest. He and Ima always found a way to fill their stomachs and their spirits.

The three disciples expressed their appreciation as they followed Lazarus down the stairs, through the kitchen door, and crowded around a small wooden table set with hand-carved cypress bowls brimming with Ima's steaming kasha. She greeted them with a nod and a shy smile, then turned to cut the men thick slabs of fresh, crusty bread.

Lazarus wiped his mouth with a small homespun cloth. "I will forever be grateful, James, that your father Joseph and Jesus became my father Eleazar's close friend. I share that same gratitude for the friendship your mother Mary enjoyed with my mother. And my sisters loved Jesus so dearly. Observing the way Jesus honored and devoted Himself to women as well as men is a lesson for all of us who followed Him."

Lazarus leaned across the table until his face was close to Peter's. "Our family is your family, and what we have is yours. Whenever you have need, you are welcome here—all of you, and any who follow *The Way*. Despite Saul of Tarsus' threats of arrest and death, our love for Jesus and faith in Him come before all else."

Peter nodded, grateful for his friend's devotion, yet at the same time pondering what their next move could be without totally jeopardizing the safety of fellow believers.

❧

Saul sat in the courtyard behind his small apartment on a low, wide bench covered with a thick scarlet cushion. As he waited for the dance of sunset in the evening sky, his thoughts turned to his parents, as they always did at the close of day.

The past days had stirred troubling thoughts he'd never considered. Had his parents heard of the Nazarene? Could it be possible that they were believers? Herod the Great's harsh tax plan had put pressure on families—and especially older members—to live close together and sometimes share homes. Although this made it easier for him to round up the followers of Jesus, it also made it more likely that his ima and abba had heard his message and fallen under his spell.

Saul reached for a glass of water purified with a small amount of wine. People were struggling to keep their ancestral lands, and scarce finances forced the faithful to pool their resources and share with one another to survive.

He'd prayed his parents were not among the destitute, but he did not know for sure. *What kind of a son am I? I must find a way to check on their welfare. My obsession to eradicate The Way has blinded me. But perhaps Stephen's execution is the blow we needed to destroy the faith of The Way.*

On the western horizon, the sky flamed orange, and Saul settled back to watch the spectacle.

Stephen's execution did not incite the riots Saul had hoped for, so he turned to a bolder choice for extermination.

He approached Caiaphas at his office near the temple mount. "I would like your approval to enlist the Temple Guard as a force to deal with *The Way*. I want to create an organized plan to bring all followers of *The Way* to justice, along with a plan of persecution."

Inasmuch as it was possible, Saul's anger had intensified to fanaticism. He had not anticipated the number of followers who had scattered throughout Judea, Samaria, and as far as Antioch, Pisidia, and Damascus.

With new fervor, Saul focused his ever-escalating rage anew on *The Way*, launching a vicious campaign in yet another attempt to destroy the faithful followers of Jesus.

♥

Saul and seven Temple Guards strode down the central Jerusalem street. Their leather-bottom sandals slapped the stone pavers and sweat dripped from their noses and chins as they approached a small home where Nazarenes were suspected to be harbored.

The guards pounded on the small wooden door as Saul yelled above the clamor of the street behind him.

"Open up now! This is Rabbi Saul of Tarsus, and I represent the interests of High Priest Caiaphas himself. I know you are providing sanctuary for Nazarenes who are members of *The Way*. Open the door immediately!"

Saul signaled two guards to circle to the back of the house to prevent escape as a female voice answered, "Please, sir, have mercy."

Saul motioned for the largest of the guards to crash through the door. Splinters flew as the massive soldier shattered the door. Pulling away the few remaining fragments of wood, Paul stepped gingerly inside, as if entering a filthy barn. He shoved a slim, frightened woman to the floor, then brushed off his hands with a sneer of derision. "Search the premises and find those deplorable heretics."

A man and woman with an infant child clinging to her mother's chest stepped out of a standing cupboard. Temple Guards seized them, dragged them outside, and handed them off to additional guards waiting to march them off to the nearby prison.

Saul exhaled with satisfaction.

Now to find the rest of these vermin.

Up and down the outskirts of Jerusalem, Saul and his men systematically searched homes and arrested dozens of men, women, and children. Surprisingly, no one denied being a follower of *The Way* to try to save their life. The task was almost too easy. Their compliance disturbed Saul. *Why do they so willingly accept their fate?*

He tried to shake off the sense of disquiet with a fresh vision of future arrests. Turning his back on Jerusalem, Saul pointed toward the villages beyond and ordered that the search be expanded in a methodically widening circle, moving outward to envelop Bethany and Bethphage.

☙

Martha was feeding chickens outside the small home she shared with her brother and sister when she spotted Temple Guards marching up the lane toward their house.

She dropped her supplies, turned, and raced toward home, shouting, "Peter, James, John! Run! Take the back trail south to Silwan and seek Yonatan Mizrahi near the Siloam necropolis. Take the provisions hidden behind the house. Lazarus, you must go with them!"

Martha worked to slow her breathing as the men scrambled out the rear door and down the path as she'd directed. They each pulled a bundle from the base of a small grove of trees, and slung them over their shoulders before they disappeared around a bend. She closed her eyes and envisioned them running, stumbling, and panting as they darted in and out of alleyways to avoid attracting attention from possible Pharisee sympathizers. She turned, closed the back door, and ordered her brother to the gathering room.

Braver than his actions would suggest, Lazarus had chosen to remain behind. None of the apostles would not be surprised that he refused to leave his Ima and sisters.

Martha took a position standing inside the front door, waiting, arms crossed. Lazarus had just taken a seat on a thickly cushioned bench near the front door when Saul and several members of the Temple Guard burst through the front door and Saul began screaming questions in Lazarus' face.

"You've been harboring fugitives from the court of the Sanhedrin. Where are they?"

Martha's heart pounded as Lazarus silently returned Saul's gaze. Saul suddenly drew back his arm and slapped Lazarus' face. Then he leaned forward, leering. "Where did your 'guests' go? Where can we find them? Tell me now and I'll spare their lives."

Martha fought the urge to strike Saul. "Leave us alone," she said through gritted teeth. "Our father passed away, and only Lazarus supports us."

As guards searched the house, Saul glared as he surveyed the room and interrogated Lazarus. Martha tried to predict the questions she might be asked as she listened to Lazarus' inquest.

Is Lazarus your name?

Who owns this house?

Who is the woman?

Are you the follower of the Nazarene called Jesus who claims to have been brought out of the tomb from death to life?"

Lazarus did not answer. Martha screamed as Saul's captain struck their prisoner in the face with the butt of his broad sabre. The blow found its mark, and blood poured from Lazarus' nose and mouth as his head thudded against the wall.

The Temple Guard leaned into Lazarus' blood-spattered face. "I say we kill you and see if your dead savior can raise you to life again. If he did it once, he can surely do it again." The guard spit onto the tiled floor at Lazarus' feet.

After a few more violent attempts to extract information from his victim, Saul gave up in disgust. "Never mind this piece of dung." He turned to Martha, who had been mentally preparing for verbal and physical abuse.

She'd knotted her hands into fists as she vowed she would never let this swine see her emotions.

"My *yakirati*, are there any other men in the house?"

"No," Martha shot back. "I told you, the only other man from our family was our abba, and he died years ago."

"Death may come to more of your family members if you continue to follow or collude with members of *The Way.*" Saul spit in her face and whirled toward the door.

"Let's go." Saul motioned to the soldiers to follow him. "Put this family on the list for later interrogation."

But before the dust could rise from Saul's sandals as he strode out the door, Martha raced to her brother's side to nurse his wounds. She would decide how to deal with Saul the assassin later.

Following Martha's instructions, Peter, James, and John hastily made their way to Sychar, Samaria to support their brothers in Christ. Here, Peter helped arrange a meeting with fellow Christians in the home of Photinia, a woman who received living water from Jesus Himself. Photine faithfully preached the gospel in her community, and as a result, Peter, James, and John found many believers in Samaria. Additionally, after the persecution following Jesus' resurrection, many believers fled from Jerusalem to Samaria.

Fearful of Saul's relentless persecution, believers went into hiding. But news of Peter and John's escape from Jerusalem renewed confidence among Jesus' followers in Samaria, who welcomed Peter and John's ministry. Thomas, who'd experienced Saul's punishing blows and become a believer under Photinia's ministry, gratefully opened his home for secret meetings.

Although the environment in Samaria was tense, Samaritan believers were united and determined to welcome and protect fellow followers of *The Way*. Peter and John were pleased to discover that their initial meeting with Samaritan believers was highly anticipated.

The meeting began positively as Samaritan believers told the apostles about their responses to the message of Jesus' atoning death and the miracles they'd witnessed under Philip's ministry.

As Peter listened to their stories, his mind envisioned other tear-streaked faces, orphaned children, widowed mothers, childless parents and grandparents. In every city it was the same, until he was certain he had no more tears. He fought back tears as he honored *these* stories of these family members in the faith and the price they paid to leave family, friends, homes, businesses, and possessions behind. Their faith humbled him—every time.

When the believers finished telling the group about their journey to faith, Peter and John led them to a local river, and, one by one, baptized them in the name of Jesus. Peter never tired of seeing each child of God rise from the water, the light of Life illuminating their faces. Once again, Peter was helpless to hold back his tears. He could scarcely see as he and John placed their hands on each newly baptized believer, and they received the Holy Spirit, identifying the Samaritan with both the apostles and the Jerusalem believers in spiritual and organizational unity.

Rumors were irrelevant. Yes, Peter had heard reports that the rapid spread of *The Way* had fanned the flames of Saul's hatred to near breakdown. Yes, he had set a plan in motion to extend his hunt beyond Judea's borders to eradicate the "heresy" of *The Way*.

But Saul, unlike believers in Jesus, could not call upon heavenly forces nor bring requests to the throne of the God of Creation. Saul's spiritual arsenal was empty. And the Pharisee had yet to come to terms with his soul and the true weight of His actions.

God alone could change this lost man's dark soul.

CHAPTER 18
"SAUL, SAUL"

Saul forced himself not to react as Caiaphas slammed his hands on the intricately carved stone table. Caiaphas lounged behind a large table scattered with scrolls and parchments as Saul stood before him in the high priest's ornate personal chamber.

"Saul, we can't stone everyone who follows the Nazarene," Caiaphas yelled. "Our prisons are full, yet you bring me requests for more warrants and soldiers so you can continue your raids. What do you expect me to do with more prisoners?" he challenged as he grabbed a fig from a silver platter and stuffed it into his mouth.

Not wanting to anger the high priest further, Saul dropped his head submissively. But *The Way* had spread rapidly from Jerusalem to Judea, Samaria, and into Syria, despite his best efforts. He needed the power of the full Sanhedrin he'd originally been given, but Caiaphas had reduced those numbers over time. Apparently, several Cretans had expressed concerns about Saul's "overzealous brutality."

He forced his tone to be conciliatory. "My Honored One, their message is vile. They proclaim that Adonai has given them a new *Way* to sacrifice for sin and are abandoning the Law. Our people have practiced the *Way of Moses* for fifteen hundred years. Yahweh Himself gave Moses the Torah and the plan for His chosen people."

Caiaphas shifted in his chair.

"Yes, Saul, but there is a limit to our power. We cannot have Pilate stepping in and taking away our authority or curtailing our ability to dictate how the masses worship."

Not to be dissuaded, Saul responded carefully. "These upstart unlearned Galileans must cease propagating this blasphemy and return to worshipping in the Temple as our people have obediently observed for generations. Their refusal is treason. They go to Temple posing as observant Jews, but the two practices are incompatible."

Caiaphas shook his head firmly. "We cannot continue to overfill prisons and expect Pilate's support. Prisons are reserved for criminals who act against Roman authority," he stated emphatically and turned away.

Yet he did not tell me to cease the raids. Caiaphas is sly. He chides and scolds but secretly agrees with my plan. He fears consequences from Pilate.

"Even though the believers originated in Galilee," Saul reminded Caiaphas, "they have not tried to proselytize other Jews, at least in Samaria. We did hear that when their disciples baptized new converts into *The Way*, a mysterious spirit came upon them, and they began to sing, dance, and spread the message to Jews loyal to Moses."

"How does this relate to what happened in Jerusalem?" Caiaphas snapped as he plopped another fig in his mouth.

"The 'cult' spread to Samaria because of the work of the so-called Holy Spirit and united the movement with the group in Jerusalem. They call the new union *ecclesia*. We must get to Damascus before this heresy spreads beyond our borders—and beyond our control. Damascus has a large population of both Jews and non-Jewish God-fearers. Reaching Damascus as soon as possible is critical if we hope to contain the spread of this evil poison."

Caiaphas stood and wiped his mouth with a cloth.

"What is your strategy for eradication of the so-called ecclesia? We can't stone all of them, nor will Rome crucify them, and our prisons won't hold their numbers. We can't charge them before

Pilate as traitors to Rome. He will ignore us, and who knows what else he will do?" Caiaphas crossed his arms and leaned toward Saul threateningly.

Saul had already thought through this answer. He smiled. "This is not a problem. I will arrest the instigators who lead them and take them to cities with major prisons: Tiberias, Shechem, Caesarea, Haifa, Sythopolis, and Caesarea Philippi." Saul was aware that Roman prisoners rot in rat-infested jails waiting for their trials.

Caiaphas continued, "As for faithful followers, we will beat them, confiscate their property, and warn them of future punishments. Give me a few weeks, and I will have these heretics pleading to return to orthodoxy."

The expression on Caiaphas' face told Saul that he had chosen his words wisely. He had presented a detailed and workable plan to the high priest, who had little tolerance for *The Way's* new threat to Judaism. Caiaphas may have been reluctant, but moments later he signed and sealed papers granting Saul's request to proceed to Damascus and carry out his plan.

Saul left the high priest's chamber elated. He could now set into motion the beginning of the end, and the heretics wouldn't be able to prepare for what was about to hit them.

૭

With extradition documents against followers of *The Way* in hand, Saul and a small band of soldiers set out at daybreak from Jerusalem to Damascus, Syria, a journey of about fourteen days. The extradition documents would be formally recognized by synagogues outside Jerusalem.

Saul smiled to himself, interpreting the good weather as God's blessing on their mission. They had quickly loaded the donkeys with provisions and the documents, then flew Caiaphas' banner, announcing their official status. To further assure their authority, a priest designated by High Priest Caiaphas accompanied them.

Saul had decided to use the long journey to think through the details of his strategy. He was also pleased to be visiting Damascus, which was said to be the longest continuously inhabited city on earth and the hub of a vast commercial trade network stretching from Mesopotamia to Anatolia and eventually to Rome.

The Damascus city planners had rebuilt the city laid out in a rectangle bisected by two parallel streets, the longer of which was called Straight Street. The city was a "cardo," with narrow, crooked streets lined with colonnades, forming a labyrinth. Houses were constructed with multiple levels and were externally unsightly. Locations in the city could be found in reference to their proximity to Straight Street.

Joseph accompanied Saul as an official member of the Temple Guard and would assure that Saul's orders were followed, and discipline was maintained. Several Roman mercenaries had been recruited to carry out beatings and arrests and do the distasteful work of spilling blood. According to rumor, Joseph had attained his childhood dream when he was appointed Captain of the Temple Guard, so Saul had no misgivings about safety or disorder.

Roman soldiers followed orders with enthusiasm. They relished mercilessness, manhandling prisoners, and using brutal flagellins when whipping. The more sadistic the punishment, the more pleasurable for Roman enforcers, and Caiaphas' letters of extradition were sufficient to empower their bloody terror.

From the beginning, the trip was taxing, forcing Saul and his men up and down steep, winding mountain trails, through disease-infested ponds, and exposed them to the oppressive heat of the lowlands and desert dehydration. Water supplies had to be preserved until they could be replenished in freshwater springs and rivers.

Thunderstorms, although a welcome relief from heat and drought, soaked supplies, spoiled food, and brought sickness. Soldiers became irritable, drunk, and violent, often breaking pottery, tearing waterskins, and spilling precious fluids.

After several days, Saul struggled to keep order and lift the spirits of his men. One sleepless night as he sat alone in his tent, he shifted his thoughts from the sagging morale of the soldiers to how to make the most of his time in Damascus and the surrounding area.

I will deliver Caiaphas' extradition letter to the rabbi of the central synagogue. He will grant my authority to carry out my plans and help me identify those in his district who have fallen victim to Galilean heresy. This will help ensure my success.

Then I will call a meeting of city elders who want to hear news from Jerusalem. I will also report on Caiaphas' approval of Stephen's stoning. When I point out that many of Stephen's followers fled to Syria to spread their poison, the city elders will join me in my mission.

With a plan settled, Saul fell into a peaceful sleep.

The early morning light slipped above the eastern horizon, illuminating fissures in the distant craggy mountains. The morning sun was warm and the air fresh following a light rain the night before. The day held promise of the journey's end, and everyone anticipated comfortable lodging and fresh food. Their steps quickened, and their spirits lifted.

Saul moved slowly along the mud-dotted road, lost in thought as they drew near Damascus. The air suddenly became muggy, and without warning, a sudden spring lightning storm struck. He ordered the men to the side of the road, but as he was speaking, a brilliant light pierced the sky with blinding intensity.

His hands flew to his face as Saul squeezed his eyes shut. Scorching heat burned the back of his hands, and he fell to his knees to evade the penetrating brilliance.

Strength drained from his body, like wine seeping from a punctured wineskin. He struggled for breath as his legs began to shake.-

I am going to die! Light this resplendent could only be Yahweh, as He appeared in the Holy of Holies! What have I done to displease my Adonai?

Terror seized Saul. The light surpassed anything earthly—it had to be a manifestation of glory. A Presence apprehended him, and he was suddenly overwhelmed by a sense of The Divine. Crushing weight compressed his heart, and with it, a penetrating awareness of his sins. They flashed through his mind in countless scenes: ego-centric facades, lies, lust, false worship, greed, envy, gluttony, pride-centered aspirations. Every moment in his life that had been motivated by self-service, selfishness, anger, and posturing flooded his memory as he lay prostrate before Yahweh. Time disappeared as his mind and heart struggle to grasp the horror of what he was seeing.

For the first time in his life, he saw the sinful bent of his heart. Remorse choked him. As he wiped tears from his eyes, they opened a sliver. More than enough.

His prayer shawl and turban lay in the dirt beside him, and his "humble," tatty undergarment was exposed. A moan rose in this throat.

This is who I am—a sinner of sinners.

At first there were no words. Simply moans until one word, then a phrase, and Saul poured out his heart in repentance, his soul stripped naked by the Light. Blinding pride, selfishness, rebellion, crushing guilt, self-hatred, judgment ...

He was terrified. Yet, wordlessly with breaths of love, the Presence comforted him.

Then overcome by his need for forgiveness yet beckoned to ask and receive by Holiness too *other* to comprehend.

Certainly, this is Adonai—the Adonai of Moses, and my Adonai. He is here, asking me to talk to Him.

With his hands shielding his eyes, Saul lifted his head.

A voice resonated from the light like echoing thunder. "Saul, Saul, why do you persecute Me?"

Breathless, *Who are you?*

"I am Jesus." A whisper, soft, loving, like the voice of Ima when he was a sick child.

Saul's heart turned to ice.

Jesus? Impossible. I felt the presence of Adonai Himself, His power, His authority. But Jesus, Who claims to be The Son of God, as those of The Way are proclaiming?

Something stirred in Saul's spirit, as if he was being drawn into Ima's arms.

"It is I. Why do you persecute Me, Saul?"

Peace.

Consolation.

Forgiveness.

The world fell away as Saul abandoned himself to the Holy Presence, to Love beyond comprehension.

Jesus' presence encompassed him, and every sorrow and sin, weight and want cried out from Saul's inmost being. Jesus hovered over him until the pain was gone. All was peace. The voice spoke again. "I have made all things new, Saul. Get up and go into the city, and you will be told what you must do."

Saul stood, struggling to understand what Jesus had asked.

What will I be told when I get to Damascus, Lord? Will I be punished for persecuting Your followers?

But the Light was gone. Saul glanced at his men. They were huddled together staring, speechless, and obviously afraid.

"What happened?" Joseph the Cyprian blurted out. "We were nearly blinded by a brilliant light and could hear a conversation, but we couldn't understand anything."

Saul could not find words to explain what he had experienced. His mind raced as he grasped for an explanation.

Why did Jesus come to me? I've been His worst enemy. Why not Gamaliel, a benevolent Pharisee? What do I tell my men? That I encountered the crucified Jesus, the Son of Adonai, who is alive? They will think I have gone mad!

Saul beckoned, and two visibly shaken guards rushed to his side, helped him to his feet, and steadied him.

His childhood friend Joseph, the Temple guard, straightened his garments and addressed him while another guard steadied him.

"Could you have been struck by lightning? The light was so blinding we had to turn our backs. But then, the brilliance lasted longer than a lightning strike."

As Saul turned his head to reply to Joseph, the world suddenly went black. He blinked to bring something—anything—into focus.

Nothing but black.

His hands flashed out to grip an arm. "I can't see! What has happened? I can't see anything or anyone!"

Is this punishment for my sin? Did the light blind me? I don't understand, Jesus. I cannot serve You this way, and I have only just come to know who You are!

As Saul struggled for answers, he was certain of only one thing. He believed in Jesus, Yahweh's Son, and he wanted to tell the world.

But what did that even mean?

And who would ever listen to him or believe him?

CHAPTER 19

DAMASCUS

Joseph was terrified. The arrogant, driven Saul of Tarsus he had always known had gone missing and been replaced by a new man totally unlike Saul.

The event on the Damascus road had inexplicably transformed Saul of Tarsus. Arrogance softened into quiet humility. Anger into calm. Demanding into gratitude. The quick judgment of hubris to listening.

Suddenly dependent upon those in his party to care for him and guide him, Saul was now speaking to those assisting him with gratitude that left everyone speechless. The proud man who lived to levy punishment could no longer fend for himself. Completing simple daily duties had become major events—all freedom had evaporated.

Saul willingly leaned his stumbling body against Joseph as they pushed toward Damascus in the cool of early morning. Joseph had made certain that Saul grasped his left arm and walked toward the center of the causeway, away from the roadside, where travelers were more susceptible to attack.

Questions pounded through Joseph's thoughts as they walked.

Where did the light come from, and whose voice spoke? What could have changed Saul so profoundly? He is not himself. Is it the shock of sudden blindness? Did the light alter his mind?

We certainly cannot return to Jerusalem with him in this condition, but where are we going now, and for what purpose?

Saul laid his hand on his friend's shoulder. "Joseph, I must tell you what happened yesterday." His tone was earnest. "It will sound as if I am mad, but I need you to trust that I speak the truth."

Joseph stopped and looked intently into Saul's face. His eyes had crusted over, and his expression was pleading. "I'm listening, and of course I trust you to speak the truth."

"While I was on the ground," Saul said, "stunned by the light, Jesus of Nazareth spoke to me and asked why I was persecuting Him."

Joseph shook his head. "This cannot be. What you are saying is not possible, Saul. Jesus of Nazareth is dead. A blow to your head must have caused delusions or a dream when you fell. I say this with respect, but what you think you saw and heard can't be real."

Even as he spoke, Joseph doubted his own words. Saul's face bore the expression of a man convinced of what he'd experienced. But Joseph saw something else—something he had not seen on Saul's face since he was in school with him. Honest transparency.

*Saul has never been one to make up stories. He's dedicated his life to eradicating Jesus' memory. So, what **really** happened?*

Saul squeezed Joseph's arm. "Joseph, the Yahweh of eternity spoke to me. You don't have to believe it, but it's true. He told me to go to Damascus and wait for further instructions, and when I rose, I was blind. I don't know if I will continue to be blind or if Yahweh will perform a miracle and restore my sight, but I am now committed to Him either way."

"You need to rest, Saul," Joseph replied, suddenly annoyed at Saul's persistence.

How can a person dedicate their life to destroying an enemy, then reverse their thinking in the blink of an eye? Either Saul is delirious, or he has spoken to the ghost of Jesus of Nazareth.

I, too, have been fascinated by what I have heard about the Nazarene for some time. But could he truly be the Messiah? And if he was, why would He appear to Saul?

The men continued to walk in silence, each occupied with his own thoughts.

The air was flat, the sun intense, and conversation sparse. Awkward silence was broken only by the sound of footsteps and an occasional bray from a donkey.

Late in the afternoon, Joseph, Saul, and their men stumbled into the outskirts of Damascus, tired, hungry, and ready for a freshly cooked meal. Joseph placed Saul under the care of another soldier while he went into the city to find an inn. Soon after heading out, he came upon a day worker who was hauling bricks on a donkey cart.

"Sir, can you direct me to an inn where my friends and I may eat and seek medical treatment for someone in need?"

The young man glanced up. "Go down to the Straight Street to the house of Judas near the East Gate. It is a large house with a gold veranda awning. He can provide whatever you need."

Joseph quickly retraced his steps and carefully guided Saul and the rest of their contingency through the town. Straight Street was crowded, as it was the city's main thoroughfare where most Damascus businesses were located. After maneuvering through shoppers and merchants, the group arrived at Judas' house. He greeted them warmly. Joseph was surprised when he invited everyone, including the soldiers, to join him for dinner.

Joseph took a seat near Saul and immediately noticed how different Syrian food was from Israeli fare. He described the various dishes to Saul, then filled Saul's bowl with the foods he requested.

Joseph successfully maneuvered the meal of eggplant, lamb, rice, chickpeas, and fava beans, but he also glanced at Saul frequently to see if he might need assistance. Again, Joseph was impressed with Saul's patience and gratitude.

How humbling it must be for a man so high-ranking to be suddenly dependent upon a soldier to guide him. Yet I have not heard one word of complaint or seen the slightest display of temper. Is this another of Saul's schemes, or is it possible that he has truly changed?

The table also offered fresh bread, lentils, cabbage, cauliflower, cucumbers, tomatoes, honey, and fruit. Everyone filled themselves with the host's bounty.

Joseph interrupted the sound of men slurping porridge and munching roasted fowl. "We haven't seen a feast like this since we left Jerusalem. This meal was welcome hospitality. The journey has been hard." He nodded in Saul's direction.

Saul's head rested on his folded hands, and his eyes were closed.

In prayer?

Later that night, Joseph mulled over his observations of Saul. One thing was becoming apparent: Saul of Tarsus *had* experienced a life-changing event on the road to Damascus. Whatever that event was, Joseph did not know. And had Saul been praying? For instructions about what to do? For the return of his sight? About his threatened ability to complete his mission without vision?

But praying to whom? Yahweh? Or the crucified Jesus, whose name he had vowed to eradicate? Or perhaps even both.

☙

Saul's blindness made him invisible to those around him. He learned much by sitting at meals and listening. The band of Jews fighting to stamp out *The Way* was fraying, and questions about what the group should do flowed through his mind like torrential spring floods. Joseph had summed it up: "If we return to Jerusalem, we face the Sanhedrin having failed our mission. For such failure, we will receive life in prison or death on a cross. It is better for me to remain with Saul and see where this strange journey takes me."

Day after day, Saul waited for direction from his newly discovered Lord. Of his own, he knew not what to do or where to go. So, he prayed for wisdom—for Adonai to show him how to equip himself for the task. He continued to fast and pray. Blindness gave him time for introspection, reflection, and prayer.

During an evening of intimate prayer with his Lord, a heavenly voice spoke to Saul in a vision. "Saul, I have directed a man named Ananias, a devout follower of *The Way*, to come to you with further instructions—your wait is over."

Further instructions? What would that mean? Saul pondered the possibilities throughout the night.

The following day around midday, he heard a sharp knock on the inn door. Moments later, Judas announced himself as he walked into the common room where Saul was seated.

"Saul, Ananias has come to visit you. He tells me that you two have not met before. I am bringing him a chair so he can sit in front of you as the two of you speak."

A hand with the thin skin and thick veins of an older man was placed in his. Ananias gripped Saul's hand tightly.

"I have been waiting for you, Saul. God directed me in a vision to meet with you and reveal instructions about what you are to do next. I did not expect a man of such power to be of small stature. This tells me a great deal about the strength of your character. I hope you do not mind that I speak freely, as I feel a special closeness to you, although we have never met."

A gentle squeeze enfolded Saul's hand. He didn't know whether to feel honored or angry at this bold man, but a spark of gratitude welled up. Ananias had been hand-picked by God to speak to him. A lump rose in Saul's throat. Again, Yahweh had personally intervened in his life. How could he not fall to his face and worship?

"I was sent to you, Saul. I was given a vision, a message from your Master."

Saul raised his head as if to search Ananias' face. What would he see if he still had his sight? Did Ananias know that Saul had received a vision of *his* coming?

"My Lord told me you were coming, Ananias."

Ananias' hand slipped from Saul's. Fingers glided across Saul's crusty, scaly eyelids. Any attempt to remove or clean the unsightly debris had brought Saul excruciating pain.

Was Ananias cupping his fingers over Saul's eyelids? That felt like the sensation.

Brilliant light flashed through his closed lids. In that instant, Saul saw Jesus, His arms outstretched and hands touching Saul's eyes. Warmth flowed through Saul's chest, then his legs and head, like a glowing ember radiating through his body.

The pain suddenly left his eyes. Saul opened them slowly, and found himself looking into the weathered face of a gray-haired elderly man. "God removed your scales."

Cupping his palms on each side of Ananias' face, Saul whispered. "You are the man I saw in my vision."

"Yes. The Master sent me. He had a second message. Together with the believers here, I am to baptize you. We can do it still today, or would you rather wait for tomorrow?"

He could not restrain himself from laughing. "Well, I see that you are a man of business, Ananias. Now! Of course, now!"

Together Saul, Ananias, and Joseph set out to find the local elders of *The Way* who were anxiously awaiting news about Saul. Although Ananias had visited Saul without fear, other believers who had seen or heard of Saul's persecution of *The Way* were less trusting. Many believed Saul's purported conversion was a ruse to draw them out.

When Saul, Ananias, and the few followers of *The Way* approached each other on the banks of the River Abana, Saul noted that Joseph remained in the background where he could quietly observe the reactions of Jesus-followers to their former persecutor. But within minutes of meeting Saul and hearing him speak about his conversion, Saul was reassured that believers were drawn by the authenticity of his message. Joseph would have to come to his own conclusion.

Saul and Ananias waded into the river until the water was waist deep. As Ananias asked questions, Saul quietly answered.

"Do you repent of your sins? Do you recognize Jesus as the Messiah and eternal atonement for your sins?"

Saul looked heavenward as tears pooled in his eyes. "Yes, I do."

A murmur—not unkind, more an utterance of awe—rippled through the crowd on shore.

Ananias placed his hands upon Saul's chest, and Saul clung to the arms of his baptizer as he was plunged beneath the waters of the slowly running river.

Spectators rejoiced as if he'd been raised from the dead. Perhaps that was an accurate description.

As the people cheered, Saul searched for his friend Joseph. But he was walking away, heading toward the inn.

Later that evening, his fast ended, Saul welcomed a full meal and, following a prayer of gratitude, scooped up lentil stew on a chunk of bread. His baptism and the return of his vision had invigorated him. He was ready to take on a new life with a new mission and a new Lord. He retired for the evening, praying and envisioning what his future might hold.

CHAPTER 20

HIS NAME IS BARNABUS

The next morning, Saul and Ananias met in the gathering room of the inn to create a plan for spreading Messiah's message. They placed pillows on two stout wooden chairs in a corner and set to work. Saul began by asking questions about the believers in Damascus: their occupations, lifestyle, ages, and family status, as well the kind of opposition believers had received and could expect from local priests. Paul also asked Ananias' opinion of how his preaching might be received and the best locations in the city for him to find receptive crowds.

The conversation lasted most of the day as Saul plied Ananias for useful information. Eventually the talk turned personal, and the innkeeper's wife brought out bowls of roasted grain and fruit, as well as fresh bread and wine.

Ananias, how did you come to believe in Jesus?"

Ananias stroked his disheveled gray beard. "It's a simple story. I am by trade a food merchant, and I often journey to Capernaum to purchase supplies. Galilee produces the finest grains and vegetables in our part of the world. When I am there, I often purchase fish at Magdala. There, I heard Jesus teach, preach, and saw him perform miracles."

Saul noted the light in Ananias' eyes as he recounted the memories.

"On one occasion Jesus was preaching in Capernaum, but

earlier, I saw him feed an enormous crowd of people with just five loaves and two fish. The people were astounded. I was especially interested because I purchase grain for bread on nearly every trip I make to Galilee."

Ananias was picking up speed. "At Capernaum, He preached that He was the bread of life and that if we eat the bread of life and drink living water, we will never be hungry or thirsty. I knew right then that I must follow this man. Later, I saw Him after His trip to Caesarea Philippi, and He revealed He had to go to the cross to pay for the sins of the world. I didn't understand then that He would defeat death and come out of the tomb."

Saul quietly digested everything Ananias was saying before he responded. "I saw Jesus heal a cripple, but I didn't believe it was a miracle. I thought He was tricking everyone. I clung to that lie, thinking I was protecting the faith Yahweh delivered to Moses. But the truth is that I never really listened to Jesus' message or evaluated His claims. I just reacted out of fear."

Ananias nodded.

"Pride and emotion blinded me. I was too busy trying to show the world that I was right—or at least certain people in the world." Silence hung in the room for several moments. "Ananias, how many believers are there in Damascus?"

"We have about forty-five in Damascus and another eighty in the villages around the city. We meet by the Abana River in open air meetings and in private homes. The Roman governor of Syria, Lucius Vitellius Veteris, who has given the authority over Damascus to Aretas IV Philopatris of Nabatea, carries out the local policies."

Ananias reclined on one elbow. "While King Aretas wields great influence, he has left us alone if we don't cause trouble. Preaching that stirs Jewish opposition is a potential danger. In past decades we've had many Roman governors, and each time we caused problems, they were removed. For now, we are safe to share our faith. The Jews only bother us if we become publicly aggressive in bringing others to our faith."

The conversation continued into the evening as Saul and Ananias discussed the most effective way to bring Jesus' message to Damascus and beyond.

The following morning, Saul was enjoying kashi on the rooftop when Joseph approached. The guard asked if he could accompany Saul to the temple to hear him tell the Jews his story of transformation from persecutor of Jesus followers to a *talmid*, or lifetime disciple, of Jesus, dedicating his life to become like his Master and propagate His message. Saul immediately smiled.

"Of course, Joseph of Cyprus. I would love to have a fellow graduate of Beit Hillel accompany me. Strangely, I am still carrying extradition letters from Caiaphas to the synagogues we will be visiting. They authorize persecution of *The Way* and denounce the founder of *The Way*, Jesus of Nazareth, as falsely claiming to be the Messiah, the Son of God."

Joseph's eyebrows raised. "In all that has happened these past days, I dismissed your original intent in coming to Damascus."

"I see that Yahweh has a unique sense of humor, sending me to Damascus with extradition papers for His Son's followers in my possession while putting the gospel message on my lips. If I carried out the intent of the letters, I would be forced to first arrest myself!" Saul threw his head back and laughed.

Joseph did not react.

"Can you imagine the shock of synagogue officials when they see me enter Jerusalem and hear me preach as a Jesus-follower? They may need the services of medico! Their only knowledge of me is that, just days ago, I was maniacally trying to eradicate both Jesus' message and His followers."

Saul looked into Joseph's eyes, trying to discern his response, but could not read his friend's stoic demeanor. Temple Guard training had served Joseph well.

More subdued, Saul said, "I will be under scrutiny, Joseph, and both Jews and members of *The Way* will be suspicious of my motives. Everyone knows I maliciously persecuted those who call on Jesus' name in Jerusalem. All will wonder if I have come to take believers prisoner, and they will assume that you are the guard assigned to physically restrain them. We will very quickly find ourselves the objects of everyone's anger and suspicion."

Saul leaned toward Joseph until their noses nearly touched. "Are you ready for *this* kind of adventure with me, my friend?"

Joseph tipped his head back and rubbed his chin, as if pondering his decision. Saul smiled, amused by the gesture.

"Yes, Saul, I'm ready. I need to find answers about Jesus, just as you did. I've been interested in the teachings of *The Way* for some time but was afraid to let anyone know, for fear I'd spend the rest of my life in prison."

Shock rippled through Saul. He'd heard earlier that his friend was intrigued by Jesus' teachings. But why *would* Joseph ever have breathed a word to *him* about it? Admitting even a slight interest would have cost their friendship and … so much more.

That's who I was—a man who would take the life of a childhood friend for pride and legalism.

The Spirit nudged him, and Saul continued.

"Joseph, you have done much for me, and I want to recognize how much you mean to me. You have played a part in my most soul-transforming days. To honor you, I want to give you the name *Barnabus*, 'son of encouragement,' if you would allow me to do so."

Joseph's eyes grew wide as a slow smile spread across his face. Saul was suddenly and painfully aware that he could not remember ever evoking such a life-giving emotion in anyone. At least not in recent memory. The thought tore at his heart as he saw the barrenness of his past.

"I will bear the name with pride," Joseph beamed. "I thankfully accept your gift."

The following day, Saul began visiting local synagogues with *Barnabus* at his side. Over and over, the reaction was the same. Audiences listened in rapt attention to the Pharisee who had ruthlessly persecuted *The Way* in Jerusalem and who was now boldly proclaiming Jesus to be the Messiah and the only hope for salvation from sin.

Daily, Saul's message grew more powerful as he preached in and around Damascus. When he wasn't teaching the gospel, he spent time ministering to widows and the poor, meeting with city officials, speaking to merchants in the marketplace, and serving the needs of the ecclesia. Believers and unbelievers trusted him and respected his passion for Jesus' message, even if they did not believe.

On more than one occasion when Saul retired to bed in the evening, he pondered his place in life. *The longer I serve among the Damascus Jews, the more I realize that my knowledge of Jesus the Messiah and His teaching is limited. I long to learn more—but how can I study what I need to learn from Jesus Himself?*

For weeks the question pulled at his heart, but there appeared to be no answer.

Then in the depths of a dream, the words of Ananias returned to him one night. "Go into the Arabian desert, where Yahweh Himself will teach you. Yahweh Himself delivered this message to me to give to you."

Saul awoke the following morning certain that Ananias' words to him were his answer.

The time had come for him to step out in faith regarding his mentor's vision. Yahweh had told him what he needed to do—go to the desert.

CHAPTER 21

ARABIAN DESERT

Saul eased the roughhewn door open slowly, then glanced back at the sound of a muffled footfall. The figure of a man was moving out of the moonlight into the shadows behind him. He quickly pushed the door shut behind him and hurried to Sere's stall. His faithful donkey was not the fastest, but he would never be able to find one stronger. Besides, he had grown attached to her over his past months of travel.

Saul was sliding the bridle over Sere's head when he heard the stable door creak open. He whirled, surprised to find Barnabus standing near the door.

"Barnabus, my friend, you frightened me. Why are you here?"

The figure took several steps closer through the darkness. "I want to go with you, Saul. I need to learn so much more from you about Jesus. And the journey through Nabataea is dangerous. Bandits roam the desert looking for vulnerable travelers. You should not go alone, and I take great joy in serving you."

Saul could hear the pleading tone of his friend's voice, and he smiled as he slung a wooden frame on Sere's back for carrying supplies. "Barnabus, I know you want to go, but I must go on this trip as Ananias directed. I will not be alone, as I am always under Yahweh's protection. I cannot be responsible for companions. I assume I will be gone for only a month. But thank you, my friend."

The men continued packing the donkey in silence. Two large

goat skins to spread on the ground for protection from moisture, woolen blankets for bedding and bartering. They also packed additional barter items: beads, small knives, tools, and cooking utensils. Final additions included a spool of camel skin thread, a spool of sisal and jute twisted into a strong cord, two awls, and grain for Sere. Currency was useless for purchasing supplies in the desert, but Ananias had insisted on giving Saul a few coins in a purse that was hidden in his girdle.

After they secured the supplies, Saul added dried mutton, matza bread, wine, and as many skins of water as Sere could carry. The desert would be dry, but travelers counted on waterfalls and springs scattered along the main routes. As Barnabus tied the final water pouches on the rear of the frame, Sere let out a loud bray and emitted a noxious burst of befouled air.

Saul struggled to maintain his dignity but was unable to hold the rising laughter that erupted so loudly that Sere startled, with wide eyes and nostrils flaring. Barnabus stepped forward, grabbed the donkey's halter, and stroked her neck as he struggled to soothe her. But instead of quieting words, all Barnabus could offer was muffled laughter as Saul wiped his eyes and tried to regain a sense of decorum. He stood quietly for a few moments, stroking Sere's nose until he was able to speak again. Saul finally turned to Barnabus.

"Barnabus, go back to Jerusalem." He forced his voice to remain steady. "I will come when I can."

Barnabus' head dropped. "I will do what you ask, but when I return, I will have to answer to the chief Temple Guard for my mission's failure. I may be in prison or dead when you come back."

Saul shifted his weight. "You are not responsible for what happened on this journey. I will send letters that state that the result was my responsibility and that you did everything possible to fulfill your job. But more importantly, Barnabus, you must remember that

Yahweh is in control. I believe that when I return, we will be reunited to serve together. This is my prayer and my hope, my brother."

With those words, Saul turned and walked toward the door, leading Sere and leaving all he had ever known and loved behind.

His journey into the desert had begun.

❧

The first day of the journey was long, tiring, and uneventful. By nightfall, Saul was exhausted and ready to set up a temporary camp for the night. He chose a spot under a small tree for protection from the cool desert night. A small fire kept the brisk evening air warm and would help provide a good night's sleep. He tied Sere to the tree so she could graze on the sparse foliage.

Saul hastily prepared a small evening meal, bedded Sere down, and nestled under his blankets under the stars.

My Lord, will you speak to me tonight? I await your instructions.

The sounds of darkness taunted Saul as he tossed and turned, awaiting a heavenly visitor.

But no visitor came. No voice spoke.

Saul's mind refused to rest. Finally, in the first glimmers of morning, exhaustion overtook him, and he remembered nothing more until the bright, hot sun beckoned him to rise. He stirred, still in the grasp of sleep's grogginess, then jolted upright.

Did my Lord not come? Did I miss Him as I slept?

Deep disappointment washed over him. He sipped watered-down wine and slowly ate a barley roll as he mulled over his conversation with Ananias.

Perhaps I misinterpreted what he said. Or maybe I haven't fully prepared myself.

179

For the next three days, Saul continued his travels in Nabataea. He laid down each night hopeful and rose each morning with questions, wondering if he was somehow failing. His rabbinic, rote prayers no longer seemed appropriate, and he spent waking moments learning how to pray to his new Master. Each new sunrise diminished his confidence that God heard him.

Do I no longer pray the Tanakh's words, promises, and exhortations? How do I approach an Adonai who guides me cares for me, and even speaks to me? I have no one to teach me, my Lord. Please help me.

A familiar text echoed through his memory:

"Be still and know that I am Yahweh."

Saul fell to his knee and cried out: "Yahweh, God of heaven and earth, what do You want from me? Am I to receive an angelic visit as Ananias told me, or was he wrong? Am I going to the right place? Have I displeased You? Where are You?"

Time ticked by as Saul waited. But the only sound was Sere snorting and scuffling as she pulled at the bridle.

Another sleepless night, tossing, turning, and staring into soul-strangling darkness.

The following day Saul straggled into the ancient capital of Nabataea—Petra. The Nabataeans had built the spectacular sandstone city by carving palaces, temples, tombs, storerooms, and stables from the soft stone cliffs.

The city was known as a haven for thieves and bandits. Saul found a room in one of the temples that he'd heard was seldom accosted by brigands. He hoped his decision would ensure his safety for at least a few nights. Once again after preparing for bed, he waited for his Lord to appear as he wordlessly pleaded for revelation. As he prayed, words of a lesson he had learned from Rabbi Akiva in Beit Midrash drifted through Saul's thoughts.

"Lack of patience can cause you to miss Yahweh's blessings."

Saul laid on his goatskin for hours thinking, pleading. He eventually recalled the story of Israel's father Jacob, who worked fourteen years to pay for Rachel to become his bride. His love for her was so strong that it seemed to him but a few days. His patience was rewarded when he finally received what he was seeking.

Be still before Yahweh and wait patiently for Him.

With a new perspective, Saul felt peace slip over him. He understood, now, that his patience was being challenged.

On his tenth day, he joined a Bedouin encampment just off the main highway along the east side of the Salt Sea. The night was calm, the night air still, and the moon dark. Saul sought permission from the Bedouin chief to lie near an occupied tent to discourage anyone with ill intent. The chief gave permission, but Saul became suspicious when he was directed to a location in the shadows. He finished his evening bread and dried mutton and was filling his goatskin pouches with spring water from a wet wadi, when he was approached by two men with head coverings wound about their faces.

"Do you think this water is free?" the taller man challenged. "What are you carrying on your donkey?"

Saul assumed his most imposing stance. "I have nothing worth stirring Yahweh's wrath." He spoke fearlessly, confident that his Lord would protect him on his divinely directed mission.

However, the bandit did not seem to fear Saul's God. He struck a fast, fierce, close-fisted blow to Saul's jaw. Saul collapsed to the ground in pain, but the thief didn't stop. He continued his sadistic beating as saliva and blood splattered from Saul's mouth and dripped down his face. Blow after blow found its mark on his prostrate body.

Saul awakened to the sound of Sere's snorts near his face. He slowly raised his throbbing head and saw the few remnants of his supplies scattered in the dim predawn light. His ribs felt as if Sere had tried to kick him back to consciousness, and he doubted that his bruised and beaten legs would hold him upright. He lowered his pulsating head slowly back to the ground.

Why, God, did You allow this to happen? What am I to do? My supplies are gone, and my broken body is bleeding. Why are You silent? Will I ever know the purpose of my miserable trip to this barren desert?

Even as his heart cried out, a promise from the Tanakh drifted through his thoughts.

"For the revelation awaits an appointed time; it speaks of the end and will not prove false. Though it lingers, wait for it; it will certainly come and will not delay."

Saul held his ribs as he cried out in the dim light. "My Lord, I don't know when You will speak to me, but I will wait and believe that You are working out Your purposes in my life—even my suffering."

Saul caught Sere's bridle and pulled her closer. With gritted teeth, he grabbed her mane, leveraged himself against her solid girth, and, with the support of the wooden frame on her back, pulled himself to a standing position. Step by step, he made his way down the road until he came upon a young Damascene husband and wife traveling to Karak who welcomed him to their roadside camp.

Saul whispered a weak but earnest psalm of praise. After a day of rest and care from the couple, he continued his journey, still battered and sore. The husband and wife sent him on his way with provisions of food, water, and grain for Sere.

Just before dawn on his thirteenth day, Saul limped into a second Bedouin camp at the edge of a small Sinai *kaphar*. The village was strategically located at the foot of Mount Horeb and well positioned on a major trade route. Small tribes of Bedouins living close to communities had a reputation for being friendly and protecting strangers. Saul counted on it.

He was warmly welcomed, and members invited him to their fire, where Saul told his story of converting from traditional Judaism to following the teachings of Jesus. Several men asked questions, expressed curiosity about Jesus' teaching, and showed openness to Saul's message.

Later, Saul rested on his remaining goatskin, covered by a blanket the couple from Damascus had given him. A thin man, Toda, who had asked several questions at the fire, called to him.

"Saul, come join my family. You can lie down beneath the outer tent canopy. It will be safer, and our fire will keep you warm."

Grateful for protection and warmth, Saul accepted, thanking God for the gift of kindness. As he spread his goat skin once again with a fire crackling warmth behind him, he recalled words about Yahweh's appearance to Moses through a burning bush.

*On this holy mountain where I stand, Yahweh appeared to Moses at the burning bush and Elohim announced He was Yahweh, Lord God of the Jews. The Law of Moses was delivered atop **this** mountain,* Saul repeated to himself in awe. *When the Israelites were complaining of thirst and passed this place during their wilderness wanderings, Moses struck the rock, and drinking water poured forth.*

Saul gazed into the flames, as his thoughts cleared. *Yahweh, You brought me to this place, at this moment in time. But why?* He suddenly felt dizzy, as if his mind could not grasp the magnitude of his question.

In the midst of his thoughts, Saul suddenly spotted a tall, dignified man dressed in a white linen robe, scarlet girdle, and a stole that hung from his neck to his knees, walking slowly toward the fire where Saul huddled. His white hair was crowned with a turban like those worn by Bedouin men, and his distinguished face was etched by time and wisdom. He greeted Saul in Greek, his voice resonating comfort.

"*Kalispera*, Saul." The stranger responded and stretched forth his hand. "My name is Yehoshua."

Saul reached forth his hand to grasp arm-in-hand in the traditional greeting. Strange … Yehoshua's hand and arm were deeply scarred.

"Please sit join me at my fire. I'm sorry, Yehoshua. I don't have money or goods to offer you," Saul responded with gentle firmness." But the expression in the man's eyes told him he was not seeking assistance. Saul continued. "I did not see you earlier. How do you know my name, and why are you greeting me in Greek, instead of Hebrew or Aramaic?"

The mystery man smiled as he folded legs and sat, and Saul's heart leaped. "Fear not, Saul. I am the one sent to you, the one you have been waiting for. Yahweh is pleased with your patience. We wanted to be sure your heart was ready. Your ministry will require many things, including patience. You must also learn to love your Lord with all your heart, soul, and mind, and love even your enemies."

This Yehoshua obviously who heard me speak when I told my stories earlier. But why did I not notice a man so distinctive in the crowd? Is he an angel, like those who appeared to the prophets? Ananias told me I would receive a heavenly vision. But would not a second vision resemble my first on the Damascus road?

Yehoshua interrupted Saul's thoughts. "I bring the message you have been awaiting, Saul. You have been chosen from the foundation of the world to be an apostle to the Gentiles."

Gentiles? Saul swallowed as he watched a tendril of smoke dissipate into the night air.

"Yahweh will share His love beyond His chosen people. Your name now becomes *Paul*."

Paul—the Greek translation of Saul. Yahweh, is this of You? Is this man truly Your messenger?

184

"You will be going beyond the Hebrew and Aramaic speaking world. We will speak more in the morning. This is your message for this moment."

For this moment. The words resonated in Paul's mind as Yehoshua turned and walked away, fading into the darkness beneath the glittering stars.

Saul sat beneath a tree, bowed his head, and slipped into deep thought, pondering the words of his visitor. *Yahweh clearly sent Yehoshua to me. I can finally rest tonight. But I do not understand—an apostle to the Gentiles? What does this mean? They are not God's chosen people and have never been part of the covenant promises of protection and favored position He made to us.*

I have so many questions. How can I trust when I know so little? But can faith be faith if we demand knowledge and full understanding? Or is true faith based upon the object of our trust? This is what The Way declares—because their Savior is Av and fully trustworthy, they can follow Him, no matter the circumstances.

This is the truth I have been searching for. I will record my journey so all the world will one day know who Jesus is.

His heart consumed by joy, Paul laid on his goat skin, pondering until peace enveloped him and his thoughts faded into night.

CHAPTER 22
THE MOUNT OF GOD

Darkness told Saul—or rather, Paul—it was the third watch. Daylight would remain hidden for another two or three hours. But for Paul, the deep sleep of night was over. Thoughts danced in his mind like feathers floating in a soft breeze, gently turning, tumbling, and finally landing.

Was Yehoshua an angel? Would he reappear? He said he had more to tell me. How long will I be with him? Will his message change my understanding of the Torah? Or the Law? And should I approach Jesus differently than I do Yahweh? There is so much to learn. I am too ignorant to even fathom what I do not know!

Questions fluttered and tumbled through Paul's thoughts until slumber again silenced his racing mind.

ᘒ

"*Kalimera, Kalimera.*" The familiar voice roused Paul. "Get up, we have a long day ahead of us."

Paul's eyes flew open. He threw off his blanket and reached for his sandals. Yehoshua was wearing the same garments as before. But this morning a skin of water hung at his side, and a sheepskin bag was slung over his shoulder.

"Come, Paul, we have a good distance to cover before we begin our discussions. The day is passing. Hurry. We will eat later."

Paul laced his sandals, then tied a few possessions in his sheepskin. "Should I bring Sere?"

"You won't need your donkey today. I have instructed Toda to care for her while we are gone, so you need not worry." Yehoshua gestured toward Toda, who was standing in the distance, waiting to be beckoned.

"We will ascend Mt. Horeb to the place where God created the Mosaic Covenant, His binding relationship, with the people of Israel. There you will receive further instructions."

Paul draped his cloak and goatskin over his shoulder and set out beside Yehoshua for the arduous walk up the back of the rugged mountain. He walked in silence, overcome with wonder that Yahweh would choose him, a man who had spitefully persecuted Jesus' followers, to be His messenger to the world. His spirit was energized with passion he had never experienced. At the same time, a familiar weight of unworthiness pressed his heart, and a long-forgotten voice echoed in his mind.

Paul struggled to keep up with Yehoshua's secure footsteps as they forged a trail among the craggy rocks. Because his weak feet were unsteady, his sandals often slipped, sending Paul sliding backwards, his fingers clawing for a handhold.

They had not ascended far when Yehoshua stopped to wait for Paul. His guide unwound the length of his scarlet girdle and secured it around Paul's waist, then his own, and knotted it firmly. They continued their ascent, Paul now anchored and borne along by the scarlet bond.

Paul immediately felt his burden ease, and his steps found purchase on the rocky soil. The climb was no longer something simply to be endured. Paul lifted his head and took in the beauty of the view.

As Yehoshua and Paul stepped onto the summit of the Holy Mountain, Yehoshua glanced around, surveying the area. "This is a good place for our discussion. I am sure you are ready to rest, and I know you have many questions." He turned toward Paul and smiled. "It is a difficult climb, yet you did not complain. You did well."

The entire fight up the mountain, Paul had fought not to gasp for air. He was accustomed to city walking and avoided mountainous journeys whenever possible. He suddenly wondered if the ascent would be a daily walk.

Yehoshua gestured to a spot a short distance away, and the two men moved to a rocky escarpment overlooking the beautiful valley. The sun was hot, so they removed their mantles and untied their waterskins. Yehoshua pulled dried goat meat, bread, and figs from his sheepskin bag and spread the food on a rock.

Paul took a deep drink as he scanned the view below, then voiced the question that had tugged hardest at his heart.

"Why did God choose *me* to be His messenger to the Gentiles? I am a Pharisee of Pharisees and have strived to keep the Law of Moses as perfectly as possible. But I know little about Gentiles, except to disdain them, as I have been taught. Why me?"

Yehoshua tore off a chunk of bread. "Pauli, what have you dreamed of most in your life? What does your heart call you to above everything else?"

Paul glanced sideways and responded slowly. "Why do you call me Pauli?

"Is not that who you often feel you are—a longing child? What does that longing child's heart ache for above all, Pauli? You are safe to say it because I already know the longings of your heart. You do not need to fear admitting that you are driven to please your abba, to finally earn his approval and love after working all your life for it. And to also find forgiveness for Cassia's death."

Paul swallowed. For a moment he felt like he might be sick. He did not want to talk about these things. He had never talked about them—these childhood ghosts—with anyone. *How does this man know my life? I have never even spoken of these things to Av.*

"What does this have to do with why God chose me to take the gospel to the Gentiles, other than to reveal my shame and confirm my unworthiness?" Paul turned his head away and choked back the lump in his throat. He felt a hand upon his shoulder.

"Yahweh, the Father of the Universe, sees you—sinless, forgiven, and worthy. He calls you His son. He chose you before you were in the belly of your mother. You have been hidden in the shadow of His hand from before time. Your abilities, experiences, and passions fit His purposes, Paul. Yes, even your past."

Yehoshua continued. "Yahweh chose *you* to fulfill His divine purpose because since you were a youth, you dreamed of serving Him, and you longed for the approval of your abba. That longing is a longing for your Heavenly Father. In Him alone you will find the purpose, fulfillment, and satisfaction you have dreamed of finding."

For a moment, Paul held his breath, awestruck as wonder, mystery, and majesty pressed him to his knees. But the voice—it brought back the memory of the speaker he had heard on the Damascus road—the voice from heaven. How could he be partnered in such divine mystery? It was beyond comprehension.

Yehoshua, continued speaking. "The message of Jesus will be given to Jews first, then to the Gentiles. You will be given power and authority to perform signs and authenticate the gospel message. Many people, particularly the Jews of old, will reject the truth of God's New Covenant—His new binding relationship to His people—but God's chosen will believe."

"But will Jews accept this new revelation?" Paul asked. "We have been taught Jewish law and tradition for hundreds of years. How could we ever reject the Tanakh?"

Paul was bewildered. "I have spent my life defending the Law and demanded rigid adherence to it. I have mastered all levels of education possible for a Jew to learn how to be true to the Law."

Yehoshua tossed a few crumbs of bread to a small bird. "Yes Paul, your training prepared you for a lifetime ministry—although you practiced it in a misguided way. You were prepared in many ways." Yehoshua smiled.

"And while the revelation will be new, it will not nullify the Tanakh. It fulfills and builds upon it. The new revelation *illuminates* the teaching of Tanakh. The New Covenant, as are all the covenants, are *contained within* the Tanakh, and they are explained *considering* the New Covenant.

"I will need many parchments to record this information," Paul observed, recognizing that the knowledge he was receiving was vital and historic.

"Yes, take notes, but when the time comes to spread this message, I will give you the words to speak and to write. For now, any notes you write will be for your personal study."

Paul turned his head and stared at Yehoshua, who had focused on the view of the valley below.

"I." He'd said "I" will give you the words to speak and write. Paul felt his heart quicken. Who is this man—a prophet, Elijah, an angel? Paul felt a stirring of wariness.

"The transition from the old way of Judaism to *The Way* will not take place overnight,"

Yehoshua continued. "Jews have worshipped in the Temple for over fifteen-hundred years. We have rested in the faith of Abraham, Isaac, and Jacob for two-thousand years. My people will need time and evidence to trust my words and works."

Paul nodded, transfixed as the magnitude of the truth seeped into his mind, then his heart. Like his encounter on the road to Damascus, what he thought could not be true, *was true*.

Jesus was alive. He had risen from the dead and was the promised Messiah!

And He had chosen Paul as His emissary to carry His message to the world.

How could he ever absorb the magnitude of these realities? Questions raced through Paul's mind as he searched the face of the man sitting beside him.

"You are Jesus of Nazareth," Paul breathed through his tears, but Yehoshua did not respond. He looked like the radiant Jesus Paul had met in his divine encounter. He would never forget that glorious, shining face. But Yehoshua looked different—he sweated and batted away insects, and his face was dirt-streaked. His skin was sun-scorched, and his skin was etched with creases, scars, and imperfections. This man could not be the radiant Jesus the Messiah, who had apprehended him on the Damascus road—could he?

Yehoshua continued. "The Tanakh's teaching of the Law and animal sacrifice for the atonement of sins ended with Jesus' death and resurrection. When the Holy Spirit descended on believers at the Feast of Pentecost, the age of the ecclesia, the body of Christ, began."

Yehoshua turned and looked at Paul, his gaze piercing.

"God has called *you* to deliver the message and help the ecclesia transition into the new age with new revelation—that *you* will help deliver. You will communicate the transition of the Holy Word from Tanakh to the New Covenant revelation. Worship will no longer take place in the Temple but in the ecclesia, my people indwelt by the Holy Spirit, not a building or synagogue. Yahweh's divine dealings with humankind will no longer be through the Law but personal faith in Jesus the Messiah's sacrifice for sin through His death and resurrection."

"But I do not know enough about this new message." Paul stated bluntly. "I have not been taught it or lived it like the disciples. It is foreign to me."

Yehoshua smiled as he tore off another hunk of bread. "Have you thought that perhaps this is why we climbed this mountain and why I am here with you? Get out one of the parchment fragments you brought with you, and we shall begin at the beginning." He laid the bread in Paul's lap. "You will need the nourishment," he said with a smile.

Paul arranged his parchment, ink well, and styli, then signaled Yehoshua with a bite of bread.

"The Law of Moses was Yahweh's most important covenant with His people—made here on this very mountain, which is why I brought you here to explain the historic New Covenant."

Paul spoke up. "Forgive me, Yehoshua, but even a young child knows the Law of Moses has been the instruction book for conduct and worship throughout the history of Judaism. Why are you telling me this?

Paul's companion smiled graciously. "Yes, I understand you know this, Paul. But we often lose true appreciation and deeper understanding for things that are overly familiar to us.

The Law of Moses was given to provide a temporary solution to sin. The blood of an animal could never atone for the sins of a man or woman. Atonement for human sin can only be accomplished by the death of a sinless human. And atonement for the sins of all humanity would require the death of a sinless human who had lived through all generations. Do you see the dilemma?"

Paul's styli froze in mid-air, and he looked up. "So, you are saying that animals are not sufficient for sacrifice for sins?" His heart began to pound.

"Not permanent forgiveness. They were required by God on a repetitive basis but sufficient only until a permanent solution could be made."

Tears formed in Yehoshua's eyes as He gestured to the towns in the valley below.

"When Moses led the children of Israel out of Egypt, they had been slaves for four-hundred years. They lacked discipline, knowledge of Yahweh, and a way to please the Divine. They were exposed to the pagan gods of Egypt and did not personally know Yahweh, the true God. Once the Jews escaped the influence of Egyptian tyranny, Yahweh gave Moses strict laws to teach them discipline, protect them, and keep their hearts attuned to purity."

Paul tried to look into his friend's eyes but could not. He fixed his eyes on a tree in the valley. "Ah, yes. I was well-schooled in those laws. They'd almost kept me from the Truth.

"Paul," Yehoshua continued, "The Law gave the people a way to access Yahweh through obedience to laws and animal sacrifice to atone for their sins. The civil, moral, and ethical laws regulating diet, worship, and feasts were designated to celebrate Yahweh's goodness. From the beginning, these laws were intended to be temporary—until the Messiah came. Now the Messiah has come."

"Good, good," Yehoshua encouraged. "God's divine grace places Gentiles on equal footing with God's chosen people—the Jews. That will be your first mission—show Jews this new divine reckoning of God's grace. Your task will be difficult, to be sure."

"I know what you say is true, but it will be difficult for us to change—especially to accept Gentiles. Jews honor Abba Abraham and have great pride as a people." Paul could foresee horror, anger, and lashing out at the message Yehoshua described.

Yet, as the wind gently stirred his hair, Paul was reassured by the words he was hearing.

I have been chosen, Paul pondered, *as Yeshua's servant. How could I ever want anything else?*

The day passed with Paul asking questions, writing notes and, Yehoshua explaining God's plan for His world. At times Paul felt like falling to his face as his mind worked to grasp spiritual concepts too high for him to attain. But it quickly became apparent to Paul that many Jews would accept the new message, while others would be outraged and reject it. No matter the level of corruption in Temple leadership, some Jews would simply hold fast to tradition.

Paul's challenge to understand the message of the gospel took on new meaning. *I finally see the answer to my childhood question. Jesus, God's Son, provided the human—yet unblemished—sacrifice needed for sin. The solution is profound! Jesus lived a sinless life and was both fully divine and fully human. The Law pointed to Jesus and the final solution to sin.*

Yehoshua took a long drink, and Paul looked up from his writing. "The things you are telling me will shake the foundation of Judaism. Too many have enshrined Judaism over Yahweh. I was one of them."

Yehoshua's face sobered. "Paul, your task will be far from easy. You will face hardships and trials. But you will also be given the authority to perform miracles to authenticate the Kingdom of God."

"Do you mean that Jesus' miracles were not just to answer prayer or relieve suffering but to demonstrate His authority and authenticate His message and authority as Son of God?"

"Yes. People who followed Him for more than the miracles heard it." Yehoshua's supportive tone felt like fresh rain on the parched soil of Paul's heart.

The evening's low clouds and fog began to engulf the mountain as the sun dropped, dimming the light. It was time to return to the Bedouin camp for a late evening meal and a good night's sleep.

As Paul and Yehoshua neared the bottom of their trail back to camp, Yehoshua lagged, and Paul was left with his thoughts.

My task is going to be difficult. After everything I did to stamp out The Way, I will be a hunted man the minute my colleagues in Jerusalem hear of my conversion. But God has brought me to this place, and I will go where He sends me and place myself in His hands.

As he approached the encampment, Paul quickened his steps at the smell of burning wood and the aroma of fresh bread and basted mutton on a spit. The Bedouins were waiting for their guest with a hearty meal. But somewhere along the final descent, Yehoshua had wordlessly departed.

CHAPTER 23

COVENANTS

Paul ran his hand across his brow and wiped away the sweat rolling toward his eyes. Tension knotted his neck as he strained against the glare of the morning sun to see down the road.

Yehoshua should be here by now. It's late into the fifth watch, and I have gone to every Bedouin tent asking about him. Why has no one seen him?

Frustrated, Paul turned and walked back to the shaded spot where he'd made his bed beneath the awning of a benevolent tribesman's tent. He pulled out a parchment fragment and recorded more of the message he'd received from Yehoshua the previous day. Time crept by. Finally, in desperation, Paul stomped off and climbed halfway up the mountain to see if he could spot his mentor. Perhaps he'd misunderstood when Yehoshua had told him they would meet on Mt. Horeb.

But his climb proved to be futile. For the remainder of the day, Paul sat beneath a sycamore tree close to the road where he could easily be spotted. He went to bed that night confused and disappointed.

The next day was no different. And the next. And the next. Paul watched and waited for Yehoshua to no avail. Each day his confusion and frustration rose. Had he done something wrong? Had he failed some test? How long was he supposed to wait—without food and dependent upon the kindness of the Bedouins?

After three days of confusion and frustration, Paul awoke to the rumbling of a small caravan of camels, carts, and wagons approaching the Sinai village and Bedouin camp from the south. He jumped to his feet.

"Who are these men?" Paul called out to a Bedouin sentinel as he quickly slipped his mantle over his shoulders and rolled up his goat skin bed.

The Bedouin deftly unwrapped the turban that snugly encircled his head and mouth.

"A caravan of merchants from Alexandria," he stated matter-of-factly. "They travel this route regularly selling papyrus panels for books, official documents, and records such as land deeds and animal bills of sale. But they also sell other supplies: grain, gold, linen, and finished goods such as glass goblets, jewelry, and stoneware. Their goods are in high demand." He raised his eyebrows and tipped his head with his final comment.

Paul thanked him and rifled through his bed roll, searching to find the few hidden coins still in his possession. With one of the coins firmly in hand, he quickly laced up his sandals and set off toward the line of wagons and merchants who were setting out their wares. Purchasing more papyrus seemed foolish, on the one hand. He had no assurance that Yehoshua would return, and he would then need them. It would be far more practical to buy food or a knife for protection when he returned to Jerusalem. What was the wisest decision?

"How much for a few panels of papyrus?" Paul asked as he approached the closest cart, hoping the cost would be reasonable. A man in a pale blue turban and embroidered vest reached behind into his cart and pulled out several qualities of papyrus leaves. Paul had always prided himself on his bartering skills, and after several minutes, he walked back toward his spot beneath the awning, smiling. He had purchased three panels at a bargain price to record more discussions with Yehoshua.

The camp was bustling with its morning routine. Fires blazed as women in gemstone- colored clothing busied themselves baking fresh bread and grinding grain. The wife of the Bedouin chief handed Paul a piece of warm bread and porridge, and he bolted them down, then walked back to his sleeping area. By the time he got there, the food was gone. He quickly cleaned up, packed Sere with the little food he had, then started up the mountain. He refused to sit idly, so he would study his parchments, meditate, pray, and wait for his mentor.

Yehoshua always knows where to find me ... oddly enough. It's ridiculous for me to go looking for him, since he could be ... anywhere.

The ascent seemed more difficult this time. Paul's sandals repeatedly slid backwards over the jagged rocks, and he was forced to re-trace his tracks. After nearly an hour, he spotted a large boulder jutting out over a depression in the side of the mountain, forming a shallow cave.

Thank You, Yahweh. A place where Sere can rest and I can spend time with You. He urged Sere into the shadow of the outcropping, watered her from his sparse supply, then sat down to meditate and pray where he would be out of the punishing heat of the sun.

"*Kalimera*, Paul."

The voice he'd come to love came from beyond the small cave, but the intense sun blinded his weak eyes when he turned his head.

Raising a hand to shade his face and blinking to clear the glare, Paul recognized the outline of his *zaqen* friend Yehoshua standing against a backdrop of blinding sunlight. Yehoshua's white garment shimmered, and an ethereal glow around his head obscured his features.

Paul squinted, and Yehoshua's features became clear.

It cannot be possible ... can it? He searched for features of the face he had seen through the bright light on the Damascus road—Jesus of Nazareth?

Paul's thoughts froze. He held his breath in reverence, as if the expulsion of air from his mortal body would violate the Holy One.

"*Kalimera*, my Master," Paul whispered, his throat tight with awe, bewilderment, and humility.

"We have much to discuss, Paul. But I prefer we talk at our spot further up the mountain." The voice resonated with comfort, authority, and a luminous quality Paul could not identify.

His hand shook as he reached for Sere's bridle and followed Yehoshua's footsteps further up Mt. Horeb.

The remainder of the climb passed quickly. Paul's thoughts dissipated like smoke into the night sky. He chided himself for his confusion as he and his Mentor settled again on the rock escarpment and Yehoshua produced a loaf of bread, dried fish, and water purified with wine.

"I hope you spent the past few days wisely, Paul. You needed time to absorb our discussions. They will be the basis for your life's work."

In his side vision Paul noted his Teacher's subtle smile, as if He was enjoying a humorous thought.

"Wisely ... yes, of course." Paul tore off a hunk of bread.

He knows I was anxious and impatient.

Yehoshua quickly summarized his previous lesson. "So, you see, Paul, Yahweh's program has always included Gentiles. The New Covenant does not require Gentiles to become Jews and offer sacrifices in the Temple. Both Jews and Gentiles will worship based on faith in Jesus' death, burial, and resurrection. The Law was put in place to bring knowledge of sin to people who had no understanding of Yahweh's holiness and the purity that holiness demands."

Paul was filling papyrus' sheets as fast as he could for later study. But the new message shattered his understanding of everything Judaism had ever taught him. He suddenly felt dizzy and looked up from his notes as if a torch had illuminated his mind.

"I ... I have overlooked this understanding of the prophets' words," Paul stammered. "But they don't mention a *new* message about the Messiah's sacrifice or *new* teaching for living holy lives or abandoning the commandments and laws of Moses. Are the commandments and the Law then rendered defective? For centuries we have centered our lives, culture, and history around the sacred Law of Moses. Our obedience to the Law of Moses demonstrates our desire to please Him. How does faith in Jesus, without obedience to the Law, works of charity, and duties, allow us to show our devotion and spirituality?"

Yehoshua clapped his hands and laughed. "Paul, your questions reveal the central issue. Let Me explain."

He adjusted His position on the blanket He'd spread for their comfort.

But I still have so many questions ... Pain shot through Paul's eyes, and he bowed his head to rub them.

"Yahweh was not finished with His promises in the Tanakh, Paul. The Prophet Jeremiah wrote, 'The day is coming,' says the LORD, 'when I will make a new covenant with the people of Israel and Judah.' The covenant is made with Israel and looks to the future for its fulfillment. It is not being fulfilled in the ecclesia, but the blood of the New Covenant is the atoning blood of Jesus. It is a promise to Yahweh's chosen people that everyone, from the least to the greatest, will know Yahweh, He will forgive their wickedness, and He will never again remember their sins."

The pain pulsed in Paul's eyes again. He reached for his discarded mantle and pulled it over his head to create a shield from the sun.

He must know I'm in pain, that my eyes are weak. I can't remain in the sunlight much longer.

Yehoshua stood and walked a short distance, then returned carrying a large juniper branch. He stood behind Paul and held it above his head to provide shade. "We will not be much longer, Paul. Just one final matter today."

He knew. In the very instant I thought it, He knew. Paul struggled to refocus on the lesson.

"On the evening of Jesus' arrest, He came together with His disciples, and after their supper Jesus took a chalice of wine and said, 'This cup is the new covenant in my blood which is shed for you as a sacrifice.' Then He invited them to drink the cup and eat the bread as a representation of His body and blood asking them to do it as often as they met together until He returned."

Until He returned? Paul's head snapped toward Yehoshua.

"What do you mean, 'until He returns? Are you saying Jesus is coming back again? I have read texts in the Tanakh that imply the Messiah will return. Will He return after I have preached to all the Jews and Gentiles? Could His coming cut short my mission? What is His purpose in coming back if His work on earth is finished?" Paul's head was spinning with this new possibility.

Yehoshua laid down the branch and placed His hands on Paul's shoulders. "God's redemptive work is done, but Jesus will return to establish His kingdom, which the leaders of Israel have rejected. When He was asked about His return, the answer was clear. 'No one knows the day nor the hour of the return of the Son of Man.'"

Paul looked up at Yehoshua, trying to sear the moment into his memory. His heart told him that his mentoring time was ending, and it would soon be time for him to teach and apply these intense lessons. With a sorrow-filled heart, Paul collected his notes.

Yehoshua disappeared while Paul was packing to return. Stumbling in the dimming light of evening, Paul made his way down the path toward the Bedouin camp, a hot meal, and the closest thing he had to a home.

Days and nights passed as Paul soaked up Yehoshua's instruction like a dry stream bed in a spring rain. He filled his parchments and bartered for more with the Bedouins. Nights brought visions and dreams.

Until the morning that Yehoshua did not appear ... and the days following.

On the fifth day Paul rose early, and with his faithful Sere, climbed Mt. Horeb with a water skin and his goatskin sleeping mat. For days he sheltered in the cave on the mountain and studied his parchments, returning to the Bedouin camp to repair tents to purchase food and supplies.

But always, whether day or night, awaiting instructions from his beloved Master.

CHAPTER 24

OLIVE TREE

The robbery had forced Paul to remain at the Bedouin camp and return to his craft as a tentmaker until he received instructions from his Master to return to Jerusalem. The little money he had brought with him had been spent on parchments and food, and his barter items had been stolen long ago. He hoped that seven or ten days of work would provide the money and supplies he needed to travel again, as well as time for Yehoshua to return.

But ten days passed without a whisper from Paul's Master, so he set to work.

Since he had no skins to work with, Paul decided to repair tents to earn the funds he would need to journey back to Jerusalem. He rose early and rounded the camp, bartering his skills for needed supplies. Leaders and members of the tribe had come to know and trust him and had seen his willingness to work. Although most Bedouin men could repair their own tents, they agreed to hire Paul to mend those of elderly tribe members and widows.

He gratefully settled into a new routine, rising early to his work and look for Yehoshua, and returning to his shaded sleeping mat to study in the heat of the afternoon. On the third day of his efforts, a boy from the camp spotted a cloud of dust on the horizon. A Bedouin sentinel set out to investigate and soon returned at a gallop. A camel train from Egypt was approaching with much-needed supplies.

Word spread through the camp like wildfire. As the dust cloud drew closer, everyone scurried to find their finest goatskins, woven blankets, and crafts to trade. The thrill of bartering—feigning anger at an asking price or selling price—excited the Bedouins, as did the promise of fresh food, spices, skins, and textiles.

Paul joined in the raucous scene. He ambled through the wagons looking for quality hides, rope, and dried fish from the Nile to purchase with his few coins. Merchants were anxious to sell their goods to enthusiastic shoppers, but Bedouin women were hard bargainers and made it difficult for the merchants to make their usual profit.

The hour passed, and the shopping ended. Paul purchased only an extra goatskin to replace the one that had been stolen from him. It was an expensive but necessary item. The caravan soon packed up and continued their journey toward Petra and beyond. The Bedouins spent the evening feasting, dancing, and making merry. Paul retired to his old goatskin mat beneath the awning and waited for the dawn of a new day.

The need for Paul's tentmaking skills grew. He often worked deep into the night to accommodate the needs of both the Bedouin camp and village dwellers. His quality workmanship created a bond of trust that gave Paul opportunities to tell the people he worked for about Jesus. Slowly, the gospel message spread throughout the region.

A few *nundinae* (market days) into his work, Paul began repairing a ragged and worn tent for his Bedouin friend Jamal, his wives Fatima, Rima, Yara, and their twelve children. They were a poor family, like most of the tribe. Paul prayed about how to balance asking for needed payment from Jamal with his desire to help a friend who had little money.

The next morning, Paul awakened to find Jamal's wife Fatima at his tent carrying a gift of exquisite baked bread and homemade stew of beans, barley, millet, lentils, and emmer. She returned every other day with a fresh meal and a smile, thanking Paul for his kindness to their family.

Once again Paul's faith strengthened as he saw God provide for His needs in response to his ardent prayers. But Fatima gifted Paul with much more than food. When he was not mending tents, he now had more time to study and earn needed money.

And return to the mountain top to wait for Yehoshua.

❧

In the month of Tishrei, a caravan arrived from Jericho with a supply of dried fruits, medicinal oils, Ahava from the Dead Sea, cooking oil, and fashionable bolts of linen cloth.

Paul had little interest in spending the few coins he had buried in the dirt beside his sleeping mat. He was more interested in news of regional politics and events.

As Paul strolled from wagon to wagon listening for bits of news, he spotted a striking woman with a compelling presence. She sold medicinal herbs, poultice powders, tea preparations, and ointments from a small table. Fascinated, he stopped at the back of the crowd that had gathered to examine her products and inquire about their healing capabilities.

The woman was responding to a question from a Bedouin mother about a poultice for her child's cough when a mocking male voice called out from the back of the crowd.

"You think you have superior healing powers because you're from Egypt! You believe Bedouins are ignorant and need your medicines because ours are not good enough. "

The crowd laughed, and Paul watched as the woman straightened her back and looked in the direction of the voice. "I do not claim to have superior healing powers," she spoke boldly. "My name is

Adriana, and I am the daughter of a medicus. My father trained me in his skills, and I am traveling to Egypt, where an outbreak of the pox has overwhelmed the people."

Her chin lifted. "The medicines that I sell at a modest cost are made from herbs and plants created by Adonai to have healing properties. I offer them to all people as I offer my life, in His name."

The crowd went silent, then slowly dispersed, as if confused by Adriana's response. Several Bedouin women remained behind to make purchases. When the last one left, Paul stepped forward tentatively. He knew a respectable woman would not feel comfortable being approached by an unknown man in public. Paul glanced around. They were within eyesight of dozens of other people at a place of business. Maintaining a respectable distance, he took a deep breath and assumed what he hoped was his most humble demeanor.

"You ... you are a follower of *The Way* ... Adriana?"

"Why, yes I am. How did you know?"

"My name is Paul, and I am also a follower of *The Way*." He looked at the ground, trying not to stare at her beauty. His work in and around the Temple had seldom put him in proximity to women.

Did I see a smile cross her lips? Paul caught himself the moment the thought flitted through his mind. *Pure idiocy to note such a thing.* He had seldom allowed himself to be in the company of women, although priests were allowed to marry. He had put away the idea of coming under the canopy long ago.

"I am Adriana, daughter of Lukas of Antioch." She spoke softly, without the boldness she had shown moments before, her eyes appropriately averted from a direct gaze.

"I do not mean to invade your privacy," he said, "but I heard you were coming from Jerusalem and assumed you are a follower of *The Way* from your conversations."

Adriana turned, her eyes meeting Paul's. "Yes," she responded quickly. Her shy manner had given way to the eagerness of a child. "I am traveling to join a small team of medicos in Egypt where there is an outbreak of the pox. People are sick and need medicine. The disease has already spread to Damascus."

Adriana handed a jar of herbs to a Bedouin woman who had been waiting, took her coin, and nodded thanks. She then addressed Paul directly.

"You call yourselves followers of *The Way*, but we call ourselves 'Christians' in Antioch because we follow our Lord Jesus Christ."

Paul jolted to attention. "Please, tell me about your 'Christian' friends in Antioch. Although I have been delayed here on a journey, I am trying to learn all I can about *The Way*."

Adriana shook her head sadly, and her chestnut eyes moistened. "Believers are receiving a backlash of Jewish and Roman anger across the empire. Christians are being imprisoned and even stoned to death."

Stoning. Stephen. His heart clenched.

"The Romans are hearing false rumors from Jewish leaders that Christ followers are raising armies to overthrow Roman rule," Adriana said in a whisper. "They use these rumors as an excuse to crucify Christ followers who are punished alongside rebel Jews who are actively trying to overthrow Roman tyranny. Most Christian believers are fleeing Jerusalem, attempting to elude a zealous Pharisee called 'Saul of Tarsus.'" Adriana dropped her head, as if the words had exhausted her.

Paul felt sick. He had not been in Jerusalem in months, but he was still being blamed for persecuting Jesus' followers. His evil actions had produced consequences that were rippling into the world far beyond his imagination.

For a moment Paul felt as if his knees might give way and he might collapse into the dirt where he belonged. That God would offer him such mercy and love felt more than his heart could bear. The thought never ceased to overwhelm him.

How could he face this woman and not tell her the truth about himself? To pretend that he was not the Saul to whom she referred was to lie.

Paul blurted out the words before reason could tell him to stop. "Please don't be frightened, Adriana. I am also a Christian. Please trust me."

Paul's hands were clasped in front of him as he implored. "My name is Paul, and I am ashamed to tell you that I was at one time the Saul of Tarsus of whom you speak."

Adriana's eyes grew wide with fear, and she grasped her upper arms as if trying to protect herself. She tried to step backwards, but her wagon blocked her.

"No! No!" She gasped as she looked for somewhere to run.

"You are safe, you are safe, Adriana! I mean you no harm, I am no longer that man!"

Paul could see the terror on her face. In an instant she could bolt, and he would never be able to speak to her again.

"As a follower of Jesus, I face the same threats from Rome that you fear—although far worse because now I am committed to Christ. I have been living among the Bedouins, who see my devotion to Jesus every day. They can tell you He is all I live for."

The fear drained from Adriana's face. At Paul's suggestion, she climbed into her wagon, where she could feel safer. He sat on the ground within speaking distance and quietly told her the story of his conversion on the road to Damascus and his baptism by Ananias in the River Abana. As he talked about Jesus, a smile slowly returned to Adriana's face. As they sat and conversed, Paul became uncomfortably aware that this was the first conversation he'd ever had alone with a woman, other than his Ima, relatives, and Sonja, their servant. Talking to Adriana felt like fresh honey to his soul.

Several of Adriana's fellow medicos, who were also believers, passed by and joined the conversation. Paul was instantly excited for the opportunity to learn about *The Way* from this group.

"How did all of you come to believe in Jesus? Did any of you see Him minister? Did you witness miracles?"

An older man spoke up. "I am Julian of Capernaum. I heard Him preach. I'm a trader in medicines and oils and joined a caravan at Jericho. I traveled from Galilee to Egypt selling and trading my goods and saw many of Jesus' miracles and heard other believers talk about His works and wonders."

Julian continued with details about Jesus—a sermon He delivered on a small mountain outside Capernaum, His miracle walking on the Sea of Tiberias, His lessons in the Capernaum synagogue, feeding a crowd of thousands, and healing lepers, the lame, and the sick.

Paul drank in every word, as he remembered listening to Jesus' voice and looking upon His face.

Paul left his new friends that evening, his enthusiasm for taking the gospel to the Gentiles fanned into a raging blaze. His work would be dangerous, but he was ready to give his life, his future, his everything to His newfound Savior.

❧

Paul sat at a borrowed workbench in the tent of a Bedouin companion. He steadied his arms as he strained to punch holes in a worn goatskin tent-covering to make room for a fresh patch. Great skill was required to sew in a new patch without ripping the existing holes in an aged skin. The morning had passed peacefully as Paul conversed with Abdu and Abdu's son Fahed about matters of faith. Their conversations had become a beloved part of Paul's daily routine.

In the early afternoon, Paul returned home to the used tent he had been given by the Bedouins and feasted on a spicy partridge stew prepared by Fatima. As he was wiping the last bits from the bowl with a chunk of barley bread, a shadow darkened the doorway of his tent. He looked up to see the familiar tall figure of Yehoshua in his white robe and scarlet girdle. Paul leaped to his feet, and his heart warmed at the sight of his mentor.

"It is time."

The days had dragged without Yehoshua. Paul could not wait to climb the mountain again and sit with his friend. He placed his bowl in a large hand-hewn pot of water and grabbed the goatskin bag of supplies he kept waiting by the tent opening. Struggling to keep his questions to himself, Paul followed Yehoshua to a quiet spot about a mille up the Holy Mount, where Yehoshua prepared a place for them to sit beneath a few straggling olive trees. Before he could spread the goatskins, Paul burst out with a question that had been troubling him for days.

"You told me I will tell Jews that the new revelation places Gentiles on equal footing with them. I don't understand how this can be. From the time of Moses, *your* chosen people rebelled against Yahweh. Are they no longer God's chosen people? Do they have a future?"

Yehoshua touched the tips of his fingers together. "You show great insight." He gestured for Paul to sit beside him.

"Israel's choice as God's people did not result in their salvation under the requirements of the Law.

Yehoshua picked up a stone and tossed it into the air, then caught it. "Has Yahweh rejected Israel as a nation and replaced them with Gentiles? In other words, has Yahweh's word failed?"

He tossed the rock again and caught it, his fingers curling around the stone until it disappeared in his hand.

"No, Yahweh's word has not failed," Yehoshua stated. The Law served its purpose. Israel failed because the people tried to use the Law to demonstrate their righteousness. Israel sought salvation by doing good deeds. Sacrifices under the Law required faith that they were a *temporary remedy* for sin until the permanent solution came with the sacrifice of the Messiah, Jesus. Righteousness comes by trusting in the substitutionary death of the Messiah, who is the *completion* of the Law.

Paul rubbed his aching head as if it would help his brain absorb this new way of thinking. But could he possibly absorb what any good Pharisee would deem heresy? The concept of Jesus as the fulfillment of the Law sounded like divine mathematics beyond his comprehension.

After clearing his throat, Paul urged Yehoshua to continue.

Yehoshua pointed to the tree above them. "Metaphorically, the people of Israel are compared to a cultivated olive tree. Because of unbelief, some, but not all, of the tree's branches were broken off, and a wild olive branch was grafted in."

Paul followed Yehoshua's gaze to the base of the tree.

"The root is Abraham and Yahweh's promise to bless all the nations of the world through Abraham. Yahweh will graft Israel back into the olive tree. Though Israel was set aside for a time, the Lord will accomplish His purposes among the nations, and then He will save Israel. Some of the olive branches have been broken off, and a wild olive shoot has been grafted in among the others and now shares the nourishing sap from the olive root. But we cannot consider grafted branches, the Gentiles, superior to original branches, Israel."

It will take time for me to absorb this profound new teaching. Paul paused in his writing as Yehoshua moved on to a more easily grasped subject, as if he knew Paul would need personal time to think about the analogy he had just heard presented.

Time passed almost unnoticed as Yehoshua taught and Paul wrote, questioned, and absorbed.

Early darkness crept in, and the small grotto glowed golden in the moonlight.

In the dusky pall, Paul glanced up from his notes to discover that Yehoshua had once again disappeared without explanation.

Paul gathered his few possessions and began his trek back down the mountain alone, faltering and occasionally losing his footing—but pressing on through the darkness.

CHAPTER 25

THE DESERT

Days passed, and desert mornings blurred into sameness. Paul slipped into a comfortable routine: rising early, praying, climbing Mt. Horeb, and absorbing Yehoshua's teaching about how Jesus' life and death offered the world a way to find peace with God.

Each day as he climbed the familiar rocky path, Paul rehearsed his questions for the day's lesson.   One morning he reached the small grotto and paused in the darkness, his legs throbbing as he allowed his aching eyes to adjust to the dimmer light.

"*Kalimera,* Paul." Yehoshua was seated on the crimson and yellow pillow that Paul had brought for his beloved teacher's comfort. It had been gifted to him by the Bedouin chief.

Exhaustion was replaced by anticipation as Paul slipped his satchel to the ground and sat on the blanket Yehoshua had spread for him. "*Kalimera,* Yehoshua. May I begin right away? I am still confused about something. Can we ever sin so much or so severely that Jesus' salvation is taken from us?"

Paul pulled his eyes away from Yehoshua's face and to the floor. *The man does not read minds, Paul. Don't be a fool. He cannot possibly know that you tossed and turned last night because your thoughts kept drifting to Cassia's dying face.*

Yehoshua pointed to an array of food spread on the blankets between them. "I've brought grapes, almonds, pears, dried lamb, fresh bread, oil, and water purified with wine. Everything you need, I have provided, Paul." Yehoshua leaned forward.

"The same is true of salvation," he continued. "A person's salvation does not depend upon how good or bad they determine their actions to be. No person can live up to God's standard, no matter how hard they try. That's why it is so important for you and your students to understand that Jesus' death atones for *all* sin for *all* time. No one must ever again try to work to be good enough. Salvation is *only* determined by faith in Jesus, and since it depends on His finished work on the cross, human effort can never undo it."

Paul pulled out a parchment and shook his head as he prepared to write. "This teaching will certainly create controversy, if not direct opposition. As Jews, we cling to the thought that our rituals and ceremonies help atone for our sins. Circumcision, for instance, always set us apart from Gentiles. It justified our reason to feel superior."

Yehoshua handed Paul the writing skin. "Yes, my friend, you are right. This is one reason why Jesus came into the world to level the ground between Jew and Gentile. Paul, a self-righteous Jew is as guilty as a Gentile in their unbelief. Jews do the very things they condemn others of doing. They will be judged based on their faith and actions and will *not* be vindicated based on their ancestry."

"All are guilty," Paul mused aloud. "And are counted righteous by faith."

He shook his head in confusion. "But how can the death of *one* man be for *all* men, when thousands of animal sacrifices over our history were insufficient?"

Yehoshua slowly brushed food crumbs from his beard, then explained that Adam introduced sin into the bloodline of all humanity because of the curse, and Jesus' death on the cross as an eternal and sinless God-man reversed the curse and provided eternal life for all believers of all ages.

Jesus' death changes everything I ever believed as a Jew. Everything. I was deceived and blind to the truth. Every time Yehoshua teaches me,

His words reveal more of my self-deception, sin, and how the choices of my past condemn me. Yet I see love in His eyes.

For the next hour the visionary explained the Tanakh's story of redemption.

Paul sat silent. Scenes of Saul, the terrorizing Pharisee, flashed through his mind. Screams of mothers torn from their children, fathers whipped to death, houses set fire, shrieks of delight from spectators as wild animals tore human flesh from bone.

Tears coursed from Paul's eyes and dripped from his beard into his trembling hands. His words came out in sobs. "My ... my Lord. I ... am so unworthy; I am the greatest of all sinners."

Yehoshua slid closer to Paul's side, and placed his hands upon Paul's shoulders.

"My dear friend." He spoke softly. "When God looks at you, He sees only Jesus' perfection. Your past is gone, and your sins have been cast as far as the East is from the West. Guilt and shame have been cast into hell." Yehoshua stooped and looked into Paul's face. "You are free, my son. The price has been paid."

Paul felt a gentle squeeze.

"You are perfect in Your Father's sight. Jesus' righteousness is yours."

Fear flashed through Paul's body. His mind told him to run, to escape. But he forced himself to keep his eyes fixed on Yehoshua's face.

Love radiated from his friend's eyes, and for a moment, Paul felt as if he wanted to throw himself into Yehoshua's arms and feel the hug he so missed from Ima and the approval he had never felt from Abba. Fear melted, and the hope of Yahweh's love and sacrifice through Jesus swept Paul away in waves of love and gratitude. He took a deep breath, savoring the peace that flooded his heart like water from a freshly dug well.

For the next moments, Saul was lost in praise as the Spirit of God lifted him into Jesus' sweet presence.

༉

Paul moaned as he gripped his head in the darkness. Through slitted eyes, he glanced around the inside of the tent. The measure of light told him it was the third watch. His body told him he was ill. Very ill. His head and body were blazing, and his head was throbbing, as though someone were pounding on the inside. Sharp pains stabbed his abdomen and stomach, sending him into retching cramps.

On his last trip up the mountain, Paul had remained with Yehoshua for several weeks. While he was away, disease had engulfed the Sinai village and the Bedouin camp, most likely carried by people in the caravan from Egypt, who had been unaware of disease or symptoms among their people.

The sick in the Bedouin camp developed skin rashes—flat, red spots that changed into raised bumps, then fluid-filled blisters that eventually became ugly scabs.

Because no one could identify the illness or where it had come from, widespread panic rocked the kingdom of Nabataea. From kings to farmers to gleaners, everyone was blaming a king, a kingdom, a tribe, or anyone for their woes.

By the second week, Paul was showing severe signs of the disease. Red spots and pus-filled boils covered his body and face. His fever rose so quickly that Yara, one of Jamal's wives, called the local *aman* to nurse Paul. Yara had purchased calamine lotion and chamomile flower buds from the caravan from Jericho. She had the *aman* apply the lotion to ease Paul's itching and chamomile flower compresses to soothe the burning and, hopefully, make him more comfortable.

218

For several days, Paul's pain was so agonizing that he rose from his sleeping mat only to relieve himself, refill his water skin, and swallow a few bites of bread or figs. His aman had become sick with the disease and immediately left for his home in the Sinai village. The Bedouins and Paul were left to care for themselves.

Late one afternoon Paul rested on his mat, trying not to disturb the painful blisters that encased his flesh, praying for God to send someone to refresh his water supply. Yara and the rest of Jamal's family had become too sick to tend to anyone. As Paul was deep in prayer, a shadow darkened his tent opening, and he heard a strange voice.

"Paul, emissary of God, my name is Abasi, and I am a medico who has been sent to you by Adriana. Our caravan is returning to Jericho and has camped outside the Sinai village. Adriana feared you might be ill and sent me to help. I have recovered from the illness and am here to assist you. May I enter?"

Thank You, Yahweh, my Provider and Hope, for hearing my prayer. Praise Your name! Your eyes are always on me, and I am never alone.

Paul responded with a moan. His lips were so scabbed with blisters that trying to speak was agonizing. The blisters continually cracked and oozed and cracked again. Even his eyelids were covered by the virulent pox.

Abasi entered and quickly examined Paul, being careful not to touch his painful sores.

"I see that your scabs have not fallen away," Abasi observed, compassion in his voice. Paul's eyelids were so heavily crusted that he did not attempt to open his eyes to look at the medico.

"It is good news, Paul. You are over the worst of the illness and will soon recover."

Abasi's words proved to be right. A few days later, Paul began to gain strength and eventually returned to his regular climbs to Mt.

Horeb. However, the illness left pitted scars on his face and body, as well as dulled vision.

℘

At the outset of his wilderness pilgrimage, Paul had anticipated he would spend a few days or weeks with Yehoshua to receive instruction from the Messiah. He was shocked when he realized that his time on Mt. Horeb had lasted nearly three years.

Yehoshua had taught him about Jesus, the New Covenant, how faith in Jesus influenced daily life, and how forgiveness through faith in Jesus impacted historical Judaism and humanity's relationship with God. During this time, Paul's tentmaking skills provided for his needs. His friendships with the Bedouins and local villagers provided him with rich resources for cultural application and pragmatic examples regarding spiritual issues. Looking back, Paul saw how God had planned this time for him as a period of rich growth both spiritually and personally.

The day came when Paul ascended the mountain for the last time with Yehoshua. His mentor and friend led him to the escarpment where they had spoken their first day. The wind rustled gently as Yehoshua turned to speak to Paul.

"The time has come for you to go to My people, Paul. I appoint you to be an apostle before you were born, and I hid you in the shadow of my hand to be a herald and a teacher to the Gentiles. Whether or not you will see Me, I will be with you always."

Paul inhaled deeply. He could feel his heart pounding. Who is Yehoshua?

"To My people ... whom I appointed ... I will be with you always."
My heart has long suspected, but to talk with and sit beside my Messiah as if He were my friend is a gift beyond comprehension.

He dropped to his knees. "My Master and Messiah," Paul sobbed.

"I am who I am." The voice spoke with bold authority that echoed into the valley below as Paul worshipped at Jesus' feet.

CHAPTER 26

JERUSALEM BOUND

Three years passed as Paul learned from Jesus and lived among the Bedouin and Sinai village communities. He made many close friends, served the people with his skills, and taught basic reading and writing to those interested in learning. His heart was torn the day he announced he would be departing. If a few years before someone had told Saul of Tarsus that he would someday love and live beside Gentiles and pagans, he would have sneered in derision.

But for the grace of God ... the grace of God.

The words rang in his ears as members of both communities gathered to express their thanks and devotion to him the morning he joined a caravan bound for Damascus. As the crowd of friends receded in the distance, Paul forced himself to tear his eyes away, turn around, and focus on the road ahead.

While his time with his Lord had infused him with life and hope, his life—like the lives of other Jesus followers—was constantly in danger. Word of his activities had surely drifted back to the city with one of the hundreds of caravanners who had heard Paul's conversion story and about the mysterious man named Yehoshua who spent time with him on Mt. Horeb.

Temple authorities would be watching for Paul's return, and skeptical believers who knew about his enthusiastic persecution of *The Way* in Jerusalem would be waiting to prove that his conversion was genuine. He would be caught between two worlds without friends and would be the object of everyone's distrust or hatred.

Paul spent the trip praying and pondering how to wisely re-enter the Damascus community. The most obvious answer seemed to be to seek out Ananias for wisdom and refuge.

Paul was delighted when Ananias discovered him standing at his door. Ananias not only embraced Paul with delight but extended a warm invitation for Paul to stay with him if he remained in the area.

The first three weeks in the city were difficult. Believers regarded him with skepticism and refused to listen to him until the disciples first authorized his message. After all, the disciples had been chosen by Jesus and were with Him throughout His ministry. Members of *The Way* in Damascus were concerned that no one could validate that Paul had been taught by Jesus, as he claimed. Even his demonstrations of Spirit-empowered miracles did not remove their skepticism.

Unsurprisingly, local priests were enraged to discover that Paul—the person they'd known as Saul—had returned and was purportedly preaching the same message taught by *The Way*. They sent word to Roman officials that Saul of Tarsus had returned, was publicly violating their beliefs, and had been rumored to have brought the pox plague to their city. To make matters even worse, the priests also accused members of *The Way* of spreading disease in their meetings. The "death plague," as the pox was called, had decimated many populations within the Roman Empire and was now, they said, threatening King Aretas's Nabatean kingdom.

Jewish priests refused to admit—especially to the Romans—that they hated Paul because he was converting Jews to what they considered a new "cult." Paul had heard reports from many people that the moment Jewish leaders had heard of his defection years before, leading priests had dedicated themselves to executing "this most dangerous man" who had once been their greatest ally.

Mounting pressure from Jews and local Syrians forced King Aretas to issue an order to arrest Paul. Knowing Paul's home was in Jerusalem, and he would likely be heading there, the king placed soldiers at every city gate in Damascus and added sentries to patrol his city walls.

Convinced by Jewish leaders of Paul's guilt, King Aretas pledged that this liar, deceiver, and man of dual identities would not escape his grasp and flee to Jerusalem.

℘

Paul paced the small room Ananias had offered him for hospitality and safe harbor. He rubbed his forehead to ease the ever-present pain in his head.

My Heavenly Av, I am so grateful for my brother's love for me. But every moment I remain here I put Ananias and the community of The Way in danger. Please help me find a way of escape from the city for their protection, and so I can fulfill Your mission for me.

Only one option remained. Paul quickly found Ananias in the gathering room to present the idea to him.

"My brother Ananias, I must ask you to call a meeting with the members of *The Way*. I want to speak to them about a plan of escape from the city. My presence has become a threat to all of you and your families, and the time has come for me to leave the city."

In the brief time Paul had been in Damascus, Paul had tried to show believers the reality of his faith. Although the Jews resolved to murder him, he remained committed to carrying Jesus' message to the world. One by one, members of the local ecclesia had come and sat at Paul's feet while he preached. Now they crowded into Ananias' home, and Paul looked on each face with affection and gratitude.

"I have come to love you all and appreciate what you have done for me in the name of the Lord. But it is now time for me to find a way of escape from Damascus for the sake of each of you and your families."

Paul heard an intake of breath.

Ananias spoke first. "Paul, we will do everything in our power with God's help to get you out of the city and on the King's highway to Jerusalem. I am asking everyone here if they have any ideas how we can do this."

Valentina, a widowed Roman-born believer spoke up. "I live on the second level where houses attach to the east wall near the East Gate—not far from here. My window allows access to the street below. The danger would be getting out the window unseen and to the ground several *pedes* below. Roman sentries patrol the wall and the outside path."

Valentina narrowed her eyes as she spoke. "If you were successful, you would need to walk or run a long distance to the Jerusalem Gate, where you can choose the King's Highway or the Via Maris to Jerusalem."

"I know the schedule of the sentries," Damen, one of the elderly believers chimed in. "I can stand outside the city wall where I often meet city officials for conversation and a goblet of wine and look for opportunities to talk about Jesus' death, burial, and resurrection. The soldiers often speak to me and won't think it odd that I am there. When the sentries have passed, I could signal you, Paul."

"If someone has a large wicker basket made of tightly woven willow rods with handles strong enough to support Paul, I think it could be done," Valentina interjected.

A man's voice called out at the back of the crowd near the door. "I have a large basket used for packing vegetables to carry on my donkey. I'm sure it is strong enough to bear Paul."

"Then we will fill in the details of the plan," Ananias concluded, "and prepare." He quickly divided the crowd into groups to pray while he, Paul, Valentina, Damen, and the man who had volunteered the basket moved into the kitchen area to refine the plan.

Paul followed Ananias and the others into the small kitchen area. Was such drama truly part of Messiah's plan—escaping from a window, hiding in a basket, employing spies, and the like? Or should he walk boldly through Damascus' gates and expect God's divine protection?

My time in the desert taught me many things, Yahweh, my God. You forced me into the desert so You could teach me to trust others and to watch You provide for me through them. But these people are my flock, and this is their plan. I put my trust in You and my brothers and sisters.

Even if it means stuffing myself inside a basket.

❧

The following evening, the sun faded in the west and cast fingerling shadows on the eastern part of the city. The lamps in Ananias' house were already lit as believers crowded inside and rehearsed their movements. Damen left the house first to take his position on the path outside the Eastern Wall.

With plans calculated and conspirators prepared, believers quietly left the house in small groups or alone. Those who remained scattered throughout the house, knelt and prayed in passionate whispers for a successful escape.

Making their way around the house under the cover of darkness, the believers darted east between buildings, down alleys, over fences, and through gates, each taking a separate course. The distance was soon conquered and, one-by-one, they arrived at Valentina's house and entered through a low wooden door. The moment the last runner passed through the door, they let go with a collective sigh as they congratulated each other for their success.

"The real danger is now before us," Ananias breathed out solemnly.

Paul and two muscular men went up the stairs to a room where a small window provided access to the alley below. The distance to the ground made it impossible for Paul to jump. A fall would put his life in deeper jeopardy.

Paul opened the window and checked to be certain he could fit through. Then he slipped in and out of the basket to make sure it was large enough. The men tied sturdy rope woven with camel hide to each handle of the basket, then anchored the other end to a ceiling beam. They held it secure as Paul listened for the sound of a whistle, then slipped the basket outside the window and climbed awkwardly in.

Outside, Damen watched until the guard disappeared beyond a shadow on the city wall. A soft whistle to the window above provided the signal for Paul to put the basket through the window.

Suddenly, Damen cried out in a raspy whisper, "Wait! The sentry is coming back. He must have heard us. Draw the basket back inside!"

The men quickly pulled the basket back over the window ledge, and Paul tumbled out and froze in the position where he fell. The sentry had come back to check a noise, and his voice wafted up through the window.

"Old man, did you hear or see anything?"

Damen responded calmly, "No one has passed. I did hear noises coming from one of the popinas wine bars on Straight Street. Maybe that is what you heard."

The sentry's shoulders relaxed. "Probably. No one would dare try to get in or out of the city right now. And I always like an excuse to snatch a drink at the popinas." He laughed as he turned and continued his rounds.

When the guard was gone and the alley empty again, Damen signaled to execute the plan. Once again, the basket slid out the window. Paul squeezed through the window gap and folded himself into the basket as the men firmly held the rope.

With a lurch, the basket slowly began to descend as the men passed the rope hand-over-hand and lowered him. Safe on the ground, Paul darted into the shadows of the southern wall and raced to the junction of the King's Highway and Via Maris, where he slipped into a group of travelers.

With Damascus behind him, Paul's return journey to Jerusalem—and his parents—had begun.

☙

A few *mīlia passuum* out of Damascus, Paul spotted a familiar figure making her way in his direction. He could not believe his eyes! Sere was headed toward him at a steady trot, loaded with supplies flopping against her sides. Young Christophe, wearing a broad smile, was leading her.

"Ananias said the Roman soldiers would look right past me if I pretended to be making my regular deliveries to widows. I came as quickly as I could. I have provisions for you from the ecclesia. The believers want you to know they are praying for your safety. Now go, before the soldiers become suspicious!"

Paul smiled as he took Sere's rope. "Toda, little one. May God bless you and your family for your kindness."

With those words, Christophe continued toward Damascus, and Paul resumed his trek toward Jerusalem. Instead of taking the Kings Highway toward the Arabian desert, he chose the Via Maris to Hazor, then straight south to the Sea of Galilee, where he hoped to catch up with believers in Capernaum and Magdala. From there he would travel around the west side of the sea to Scythopolis and follow the Jordan River to Jericho and up to Jerusalem.

Paul chose his route to avoid the dangers of brigands seeking to fill their thieving coffers and Roman soldiers looking for sport. Unlike traveling the barren desert floor, the two-day walk encompassed dry grasslands and well-traveled highways.

Paul walked briskly, his legs cramping from time to time and his feet burning from the glaring stone highway. Scattered high clouds gave occasional shade but heat reflected relentlessly from the road. Night fell at last, and Paul looked for other travelers to join when preparing his camp.

A fire in the distance called to him. Paul joined a small group journeying from Jerusalem that had gathered to talk and eat around the warmth of the flames. He rolled out his goatskin and blanket beneath a juniper tree and settled in for the night.

Although Paul's body was weary, his mind refused to rest. His thoughts ran in circles, replaying the revelations he'd received at Mt. Horeb, his rejection in Damascus, and the task before him. Would faithful Jews accept Yahweh's new revelation? Exhausted, Paul reminded himself that the battle belonged to the Lord. His job was to be faithful and to trust.

I am in Your hands, and You will give me the power of Your Spirit to lead Your chosen ones to The Way. I cannot do this in my power, Yahweh—only through Your wisdom and Your Spirit.

The following day he arrived at Capernaum and headed for the city center to find believers. The streets were filled with shoppers fighting to be heard, screaming merchants hawking their goods, and irritated passersby. Paul searched the crowd for signs of believers, knowing he would put their lives in jeopardy if he identified them. However, most members of *The Way* valued their faith enough to risk arrest to share their message with anyone who'd listen. Besides, the villages around the sea were a hotbed for *The Way* because Jesus had spent most of His earthly ministry in this area.

Word spread quickly among the believers that Saul of Tarsus, now calling himself Paul, was asking questions about the whereabouts of followers of *The Way*. Paul heard that some believers were skeptical, thinking he was trying to ferret out believers to turn them over for persecution. Others believed his conversion was genuine, but everyone agreed they must be cautious and insisted no one provide information about other believers.

It soon became obvious that Paul must first establish his credibility in Jerusalem to become accepted among members of *The Way* outside the Holy City. Only then could he begin to share the marvelous message with which he had been entrusted. Once he recognized the path he must take, he decided he would cease seeking believers outside of Jerusalem.

Paul hurriedly gathered supplies, packed Sere, and re-routed toward the destination where his true journey would begin.

CHAPTER 27

THE HOLY CITY

Paul sat across a rough wooden table watching his beloved friend Barnabus mop up the last vestiges of partridge stew with a chunk of bread. Stray crumbs clung to Barnabus' gray-streaked beard. When Paul first returned to Jerusalem, he was shocked to learn that his dear friend was alive and well. Paul's letter had spared his ministry companion's life, and after months in jail and repeated beatings, the former Temple Guard had been released and found sanctuary in the home of his parents, who had secretly come to faith in Jesus.

Thank You, my Lord, for one faithful friend—one believer in the city of Jerusalem who does not see me as a threat to their safety and who remained faithful to me despite persecution. Please bless him abundantly, and open a way for me to preach the message You entrusted to me in this beloved city.

Paul took a few bites of the dinner Barnabus' Ima had so graciously prepared for them. Did she, like his friend, perceive his discouragement?

After years of hoping and waiting, Paul finally passed through Jerusalem's gates once again. His heart ached to preach to his childhood community. But instead, he found himself shunned, scorned, and pursued. The alienation he faced in Jerusalem was twin to the rejection he'd faced in Damascus, but the sting went deeper. Jerusalem was his home. And his Christ-driven compassion, love, and trust was causing many believers in *The Way* to fear he was subversively cultivating their affection.

Jews vehemently hated him as a traitor to the Torah and were demanding his death. Even the disciples doubted his conversion. Only Paul's longtime friend Barnabas had welcomed him, rejoiced over his arrival, and was enthused to hear Paul talk about the New Covenant teaching on Mt. Horeb.

Paul took a bite of broth-soaked bread as Barnabus broke the silence.

"Paul, I think you should tell your story first to individual believers instead of crowds. I believe people are far more receptive when they are alone or with a few friends. People are willing to listen with open minds in a private setting more than in a crowd."

The thought certainly had merit. "I think you're right, Barnabus. I should use this approach in Jerusalem."

Barnabus set down his cup. "I've wanted to discuss another subject with you. In the past months I've observed that my cousin John Mark has the unique ability to preach powerfully and succinctly. He was converted at the feast of Pentecost three years ago and has been spreading the gospel message throughout Judea."

Paul nodded. *Good to hear.*

"However, I'm concerned about one aspect of his teaching. He insists that circumcising Gentiles is a prerequisite for becoming a follower of *The Way*. Is this your understanding of what Jesus taught?"

Paul could feel blood rising to his face as anger flashed through him. This was *not* his understanding. He thought his mission was to teach the truth of the gospel, but apparently it was also to correct false doctrine.

He drew a deep breath as a voice whispered, *Yes, it **is** your mission to correct false doctrine. Correction is part of teaching. You must be patient with those new to the faith. You, Paul, are in no position to judge those who need patience and instruction.*

Feeling the sting of rebuke, Paul adjusted his tone, and his passion urged him on. "Jews and Gentiles have liberty to approach God *directly*. Jesus' sacrifice superseded and completed the Law of Moses, making Jews and Gentiles equals on the same footing before Yahweh."

He saw Barnabus' eyebrows lift, and Paul felt a smile tug his lips.

"Circumcision is a *sign for Jews*, not Gentile believers, Barnabus. Baptism is *the new sign* that Jewish and Gentile believers are identifying with Jesus and the New Covenant gospel message. Unfortunately, John Mark is wrong, but I'm here to help clarify matters like these."

Barnabus nodded. "I will try to talk to him and correct his thinking on this, but he is headstrong. John Mark does not even eat with Gentiles unless they are circumcised. To be honest, his arguments can sound persuasive, and he has persuaded many."

Paul looked away as a rush of guilt washed over him. How many members of *The Way* lost their lives because of *his* persuasive arguments? How many families and innocent children had been killed?

"Unfortunately, my friend, many things that sound reasonable do not align with what God says about a matter. God spoke directly to me about this issue so there would be no confusion. Barnabus, I would like to meet with John Mark and explain the truth as God delivered it to me. Nothing can be allowed to supersede His word. This teaching is not a matter of my opinion."

Barnabus nodded again. "I understand. God taught this *directly to you*. What John Mark thinks or believes is irrelevant if it does not agree with what God communicated."

"Exactly." Paul's mouth was firm. "But people *must* understand that the issue is not my opinion or John Mark's. The question is *only* what God says."

"I could not agree with you more, Paul." Barnabus spoke softly as he rose and walked toward the door. "But I believe John Mark sees the question as whether you or he speaks on God's behalf. He has turned the discussion into a schoolyard game of choosing sides. Of course, he sees you as somewhat of an interloper, not one of the original disciples who learned from Jesus." Barnabus turned and disappeared out the door.

An interloper? Was this how division was going to come into the ecclesia—with one believer accusing another's veracity, when the only issue was God's word on the matter?

Much to Paul's surprise, John Mark agreed to a meeting and arrived promptly the following evening as requested. Paul had arranged comfortable seating on the rooftop, where they could enjoy the cool of the day with a cup of wine, fresh bread, and herbed oil. Barnabus listened quietly as Paul explained Jesus' teaching on salvation by faith alone. John Mark asked a few questions, and when he left, he reassured Paul he would think seriously on this matter of Paul' revolutionary teaching. Paul sensed sincerity in his colleague's spirit, yet, as John Mark left, Paul also felt a shadow of doubt.

The following day, Barnabus sent an official statement to the disciples and followers of *The Way* that reassured them of the authenticity of Paul's conversion. Since Barnabus had separated from Paul in Damascus and been freed from prison, he'd become a devoted disciple and often spoke of Paul's miraculous conversion and life change. Barnabus' recommendation helped break down walls of fear and helped Jerusalem believers trust Paul.

He could not find appropriate words to thank his friend and co-minister.

Paul was further encouraged when Peter agreed to meet with him so the two men could learn from and motivate one another in God. For fifteen days, Peter taught Paul about the times he'd spent with the earthly Jesus, and Paul taught Peter the nature of the New Covenant as delivered to him by their Lord.

Paul also met with James, the leader of the Jerusalem church. However, Paul was adamant that he did not want to meet with the other apostles, after hearing that many still distrusted him. He felt it best that reports of his character and teaching be carried back to skeptical church leaders by Peter, Barnabus, and other believers, rather than forcing himself upon those who doubted him.

One afternoon Peter and Paul met at a popular agora where both Jewish and Gentile members of *The Way* met to eat their noon meal. However, while many Jewish and Gentile believers ate together, some Jews refused to eat with Jewish believers, even though they shared faith in Christ. During his days with Peter, Paul observed that his colleague and friend was struggling to understand the new relationship between Jews and Gentiles. Although Peter believed Paul's teaching about equal standing between Jews and Gentiles, he was confused about how to apply the teaching in daily life. For instance, Peter willingly ate with Gentiles, but when believing Jews came to the table, he separated himself from those who were circumcised.

Other Jews acted hypocritically as well, so that even Barnabus was beginning to question the role of religious liberty. Confusion about the relationship between Jewish and Gentile believers was creating an adversarial atmosphere among believers.

With a broken heart Paul, fearlessly proclaimed the Gospel of Jesus and the New Covenant to the Hebrew Jewish community, as well as to Grecian Jews. Hebrew Jews prided themselves on being born in Israel, living continuously in the land, and speaking Hebrew. Grecian Jews lived outside the land, spoke Greek, the Septuagint Scriptures, and were schooled in Hellenistic rhetoric. These deep-seated differences led to even more division among believers after they converted to *The Way*.

The controversy reached a peak one day as Paul was debating and preaching to Grecian Jews. The crowd grew angry and rejected his message. In a state of uncontrollable rage, they attempted to kill Paul. His reputation as a persecutor had poisoned people's reason and ability to listen to him rationally. Jerusalem turned against him. His brief time of preaching in the Holy City drew to an abrupt end when religious authorities issued his death warrant.

Contention in the ecclesia grew hotter by the day, fanned by pride, power mongering, and factionalism. Fearing for his life, Paul agreed to allow "underground" believers make plans to smuggle him out of Jerusalem to Caesarea, hoping to secretly transport him to Tarsus and away from the dangers of the city he loved.

And—if God permitted—return to see his beloved Ima and Abba, whom he had not seen or spoken to since he had left to study at the School of Hillel under Rabbi Gamaliel.

But would they still welcome a son who had left the priesthood and his Jewish heritage? The question plagued him, yet Paul found no one he could entrust with his burden.

ↄ

Paul turned to Barnabus as they ate a hasty midday meal. "I've decided I would like John Mark to accompany me to Tarsus. This will give me time to communicate to him what Jesus taught me on Mt. Horeb. As a key member of the ecclesia and a gifted preacher, John Mark must have a clear understanding of God's word. I need to make sure he receives it."

Barnabas shook his head. "He is a busy businessman and may find it difficult to leave Judea on such short notice, but, of course, I will ask and see what he says." He carefully wiped his hands. "And then, there is the possibility that he simply will not want to go."

Paul leaned forward. "I'm relying on your influence to persuade him, Barnabus. I must leave Jerusalem immediately, and I cannot take time to instruct him here."

Barnabus nodded, his deep brown eyes somber. "I will do all I can."

The next day dawned clear. Paul gathered his few belongings and headed to the Caesarean port to set sail, praying every footstep of the way. By the time he got there, Barnabus had already arrived. A reluctant John Mark was with him, prepared to set sail to Tarsus. Paul inhaled a sigh of gratitude.

He and John Mark quickly secured passage in the two-masted merchant ship, *Gaulus,* which was loaded with grain from Egypt. Built to be seaworthy, the bow came to a point and the stern was square, with the sternpost marked by a swan's head.

As they waited to board, the first mate, who had been overseeing the loading of supplies, paused briefly beside the small group of passengers, and proudly provided details about the *Gaulus.* On the deck below the midship mast, a large galley kitchen, sleeping quarters, and grain storage were located, with the cabin at the stern. The bow was concave, due to the cutwater, which was a structural feature that improved the nautical speed and efficiency of the vessel. The limited number of passengers slept below deck in crudely stacked beds and hemp hammocks.

Paul watched from the deck as the ship took on dried fruits, medicinal oils, and goatskins from Israel before shoving off with winds in full force. They would follow the Pole star, keeping as close to the mainland as possible as they proceeded to the Isle of Cyprus. Ship captains feared pirates in the waters between Caesarea and Cyprus, so the *Gaulus* would stop in Cyprus to unload grain and get updated reports about pirates in the waters ahead.

The day promised a smooth voyage from Port Caesarea to Port Mersin in the Cilicia Province, and brisk winds moved the ship swiftly through the Mediterranean waters. Paul and John Mark chose hemp hammocks near the galley entrance. Their beds swayed with the motion of the vessel and the creaking of beams. Paul hoped the relentless swinging, though gentle, would not make him sick.

After the men had taken time to stow their few belongings, Paul turned their casual conversation to more serious matters. "John Mark, I have spoken with Barnabus about your excellent work as an evangelist for *The Way*. Your enthusiasm is commendable, and your love for both Jews and Gentiles is obvious. However, your knowledge is limited, which is to be expected. But because you lack teaching in important mattes, your judgment is often misguided."

"How so?" John Mark retorted, and Paul observed Barnabus' eyebrows narrow, as well as offense and pride in his tone.

"I have worked alongside Peter, James, and the other apostles since Jesus' death and resurrection. When you arrived, Paul, you refused to speak with the apostles, except for James and Peter. I learned everything I know from these men, and they were personally taught by our Lord Jesus while He was on earth."

Paul paused to silently pray and quiet his spirit, then continued. "I am grateful for these men and all they have taught you. But God has given additional revelation since Jesus ascended.

"As I was traveling to Damascus with the purpose of persecuting believers there, Jesus Himself appeared to me in a brilliant light and spoke to me. He struck me blind for three days to humble me and come to a place where I could hear His voice. When I recognized that I was chief among sinners and Jesus had died for me, as well as the world, I fell at His feet."

John Mark had no doubt heard the story—or bits of it—before. But Paul felt compelled to repeat it in hopes the man would sense the unfolding details as Paul had experienced them.

"I was directed to Mt. Horeb, where the Lord taught me for three years. He told me He had chosen me from the foundations of the earth to be a bridge that would bring Jews and Gentiles to knowledge of their equality in the New Covenant."

Silence hung between them as Paul waited for a response.

"What evidence do you have that *you* were chosen to be this 'bridge' between Jews and Gentiles and bring special knowledge of a New Covenant?" John Mark demanded.

Paul sucked in his breath. *Does he not recognize that this matter is not about me—that my authority is given by Yahweh? The man is impertinent.* His hammock swung back and forth as Paul reflected. *But I have often argued that unchallenged views create gullibility, rumor, and false interpretations. Perhaps John Mark's question is an opportunity.*

Paul rested his hands on his stomach and placed his fingertips together. "You are wise to ask for evidence. You do not know me and have not had an opportunity to judge my character for yourself. It appears that the Spirit of God has not yet directed you to accept my words as truth, so your mind is not settled."

John Mark snorted in response.

Paul chose to ignore it. "We have been given an opportunity on this journey. Let us agree to respect one another's views as we discuss, debate, and pray about where we disagree in Jesus' teachings'. Together, we will look at what the Lord has said. And as to your question about evidence, God has gifted me with the ability to perform signs and wonders, and I pray that you will accept those signs as from Him when you see them."

After a long pause, John Mark agreed, reluctance evident in his subdued tone. Paul decided to defer further discussion. Words sown in hard soil would not produce fruit.

Over the next days, the men were confined to the lower deck.

They ate their meals, talked about life, the challenges of seafaring, argued their views, and often sparred—most often respectfully—late into the night.

Disagreement flared into a blaze one evening. John Mark's condescending, arrogant manner convinced Paul that he was not merely questioning Paul's views, he was challenging Paul's commission as a preacher of the gospel.

John Mark bristled at every attempt Paul made to instruct him in God's revelation on Mt. Horeb.

With yet another disagreement ending with challenges to Paul's authority, he could do nothing but trust the matter to God's hands and relinquish his worries to the realms of restless sleep.

જ

Paul stood at the rail, staring out to sea. Soothing sounds of water caressed the hull as a sail above gently flapped in the breeze. Suddenly, the loud clanging of the ship's bell interrupted the peace as the first mate's whistle penetrated the *whoosh* of the ship cutting through water.

"All hands on deck!" The crew scurried into place like rats to spilled barley. At the rail, Paul spotted a small, agile craft on the horizon closing fast.

The ship's flag identified the vessel as a merchant ship that carried fresh foods and supplies to ports. However, the wary first mate had announced a warning, concerned that the ship might be a pirate rig.

Pirate ships in these waters often masqueraded as legitimate merchants bearing needed supplies or exotic merchandise. If the unknown ship came close enough, pirates boarded and pillaged the unsuspecting vessel. Silician pirates working for the Roman Empire were notorious in the Mediterranean Sea for stealing crews or passengers and selling them into slavery. The region's rocky southern coast and many inlets made the area easy for escape.

Paul watched as the captain of the *Gaulus* made multiple attempts to out-maneuver the smaller vessel. All efforts failed. Paul listened closely to conversations on deck as the ship drew closer. Apparently, this craft had a reputation for searching out slaves and bounty—especially gold. And from what Paul could determine, their captain was about to be forced to allow the pirate crew to board the *Gaulus*.

Common sense told Paul to go below deck and hide. But a voice inside his head told him to remain on deck and find his protection in God. He was not to scurry of to hide like a rat.

Paul stood his ground as the pirates tied their boat to the *Gaulus*, and half a dozen knife-armed men boarded.

Holding the *Gaulus'* crew at bay, the pirates pillaged the ship's galley, personal satchels, then lined up and inspected the crew and passengers for potential slaves. Paul, who was considered too fragile, was overlooked; however, younger, healthy John Mark and several crew members were identified as good candidates for the slave market, bound, and tied together.

The squirming John Mark and other captives struggled to get free as the laughing pirates spat upon, beat, and kicked the prisoners.

In the distance, a spot appeared on the horizon, then slowly grew. One of the pirates suddenly cried out, "A Roman ship is approaching."

All eyes fixed on the growing object, which could now be seen as a large and well-manned Roman frigate.

The pirate crew quickly gathered all the bounty they could carry, scrambled back to their ship, untied the ropes, and launched off, most likely heading for safety at the Mersin Port off the coast of Asia Minor. Taking advantage of the full winds and the small size of their craft, the pirate ship quickly passed out of sight.

But the instant the pirates scrambled back to their own ship, Paul rushed to John Mark's side. His companion had suffered severe bruises to his face and arms, but before Paul had time to fully assess the wounds, crew members from the Gaulus swept John Mark off to lower quarters, along with other injured passengers.

Paul stood on deck and waited for the *Gaulus'* crew check out the injured below. The captain announced that they would continue their voyage with a brief stop at Cyprus to replenish the supplies stolen by the pirates. Soon the crew returned and took up their posts. Most of the injured passengers followed behind them, albeit slowly.

Paul waited patiently until it became clear that John Mark would not be returning to the deck. Undeterred, Paul went down to John Mark's hammock and stood at his side. His companion was lying facing the hull of the ship.

"My brother, I am here to see how you are feeling, if you are in pain, or if I can bring you water or food or just sit with you." Paul clung to his empty hammock above John Mark and waited.

Silence.

How do I respond? What does Your love look like, Jesus? Silent in suffering. Wordless before false accusations. Relentlessly offering hope. Forgiving freely. My gracious and merciful Master, give me Your love to do Your work and Your eyes to see how to help my brother John Mark. Perhaps this pirate incursion can be used to soften his spirit toward me. Give me grace for what I do not understand, mercy for my judgmental heart, and forgiveness for his blind willfulness that is so like my own.

Paul took off his mantle and draped it gently over John Mark's body and laid several dried figs close to his hand. For now, his prayers and ministering presence at his friend's side was all he could do.

CHAPTER 28

HOMECOMING

As the *Gaulus* slid in beside the dock at the Port of Mersin, questions tumbled through Paul's mind. He had not seen his parents since they had moved back to Tarsus. From the moment the journey became reality, he had refused to think about possibilities of meeting them once again. They may have moved or might be dead. He might not be able to find them at all.

Paul impatiently assessed the line of passengers ahead of them signing off the ship with the first mate.

What will my mother and father think of "Paul," who is no longer "Saul" and who walked away from their faith? Will they allow me to enter their home or report me to Jewish authorities? Or denounce me altogether?

Paul sucked in a ragged breath as he signed off with the first mate and set out to find his parents' home. A sullen John Mark, however, excused himself to find passage back to Jerusalem.

Somewhere ahead of Paul, a voice bellowed. "Look what the goats are butting off the deck and onto our shores!"

Paul burst into laughter. The jest could have come from only one person—Reuben. His childhood friend had relished teasing Paul with boyish, humorous barbs.

"I hear the voice of a smelly camel," Paul called back as he threaded his way through the crowd toward his beloved childhood companion, who irreverently speeded up his walk to a near-run until Reuben nearly knocked Paul off his feet in greeting. Any sense of decorum was lost in the raucous laughter of two old friends as passersby looked on and shared the moment of joy.

In the mayhem of greeting Reuben, Paul observed John Mark watching at a distance with a look of disdain as he waited to board a ship returning to Jerusalem. As requested, he had accompanied Paul to Tarsus, fulfilled his duty, and was returning as quickly as possible, his objections to salvation by faith alone staunchly unchanged.

Paul gathered his few possessions and set out with Reuben toward his parents' home. He briefly explained the circumstances of his name change as they walked, and Reuben did not question him. They passed through the Cilician Gate that connected Tumulus to Tarsus, journeyed a short distance further, and soon turned up a narrow lane leading to Paul's beloved childhood home. They had somehow managed to retain their homestead while living briefly in Jerusalem.

As familiar smells overwhelmed Paul, long-forgotten memories and a tumult of images and emotions washed over him.

Working beside Abba as he taught me how to stitch. Refining tasks repeatedly until they were completed with excellence—to the glory of Yahweh. The smell of Ima's bread and lentil stew. And learning to read the Septuagint, as well as the Hebrew Tanakh sitting under Rabbi Akiva, because Abba believed the world would eventually read Greek, instead of Hebrew.

And today I can tell Abba that I speak all over the world. That I have mastered Greek, and he was right—I must speak it everywhere I go.

If he will allow me to see him. Or if I have ultimately disgraced him.

Reuben bid Paul a quick farewell, then turned in the direction of his home, as Paul tried to push the mountain of growing worries from his mind.

Have Ima and Abba heard about my conversion? Do they know the teachings of Jesus? Will they reject me? Abba is a conservative Pharisee who tolerates only a strict interpretation of Torah. Will he watch me taken from his home in chains? Are they both even still living? Did I abandon them as a son—to die without my protection and care?

But before Paul could knock on the ornate oak door, it suddenly swung open. Ima stood before him, her face deeply etched with worry lines. She started to speak, then stopped as recognition lit her face. She reached for Paul and held him in a long embrace as tears flowed down her cheeks, creating dark stains on Paul's mantle.

Ima's age had not diminished her beauty, although her raven hair and flawless complexion had given way to the passing years. Her movements were slower, and her walk was impaired by a slight limp, but Paul could see the same beautiful woman and gentle spirit. As a child, he had never heard Ima complain, gossip, or use harsh words. He remembered only the gentle eyes and spirit of a godly mother.

"My Saul, my Saul, you are an answer to my prayers. Come in. Are you hungry? Let me get you some porridge and bread, and we have dates and nuts."

Paul's strained relationship with his father made the reunion awkward. *Will Abba refuse to see me? Has the darkness of death called him?*

"He is…alive still?"

She paused. "Yes. Please, eat. We will talk about him. I'm sure he longs to see you, as I did."

Paul could not refuse her. He sat down and dutifully ate everything she placed before him. After a few awkward pauses he asked the unspoken question they both felt.

"Where is Abba?" Paul had seen no sign of him since he'd entered the house. Ima stared at her knotted hands.

"Your abba has been afflicted with sickness for quite some time and continues to grow weaker. I will go and tell him you are here." Ima turned and walked slowly toward the room she shared with Abba. Paul clenched his hands as he watched her slow, tentative steps.

A moment later she returned, her lips quivering. "Saul, I am sorry. Abba does not want to see you. Your conversion broke his heart. You know how devoted he is to Yahweh and the Torah."

Paul took her face in his hands. "My Ima, you, more than anyone, know how dedicated I have always been to the Torah and its demands. From the time I was a child, this passion has driven me."

He searched her face. How could he make her understand? "Turning my back on all I believed and fought for would have been impossible for me—apart for a miracle from Yahweh Himself. I experienced that miracle on a trip to Damascus to destroy the new sect of Jews who believe that Jesus of Nazareth fulfilled the Tanakh's prophecy of a coming Messiah. I *saw* the risen Jesus *myself.* He is alive and the Messiah we have been waiting for."

Ima gently pulled his hands from her face. "My son, I want to believe you experienced a miracle from Yahweh, but what you teach disrupts all I have ever known and believed. I will try to convince your father to see you. His illness has made him short-tempered and cruel. Of course, we have room here, and you are welcome to stay. I will see that you are not subjected to his tyrannical fits of anger."

Paul's stomach felt sick, and his heart throbbed in pain. Abba was dangerously sick, his mind twisted by pain and disease, and Ima had worn herself to a shadow caring for him. His ministry, at least for a time, would require caring for his Ima and abba. He could not change Abba's heart, but he could lift the burden of his care for Ima.

"I must take this to my Heavenly Father in prayer, Ima, to be confident I move ahead doing His will for you and for Abba."

Several days later, with confirmation from the Holy Spirit, Paul moved in with his parents and settled into daily life in Tarsus. He established an income repairing tents in his abba's shop, and he often visited Reuben. They became reacquainted, frequently talking about the past twenty years of one another's lives.

Reuben never asked about Paul's conversion from Judaism to following *The Way*. Instead, he talked about his life, family, and his job as the first mate on a small merchant ship called *Victoria*. He'd traveled as far as Egypt and had made one trip to Rome. Reuben liked his job. Being a first mate offered a life of adventure and was quite profitable. He was willing to take the risks of attacks, diseases, and long voyages to be able to provide well for his family.

The more Paul and Reuben talked, the more Paul realized he no longer shared much in common with his friend. He searched for a topic that would open the conversation to talking about his life mission and the gospel. The opportunity unfolded naturally as they were talking one evening after eating together and sharing childhood memories.

"Reuben, do you remember the day you and I went to the pagan temple?" Paul still found it difficult to think about that day. The memory haunted him. *Is Reuben as troubled by that day as I am? Will I ever be able to rid myself of the guilt I carry for what we witnessed ... as if I participated?*

Reuben let out a hearty laugh. "Of course. For years I've told people about how we witnessed that horrible execution. But the horror faded as time passed. Now I look back and see only a childhood adventure."

Paul stared at his friend, surprised by his answer. "It was much more than a childhood adventure for me.

Paul felt his heart quicken. "The event overshadowed my mind for years. I could not get over the horror of it and how a religious sect could justify slaughter. I questioned my teachers in Beit Midrash and Beit Hillel. They all agreed that human sacrifice was wrong. Pagans did it, but Yahweh certainly condemned it."

Paul leaned forward on the cushions where he sat in the common room. "But in my studies, I learned that while God condemned pagan human sacrifice to their gods, He did not reject the idea of human sacrifice for sin. He asked Abraham to offer his son as a sacrifice but then at the last moment provided a substitute. This happened on the very site of our Temple in Jerusalem, which I can only believe was intentional."

Paul had hoped their childhood experience would draw Reuben into a spiritual conversation, and Reuben's face told Paul he had his friend's full attention.

"Should I call you Pauli, as I knew you? Or Saul or Paul?" Reuben asked, his awkwardness revealed in his averted eyes.

"That's alright, you knew me as Saul and Pauli. I want to be known as Paul, the name that identifies me with Jesus." Paul clasped his hands. "I wish I could find words adequate to my experience. I searched for decades, Reuben, looking for Yahweh. And when the answer came to life before my own eyes, I refused to accept it until Yahweh literally apprehended me—appeared before me and shook my life to the core."

Reuben sat speechless as Paul told what he'd learned about Jesus in the intervening years.

Reuben ran his hands through his hair, then, his face slowly broke into a smiled. "I heard about this new form of Judaism from Jews who were fleeing Jerusalem and settled here in Tarsus. They called their persecutor 'Saul of Tarsus.' I always knew of your zeal for Judaism, but I had no idea it would so consume you that you would commit the atrocities I heard attributed to you."

Paul lowered his head. "I pursued my earlier faith, in part, out of pride. Jesus has forgiven me of the many sins of my past, but the consequences live on in the lives of the families and loved ones I am responsible for torturing and killing. I will never stop being amazed, humbled, and grateful that Av has chosen to partner with me in His plan for redemption."

Paul investigated Reuben's eyes, searching his face and then challenging him. "Where is your heart regarding Jesus and the things of which I have spoken?"

Reuben's eyes lit up. "Your words confirm my recent thoughts that *The Way* is *Yahweh's way*."

Paul's soul felt like it had inhaled a deep breath of air.

Thank You, Heavenly Father, for preparing Reuben's heart long before I ever knew I would see him again. Thank You for going before us and walking behind us and hemming us in.

When Paul departed that night to return to his parents' home, a new bond had been forged between himself and Reuben—a tie rooted in brotherhood in Jesus.

❧

The Jews in Tarsus were aware of the growing influence of *The Way.* Paul was not only denied entrance to synagogues, but he was also rebuffed at every attempt to proclaim his message. Open hostility followed him as he extended his attempts at evangelism beyond the city limits of Tarsus. Merchants refused to serve him, and he daily faced verbal abuse. But Paul's greatest concern was that zealous Jews were shunning his Ima because of *his* devotion to the new gospel message.

Because Paul's abba was gravely ill, he took over the tentmaking business to help support Ima. While living among the Bedouins, Paul had not only refined his skills, but also borrowed techniques from the travelers who passed through the area. Although he was denounced for his religious views, a steady flow of trade came Paul's way because of his unique and excellent skills. He also found steady trade among Gentile farmers and shepherds who were dissatisfied with the silence of Roman gods and were willing to listen to the gospel message.

⌘

Paul sat in the front courtyard in the shade of an olive tree, where his eyes were protected. He hummed quietly as he stitched a section of a new goatskin tent for a Gentile patron who needed his project finished quickly. Corners were always particularly difficult, and he reminded himself to carefully reinforce them before continuing.

Suddenly, Ima burst through the front door. "Come quickly, Saul, it's your abba!" She motioned as she ran back into the house.

Paul raced to the small room off the kitchen that Abba and Ima shared and pulled his abba to his chest. His cheek was cold, and no heartbeat throbbed against his own. He was too late.

Paul lowered the body slowly to the bed as he heard a wail of sorrow behind him.

Why God? I never got the chance to see or speak to him when I came home! I wanted to talk to him about Jesus! I wanted to tell him the truth about who You are and what You did for us. You are a just God, and yet here lies my abba, dead, unable to hear about how You changed my life. You chose me to tell the world the gospel, yet You would not let me tell my abba?"

Tears blurred Paul's eyes and coursed down his cheeks. His sadness flamed into anger. He grabbed his tunic and ripped it from top to bottom, then turned to the wall and began striking it with his fists. He cried out, the words indistinct, as he pounded. Blood from his hands streaked the rough mud plaster.

Behind him, Paul felt Ima's hands rest tenderly on his shoulders.

"Abba loved you very much, Saul. It is not your fault he was a proud, stubborn man and wasted precious time. You did nothing wrong. And you cannot point a finger at Av. Abba often asked about you and your message. We had long conversations about the beliefs of *The Way* before you came back. Neither you nor I know what he believed, but he listened far more than you know. He had time to decide if he wanted to follow Jesus."

Paul turned away from the wall. "When I was a child, I never sensed that I did anything to his satisfaction, and even as an adult and a priest, I felt like I needed to earn his approval."

Paul touched Ima's cheek as scenes from childhood flashed through his mind.

"Then when I finally found the truth and had nothing to prove, Abba refused to speak to me." He dropped his gaze. "I wanted him to see that I know who I am now. I'm accepted by God Himself." Paul pushed away the swelling emotion.

His ima did what imas do. With a voice of an angel, she consoled her son, "Yahweh knows your heart, my son, and His plan for you will change the world. He has called you to be His witness for this time and to the Gentile people. God's plan will be fulfilled. Trust Him to care for your Abba."

Paul rested his head on Ima's shoulder, comforted by her words, but his heart still ached. Together they held each other as tears flowed, and together they tended to Abba's body. Before they left the room, Paul turned to his Ima one more time.

"Ima, be reassured that I will always provide for your care. Thank you for your comfort and wisdom."

Paul touched the shroud covering his abba's body. "May you find rest in Jesus, Abba."

☙

Paul sat in the common room of his parents' home, parchments surrounding him on the floor. Grief had consumed him in the days following Abba's death, and he'd sought refuge in the sacred messages he had transcribed during his days with Jesus on Mt. Horeb. As he'd read and studied, the words had come alive, comforting him in a way he had never experienced and could not explain. The Spirit of God had also spoken specifically: the time had come for him to begin preaching God's message.

Paul gathered his parchments, placed them in a goatskin satchel, and hung it at his side. He told Ima he would return shortly, then left the house and walked toward Reuben's home. *I want to preach first to believers here in Tarsus, but I need Reuben's help.*

As soon as he arrived at Reuben's home, Paul presented his plan. "The Spirit of God has told me to begin preaching, and I want to start in Tarsus. I'm asking you to contact believers in the area and invite them to come to a class where I will teach them about Yahweh's plan for His people."

He patted the goatskin at his side. "I've been studying the parchments that I transcribed during my encounters with Jesus in the desert. I've prayed and called upon Yahweh and written my thoughts and conclusions as the Spirit guided me. I hope someday to sew these parchments together to form a scroll, but it is difficult for me to read and write since the pox harmed my eyes. My weak eyes are like a thorn in my flesh."

"Of course, I can ask the believers," Reuben responded hesitantly. "But I don't know how many will feel safe with you, much less want to hear you preach. Many are still unconvinced of your conversion. I think the biggest advantage is that almost everyone is at least curious about what you have to say. I will go ahead and spread word about a meeting time and location where a crowd would not be subject to scrutiny from Jewish leaders."

Twelve days later, on a quiet Sabbath evening, believers arrived at Paul's mother's modest home one at a time or in twos, carrying food, and entering from both the front door and the rear. As Jewish believers, they first observed the tradition of the Shabbat meal and provided for the needs of the grieving widow.

Twenty or more crowded into the house to eat. When they finished, Reuben herded them into the common room and introduced Paul, who began his lesson. Men sat on the gathering room floor, and women listened from the kitchen. Paul sat on a stool between the two. Both rooms were dimly illuminated by candles placed in wall niches.

Paul began with a scene from the Shabbat. "Jesus met with the disciples on the night before He was crucified and instructed them to use common bread and wine from the Shabbat meal to remember his life and sacrifice for them. If Christians had disputes, they were required to seek forgiveness before they partook of the commemorative elements."

Some people nodded and others remained unmoved, but Paul continued to describe the vital ceremony of remembrance and confession Jesus had asked the ecclesia to continue in His remembrance.

A young man in fisherman's clothing spoke. "Do our blessings come because of our faithfulness to Torah? We surely can't do whatever we want and be acceptable to God. What laws must we obey?"

Paul nodded as the young man spoke. "I thank you for thoughtful questions that will help everyone here understand Yahweh's purposes," Paul responded.

"This question troubled me for many years as well. Because my life was chained to the Law, I hated anyone who broke the Law as my sworn enemy."

Paul was sure the sorrow for his past was etched upon on his face. "Now I understand everyone is chained by the Law. None of us can keep it. Yahweh provided a way through Jesus' sacrifice so the world can be set free from sin. We were once slaves to the law, but we are liberated through Jesus."

The young man scratched his head. "Paul, do you mean God will not condemn us, regardless of what we do?"

Paul sensed the motive behind the young man's observation. "No! It does not mean that we are free to live a life of debauchery, but rather, our freedom enables us to freely serve and obey our Master in love—immorality is never condoned."

A middle-aged woman with striking white hair and stately clothing asked, "As Gentiles, how do we enter into God's blessings?"

Paul smiled. He felt like the most favored of God's children to be able to announce to the world the new, revolutionary shared status of Jew and Gentile. "This union of Gentile and Jew has been accomplished through Jesus' sacrifice and resurrection—for both Jew and Gentile. Both now stand united as God's children through a new revelation, although blessings on Gentiles have always been part of Hebrew Scripture. The fact of blessing was revealed to Abraham when Yahweh spoke the words, 'In thee Israel will all the nations of the earth be blessed.' God declares this is His plan for all humankind to demonstrate His glory."

Before the group dismissed that night, they discussed the risks of being caught and agreed that they would change the location of their meeting every week and pass news to one another through a relay system. Everyone agreed that this would be the safest way to proceed, and they decided whose home could accommodate a meeting the following week. By the time the group disbanded, Paul was already planning how to continue developing his theological framework from his parchment notes—and as God gave him more revelation.

Over the next months the Sabbath meeting flourished. A core

group of believers faithfully attended every week and brought other Jews who were interested in *The Way*. But a fearful skeptic left a meeting one evening and talked about his observations in several public locations. Within days, information about Paul's meetings with the *ecclesia* reached the ears of the local rabbi, Aharon, who called upon rabid Jewish fanatics to discourage Paul from continuing to teach his heresy.

One evening as Paul exited a home after a meeting, Aharon's associates attacked him and threw him to the ground. The men took turns kicking and punching Paul, then pummeled his face with branches from a nearby eucalyptus tree, and left him bleeding and fighting for air.

It appeared that the attack was intended to warn believers of the vehement hatred against followers of *The Way*, Paul's commitment, and Jesus' message. In response, church leaders developed additional covert measures, but despite their efforts, Paul continued to face both public and furtive threats and abuse.

Paul's time in Tarsus continued to be torn by the joy of studying and preaching God's Word and the heartache of grief, mistreatment, and misunderstanding. Members of his extended family disowned him, his enemies repeatedly and maliciously beat him, and he was tormented with recurring struggles with malaria, his diseased eyes, and other ailments.

Nevertheless, Paul pressed into his call, deepening his understanding of Scripture through study, prayer, and writing. Led by the Spirit, he remained in Cilicia and Syria to prepare for an unknown future ministry that God had whispered to his heart.

CHAPTER 29

DREAM TEAM

I'm looking for Saul of Tarsus. Do you know him?" Barnabus called out to the captain on the deck of the *Victoria* as he made his way hastily down the dock.

"Never heard of him," the captain spit back.

Barnabus continued his inquiries as he made his way along the wharf, stopping passersby and calling out to anyone on or around the ships that were docked in the harbor. Many had heard the name but did not know where he could be found.

Finding no success, he headed for the Tarsus town center where he could locate the popinas, where men from the community gathered to enjoy a cup of wine and town news.

Those there who had heard of Saul of Tarsus had no knowledge of his family or where in the city he may have lived. Or perhaps they were protecting the family from an unknown inquirer.

Barnabus refused to give up. After all, he'd traveled from Jerusalem to Tarsus by way of Antioch, crossing the Gulf of Iskenderun to find his friend. He wasn't going to turn around and go home without answers.

I must try to locate members of The Way, but I need to do so without referring to their faith and putting them at risk. Perhaps Paul was arrested for preaching.

Tentatively, Barnabus approached a vegetable merchant selling his goods in the street and inquired about the location of the Tarsus prison. The man gave him directions, and a short time later Barnabus rounded a corner and spotted the imposing stone building. He prayed that Paul was not confined inside. Even men with the heartiest constitutions often succumbed to the filthy conditions, savage punishments, and lack of food and water in Roman prisons.

Barnabus took a deep breath and entered the outer court that led to the prison office. He approached a clerk, and in his best Latin told him that he was searching for Saul of Tarsus.

"What are his charges?" the clerk shot back. "Are you related to him? Do you have knowledge of his crimes?"

Barnabus' bravado dissolved. "No, I have no knowledge of his crimes or if he is even here. I traveled a great distance to meet this man to discuss employment, but I have been unable to find him. I've searched everywhere and decided to check the prison before I gave up. He is *not* a criminal, but I thought he may have been beaten or robbed."

"And what?" the clerk leered at him. "Take him home? Tell us what a good man he is? Do you think I'm a fool?"

As the clerk's words rose in anger, Barnabus exited the room and headed back toward the wharf, trying not to look as if he was fleeing. With no idea where to look for Paul's parents, he returned to the docks to search the crowds along the wharf again, stationing himself near the *Victoria*.

As he watched, a boatman headed up the gangplank to board.

Dear Lord, help me be bold, and direct me to the right people.

Clinging to his prayer, Barnabus called out. "Sir, do you know a man called Saul of Tarsus? I am searching for him on matters of business."

The boatman stopped and looked back at Barnabus. "No, I do not, but I will ask the first mate. He's lived in Tarsus since he was a boy. He's right there, on the bow." The boatman pointed.

The first mate shouted from the bow, "I heard you. Who are you and what do you want?"

Barnabus could hear caution in the first mate's tone. He obviously wanted to protect Paul.

"I am Barnabus, Saul's longtime friend from Cyprus, and I have come from Antioch, Syria, to offer him a job. I know him as Paul."

The man left his post and came down the gangway. "My name is Reuben," he said in a low voice, "a follower of Paul's teaching. I know him well and where he lives. Follow me and I will take you to him." Barnabus felt the fear drain from his body, and his muscles relaxed.

The two hurried from Port Mersin to Tarsus as Barnabus quizzed his traveling companion about Paul. They had not walked far before Reuben pointed to the large home belonging to Paul's parents. Barnabus' heart quickened as he knocked and announced his name. Almost instantly, Paul threw open the door, and the men embraced, pounding each other on the back with closed fists.

"What are you doing here?" Paul asked, incredulously. "Is there trouble in Jerusalem or among *The Way* in Judea?"

Barnabus' countenance turned somber. "I don't have time to explain completely right now. I have come from Antioch with an urgent message." He struggled for control.

"Paul, the ecclesia in Jerusalem asked me to travel to Antioch to encourage believers there. I did and was encouraged to find them welcoming both Jews and Gentiles into their community. But Hellenistic Jews are insisting on their superior standing among the Jews and Gentiles. Followers lack accurate teaching about the equal relationship between Jewish and Gentile believers. Unfortunately, the new ecclesia is in danger of splitting."

Paul dropped his head. "I am not surprised by this tragic news. It's difficult to let go of the concept Jews were incorrectly taught—that keeping the Law places responsibility for our atonement upon our shoulders. I personally know this struggle. I will prepare to go with you."

Paul motioned for them to come in. "Ima will happily prepare an early *cena* for you. She has been making lentil soup. Come, sit. I can serve you wine or *posca* if you prefer vinegar and water. Ima adds her own touch to the posca with herbs and spices."

Paul discreetly pulled Reuben aside. "My friend, I must ask a favor of you. I must leave on this trip, but I need someone to oversee the care of my Ima. Can you and your wife do this for me?" Paul implored. "I know I am asking an enormous favor ...." His voice trailed off as Reuben patted him on the arm.

"Not a word, Paul. It is done for however long it takes. We will care for her as if she were our own Ima. Go and let your heart rest at peace." Reuben took Paul by both shoulders and squeezed them, then released him. The two returned to the table and slipped into the flow of conversation.

Barnabus and Reuben enjoyed Ima's soup, bread, and posca while Paul gathered his clothes and necessities for the trip to Antioch. Barnabus had already booked passage for himself. It was important to get to the harbor as soon as possible to reserve a spot on the same ship for Paul. Rumor was circulating that the port would be closing for winter any day and the last ship would be sailing soon. The men finished their meals and said their goodbyes as quickly as possible, then headed toward the docks.

Walking south, Paul could see a red sky as the sun set in the west, indicating high pressure, stable air, and good sailing weather. Before darkness overtook the light, they made their way nearly to Port Mersin. Reuben and Paul said sorrowful goodbyes before they reached the wharf.

Good weather encouraged the captain to set sail that evening toward the port at Seleucia Pieria and head up the Orontes River. By nightfall the ship was underway. The stern cut through the water, and steady gales promised for a smooth and speedy trip. Both men hoped to get precious sleep that night, but it eluded them. Instead, Barnabus gave Paul an update on the ecclesia in Jerusalem and its spread into Antioch.

Swaying in his hammock, Barnabus summarized the highlights. "Philip spent most of his ministry among the Hellenistic Jews in Samaria. One of his converts, Proclus, came to Antioch and insisted on circumcising Gentiles who want to follow Jesus. And while James and Peter preached that the New Covenant fulfilled the Old Covenant, their explanations caused confusion."

Paul leaned forward, "What caused this?"

"While he was ministering in Caesarea, Peter had a vision in which God declared all food items clean, meaning that both Jewish and Gentile believers could eat what was previously declared unclean in the Mosaic Law. A new day had arrived— God's children were now living under the New Covenant."

Paul considered the chaos that might have stirred and waited for Barnabus to say more. He didn't need to wait long.

"The leaders of the ecclesia believe you are best qualified to head the teaching ministry in Antioch. They need a leadership model for their ecclesia for other groups to follow. They're a great light in the Church, and their witness must be preserved with pure doctrine."

"I understand." *The ecclesia must understand that their future will rise or fall on their clear understanding of their faith—unrelated to their feelings or their preferences.*

On the third morning, Barnabus and Paul docked at Antioch. As they waited to leave the ship, Paul looked out upon the city. Antioch was positioned on the Silk Road. The heavy traffic had provided great wealth for the city, but also great excess and corruption. The residents enjoyed Roman citizenship, which allowed them a lifestyle of extravagance.

A large Jewish community existed in Antioch, and their beliefs had spread to many Gentiles, making the city a favorable location for the first Jewish-Gentile Christian church and community.

But a Jewish-Gentile collaboration would not be easy. Cultural barriers existed that would be difficult to overcome. Jews held deeply rooted biases against Gentiles, as Paul once had, that would take conscious effort to eliminate—even among leadership. The New Covenant was a radical new way of looking at life, faith, self, and others.

Paul was certain conflict lay ahead. He just couldn't be sure where and when it would arise. And how could he—a man who had worshipped the Law antagonized and persecuted Jesus' followers—gain trust and stir wonder and faith in God's gift of salvation through Jesus alone?

He knew he could not rely upon his knowledge or ability to speak. His only hope was laying aside himself so that the Spirit of God could freely work.

CHAPTER 30

"CHRISTIANS"

Barnabus knew Antioch well. He led Paul into the walled city through the southern Daphne Gate and down the ten-mille passus long colonnaded Tiberius Street to the old city. There they passed the royal palace and principal administrative offices, which took them to the other side of the stadium and gymnasium and into a modest residential section of the town. They soon turned into a mosaic tiled courtyard. Barnabus knocked on the large cedar door of a two-story stone home covered with green ivy and offset by a garden of local plants.

The door swung open and a man with a streaked gray beard, round and ruddy face, and receding hairline greeted Barnabus and invited the two visitors inside. Their host was dressed in finely woven linen, and a royal sash encircled his full girth.

"This is Saul of Tarsus," Barnabus gestured, "who now goes by his Greek name, Paul. Paul, you remember I told you about Lukas, a medico who grew up in the household of his patron, Theophilus, Roman governor of Antioch. Lukas, this is Saul, and you must forgive me for boasting a bit about your medical studies in Alexandria and surgical expertise, as well as your worldwide travels as a historian and researcher."

Lukas shook his head modestly. "If I boast, I find that it must be in what Jesus has done for me and that He has permitted me to become part of *The Way* and spread His message."

Paul nodded. "Yes, Barnabus has spoken highly of you. I also heard of you from your daughter, Adriana, who I met in Arabia when she was working as a medico, and I was studying God's word. Thank you, Lukas, for graciously hosting us in your home."

Lukas nodded his head humbly. "Your presence is a gift to me. And you are too kind. Yes, I am a follower of *The Way*, but here in Antioch we call ourselves "Christians" to honor our Lord and Savior Jesus Christ. The term does not inflame our municipal authorities. They see us as a Jewish sect and not a danger to Roman rule." He directed Paul and Barnabus to chairs in a large, well-appointed gathering room.

Paul offered his gratitude for the news as well as the invitation.

"The Jews here have no special bond with the magistrate," Lukas said, "so authorities do not challenge our right to worship. Most people who live in Antioch are pagans, so we have rich opportunities for sharing the gospel. And, Paul, I am very much looking forward to time to talk to you about what you learned from our risen Lord during your time in the desert with Him. But you have come, of course, because of the division we are experiencing."

Paul nodded. "I understand the temptation to view Hellenists as having a lower status than God's chosen people, but this condescending attitude results in arrogance and sinful, divisional choices in living, such as regarding circumcision as an essential accompaniment to salvation by faith. Pride is also the root of the dispute about what to eat and with whom believing Jews should associate."

The three men sat deep in discussion until late into the night. Paul retired to bed thanking God for wise counselors he could lean upon.

The following day, he rose early and made his way to the agora with Barnabus, where he planned to preach the gospel. Most who gathered to listen were Greek Hellenists who were drawn to the monotheistic Jewish faith, rather than the polytheistic traditions of Romans and Greeks. Paul emphasized God's justice and love and that He created all things and ruled as King of the Universe.

As he preached, Paul noticed a thin young man listening, earnest eagerness distinguishing his expression. After the crowd dispersed, the youth approached him.

"My name is Titus, and I want to know more about Jesus. I am a Greek and have never worshipped a Jewish God or a Christian God. As I listened today, my heart was warmed, and I believed … that Jesus offers forgiveness for my sins. What must I do to become a Christian?"

Paul's heart exploded with joy. His first Antioch Gentile asking to come to faith in Jesus. Words couldn't express his gratitude for the role God had entrusted to him.

Paul was quiet when he returned from the agora later that afternoon, overwhelmed that he had introduced his first Antioch Gentile to faith in Jesus and all the life changes he was seeing. Every person was different—their background and needs, their experiences, the community they lived in. They were all part of a mosaic that would span centuries and cultures. His experience that day reminded Paul that he needed to apply great wisdom as he presented the gospel in each new city.

After returning home that night, Paul decided he would learn about the lives and faith of the Christians in the Antioch ecclesia. To help him meet that goal, he would begin to meet for meals, evening lessons, and worship with believers in their homes. As he got to know them, he would seek God's guidance regarding who he should appoint as leaders and anointed elders. With these strategies in place, Paul then asked Barnabus and Lukas to meet with him and discuss his observations and ideas.

"The Christians here need sound teaching, a leadership model, and instruction about Christian principles of holy living and why to avoid the legalism of Judaism. It's important that they not only understand salvation by faith, but how to live out their faith in daily life. Clear teaching will help people from developing misconceptions and correct misunderstandings."

Saying it aloud reinforced Paul's conviction that young believers needed a unified body of instruction.

"I'm impressed that your followers are so solid in their beliefs, despite limited leadership. We need to appoint elders and teach them what Christ-like guidance looks like and the servant heart that motivates it."

Paul also asked Lukas and Barnabus if they would meet with him on the first day of the week. He explained that Christians in Antioch worshiped on the first day of the week rather than the Sabbath, in honor of the resurrection of their Savior on the first day.

"My mission is to equip Christ followers to do the work of evangelists," Paul explained. The rapid growth of your ecclesia has proven they desire to spread the gospel. We need to gather believers to formally initiate our mission as the ecclesia in Jerusalem instructed. I will anoint leadership at that meeting."

Lukas, who had been standing at one side of the gathering room, spoke up. "My house is the largest, and we have too many believers to fit into most homes. We have inquired of the rabbis if we could use the synagogue, but we have always been refused, of course, since many of our early converts left the synagogue."

Paul nodded, "Yes, of course. Then we will implement a different plan. Perhaps a better one. We will systematically visit the house churches and appoint an elder for each house. This will give them greater autonomy in meeting individually and provide greater protection if believers face persecution. Each 'church' will not be linked to the larger group. We will be looking for elders with specific spiritual and character qualities, as instructed by our Lord."

On a parchment that he had laid out on a table in front of him, Paul began to list the qualities God desires in elders of His church—irreproachable character, respectful, honorable, temperate, disciplined, holy, and additional qualities. Then, with the parchments in hand, Paul and Barnabus visited five house churches and appointed elders, based on the qualities they had listed.

The ceremony was simple. Prayer for each candidate, then Paul anointed them with oil, and both Barnabus and Paul laid hands on them. Paul concluded with a charge to hold fast the principles of eldership and a charge to the church to hold the office in high regard and commit to accountability to their ordained leaders.

While the process might have appeared easy, Paul returned to Lukas' home following the ordination of Antioch's elders and pondered the work they had done. As he prayed, he glimpsed a vision of a throng of countless worshippers gathered around the throne of Jesus, bowing and praising Him. Peter, Stephen, Paul, the disciples and apostles sat at Jesus' feet, pouring out love for their Savior

As he watched the vision, Paul' heart leapt.

Through the power of Your Spirit, we will take Your story of redemption to every corner of the earth, dear Master.

Tears streamed down his face, and he let them flow. *To serve You is the joy I have sought all my life, Av. Your perfect love heals every ache I have felt since childhood and wraps me in peace. Thank You for loving us so much that You sent Your Son to earth to humble Himself and become a man to die for us—so we could one day live with You.*

❦

Paul sat at the table in Lukas' home where meals were typically eaten, and waited for his good friend and host to appear. The day would be busy as he, Lukas, and Barnabas traveled to several nearby churches to reinforce previous instruction on offering petition, prayers, and intercession for all people, including those in authority; and to live peaceful, quiet, godly, and holy lives.

He and Barnabus had spent the past year teaching and building home churches in Antioch. The number of believers had steadily multiplied, and many Christians had dispersed to other cities, where they carried the gospel. Those cities now boasted small ecclesia and leadership of their own. The time had come to discuss whether their mission in Antioch was complete.

Barnabus soon joined Paul and Lukas at the table, and a servant girl brought warm kashi, milk, and assorted fruits and bread.

Paul began the discussion. "You all know that Barnabus and I have used our time in Antioch to strengthen the ecclesia—but we have also been preparing for an itinerant ministry throughout the Roman Empire. As we neared the end of a year in Antioch, we discussed whether our mission here was complete. We are still unsure and seek your corporate wisdom."

The group conferred late into the night, praying, discussing, and reading God's Word for guidance. But late that night the men still had not come to a clear consensus. So together, they decided to continue their work among the Antioch Christians while praying for further direction and listening intently for the voice of the Holy Spirit.

⟡

Lukas laid down a stone mortar and pestle that had captured his attention. He quickly stepped away from the vendor's table in time to catch sight of a small man walking into the central agora, proclaiming himself a prophet. His unkempt hair, disheveled clothing, and shagged beard were reminiscent of the great prophet John the Baptist, and he was waving a large staff. His disconcerting message had obviously caused a stir among the merchants and shoppers, who weren't sure whether to fear him or to ignore him. However, his jarring prophecy had secured their attention.

Everyone stood silent, trying to determine if the man was a devil or could possibly have received a message from God. Suddenly, several soldiers stationed in the agora to prevent thieves, pickpockets, and troublemakers from creating problems, began laughing and ridiculing the man who called himself Agabus.

"This man is a fake and a charlatan. Pay him no mind. Let's see if his god can predict our future. Agabus! Is fortune in my future? What, no answer? If you are fools, rush to the market and fill your cupboards with grain—Agabus has told us that doom is coming!"

Agabus' words stirred Lukas' memory of Joseph's prophecy of famine in Egypt. Those who had heard Joseph's message had wisely acknowledged it.

We should heed this man's warning, as well. I sense the Holy Spirit is moving him to speak.

Lukas quickly left the agora and returned home. He relayed the prophecy to Paul and Barnabus, who responded with concern. They quickly communicated the message to the home churches. In response, believers in Antioch corporately gathered money to send to Christians in Judea.

With purses of money stitched in the linings of their satchels, clothing, and bedding, Paul and Barnabus headed for the wharf to board a ship for Jerusalem, carrying Antioch's gift of financial blessing.

Their gift proved to be timely. Famine did come, and the Roman Emperor had stored food, but it was being sold at market-gouging prices. The gift from the Antioch church provided needed funds for Judean Christians to purchase much-needed food. Their display of generosity was a visible act of unity and commitment between Judean Jews and Antiochian Gentile believers to those in Jerusalem and beyond—and a dynamic, visible demonstration of Jesus' love at work in His people.

CHAPTER 31

SAILING

Paul stood beside Barnabus at Port Pieria on the deck of the *Minerva*, a merchant ship that transported both cargo and passengers. The morning air was crisp, but as Paul surveyed the outlying waters, he scowled as he spotted high, dark clouds to the north.

A storm was brewing, and the waters would soon grow choppy with rising swells that would make it difficult for ships to navigate safely. The port would most likely remain open for only a short time. Their ship needed to depart as quickly as possible if they hoped to set sail and not be delayed at the port an additional day.

The Port of Pieria had been created by a river that enlarged at the mouth into a natural basin. The city was first built on a rocky outcrop that projected from Mt. Coryphaeus, then spread to the narrow plain below from the point where the Orontes river flowed into the Mediterranean.

"Don't worry," Barnabus offered, obviously reading Paul's concern. "God has an appointment for us in Jerusalem, and we will not be denied."

Moments later, the ship's captain bellowed to the crew. "Cast off! If we can get past the first swells and use the tunneling winds to our advantage through the pounding Cyprus waters, we may have a chance to complete our journey. If not, we will dock at Cyprus and our trip will be delayed—perhaps for several days. Get moving, boatmen, or I will have you all thrown into the sea!"

With the crew motivated by the captain's threat, the ship cast off, and Paul heaved a sigh of relief. They had not been delayed, but they would most certainly face rough seas ahead. He hoped that the crew had strong, seasoned constitutions, and he sent up prayers for safe passage for all aboard as he and Barnabus went below to secure their belongings.

The merchant ship depended on the wind power generated by two masts, with a large square sail in the center of the ship and a small triangular sail at the bow. They also used a small crew of slave oarsmen. The ship was transporting olive oil and wine from Greece, as well as iron and copper headed to Egypt's Nile Valley. They planned to return to the Port of Pieria with a load of Egypt's grain. Due to design and cargo weight, the ship was slow and cumbersome. Because it frequently anchored in ports, it was designed with a V-shaped hull and ballast for added stability. Double planking strengthened the hull, allowing the vessel to transport heavy cargo.

Although the skies looked ominous, the trip began smoothly and without incident. Seamen were always prepared for rough waters. But soon a maelstrom broke with sudden violence, and clouds shrouded the ship in impenetrable darkness and blinding rain. The crew had no hope of guidance from the Pole Star. Wind screamed and the crew became deaf to commands and orders as the waters crashed and boiled into foam. Three water-soaked veteran sailors struggled and clung to one another as they strained to lower and fold the sails at the base of the thick masts and lash them down. The waves crashing across the deck threatened to snap the masts like sticks and smash the double-plank floors.

Paul and Barnabus lashed themselves to a supporting rail near the stairs that led to the lower deck. They watched, aghast, as the crew and captain disintegrated into panic. Paul tried to comfort Barnabus, who was staring into the gale, but the wind whipped Paul's words away before they could reach his friend, though pressed into his side.

Suddenly, a wave taller than a tree crashed across the deck, and Paul and Barnabus were deluged by a force so strong it felt as if it was pulling flesh from Paul's bones. What seemed like an eternity later, the waters parted, and Paul gasped for breath and struggled to get his bearings. Was the ship still intact? Had he and Barnabus been torn from the railing?

And then … a scream like no other Paul had ever heard.

"Has God abandoned us?" The fear in Barnabus' scream echoed the terror in Cassia's cries as the priests had dragged her toward the altar.

Paul forced himself to hold his tongue from rebuking his petrified friend. What to say that was both true and comforting and would not sound condescending to one utterly terrorized—and with justifiable fear?

"Barnabus, my friend, look at me. I am right here beside you." Barnabus unburied his head from Paul's shoulder as the wind slammed rain into their faces.

Yelling at the top of his voice. "We must not let fear control us."

Paul crashed to the floor as the waters washed across the deck. He managed to cling to slat on the deck. He called out again, "Our God is right here with us. He's in control of this storm, even though everything looks and feels out of control to us."

"It doesn't *feel* like anything is in control right now," he hollered over the shrieking wind.

Paul glanced to the deck below. The blankets on their hammocks were soaked, and debris in water on the lower deck sloshed from side to side with the motion of the ship. But Paul's satchel was still securely hanging from the peg where he had hung it. The parchments were safe.

Experienced seamen were on their knees on both decks of the ship, preparing to face their gods. Other crew members were fighting valiantly to maintain control of the vessel amid the raging storm. Paul refused to despair, choosing to be confident that he and Barnabus would walk away from the ship at the end of their journey with their faith strengthened, their lives secure in God's hands. Just as suddenly as the storm had erupted, the winds dissolved, the sea calmed, and peace returned.

The tempest was over, but the test was not. Paul and Barnabus had been graced with reprieve, but a voice in Paul's spirit whispered for him to strengthen himself in the power of the Lord, for the trials had only begun.

CHAPTER 32

BON VOYAGE

Paul sat on a crude bench beside Barnabus at the far end of a large shed. Crispus, a new believer, used the building attached to his house as a stable. But with his flocks currently in his pastures fattening up, the shed was available for meeting space for the ecclesia.

The stable buzzed with whispers and hushed voices. Elders from all six Antioch, Syria house churches had gathered, along with Barnabus, Paul, Philip, and John Mark, to await the Holy Spirit's direction in appointing the first team to launch a missionary expedition to Galatia.

Barnabus had opened the meeting with group prayer for God's direction, and then the men had divided into twos or threes, asking Yahweh to show them His choice for team members. Paul, Barnabus, Philip, and John Mark prayed together and conferred with the other group members as they finished.

When all group leaders had reported the leading of the Spirit of God, Philip stood. "The Holy Spirit has spoken in answer to our prayers. He has chosen Barnabus and Paul for God's mission."

Paul's heart skipped a beat. The news was what he wanted— the call he felt God had placed upon his life. He also knew the harsh realities that would come with the task. More isolation and persecution. But no cost was too high for his Lord. Even death would be gain.

The elders circled Paul and Barnabus to lay hands on them and pray, signifying their support for the men and their mission. Words and gestures of affirmation spilled from their lips.

Quietly, Barnabus turned to Paul. "I would like to take John Mark with us."

Paul hesitated. John Mark's attitude toward leadership had been disappointing. Paul feared dissension, but he also wanted to give John Mark an opportunity to learn and grow. "I will agree, but I would like to take Tertius as well. Since becoming a believer, he has served as a scribe for the church in Jerusalem, and he has proven faithful helping me with my correspondence and copying my notes. Unfortunately, since I was ill with the pox, I have not been able to depend upon my eyesight. He would be a great help to me."

Barnabus agreed, and it was decided that Tertius would accompany Paul. The rest of the meeting was spent finalizing plans for Paul and Barnabus to teach new Christians the tenets of the gospel message.

In the early hours of a promising spring morning, the men set out on the ten mille overland route to the port of Seleucia Pieria. The first day's route crossed the Orontes, climbed winding trails, and traversed rough territory.

The following day, they booked passage to Salamis, Cyprus, but changing weather delayed the ship's departure for three days. They used the time to talk about the gospel to the seamen on the wharf, and after a three-day wait, were off to Cyprus, the crossroads of the ancient world.

Paul was excited about spreading the gospel in Cyprus. Situated in the Mediterranean, Cyprus was well suited for international commerce. Barnabus was also a native of the port city of Salamis and knew the island well. A large Jewish community had moved to Salamis after Augustus Caesar had leased the salt mines to King Herod the Great. The first believers arrived shortly after the outbreak of the Jerusalem persecutions. It would be an excellent learning opportunity to spend time with these members of *The Way.*

After landing at Port Salamis, the men stepped off the ship—their first steps bringing the Roman Empire the gospel. Paul could hardly contain his joy as he headed toward the home of the well-known Cypriot disciple Manean, where he had been invited to stay.

Barnabus and Paul immediately set to work preaching their message to Jewish congregations, encouraging early converts, and openly inviting Gentiles to follow the gospel. Then they headed to Paphos on the other side of Cyprus, the seat of the provincial government, and spread the good news in synagogues along the way.

Barnabus visited his family in Salamis while Paul, Tertius, and John Mark visited the synagogue. To their surprise, their message was met with mixed success.

Paul witnessed a young Jewish widow, who had just lost her husband. As he had preached, she had hung onto every word he said. And when he concluded his message, the widow stepped forward, her two children clinging to her skirt. With tears in her eyes, she proclaimed her acceptance of his message about Jesus. To Paul's surprise others followed.

Many of the men became violent: yelling and screaming at Paul. Their ugly grimaces became contorted and red as one synagogue leader shouted insults. "Take your savior and *sin-condoning* message and go back to where you came from. Our God has no place for religion that denies the Law of Moses and the practice of god-fearing Jews. We have no God but Yahweh."

After a few days, the team pressed on and reached Lapithus during their annual idol festival. Paul saw the timing of their arrival as providential.

He headed for the main agora in the middle of the city, raised his hand, and began to speak. Crowds gathered around him as he boldly shouted above the noise.

"Men and women of Lapithus, what agreement is there between the temple of the living God and idols? When you become a follower of Jesus Christ, your sins are forever paid for by His finished work as a sacrifice on the cross. We know God was pleased because He raised Jesus from the grave. Christ lives in us. We are the temple of the living God. As God has said: 'I will live with them and walk among them, and I will be their God, and they will be my people.' You must stop worshiping demons and idols of gold, silver, bronze, stone, and wood—idols that cannot see or hear or walk."

As Paul paused, the men in the crowd rose and rushed toward him to beat him, crying out "We cannot tolerate this blasphemy. These men must be cast into prison."

Another person who was standing by joined in, "Take them—now. They will corrupt our gods and way of life."

Barnabus, Tertius, and John Mark, who were standing near Paul's side, quickly dragged him to safety. Plautia, a widow Barnabus had witnessed to earlier that morning, motioned the fleeing apostles to enter her home, which was located down an alley off the main street. As she slammed the door closed behind them, they fell to the floor, exhausted.

Paul gasped for air. "Thank you, Plautia, you are God's servant. May He bless your home and provide all you need."

At nightfall, the men crept out of the city and continued to Ledrians, which was known to be a bastion for fanatical Jews. The crowd there cut Paul's words short, so he brushed the dust from his feet and moved on to Lampadistus. He would not waste his time on those who had hardened their hearts to the truth.

Each night Tertius recopied the words he'd noted as Paul

preached that day. The longer Tertius worked with Paul, the more Paul's appreciation grew for the young scribe. Tertius demonstrated a desire for excellence in all Paul asked him to do. He was an exceptional scribe, and his letters were perfectly formed in a large enough hand for Paul to read.

But John Mark? Paul rested his head in his hands for a moment. He was aware that John Mark seemed to be reluctant to join in the celebration of new believers, and that gave him pause. *Is John Mark tracking with the same message we are preaching?*

After several weeks of frustrating ministry, the men arrived at Paphos, which included a well-established Jewish population. Paul knew that the proconsul, Sergius Paulus, had heard of his preaching and had expressed a genuine interest in his message. Anxious for a face-to-face meeting, Sergius had sent for Paul and Barnabus. They quickly came to the city administrative offices to visit with the governor, and Sergius enthusiastically accepted the gospel message as soon as Paul finished preaching.

Delighted, Paul was preparing to transition to a discussion about spiritual matters with Sergius when their meeting was suddenly interrupted. A Jewish sorcerer named Bar-Jesus (Elymas, the sorcerer), stormed into the room and urged the proconsul not to listen to Paul's words. Paul was enraged at the man's obvious efforts to subvert his interaction with Sergius and the governor's accepting the gospel.

Before Elymas could finish his rant, Paul exposed him. "You are a child of the devil and an enemy of everything that is true and right! Your heart spills over with deceit and trickery. Will you never stop perverting the righteous ways of the Lord?"

Paul raised his hands toward heaven in a gesture of authority. "Elymas, you will be stricken with blindness, unable to see even the light of the sun!"

Sergius gasped as he heard the curse. "Never have I heard a man claim authority to make someone blind as a consequence for their sins!" But when he glanced back to Elymas, the sorcerer lay crumpled on the floor, his hands covering his eyes. Authorities called a guide to lead him from the room.

The sorcerer had lost his sight. The proconsul, stunned by the event, asked Paul to explain what had just happened. Paul sat with Sergius Paulus and explained that he performed signs and wonders to authenticate that his message was from God—not simply to ease pain and suffering or mystify people.

Before they left, Sergius Paulus expressed deep gratitude to Paul, Barnabus, and Tertius, insisting that if they ever needed anything, he would be happy to help, and that he, too believed in the power of Jesus to change lives.

That night, Paul called Tertius to come to record notes of the day's events. Paul rehearsed the fruits and frustrations of the day as they settled into comfortable guest chairs in Lukas' gathering room. A complete report must be prepared for the leaders of the Jerusalem church, and Paul was pleased with the performance of Barnabus and Tertius.

But he was growing more and more frustrated with the reluctance of John Mark to fully embrace the ministry task they were charged with. He hesitated to put it in the report, but he thought, *John Mark has followed us but has added some elements to our message. He has undermined our teaching with a constant refrain of adding some merits in circumcision and insisting on the values of keeping the Law.*

As they discussed their troubles and frustrations, Paul recalled Jesus' last words to him, "I will be with you in all your experiences and the messages you speak." Paul smiled and looked around the table. Isn't this all we need to know? Jesus is with us. We know where we need to go and the priorities of our message: Salvation by faith in Jesus alone for Jews and Gentiles alike."

CHAPTER 33

GENTILE CHURCH

John Mark chose to return to Jerusalem, and Paul—with deep pain for the loss—released his brother into God's hands. Again, the group set out by ship, sailing from Paphos to Perga, Pamphylia. The day was sunny, and mild winds hinted at a quick three-day trip. Paul stood on deck, watching the ship slice through the white-crested waves as he prayed for John Mark and pain flooded his heart.

The ship rushed forward as the wind billowed the sails. Paul stared into the deep blue of the sea as the wind tousled his hair and cooled his brow. Unwelcome heat would come soon. Right now he could enjoy freedom from the suffocating heat of land travel.

On the third day of the voyage, the snow-crested, craggy peaks and clear lakes of the Tarsus Mountains came into distant view as the ship approached the harbor of Perga, and Paul and Barnabas would soon begin the next difficult leg of their God-ordained trip.

Although the beauty was irresistible, Paul knew that the geography of the region would be inhospitable. Swamps, high humidity, and difficult waterways often required ships to be towed to Perga's docks. Nevertheless, the merchants' and hunters' paradise provided prosperity to the area. Perga boasted the infamous temple of Artemis, goddess of wild animals, the hunt, vegetation, of chastity, and childbirth.

Paul's thoughts turned toward the narrow passes of the Tarsus Mountain chain. The two men were happy to trade the hot and humid malaria-infested weather of the coastal plain for fresh mountain air. They needed to leave quickly to be sure they arrived in Pisidian, Antioch, before bitter winds, torrid rains, and muddy roads hindered their progress.

The difficult trip would take them over rough terrain that included many ravine crossings known for thieves' ambushes. Smaller groups often joined larger parties for protection on the difficult and dangerous journey.

Paul and Barnabus joined a group of families traveling to Antioch, Pisidia. Even on sunny days, the deep, savage gorges lay in darkness. The passes were bordered by fir trees and sloped steeply to rivers below. After ten days walking through challenging territory, fighting sheep for trail space, and sharing the primitive road with other travelers and wooden-wheeled carts, the men finally reached the city of Antioch, Pisidia. The nights of camping and delays by local customs officers and tax agents were finally over—at least for a time.

Antioch, Pisidia, lay ahead on the slope of a mountain overlooking a fertile valley beside the River Anthias. The city was founded by Seleucus and named after his father, Antiochus. Its name—Antioch, Pisidia—distinguished it from other cities of similar name. Many years before Paul's time, the consul, Publius Sulpicius Quirinius, left no man free and forced younger citizens to adopt Roman customs. Quirinius was eventually transferred to Syria, where he ordered the great census at the time of Jesus's birth.

The men chose to go to Antioch, rather than to the more populated cities of Sagalassos or Cremna. A member of one of the most influential families in Antioch was a relative of Sergius Paulus, who Paul had led to faith in Jesus in Paphos. Because of this connection, Paul would receive access to Antioch's most prominent citizens for support. They would be the first in the city to hear his story of conversion on the Damascus road.

Paul and Barnabus began preaching in the Antioch synagogues as Tertius made notes. But the gospel message challenged Barnabus' thinking on a new level, and Paul noticed Barnabus draw aside for regular private times of reflection. His deeply committed Jewish upbringing was being uniquely confronted, and Paul prayed that the steady diet of Christian teaching would stir personal learning for Barnabus—and that one day he might commit what God was teaching him to writing, as Paul was doing.

But their ministry in the synagogue did not meet with the success Paul had prayed for. At first the crowd listened as Paul summarized the Old Testament and God's choice of Israel for His plan of redemption. He then went on to preach that God had sent His Son Jesus to be the Savior of the world, but the Jews and their rulers did not recognize Jesus and condemned Him, which fulfilled the words of the prophets. Finding no proper grounds for a death sentence, the Jews asked Pilate to order His execution. When all was fulfilled that was written about Him, they took Him down from the cross and laid Him in a tomb.

As he stood before Antioch's Jewish citizens, Paul stated that God had raised Jesus from the dead, that he was seen by those who had traveled with him, and that God spoke the words "You are my Son; today I have become your Father" before a crowd of witnesses.

Finally, Paul added that forgiveness of sins comes through Jesus and that everyone who believes is set free from every sin, a justification people were not able to obtain under the Law of Moses.

Then he dismissed the stunned crowd until the following Sabbath, to hear the conclusion of his sermon.

CHAPTER 34

EMBATTLED

Paul stood along Iconium's crowded Harbor Street. Nearly the whole city had gathered to hear him give the conclusion to the sermon he had presented the week before. The word he'd picked up as he'd listened to the conversations of those standing in the crowds told him that Jewish leaders were jealous of the numbers of people who were coming to listen to him and growing even more opposed to anything Paul might say.

He planned to directly confront both Jewish leaders and the people today. Paul stepped out into the agitated crowd and, in a voice that carried above the crowd, identified himself and began.

"I spoke the word of God to Jews first. You rejected it and God's gift of eternal life. So, I now turn from you and offer God's message to the Gentiles."

The throng erupted in shouting. The Jews were infuriated at such a disgraceful response. Gentiles screamed in delight that the apostles were bringing the Word of the Lord directly to them. They quickly took every opportunity to congregate and listen, and the Word quickly spread to Gentiles throughout the region. Soon, the first Gentile church was established, separate from the Jewish community.

However, to Paul's grave disappointment, the influential families of the city he had counted on for support sided with the Jews and were angered by Gentile church growth. Shockingly, he and Barnabus were driven from the city by stoning at the hands of women of high standing and the city's leading men.

Paul was greatly distressed, but those who refused to listen and divide the ecclesia were accountable to God, not him.

With Antioch behind them, Paul and Barnabus set out on the military road for Iconium, disappointed but undaunted.

℃

Above the noise of Iconium's crowded Harbor Street, Paul heard the voice.

"Mercy, mercy! Have mercy on a blind man!"

The words struck Paul's heart. He knew too well what it meant to sit in silence as the world passed by and how it felt to rely upon others for his every need. He looked in the direction of the voice and spotted a blind beggar sitting at the side of the road a short distance ahead.

"I must speak to him," Paul said to Barnabus and Tertius as he pushed through the crowd to the side of the road. He leaned down and took the man's hand.

"How long have you been blind, sir?"

"As a child, I had the pox, and it scarred my face and took my vision. My parents cared for me until they died in a wagon accident many years ago."

The pox. I could have lost my sight like this man and been left in darkness for the rest of my life. Paul squeezed the man's hand, and an unsettling mix of gratitude, guilt, and compassion washed over him.

"I am so sorry for the loss of your parents," Paul spoke gently. "I can only imagine the shattering grief their deaths would have caused you. What is your name, sir?"

"My name is Elias, but why do you ask? No one ever asks the name of the blind beggar. They either pretend they don't see me or give a small coin to ease their conscience as they pass."

Paul squeezed the man's hand again. "I ask your name because Yahweh calls you by name. Do you know God, Elias?"

Elias tilted his head, his expression troubled. "I'm not sure anyone can 'know' God, but I go to the synagogue every Sabbath and try to be a good person."

Paul sat down next to Elias, and he felt Barnabus' and Tertius' watching him. He glanced. Their eyes showed curiosity. Paul told his story of rising to a position of authority among the Pharisees, then meeting Jesus on the road to Damascus, followed by Paul's brief blindness. His experience of coming face-to-face with the Messiah, God's own Son, poured from his lips as Elias listened in amazement.

Then Paul placed his fingers on the man's sightless, closed eyes and quietly prayed. When he finished, he spoke directly to Elias. "Open your eyes and go directly to the synagogue and tell the priest the sign you received in the name of Jesus."

Elias opened his eyes. He blinked. When he opened them a third time, they grew wide with wonder.

"I can see!" Elias jumped to his feet. "I can see! Praise Yahweh, I can see!"

Elias grasped Paul's hand, then in a frenzy of joy, ran off in the direction of the synagogue, yelling and waving his arms as he ran. Paul rose and headed toward the agora to preach. Barnabus and Tertius followed him, speechless.

The synagogue was a focal point in the small village of Iconium, which was in the central plateau of the Lycaonian Province. The city was set in the middle of a large, fertile plain that stretched to the north and east. Well-watered and surrounded by alluvial soil, it produced grains, plums, and apricots in a moderate summer climate. The high elevation was well-suited as a location for a major highway that connected the East and West.

The following Sabbath, Paul and Barnabus visited the Iconium synagogue. Immediately, Paul sensed that the priest, whom Elias had dutifully told about his healing, was waiting to test Paul's authority as a healer. The priest invited Paul to preach and explain the source of his authority for his healing power, but Paul's spirit told him the invitation was a trap.

My Master and Savior, thank You for this opportunity to share the gospel at the invitation of Iconium's priest. Only You could have provided a venue with the sanction of a Jewish official. Give me Your wisdom, Your power, and Your words as I share the good news of Your Son.

Paul watched the synagogue priest respond in amazement as Paul clearly and scripturally explained the source of his authority, as well as his healing power. He spoke repeatedly of his experiences with Jesus on the Damascus road, as well as on Mount Horeb.

Not only did Paul pass the test, after listening to his message, many Jews and Gentiles believed the gospel message.

Sabbath after Sabbath, Paul and Barnabus returned to preach in the synagogue. During the week, they preached in the local agora. The three-man team that included Tertius remained in Iconium for several months, preaching among the Jews and Gentiles and seeing many people come to faith in Jesus.

But opposition crept in as unbelieving Jews stirred discord among the Gentiles and fanned flames of deception and falsehood. Those who disagreed with the apostles sowed lies that Paul and Barnabus were sorcerers. When the apostles demonstrated their authority through signs and wonders, their challengers discredited their miracles, accusing them of witchcraft. As time passed, rivals and intolerance grew.

The apostles eventually discovered that plots against them had been set in motion the very first day of their ministry in Iconium. Contention grew to an inferno, and Paul, Barnabus, and Tertius entered a period of focused prayer about their life-threatening situation.

Their answer came quickly in the form of a reported plan to stone them. With the plot against their life revealed, the apostles fled Iconium and took the gospel message to Lystra and Derbe.

☙

Instead of going first to Lystra's synagogue, this time Paul decided to preach in the agora in the center of town, where large crowds gathered. This placed him directly among the people and away from entanglements with synagogue officials. He had learned that one reason people were not accepting the gospel was because false teachers were preaching competing "gospels," often where large crowds gathered. However, miracles were a vital part of their apostolic ministry. They gave evidence of God's authority and uniquely authenticated Paul's message.

Lystra served as a market town of Lycaonia in south central Asia Minor. Lycaonia was a rural area which was less affected by Hellenization than other regions. Inhabitants of Lystra spoke the ancient language of the region, Lycaonian, rather than the more widespread Greek. In 6 BC, Augustus made Lystra a Roman colony to protect trade routes into the Tarsus Mountains, and a Roman Imperial Road was built between Lystra and Pisidian, Antioch.

Along the roadside as he approached the entrance to the agora, Paul spotted a crippled man sitting and begging. A make-shift staff lay on the ground at his side. The man noticed Paul look at him and cried out, "Sir, I see that you and your friend are God-fearing men. Can you spare a few coins for a hungry beggar?"

Paul drew closer so he could speak privately to the man. "How did you come to be lame, sir?" he asked.

The man looked up at him, surprised. "My Ima was attacked and beaten on the trail to Antioch when I was in her womb. She later died in childbirth, and I was born with a severely deformed leg."

Although Paul's legs had always been weak, despite his physical struggles as a child, his parents had loved him and supported him. His heart moved, and he took the man's hands.

"Stand up and walk."

Immediately, the young man's legs straightened, and fear washed over his face.

Squeezing the man's hands, Paul said, "Look at me. You have begged Yahweh for a miracle. He hears your prayers. All of them. Stand up."

He pulled on the man's hands gently, and he rose to his feet, his eyes wide with a mix of terror and exhilaration. He took a few tentative steps, then began jumping and dancing as he shouted with joy.

Reaching out, Paul caught his arm. "Go to the synagogue and tell the priest what has happened."

People in the crowds saw what Paul had done, and they shouted in Lycaonian, "The gods have come down to us in human form!" They called Paul *Hermes*, the chief speaker of their gods, and they called Barnabus *Zeus*, the chief of their gods. Sometime later, the priest of the god Zeus, whose temple was outside the city, brought oxen and garlands to the city gates to offer sacrifices to Paul and Barnabus.

When they realized the priest's intent, Paul and Barnabus tore their clothes as a sign of horror and grief. They ran among the people, crying out, "Sirs, why do you do these things? We are men of like passions to you. We preach unto you that you should turn from these false vanities unto the living God, which made heaven, and earth, and the sea, and all things that are therein."

Even after Paul made his fervent denial, he and the other apostles struggled to convince the Lyconians not to offer sacrifices to them. Jews from Antioch and Iconium were inciting the crowd, angering them against Paul and his team. Emotions boiled over among the throng, and they chased Paul and his company out of town, stoning them until they were assumed dead.

After the crowd drifted away, Paul tended to the battered and bloody bodies of Barnabus and Tertius. He found solace knowing that God's message had been delivered, and it would find seed in ways that only his Master would ever know. Their task was spreading the gospel, and they had succeeded. Their visible "success" was summed up in three members of one family: a young convert named Timothy, his grandmother Lois, and his mother Eunice.

The next morning, the bruised and bloody *talmidim,* lifetime disciples of their Master who pledged their all, struck out for Derbe, an insignificant city in the region of Lycaonia, and about a day's walk. Derbe sat on a major route connecting Iconium to Laranda and was about twenty-five mille from Lystra. The city became part of the province of Galatia and was given great privileges under the Emperor.

The missionary team preached the gospel in Derbe with no persecution and won many disciples. Then they returned to Lystra, Iconium, and Antioch, strengthening the disciples, encouraging them to remain true to the faith, and appointing elders in every city. Upon their return they also visited the thriving port town of Attalia.

The door had been opened to the Gentiles. Paul, Barnabus, and Tertius had successfully carried out their mission, although the victories had come at great price.

Yet Paul was certain that the greatest battle was still to be won—in Jerusalem, among fellow members of *The Way* who needed to learn how to lay down their preferences and personal choices to demonstrate Jesus' love in a hopeless world.

CHAPTER 35

ILLUMINATING GRACE

James sat at his writing desk, his head in his hands, and his stylus and ink well shoved to the side. His letter to the Jews scattered throughout the Roman Empire was proving to be more difficult to write than he had thought. Two questions gripped his mind: *Would the new ecclesia endure? And would the debate about the necessity of circumcision and clinging to the Mosaic Law cause a division? Surely these things are not what the Lord wants.*

James knew that many members of *The Way* saw him as a leader and admired him for growing up alongside Jesus, but he never spoke to anyone about the pressures of being raised in the same household as the Messiah. He'd felt reservations when leaders appointed him to be the first head of the Jerusalem ecclesia, whose primary constituency was Hebrew Christians.

James prided himself in his strong work ethic. But he knew he had a temper and strong opinions—often expressed inappropriately. He'd felt the sting of comparison when Jesus had confirmed Peter as the "Rock of the Church," and, because of his pride, he'd carried those wounds too long.

Peter and he, along with the other disciples, had been commissioned to carry the gospel message to the uttermost parts of the earth. As part of the new ecclesia structure, James assumed responsibility as de facto head of the Church in Jerusalem, and he and Paul quickly became regarded as leaders.

He reached for a sip of purified water to slake his parched throat and stave off the heat. He had never sought leadership and its accompanying battles. The controversy over the nature of the gospel was dividing the Church, and it troubled him. He believed felt it was vital that the Jerusalem Council discuss the issue and bring needed resolution. Many people mistakenly believed he sympathized with Jewish Christians who wanted to keep practices of the Law in force for Gentiles. Their opinions of him were not the issue. Paul, who had been instructed by Jesus Himself, taught that Gentiles were not restricted by Jewish Law. Salvation came through faith alone. The church could not compromise on this.

While he embraced Paul's new emphasis on Christian liberty, James was concerned about new converts excusing and justifying their sin because they were saved by God's grace. *Surely*, James reasoned, *God wants purity in Christian living. Could salvation come by faith alone and Jesus' followers still be expected to live pure lives?*

James asked his servant to fetch his companion, John Mark, an elder in the Jerusalem church who was in Caesarea in Jerusalem, staying in his mother's home.

As James was partaking of his cena at his simple desk in the gathering room, John Mark entered.

"John Mark, do you care to join me in a simple midday meal? Thank you for coming on such short notice."

John Mark declined all but water, and James continued.

"I will not waste time and get to the point. You spent time with Paul and Barnabas on their trip to Asia Minor and heard their preaching, and I want you to summarize their message."

Mark hesitated, placing his hand on his chest. "I was concerned about the emphasis Paul gave in a message that seemed to suggest that one is free to sin as long as he accepts Jesus's sacrifice for iniquity and the grace that applies it."

Mark looked away. "I discussed this with Paul because I also saw controversial implications that did not seem to consider other aspects of God's revelation to us. Paul reports he received his teaching from Jesus himself. But I don't think God can reveal one message in the Torah and another to Paul."

James rubbed his beard. "Your cousin Barnabas was with Paul. Was he teaching the same things?"

"Yes, which puzzles me. Barnabas is of the bloodline of Jewish priests. As a boy, he joined Jesus' father, Joseph, in an in-depth study of the Day of Atonement, then dedicated his life to following the sacrificial system."

Mark paused for a moment, fingering the leather scripture box bound to the back of his hand, and continued. "Yet, Barnabas accepted Paul's emphasis. It was unsettling, so I left before the trip was finished. I'm still confused about whether a Gentile must become a Jew by circumcision before he becomes a Christian."

James paused to absorb Mark's comments, then replied. "You are not alone in your confusion. I am hearing that many scattered Jews are looking for clarity as well. I have decided to write a letter to see if I can bring a unified understanding of the new message to the ecclesia before we splinter before the eyes of a dying world."

Mark shook his head. "I know you mean well, James, but I do not know if you are aware of how stubborn and uncompromising Paul can be. When we discussed these issues, he never listened to me. He ignored me or dismissed my thinking as an immature youth."

James could see the hurt and rejection etched on Mark's face. "You must try to be patient with Paul. Remember, he was he fiercest opponent of Christianity we ever faced and responsible for the death of countless followers of *The Way*. Then, as he was traveling to carry out his greatest purge ever, Jesus Himself met him face-to-face and revealed who He was. No man alive carries a greater awareness of sin and guilt than Paul. And neither does any other man know freedom in Jesus as he does. Our Paul, who was Saul, carries his weight of responsibility with singular insight. These things have molded him into the *fiercest* follower of Jesus and most exemplary expression of Christianity."

Mark hung his head. "I know. But is it possible to carry *liberty* too far?"

James responded quickly. "In my letter to all Christian Jews, I want them to see the relationship between salvation by grace apart from the Law and good works described in the Law."

"So, what is the difference between faith and good works of the Law?"

James picked up a fig from the bowl in front of him. "Mark, if you say to me 'I like figs,' but you never eat them, how can I *know* you like figs? But if I tell you 'I like figs' and you observe me regularly eating figs, you know with certainty that I like figs because it's obvious to see from my life. The same is true with the relationship between faith and good deeds."

Mark smiled at James' simple expression of a new truth. "If I say I follow Jesus, you will see the evidence every day in the way I live! Write it James. Write it for all to read. I am beginning to understand. Maybe Paul was right."

Pleading with his friend for prayers, James asked Mark to leave. Like a mother ready to be delivered, he knew the time had come and he needed to be alone.

At the close of the door, James picked up his stylus and dipped it in the inkwell. His lips moved as he asked God to guide the words he wrote so they would be His. Humbly, James committed every word of his letter to Adonai.

In meticulous letters, he penned, "Count it pure joy, my brothers, whenever you face trials of many kinds ...."

His words flowed like the Jordan River in rainy season. He hesitated and listened for the voice, praying and stilling his thoughts until the Presence flowed through him again. James continued until the strain of sitting and penning forced him to his bed. For the next two days he wrote as the Spirit of God led, stopping only occasionally to eat, sleep, and attend synagogue on the Sabbath. But the spiritual and physical demands of writing were quickly overshadowing his resolve.

Several days later at the rooster's crow, James rose quickly, dressed, and ate a hearty breakfast. Then he sat in his room in prayer as he pondered the spiritual and physical demands of writing. After a time, he grabbed a piece of bread on his way out the door, then made his way through the empty streets of Jerusalem to the house of John Mark's mother. Earlier, he had sent his servant to call two believers, Eli and Ezra, trained scribes, to meet him there to discuss a potential business partnership. James knew the young men to be of good reputation and reliable workers.

Soon after James arrived, Eli and Ezra joined him and John Mark in the spacious gathering room, sat on pillows across from them, and waited politely for James to reveal his proposition.

Eli sat on a low hassock made of neatly stacked wide pillows. His long legs were bent beneath his sand-colored tunic, and his knees nearly reached chin. He was the son of an honorable Jerusalem mason and had learned to be a scribe in beit Hillel. His penmanship was impeccable, and his newly found faith in Jesus was widely known in Jerusalem. Ezra offered similarly impressive credentials and skill in writing.

"I have asked you here today to propose your working as my amanuenses in my writing. I am finding the work physically taxing and taking more time than I expected."

"Please tell us more," Eli responded.

"I fear a storm is brewing in the ecclesia regarding the message of the gospel. I am fearful that the body will divide into a Jewish ecclesia and a Gentile ecclesia. I have written a letter to Hellenistic Jewish believers living outside Judea to provide evidence that Jews and Gentiles can believe the same message, love one another, and function as one body."

Eli and Ezra listened, both with eyebrows tented, as James continued

"However, to more effectively get the message to members of the ecclesia who so are so widely scattered, I would like to partner with you men of shared faith to reproduce my letter."

Eli and Ezra looked back at James, in astonishment that slowly dissolved into smiles.

"As I complete each leaf of papyrus, your task would be to copy the page precisely. When we finish, curriers would take the completed letters to congregations outside Judea and beyond. By duplicating my efforts through scribes, the message of Jesus can be taken further, faster."

The men nodded and expressed their appreciation for being selected for such a vital mission. After a brief discussion of responsibilities and payment, the decision was finalized.

"Our work will begin tomorrow in my home," James summed up. "This will give me time to secure supplies and arrange the gathering room to accommodate us. I am greatly enthused about our partnership in the gospel."

ε৯

By the time Eli and Ezra arrived the next morning, James had arranged extra supplies in his sleeping quarters and moved his eating table and benches into the gathering room to make space for his amanuenses to work. He had even set out roasted grain, dried fruit, and drinking glasses and light wine in the kitchen.

James began writing while the scribes gathered their parchments and arranged their inkwells, sharpened and inked their styli, and waited for James to complete the first leaves. Before long, Ezra and Eli were copying the words James had written, as moved by the Holy Spirit.

James continued writing, listening, thinking, listening ... borne along in a heavenly dance.

Address faith and works. Faith in Jesus' sacrifice is the requirement for forgiveness and reconciliation. Yet do not neglect the application of faith in doing good deeds.

"What good is it, my brothers, if a man claims to have faith but has no deeds ..."

True faith is more than intellectual and emotional assent; true faith produces works. Good deeds don't save; they are the outcome of true faith in Christ.

His hand and words were his own, yet even as ye wrote, drawn from somewhere deep inside him that was Beyond and more deeply himself than he had ever known.

At times, his writing was furious, as he felt the Spirit direct him.

"To be friends with the world is to hate God ..."

At other times the pen moved as if at the beckon of the wind.

James put down the stylus looked at Eli, who had fallen into a half sleep.

"Eli, as I write, I have been forced to contemplate the past twenty-some years of my life. My eldest brother Jesus was unlike my other siblings, and I wasted years on envy and bitterness, only to realize *after* Jesus' death that He was the Messiah. My regret for the years I disdained my brother ran so deep that it had pressed me almost to despair. Now He is my Savior, and not just mine but the world's. My awe of Him is so great as to defy words, my love so profound that I will spend the rest of my life trying to express it. To be charged with taking His message to the world is the most humbling task man could ever know. What a wonderful God, and He is ours!" James felt tears rolling down his face, and he let them flow.

Eli moved over to James's table and laid his hand upon James' shoulder. "I know you do not know Ezra and me well, James, but we all feel overwhelmed to think that we have walked with God and taken it for granted. While we do not share your sorrow, we know it in part, and we are sorry." Ezra nodded, his eyes compassionate.

"I am fine, gentlemen. I find that writing about my earthy brother as the Savior is also somehow writing about me and my sin and how much He loved me despite myself. And I feel Paul's pain and guilt from his past. He has said he is the greatest of all sinners. I believe it, but praise God, he is now a new creation, purposed by Av Himself for great things."

But as fatigue began to pull at his body, James ended the writing session and sent Ezra and Eli home to their families. James crawled into bed without worry. The epistle had not been his own but written at the prompting of the Holy Spirit. The message had come from God and communicated His mind regarding the guidelines for Christians who were now to unite under one ecclesia. His letter of concern and clarification would provide evidence to all Christians to unite under one ecclesia.

CHAPTER 36

LAW AND LIBERTY

Call my amanuensis!" the Apostle Paul bellowed as he pounded his desk with his walking staff. "I must write a charge to the Galatians. I have barely returned from my maggot-infested cell to hear that someone has been preaching a contrary message to the Galatian ecclesia. Whoever is teaching this 'other gospel,' let him enter the gates of hades."

A decade had passed since the birth of the church. Communicating God's New Covenant through the written word was still in its infancy. James had completed the first letter of the new era, appropriately called *James to Jewish Christians Everywhere*. However, Paul knew that the question of salvation by faith, the relationship of works to salvation, the role of the Law of Moses, and the place of circumcision within the faith still confused believers.

Paul and Barnabus would certainly be chosen to attend the council and relate the successes of their missionary journey, as well as help make strategic decisions. And that would include defending salvation by faith, apart from works.

Paul had reined in his anger and stood beside his desk. "Tertius, bring the parchments you copied while on our trip to Galatia. My notes will provide insights to help me write the epistle to the Galatians.

Paul laid his hand on his friend's arm. "And Tertius, I am sorry for my outburst of anger."

Although it was hard for him to admit, Paul struggled with a quick temper when he confronted false teaching or when the authority of God's word was challenged. His assurance in *his* authority was not confidence in himself, but in the role God had assigned him, with commensurate authority. But at times he still had to rein in his compulsion to be right to satisfy his pride. His poor vision, weak legs, and small stature were all Yahweh's daily reminders of his limitations and God's grace.

The initial words of Paul's epistle evidenced his anger: "You foolish Galatians."

He paced the stone floor as he fought to contain his anger. He had heard the rumor more than once that certain Galatians were abandoning the apostles' teaching.

What are they thinking? I clearly taught them the message the Lord Jesus delivered to me in the wilderness. How could they so quickly desert His teaching? Who led them astray?

Acutely aware of the infancy of the church in Galatia and the persistence of deceptive religious instructors, Paul had repeatedly warned the church about false teachers before he'd left on his missionary journey. He had repeatedly distinguished between truth and untruth, and anger against the Galatians' betrayal of Jesus's message burned deeply in his heart.But false teachers had followed closely on Paul's heels, demanding that believers add the Law to their new-found faith to receive God's full blessing.

I can tolerate no excuse for their abdication of their instruction. They joyfully accepted the message of the crucified Christ and received the Holy Spirit. They accepted my teaching as the word of God, knowing I delivered to them the message I personally received from Him. Now they have added to the gospel message to follow a charlatan!

These false teachers preach a gospel of works to avoid being persecuted for the cross of Christ and to cull favor with Jewish religious leaders.

With these thoughts swirling, Paul barked orders at his amanuensis to begin taking dictation. Tertius stood by, watching wordlessly, but his expression told Paul that his friend knew he expected silence.

Paul hesitated as a voice whispered in his head. *Is your anger an impediment to loving others well, Paul?*

A picture of the face of a priest slashing the throat of an innocent girl flashed through his mind.

Care deeply about what your anger does to you and others, Paul. Accept that all your sins have been forgiven, and forgive others from a humble heart.

He stood, his head bowed, as moments ticked by. When the weight of pride lifted, he looked up and turned toward his amanuensis.

"Please forgive my angry outbursts, Tertius. They are self-indulgent and wrong. I had no right to speak in that manner." Then Paul quietly returned to his work, his heart contrite.

Late in the afternoon, pounding on the front door broke Paul's concentration. A servant opened it, and a hooded man stood outside.

"Is Paul, formerly known as Saul of Tarsus, here?" The voice was hushed.

The servant girl hesitated. "Who asks to speak to him?"

"I am Ezra from Jerusalem with a message from James, the brother of Jesus."

Paul called out for the girl to invite Ezra in, and she led him into the gathering room where Paul was seated at a desk, writing.

"Paul, I have brought a letter from James that is circulating throughout the followers of *The Way*. He wrote the letter considering the upcoming Jerusalem council. I have been asked to wait until you finish reading it, then take it to others who are awaiting word from Jerusalem."

"I commend your diligence, Ezra," Paul responded. But perhaps you could stay the night, which would give Tertius time to read the letter to me since my eyes are so poor and make a copy for the churches here in Antioch. Would this be acceptable?"

Ezra agreed, and later that evening Paul listened attentively as Tertius read James' epistle to him. He slept restlessly.

Paul rose in the morning with concerns about new believers potentially misunderstanding James' epistle. While what James wrote was certainly accurate, Paul believed the epistle left vital teachings unaddressed. He stepped outside into the early morning sunshine to help sort out his thoughts.

Some readers may not fully understand James' message. He and I teach the same Spirit and the same God. In that regard, our messages are the same. However, I need to more fully explain the grace of God and the pure gospel message to balance the functions of law and grace.

It's important that James and I get together in Jerusalem and discuss the intent of his message before the council meets so that we are not seen to be opposing each other.

The Galatian ecclesia had tried to discredit Paul's person and attack his message. They believed it was necessary to add to Paul's message for it to be a "full gospel." In response, Paul's epistle explained the doctrines of justification by faith and sanctification by faith.

The central issue was a new concept for those who had for centuries lived under the Law: liberty in Jesus and freedom based upon individual justification. The Galatians needed to understand that sanctification is *applied* to the life of a believer, not earned. To convince them of this, Paul explained that the Abrahamic Covenant was based on faith and not on works.

The emerging question for the ecclesia was becoming more and more evident: How do believers live out their new faith? Do they add elements of Old Testament Law, such as deeds or circumcision?

Paul began dictating, and Tertius noted every word.

Paul opened the letter by establishing both his legitimacy as an apostle of Jesus Christ and the authority of his message as Jesus' apostle. His opening comments were harsh, "I am astonished that you are so quickly deserting the one who called you to live in the grace of Christ and are turning to a different gospel—which is really no gospel at all."

He followed by condemning their behavior with a curse, then cited the source of his authority: God.

"I did not receive the gospel from any man, nor was I taught it; rather, I received it by revelation from Jesus Christ."

Paul's response to his critics was unequivocal: "I admit that I failed in the past when I persecuted Christians, but I rejoice that, by the grace of God, I was converted from Judaism to Christianity and commissioned as an apostle of Jesus Christ Himself. I did not confer with any human authority, including the apostles in Jerusalem. My authority came from my encounter with Jesus in the Arabian desert on Mt. Horeb. My message has divine origin and authority."

Paul then summarized the thesis of his message in a single statement: "I do not set aside the grace of God, for if righteousness could be gained through the law, Christ died for nothing."

Paul straightened up. "Did you write that down, Tertius? That is as clear as I can make it. Salvation and sanctification are by faith alone but are expressed in actions."

Paul withdrew his stylus from the papyrus leaf and handed it to Tertius. The handle of the stylus was dripping with ink. Paul had jammed the instrument in the inkwell and splashed the fluid in all directions. Paul called a servant girl who came and quickly wiped up the spill.

Paul caught Tertius' grin. His amanuensis knew him well enough to know that Paul's raw emotions had spilled over into his writing. When the blots had been removed, Paul returned to his writing. Tears formed in his eyes as he penned the words "Clearly no one is justified before God by the law, because 'The righteous shall live by faith.' Everyone else is under the curse of the Law and can be redeemed by Christ who became a curse for all who believe."

☙

The afternoon calm was interrupted by the sound of doors being kicked in, followed by cries in the street. Ezra had been shopping in the local market when the chaos erupted, and he and rushed into the house where Paul and Tertius were writing.

"Quick, grab your things! We must leave immediately. Chief Magistrate Silius has sent his soldiers to find us. He was told that someone in this district was writing subversive pamphlets against Rome. They are searching every house."

Paul, Tertius, and Barnabus, who rushed out of Paul's sleeping quarters, swept the papyrus leaves, styli and inkwells into pouches and satchels. Ink spilled and leaves crumpled as supplies were stuffed in. Items hung precariously from the gaping bags as the men grabbed their cloaks and exited the rear door into the alley and the pandemonium in the streets.

Paul suddenly stopped. "I left my last parchment on the table and must run back and get it. Go ahead, I'll join you as soon as I can."

Barnabas cried out, "We will go to "Rufus' unoccupied house where *The Way* meets and wait for you there. Come as quickly as you can. We will be safe there until the searches are over."

With no time to express their objections, Barnabus and Tertius rushed down the alley and into the broader streets. Eventually they came to the unoccupied house that was owned by Rufus, a member of *The Way*, who made the large home available for use by the ecclesia. The men could safely shelter there until the searches were over.

As they entered a rear door to the house, Tertius whispered, "Where is Paul? Shouldn't he be following closely behind us?"

"I don't know," Barnabus answered. "I have not seen him, and I have been glancing back to make sure that he is safe. We must pray that he has not been arrested." Barnabus' face was lined with worry.

The two men took shifts—one standing near the door watching for Paul while the other prayed.

By afternoon, Paul had not come. And by late evening he had not appeared. Gravely concerned, Barnabus and Tertius continued their prayer watch through the night hours.

As light was dawning the next morning, Tertius spotted the figure of a man in the distance, slowly limping down the center of the road.

"Barnabus!" he called out, "I see him, and he's injured. I'm going to get him."

Tertius raced from the house and nearly knocked Paul to the ground with his embrace.

"Gently, my brother. The guards saw my writing materials and dragged me into prison," Paul said. "They didn't believe me when I told them I wasn't writing subversive material. They beat me to get me to confess. When I showed them blank parchments to prove my innocence, they beat me again then released me. Thank God that you took those that were written upon, and I did not find the one I was certain I left on my writing table."

Tertius gently helped Paul back to the house where he and Barnabus had hidden, then found medical supplies to bind Paul's wounds. After he returned and applied healing ointment and bandages, the men slowly made their way back to the house to assess the damage. It had obviously been searched. Items had been tossed to the floor and scattered, but nothing appeared to be broken or damaged. They praised God together, and Tertius slipped away for a time of private prayer to thank God for sparing the life of Paul.

No one had eaten anything since the previous day, and Barnabus prepared a meal to slake their ravenous hunger. Tertius set to work putting the house back in order: setting up tables and chairs, clearing the floor of ink and debris, gathering and ordering the parchments, and preparing the styli for the next session of writing. Paul was ordered to rest.

Evening was drawing near, and golden light poured through the small windows of the work room. It was time for bread and porridge, gratitude, and reflection with their God.

CHAPTER 37
JERUSALEM COUNCIL

Paul sat in the open courtyard of Lukas of Antioch's house. The idyllic evening offered a rare opportunity for reflection, prayer, and grief as he pondered the discord that had so quickly beset the ecclesia. Believers had lost sight of Jesus as they contended for frayed rags of the Law. The gospel of freedom was being consumed by a spirit of legalism, works, and pride. The fading sun cast soft shadows on the stones behind him, as Paul closed his eyes, and a fresh breeze brushed his face.

A man who had been slowly making his way down the street stopped at the gate and called out to Paul. "Good evening, sir. I am searching for Barnabus of Cyprus and Paul, who comes from Tarsus. I was told they are staying here."

Paul eyed the man suspiciously. He did not appear familiar. "You may approach, but who may I say is looking for Paul and Barnabus?"

The man entered and crossed the courtyard, then bowed slightly. "I am Mateo from Jerusalem with an important message for them." The visitor looked eager and sincere.

"I am Paul of Tarsus. What message do you bring?"

"I have been sent with the authority of the Jerusalem ecclesia. They are requesting that Barnabus and you come to Jerusalem to answer charges."

Paul raised his eyebrows. "Charges? What charges could they possibly be bringing?"

Mateo stepped a few paces closer. "I would prefer to come inside and discuss the matter in private, rather than here in the open, where itching ears could easily turn our conversation into destructive gossip. Do you agree?"

Paul nodded as he stood. "Yes, of course. I'll ask Barnabus to join us and have my amanuensis take notes."

Paul directed Mateo inside to a chair. Barnabus and Tertius joined them in the gathering room. Paul worked hard to hold his tongue and to disguise that he was doing so.

Charges? What charges could the ecclesia in Jerusalem possibly bring against us? He stewed as the men settled in and a servant girl brought cups of wine.

What is under scrutiny—our message or our actions? Has Peter brought accusations against me, or is James fearful that my message has gone astray? His epistle did not show evidence of contradicting mine.

Barnabus quickly initiated the conversation. "Mateo, we are unaware that we have had any disagreement with Jerusalem. Why were we not given an opportunity to discuss the concerns before being formally brought under charges? A process that begins with charges is shortsighted, to say the least."

Mateo tilted his head, then nodded. "Gentiles have rapidly accepted the gospel message in Antioch, Cyprus, and Galatia, and this has caused concerns among conservative Jewish Christians. Peter's vision in the house of Cornelius authorized him to declare all things clean."

He took a sip of wine and continued. "Jewish Christians reason that Gentiles will soon outnumber Jewish believers and weaken the moral standards of *The Way*—especially regarding fornication. This problem could be rectified by requiring Gentiles to be circumcised and assume the obligations of the Law. However, these obligations are not required outside the Jerusalem church. A council is the only way to clarify this matter. Thus, the charges."

Paul rose from his chair, his eyes drilling into Mateo's. "Peter and James may lead the church in Jerusalem and have the authority to call a Church conference. But they do not have authority over the revelation God gave me in the desert. My authority was established when Jesus Himself appointed me as Apostle to the Gentiles. I stand on those credentials. And I will preach and teach *nothing* but His revelation. *Nothing*—do you understand? Not Jesus' blood atonement for our sins *plus* the Law. Salvation comes through Jesus *alone*."

Mateo swallowed, then took a sip of his wine. "I bring greetings from Peter and James, who ask you to join them in a council of leaders, apostles, and elders to unify the gospel message. The council is in response to the growing number of Jewish Christians who insist that Gentile Christians must be circumcised and follow a kosher diet."

Paul felt Barnabus' eyes rest on him. His precious friend knew him better than anyone.

Can Barnabus see that my heart is inflamed at the suggestion of a council on these matters? I have presented clear instruction on Christian freedom everywhere I have preached! Freedom from salvation by works is the cornerstone of the Gospel delivered to me by Jesus Himself!

Paul forced himself to be seated. "It appears that the real question under consideration is the authority supporting my teaching. Let us not play games. That is the core issue at hand."

Mateo changed position in his chair as droplets of perspiration formed on his brow. "I … I must not be making myself clear. This is not an excommunication trial. Leaders are seeking your input in the discussions. We are simply seeking unity on issues that have divided us. For instance, John Mark—"

John Mark's name stirred Paul's immediate response as he cut Mateo off. "Yes, of course, John Mark. And now we get to the root of the matter—John Mark's arrogant spirit and disagreement with my teaching. He possessed a proud, unteachable spirit. He was argumentative and intolerant, and we were fortunate when he left our missionary tour, as he insisted on teaching a gospel of works, rather than the Gospel delivered by our Lord Himself on Mt. Horeb."

Not even the men's breath dared pierce the silence until Paul spoke again.

"Yes, Mateo we will go to Jerusalem for the so-called 'discussions.' When are they scheduled?"

"The council will meet as soon as you arrive. I will leave immediately and tell them you are coming. You will be hosted in the home of Silas and his brother Barsabbas, who are leaders in the Jerusalem ecclesia. Their home overlooks the Temple Mount."

I must go. The ecclesia cannot be divided. We need to learn to love as Jesus loved. The Way will never survive a Jewish church and a Gentile church, and a divided Church would have nothing to say to the world— nothing. We must remain united. I will do all in my power, with God's help, to prevent division. I won't allow James and Peter to make this council about my authority. I must make them understand that it is about faithfulness to Jesus' message and His words only.

"Tell Peter and James that Barnabus and I will bring Lukas, Titus, Tertius, and perhaps a few of our elders. We want the council to hear their stories from their lips. My brother Barnabus will present our case."

ও

Paul slept at peace that night, knowing division among the ecclesia would finally be formally addressed.

The following day he rose early to rouse Barnabus. "We must

get on the road at first light. We do not have much time to prepare for the ten-day trip to Jerusalem, and we need to leave as soon as possible. I will wake Tertius, and you wake Titus."

"Why are we taking Titus?"

"Because he is an excellent example of a godly, uncircumcised Gentile who loves and serves Jesus, and he will gladly share his faith with members of the council," Paul stated firmly. "His life demonstrates our case."

Barnabus seemed lost in thought. "Of course, he's faithfully supported our missionary work. And I assume the other men have been asked to accompany us to speak, if needed, and to add to the vote."

Paul crossed his arms. "It would not be appropriate if most of the voting members of the council were from the Jerusalem church. A fair vote should allow equal representation from all participating churches." Paul shifted the weight of a goatskin bag that hung from his shoulder.

The men set to work packing the donkey with clothing, food, and provisions for the journey. Before long, they secured the final bag, and the trip to Jerusalem was underway.

The main route to Jerusalem ran through Syria, Phoenicia, and Samaria. Because Paul was a Roman citizen, he and his companions were not required to pay road taxes at every town or river crossing. The group stopped to visit churches along the way and listened to stories of Gentile conversions. Tertius recorded the experiences of new believers for a special presentation at the council.

As the sun was setting on their tenth day, the weary travelers arrived in the Holy City and sought out the home of Silas and his brother Barsabbas. After a quick meal, they retired for the night in preparation for what the next day might hold.

Paul, however, found a spot outside the stable where the animals had been sheltered. He leaned on a wall and gazed up at the stars. The focus of the council's attention was upon him, and he would face accusations and hostility. He was responsible for representing and protecting the message Jesus gave him on Mt. Horeb. As Paul watched the stars flicker overhead, Yahweh reminded him that He was Paul's defender, and he had no need to fear.

Paul awoke to the clamor of creaking carts, clattering hooves, bustling crowds, and grunting camels.

The men ate a quick breakfast and walked to the large guest room in the Essene district on Mt. Zion where many of Jesus' followers had gathered. For Paul, the location was bittersweet. This was the room where the Lord had eaten His last supper with His disciples, and it served as a secret meeting room for members of *The Way* to worship. Because the room was in the Essene district, it was not under strict observation by Jewish authorities. Many within the community, however, had become Christians, and a believer regularly donated the space for use by the ecclesia.

The room had been prepared. The walls were lined with benches, and center rows faced a table and chairs reserved for speakers and moderators.

As Paul entered with Barnabus, he noted that Peter and James had already taken seats at the front table. Paul and Barnabus' guests were directed to benches against the wall, and the two were ushered to the speakers' table.

Paul had not seen Peter for several years. His body was still muscled from years of dragging fishing nets. His face bore the wrinkles of age, his once-full head of hair had thinned, but his smile remained the same—open and welcoming.

Paul was suddenly aware of his own appearance, face ravaged by pox scars and beatings. His shoulders had rounded after years of illness, scourging, and the rigors of travel. But no matter, he was God's spokesman for the Gospel of freedom for the Gentiles—and for the world. The Spirit of God would direct his words. He was ready. He had not come to please anyone in the room—only His Master.

The council marshal pounded a staff on the floor and called the meeting to session. "Let us pray for God's guidance in and over these proceedings." Men scattered about the room directed prayers to Av for peace, order, wisdom, and direction, and Paul quietly joined them.

He opened his eyes and scanned the room, recognizing many of the men as legalistic Jews from Judea who taught that circumcision was necessary for salvation. They were rigidly ritualistic traditionalists who fought to defend core tenets of Judaism. They were steeped in the traditional teachings of Moses, and undoubtedly regarded Paul as a radical rebel whose form of Christianity lowered moral standards.

Paul shook his head. How had the Gospel of Jesus so quickly become tainted? Religious zealots refused to socially interact with the uncircumcised, which included the Lord's supper. Rules superseded Jesus' command to love God with all one's heart, soul, and mind and love one's neighbor as they, themselves, desired to be loved. Instead, they had turned Christianity into a new sect of Judaism with the same requirements of the Law Christ had already fulfilled.

How ironic that most of these legalists were former Pharisees—like he once was—who already believed in resurrection. They converted to Christianity without abandoning their basic beliefs. Believing in Jesus' resurrection and accepting Him as Messiah was a short jump—if the Law remained intact.

The council marshall announced that the proceedings would consist of three public sessions and one private council meeting. The first public session would set the stage. The second meeting would set forth the arguments to be discussed. And the third meeting would be a deliberation of the issue, as well as tending to routine matters of church business.

The marshall took his seat. James rose to begin the first session.

He cleared his throat. "Many Jewish believers in Samaria and Jerusalem insist that Gentile Christianity accept circumcision, follow kosher diets, and reject fornication. Others among us believe that elements of the Law are not necessary to Jesus' message of the Gospel."

Paul stood and waited for James to recognize him. He spoke firmly, but could not tame the emotion that edged his voice. "I condemn, in the strongest terms, those who sent your disciples to Antioch and Galatia to *oppose* the message we brought to the Gentiles. We preached the pure gospel of grace and freedom from the yoke of the Law received from God's mouth as He spoke it to me in person on Mt. Horeb."

Paul's voice grew louder. "Faith in Jesus our Messiah for both Jews and Gentiles frees us from the penalty of sin. We are no longer slaves who work out our salvation by following the Law! You desire laws because you can look at your conduct and take pride in *false* spirituality, based on your works. I, Saul of Tarsus—once a persecutor of *The Way*—know this more than anyone. I am the chief of sinners."

He pounded his fist against his chest. "Can you not see? We come to Jesus with *our nothing* to receive *His everything*—spiritual riches that cannot be purchased with circumcision or dietary restrictions. We have nothing to offer but faith, which is God's gift, and our broken, penitent hearts."

He scanned the room, overcome with passion but also moved by compassion for those who did not yet understand. "Do not profane the gift of God's mercy and grace by trying to add paltry human effort. Jesus did not die so you would continue to rely upon your own efforts. He died, rather, that you would fall on your face before Him because of what He has done *for you*."

Paul's voice had quieted. He lowered himself slowly onto the bench and wiped his eyes. The room was silent, but Paul felt every gaze upon him. Barnabus placed a hand on his shoulder.

James finally broke the silence. "Thank you, Paul. Your passion for the gospel and your love for our Savior are evident to everyone. I stand humbled in your presence. I must also say that I am sorry for the destructive behavior of our brothers who came to the church at Antioch preaching 'another gospel' after you had instructed them."

James drew a deep breath. "Rest assured, it was not me. I can also confidently say it was not Peter. He was commissioned to minister among the Jews but has no such misconceptions about the essence of the gospel. Remember, he received a divine message at Cornelius' house that called for the end of clean and unclean distinctions. I cannot cast light on who this may have been."

Peter stood and led a short discussion among the attendees that demonstrated the schism among those present. Many spoke up in defense of Paul's teaching. Others remained silent or voiced their support for Gentile circumcision and the Jewish food laws. Late in the evening, the marshal adjourned for the day. He charged those present to continue to consider the issue privately through prayer and fasting.

After a restless night, Paul and Barnabus returned to the hall. As others entered, their conversations and facial expressions made it apparent they had formulated opinions and were prepared for debate.

Following opening prayer, Nicolaus of Antioch, a Hellenist elder, immediately challenged James' denial of deceptive behavior. "I am still curious about who sent Pharisaic Christian zealots to Antioch to preach the heresy of circumcision. James had the authority to commission such a mission."

Barnabus jumped to his feet. "James is *not* a liar. If he says he did not do something, he did not do it. He is a man of his word.

Your charge is unsubstantiated. If you have witnesses, call them. Otherwise, sit down and be silent."

Nicolaus stood his ground. "Then it must be Peter. He is as changeable as the wind."

Paul gritted his teeth, and Barnabus reached over and grasped his arm.

"He says he has done something, and then when confronted, he changes his mind," Nicolaus carried on. "Look what he did in Antioch. Paul had to oppose him to his face."

Paul drew in his breath as Nicolaus continued.

"Peter used to eat with the Gentiles. But when Paul arrived, he separated himself from them. Was he suddenly afraid of Gentiles who had not been circumcised? Was he ashamed of his friendship with them? Soon other Jews joined him in his hypocrisy, so that by their hypocrisy even Barnabus was led astray."

Paul's spirit sank. What had brought such division into the midst of Jesus' followers?

Mistrust.

Accusations.

Pride.

Anger.

Bitterness.

Unforgiveness.

A vision of Jesus' face flashed through Paul's mind. His friend, his Savior, was weeping.

Barnabus suddenly rose to his feet. "Yes, Peter did withdraw from uncircumcised Gentiles, and he willingly accepted responsibility for that poor choice. Since then, he has shown strong support that faith in Jesus alone saves and that by faith we walk in the Spirit."

Paul glanced around the room and noted that many in the crowd were nodding their heads in approval. His shoulders relaxed. Perhaps those present were more open to reason than he had thought—or perhaps, they were beginning to see the light.

The day continued with heated debate of the issues. Sometimes voices were loud and tempers flared. Everyone was hot, tired, hungry, frustrated, and their actions and words told Paul they simply wanted the matter settled and over. Several times throughout the proceedings, he stepped outside to escape the "discussions" and pray in solitude. By the end of the day, little progress had been made, and Peter dismissed the delegates with an admonition to lay down their pride and seek God's heart.

The next morning, Paul entered the room exhausted but encouraged after a night of prayer and fellowship with the Spirit of God. Attendees entered quietly, and few spoke to one another. The marshall opened the meeting with a prayer for wisdom and unity. Peter was granted permission to speak first, and Paul sent prayers heavenward for all gathered.

Peter looked out across the room. "Brothers, you know that God chose that the Gentiles would hear the gospel message from my lips. God, who knows the heart, accepted them by giving them the Holy Spirit, just as He did to us. He did not discriminate between them and us, for *He* purified their hearts by *faith*. Now then, why do you test God by putting on the necks of Gentiles a yoke that neither we nor our ancestors have been able to bear? No! It is through the grace of our Lord Jesus that we are saved, just as they are."

Paul sat, unmoving, as Barnabus squeezed his shoulder in encouragement. Heads in front of them bobbed their affirmation. Paul scanned the room. The murmurs now seemed those of agreement and congeniality. Several individuals stepped to the table to express thanks to Peter.

Be strong and immovable, Paul, always abounding in the work of the Lord.

"Yes, my Master," Paul whispered as Peter called Barnabus and him to the table. Paul signaled to Barnabus to speak first, and the assembly listened intently as he told of miraculous signs and wonders done among the Gentiles in Cyprus, Antioch, and Galatia. Everyone in the room sat transfixed as Barnabus told story after story of God's moving among the Gentiles. Then he sat and motioned to Paul, who slowly stood. He paused and waited until the prodding urged him on.

"As you all know, Barnabus and I have spent the last several years preaching Christ's message to Gentiles in Cyprus, Antioch, and Galatia. We praise God that He called out for Himself many Gentile believers, and they have faithfully followed our Savior. God confirmed our message with signs and wonders among Gentile believers. Tying the gospel message to the Law rejects God's redemptive work among the Gentiles and keeps them bound to the Law that the Jews themselves corrupted."

Peter rose and interrupted. "I would like to add to what Paul has said. You may remember my experience in Caesarea in the house of Cornelius. I have spoken of it before. I received a vision at midday and saw heaven open and something like a large sheet being let down to earth by its four corners. The sheet contained all kinds of four-footed animals, as well as reptiles and birds. A voice instructed me, 'Get up, Peter. Kill and eat.' "I answered as a faithful Jew. 'Surely not, Lord! I have never eaten anything impure or unclean.'"

Peter cleared his throat. "The voice spoke a second time, 'Do not call anything impure that God has made clean.' To make sure I understood, the voice repeated the words three times. The vision puzzled me but in the following days, the meaning became clear. It is against our law for a Jew to associate with a Gentile. God had shown me that I should not call anyone impure or unclean. I realized that God does not show favoritism. He accepts from every nation those who fear Him and do what is right."

Peter and Paul returned to their seats as James took the floor once again.

"I wish to thank Barnabus, Paul, and Peter for their statements in our council. They have spread the gospel among Jews and Gentiles equally and have seen God's blessing with their own eyes. While I have spent most of my time in Jerusalem administering the affairs of the church and looking after the needs of believers, it's important that everyone know that I support Peter and Paul's arguments. The message of God's blessing and salvation to Gentiles is not new. What *is* new is that Christ's death and resurrection has made forgiveness and redemption permanent, not temporary, as it was with animal sacrifices."

Paul's heart warmed at James's words.

"God's word tells us:

'After this I will retur and rebuild David's fallen tent.
Its ruins I will rebuild, and I will restore it, that the rest
of mankind may seek the Lord, even all the Gentiles who
bear my name, says the Lord, who does these things—
things known from long ago.'"

For the first time in a long while, Paul felt supported by his brothers in Jerusalem. The confirmation that God has spoken similarly on these issues strengthened him.

"It is my judgment, therefore," James said, "that we should not make it difficult for Gentiles who are turning to God. Instead, we should write to them, telling them to abstain from food polluted by idols, from sexual immorality, from the meat of strangled animals and from blood."

James turned the meeting over to the marshal who adjourned the council until the following day.

Barnabus' hand rested on Paul's shoulder again. "Do you think everyone understands the magnitude of what just happened?" Barnabus whispered as they walked toward the door.

Paul shook his head noncommittally. "I hope and pray so, but I doubt that any of us truly understand. Yahweh's ways are too far above us. He is 'other' from human logic. But I am grateful that the essential nature of salvation by faith alone in Jesus' death on the cross was affirmed in our decision. We go forth today united in our faith: God's Son came to earth and died … so we can truly be free."

Barnabus stepped through the door and descended the stairs, followed by Paul, who paused to scan the crowded city street.

"But more importantly, my friend Barnabus, we preserved the message of the Gospel for generations to come."

CHAPTER 38

SHARD OF GLASS

Paul raised his tunic to avoid stumbling on the protruding paving stones in the road. With his other hand, he lightly gripped the arm of Linus, a faithful but overbearing elder in the Jerusalem church. The council meeting had drained Paul's energy, and more than anything he wanted time alone with his Lord to pour out his heart, rest in the Spirit, and be refreshed. But Linus had pleaded with him to spend the night with him and his wife Taryn in their home in lower Jerusalem while they waited for the final rendering of the Council.

Paul's mind rehearsed the events of the past several days. He was not overly concerned with the flaring tempers, accusations, and debates. As the council had drawn to a close, people had set aside their opinions, grudges, bruised feelings, and pride. With few exceptions, everyone had agreed upon a unified message of the gospel and a united ecclesia. Jesus' death was more than enough to pay for the sins of the world. The decision and official decree would be issued the following day.

For a moment he lifted his gaze from his feet to the city around him. In the distance he spotted the blurred features of the Temple Mount. He waited for the echo of his father's accusing voice, but his mind instead echoed with the words, "Well done, my good and faithful servant."

Again, Paul glanced at the uneven stones in the road as Linus droned on about the council. But only whispers of affirmation and love echoed through Paul's head. Certainty rooted deeply in him that from the dawn of eternity, God had hidden him in the shadow of His hand. That truth was his security and his identity.

He wondered what influence the council's decision would have on his future ministry. He did not know, but he did know that he would never stop sharing the gospel. This was his life.

His thoughts were interrupted when Linus called out in front of a modest two-story stone home to announce their arrival. His wife, Taryn, quickly greeted them and announced that their evening meal would be ready soon.

Taryn's gracious, warm smile counterbalanced her husband's brusque manner. Linus led Paul to a long, low couch in the gathering room and sat at one end while motioning to Paul to sit at the other. After an awkward silence, Linus seemed he could hold his tongue no longer.

"Paul, what will you do if the Council decides against James, Barnabus, Peter, and you tomorrow?"

"I would disagree with the way you've stated the question," Paul replied. "The Council is not deciding about me, James, Barnabus, or Peter. The question is about the nature of the gospel message. Did Jesus speak to me in the wilderness, and was I with Him, face-to-face for three years? Was the reason for this appointed time to deliver a message to me about God's New Covenant relationship with us? We possess God's Word, Linus, and the task of the Council was to determine whether or not to carry it out."

The man's thick eyebrows danced on his forehead. But Paul would not be deterred.

"We don't know what the decision will be, but we are all of one baptism and one Spirit. The Spirit of God who indwells those who have trusted Christ will bring us to a conclusion in agreement with our Heavenly Father's will."

Linus, wide-eyed, sat unmoving, as if searching for the right words. At that moment, Taryn slipped into the room and announced that the meal was ready.

The men seated themselves at a plank table. Paul offered a prayer of thanks for the food that Taryn had prepared: fresh barley bread with olive oil, vegetable soup, and a wooden platter with figs, pomegranate, dates, almonds, and olives. Wine had already been poured. After the men began their meal, Taryn joined them.

Several bites of bread and savory soup later, Paul lifted his head and asked, "Do you have any children? If so, they are very well behaved."

Linus and Taryn froze. Taryn's spoon fell back into her bowl, splashing broth against her pale blue mantle. Her hand remained suspended in space, trembling. The silence stretched on painfully. She began to weep, her shoulders shaking. Linus dropped his head, his usual rock-like composure reduced to immobility.

Paul forced himself to let the quiet breathe for however long required. After a few moments Taryn spoke, her voice trembling as she stared at her bowl. "Paul, we are honored to have you share a meal at our table. I … I apologize … I did not know you were … You are a great man of … faith and servant of God. But your presence stirs heart crushing and terrifying memories for us."

For an instant Paul was confused, then aghast as he recognized the pain and terror he had seen before in the faces of believers he had met. For a moment he could not breathe.

Is this what You came to experience, Jesus, and to bear for us? This guilt that outstrips remorse and suffering that surpasses pain? My God, my God, what wondrous grace is the glory of Your cross?

Paul knew the next words—or some form of them. He braced himself to hear them from this gentle, tattered voice.

"Years ago, you came to our home and arrested us for being members of *The Way*—but not just us, our nine-year-old son as well. We were separated and repeatedly whipped. Linus and I barely survived. Our son did not. He died in my arms and was dragged away from me by the Temple Guard."

Taryn's eyes dropped, and she stopped speaking, but her body shook.

Paul reached for a cloth inside his mantle to wipe the tears from his face. His mother had given him several strips of soft fabric she had stitched from remnants of his father's favorite garments. How poignant that this would be the cloth that caught his tears of regret and sorrow.

"No word I could ever offer can express my remorse for the suffering and loss I have caused you," he said. "If giving my life for your son could bring him back, I would willingly do so. Images of my past actions continually haunt me. I am truly the worst of sinners and sit here in your presence today only by the grace of God."

Linus looked Paul in the eyes. "We forgave you long ago, Paul. Finding you at our door today surprised Taryn. You can imagine how difficult that must have been. And although we still grieve Ethan's loss deeply, God blessed us with a second child. She is sleeping contentedly on our bed and will wake soon."

"A daughter?" Paul asked as he prayed for guidance about what to say next.

"Yes," Linus spoke with an Abba's proud smile. "Cassia is a precious baby who adores her Abba already. I hear her waking in the next room. Taryn, could you go get her?"

Paul struggled not to choke on his sip of wine. "Cassia … your daughter's name is Cassia?"

"Yes," Linus said glowingly. "Taryn chose the name. She thought it was beautiful and unique. You do not often hear it."

"No, that is true," Paul said quietly as Taryn laid the child in her abba's arms. Paul stared, drinking in the picture as Linus traced the shape of his daughter's face and whispered to her.

"Would you like to hold her?" he offered.

Paul shook his head. "I would much rather watch her Abba love on her and observe the joy on his face at his daughter's mere existence." Paul drank in the picture of Linus beaming, gazing at his daughter's face and whispering to her. Paul forced his mind to focus on the child, as the haunting face from the past fought to seize his thoughts.

Beautiful Cassia, safe in Abba's arms, safe in Abba's arms.

Paul's heart flooded with gratitude for the reality of forgiveness. The image of the helpless slave girl Cassia's eyes that had tormented him for so long began to fade as he looked into the beautiful eyes of the newborn, Cassia. One life had blurred his vision; the eyes of this beautiful new life was filled with hope for redemption and anticipation of a full life.

A vision of the Love of Loves burst into brilliant illumination in Paul's heart—that God, through Jesus, made us His children and loves us all with the same love that binds Him to His Son. The look on Linus' face, gazing so lovingly at tiny Cassia, was barely a glimmer of Yahweh's love for us. With no other way to redeem humanity, God Almighty sent Jesus to suffer and die for us. Paul had seen a mere reflection, and he was undone. He couldn't help reflecting on the irony: *The helpless slave Cassia's sacrifice was for herd revenge; Christ's sacrifice was for personal redemption for newborn Cassia.*

Paul rose. "Linus, I do not mean to impose, but I would like to spend some time alone on your rooftop with Yahweh before I retire. Please excuse me." He quickly slipped out the front door as Linus carefully stood and pulled Taryn into his free arm.

Paul mounted the stairs at the side of the house near the kitchen entry. The evening air had cooled, and a gentle breeze brushed Paul's face. He stood atop the house and watched the sun slip behind the Mount of Olives as fading sunlight splayed orange hues against the Temple, illuminating radiant white marble, gold, and bronze entrance doors. As the sun sank lower, the Temple's stones melted into brilliant red.

The noises of the afternoon faded to the quiet cadence of evening—occasional bird songs, a cart passing below, an Ima calling for a wayward child, the conversation of passersby in the street.

Paul pulled out the familiar wrinkled cloth. He fingered it gently. His abba *had* loved him. But how hard for him to see it through the eyes of a child with limited vision. Abba's discipline had been love. His watchfulness had been love. His desire for the best had been love. Pauli had never seen it until he saw an abba's love shining from the face of Linus.

"How hard for all of us, God, with our distorted vision, to see how much You love us. We are so blinded by our pride and sin. Yahweh, my God, how can I look at Your glorious Temple and not be moved with thanks that motivates all I say and do?"

The cloth dabbed at another rush of tears.

"As I look out over the Holy City, I am overwhelmed by Your love for us from before time. I do not know what will happen tomorrow, but I will press forward to complete Your calling upon my life and to run my race with excellence. I will, no doubt, face the wrath of those blinded by unbelief. For me to live is Christ and to die is gain. I will live out my days preaching the gospel delivered to me by Jesus and Your love for us that would pay that price to have us near You."

He lifted his face to the skies.

"You have healed every ache in my heart and given me peace I didn't know was possible. You came to me on Mt. Horeb and taught me about scripture and how to know You, but my most precious gift is that You gave me a relationship with You through Jesus."

"And that's all anyone really needs."

EPILOGUE

Paul spent the next years facing persecution, hatred, misunderstanding, and jail time, but he continued a life of dedicated ministry as recorded in the New Testament.

The rift between John Mark and Paul was healed in later years as Paul found him useful for his later ministry (2 Timothy 4:11). John Mark wrote the Gospel of Mark, which many scholars believe to be the first Gospel written (AD 50s?).

Barnabus continued to minister as an apostolic legate, and some scholars believe he authored the book of Hebrews.

By AD 180, the greatest number of Christians lived in Asia Minor and along the Aegean coast in Greece. By 325, the strength of the established church was centered in Asia Minor, where all the major church councils convened. Egypt, early in the timeline of church history, had a large Jewish population, and a Christian church soon developed in Alexandria.

The need for Scripture fueled quick copying to pass on these precious documents to eager followers to share with new congregations. This growth meant that the supply of copies multiplied, crisscrossed the Roman Empire, were compared with other copies being circulated, and were edited. John, writing in the Book of Revelation (late in Nero's reign AD 54-68 or Domitian's reign 81-96; possibly Vespasian's reign 69-79) less than fifty years after the gospel had first been presented, addressed seven churches of Asia Minor. For the first 300 years of church growth, congregations in Asia Minor and Greece exerted the greatest force in Christianity.

As Christianity spread throughout the empire into Rome, North Africa, and Egypt, the New Testament documents were translated into Latin, Coptic, Syriac, and other languages. After AD 325, the Church in Rome continued to be a significant force during the next centuries.

As of this writing, there are more than 2.5 billion Christians worldwide, representing over 30% of the world's population. God's message is available to all.

From a small, local Jewish sect to worldwide Christianity.

CAST OF CHARACTERS

Abner	Cripple healed by the Galilean
Adriana	Daughter of Lukas of Antioch
Aegeus	Elder, Church of Aleppo
Amira	Paul's sister
Andrew	Disciple
Aretas IV Philopatris	King of Nabataea
Asher of Adana	Saul's friend at Beit Midrash in Tarsus
Athenodorus	A teacher at the Tarsus University
Atticus	Elder, Stadium Church
Barnabus	Friend of Paul from childhood to end
Bartholomew	Disciple
Benjamin	Father of Saul
Caleb	Leader of group of Essenes
Cassia	Slave girl that Saul witnessed being sacrificed and newborn to Linus
Cassius	Elder, Church of Mt. Staurin
Chanoch	Fellow student at Beit Hillel
Christia	Boy leading Paul out of Damascus
Cilicia	Province of Tarsus
Damen	Assisted Paul's escape from Damascus
Didymus	Called doubting Thomas, a disciple
Drusilla	Daughter of Philip the evangelist
Eli	James' amanuensis
Erastus	Elder, Church of Orontes
Ezra	James' amanuensis

Gamaliel ha-Zaqen	Teacher at Jerusalem yeshiva
Gaulus	Name of ship Paul and John Mark sailed from Caesarea
Hiram	Reuben's Jewish father
Nicolaus of Antioch	A hellenistic Christian and Jerusalem elder
Jamal	Paul's host at Bedouin camp; father of Fatima, Rima and Yara
Reuben	Paul's childhood classmate
Johanan Ben Arza	Captain of the Temple Guard
Yehoshua	Name of strange otherworldly man at Mt. Horeb
Linus	Jerusalem elder who hosted Paul at Jerusalem Council
Lukas	A medicos living in Antioch, Syria Elder of Antioch Church
Lukas of Antioch	Elder, Church of Antioch
Manaen, Essene	Elder, Stadium Church
Mateo	Emissary from Jerusalem Church
Photinia	The woman who received the living water
Sceva	Elder, Church of Daphne
Silas and Barsabbas	Elders in Jerusalem who delivered council's decision
Silium	Chief Magistrate, Antioch
Symeon Niger	Elder Church of Mt. Staurin
Nicolas	First Gentile convert to Judaism and then converted to *The Way*
Rabbi Aharon	Saul family rabbi in Tarsus
Rabbi Akiva	Saul's Beit Midrash teacher
Peter	Founder of *The Way* and apostle
Proclus	Disciple of Philip spreading circumcision for Gentiles

Sarah	Mother of Saul
Saul	Gaius Julius Paulus Paul's full birth name
Sonja	Early family slave girl
Tertius	Paul's Amanuensis
Uziel	Student at Beit Hillel
Valentina	Assisted Paul in escape from Damascus
Victoria	Name of ship—Reuben, First Mate
Yacov	Father of Stephen, the martyr
Yara	Wife of Jamal (Bedouin)

A CHRONOLOGY OF EARLY CHRISTIANITY

6-4 BC
> The Birth of Jesus
> Death of Herod

AD 3-19
> Birth of Paul 3-5
> Paul in Tarsus 5-18

20–30
> Paul studies in Jerusalem under Gamaliel (23-27)
> > Paul (18) Jesus (25)
> Paul works as intern (27-28)
> Jesus baptized (29) Paul (26) Jesus (34)
> Ministry of Jesus (29-33) Paul (26-29) Jesus (34-37)
> Paul teaches in Beit Midrash (28-3) (31–35)
> Death of Jesus AD (33) Jesus aged (35-38)
> Pentecost (33) Paul aged (29-32)
> Paul persecuting the Church (34-35)

35–40
> Stephen martyred (35) (Acts 7:57–60)
> Conversion of Paul (35–38 [?]) (Acts 9:1–19)

Rule of Caligula (37–41)

Paul's trip to Arabia (35–38) (9:23; Galatians 1:17)

Paul's trip to Jerusalem (38) (Acts 9:26–29)

Paul's trip to Tarsus, Cilicia (38–43) (9:30)

41–50

Rule of Claudius (41–54)

Paul's trip to Antioch, Syria, at the invitation of Barnabus 43
    (Acts 11:25–26)

Herod's death (44) (Acts 12:25–26)

Epistle of James (45–49?)

Paul's first missionary journey (46–49)
    (Acts 13:2—14:28)

Paul's second visit to Jerusalem (for Jerusalem offering) (49)
    (Acts 11:29–30)

Writing of Galatians from Antioch, Syria (49)

Jerusalem Council (50)

51–60

Paul's second missionary journey (51–54)
    (Acts 15:1–29)

Paul appears before Gallio (51/52) (Acts 18:12–17)

Writing of 1 and 2 Thessalonians from Corinth (52–53)

Rule of Nero (54–68)

Paul's third missionary journey (54–58)
    (Acts 18:23—21:17)

Writing of 1 Corinthians from Ephesus (57)

Writing of 2 Corinthians from Macedonia (57)

Arrest in Jerusalem (57) (Acts 21:27—22:30)

Imprisonment in Caesarea (57–59) (Acts 23:23—26:32)

Writing of Romans from Greece (58/59)

Journey to Rome (60–61) (Acts 27:1—28:16)

61–70

First Roman imprisonment (61–63)

Writing of Philippians from Rome (61–62)

Writing of Colossians from Rome (61– 62)

Writing of Ephesians from Rome (61–62)

Writing of Philemon from Rome (63)

Release from prison (64?)

Writing of 1 Timothy from Macedonia (Philippi) (67)

Writing of Titus from Ephesus(?) (67) (2 Timothy 4:20)

Second Roman imprisonment (68) (2 Timothy 4:6–3)

Writing of 2 Timothy from Roman Prison (68)
(2 Timothy 4:6)

Paul's trial and execution (68)

Writing of Matthew, Mark, Luke, and John(?)

Writing of Revelation (65-68?)

71–80

Jewish revolt in Jerusalem (fall of Jerusalem and
Temple destroyed) (66–70)

Rule of Vespasian (69–79) (Writing of Revelation?)

Rule of Titus (79–81)

81–120

Council of Yavneh (90)

Rule of Domitian (81–96) (Writing of Revelation?)

Rule of Nerva (96–98)

Rule of Trajan (98–117)

ACKNOWLEDGMENTS

No book could be produced without the influence and efforts of many gifted men and women. This book is no exception. From authors' backgrounds, influences, and experiences to editors, designers, artists, and administrators, books take form and are published. We wish to acknowledge some of those dedicated people.

Our special thanks to artist Ron Waalkes whose oil paintings of Paul's encounter on the road to Damascus, his depiction of the village and Bedouin camp at the foot of Mt Sinai, and his map of Damascus inspired the scenes in this book.

Thanks to Cynthia Ruchti whose editorial comments and suggestions enhanced the final product. The time she spent to invest in this book was beyond generous.

Thanks to our literary agent, Pete Ford, Credo Communications, for his work on our behalf in manuscript preparation and presentation to secure a publisher.

And of course, I, Don, wish to thank my co-writer, Shelly Beach, who agreed to join me in this adventure. Her writing gifts and willingness to devote a vast amount of time to make this book possible was inspiring. The same is true for me, Shelly. It has been my pleasure to partner with Don on numerous writing endeavors over the years. This book on the life of Paul is a special gift, and working with Don is a delight.

Shelly and I want to express our thanks to Dan Beach and Carol Brake for their loving support in our project.

MEET THE AUTHORS

Donald L. Brake Sr. holds a Ph.D. from Dallas Theological Seminary and is dean emeritus at Multnomah Biblical Seminary, Multnomah University. His experience as president of the Jerusalem University College and experience leading tours in Israel, Greece, and Turkey have given him insight into the historical and geographical background of Israel and the New Testament. He is also a collector of rare Bibles and manuscripts from the second to twentieth centuries. His books include *A Visual History of the English Bible in 2008, A Visual History of the King James Bible* in 2011 (cowritten with Shelly Beach), *Jesus, a Visual History* with Todd Bolen, published in 2014 by Zondervan Academic, as well as a novel, *They Called Him Yeshua,* with co-writer Shelly Beach, published in 2019. Don and his wife Carol live in Lewisville, Texas.

Shelly Beach is a multiple award-winning author of more than twelve books of both fiction and nonfiction. She served as managing editor of Zondervan's *Hope in the Mourning Bible* (2013) and was one of three writers of Zondervan's *NIV Stewardship Bible*, as well as a contributor to *Tyndale's Mosaic Bible.* She also serves as a compilation editor for *Guideposts* and a writing consultant and

mentor at Shelly Beach Communications. She holds and M.R.E. from Grand Rapids Theological Seminary and is cofounder of the Breath Writer's Conference (MI) and the Cedar Falls Christian Writer's Workshop (IA). Shelly speaks nationally on caregiving, post-traumatic stress, faith, and writing. She and her husband Dan have two adult children and live in Iowa.

www.ingramcontent.com/pod-product-compliance
Lightning Source LLC
Chambersburg PA
CBHW060355260626
47160CB00006B/2323